Agatha Christie is known throughout the world as the Queen of Crime. Her books have sold over a billion copies in English with another billion in foreign languages. She is the most widely published author of all time and in any language, outsold only by the Bible and Shakespeare. She is the author of 80 crime novels and short story collections, 19 plays, and six novels written under the name of Mary Westmacott.

Agatha Christie's first novel, *The Mysterious Affair at Styles*, was written towards the end of the First World War, in which she served as a VAD. In it she created Hercule Poirot, the little Belgian detective who was destined to become the most popular detective in crime fiction since Sherlock Holmes. It was eventually published by The Bodley Head in 1920.

In 1926, after averaging a book a year, Agatha Christie wrote her masterpiece. *The Murder of Roger Ackroyd* was the first of her books to be published by Collins and marked the beginning of an author–publisher relationship which lasted for 50 years and well over 70 books. *The Murder of Roger Ackroyd* was also the first of Agatha Christie's books to be dramatized – under the name *Alibi* – and to have a successful run in London's West End. *The Mousetrap*, her most famous play of all, opened in 1952 and is the longest-running play in history.

Agatha Christie was made a Dame in 1971. She died in 1976, since when a number of books have been published posthumously: the bestselling novel *Sleeping Murder* appeared later that year, followed by her autobiography and the short story collections *Miss Marple's Final Cases*, *Problem at Pollensa Bay* and *While the Light Lasts*. In 1998 *Black Coffee* was the first of her plays to be novelized by another author, Charles Osborne.

THE AGATHA CHRISTIE COLLECTION

The Man in the Brown Suit
The Secret of Chimneys
The Seven Dials Mystery
The Mysterious Mr Quin
The Sittaford Mystery
The Hound of Death
The Listerdale Mystery
Why Didn't They Ask Evans?
Parker Pyne Investigates
Murder is Easy
And Then There Were None
Towards Zero
Death Comes as the End
Sparkling Cyanide
Crooked House
They Came to Baghdad
Destination Unknown
Ordeal by Innocence
The Pale Horse
Endless Night
Passenger to Frankfurt
Problem at Pollensa Bay
While the Light Lasts

Poirot
The Mysterious Affair at Styles
The Murder on the Links
Poirot Investigates
The Murder of Roger Ackroyd
The Big Four
The Mystery of the Blue Train
Peril at End House
Lord Edgware Dies
Murder on the Orient Express
Three-Act Tragedy
Death in the Clouds
The ABC Murders
Murder in Mesopotamia
Cards on the Table
Murder in the Mews
Dumb Witness
Death on the Nile
Appointment With Death
Hercule Poirot's Christmas
Sad Cypress
One, Two, Buckle My Shoe
Evil Under the Sun
Five Little Pigs
The Hollow
The Labours of Hercules
Taken at the Flood
Mrs McGinty's Dead
After the Funeral
Hickory Dickory Dock

Dead Man's Folly
Cat Among the Pigeons
The Adventure of the Christmas Pudding
The Clocks
Third Girl
Hallowe'en Party
Elephants Can Remember
Poirot's Early Cases
Curtain: Poirot's Last Case

Marple
The Murder at the Vicarage
The Thirteen Problems
The Body in the Library
The Moving Finger
A Murder is Announced
They Do It With Mirrors
A Pocket Full of Rye
4.50 from Paddington
The Mirror Crack'd from Side to Side
A Caribbean Mystery
At Bertram's Hotel
Nemesis
Sleeping Murder
Miss Marple's Final Cases

Tommy & Tuppence
The Secret Adversary
Partners in Crime
N or M?
By the Pricking of My Thumbs
Postern of Fate

Published as Mary Westmacott
Giant's Bread
Unfinished Portrait
Absent in the Spring
The Rose and the Yew Tree
A Daughter's a Daughter
The Burden

Memoirs
An Autobiography
Come, Tell Me How You Live

Play Collections
The Mousetrap and Selected Plays
Witness for the Prosecution
and Selected Plays

Play Adaptations by Charles Osborne
Black Coffee (Poirot)
Spider's Web
The Unexpected Guest

Agatha Christie

POIROT
THE POST-WAR YEARS

•

AFTER THE FUNERAL

•

HICKORY DICKORY DOCK

•

CAT AMONG THE PIGEONS

•

THE CLOCKS

•

HarperCollins*Publishers*

HarperCollins*Publishers*
77–85 Fulham Palace Road,
Hammersmith, London W6 8JB
www.harpercollins.co.uk

This edition first published 2005
1

ISBN 0 00 719066 2

Typeset in Plantin Light and Gill Sans by
Palimpsest Book Production Limited,
Polmont, Stirlingshire

Printed and bound in Great Britain by
Clays Ltd, St Ives plc

CONTENTS

AFTER THE FUNERAL

For James
in memory of happy days
at Abney

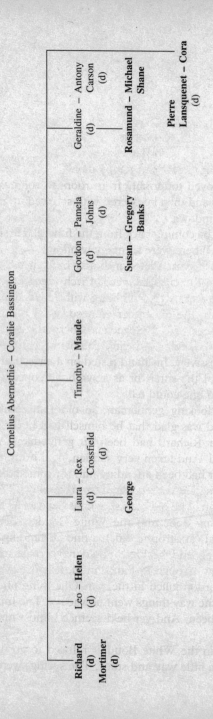

The Abernethie Family

Those designated in **bold** were present at the funeral of
Richard Abernethie

I

Old Lanscombe moved totteringly from room to room, pulling up the blinds. Now and then he peered with screwed up rheumy eyes through the windows.

Soon they would be coming back from the funeral. He shuffled along a little faster. There were so many windows.

Enderby Hall was a vast Victorian house built in the Gothic style. In every room the curtains were of rich faded brocade or velvet. Some of the walls were still hung with faded silk. In the green drawing-room, the old butler glanced up at the portrait above the mantelpiece of old Cornelius Abernethie for whom Enderby Hall had been built. Cornelius Abernethie's brown beard stuck forward aggressively, his hand rested on a terrestrial globe, whether by desire of the sitter, or as a symbolic conceit on the part of the artist, no one could tell.

A very forceful looking gentleman, so old Lanscombe had always thought, and was glad that he himself had never known him personally. Mr Richard had been *his* gentleman. A good master, Mr Richard. And taken very sudden, he'd been, though of course the doctor had been attending him for some little time. Ah, but the master had never recovered from the shock of young Mr Mortimer's death. The old man shook his head as he hurried through a connecting door into the White Boudoir. Terrible, that had been, a real catastrophe. Such a fine upstanding young gentleman, so strong and healthy. You'd never have thought such a thing likely to happen to him. Pitiful, it had been, quite pitiful. And Mr Gordon killed in the war. One thing on top of another. That was the way things went nowadays. Too much for the master, it had been. And yet he'd seemed almost himself a week ago.

The third blind in the White Boudoir refused to go up as it should. It went up a little way and stuck. The springs were weak

– that's what it was – very old, these blinds were, like everything else in the house. And you couldn't get these old things mended nowadays. Too old-fashioned, that's what they'd say, shaking their heads in that silly superior way – as if the old things weren't a great deal better than the new ones! *He* could tell them that! Gimcrack, half the new stuff was – came to pieces in your hands. The material wasn't good, or the craftsmanship either. Oh yes, *he* could tell them.

Couldn't do anything about this blind unless he got the steps. He didn't like climbing up the steps much, these days, made him come over giddy. Anyway, he'd leave the blind for now. It didn't matter, since the White Boudoir didn't face the front of the house where it would be seen as the cars came back from the funeral – and it wasn't as though the room was ever used nowadays. It was a lady's room, this, and there hadn't been a lady at Enderby for a long time now. A pity Mr Mortimer hadn't married. Always going off to Norway for fishing and to Scotland for shooting and to Switzerland for those winter sports, instead of marrying some nice young lady and settling down at home with children running about the house. It was a long time since there had been any children in the house.

And Lanscombe's mind went ranging back to a time that stood out clearly and distinctly – much more distinctly than the last twenty years or so, which were all blurred and confused and he couldn't really remember who had come and gone or indeed what they looked like. But he could remember the old days well enough.

More like a father to those young brothers and sisters of his, Mr Richard had been. Twenty-four when his father had died, and he'd pitched in right away to the business, going off every day as punctual as clockwork, and keeping the house running and everything as lavish as it could be. A very happy household with all those young ladies and gentlemen growing up. Fights and quarrels now and again, of course, and those governesses had had a bad time of it! Poor-spirited creatures, governesses, Lanscombe had always despised them. Very spirited the young ladies had been. Miss Geraldine in particular. Miss Cora, too, although she was so much younger. And now Mr Leo was dead, and Miss Laura gone too. And Mr Timothy such a sad invalid.

And Miss Geraldine dying somewhere abroad. And Mr Gordon killed in the war. Although he was the eldest, Mr Richard himself turned out the strongest of the lot. Outlived them all, he had – at least not quite because Mr Timothy was still alive and little Miss Cora who'd married that unpleasant artist chap. Twenty-five years since he'd seen her and she'd been a pretty young girl when she went off with that chap, and now he'd hardly have known her, grown so stout – and so arty-crafty in her dress! A Frenchman her husband had been, or nearly a Frenchman – and no good ever came of marrying one of *them*! But Miss Cora had always been a bit – well *simple like* you'd call it if she'd lived in a village. Always one of them in a family.

She'd remembered *him* all right. 'Why, it's Lanscombe!' she'd said and seemed ever so pleased to see him. Ah, they'd all been fond of him in the old days and when there was a dinner party they'd crept down to the pantry and he'd given them jelly and Charlotte Russe when it came out of the dining-room. They'd all known old Lanscombe, and now there was hardly anyone who remembered. Just the younger lot whom he could never keep clear in his mind and who just thought of him as a butler who'd been there a long time. A lot of strangers, he had thought, when they all arrived for the funeral – and a seedy lot of strangers at that!

Not Mrs Leo – she was different. She and Mr Leo had come here off and on ever since Mr Leo married. She was a nice lady, Mrs Leo – a *real* lady. Wore proper clothes and did her hair well and looked what she was. And the master had always been fond of her. A pity that she and Mr Leo had never had any children . . .

Lanscombe roused himself; what was he doing standing here and dreaming about old days with so much to be done? The blinds were all attended to on the ground floor now, and he'd told Janet to go upstairs and do the bedrooms. He and Janet and the cook had gone to the funeral service in the church but instead of going on to the Crematorium they'd driven back to the house to get the blinds up and the lunch ready. Cold lunch, of course, it had to be. Ham and chicken and tongue and salad. With cold lemon soufflé and apple tart to follow. Hot soup first – and he'd better go along and see that Marjorie had got it on ready to serve, for they'd be back in a minute or two now for certain.

Lanscombe broke into a shuffling trot across the room. His gaze, abstracted and uncurious, just swept up to the picture over this mantelpiece – the companion portrait to the one in the green drawing-room. It was a nice painting of white satin and pearls. The human being round whom they were draped and clasped was not nearly so impressive. Meek features, a rosebud mouth, hair parted in the middle. A woman both modest and unassuming. The only thing really worthy of note about Mrs Cornelius Abernethie had been her name – Coralie.

For over sixty years after their original appearance, Coral Cornplasters and the allied 'Coral' foot preparations still held their own. Whether there had ever been anything outstanding about Coral Cornplasters nobody could say – but they had appealed to the public fancy. On a foundation of Coral Cornplasters there had arisen this neo-Gothic palace, its acres of gardens, and the money that had paid out an income to seven sons and daughters and had allowed Richard Abernethie to die three days ago a very rich man.

II

Looking into the kitchen with a word of admonition, Lanscombe was snapped at by Marjorie, the cook. Marjorie was young, only twenty-seven, and was a constant irritation to Lanscombe as being so far removed from what his conception of a proper cook should be. She had no dignity and no proper appreciation of his, Lanscombe's, position. She frequently called the house 'a proper old mausoleum' and complained of the immense area of the kitchen, scullery and larder, saying that it was a 'day's walk to get round them all'. She had been at Enderby two years and only stayed because in the first place the money was good, and in the second because Mr Abernethie had really appreciated her cooking. She cooked very well. Janet, who stood by the kitchen table, refreshing herself with a cup of tea, was an elderly housemaid who, although enjoying frequent acid disputes with Lanscombe, was nevertheless usually in alliance with him against the younger generation as represented by Marjorie. The fourth person in the kitchen was Mrs Jacks, who 'came in' to lend assistance where it was wanted and who had much enjoyed the funeral.

'Beautiful it was,' she said with a decorous sniff as she replenished her cup. 'Nineteen cars and the church quite full and the Canon read the service beautiful, I thought. A nice fine day for it, too. Ah, poor dear Mr Abernethie, there's not many like him left in the world. Respected by all, he was.'

There was the note of a horn and the sound of a car coming up the drive, and Mrs Jacks put down her cup and exclaimed: 'Here they are.'

Marjorie turned up the gas under her large saucepan of creamy chicken soup. The large kitchen range of the days of Victorian grandeur stood cold and unused, like an altar to the past.

The cars drove up one after the other and the people issuing from them in their black clothes moved rather uncertainly across the hall and into the big green drawing-room. In the big steel grate a fire was burning, tribute to the first chill of the autumn days and calculated to counteract the further chill of standing about at a funeral.

Lanscombe entered the room, offering glasses of sherry on a silver tray.

Mr Entwhistle, senior partner of the old and respected firm of Bollard, Entwhistle, Entwhistle and Bollard, stood with his back to the fireplace warming himself. He accepted a glass of sherry, and surveyed the company with his shrewd lawyer's gaze. Not all of them were personally known to him, and he was under the necessity of sorting them out, so to speak. Introductions before the departure for the funeral had been hushed and perfunctory.

Appraising old Lanscombe first, Mr Entwhistle thought to himself, 'Getting very shaky, poor old chap – going on for ninety I shouldn't wonder. Well, he'll have that nice little annuity. Nothing for *him* to worry about. Faithful soul. No such thing as old-fashioned service nowadays. Household helps and baby sitters, God help us all! A sad world. Just as well, perhaps, poor Richard didn't last his full time. He hadn't much to live for.'

To Mr Entwhistle, who was seventy-two, Richard Abernethie's death at sixty-eight was definitely that of a man dead before his time. Mr Entwhistle had retired from active business two years ago, but as executor of Richard Abernethie's will and in respect of one of his oldest clients who was also a personal friend, he had made the journey to the North.

Reflecting in his own mind on the provisions of the will, he mentally appraised the family.

Mrs Leo, Helen, he knew well, of course. A very charming woman for whom he had both liking and respect. His eyes dwelt approvingly on her now as she stood near one of the windows. Black suited her. She had kept her figure well. He liked the clear cut features, the springing line of grey hair back from her temples and the eyes that had once been likened to cornflowers and which were still quite vividly blue.

How old was Helen now? About fifty-one or -two, he supposed. Strange that she had never married again after Leo's death. An attractive woman. Ah, but they had been very devoted, those two.

His eyes went on to Mrs Timothy. He had never known her very well. Black didn't suit her – country tweeds were her wear. A big sensible capable-looking woman. She'd always been a good devoted wife to Timothy. Looking after his health, fussing over him – fussing over him a bit too much, probably. Was there really anything the matter with Timothy? Just a hypochondriac, Mr Entwhistle suspected. Richard Abernethie had suspected so, too. 'Weak chest, of course, when he was a boy,' he had said. 'But blest if I think there's much wrong with him now.' Oh well, everybody had to have some hobby. Timothy's hobby was the all absorbing one of his own health. Was Mrs Tim taken in? Probably not – but women never admitted that sort of thing. Timothy must be quite comfortably off. He'd never been a spendthrift. However, the extra would not come amiss – not in these days of taxation. He'd probably had to retrench his scale of living a good deal since the war.

Mr Entwhistle transferred his attention to George Crossfield, Laura's son. Dubious sort of fellow Laura had married. Nobody had ever known much about him. A stockbroker he had called himself. Young George was in a solicitor's office – not a very reputable firm. Good-looking young fellow – but something a little shifty about him. He couldn't have too much to live on. Laura had been a complete fool over her investments. She'd left next to nothing when she died five years ago. A handsome romantic girl she'd been, but no money sense.

Mr Entwhistle's eyes went on from George Crossfield. Which

of the two girls was which? Ah yes, that was Rosamund, Geraldine's daughter, looking at the wax flowers on the malachite table. Pretty girl, beautiful, in fact – rather a silly face. On the stage. Repertory companies or some nonsense like that. Had married an actor, too. Good-looking fellow. '*And* knows he is,' thought Mr Entwhistle, who was prejudiced against the stage as a profession. 'Wonder what sort of a background *he* has and where he comes from.'

He looked disapprovingly at Michael Shane with his fair hair and his haggard charm.

Now Susan, Gordon's daughter, would do much better on the stage than Rosamund. More personality. A little too much personality for everyday life, perhaps. She was quite near him and Mr Entwhistle studied her covertly. Dark hair, hazel – almost golden – eyes, a sulky attractive mouth. Beside her was the husband she had just married – a chemist's assistant, he understood. Really, a chemist's assistant! In Mr Entwhistle's creed girls did not marry young men who served behind a counter. But now of course, they married *anybody*! The young man, who had a pale nondescript face and sandy hair, seemed very ill at ease. Mr Entwhistle wondered why, but decided charitably that it was the strain of meeting so many of his wife's relations.

Last in his survey Mr Entwhistle came to Cora Lansquenet. There was a certain justice in that, for Cora had decidedly been an afterthought in the family. Richard's youngest sister, she had been born when her mother was just on fifty, and that meek woman had not survived her tenth pregnancy (three children had died in infancy). Poor little Cora! All her life, Cora had been rather an embarrassment, growing up tall and gawky, and given to blurting out remarks that had always better have remained unsaid. All her elder brothers and sisters had been very kind to Cora, atoning for her deficiencies and covering her social mistakes. It had never really occurred to anyone that Cora would marry. She had not been a very attractive girl, and her rather obvious advances to visiting young men had usually caused the latter to retreat in some alarm. And then, Mr Entwhistle mused, there had come the Lansquenet business – Pierre Lansquenet, half French, whom she had come across in an Art school where she had been having very correct lessons in painting flowers in water colours. But somehow she had got into the Life class and there she had met Pierre Lansquenet and had come home and announced her intention of marrying him. Richard Abernethie had put his foot down – he hadn't liked what he saw of Pierre Lansquenet and suspected that the young man was really in search of a rich wife. But whilst he was making a few researches into Lansquenet's antecedents, Cora had bolted with the fellow and married him out of hand. They had spent most of their married life in Brittany and Cornwall and other painters' conventional haunts. Lansquenet had been a very bad painter and not, by all accounts, a very nice man, but Cora had remained devoted to him and had never forgiven her family for their attitude to him. Richard had generously made his young sister an allowance and on that they had, so Mr Entwhistle believed, lived. He doubted if Lansquenet had ever earned any money at all. He must have been dead now twelve years or more, thought Mr Entwhistle. And now here was his widow, rather cushion-like in shape and dressed in wispy artistic black with festoons of jet beads, back in the home of her girlhood, moving about and touching things and exclaiming with pleasure when she recalled some childish memory. She made very little pretence of grief at her brother's death. But then, Mr Entwhistle reflected, Cora had never pretended.

Re-entering the room Lanscombe murmured in muted tones suitable to the occasion:

'Luncheon is served.'

CHAPTER 2

After the delicious chicken soup, and plenty of cold viands accompanied by an excellent Chablis, the funeral atmosphere lightened. Nobody had really felt any deep grief for Richard Abernethie's death since none of them had had any close ties with him. Their behaviour had been suitably decorous and subdued (with the exception of the uninhibited Cora who was clearly enjoying herself) but it was now felt that the decencies had been observed and that normal conversation could be resumed. Mr Entwhistle encouraged this attitude. He was experienced in funerals and knew exactly how to set correct funeral timing.

After the meal was over, Lanscombe indicated the library for coffee. This was his feeling for niceties. The time had come when business – in other words, The Will – would be discussed. The library had the proper atmosphere for that, with its bookshelves and its heavy red velvet curtains. He served coffee to them there and then withdrew, closing the door.

After a few desultory remarks, everyone began to look tentatively at Mr Entwhistle. He responded promptly after glancing at his watch.

'I have to catch the 3.30 train,' he began.

Others, it seemed, also had to catch that train.

'As you know,' said Mr Entwhistle, 'I am the executor of Richard Abernethie's will –'

He was interrupted.

'*I* didn't know,' said Cora Lansquenet brightly. 'Are you? Did he leave me anything?'

Not for the first time, Mr Entwhistle felt that Cora was too apt to speak out of turn.

Bending a repressive glance at her he continued:

'Up to a year ago, Richard Abernethie's will was very simple. Subject to certain legacies he left everything to his son Mortimer.'

'Poor Mortimer,' said Cora. 'I do think all this infantile paralysis is *dreadful.*'

'Mortimer's death, coming so suddenly and tragically, was a great blow to Richard. It took him some months to rally from it. I pointed out to him that it might be advisable for him to make new testamentary dispositions.'

Maude Abernethie asked in her deep voice:

'What would have happened if he *hadn't* made a new will? Would it – would it all have gone to Timothy – as the next of kin, I mean?'

Mr Entwhistle opened his mouth to give a disquisition on the subject of next of kin, thought better of it, and said crisply:

'On my advice, Richard decided to make a new will. First of all, however, he decided to get better acquainted with the younger generation.'

'He had us upon appro,' said Susan with a sudden rich laugh. 'First George and then Greg and me, and then Rosamund and Michael.'

Gregory Banks said sharply, his thin face flushing:

'I don't think you ought to put it like that, Susan. On appro, indeed!'

'But that was what it was, wasn't it, Mr Entwhistle?'

'Did he leave *me* anything?' repeated Cora.

Mr Entwhistle coughed and spoke rather coldly:

'I propose to send you all copies of the will. I can read it to you in full now if you like but its legal phraseology may seem to you rather obscure. Briefly it amounts to this: After certain small bequests and a substantial legacy to Lanscombe to purchase an annuity, the bulk of the estate – a very considerable one – is to be divided into six equal portions. Four of these, after all duties are paid, are to go to Richard's brother Timothy, his nephew George Crossfield, his niece Susan Banks, and his niece Rosamund Shane. The other two portions are to be held upon trust and the income from them paid to Mrs Helen Abernethie, the widow of his brother Leo; and to his sister Mrs Cora Lansquenet, during their lifetime. The capital after their death to be divided between the other four beneficiaries or their issue.'

'That's *very* nice!' said Cora Lansquenet with real appreciation. 'An income! How much?'

'I – er – can't say exactly at present. Death duties, of course, will be heavy and –'

'Can't you give me any idea?'

Mr Entwhistle realized that Cora must be appeased.

'Possibly somewhere in the neighbourhood of three to four thousand a year.'

'Goody!' said Cora. 'I shall go to Capri.'

Helen Abernethie said softly:

'How very kind and generous of Richard. I do appreciate his affection towards me.'

'He was very fond of you,' said Mr Entwhistle. 'Leo was his favourite brother and your visits to him were always much appreciated after Leo died.'

Helen said regretfully:

'I wish I had realized how ill he was – I came up to see him not long before he died, but although I knew he *had* been ill, I did not think it was serious.'

'It was always serious,' said Mr Entwhistle. 'But he did not want it talked about and I do not believe that anybody expected the end to come as soon as it did. The doctor was quite surprised, I know.'

'"*Suddenly, at his residence*" that's what it said in the paper,' said Cora, nodding her head. 'I wondered then.'

'It was a shock to all of us,' said Maude Abernethie. 'It upset poor Timothy dreadfully. So sudden, he kept saying. So *sudden.*'

'Still, it's been hushed up very nicely, hasn't it?' said Cora.

Everybody stared at her and she seemed a little flustered.

'I think you're all quite right,' she said hurriedly. '*Quite* right. I mean – it can't do any good – making it public. Very unpleasant for everybody. It should be kept strictly in the family.'

The faces turned towards her looked even more blank.

Mr Entwhistle leaned forward:

'Really, Cora, I'm afraid I don't quite understand what you mean.'

Cora Lansquenet looked round at the family in wide-eyed surprise. She tilted her head on one side with a bird-like movement.

'But he *was* murdered, wasn't he?' she said.

CHAPTER 3

I

Travelling to London in the corner of a first-class carriage Mr Entwhistle gave himself up to somewhat uneasy thought over that extraordinary remark made by Cora Lansquenet. Of course Cora was a rather unbalanced and excessively stupid woman, and she had been noted, even as a girl, for the embarrassing manner in which she had blurted out unwelcome truths. At least, he didn't mean *truths* – that was *quite* the wrong word to use. Awkward statements – that was a much better term.

In his mind he went back over the immediate sequence to that unfortunate remark. The combined stare of many startled and disapproving eyes had roused Cora to a sense of the enormity of what she had said.

Maude had exclaimed, '*Really*, Cora!' George had said, 'My dear Aunt Cora.' Somebody else had said, 'What *do* you mean?'

And at once Cora Lansquenet, abashed, and convicted of enormity, had burst into fluttering phrases.

'Oh I'm sorry – I didn't mean – oh, of course, it was very stupid of me, but I did think from what he said – Oh, of course I know it's quite all right, but his death was so *sudden* – please forget that I said anything at all – I didn't mean to be so stupid – I know I'm always saying the wrong thing.'

And then the momentary upset had died down and there had been a practical discussion about the disposition of the late Richard Abernethie's personal effects. The house and its contents, Mr Entwhistle supplemented, would be put up for sale.

Cora's unfortunate gaffe had been forgotten. After all, Cora had always been, if not subnormal, at any rate embarrassingly naïve. She had never had any idea of what should or should not be said. At nineteen it had not mattered so much. The mannerisms of an *enfant terrible* can persist to then, but an *enfant terrible* of nearly fifty is decidedly disconcerting. To blurt out unwelcome truths –

Mr Entwhistle's train of thought came to an abrupt check. It was the second time that that disturbing word had occurred. *Truths*. And why was it so disturbing? Because, of course, that had always been at the bottom of the embarrassment that Cora's outspoken comments had caused. It was because her naïve statements had been either true or had contained some grain of truth that they had been so embarrassing!

Although in the plump woman of forty-nine, Mr Entwhistle had been able to see little resemblance to the gawky girl of earlier days, certain of Cora's mannerisms had persisted – the slight bird-like twist of the head as she brought out a particularly outrageous remark – a kind of air of pleased expectancy. In just such a way had Cora once commented on the figure of the kitchen-maid. 'Mollie can hardly get near the kitchen table, her stomach sticks out so. It's only been like that the last month or two. I wonder *why* she's getting so fat?'

Cora had been quickly hushed. The Abernethie household was Victorian in tone. The kitchen-maid had disappeared from the premises the next day, and after due inquiry the second gardener had been ordered to make an honest woman of her and had been presented with a cottage in which to do so.

Far-off memories – but they had their point . . .

Mr Entwhistle examined his uneasiness more closely. What was there in Cora's ridiculous remarks that had remained to tease his subconscious in this manner? Presently he isolated two phrases. 'I did think from what he said –' and 'his death was so sudden . . .'

Mr Entwhistle examined that last remark first. Yes, Richard's death could, in a fashion, be considered sudden. Mr Entwhistle had discussed Richard's health both with Richard himself and with his doctor. The latter had indicated plainly that a long life could not be expected. If Mr Abernethie took reasonable care of himself he might live two or even three years. Perhaps longer – but that was unlikely. In any case the doctor had anticipated no collapse in the near future.

Well, the doctor had been wrong – but doctors, as they were the first to admit themselves, could never be sure about the individual reaction of a patient to disease. Cases given up, unexpectedly recovered. Patients on the way to recovery relapsed and died. So much depended on the vitality of the patient. On his own inner urge to live

And Richard Abernethie, though a strong and vigorous man, had had no great incentive to live.

For six months previously his only surviving son, Mortimer, had contracted infantile paralysis and had died within a week. His death had been a shock greatly augmented by the fact that he had been such a particularly strong and vital young man. A keen sportsman, he was also a good athlete and was one of those people of whom it was said that he had never had a day's illness in his life. He was on the point of becoming engaged to a very charming girl and his father's hopes for the future were centred in this dearly loved and thoroughly satisfactory son of his.

Instead had come tragedy. And besides the sense of personal loss, the future had held little to stir Richard Abernethie's interest. One son had died in infancy, the second without issue. He had no grandchildren. There was, in fact, no one of the Abernethie name to come after him, and he was the holder of a vast fortune with wide business interests which he himself still controlled to a certain extent. Who was to succeed to that fortune and to the control of those interests?

That this had worried Richard deeply, Entwhistle knew. His only surviving brother was very much of an invalid. There remained the younger generation. It had been in Richard's mind, the lawyer thought, though his friend had not actually said so, to choose one definite successor, though minor legacies would probably have been made. Anyway, as Entwhistle knew, within the last six months Richard Abernethie had invited to stay with him, in succession, his nephew George, his niece Susan and her husband, his niece Rosamund and her husband, and his sister-in-law, Mrs Leo Abernethie. It was amongst the first three, so the lawyer thought, that Abernethie had looked for his successor. Helen Abernethie, he thought, had been asked out of personal affection and even possibly as someone to consult, for Richard had always held a high opinion of her good sense and practical judgement. Mr Entwhistle also remembered that sometime during that six months period Richard had paid a short visit to his brother Timothy.

The net result had been the will which the lawyer now carried in his brief-case. An equable distribution of property. The only conclusion that could be drawn, therefore, was that he had been disappointed both in his nephew, and in his nieces or perhaps in his nieces' husbands.

As far as Mr Entwhistle knew, he had not invited his sister, Cora Lansquenet, to visit him – and that brought the lawyer back to that first disturbing phrase that Cora had let slip so incoherently – 'but I did think from what he *said* –'

What had Richard Abernethie said? And when had he said it? If Cora had not been to Enderby, then Richard Abernethie must have visited her at the artistic village in Berkshire where she had a cottage. Or was it something that Richard had said in a letter?

Mr Entwhistle frowned. Cora, of course, was a very stupid woman. She could easily have misinterpreted a phrase, and twisted its meaning. But he did wonder what the phrase could have been . . .

There was enough uneasiness in him to make him consider the possibility of approaching Mrs Lansquenet on the subject. Not too soon. Better not make it seem of importance. But he *would* like to know just what it was that Richard Abernethie had said to her which had led her to pipe up so briskly with that outrageous question:

'*But he was murdered, wasn't he?*'

II

In a third-class carriage, farther along the train, Gregory Banks said to his wife:

'That aunt of yours must be completely bats!'

'Aunt Cora?' Susan was vague. 'Oh, yes, I believe she was always a bit simple or something.'

George Crossfield, sitting opposite, said sharply:

'She really ought to be stopped from going about saying things like that. It might put ideas into people's heads.'

Rosamund Shane, intent on outlining the cupid's bow of her mouth with lipstick, murmured vaguely:

'I don't suppose anyone would pay any attention to what a frump like that says. The most peculiar clothes and lashings and lashings of jet –'

'Well, I think it ought to be stopped,' said George.

'All right, darling,' laughed Rosamund, putting away her lipstick and contemplating her image with satisfaction in the mirror. 'You stop it.'

Her husband said unexpectedly:

'I think George is right. It's so easy to set people talking.'

'Well, would it matter?' Rosamund contemplated the question. The cupid's bow lifted at the corners in a smile. 'It might really be rather fun.'

'Fun?' Four voices spoke.

'Having a murder in the family,' said Rosamund. 'Thrilling, you know!'

It occurred to that nervous and unhappy young man Gregory Banks that Susan's cousin, setting aside her attractive exterior, might have some faint points of resemblance to her Aunt Cora. Her next words rather confirmed his impression.

'If he was murdered,' said Rosamund, 'who do you think did it?'

Her gaze travelled thoughtfully round the carriage.

'His death has been awfully convenient for all of us,' she said thoughtfully. 'Michael and I are absolutely on our beam ends.

Mick's had a really good part offered to him in the Sandbourne show if he can afford to wait for it. Now we'll be in clover. We'll be able to back our own show if we want to. As a matter of fact there's a play with a simply wonderful part –'

Nobody listened to Rosamund's ecstatic disquisition. Their attention had shifted to their own immediate future.

'Touch and go,' thought George to himself. 'Now I can put that money back and nobody will ever know . . . But it's been a near shave.'

Gregory closed his eyes as he lay back against the seat. Escape from bondage.

Susan said in her clear rather hard voice, 'I'm very sorry, of course, for poor old Uncle Richard. But then he *was* very old, and Mortimer had died, and he'd nothing to live for and it would have been awful for him to go on as an invalid year after year. *Much* better for him to pop off suddenly like this with no fuss.'

Her hard confident young eyes softened as they watched her husband's absorbed face. She adored Greg. She sensed vaguely that Greg cared for her less than she cared for him – but that only strengthened her passion. Greg was hers, she'd do anything for him. Anything at all . . .

III

Maude Abernethie, changing her dress for dinner at Enderby (for she was staying the night), wondered if she ought to have offered to stay longer to help Helen out with the sorting and clearing of the house. There would be all Richard's personal things . . . There might be letters . . . All important papers, she supposed, had already been taken possession of by Mr Entwhistle. And it really was necessary for her to get back to Timothy as soon as possible. He fretted so when she was not there to look after him. She hoped he would be pleased about the will and not annoyed. He had expected, she knew, that most of Richard's fortune would come to *him*. After all, he was the only surviving Abernethie. Richard could surely have trusted *him* to look after the younger generation. Yes, she was afraid Timothy *would* be annoyed . . . And that was so bad for his digestion. And really, when he was annoyed, Timothy could become quite unreasonable. There were times when he seemed to lose his sense of proportion . . . She wondered if she ought to speak to Dr Barton about it . . . Those sleeping pills – Timothy had been taking far too many of them lately – he got so angry when she wanted to keep the bottle for him. But they could be dangerous – Dr Barton had said so – you could get drowsy and forget you'd taken them – and then take more. And then anything might happen! There certainly weren't as many left in the bottle as there ought to be . . . Timothy was really very naughty about medicines. He wouldn't listen to her . . . He was very difficult sometimes.

She sighed – then brightened. Things were going to be much easier now. The garden, for instance –

IV

Helen Abernethie sat by the fire in the green drawing-room waiting for Maude to come down to dinner.

She looked round her, remembering old days here with Leo and the others. It had been a happy house. But a house like this needed *people*. It needed children and servants and big meals and plenty of roaring fires in winter. It had been a sad house when it had been lived in by one old man who had lost his son . . .

Who would buy it, she wondered? Would it be turned into an hotel, or an institute, or perhaps one of those hostels for young people? That was what happened to these vast houses nowadays. No one would buy them to live in. It would be pulled down, perhaps, and the whole estate built over. It made her sad to think of that, but she pushed the sadness aside resolutely. It did one no good to dwell on the past. This house, and happy days here, and Richard, and Leo, all that was good, but it was over. She had her own interests . . . And now, with the income Richard had left her, she would be able to keep on the villa in Cyprus and do all the things she had planned to do.

How worried she had been lately over money – taxation – all those investments going wrong . . . Now, thanks to Richard's money, all that was over . . .

Poor Richard. To die in his sleep like that had been really a great mercy . . . *Suddenly on the 22nd* – she supposed that that was what had put the idea into Cora's head. Really Cora was outrageous! She always had been. Helen remembered meeting her once abroad, soon after her marriage to Pierre Lansquenet. She had been particularly foolish and fatuous that day, twisting her head sideways, and making dogmatic statements about painting, and particularly about her husband's painting, which must have been most uncomfortable for him. No man could like his wife appearing such a fool. And Cora was a fool! Oh, well, poor thing, she couldn't help it, and that husband of hers hadn't treated her too well.

Helen's gaze rested absently on a bouquet of wax flowers that stood on a round malachite table. Cora had been sitting beside it when they had all been sitting round waiting to start for the church. She had been full of reminiscences and delighted recognitions of various things and was clearly so pleased at being back in her old home that she had completely lost sight of the reason for which they were assembled.

'But perhaps,' thought Helen, 'she was just less of a hypocrite than the rest of us . . .'

Cora had never been one for observing the conventions. Look at the way she had plumped out that question: 'But he *was* murdered, wasn't he?'

The faces all round, startled, shocked, staring at her! Such a variety of expressions there must have been on those faces . . .

And suddenly, seeing the picture clearly in her mind, Helen frowned . . . There was something wrong with that picture . . .

Something . . . ?

Somebody . . . ?

Was it an expression on someone's face? Was that it? Something that – how could she put it? – ought not to have been there . . . ?

She didn't know . . . she couldn't place it . . . but there had been something – somewhere – *wrong*.

V

Meanwhile, in the buffet at Swindon, a lady in wispy mourning and festoons of jet was eating bath buns and drinking tea and looking forward to the future. She had no premonitions of disaster. She was happy.

These cross-country journeys were certainly tiring. It would have been easier to get back to Lytchett St Mary via London – and not so very much more expensive. Ah, but expense didn't matter now. Still, she would have had to travel with the family – probably having to talk all the way. Too much of an effort.

No, better to go home cross-country. These bath buns were really excellent. Extraordinary how hungry a funeral made you feel. The soup at Enderby had been delicious – and so was the cold soufflé.

How smug people were – and what hypocrites! All those faces – when she'd said that about murder! The way they'd all looked at her!

Well, it had been the right thing to say. She nodded her head in satisfied approval of herself. Yes, it had been the right thing to do.

She glanced up at the clock. Five minutes before her train went. She drank up her tea. Not very good tea. She made a grimace.

For a moment or two she sat dreaming. Dreaming of the future unfolding before her . . . She smiled like a happy child.

She was really going to enjoy herself at last . . . She went out to the small branch line train busily making plans . . .

CHAPTER 4

I

Mr Entwhistle passed a very restless night. He felt so tired and so unwell in the morning that he did not get up.

His sister, who kept house for him, brought up his breakfast on a tray and explained to him severely how wrong he had been to go gadding off to the North of England at his age and in his frail state of health.

Mr Entwhistle contented himself with saying that Richard Abernethie had been a very old friend.

'Funerals!' said his sister with deep disapproval. 'Funerals are absolutely fatal for a man of your age! You'll be taken off as suddenly as your precious Mr Abernethie was if you don't take more care of yourself.'

The word 'suddenly' made Mr Entwhistle wince. It also silenced him. He did not argue.

He was well aware of what had made him flinch at the word *suddenly*.

Cora Lansquenet! What she had suggested was definitely quite impossible, but all the same he would like to find out exactly why she had suggested it. Yes, he would go down to Lytchett St Mary and see her. He could pretend that it was business connected with probate, that he needed her signature. No need to let her guess that he had paid any attention to her silly remark. But he would go down and see her – and he would do it soon.

He finished his breakfast and lay back on his pillows and read *The Times*. He found *The Times* very soothing.

It was about a quarter to six that evening when his telephone rang.

He picked it up. The voice at the other end of the wire was that of Mr James Parrott, the present second partner of Bollard, Entwhistle, Entwhistle and Bollard.

'Look here, Entwhistle,' said Mr Parrott, 'I've just been rung up by the police from a place called Lytchett St Mary.'

'Lytchett St Mary?'

'Yes. It seems –' Mr Parrott paused a moment. He seemed embarrassed. 'It's about a Mrs Cora Lansquenet. Wasn't she one of the heirs of the Abernethie estate?'

'Yes, of course. I saw her at the funeral yesterday.'

'Oh? She was at the funeral, was she?'

'Yes. What about her?'

'Well,' Mr Parrott sounded apologetic. 'She's – it's really *most* extraordinary – she's been well – *murdered.*'

Mr Parrott said the last word with the uttermost deprecation. It was not the sort of word, he suggested, that ought to mean anything to the firm of Bollard, Entwhistle, Entwhistle and Bollard.

'*Murdered?*'

'Yes – yes – I'm afraid so. Well, I mean, there's no doubt about it.'

'How did the police get on to us?'

'Her companion, or housekeeper, or whatever she is – a Miss Gilchrist. The police asked for the name of her nearest relative or her solicitors. And this Miss Gilchrist seemed rather doubtful about relatives and their addresses, but she knew about us. So they got through at once.'

'What makes them think she was murdered?' demanded Mr Entwhistle.

Mr Parrott sounded apologetic again.

'Oh well, it seems there can't be any doubt about *that* – I mean it was a hatchet or something of that kind – a very violent sort of crime.'

'Robbery?'

'That's the idea. A window was smashed and there are some trinkets missing and drawers pulled out and all that, but the police seem to think there might be something – well – phony about it.'

'What time did it happen?'

'Some time between two and four-thirty this afternoon.'

'Where was the housekeeper?'

'Changing library books in Reading. She got back about five o'clock and found Mrs Lansquenet dead. The police want to know if we've any idea of who could have been likely to attack her. I said,' Mr Parrott's voice sounded outraged, 'that I thought it was a most unlikely thing to happen.'

'Yes, of course.'

'It *must* be some half-witted local oaf – who thought there might be something to steal and then lost his head and attacked her. That must be it – eh, don't you think so, Entwhistle?'

'Yes, yes . . .' Mr Entwhistle spoke absentmindedly.

Parrott was right, he told himself. That was what must have happened . . .

But uncomfortably he heard Cora's voice saying brightly:

'*He was murdered, wasn't he?*'

Such a fool, Cora. Always had been. Rushing in where angels fear to tread . . . Blurting out unpleasant truths . . .

Truths!

That blasted word again . . .

II

Mr Entwhistle and Inspector Morton looked at each other appraisingly.

In his neat precise manner Mr Entwhistle had placed at the Inspector's disposal all the relevant facts about Cora Lansquenet. Her upbringing, her marriage, her widowhood, her financial position, her relatives.

'Mr Timothy Abernethie is her only surviving brother and her next of kin, but he is a recluse and an invalid, and is quite unable to leave home. He has empowered me to act for him and to make all such arrangements as may be necessary.'

The Inspector nodded. It was a relief for him to have this shrewd elderly solicitor to deal with. Moreover he hoped that the lawyer might be able to give him some assistance in solving what was beginning to look like a rather puzzling problem.

He said:

'I understand from Miss Gilchrist that Mrs Lansquenet had been North, to the funeral of an elder brother, on the day before her death?'

'That is so, Inspector. I myself was there.'

'There was nothing unusual in her manner – nothing strange – or apprehensive?'

Mr Entwhistle raised his eyebrows in well-simulated surprise.

'Is it customary for there to be something strange in the manner of a person who is shortly to be murdered?' he asked.

The Inspector smiled rather ruefully.

'I'm not thinking of her being "fey" or having a premonition. No, I'm just hunting around for something – well, something out of the ordinary.'

'I don't think I quite understand you, Inspector,' said Mr Entwhistle.

'It's not a very easy case to understand, Mr Entwhistle. Say someone watched the Gilchrist woman come out of the house at about two o'clock and go along to the village and the bus stop. This someone then deliberately takes the hatchet that was lying by the woodshed, smashes the kitchen window with it, gets into the house, goes upstairs, attacks Mrs Lansquenet with the hatchet – and attacks her savagely. Six or eight blows were struck.' Mr Entwhistle flinched – 'Oh, yes, quite a brutal crime. Then the intruder pulls out a few drawers, scoops up a few trinkets – worth perhaps a tenner in all, and clears off.'

'She was in bed?'

'Yes. It seems she returned late from the North the night before, exhausted and very excited. She'd come into some legacy as I understand?'

'Yes.'

'She slept very badly and woke with a terrible headache. She had several cups of tea and took some dope for her head and then told Miss Gilchrist not to disturb her till lunch-time. She felt no better and decided to take two sleeping pills. She then sent Miss Gilchrist into Reading by the bus to change some library books. She'd have been drowsy, if not already asleep, when this man broke in. He could have taken what he wanted by means of threats, or he could easily have gagged her. A hatchet, deliberately taken up with him from outside, seems excessive.'

'He may just have meant to threaten her with it,' Mr Entwhistle suggested. 'If she showed fight then –'

'According to the medical evidence there is no sign that she did. Everything seems to show that she was lying on her side sleeping peacefully when she was attacked.'

Mr Entwhistle shifted uneasily in his chair.

'One does hear of these brutal and rather senseless murders,' he pointed out.

'Oh yes, yes, that's probably what it will turn out to be. There's an alert out, of course, for any suspicious character. Nobody local is concerned, we're pretty sure of that. The locals are all accounted for satisfactorily. Most people are at work at that time of day. Of course her cottage is up a lane outside the village proper. Anyone could get there easily without being seen. There's a maze of lanes all round the village. It was a fine morning and there has been no rain for some days, so there aren't any distinctive car tracks to go by – in case anyone came by car.'

'You think someone came by car?' Mr Entwhistle asked sharply.

The Inspector shrugged his shoulders. 'I don't know. All I'm saying is there are curious features about the case. These, for instance –' He shoved across his desk a handful of things – a trefoil-shaped brooch with small pearls, a brooch set with amethysts, a small string of pearls, and a garnet bracelet.

'Those are the things that were taken from her jewel box. They were found just outside the house shoved into a bush.'

'Yes – yes, that *is* rather curious. Perhaps if her assailant was frightened at what he had done –'

'Quite. But he would probably then have left them upstairs in her room . . . Of course a panic may have come over him between the bedroom and the front gate.'

Mr Entwhistle said quietly:

'Or they may, as you are suggesting, have only been taken as a blind.'

'Yes, several possibilities . . . Of course this Gilchrist woman may have done it. Two women living alone together – you never know what quarrels or resentments or passions may have been aroused. Oh yes, we're taking that possibility into consideration as well. But it doesn't seem very likely. From all accounts they were on quite amicable terms.' He paused before going on. 'According to you, nobody stands to gain by Mrs Lansquenet's death?'

The lawyer shifted uneasily.

'I didn't quite say that.'

Inspector Morton looked up sharply.

'I thought you said that Mrs Lansquenet's source of income was an allowance made to her by her brother and that as far as you knew she had no property or means of her own.'

'That is so. Her husband died a bankrupt, and from what I knew of her as a girl and since, I should be surprised if she had ever saved or accumulated any money.

'The cottage itself is rented, not her own, and the few sticks of furniture aren't anything to write home about, even in these days. Some spurious "cottage oak" and some arty painted stuff. Whoever she's left them to won't gain much – if she's made a will, that is to say.'

Mr Entwhistle shook his head.

'I know nothing about her will. I had not seen her for many years, you must understand.'

'Then, what exactly did you mean just now? You had something in mind, I think?'

'Yes. Yes, I did. I wished to be strictly accurate.'

'Were you referring to the legacy you mentioned? The one that her brother left her? Had she the power to dispose of that by will?'

'No, not in the sense you mean. She had no power to dispose of the capital. Now that she is dead, it will be divided amongst the five other beneficiaries of Richard Abernethie's will. That is what I meant. All five of them will benefit automatically by her death.'

The Inspector looked disappointed.

'Oh, I thought we were on to something. Well, there certainly seems no motive there for anyone to come and swipe her with a hatchet. Looks as though it's some chap with a screw loose – one of these adolescent criminals, perhaps – a lot of them about. And then he lost his nerve and bushed the trinkets and ran . . . Yes, it must be that. Unless it's the highly respectable Miss Gilchrist, and I must say that seems unlikely.'

'When did she find the body?'

'Not until just about five o'clock. She came back from Reading by the 4.50 bus. She arrived back at the cottage, let herself in by the front door, and went into the kitchen and put the kettle on for tea. There was no sound from Mrs Lansquenet's room, but Miss Gilchrist assumed that she was still sleeping. Then Miss Gilchrist noticed the kitchen window; the glass was all over the floor. Even then, she thought at first it might have been done by a boy with a ball or a catapult. She went upstairs and peeped very gently into Mrs Lansquenet's room to see if she were asleep or if she was ready for some tea. Then of course, she let loose, shrieked, and rushed down the lane to the nearest neighbour. Her story seems perfectly consistent and there was no trace of blood in her room or in the bathroom, or on her clothes. No. I don't think Miss Gilchrist had anything to do with it. The doctor got there at half-past five. He puts the time of death not later than four-thirty – and probably much nearer two o'clock, so it looks as though whoever it was, was hanging round waiting for Miss Gilchrist to leave the cottage.'

The lawyer's face twitched slightly. Inspector Morton went on: 'You'll be going to see Miss Gilchrist, I suppose?'

'I thought of doing so.'

'I should be glad if you would. She's told us, I think, everything that she can, but you never know. Sometimes, in conversation, some point or other may crop up. She's a trifle old maidish – but quite a sensible, practical woman – and she's really been most helpful and efficient.'

He paused and then said:

'The body's at the mortuary. If you would like to see it –'

Mr Entwhistle assented, though with no enthusiasm.

Some few minutes later he stood looking down at the mortal remains of Cora Lansquenet. She had been savagely attacked and the henna dyed fringe was clotted and stiffened with blood. Mr Entwhistle's lips tightened and he looked away queasily.

Poor little Cora. How eager she had been the day before yesterday to know whether her brother had left her anything. What rosy anticipations she must have had of the future. What a lot of silly things she could have done – and enjoyed doing – with the money.

Poor Cora . . . How short a time those anticipations had lasted.

No one had gained by her death – not even the brutal assailant who had thrust away those trinkets as he fled. Five people had a few thousands more of capital – but the capital they had already received was probably more than sufficient for them. No, there could be no motive there.

Funny that murder should have been running in Cora's mind the very day before she herself was murdered.

'*He was murdered, wasn't he?*'

Such a ridiculous thing to say. Ridiculous! Quite ridiculous! Much too ridiculous to mention to Inspector Morton.

Of course, after he had seen Miss Gilchrist . . .

Supposing that Miss Gilchrist, although it was unlikely, could throw any light on what Richard had said to Cora.

'*I thought from what he said –*' What *had* Richard said?

'I must see Miss Gilchrist at once,' said Mr Entwhistle to himself.

III

Miss Gilchrist was a spare faded-looking woman with short, iron-grey hair. She had one of those indeterminate faces that women around fifty so often acquire.

She greeted Mr Entwhistle warmly.

'I'm *so* glad you have come, Mr Entwhistle. I really know so *little* about Mrs Lansquenet's family, and of course I've never, never had anything to do with a *murder* before. It's too dreadful!'

Mr Entwhistle felt quite sure that Miss Gilchrist had never before had anything to do with murder. Indeed, her reaction to it was very much that of his partner.

'One *reads* about them, of course,' said Miss Gilchrist, relegating crimes to their proper sphere. 'And even *that* I'm not very fond of doing. So *sordid*, most of them.'

Following her into the sitting-room Mr Entwhistle was looking sharply about him. There was a strong smell of oil paint. The cottage was overcrowded, less by furniture, which was much as Inspector Morton had described it, than by pictures. The walls were covered with pictures, mostly very dark and dirty oil paintings. But there were water-colour sketches as well, and one or two still lifes. Smaller pictures were stacked on the window-seat.

'Mrs Lansquenet used to buy them at sales,' Miss Gilchrist explained. 'It was a great interest to her, poor dear. She went to all the sales round about. Pictures go so cheap, nowadays, a mere song. She never paid more than a pound for any of them, sometimes only a few shillings, and there was a wonderful chance, she always said, of picking up something worth while. She used to say that this was an Italian Primitive that might be worth a lot of money.'

Mr Entwhistle looked at the Italian Primitive pointed out to him dubiously. Cora, he reflected, had never really known anything about pictures. He'd eat his hat if any of these daubs were worth a five pound note!

'Of course,' said Miss Gilchrist, noticing his expression, and quick to sense his reaction, 'I don't know much myself, though my father was a painter – not a very successful one, I'm afraid. But I used to do water-colours myself as a girl and I heard a lot of talk about painting and that made it nice for Mrs Lansquenet to have someone she could talk to about painting and who'd understand. Poor dear soul, she cared so much about artistic things.'

'You were fond of her?'

A foolish question, he told himself. Could she possibly answer 'no'? Cora, he thought, must have been a tiresome woman to live with.

'Oh *yes*,' said Miss Gilchrist. 'We got on *very* well together. In some ways, you know, Mrs Lansquenet was just like a child. She said anything that came into her head. I don't know that her *judgement* was always very good –'

One does not say of the dead – 'She was a thoroughly silly woman' – Mr Entwhistle said, 'She was not in any sense an intellectual woman.'

'No – no – perhaps not. But she was very shrewd, Mr

Entwhistle. Really very shrewd. It quite surprised me sometimes – how she managed to hit the nail on the head.'

Mr Entwhistle looked at Miss Gilchrist with more interest. He thought that she was no fool herself.

'You were with Mrs Lansquenet for some years, I think?'

'Three and a half.'

'You – er – acted as companion and also did the – er – well – looked after the house?'

It was evident that he had touched on a delicate subject. Miss Gilchrist flushed a little.

'Oh yes, indeed. I did most of the cooking – I *quite* enjoy cooking – and did some dusting and light housework. None of the *rough*, of course.' Miss Gilchrist's tone expressed a firm principle. Mr Entwhistle, who had no idea what 'the rough' was, made a soothing murmur.

'Mrs Panter from the village came in for that. Twice a week regularly. You see, Mr Entwhistle, I could not have contemplated being in any way a *servant*. When my little tea-shop failed – such a disaster – it was the war, you know. A delightful place. I called it the Willow Tree and all the china was blue willow pattern – sweetly pretty – and the cakes *really* good – I've always had a hand with cakes and scones. Yes, I was doing really well and then the war came and supplies were cut down and the whole thing went bankrupt – a war casualty, that is what I always say, and I try to think of it like that. I lost the little money my father left me that I had invested in it, and of course I had to look round for something to do. I'd never been trained for anything. So I went to one lady but it didn't answer at all – she was so rude and overbearing – and then I did some office work – but I didn't like that at all, and then I came to Mrs Lansquenet and we suited each other from the start – her husband being an artist and everything.' Miss Gilchrist came to a breathless stop and added mournfully: 'But how I loved my dear, dear little tea-shop. Such *nice* people used to come to it!'

Looking at Miss Gilchrist, Mr Entwhistle felt a sudden stab of recognition – a composite picture of hundreds of ladylike figures approaching him in numerous Bay Trees, Ginger Cats, Blue Parrots, Willow Trees and Cosy Corners, all chastely encased in blue or pink or orange overalls and taking orders for pots of china tea and cakes. Miss Gilchrist had a Spiritual Home –

a lady-like tea-shop of Ye Olde Worlde variety with a suitable genteel clientèle. There must, he thought, be large numbers of Miss Gilchrists all over the country, all looking much alike with mild patient faces and obstinate upper lips and slightly wispy grey hair.

Miss Gilchrist went on:

'But really I must not talk about myself. The police have been very kind and considerate. Very kind indeed. An Inspector Morton came over from headquarters and he was *most* understanding. He even arranged for me to go and spend the night at Mrs Lake's down the lane but I said "No." I felt it my duty to stay here with all Mrs Lansquenet's nice things in the house. They took the – the –' Miss Gilchrist gulped a little – 'the body away, of course, and locked up the room, and the Inspector told me there would be a constable on duty in the kitchen all night – because of the broken window – it has been reglazed this morning, I am glad to say – where was I? Oh yes, so I said I should be *quite* all right in my own room, though I must confess I *did* pull the chest of drawers across the door and put a big jug of water on the window-sill. One never knows – and if by any chance it *was* a maniac – one does hear of such things . . .'

Here Miss Gilchrist ran down. Mr Entwhistle said quickly:

'I am in possession of all the main facts. Inspector Morton gave them to me. But if it would not distress you too much to give me your own account –?'

'Of course, Mr Entwhistle. I know *just* what you feel. The police are so impersonal, are they not? Rightly so, of course.'

'Mrs Lansquenet got back from the funeral the night before last,' Mr Entwhistle prompted.

'Yes, her train didn't get in until quite late. I had ordered a taxi to meet it as she told me to. She was very tired, poor dear – as was only natural – but on the whole she was in quite good spirits.'

'Yes, yes. Did she talk about the funeral at all?'

'Just a little. I gave her a cup of hot milk – she didn't want anything else – and she told me that the church had been quite full and lots and lots of flowers – oh! and she said that she was sorry not to have seen her other brother – Timothy – was it?'

'Yes, Timothy.'

'She said it was over twenty years since she had seen him and that she hoped he would have been there, but she quite realized he would have thought it better not to come under the circumstances, but that his wife was there and that she'd never been able to stand Maude – oh dear, I *do* beg your pardon, Mr Entwhistle – it just slipped out – I never meant –'

'Not at all. Not at all,' said Mr Entwhistle encouragingly. 'I am no relation, you know. And I believe that Cora and her sister-in-law never hit it off very well.'

'Well, she almost said as much. "I always knew Maude would grow into one of those bossy interfering women," is what she said. And then she was very tired and said she'd go to bed at once – I'd got her hot-water bottle in all ready – and she went up.'

'She said nothing else that you can remember specially?'

'She had no *premonition*, Mr Entwhistle, if that is what you mean. I'm sure of that. She was really, you know, in remarkably good spirits – apart from tiredness and the – the sad occasion. She asked me how I'd like to go to Capri. To Capri! Of course I said it would be too wonderful – it's a thing I'd never dreamed I'd ever do – and she said, "We'll go!" Just like that. I gathered – of course it wasn't actually *mentioned* – that her brother had left her an annuity or something of the kind.'

Mr Entwhistle nodded.

'Poor dear. Well, I'm glad she had the pleasure of planning – at all events.' Miss Gilchrist sighed and murmured wistfully, 'I don't suppose I shall ever go to Capri now . . .'

'And the next morning?' Mr Entwhistle prompted, oblivious of Miss Gilchrist's disappointments.

'The next morning Mrs Lansquenet wasn't at all well. Really, she looked dreadful. She'd hardly slept at all, she told me. Nightmares. "It's because you were overtired yesterday," I told her, and she said maybe it was. She had her breakfast in bed, and she didn't get up all the morning, but at lunch-time she told me that she still hadn't been able to sleep. "I feel so restless," she said. "I keep thinking of things and wondering." And then she said she'd take some sleeping tablets and try and get a good sleep in the afternoon. And she wanted me to go over by bus to Reading and change her two library books, because she'd finished them both on the train journey and she hadn't got anything to read. Usually two books lasted her nearly a week. So I went off just after two and that – and that – was the last time –' Miss Gilchrist began to sniff. 'She must have been asleep, you know. She wouldn't have heard anything and the Inspector assures me that she didn't suffer . . . He thinks the first blow killed her. Oh dear, it makes me quite sick even to *think* of it!'

'Please, please. I've no wish to take you any further over what happened. All I wanted was to hear what you could tell me about Mrs Lansquenet before the tragedy.'

'Very natural, I'm sure. Do tell her relations that apart from having such a bad night she was really very happy and looking forward to the future.'

Mr Entwhistle paused before asking his next question. He wanted to be careful not to lead the witness.

'She did not mention any of her relations in particular?'

'No, no, I don't think so.' Miss Gilchrist considered. 'Except what she said about being sorry not to see her brother Timothy.'

'She did not speak at all about her brother's decease? The – er – cause of it? Anything like that?'

'No.'

There was no sign of alertness in Miss Gilchrist's face. Mr Entwhistle felt certain there would have been if Cora had plumped out her verdict of murder.

'He'd been ill for some time, I think,' said Miss Gilchrist vaguely, 'though I must say I was surprised to hear it. He looked so very vigorous.'

Mr Entwhistle said quickly:

'You saw him – when?'

'When he came down here to see Mrs Lansquenet. Let me see – that was about three weeks ago.'

'Did he stay here?'

'Oh – no – just came for luncheon. It was quite a surprise. Mrs Lansquenet hadn't expected him. I gather there had been some family disagreement. She hadn't seen him for years, she told me.'

'Yes, that is so.'

'It quite upset her – seeing him again – and probably realizing how ill he was –'

'She knew he was ill?'

'Oh yes, I remember quite well. Because I wondered – only in my own mind, you understand – if perhaps Mr Abernethie might be suffering from softening of the brain. An aunt of mine –'

Mr Entwhistle deftly side-tracked the aunt.

'Something Mrs Lansquenet said caused you to think of softening of the brain?'

'Yes. Mrs Lansquenet said something like "Poor Richard. Mortimer's death must have aged him a lot. He sounds quite senile. All these fancies about persecution and that someone is poisoning him. Old people get like that." And of course, as I knew, that is only too *true*. This aunt that I was telling you about – was convinced the servants were trying to poison her in her food and at last would eat only boiled eggs – because, she said, you couldn't get inside a boiled egg to poison it. We humoured her, but if it had been nowadays I don't know *what* we should have done. With eggs so scarce and mostly foreign at that, so that boiling is always risky.'

Mr Entwhistle listened to the saga of Miss Gilchrist's aunt with deaf ears. He was very much disturbed.

He said at last, when Miss Gilchrist had twittered into silence:

'I suppose Mrs Lansquenet didn't take all this too seriously?'

'Oh no, Mr Entwhistle, she *quite* understood.'

Mr Entwhistle found that remark disturbing too, though not quite in the sense in which Miss Gilchrist had used it.

Had Cora Lansquenet understood? Not then, perhaps, but later. Had she understood only too well?

Mr Entwhistle knew that there had been no senility about Richard Abernethie. Richard had been in full possession of his faculties. He was not the man to have persecution mania in any form. He was, as he always had been, a hard-headed business man – and his illness made no difference in that respect.

It seemed extraordinary that he should have spoken to his sister in the terms that he had. But perhaps Cora, with her odd childlike shrewdness, had read between the lines, and had crossed the t's and dotted the i's of what Richard Abernethie had actually said.

In most ways, thought Mr Entwhistle, Cora had been a complete fool. She had no judgement, no balance, and a crude childish point of view, but she had also the child's uncanny knack of sometimes hitting the nail on the head in a way that seemed quite startling.

Mr Entwhistle left it at that. Miss Gilchrist, he thought, knew no more than she had told him. He asked whether she knew if Cora Lansquenet had left a will. Miss Gilchrist replied promptly that Mrs Lansquenet's will was at the Bank.

With that and after making certain further arrangements he took his leave. He insisted on Miss Gilchrist's accepting a small sum in cash to defray present expenses and told her he would communicate with her again, and in the meantime he would be grateful if she would stay on at the cottage while she was looking about for a new post. That would be, Miss Gilchrist said, a great convenience and really she was not at all nervous.

He was unable to escape without being shown round the cottage by Miss Gilchrist, and introduced to various pictures by the late Pierre Lansquenet which were crowded into the small dining-room and which made Mr Entwhistle flinch – they were mostly nudes executed with a singular lack of draughtsmanship but with much fidelity to detail. He was also made to admire various small oil sketches of picturesque fishing ports done by Cora herself.

'Polperro,' said Miss Gilchrist proudly. 'We were there last year and Mrs Lansquenet was delighted with its picturesqueness.'

Mr Entwhistle, viewing Polperro from the south-west, from the north-west, and presumably from the several other points of the compass, agreed that Mrs Lansquenet had certainly been enthusiastic.

'Mrs Lansquenet promised to leave me her sketches,' said Miss Gilchrist wistfully. 'I admired them so much. One can really see the waves breaking in this one, can't one? Even if she forgot, I might perhaps have just *one* as a souvenir, do you think?'

'I'm sure that could be arranged,' said Mr Entwhistle graciously.

He made a few further arrangements and then left to interview the Bank Manager and to have a further consultation with Inspector Morton.

CHAPTER 5

I

'Worn out,' that's what you are,' said Miss Entwhistle in the indignant and bullying tones adopted by devoted sisters towards brothers for whom they keep house. 'You shouldn't do it, at your age. What's it all got to do with you, I'd like to know? You've retired, haven't you?'

Mr Entwhistle said mildly that Richard Abernethie had been one of his oldest friends.

'I dare say. But Richard Abernethie's dead, isn't he? So I see no reason for you to go mixing yourself up in things that are no concern of yours and catching your death of cold in these nasty draughty railway trains. And murder, too! I can't see why they sent for you at all.'

'They communicated with me because there was a letter in the cottage signed by me, telling Cora the arrangements for the funeral.'

'Funerals! One funeral after another, and that reminds me. Another of these precious Abernethies has been ringing you up – Timothy, I think he said. From somewhere in Yorkshire – and *that's* about a funeral, too! Said he'd ring again later.'

A personal call for Mr Entwhistle came through that evening. Taking it, he heard Maude Abernethie's voice at the other end.

'Thank goodness I've got hold of you at last! Timothy has been in the most terrible state. This news about Cora has upset him dreadfully.'

'Quite understandable,' said Mr Entwhistle.

'What did you say?'

'I said it was quite understandable.'

'I suppose so.' Maude sounded more than doubtful. 'Do you mean to say it was really murder?'

('*It was murder, wasn't it?*' Cora had said. But this time there was no hesitation about the answer.)

'Yes, it was murder,' said Mr Entwhistle.

'And with a hatchet, so the papers say?'

'Yes.'

'It seems *quite* incredible to me,' said Maude, 'that Timothy's sister – his own sister – can have been murdered with a *hatchet*!'

It seemed no less incredible to Mr Entwhistle. Timothy's life was so remote from violence that even his relations, one felt, ought to be equally exempt.

'I'm afraid one has to face the fact,' said Mr Entwhistle mildly.

'I am really *very* worried about Timothy. It's so bad for him, all this! I've got him to bed now but he insists on my persuading you to come up and see him. He wants to know a hundred things – whether there will be an inquest, and who ought to attend, and how soon after that the funeral can take place, and where, and what funds there are, and if Cora expressed any wishes about being cremated or what, and if she left a will –'

Mr Entwhistle interrupted before the catalogue got too long.

'There is a will, yes. She left Timothy her executor.'

'Oh dear, I'm afraid Timothy can't undertake anything –'

'The firm will attend to all the necessary business. The will's very simple. She left her own sketches and an amethyst brooch to her companion, Miss Gilchrist, and everything else to Susan.'

'To Susan? Now I wonder why Susan? I don't believe she ever saw Susan – not since she was a baby anyway.'

'I imagine that it was because Susan was reported to have made a marriage not wholly pleasing to the family.'

Maude snorted.

'Even Gregory is a great deal better than Pierre Lansquenet ever was! Of course marrying a man who serves in a shop would have been unheard of in my day – but a chemist's shop is much better than a haberdasher's – and at least Gregory seems quite respectable.' She paused and added: 'Does this mean that Susan gets the income Richard left to Cora?'

'Oh no. The capital of that will be divided according to the instructions of Richard's will. No, poor Cora had only a few hundred pounds and the furniture of her cottage to leave. When outstanding debts are paid and the furniture sold I doubt if the whole thing will amount to more than at most five hundred pounds.' He went on: 'There will have to be an inquest, of course. That is fixed for next Thursday. If Timothy is agreeable, we'll send down young Lloyd to watch the proceedings on behalf of the family.' He added apologetically: 'I'm afraid it may attract some notoriety owing to the – er – circumstances.'

'How very unpleasant! Have they caught the wretch who did it?'

'Not yet.'

'One of these dreadful half-baked young men who go about the country roving and murdering, I suppose. The police are so incompetent.'

'No, no,' said Mr Entwhistle. 'The police are by no means incompetent. Don't imagine that, for a moment.'

'Well, it all seems to me quite extraordinary. And *so* bad for Timothy. I suppose you couldn't possibly come down here, Mr Entwhistle? I should be *most* grateful if you could. I think Timothy's mind might be set at rest if you were here to reassure him.'

Mr Entwhistle was silent for a moment. The invitation was not unwelcome.

'There is something in what you say,' he admitted. 'And I shall need Timothy's signature as executor to certain documents. Yes, I think it might be quite a good thing.'

'That is splendid. I am so relieved. Tomorrow? And you'll stay the night? The best train is the 11.20 from St Pancras.'

'It will have to be an afternoon train, I'm afraid. I have,' said Mr Entwhistle, 'other business in the morning . . .'

II

George Crossfield greeted Mr Entwhistle heartily but with, perhaps, just a shade of surprise.

Mr Entwhistle said, in an explanatory way, although it really explained nothing:

'I've just come up from Lytchett St Mary.'

'Then it really was Aunt Cora? I read about it in the papers and I just couldn't believe it. I thought it must be someone of the same name.'

'Lansquenet is not a common name.'

'No, of course it isn't. I suppose there is a natural aversion to believing that anyone of one's own family can be murdered. Sounds to me rather like that case last month on Dartmoor.'

'Does it?'

'Yes. Same circumstances. Cottage in a lonely position. Two elderly women living together. Amount of cash taken really quite pitifully inadequate one would think.'

'The value of money is always relative,' said Mr Entwhistle. 'It is the need that counts.'

'Yes – yes, I suppose you're right.'

'If you need ten pounds desperately – then fifteen is more than adequate. And inversely so. If your need is for a hundred pounds, forty-five would be worse than useless. And if it's thousands you need, then hundreds are not enough.'

George said with a sudden flicker of the eyes: 'I'd say *any* money came in useful these days. Everyone's hard up.'

'But not *desperate*,' Mr Entwhistle pointed out. 'It's the desperation that counts.'

'Are you thinking of something in particular?'

'Oh no, not at all.' He paused then went on: 'It will be a little time before the estate is settled; would it be convenient for you to have an advance?'

'As a matter of fact, I *was* going to raise the subject. However, I saw the Bank this morning and referred them to you and they were quite obliging about an overdraft.'

Again there came that flicker in George's eyes, and Mr Entwhistle, from the depths of his experience, recognized it. George, he felt certain, had been, if not desperate, then in very sore straits for money. He knew at that moment, what he had felt subconsciously all along, that in money matters he would not trust George. He wondered if old Richard Abernethie, who also had had great experience in judging men, had felt that. Mr Entwhistle was also sure that after Mortimer's death, Abernethie had formed the intention of making George his heir. George was not an Abernethie, but he was the only male of the younger generation. He was the natural successor to Mortimer. Richard Abernethie had sent for George, had had him staying in the house for some days. It seemed probable that at the end of the visit the older man had not found George satisfactory. Had he felt instinctively, as Mr Entwhistle felt, that George was not straight? George's father, so the family had thought, had been a poor choice on Laura's part. A stockbroker who had had other rather mysterious activities.

George took after his father rather than after the Abernethies.

Perhaps misinterpreting the old lawyer's silence, George said with an uneasy laugh:

'Truth is, I've not been very lucky with my investments lately. I took a bit of a risk and it didn't come off. More or less cleaned me out. But I'll be able to recoup myself now. All one needs is a bit of capital. Ardens Consolidated are pretty good, don't you think?'

Mr Entwhistle neither agreed nor dissented. He was wondering if by any chance George had been speculating with money that belonged to clients and not with his own? If George had been in danger of criminal prosecution –

Mr Entwhistle said precisely:

'I tried to reach you the day after the funeral, but I suppose you weren't in the office.'

'Did you? They never told me. As a matter of fact, I thought I was entitled to a day off after the good news!'

'The good news?'

George reddened.

'Oh look here, I didn't mean Uncle Richard's death. But knowing you've come into money does give one a bit of a kick. One feels one must celebrate. As a matter of fact I went to Hurst Park. Backed two winners. It never rains but it pours! If your luck's in, it's in! Only a matter of fifty quid, but it all helps.'

'Oh yes,' said Mr Entwhistle. 'It all helps. And there will now be an additional sum coming to you as a result of your Aunt Cora's death.'

George looked concerned.

'Poor old girl,' he said. 'It does seem rotten luck, doesn't it? Probably just when she was all set to enjoy herself.'

'Let us hope the police will find the person responsible for her death,' said Mr Entwhistle.

'I expect they'll get him all right. They're good, our police. They round up all the undesirables in the neighbourhood and go through 'em with a tooth comb – make them account for their actions at the time it happened.'

'Not so easy if a little time has elapsed,' said Mr Entwhistle. He gave a wintry little smile that indicated he was about to make a joke. 'I myself was in Hatchard's bookshop at 3.30 on the day in question. Should I remember that if I were questioned by the police in ten days' time? I very much doubt it. And you, George, you were at Hurst Park. Would you remember which day you went to the races in – say – a month's time?'

'Oh I could fix it by the funeral – the day after.'

'True – true. And then you backed a couple of winners. Another aid to memory. One seldom forgets the names of a horse on which one has won money. Which were they, by the way?'

'Let me see. Gaymarck and Frogg II. Yes, I shan't forget them in a hurry.'

Mr Entwhistle gave his dry little cackle of laughter and took his leave.

III

'It's lovely to see you, of course,' said Rosamund without any marked enthusiasm. 'But it's frightfully early in the morning.'

She yawned heavily.

'It's eleven o'clock,' said Mr Entwhistle.

Rosamund yawned again. She said apologetically:

'We had the hell of a party last night. Far too much to drink. Michael's got a terrible hangover still.'

Michael appeared at this moment, also yawning. He had a cup of black coffee in his hand and was wearing a very smart dressing-gown. He looked haggard and attractive – and his smile had the usual charm. Rosamund was wearing a black skirt, a rather dirty yellow pullover, and nothing else as far as Mr Entwhistle could judge.

The precise and fastidious lawyer did not approve at all of the young Shanes' way of living. The rather ramshackle flat on the first floor of a Chelsea house – the bottles and glasses and cigarette ends that lay about in profusion – the stale air, and the general air of dust and dishevelment.

In the midst of this discouraging setting Rosamund and Michael bloomed with their wonderful good looks. They were certainly a very handsome couple and they seemed, Mr Entwhistle thought, very fond of each other. Rosamund was certainly adoringly fond of Michael.

'Darling,' she said. 'Do you think just a teeny sip of champagne? Just to pull us together and toast the future. Oh, Mr

Entwhistle, it really is the most marvellous luck Uncle Richard leaving us all that lovely money just now –'

Mr Entwhistle noted the quick, almost scowling, frown that Michael gave, but Rosamund went on serenely:

'Because there's the most wonderful chance of a play. Michael's got an option on it. It's a most wonderful part for him and even a small part for me, too. It's about one of these young criminals, you know, they are really saints – it's absolutely full of the latest modern ideas.'

'So it would seem,' said Mr Entwhistle stiffly.

'He robs, you know, and he kills, and he's hounded by the police and by society – and then in the end, he does a miracle.'

Mr Entwhistle sat in outraged silence. Pernicious nonsense these young fools talked! *And* wrote.

Not that Michael Shane was talking much. There was still a faint scowl on his face.

'Mr Entwhistle doesn't want to hear all our rhapsodies, Rosamund,' he said. 'Shut up for a bit and let him tell us why he's come to see us.'

'There are just one or two little matters to straighten out,' said Mr Entwhistle. 'I have just come back from Lytchett St Mary.'

'Then it *was* Aunt Cora who was murdered? We saw it in the paper. And I said it must be because it's a very uncommon name. Poor old Aunt Cora. I was looking at her at the funeral that day and thinking what a frump she was and that really one might as well be dead if one looked like that – and now she *is* dead. They absolutely wouldn't *believe* it last night when I told them that that murder with the hatchet in the paper was actually *my aunt*! They just laughed, didn't they, Michael?'

Michael Shane did not reply and Rosamund with every appearance of enjoyment said:

'Two murders one after another. It's almost too much, isn't it?'

'Don't be a fool, Rosamund, your Uncle Richard wasn't murdered.'

'Well, Cora thought he was.'

Mr Entwhistle intervened to ask:

'You came back to London after the funeral, didn't you?'

'Yes, we came by the same train as you did.'

'Of course . . . Of course. I ask because I tried to get hold of you,' he shot a quick glance at the telephone – 'on the following day – several times in fact, and couldn't get an answer.'

'Oh dear – I'm so sorry. What were we doing that day? The day before yesterday. We were here until about twelve, weren't we? And then you went round to try and get hold of Rosenheim and you went on to lunch with Oscar and I went out to see if I could get some nylons and round the shops. I was to meet Janet but we missed each other. Yes, I had a lovely afternoon shopping – and then we dined at the *Castile*. We got back here about ten o'clock, I suppose.'

'About that,' said Michael. He was looking thoughtfully at Mr Entwhistle. 'What did you want to get hold of us for, sir?'

'Oh! Just some points that had arisen about Richard Abernethie's estate – papers to sign – all that.'

Rosamund asked: 'Do we get the money now, or not for ages?'

'I'm afraid,' said Mr Entwhistle, 'that the law is prone to delays.'

'But we can get an advance, can't we?' Rosamund looked alarmed. 'Michael said we could. Actually it's terribly important. Because of the play.'

Michael said pleasantly:

'Oh, there's no real hurry. It's just a question of deciding whether or not to take up the option.'

'It will be quite easy to advance you some money,' said Mr Entwhistle. 'As much as you need.'

'Then that's all right.' Rosamund gave a sigh of relief. She added as an afterthought: 'Did Aunt Cora leave any money?'

'A little. She left it to your Cousin Susan.'

'Why Susan, I should like to know! Is it much?'

'A few hundred pounds and some furniture.'

'Nice furniture?'

'No,' said Mr Entwhistle.

Rosamund lost interest. 'It's all very odd, isn't it?' she said. 'There was Cora, after the funeral, suddenly coming out with

"He *was* murdered!" and then, the very next day, *she* goes and gets *herself* murdered? I mean, it is *odd*, isn't it?'

There was a moment's rather uncomfortable silence before Mr Entwhistle said quietly:

'Yes, it is indeed very odd . . .'

IV

Mr Entwhistle studied Susan Banks as she leant forward across the table talking in her animated manner.

None of the loveliness of Rosamund here. But it was an attractive face and its attraction lay, Mr Entwhistle decided, in its vitality. The curves of the mouth were rich and full. It was a woman's mouth and her body was very decidedly a woman's – emphatically so. Yet in many ways Susan reminded him of her uncle, Richard Abernethie. The shape of her head, the line of her jaw, the deep-set reflective eyes. She had the same kind of dominant personality that Richard had had, the same driving energy, the same foresightedness and forthright judgement. Of the three members of the younger generation she alone seemed to be made of the metal that had raised up the vast Abernethie fortunes. Had Richard recognized in this niece a kindred spirit to his own? Mr Entwhistle thought he must have done. Richard had always had a keen appreciation of character. Here, surely, were exactly the qualities of which he was in search. And yet, in his will, Richard Abernethie had made no distinction in her favour. Distrustful, as Mr Entwhistle believed, of George, passing over that lovely dimwit, Rosamund – could he not have found in Susan what he was seeking – an heir of his own mettle?

If not, the cause must be – yes, it followed logically – the husband . . .

Mr Entwhistle's eyes slid gently over Susan's shoulder to where Gregory Banks stood absently whittling at a pencil.

A thin, pale, nondescript young man with reddish sandy hair. So overshadowed by Susan's colourful personality that it was difficult to realize what he himself was really like. Nothing to take hold of in the fellow – quite pleasant, ready to be agreeable – a 'yes' man, as the modern term went. And yet that did not seem to describe him satisfactorily. There was something vaguely disquieting about the unobtrusiveness of Gregory Banks. He had been an unsuitable match – yet Susan had insisted on marrying him – had overborne all opposition – why? What had she seen in him?

And now, six months after the marriage – 'She's crazy about the fellow,' Mr Entwhistle said to himself. He knew the signs. A large number of wives with matrimonial troubles had passed through the office of Bollard, Entwhistle, Entwhistle and Bollard. Wives madly devoted to unsatisfactory and often what appeared quite unprepossessing husbands, wives contemptuous of, and bored by, apparently attractive and impeccable husbands. What any woman saw in some particular man was beyond the comprehension of the average intelligent male. It just was so. A woman who could be intelligent about everything else in the world could be a complete fool when it came to some particular man. Susan, thought Mr Entwhistle, was one of those women. For her the world revolved around Greg. And that had its dangers in more ways than one.

Susan was talking with emphasis and indignation.

'– because it *is* disgraceful. You remember that woman who was murdered in Yorkshire last year? Nobody was ever arrested. And the old woman in the sweet shop who was killed with a crowbar. They detained some man, and then they let him go!'

'There has to be evidence, my dear,' said Mr Entwhistle.

Susan paid no attention.

'And that other case – a retired nurse – that was a hatchet or an axe – just like Aunt Cora.'

'Dear me, you appear to have made quite a study of these crimes, Susan,' said Mr Entwhistle mildly.

'Naturally one remembers these things – and when someone in one's own family is killed – and in very much the same way – well, it shows that there must be a lot of these sorts of people going round the countryside, breaking into places and attacking lonely women – and that the police just don't *bother*!'

Mr Entwhistle shook his head.

'Don't belittle the police, Susan. They are a very shrewd and patient body of men – persistent, too. Just because it isn't still mentioned in the newspapers doesn't mean that a case is closed. Far from it.'

'And yet there are hundreds of unsolved crimes every year.'

'Hundreds?' Mr Entwhistle looked dubious. 'A certain number, yes. But there are many occasions when the police know who has committed a crime but where the evidence is insufficient for a prosecution.'

'I don't believe it,' said Susan. 'I believe if you knew definitely *who* committed a crime you could always get the evidence.'

'I wonder now.' Mr Entwhistle sounded thoughtful. 'I very much wonder . . .'

'Have they any idea *at all* – in Aunt Cora's case – of who it might be?'

'That I couldn't say. Not as far as I know. But they would hardly confide in me – and it's early days yet – the murder took place only the day before yesterday, remember.'

'It's definitely got to be a certain kind of person,' Susan mused. 'A brutal, perhaps slightly half-witted type – a discharged soldier or a gaol bird. I mean, using a hatchet like that.'

Looking slightly quizzical, Mr Entwhistle raised his eyebrows and murmured:

> '*Lizzie Borden with an axe*
> *Gave her father fifty whacks.*
> *When she saw what she had done*
> *She gave her mother fifty-one.*'

'Oh,' Susan flushed angrily, 'Cora hadn't got any relations living with her – unless you mean the companion. And anyway Lizzie Borden was acquitted. Nobody knows for certain she killed her father and stepmother.'

'The rhyme is quite definitely libellous,' Mr Entwhistle agreed.

'You mean the companion *did* do it? Did Cora leave her anything?'

'An amethyst brooch of no great value and some sketches of fishing villages of sentimental value only.'

'One has to have a motive for murder – unless one is half-witted.'

Mr Entwhistle gave a little chuckle.

'As far as one can see, the only person who had a motive is *you*, my dear Susan.'

'What's that?' Greg moved forward suddenly. He was like a sleeper coming awake. An ugly light showed in his eyes. He was suddenly no longer a negligible feature in the background. 'What's Sue got to do with it? What do you mean – saying things like that?'

Susan said sharply:

'Shut up, Greg. Mr Entwhistle doesn't mean anything –'

'Just my little joke,' said Mr Entwhistle apologetically. 'Not in the best taste, I'm afraid. Cora left her estate, such as it was, to you, Susan. But to a young lady who has just inherited several hundred thousand pounds, an estate, amounting at the most to a few hundreds, can hardly be said to represent a motive for murder.'

'She left her money to me?' Susan sounded surprised. 'How extraordinary. She didn't even know me! Why did she do it, do you think?'

'I think she had heard rumours that there had been a little difficulty – er – over your marriage.' Greg, back again at sharpening his pencil, scowled. 'There had been a certain amount of trouble over her own marriage – and I think she experienced a fellow feeling.'

Susan asked with a certain amount of interest:

'She married an artist, didn't she, whom none of the family liked? Was he a good artist?'

Mr Entwhistle shook his head very decidedly.

'Are there any of his paintings in the cottage?'

'Yes.'

Then I shall judge for myself,' said Susan.

Mr Entwhistle smiled at the resolute tilt of Susan's chin.

'So be it. Doubtless I am an old fogey and hopelessly old-fashioned in matters of art, but I really don't think you will dispute my verdict.'

'I suppose I ought to go down there, anyway? And look over what there is. Is there anybody there now?'

'I have arranged with Miss Gilchrist to remain there until further notice.'

Greg said: 'She must have a pretty good nerve – to stay in a cottage where a murder's been committed.'

'Miss Gilchrist is quite a sensible woman, I should say. Besides,' added the lawyer drily, 'I don't think she has anywhere else to go until she gets another situation.'

'So Aunt Cora's death left her high and dry? Did she – were she and Aunt Cora – on intimate terms –?'

Mr Entwhistle looked at her rather curiously, wondering just what exactly was in her mind.

'Moderately so, I imagine,' he said. 'She never treated Miss Gilchrist as a servant.'

'Treated her a damned sight worse, I dare say,' said Susan. 'These wretched so called "ladies" are the ones who get it taken out of them nowadays. I'll try and find her a decent post somewhere. It won't be difficult. Anyone who's willing to do a bit of housework and cook is worth their weight in gold – she does cook, doesn't she?'

'Oh yes. I gather it is something she called, er "*the rough*" that she objected to. I'm afraid I don't quite know what "the rough" is.'

Susan appeared to be a good deal amused.

Mr Entwhistle, glancing at his watch, said:

'Your aunt left Timothy her executor.'

'Timothy,' said Susan with scorn. 'Uncle Timothy is practically a myth. Nobody ever sees him.'

'Quite.' Mr Entwhistle glanced at his watch. 'I am travelling up to see him this afternoon. I will acquaint him with your decision to go down to the cottage.'

'It will only take me a day or two, I imagine. I don't want to be long away from London. I've got various schemes in hand. I'm going into business.'

Mr Entwhistle looked round him at the cramped sitting-room of the tiny flat. Greg and Susan were evidently hard up. Her father, he knew, had run through most of his money. He had left his daughter badly off.

'What are your plans for the future, if I may ask?'

'I've got my eye on some premises in Cardigan Street. I suppose, if necessary, you can advance me some money? I may have to pay a deposit.'

'That can be managed,' said Mr Entwhistle. 'I rang you up the day after the funeral several times – but could get no answer. I thought perhaps you might care for an advance. I wondered whether you might perhaps have gone out of Town.'

'Oh no,' said Susan quickly. 'We were in all day. Both of us. We didn't go out at all.'

Greg said gently: 'You know Susan, I think our telephone must have been out of order that day. You remember how I couldn't get through to Hard and Co. in the afternoon. I meant to report it, but it was all right the next morning.'

'Telephones,' said Mr Entwhistle, 'can be very unreliable sometimes.'

Susan said suddenly:

'How did Aunt Cora know about our marriage? It was at a Registry Office and we didn't tell anyone until afterwards!'

'I fancy Richard may have told her about it. She remade her will about three weeks ago (it was formerly in favour of the Theosophical Society) – just about the time he had been down to see her.'

Susan looked startled.

'Did Uncle Richard go down to see her? I'd no idea of that?'

'I hadn't any idea of it myself,' said Mr Entwhistle.

'So that was when –'

'When what?'

'Nothing,' said Susan.

CHAPTER 6

I

'Very good of you to come along,' said Maude gruffly, as she greeted Mr Entwhistle on the platform of Bayham Compton station. 'I can assure you that both Timothy and I much appreciate it. Of course the truth is that Richard's death was the worst thing possible for Timothy.'

Mr Entwhistle had not yet considered his friend's death from this particular angle. But it was, he saw, the only angle from which Mrs Timothy Abernethie was likely to regard it.

As they proceeded towards the exit, Maude developed the theme.

'To begin with, it was a *shock* – Timothy was really very attached to Richard. And then unfortunately it put the idea of death into Timothy's head. Being such an invalid has made him rather nervous about himself. He realized that he was the only one of the brothers left alive – and he started saying that he'd be the next to go – and that it wouldn't be long now – all very morbid talk, as I told him.'

They emerged from the station and Maude led the way to a dilapidated car of almost fabulous antiquity.

'Sorry about our old rattletrap,' she said. 'We've wanted a new car for years, but really we couldn't afford it. This has had a new engine twice – and these old cars really stand up to a lot of hard work.

'I hope it will start,' she added. 'Sometimes one has to wind it.'

She pressed the starter several times but only a meaningless whirr resulted. Mr Entwhistle, who had never wound a car in his life, felt rather apprehensive, but Maude herself descended, inserted the starting handle and with a vigorous couple of turns woke the motor to life. It was fortunate, Mr Entwhistle reflected, that Maude was such a powerfully built woman.

'That's that,' she said. 'The old brute's been playing me up lately. Did it when I was coming back after the funeral. Had to walk a couple of miles to the nearest garage and they weren't good for much – just a village affair. I had to put up at the local inn while they tinkered at it. Of course *that* upset Timothy, too. I had to phone through to him and tell him I couldn't be back till the next day. Fussed him terribly. One tries to keep things from him as much as possible – but some things one can't do anything about – Cora's murder, for instance. I had to send for Dr Barton to give him a sedative. Things like murder are too much for a man in Timothy's state of health. I gather Cora was always a fool.'

Mr Entwhistle digested this remark in silence. The inference was not quite clear to him.

'I don't think I'd seen Cora since our marriage,' said Maude. 'I didn't like to say to Timothy at the time: "Your youngest sister's batty," not just like that. But it's what I *thought*. There she was saying the most extraordinary things! One didn't know whether to resent them or whether to laugh. I suppose the truth is she lived in a kind of imaginary world of her own – full of melodrama and fantastic ideas about other people. Well, poor soul, she's paid for it now. She didn't have any protégés, did she?'

'Protégés? What do you mean?'

'I just wondered. Some young cadging artist, or musician – or something of that kind. Someone she might have let in that day, and who killed her for her loose cash. Perhaps an adolescent – they're so queer at that age sometimes – especially if they're the neurotic arty type. I mean, it seems so odd to break in and murder her in the middle of the afternoon. If you break into a house surely you'd do it at night.'

'There would have been two women there then.'

'Oh yes, the companion. But really I can't believe that anyone would deliberately wait until she was out of the way and then break in and attack Cora. What for? He can't have expected she'd have any cash or stuff to speak of, and there must have been times when both the women were out and the house was empty. That would have been much safer. It seems so stupid to go and commit a murder unless it's absolutely necessary.'

'And Cora's murder, you feel, was unnecessary?'

'It all seems so stupid.'

Should murder make sense? Mr Entwhistle wondered. Academically the answer was yes. But many pointless crimes were on record. It depended, Mr Entwhistle reflected, on the mentality of the murderer.

What did he really know about murderers and their mental processes? Very little. His firm had never had a criminal practice. He was no student of criminology himself. Murderers, as far as he could judge, seemed to be of all sorts and kinds. Some had had overweening vanity, some had had a lust for power, some, like Seddon, had been mean and avaricious, others, like Smith and Rowse, had had an incredible fascination for women; some, like Armstrong, had been pleasant fellows to meet. Edith Thompson had lived in a world of violent unreality, Nurse Waddington had put her elderly patients out of the way with business-like cheerfulness.

Maude's voice broke into his meditations.

'If I could only keep the newspapers from Timothy! But he will insist on reading them – and then, of course, it upsets him. You do understand, don't you, Mr Entwhistle, that there can be *no question* of Timothy's attending the inquest? If necessary, Dr Barton can write out a certificate or whatever it is.'

'You can set your mind at rest about that.'

'Thank goodness!'

They turned in through the gates of Stansfield Grange, and up a neglected drive. It had been an attractive small property once – but had now a doleful and neglected appearance. Maude sighed as she said:

'We had to let this go to seed during the war. Both gardeners called up. And now we've only got one old man – and he's not much good. Wages have gone up so terribly. I must say it's a blessing to realize that we'll be able to spend a little money on the place now. We're both so fond of it. I was really afraid that we might have to sell it . . . Not that I suggested anything of the kind to Timothy. It would have upset him – dreadfully.'

They drew up before the portico of a very old Georgian house which badly needed a coat of paint.

'No servants,' said Maude bitterly, as she led the way in. 'Just a couple of women who come in. We had a resident maid until a month ago – slightly hunchbacked and terribly adenoidal and in many ways not too bright, but she was *there* which was such a comfort – and quite good at plain cooking. And would you believe it, she gave notice and went to a fool of a woman who keeps six Pekinese dogs (it's a larger house than this and more work) because she was "so fond of little doggies," she said. Dogs, indeed! Being sick and making messes all the time I've no doubt! Really, these girls are *mental*! So there we are, and if I have to go out any afternoon, Timothy is left quite alone in the house and if anything should happen, how could he get help? Though I do leave the telephone close by his chair so that if he felt faint he could dial Dr Barton immediately.'

Maude led the way into the drawing-room where tea was laid ready by the fireplace, and establishing Mr Entwhistle there, disappeared, presumably to the back regions. She returned in a few minutes' time with a teapot and silver kettle, and proceeded to minister to Mr Entwhistle's needs. It was a good tea with home-made cake and fresh buns. Mr Entwhistle murmured:

'What about Timothy?' and Maude explained briskly that she had taken Timothy his tray before she set out for the station.

'And now,' said Maude, 'he will have had his little nap and it will be the best time for him to see you. Do try and not let him excite himself too much.'

Mr Entwhistle assured her that he would exercise every precaution.

Studying her in the flickering firelight, he was seized by a feeling of compassion. This big, stalwart matter-of-fact woman, so healthy, so vigorous, so full of common sense, and yet so strangely, almost pitifully, vulnerable in one spot. Her love for her husband was maternal love, Mr Entwhistle decided. Maude Abernethie had borne no child and she was a woman built for motherhood. Her invalid husband had become her child, to be shielded, guarded, watched over. And perhaps, being the stronger character of the two, she had unconsciously imposed on him a state of invalidism greater than might otherwise have been the case.

'Poor Mrs Tim,' thought Mr Entwhistle to himself.

II

'Good of you to come, Entwhistle.'

Timothy raised himself up in his chair as he held out a hand. He was a big man with a marked resemblance to his brother Richard. But what was strength in Richard, in Timothy was weakness. The mouth was irresolute, the chin very slightly receding, the eyes less deep-set. Lines of peevish irritability showed on his forehead.

His invalid status was emphasized by the rug across his knees and a positive pharmacopoeia of little bottles and boxes, on a table at his right hand.

'I mustn't exert myself,' he said warningly. 'Doctor's forbidden it. Keeps telling me not to worry! Worry! If *he'd* had a murder in his family *he'd* do a bit of worrying, I bet! It's too much for a man – first Richard's death – then hearing all about his funeral and his will – what a will! – and on top of that poor little Cora killed with a hatchet. Hatchet! ugh! This country's full of gangsters nowadays – thugs – left over from the war! Going about killing defenceless women. Nobody's got the guts to put these things down – to take a strong hand. What's the country coming to, I'd like to know? What's the damned country coming to?'

Mr Entwhistle was familiar with this gambit. It was a question almost invariably asked sooner or later by his clients for the last twenty years and he had his routine for answering it. The non-committal words he uttered could have been classified under the heading of soothing noises.

'It all began with that damned Labour Government,' said Timothy. 'Sending the whole country to blazes. And the Government we've got now is no better. Mealy-mouthed, milk-and-water socialists! Look at the state *we're* in! Can't get a decent gardener, can't get servants – poor Maude here has to work herself to a shadow messing about in the kitchen (by the way, I think a custard pudding would go well with the sole tonight, my dear – and perhaps a little clear soup first?). I've got to keep my strength up – Doctor Barton said so – let me see, where was I? Oh yes, *Cora*. It's a shock, I can tell you, to a man when he hears his sister – his own sister – has been *murdered*! Why, I had palpitations for twenty minutes! You'll have to attend to everything for me, Entwhistle. *I* can't go to the inquest or be bothered by business of any kind connected with Cora's estate. I want to forget the whole thing. What happened, by the way, to Cora's share of Richard's money? Comes to me, I suppose?'

Murmuring something about clearing away tea, Maude left the room.

Timothy lay back in his chair and said:

'Good thing to get rid of the women. Now we can talk business without any silly interruptions.'

'The sum left in trust for Cora,' said Mr Entwhistle, 'goes equally to you and the nieces and nephew.'

'But look here,' Timothy's cheeks assumed a purplish hue of indignation. 'Surely I'm her next of kin? Only surviving brother.'

Mr Entwhistle explained with some care the exact provisions of Richard Abernethie's will, reminding Timothy gently that he had had a copy sent him.

'Don't expect me to understand all that legal jargon, do you?' said Timothy ungratefully. 'You lawyers! Matter of fact,

I couldn't believe it when Maude came home and told me the gist of it. Thought she'd got it wrong. Women are never clear headed. Best woman in the world, Maude – but women don't understand finance. I don't believe Maude even realizes that if Richard hadn't died when he did, we might have had to clear out of here. Fact!'

'Surely if you had applied to Richard –'

Timothy gave a short bark of harsh laughter.

'That's not my style. Our father left us all a perfectly reasonable share of his money – that is, if we didn't want to go into the family concern. I didn't. I've a soul above cornplasters, Entwhistle! Richard took my attitude a bit hard. Well, what with taxes, depreciation of income, one thing and another – it hasn't been easy to keep things going. I've had to realize a good deal of capital. Best thing to do these days. I did hint once to Richard that this place was getting a bit hard to run. He took the attitude that we'd be much better off in a smaller place altogether. Easier for Maude, he said, more labour saving – labour saving, what a term! Oh no, I wouldn't have asked Richard for help. But I can tell you, Entwhistle, that the worry affected my health most unfavourably. A man in my state of health oughtn't to have to worry. Then Richard died and though of course naturally I was cut up about it – my brother and all that – I couldn't help feeling relieved about future prospects. Yes, it's all plain sailing now – and a great relief. Get the house painted – get a couple of really good men on the garden – you can get them at a price. Restock the rose garden completely. And – where was I –'

'Detailing your future plans.'

'Yes, yes – but I mustn't bother you with all that. What did hurt me – and hurt me cruelly – were the terms of Richard's will.'

'Indeed?' Mr Entwhistle looked inquiring. 'They were not – as you expected?'

'I should say they weren't! Naturally, after Mortimer's death, I assumed that Richard would leave everything to *me*.'

'Ah – did he – ever – indicate that to you?'

'He never said so – not in so many words. Reticent sort of chap, Richard. But he asked himself here – not long after Mortimer's death. Wanted to talk over family affairs generally. We discussed young George – and the girls and their husbands. Wanted to know my views – not that I could tell him much. I'm an invalid and I don't get about, and Maudie and I live out of the world. Rotten silly marriages both of those girls made, if you ask me. Well, I ask you, Entwhistle, naturally I thought he was consulting me as the head of the family after he was gone and naturally I thought the control of the money would be mine. Richard could surely trust me to do the right thing by the younger generation. And to look after poor old Cora. Dash it all, Entwhistle, I'm an Abernethie – the last Abernethie. Full control should have been left in my hands.'

In his excitement Timothy had kicked aside his rug and had sat up in his chair. There were no signs of weakness or fragility about him. He looked, Mr Entwhistle thought, a perfectly healthy man, even if a slightly excitable one. Moreover the old lawyer realized very clearly that Timothy Abernethie had probably always been secretly jealous of his brother Richard. They had been sufficiently alike for Timothy to resent his brother's strength of character and firm grasp of affairs. When Richard had died, Timothy had exulted in the prospect of succeeding at this late date to the power to control the destinies of others.

Richard Abernethie had not given him that power. Had he thought of doing so and then decided against it?

A sudden squalling of cats in the garden brought Timothy up out of his chair. Rushing to the window he threw up the sash, bawled out, 'Stop it, you!' and picking up a large book hurled it out at the marauders.

'Beastly cats,' he grumbled, returning to his visitor. 'Ruin the flower beds and I can't stand that damned yowling.'

He sat down again and asked:

'Have a drink, Entwhistle?'

'Not quite so soon. Maude has just given me an excellent tea.'

Timothy grunted.

'Capable woman. Maude. But she does too much. Even has to muck about with the inside of that old car of ours – she's quite a mechanic in her way, you know.'

'I hear she had a breakdown coming back from the funeral?'

'Yes. Car conked out. She had the sense to telephone through about it, in case I should be anxious, but that ass of a daily woman of ours wrote down the message in a way that didn't make sense. I was out getting a bit of fresh air – I'm advised by the doctor to take what exercise I can if I feel like it – I got back from my walk to find scrawled on a bit of paper: "Madame's sorry car gone wrong got to stay night." Naturally I thought she was still at Enderby. Put a call through and found Maude had left that morning. Might have had the breakdown *anywhere*! Pretty kettle of fish! Fool of a daily woman only left me a lumpy macaroni cheese for supper. I had to go down to the kitchen and warm it up *myself – and* make myself a cup of tea – to say nothing of stoking the boiler. I might have had a heart attack – but does that class of woman care? Not she! With any decent feelings she'd have come back that evening and looked after me properly. No loyalty any more in the lower classes –'

He brooded sadly.

'I don't know how much Maude told you about the funeral and the relatives,' said Mr Entwhistle. 'Cora produced rather an awkward moment. Said brightly that Richard had been murdered, hadn't he? Perhaps Maude told you.'

Timothy chuckled easily.

'Oh yes, I heard about that. Everybody looked down their noses and pretended to be shocked. Just the sort of thing Cora would say! You know how she always managed to put her foot in it when she was a girl, Entwhistle? Said something at our wedding that upset Maude, I remember. Maude never cared for her very much. Yes, Maude rang me up that evening after the funeral to know if I was all right and if Mrs Jones had come in to give me my evening meal and then she told me it had all gone off very well, and I said "What about the will?" and she tried to hedge a bit, but of course I had the truth out of her. I couldn't believe it, and I said she must have made a mistake, but she stuck to it. It hurt me, Entwhistle – it really *wounded* me, if you know what I mean. If you ask me, it was just *spite* on Richard's part. I know one shouldn't speak ill of the dead, but, upon my word –'

Timothy continued on this theme for some time.

Then Maude came back into the room and said firmly:

'I think, dear, Mr Entwhistle has been with you quite long enough. You really *must* rest. If you have settled everything –'

'Oh, we've settled things. I leave it all to you, Entwhistle. Let me know when they catch the fellow – if they ever do.

I've no faith in the police nowadays – the Chief Constables aren't the right type. You'll see to the – er – interment – won't you? We shan't be able to come, I'm afraid. But order an expensive wreath – and there must be a proper stone put up in due course – she'll be buried locally, I suppose? No point in bringing her North and I've no idea where Lansquenet is buried, somewhere in France I believe. I don't know what one puts on a stone when it's murder . . . Can't very well say "entered into rest" or anything like that. One will have to choose a text – something appropriate. R.I.P.? No, that's only for Catholics.'

'O Lord, thou has seen my wrong. Judge thou my case,' murmured Mr Entwhistle.

The startled glance Timothy bent on him made Mr Entwhistle smile faintly.

'From Lamentations,' he said. 'It seems appropriate if somewhat melodramatic. However, it will be some time before the question of the Memorial stone comes up. The – er – ground has to settle, you know. Now don't worry about anything. We will deal with things and keep you fully informed.'

Mr Entwhistle left for London by the breakfast train on the following morning.

When he got home, after a little hesitation, he rang up a friend of his.

CHAPTER 7

'I can't tell you how much I appreciate your invitation.'

Mr Entwhistle pressed his host's hand warmly.

Hercule Poirot gestured hospitably to a chair by the fire.

Mr Entwhistle sighed as he sat down.

On one side of the room a table was laid for two.

'I returned from the country this morning,' he said.

'And you have a matter on which you wish to consult me?'

'Yes. It's a long rambling story, I'm afraid.'

'Then we will not have it until after we have dined. Georges?'

The efficient Georges materialized with some pâté de foie gras accompanied by hot toast in a napkin.

'We will have our pâté by the fire,' said Poirot. 'Afterwards we will move to the table.'

It was an hour and a half later that Mr Entwhistle stretched himself comfortably out in his chair and sighed a contented sigh.

'You certainly know how to do yourself well, Poirot. Trust a Frenchman.'

'I am a Belgian. But the rest of your remark applies. At my age the chief pleasure, almost the *only* pleasure that still remains, is the pleasure of the table. Mercifully I have an excellent stomach.'

'Ah,' murmured Mr Entwhistle.

They had dined off sole veronique, followed by escalope de veau milanaise, proceeding to poire flambée with ice-cream.

They had drunk a Pouilly Fuissé followed by a Corton, and a very good port now reposed at Mr Entwhistle's elbow. Poirot, who did not care for port, was sipping Crème de Cacao.

'I don't know,' murmured Mr Entwhistle reminiscently, 'how you manage to get hold of an escalope like that! It melted in the mouth!'

'I have a friend who is a Continental butcher. For him I solve a small domestic problem. He is appreciative – and ever since then he is most sympathetic to me in the matters of the stomach.'

'A domestic problem,' Mr Entwhistle sighed. 'I wish you had not reminded me . . . This is such a perfect moment . . .'

'Prolong it, my friend. We will have presently the demitasse and the fine brandy, and then, when digestion is peacefully under way, *then* you shall tell why you need my advice.'

The clock struck the half hour after nine before Mr Entwhistle stirred in his chair. The psychological moment had come. He no longer felt reluctant to bring forth his perplexities – he was eager to do so.

'I don't know,' he said, 'whether I'm making the most colossal fool of myself. In any case I don't see that there's anything that can possibly be done. But I'd like to put the facts before you, and I'd like to know what you think.'

He paused for a moment or two, then in his dry meticulous way, he told his story. His trained legal brain enabled him to put the facts clearly, to leave nothing out, and to add nothing extraneous. It was a clear succinct account, and as such appreciated by the little elderly man with the egg-shaped head who sat listening to him.

When he had finished there was a pause. Mr Entwhistle was prepared to answer questions, but for some few moments no question came. Hercule Poirot was reviewing the evidence.

He said at last:

'It seems very clear. You have in your mind the suspicion that your friend, Richard Abernethie, may have been murdered? That suspicion, or assumption, rests on the basis of one thing only – *the words spoken by Cora Lansquenet at Richard Abernethie's funeral*. Take those away – and there is nothing left. The fact that she herself was murdered the day afterwards may be the purest coincidence. It is true that Richard Abernethie died suddenly, but he was attended by a reputable doctor who knew him well, and that doctor had no suspicions and gave a death certificate. Was Richard buried or cremated?'

'Cremated – according to his own request.'

'Yes, that is the law. And it means that a second doctor signed the certificate – but there would be no difficulty about that. So we come back to the essential point, *what Cora Lansquenet said*. You were there and you heard her. She said: "But he was murdered, wasn't he?"'

'Yes.'

'And the real point is – that you believe she was speaking the truth.'

The lawyer hesitated for a moment, then he said:

'Yes, I do.'

'Why?'

'Why?' Entwhistle repeated the word, slightly puzzled.

'But yes, *why*? Is it because, already, deep down, you had an uneasiness about the manner of Richard's death?'

The lawyer shook his head. 'No, no, not in the least.'

'Then it is because of *her* – of Cora herself. You knew her well?'

'I had not seen her for – oh – over twenty years.'

'Would you have known her if you had met her in the street?'

Mr Entwhistle reflected.

'I might have passed her by in the street without recognizing her. She was a thin slip of a girl when I saw her last and she had turned into a stout, shabby, middle-aged woman. But I think that the moment I spoke to her face to face I should have recognized her. She wore her hair in the same way, a bang cut straight across the forehead, and she had a trick of peering up at you through her fringe like a rather shy animal, and she had a very characteristic, abrupt way of talking, and a way of putting her head on one side and then coming out with something quite outrageous. She had *character*, you see, and character is always highly individual.'

'She was, in fact, the same Cora you had known years ago. And she still said outrageous things! The things, the outrageous things, she had said in the past – were they usually – justified?'

'That was always the awkward thing about Cora. When truth would have been better left unspoken, she spoke it.'

'And that characteristic remained unchanged. Richard Abernethie was murdered – so Cora at once mentioned the fact.'

Mr Entwhistle stirred.

'You think he *was* murdered?'

'Oh, no, no, my friend, we cannot go so fast. We agree on this – Cora *thought* he had been murdered. She was quite sure he had been murdered. It was, to her, more a certainty than a surmise. And so, we come to this, *she must have had some reason for the belief.* We agree, by your knowledge of her, that it was not just a bit of mischief making. Now tell me – when she said what she did, there was, at once, a kind of chorus of protest – that is right?'

'Quite right.'

'And she then became confused, abashed, and retreated from the position – saying – as far as you can remember, something like "But I thought – from what he told me –"'

The lawyer nodded.

'I wish I could remember more clearly. But I am fairly sure of that. She used the words "he told me" or "he said –"'

'And the matter was then smoothed over and everyone spoke of something else. You can remember, looking back, no special expression on anyone's face? Anything that remains in your memory as – shall we say – *unusual*?'

'No.'

'And the very next day, *Cora is killed* – and you ask yourself: "Can it be cause and effect?"'

The lawyer stirred.

'I suppose that seems to you quite fantastic?'

'Not at all,' said Poirot. 'Given that the original assumption is correct, it is logical. The perfect murder, the murder of Richard Abernethie, has been committed, all has gone off smoothly – and suddenly it appears that there is one person who has a knowledge of the truth! Clearly that person must be silenced *as quickly as possible*.'

'Then you do think that – it was murder?'

Poirot said gravely:

'I think, *mon cher*, exactly as you thought – that there is a case for investigation. Have you taken any steps? You have spoken of these matters to the police?'

'No.' Mr Entwhistle shook his head. 'It did not seem to me that any good purpose could be achieved. My position is that I represent the family. If Richard Abernethie was murdered, there seems only one method by which it could be done.'

'By poison?'

'Exactly. *And the body has been cremated.* There is now no evidence available. But I decided that I, myself, *must* be satisfied on the point. That is why, Poirot, I have come to *you*.'

'Who was in the house at the time of his death?'

'An old butler who has been with him for years, a cook and a housemaid. It would seem, perhaps, as though it must necessarily be one of them –'

'Ah! do not try to pull the wool upon my eyes. This Cora, she knows Richard Abernethie was killed, yet she acquiesces in the hushing up. She says, "I think you are all quite right." Therefore it *must* be one of the family who is concerned, someone whom the victim himself might prefer not to have openly accused. Otherwise, since Cora was fond of her brother, she would not agree to let the sleeping murderer lie. You agree to that, yes?'

'It was the way I reasoned – yes,' confessed Mr Entwhistle. 'Though how any of the family could possibly –'

Poirot cut him short.

'Where poison is concerned there are all sorts of possibilities. It must, presumably, have been a narcotic of some sort if he died in his sleep and if there were no suspicious appearances. Possibly he was already having some narcotic administered to him.'

'In any case,' said Mr Entwhistle, 'the *how* hardly matters. We shall never be able to prove anything.'

'In the case of Richard Abernethie, no. But the murder of Cora Lansquenet is different. Once we know "who" then evidence ought to be possible to get.' He added with a sharp glance, 'You have, perhaps, already done something.'

'Very little. My purpose was mainly, I think, *elimination*. It is distasteful to me to think that one of the Abernethie family is a murderer. I still can't quite believe it. I hoped that by a few apparently idle questions I could exonerate certain members of the family beyond question. Perhaps, who knows, *all* of them? In which case, Cora would have been wrong in her assumption and her own death could be ascribed to some casual prowler who broke in. After all, the issue is very simple. What were the members of the Abernethie family doing on the afternoon that Cora Lansquenet was killed?'

'*Eh bien,*' said Poirot, 'what were they doing?'

'George Crossfield was at Hurst Park races. Rosamund Shane was out shopping in London. Her husband – for one must include husbands –'

'Assuredly.'

'Her husband was fixing up a deal about an option on a play, Susan and Gregory Banks were at home all day, Timothy Abernethie, who is an invalid, was at his home in Yorkshire, and his wife was driving herself home from Enderby.'

He stopped.

Hercule Poirot looked at him and nodded comprehendingly.

'Yes, that is what they *say*. And is it all true?'

'I simply don't know, Poirot. Some of the statements are capable of proof or disproof – but it would be difficult to do so without showing one's hand pretty plainly. In fact to do so would be tantamount to an accusation. I will simply tell you certain conclusions of my own. George *may* have been at Hurst Park races, but I do not think he was. He was rash enough to boast that he had backed a couple of winners. It is my experience that so many offenders against the law ruin their own case by saying too much. I asked him the name of the winners, and he gave the names of two horses without any apparent hesitation. Both of them, I found, had been heavily tipped on the day in question and one had duly won. The other, though an odds on favourite, had unaccountably failed even to get a place.'

'Interesting. Had this George any urgent need for money at the time of his uncle's death?'

'It is my impression that his need was very urgent. I have no evidence for saying so, but I strongly suspect that he has been speculating with his clients' funds and that he was in danger of prosecution. It is only my impression but I have some experience in these matters. Defaulting solicitors, I regret to say, are not entirely uncommon. I can only tell you that I would not have cared to entrust my own funds to George, and I suspect that Richard Abernethie, a very shrewd judge of men, was dissatisfied with his nephew and placed no reliance on him.

'His mother,' the lawyer continued, 'was a good-looking rather foolish girl and she married a man of what I should call dubious character.' He sighed. 'The Abernethie girls were not good choosers.'

He paused and then went on:

'As for Rosamund, she is a lovely nitwit. I really cannot see her smashing Cora's head in with a hatchet! Her husband, Michael Shane, is something of a dark horse – he's a man with ambition and also a man of overweening vanity I should say. But really I know very little about him. I have no reason to suspect him of a brutal crime or of a carefully planned poisoning, but until I know that he really was doing what he says he was doing I cannot rule him out.'

'But you have no doubts about the wife?'

'No – no – there is a certain rather startling callousness . . . but no, I really cannot envisage the hatchet. She is a fragile looking creature.'

'And beautiful!' said Poirot with a faint cynical smile. 'And the other niece?'

'Susan? She is a very different type from Rosamund – a girl of remarkable ability, I should say. She and her husband were at home together that day. I said (falsely) that I had tried to get them on the telephone on the afternoon in question. Greg said very quickly that the telephone had been out of order all day. He had tried to get someone and failed.'

'So again it is not conclusive . . . You cannot eliminate as you hoped to do . . . What is the husband like?'

'I find him hard to make out. He has a somewhat unpleasing personality though one cannot say exactly why he makes this impression. As for Susan –'

'Yes?'

'Susan reminds me of her uncle. She has the vigour, the drive, the mental capacity of Richard Abernethie. It may be my fancy that she lacks some of the kindliness and the warmth of my old friend.'

'Women are never kind,' remarked Poirot. 'Though they can sometimes be tender. She loves her husband?'

'Devotedly, I should say. But really, Poirot, I can't believe – I *won't* believe for one moment that Susan –'

'You prefer George?' said Poirot. 'It is natural! As for me, I am not so sentimental about beautiful young ladies. Now tell me about your visit to the older generation?'

Mr Entwhistle described his visit to Timothy and Maude at some length. Poirot summarized the result.

'So Mrs Abernethie is a good mechanic. She knows all about the inside of a car. And Mr Abernethie is not the invalid he likes to think himself. He goes out for walks and is, according to you, capable of vigorous action. He is also a bit of an egomaniac and he resented his brother's success and superior character.'

'He spoke very affectionately of Cora.'

'And ridiculed her silly remark after the funeral. What of the sixth beneficiary?'

'Helen? Mrs Leo? I do not suspect her for a moment. In any case, her innocence will be easy to prove. She was at Enderby. With three servants in the house.'

'*Eh bien*, my friend,' said Poirot. 'Let us be practical. What do you want me to do?'

'I want to know the truth, Poirot.'

'Yes. Yes, I should feel the same in your place.'

'And you're the man to find it out for me. I know you don't take cases any more, but I ask you to take this one. This is a matter of business. I will be responsible for your fees. Come now, money is always useful.'

Poirot grinned.

'Not if it all goes in the taxes! But I will admit, your problem interests me! Because it is not easy . . . It is all so nebulous . . . One thing, my friend, had better be done by you. After that, I will occupy myself of everything. But I think it will be best if you yourself seek out the doctor who attended Mr Richard Abernethie. You know him?'

'Slightly.'

'What is he like?'

'Middle-aged G.P. Quite competent. On very friendly terms with Richard. A thoroughly good fellow.'

'Then seek him out. He will speak more freely to you than to me. Ask him about Mr Abernethie's illness. Find out what medicines Mr Abernethie was taking at the time of his death and before. Find out if Richard Abernethie ever said anything to his doctor about fancying himself being poisoned. By the way, this Miss Gilchrist is sure that he used the term *poisoned* in talking to his sister?'

Mr Entwhistle reflected.

'It was the word she used – but she is the type of witness who often changes the actual words used, because she is convinced she is keeping to the sense of them. If Richard had said he was afraid someone wanted to kill him, Miss Gilchrist might have assumed poison because she connected his fears with those of an aunt of hers who thought her food was being tampered with. I can take up the point with her again some time.'

'Yes. Or I will do so.' He paused and then said in a different voice: 'Has it occurred to you, my friend, that your Miss Gilchrist may be in some danger herself?'

Mr Entwhistle looked surprised.

'I can't say that it had.'

'But, yes. Cora voiced her suspicions on the day of the funeral. The question in the murderer's mind will be, did she voice them to anybody when she first heard of Richard's death? And the most likely person for her to have spoken to about them will be Miss Gilchrist. I think, *mon cher*, that she had better not remain alone in that cottage.'

'I believe Susan is going down.'

'Ah, so Mrs Banks is going down?'

'She wants to look through Cora's things.'

'I see . . . I see . . . Well, my friend, do what I have asked of you. You might also prepare Mrs Abernethie – Mrs Leo Abernethie, for the possibility that I may arrive in the house. We will see. From now on I occupy myself of everything.'

And Poirot twirled his moustaches with enormous energy.

CHAPTER 8

I

Mr Entwhistle looked at Dr Larraby thoughtfully.

He had had a lifetime of experience in summing people up. There had been frequent occasions on which it had been necessary to tackle a difficult situation or a delicate subject. Mr Entwhistle was an adept by now in the art of how exactly to make the proper approach. How would it be best to tackle Dr Larraby on what was certainly a very difficult subject and one which the doctor might very well resent as reflecting upon his own professional skill?

Frankness, Mr Entwhistle thought – or at least a modified frankness. To say that suspicions had arisen because of a haphazard suggestion thrown out by a silly woman would be ill-advised. Dr Larraby had not known Cora.

Mr Entwhistle cleared his throat and plunged bravely.

'I want to consult you on a very delicate matter,' he said. 'You may be offended, but I sincerely hope not. You are a sensible man and you will realize, I'm sure, that a – er – preposterous suggestion is best dealt with by finding a reasonable answer and not by condemning it out of hand. It concerns my client, the late Mr Abernethie. I'll ask you my question flat out. Are you certain, *absolutely certain*, that he died what is termed a natural death?'

Dr Larraby's good-humoured, rubicund middle-aged face turned in astonishment on his questioner.

'What on earth – Of course he did. I gave a certificate, didn't I? If I hadn't been satisfied –'

Mr Entwhistle cut in adroitly:

'Naturally, naturally. I assure you that I am not assuming anything to the contrary. But I would be glad to have your positive assurance – in face of the – er – rumours that are flying around.'

'Rumours? What rumours?'

'One doesn't know quite how these things start,' said Mr Entwhistle mendaciously. 'But my feeling is that they should be stopped – authoritatively, if possible.'

'Abernethie was a sick man. He was suffering from a disease that would have proved fatal within, I should say, at the earliest, two years. It might have come much sooner. His son's death had weakened his will to live, and his powers of resistance. I admit that I did not expect his death to come so soon, or indeed so suddenly, but there are precedents – plenty of precedents. Any medical man who predicts exactly when a patient will die, or exactly how long he will live, is bound to make a fool of himself. The human factor is always incalculable. The weak have often unexpected powers of resistance, the strong sometimes succumb.'

'I understand all that. I am not doubting your diagnosis. Mr Abernethie was, shall we say (rather melodramatically, I'm afraid) under sentence of death. All I'm asking you is, is it quite possible that a man, knowing or suspecting that he is doomed, might of his own accord shorten that period of life? Or that someone else might do it for him?'

Dr Larraby frowned.

'Suicide, you mean? Abernethie wasn't a suicidal type.'

'I see. You can assure me, medically speaking, that such a suggestion is impossible.'

The doctor stirred uneasily.

'I wouldn't use the word impossible. After his son's death life no longer held the interest for Abernethie that it had done. I certainly don't feel that suicide is likely – but I can't say that it's *impossible*.'

'You are speaking from the psychological angle. When I say medically, I really meant: do the circumstances of his death make such a suggestion impossible?'

'No, oh no. No, I can't say that. He died in his sleep, as people often do. There was no reason to suspect suicide, no evidence of his state of mind. If one were to demand an autopsy every time a man who is seriously ill died in his sleep –'

The doctor's face was getting redder and redder. Mr Entwhistle hastened to interpose.

'Of course. Of course. But if there *had* been evidence – evidence of which you yourself were not aware? If, for instance, he had said something to someone –'

'Indicating that he was contemplating suicide? Did he? I must say it surprises me.'

'But if it *were* so – my case is purely hypothetical – could you rule out the possibility?'

Dr Larraby said slowly:

'No – not – I could not do that. But I say again. I should be very much surprised.'

Mr Entwhistle hastened to follow up his advantage.

'If, then, we assume that his death was *not* natural – all this is *purely* hypothetical – what could have caused it? What kind of a drug, I mean?'

'Several. Some kind of a narcotic would be indicated. There was no sign of cyanosis, the attitude was quite peaceful.'

'He had sleeping draughts or pills? Something of that kind.'

'Yes. I had prescribed Slumberyl – a very safe and dependable hypnotic. He did not take it every night. And he only had a small bottle of tablets at a time. Three or even four times the prescribed dose would not have caused death. In fact, I remember seeing the bottle on his wash-stand after his death still nearly full.'

'What else had you prescribed for him?'

'Various things – a medicine containing a small quantity of morphia to be taken when he had an attack of pain. Some vitamin capsules. An indigestion mixture.'

Mr Entwhistle interrupted.

'Vitamin capsules? I think I was once prescribed a course of those. Small round capsules of gelatine.'

'Yes. Containing adexoline.'

'Could anything else have been introduced into – say – one of those capsules?'

'Something lethal, you mean?' The doctor was looking more and more surprised. 'But surely no man would ever – look here, Entwhistle, what are you getting at? My God, man, are you suggesting *murder*?'

'I don't quite know what I'm suggesting . . . I just want to know what would be *possible*.'

'But what evidence have you for even suggesting such a thing?'

'I haven't any evidence,' said Mr Entwhistle in a tired voice. 'Mr Abernethie is dead – and the person to whom he spoke is also dead. The whole thing is rumour – vague, unsatisfactory rumour, and I want to scotch it if I can. If you tell me that no one could possibly have poisoned Abernethie in any way whatsoever, I'll be delighted! It would be a big weight off my mind, I can assure you.'

Dr Larraby got up and walked up and down.

'I can't tell you what you want me to tell you,' he said at last. 'I wish I could. Of course it could have been done. Anybody could have extracted the oil from a capsule and replaced it with – say – pure nicotine or half a dozen other things. Or something could have been put in his food or drink? Isn't that more likely?'

'Possibly. But you see, there were only the servants in the house when he died – and I don't think it was any of them – in fact I'm quite sure it wasn't. So I'm looking for some delayed action possibility. There's no drug, I suppose, that you can administer and then the person dies weeks later?'

'A convenient idea – but untenable, I'm afraid,' said the doctor drily. 'I know you're a reasonable person, Entwhistle, but who *is* making this suggestion? It seems to me wildly far fetched.'

'Abernethie never said anything to you? Never hinted that one of his relations might be wanting him out of the way?'

The doctor looked at him curiously.

'No, he never said anything to me. Are you sure, Entwhistle, that somebody hasn't been – well, playing up the sensational? Some hysterical subjects can give an appearance of being quite reasonable and normal, you know.'

'I hope it was like that. It might well be.'

'Let me understand. Someone claims that Abernethie told her – it was a woman, I suppose?'

'Oh yes, it was a woman.'

'– told her someone was trying to kill him?'

Cornered, Mr Entwhistle reluctantly told the tale of Cora's remark at the funeral. Dr Larraby's face lightened.

'My dear fellow. I shouldn't pay any attention! The explanation is quite simple. The woman's at a certain time of life – craving for sensation, unbalanced, unreliable – might say anything. They do, you know!'

Mr Entwhistle resented the doctor's easy assumption. He himself had had to deal with plenty of sensation-hunting and hysterical women.

'You may be quite right,' he said, rising. 'Unfortunately we can't tackle her on the subject, as she's been murdered herself.'

'What's that – murdered?' Dr Larraby looked as though he had grave suspicions of Mr Entwhistle's own stability of mind.

'You've probably read about it in the paper. Mrs Lansquenet at Lytchett St Mary in Berkshire.'

'Of course – I'd no idea she was a relation of Richard Abernethie's!' Dr Larraby was looking quite shaken.

Feeling that he had revenged himself for the doctor's professional superiority, and unhappily conscious that his own suspicions had not been assuaged as a result of the visit, Mr Entwhistle took his leave.

II

Back at Enderby, Mr Entwhistle decided to talk to Lanscombe.

He started by asking the old butler what his plans were.

'Mrs Leo has asked me to stay on here until the house is sold, sir, and I'm sure I shall be very pleased to oblige her. We are all very fond of Mrs Leo.' He sighed. 'I feel it very much, sir, if you will excuse me mentioning it, that the house has to be sold. I've known it for so very many years, and seen all the young ladies and gentlemen grow up in it. I always thought that Mr Mortimer would come here after his father and perhaps bring up a family here, too. It was arranged, sir, that I should go to the North Lodge when I got past doing my work here. A very nice little place, the North Lodge – and I looked forward to having it very spick and span. But I suppose that's all over now.'

'I'm afraid so, Lanscombe. The estate will have to be sold together. But with your legacy –'

'Oh I'm not complaining, sir, and I'm very sensible of Mr Abernethie's generosity. I'm well provided for, but it's not so easy to find a little place to buy nowadays and though my married niece has asked me to make my home with them, well, it won't be quite the same thing as living on the estate.'

'I know,' said Mr Entwhistle. 'It's a hard new world for us old fellows. I wish I'd seen more of my old friend before he went. How did he seem those last few months?'

'Well, he wasn't himself, sir, not since Mr Mortimer's death.'

'No, it broke him up. And then he was a sick man – sick men have strange fancies sometimes. I imagine Mr Abernethie suffered from that sort of thing in his last days. He spoke of enemies sometimes, of somebody wishing to do him harm – perhaps? He may even have thought his food was being tampered with?'

Old Lanscombe looked surprised – surprised and offended.

'I cannot recall anything of that kind, sir.'

Entwhistle looked at him keenly.

'You're a very loyal servant, Lanscombe, I know that. But such fancies on Mr Abernethie's part would be quite – er – unimportant – a natural symptom in some – er diseases.'

'Indeed, sir? I can only say Mr Abernethie never said anything like that to me, or in my hearing.'

Mr Entwhistle slid gently to another subject.

'He had some of his family down to stay with him, didn't he, before he died. His nephew and his two nieces and their husbands?'

'Yes, sir, that is so.'

'Was he satisfied with those visits? Or was he disappointed?

Lanscombe's eyes became remote, his old back stiffened.

'I really could not say, sir.'

'I think you could, you know,' said Mr Entwhistle gently. 'It's not your place to say anything of that kind – that's what you really mean. But there are times when one has to do violence to one's senses of what is fitting. I was one of your master's oldest friends. I cared for him very much. So did you. That's why I'm asking you for your opinion as a *man*, not as a butler.'

Lanscombe was silent for a moment, then he said in a colour-less voice:

'Is there anything – wrong, sir?'

Mr Entwhistle replied truthfully.

'I don't know,' he said. 'I hope not. I would like to make sure. Have you felt yourself that something was – wrong?'

'Only since the funeral, sir. And I couldn't say exactly what it is. But Mrs Leo and Mrs Timothy, too, they didn't seem quite themselves that evening after the others had gone.'

'You know the contents of the will?'

'Yes, sir. Mrs Leo thought I would like to know. It seemed to me, if I may permit myself to comment, a very fair will.'

'Yes, it was a fair will. Equal benefits. But it is not, I think, the will that Mr Abernethie originally intended to make after his son died. Will you answer now the question that I asked you just now?'

'As a matter of personal opinion –'

'Yes, yes, that is understood.'

'The master, sir, was very much disappointed after Mr George had been here . . . He had hoped, I think, that Mr George might resemble Mr Mortimer. Mr George, if I may say so, did not come up to standard. Miss Laura's husband was always considered unsatisfactory, and I'm afraid Mr George took after him.' Lanscombe paused and then went on, 'Then the young ladies came with their husbands. Miss Susan he took to at once – a very spirited and handsome young lady, but it's my opinion he couldn't abide her husband. Young ladies make funny choices nowadays, sir.'

'And the other couple?'

'I couldn't say much about that. A very pleasant and good-looking young pair. I think the master enjoyed having them here – but I don't think –' The old man hesitated.

'Yes, Lanscombe?'

'Well, the master had never been much struck with the stage. He said to me one day, "I can't understand why anyone gets stage-struck. It's a foolish kind of life. Seems to deprive people of what little sense they have. I don't know what it does to your moral sense. You certainly lose your sense of proportion." Of course he wasn't referring directly –'

'No, no, I quite understand. Now after these visits, Mr Abernethie himself went away – first to his brother, and afterwards to his sister Mrs Lansquenet.'

'That I did not know, sir. I mean he mentioned to me that he was going to Mr Timothy and afterwards to Something St Mary.'

'That is right. Can you remember anything he said on his return in regard to those visits?'

Lanscombe reflected.

'I really don't know – nothing direct. He was glad to be back. Travelling and staying in strange houses tired him very much – that I do remember his saying.'

'Nothing else? Nothing about either of them?'

Lanscombe frowned.

'The master used to – well, to *murmur*, if you get my meaning – speaking to me and yet more to himself – hardly noticing I was there – because he knew me so well.'

'Knew you and trusted you, yes.'

'But my recollection is very vague as to what he said – something about he couldn't think what he'd done with his money – that was Mr Timothy, I take it. And then he said something about, "Women can be fools in ninety-nine different ways but be pretty shrewd in the hundredth." Oh yes, and he said, "You can only say what you really think to someone of your own generation. They don't think you're fancying things as the younger ones do." And later he said – but I don't know in what connection – "It's not very nice to have to set traps for people, but I don't see what else I can do." But I think it possible, sir, that he may have been thinking of the second gardener – a question of the peaches being taken.'

But Mr Entwhistle did not think that it was the second gardener who had been in Richard Abernethie's mind. After a few more questions he let Lanscombe go and reflected on what he had learned. Nothing, really – nothing, that is, that he had not deduced before. Yet there were suggestive points. It was not his sister-in-law, Maude, but his sister Cora of whom he had been thinking when he made the remark about women who were fools and yet shrewd. And it was to her that he had confided his 'fancies'. And he had spoken of setting a trap. For whom?

III

Mr Entwhistle had meditated a good deal over how much he should tell Helen. In the end he decided he should take her wholly into his confidence.

First he thanked her for sorting out Richard's things and for making various household arrangements. The house had been advertised for sale and there were one or two prospective buyers who would shortly be coming to look over it.

'Private buyers?'

'I'm afraid not. The Y.W.C.A. are considering it, and there is a young people's club, and the Trustees of the Jefferson Trust are looking for a suitable place to house their Collection.'

'It seems sad that the house will not be lived in, but of course it is not a practicable proposition nowadays.'

'I am going to ask you if it would be possible for you to remain here until the house is sold. Or would it be a great inconvenience?'

'No – actually it would suit me very well. I don't want to go to Cyprus until May, and I much prefer being here than being in London as I had planned. I love this house, you know; Leo loved it, and we were always happy when we were here together.'

'There is another reason why I should be grateful if you would stay on. There is a friend of mine, a man called Hercule Poirot –'

Helen said sharply: 'Hercule Poirot? Then you think –'

'You know of him?'

'Yes. Some friends of mine – but I imagined that he was dead long ago.'

'He is very much alive. Not young, of course.'

'No, he could hardly be young.'

She spoke mechanically. Her face was white and strained. She said with an effort:

'You think – that Cora was right? That Richard was – *murdered*?'

Mr Entwhistle unburdened himself. It was a pleasure to unburden himself to Helen with her clear calm mind.

When he had finished she said:

'One ought to feel it's fantastic – but one doesn't. Maude and I, that night after the funeral – it was in both our minds, I'm sure. Saying to ourselves what a silly woman Cora was – and yet being uneasy. And then – Cora was killed – and I told myself it was just coincidence – and of course it may be – but oh! if one can only be sure. It's all so difficult.'

'Yes, it's difficult. But Poirot is a man of great originality and he has something really approaching genius. He understands perfectly what we need – assurance that the whole thing is a mare's nest.'

'And suppose it isn't?'

'What makes you say that?' asked Mr Entwhistle sharply.

'I don't know. I've been uneasy . . . Not just about what Cora said that day – something else. Something that I felt at the time to be wrong.'

'Wrong? In what way?'

'That's just it. I don't know.'

'You mean it was something about one of the people in the room?'

'Yes – yes – something of that kind. But I don't know who or what . . . Oh that sounds absurd –'

'Not at all. It is interesting – very interesting. You are not a fool, Helen. If you noticed something, that something has significance.'

'Yes, but I can't remember what it *was*. The more I think –'

'Don't think. That is the wrong way to bring anything back. Let it go. Sooner or later it will flash into your mind. And when it does – let me know – at once.'

'I will.'

CHAPTER 9

Miss Gilchrist pulled her black hat down firmly on her head and tucked in a wisp of grey hair. The inquest was set for twelve o'clock and it was not quite twenty past eleven. Her grey coat and skirt looked quite nice, she thought, and she had bought herself a black blouse. She wished she could have been all in black, but that would have been far beyond her means. She looked round the small neat bedroom and at the walls hung with representations of Brixham Harbour, Cockington Forge, Anstey's Cove, Kyance Cove, Polflexan Harbour, Babbacombe Bay, etc., all signed in a dashing way, Cora Lansquenet. Her eyes rested with particular fondness on Polflexan Harbour. On the chest of drawers a faded photograph carefully framed represented the Willow Tree tea-shop. Miss Gilchrist looked at it lovingly and sighed.

She was disturbed from her reverie by the sound of the door bell below.

'Dear me,' murmured Miss Gilchrist, 'I wonder who –'

She went out of her room and down the rather rickety stairs. The bell sounded again and there was a sharp knock.

For some reason Miss Gilchrist felt nervous. For a moment or two her steps slowed up, then she went rather unwillingly to the door, adjuring herself not to be so silly.

A young woman dressed smartly in black and carrying a small suitcase was standing on the step. She noticed the alarmed look on Miss Gilchrist's face and said quickly:

'Miss Gilchrist? I am Mrs Lansquenet's niece – Susan Banks.'

'Oh dear, yes, of course. I didn't know. Do come in, Mrs Banks. Mind the hall-stand – it sticks out a little. In here, yes. I didn't know you were coming down for the inquest. I'd have had something ready – some coffee or something.'

Susan Banks said briskly:

'I don't want anything. I'm so sorry if I startled you.'

'Well, you know you *did*, in a way. It's very silly of me. I'm not usually nervous. In fact I told the lawyer that I *wasn't* nervous, and that I wouldn't be nervous staying on here alone, and really I'm *not* nervous. Only – perhaps it's just the inquest and – and thinking of things, but I have been jumpy all this morning, just about half an hour ago the bell rang and I could hardly bring myself to open the door – which was really very stupid and so unlikely that a murderer would come *back* – and why should he? – and actually it was only a nun, collecting for an orphanage – and I was so relieved I gave her two shillings although I'm *not* a Roman Catholic and indeed have no sympathy with the Roman Church and all these monks and nuns although I believe the Little Sisters of the Poor really do good work. But do please sit down, Mrs – Mrs –'

'Banks.'

'Yes, of course, Banks. Did you come down by train?'

'No, I drove down. The lane seemed so narrow I ran the car on a little way and found a sort of old quarry I backed it into.'

'This lane is very narrow, but there's hardly ever any traffic along here. It's rather a lonely road.'

Miss Gilchrist gave a little shiver as she said those last words.

Susan Banks was looking round the room.

'Poor old Aunt Cora,' she said. 'She left what she had to me, you know.'

'Yes, I know. Mr Entwhistle told me. I expect you'll be glad of the furniture. You're newly married, I understand, and furnishing is such an expense nowadays. Mrs Lansquenet had some very nice things.'

Susan did not agree. Cora had had no taste for the antique. The contents varied between 'modernistic' pieces and the 'arty' type.

'I shan't want any of the furniture,' she said. 'I've got my own, you know. I shall put it up for auction. Unless – is there any of it you would like? I'd be very glad . . .'

She stopped, a little embarrassed. But Miss Gilchrist was not at all embarrassed. She beamed.

'Now really, that's *very* kind of you, Mrs Banks – yes, very kind indeed. I really do appreciate it. But actually, you know, I have my own things. I put them in store in case – some day – I should need them. There are some pictures my father left too. I had a small tea-shop at one time, you know – but then the war came – it was all very unfortunate. But I didn't sell up everything, because I did hope to have my own little home again one day, so I put the best things in store with my father's pictures and some relics of our old home. But I *would* like very much, if you *really* wouldn't mind, to have that little painted tea table of dear Mrs Lansquenet's. Such a pretty thing and we always had tea on it.'

Susan, looking with a slight shudder at a small green table painted with large purple clematis, said quickly that she would be delighted for Miss Gilchrist to have it.

'Thank you *very* much, Mrs Banks. I feel a little greedy. I've got all her beautiful pictures, you know, and a lovely amethyst brooch, but I feel that perhaps I ought to give *that* back to you.'

'No, no, indeed.'

'You'll want to go through her things? After the inquest, perhaps?'

'I thought I'd stay here a couple of days, go through things, and clear everything up.'

'Sleep here, you mean?'

'Yes. Is there any difficulty?'

'Oh no, Mrs Banks, of course not. I'll put fresh sheets on my bed, and I can doss down here on the couch quite well.'

'But there's Aunt Cora's room, isn't there? I can sleep in that.'

'You – you wouldn't mind?'

'You mean because she was murdered there? Oh no, I wouldn't mind. I'm very tough, Miss Gilchrist. It's been – I mean – It's all right again?'

Miss Gilchrist understood the question.

'Oh *yes*, Mrs Banks. All the blankets sent away to the cleaners and Mrs Panter and I scrubbed the whole room out thoroughly. And there are plenty of spare blankets. But come up and see for yourself.'

She led the way upstairs and Susan followed her.

The room where Cora Lansquenet had died was clean and fresh and curiously devoid of any sinister atmosphere. Like the sitting-room it contained a mixture of modern utility and elaborately painted furniture. It represented Cora's cheerful tasteless personality. Over the mantelpiece an oil painting showed a buxom young woman about to enter her bath.

Susan gave a slight shudder as she looked at it and Miss Gilchrist said:

'That was painted by Mrs Lansquenet's husband. There are a lot more of his pictures in the dining-room downstairs.'

'How terrible.'

'Well, I don't care very much for that style of painting *myself* – but Mrs Lansquenet was very proud of her husband as an artist and thought that his work was sadly unappreciated.'

'Where are Aunt Cora's own pictures?'

'In my room. Would you like to see them?'

Miss Gilchrist displayed her treasures proudly.

Susan remarked that Aunt Cora seemed to have been fond of sea coast resorts.

'Oh yes. You see, she lived for many years with Mr Lansquenet at a small fishing village in Brittany. Fishing boats are always so picturesque, are they not?'

'Obviously,' Susan murmured. A whole series of picture postcards could, she thought, have been made from Cora Lansquenet's paintings which were faithful to detail and very highly coloured. They gave rise to the suspicion that they might actually have been painted from picture postcards.

But when she hazarded this opinion Miss Gilchrist was indignant. Mrs Lansquenet *always* painted from Nature! Indeed, once she had had a touch of the sun from reluctance to leave a subject when the light was just right.

'Mrs Lansquenet was a real artist,' said Miss Gilchrist reproachfully.

She glanced at her watch and Susan said quickly:

'Yes, we ought to start for the inquest. Is it far? Shall I get the car?'

It was only five minutes' walk, Miss Gilchrist assured her. So they set out together on foot. Mr Entwhistle, who had come down by train, met them and shepherded them into the Village Hall.

There seemed to be a large number of strangers present. The inquest was not sensational. There was evidence of the identification of the deceased. Medical evidence as to the nature of the wounds that had killed her. There were no signs of a struggle. Deceased was probably under a narcotic at the time she was attacked and would have been taken quite unawares. Death was unlikely to have occurred later than four-thirty. Between two and four-thirty was the nearest approximation. Miss Gilchrist testified to finding the body. A police constable and Inspector Morton gave their evidence. The Coroner summed up briefly. The jury made no bones about the verdict. '*Murder by some person or persons unknown.*'

It was over. They came out again into the sunlight. Half a dozen cameras clicked. Mr Entwhistle shepherded Susan and Miss Gilchrist into the King's Arms, where he had taken the precaution to arrange for lunch to be served in a private room behind the bar.

'Not a very good lunch,' he said apologetically.

But the lunch was not at all bad. Miss Gilchrist sniffed a little and murmured that 'it was all so dreadful,' but cheered up and tackled the Irish stew with appetite after Mr Entwhistle had insisted on her drinking a glass of sherry. He said to Susan:

'I'd no idea you were coming down today, Susan. We could have come together.'

'I know I said I wouldn't. But it seemed rather mean for none of the family to be there. I rang up George but he said he was very busy and couldn't possibly make it, and Rosamund had an audition and Uncle Timothy, of course, is a crock. So it had to be me.'

'Your husband didn't come with you?'

'Greg had to settle up with his tiresome shop.'

Seeing a startled look in Miss Gilchrist's eye, Susan said: 'My husband works in a chemist's shop.'

A husband in retail trade did not quite square with Miss Gilchrist's impression of Susan's smartness, but she said valiantly: 'Oh yes, just like Keats.'

'Greg's no poet,' said Susan.

She added:

'We've got great plans for the future – a double-barrelled establishment – Cosmetics and Beauty parlour and a laboratory for special preparations.'

'That will be much nicer,' said Miss Gilchrist approvingly. 'Something like Elizabeth Arden who is really a Countess, so I have been told – or is that Helena Rubenstein? In any case,' she added kindly, 'a pharmacist's is not in the least like an ordinary shop – a *draper*, for instance, or a *grocer*.'

'You kept a tea-shop, you said, didn't you?'

'Yes, indeed,' Miss Gilchrist's face lit up. That the Willow Tree had ever been 'trade' in the sense that a shop was trade, would never have occurred to her. To keep a tea-shop was in her mind the essence of gentility. She started telling Susan about the Willow Tree.

Mr Entwhistle, who had heard about it before, let his mind drift to other matters. When Susan had spoken to him twice without his answering he hurriedly apologized.

'Forgive me, my dear, I was thinking, as a matter of fact, about your Uncle Timothy. I am a little worried.'

'About Uncle Timothy? I shouldn't be. I don't believe really there's anything the matter with him. He's just a hypochondriac.'

'Yes – yes, you may be right. I confess it was not his health that was worrying me. It's Mrs Timothy. Apparently she's fallen downstairs and twisted her ankle. She's laid up and your uncle is in a terrible state.'

'Because he'll have to look after her instead of the other way about? Do him a lot of good,' said Susan.

'Yes – yes, I dare say. But will your poor aunt *get* any looking after? That is really the question. With no servants in the house?'

'Life is really hell for elderly people,' said Susan. 'They live in a kind of Georgian Manor house, don't they?'

Mr Entwhistle nodded.

They came rather warily out of the King's Arms, but the Press seemed to have dispersed.

A couple of reporters were lying in wait for Susan by the cottage door. Shepherded by Mr Entwhistle she said a few necessary and non-committal words. Then she and Miss Gilchrist went into the cottage and Mr Entwhistle returned to the King's Arms where he had booked a room. The funeral was to be on the following day.

'My car's still in the quarry,' said Susan. 'I'd forgotten about it. I'll drive it along to the village later.'

Miss Gilchrist said anxiously:

'Not too late. You won't go out after dark, will you?'

Susan looked at her and laughed.

'You don't think there's a murderer still hanging about, do you?'

'No – no, I suppose not.' Miss Gilchrist looked embarrassed.

'But it's exactly what she does think, thought Susan. 'How amazing!'

Miss Gilchrist had vanished towards the kitchen.

'I'm sure you'd like tea early. In about half an hour, do you think, Mrs Banks?'

Susan thought that tea at half-past three was overdoing it, but she was charitable enough to realize that 'a nice cup of tea' was Miss Gilchrist's idea of restoration for the nerves and she had her own reasons for wishing to please Miss Gilchrist, so she said:

'Whenever you like, Miss Gilchrist.'

A happy clatter of kitchen implements began and Susan went into the sitting-room. She had only been there a few minutes when the bell sounded and was succeeded by a very precise little rat-tat-tat.

Susan came out into the hall and Miss Gilchrist appeared at the kitchen door wearing an apron and wiping floury hands on it.

'Oh dear, who do you think that can be?'

'More reporters, I expect,' said Susan.

'Oh dear, how annoying for you, Mrs Banks.'

'Oh well, never mind, I'll attend to it.'

'I was just going to make a few scones for tea.'

Susan went towards the front door and Miss Gilchrist hovered uncertainly. Susan wondered whether she thought a man with a hatchet was waiting outside.

The visitor, however, proved to be an elderly gentleman who raised his hat when Susan opened the door and said, beaming at her in avuncular style:

'Mrs Banks, I think?'

'Yes.'

'My name is Guthrie – Alexander Guthrie. I was a friend – a very old friend, of Mrs Lansquenet's. You, I think, are her niece, formerly Miss Susan Abernethie?'

'That's quite right.'

'Then since we know who we are, I may come in?'

'Of course.'

Mr Guthrie wiped his feet carefully on the mat, stepped inside, divested himself of his overcoat, laid it down with his hat on a small oak chest and followed Susan into the sitting-room.

'This is a melancholy occasion,' said Mr Guthrie, to whom melancholy did not seem to come naturally, his own inclination being to beam. 'Yes, a very melancholy occasion. I was in this part of the world and I felt the least I could do was to attend the inquest – and of course the funeral. Poor Cora – poor foolish Cora. I have known her, my dear Mrs Banks, since the early days of her marriage. A high-spirited girl – and she took art very seriously – took Pierre Lansquenet seriously, too – as an artist, I mean. All things considered he didn't make her too bad a husband. He strayed, if you know what I mean, yes, he strayed – but fortunately Cora took it as part of the artistic temperament. He was an artist and therefore immoral! In fact, I'm not sure she didn't go further: he was immoral and therefore he must be an artist! No kind of sense in artistic matters, poor Cora – though in other ways, mind you, Cora had a lot of sense – yes, a surprising lot of sense.'

'That's what everybody seems to say,' said Susan. 'I didn't really know her.'

'No, no, cut herself off from her family because they didn't appreciate her precious Pierre. She was never a pretty girl – but she had *something*. She was good company! You never knew what she'd say next and you never knew if her naïveté was genuine or whether she was doing it deliberately. She made us all laugh a good deal. The eternal child – that's what we always felt about her. And really the last time I saw her (I have seen her from time to time since Pierre died) she struck me as still behaving very much like a child.'

Susan offered Mr Guthrie a cigarette, but the old gentleman shook his head.

'No thank you, my dear. I don't smoke. You must wonder why I've come? To tell you the truth I was feeling rather conscience-stricken. I promised Cora to come and see her some weeks ago. I usually called upon her once a year, and just lately she'd taken up the hobby of buying pictures at local sales, and wanted me to look at some of them. My profession is that of art critic, you know. Of course most of Cora's purchases were horrible daubs, but take it all in all, it isn't such a bad speculation. Pictures go for next to nothing at these country sales and the frames alone are worth more than you pay for the picture. Naturally any important sale is attended by dealers and one isn't likely to get hold of masterpieces. But only the other day, a small Cuyp was knocked down for a few pounds at a farmhouse sale. The history of it was quite interesting. It had been given to an old nurse by the family she had served faithfully for many years – they had no idea of its value. Old nurse gave it to a farmer nephew who liked the horse in it but thought it was a dirty old thing! Yes, yes, these things sometimes happen, and Cora was convinced that she had an eye for pictures. She hadn't of course. Wanted me to come and look at a Rembrandt she had picked up last year. A Rembrandt! Not even a respectable copy of one! But she had got hold of a quite nice Bartolozzi engraving – damp spotted unfortunately. I sold it for her for thirty pounds and of course that spurred her on. She wrote to me with great gusto about an Italian Primitive she had bought at some sale and I promised I'd come along and see it.'

'That's it over there, I expect,' said Susan, gesturing to the wall behind him.

Mr Guthrie got up, put on a pair of spectacles, and went over to study the picture.

'Poor dear Cora,' he said at last.

'There are a lot more,' said Susan.

Mr Guthrie proceeded to a leisurely inspection of the art treasures acquired by the hopeful Mrs Lansquenet. Occasionally he said, 'Tchk, Tchk,' occasionally he sighed.

Finally he removed his spectacles.

'Dirt,' he said, 'is a wonderful thing, Mrs Banks! It gives a patina of romance to the most horrible examples of the painter's art. I'm afraid that Bartolozzi was beginner's luck. Poor Cora. Still, it gave her an interest in life. I am really thankful that I did not have to disillusion her.'

'There are some pictures in the dining-room,' said Susan, 'but I think they are all her husband's work.'

Mr Guthrie shuddered slightly and held up a protesting hand.

'Do not force me to look at those again. Life classes have much to answer for! I always tried to spare Cora's feelings. A devoted wife – a very devoted wife. Well, dear Mrs Banks, I must not take up more of your time.'

'Oh, do stay and have some tea. I think it's nearly ready.'

'That is very kind of you.' Mr Guthrie sat down again promptly.

'I'll just go and see.'

In the kitchen, Miss Gilchrist was just lifting a last batch of scones from the oven. The tea-tray stood ready and the kettle was just gently rattling its lid.

'There's a Mr Guthrie here, and I've asked him to stay for tea.'

'Mr Guthrie? Oh, yes, he was a great friend of dear Mrs Lansquenet's. He's the celebrated art critic. How fortunate; I've made a nice lot of scones and that's some homemade strawberry jam, and I just whipped up some little drop cakes. I'll just make the tea – I've warmed the pot. Oh, please, Mrs Banks, don't carry that heavy tray. I can manage *everything*.'

However, Susan took in the tray and Miss Gilchrist followed with teapot and kettle, greeted Mr Guthrie, and they set to.

'Hot scones, that *is* a treat,' said Mr Guthrie, 'and what delicious jam! Really, the stuff one buys nowadays.'

Miss Gilchrist was flushed and delighted. The little cakes were excellent and so were the scones, and everyone did justice to them. The ghost of the Willow Tree hung over the party. Here, it was clear, Miss Gilchrist was in her element.

'Well, thank you, perhaps I will,' said Mr Guthrie as he

accepted the last cake, pressed upon him by Miss Gilchrist. 'I do feel rather guilty, though – enjoying my tea here, where poor Cora was so brutally murdered.'

Miss Gilchrist displayed an unexpected Victorian reaction to this.

'Oh, but Mrs Lansquenet would have wished you to take a good tea. You've got to keep your strength up.'

'Yes, yes, perhaps you are right. The fact is, you know, that one cannot really bring oneself to believe that someone you knew – actually knew – *can* have been murdered!'

'I agree,' said Susan. 'It just seems – fantastic.'

'And certainly not by some casual tramp who broke in and attacked her. I *can* imagine, you know, reasons why Cora might have been murdered –'

Susan said quickly, 'Can you? What reasons?'

'Well, she wasn't discreet,' said Mr Guthrie. 'Cora was never discreet. And she enjoyed – how shall I put it – showing how sharp she could be? Like a child who's got hold of somebody's secret. If Cora got hold of a secret she'd want to talk about it. Even if she promised not to, she'd still do it. She wouldn't be able to help herself.'

Susan did not speak. Miss Gilchrist did not either. She looked worried. Mr Guthrie went on:

'Yes, a little dose of arsenic in a cup of tea – *that* would not have surprised me, or a box of chocolates by post. But sordid robbery and assault – that seems highly incongruous. I may be wrong but I should have thought she had very little to take that would be worth a burglar's while. She didn't keep much money in the house, did she?'

Miss Gilchrist said, 'Very little.'

Mr Guthrie sighed and rose to his feet.

'Ah! well, there's a lot of lawlessness about since the war. Times have changed.'

Thanking them for the tea he took a polite farewell of the two women. Miss Gilchrist saw him out and helped him on with his overcoat. From the window of the sitting-room, Susan watched him trot briskly down the front path to the gate.

Miss Gilchrist came back into the room with a small parcel in her hand.

'The postman must have been while we were at the inquest. He pushed it through the letter-box and it had fallen in the corner behind the door. Now I wonder – why, of course, it must be wedding cake.'

Happily Miss Gilchrist ripped off the paper. Inside was a small white box tied with silver ribbon.

'It is!' She pulled off the ribbon, inside was a modest wedge of rich cake with almond paste and white icing. 'How nice! Now who –' She consulted the card attached. '*John and Mary*. Now who *can* that be? How silly to put no surname.'

Susan, rousing herself from contemplation, said vaguely:

'It's quite difficult sometimes with people just using Christian names. I got a postcard the other day signed Joan. I counted up I knew eight Joans – and with telephoning so much, one often doesn't know their handwriting.'

Miss Gilchrist was happily going over the possible Johns and Marys of her acquaintance.

'It might be Dorothy's daughter – *her* name was Mary, but I hadn't heard of an engagement, still less of a marriage. Then there's little John Banfield – I suppose he's grown up and old enough to be married – or the Enfield girl – no, her name was Margaret. No address or anything. Oh well, I dare say it will come to me . . .'

She picked up the tray and went out to the kitchen.

Susan roused herself and said:

'Well – I suppose I'd better go and put the car somewhere.'

CHAPTER 10

Susan retrieved the car from the quarry where she had left it and drove it into the village. There was a petrol pump but no garage and she was advised to take it to the King's Arms. They had room for it there and she left it by a big Daimler which was preparing to go out. It was chauffeur driven and inside it, very much muffled up, was an elderly foreign gentleman with a large moustache.

The boy to whom Susan was talking about the car was staring at her with such rapt attention that he did not seem to be taking in half of what she said.

Finally he said in an awe-stricken voice:

'You're her niece, aren't you?'

'What?'

'You're the victim's niece,' the boy repeated with relish.

'Oh – yes – yes, I am.'

'Ar! Wondered where I'd seen you before.'

'Ghoul,' thought Susan as she retraced her steps to the cottage.

Miss Gilchrist greeted her with:

'Oh, you're safely back,' in tones of relief which further annoyed her. Miss Gilchrist added anxiously:

'You *can* eat spaghetti, can't you? I thought for tonight –'

'Oh yes, anything. I don't want much.'

'I really flatter myself that I can make a very tasty spaghetti *au gratin.*'

The boast was not an idle one. Miss Gilchrist, Susan reflected, was really an excellent cook. Susan offered to help wash up but Miss Gilchrist, though clearly gratified by the offer, assured Susan that there was very little to do.

She came in a little while after with coffee. The coffee was less excellent, being decidedly weak. Miss Gilchrist offered Susan a piece of the wedding cake which Susan refused.

'It's really very good cake,' Miss Gilchrist insisted, tasting it. She had settled to her own satisfaction that it must have been sent by someone whom she alluded to as 'dear Ellen's daughter who I know was engaged to be married but I can't remember her name.'

Susan let Miss Gilchrist chirrup away into silence before starting her own subject of conversation. This moment, after supper, sitting before the fire, was a companionable one.

She said at last:

'My Uncle Richard came down here before he died, didn't he?'

'Yes, he did.'

'When was that exactly?'

'Let me see – it must have been one, two – nearly three weeks before his death was announced.'

'Did he seem – ill?'

'Well, no, I wouldn't say he seemed exactly ill. He had a very hearty vigorous manner. Mrs Lansquenet was very surprised to see him. She said, "Well, really, Richard, after all these years!" and he said, "I came to see for myself exactly how things are with you." And Mrs Lansquenet said, "*I*'m all right." I think, you know, she was a teeny bit offended by his turning up so casually – after the long break. Anyway Mr Abernethie said, "No use keeping up old grievances. You and I and Timothy are the only ones left – and nobody can talk to Timothy except about his own health." And he said, "Pierre seems to have made you happy, so it seems I was in the wrong. There, will that content you?" Very nicely he said it. A handsome man, though elderly, of course.'

'How long was he here?'

'He stayed for lunch. Beef olives, I made. Fortunately it was the day the butcher called.'

Miss Gilchrist's memory seemed to be almost wholly culinary.

'They seemed to be getting on well together?'

'Oh, yes.'

Susan paused and then said:

'Was Aunt Cora surprised when – he died?'

'Oh yes, it was quite sudden, wasn't it?'

'Yes, it was sudden . . . I mean – she *was* surprised. He hadn't given her any indication how ill he was.'

'Oh – I see what you mean.' Miss Gilchrist paused a moment. 'No, no, I think perhaps you are right. She did say that he had got very old – I think she said senile . . .'

'But *you* didn't think he was senile?'

'Well, not to *look* at. But I didn't talk to him much, naturally I left them alone together.'

Susan looked at Miss Gilchrist speculatively. Was Miss Gilchrist the kind of woman who listened at doors? She was honest, Susan felt sure, she wouldn't ever pilfer, or cheat over the housekeeping, or open letters. But inquisitiveness can drape itself in a mantle of rectitude. Miss Gilchrist might have found it necessary to garden near an open window, or to dust the hall . . . That would be within the permitted lengths. And then, of course, she could not have helped hearing something . . .

'You didn't hear any of their conversation?' Susan asked.

Too abrupt. Miss Gilchrist flushed angrily.

'No, indeed, Mrs Banks. It has never been my custom to listen at doors!'

That means she does, thought Susan, otherwise she'd just say 'No.'

Aloud she said: 'I'm so sorry, Miss Gilchrist. I didn't mean it that way. But sometimes, in these small flimsily built cottages, one simply can't help overhearing nearly everything that goes on, and now that they are both dead, it's really rather important to the family to know just what was said at that meeting between them.'

The cottage was anything but flimsily built – it dated from a sturdier era of building, but Miss Gilchrist accepted the bait, and rose to the suggestion held out.

'Of course what you say is quite true, Mrs Banks – this *is* a very small place and I do appreciate that you would want to know what passed between them, but really I'm afraid I can't help very much. I think they were talking about Mr Abernethie's health – and certain – well, *fancies* he had. He didn't look it, but he must have been a sick man and as is so often the case, he put his ill-health down to *outside agencies*. A common symptom, I believe. My aunt –'

Miss Gilchrist described her aunt.

Susan, like Mr Entwhistle, side-tracked the aunt.

'Yes,' she said. 'That is just what we thought. My uncle's servants were all very attached to him and naturally they are upset by his thinking –' She paused.

'Oh, of course! Servants are *very* touchy about anything of that kind. I remember that my aunt –'

Again Susan interrupted.

'It *was* the servants he suspected, I suppose? Of poisoning him, I mean?'

'I don't know . . . I – really –'

Susan noted her confusion.

'It wasn't the servants. Was it one particular person?'

'I don't know, Mrs Banks. Really I don't know –'

But her eye avoided Susan's. Susan thought to herself that Miss Gilchrist knew more than she was willing to admit.

It was possible that Miss Gilchrist knew a good deal . . .

Deciding not to press the point for the moment, Susan said:

'What are your own plans for the future, Miss Gilchrist?'

'Well, really, I was going to speak to you about that, Mrs Banks. I told Mr Entwhistle I would be willing to stay on until everything here was cleared up.'

'I know. I'm very grateful.'

'And I wanted to ask you how long that was likely to be, because, of course, I must start looking about for another post.'

Susan considered.

'There's really not very much to be done here. In a couple of days I can get things sorted out and notify the auctioneer.'

'You have decided to sell up everything, then?'

'Yes. I don't suppose there will be any difficulty in letting the cottage?'

'*Oh, no* – people will queue up for it, I'm sure. There are so few cottages to rent. One nearly always has to buy.'

'So it's all very simple, you see.' Susan hesitated a moment before saying, 'I wanted to tell you – that I hope you'll accept three months' salary.'

'That's very generous of you, I'm sure, Mrs Banks. I do appreciate it. And you would be prepared to – I mean I could ask you – if necessary – to – to recommend me? To say that I had been with a relation of yours and that I had – proved satisfactory?'

'Oh, of course.'

'I don't know whether I ought to ask it.' Miss Gilchrist's hands began to shake and she tried to steady her voice. 'But would it be possible not to – to mention the circumstances – or even the *name*?'

Susan stared.

'I don't understand.'

'That's because you haven't thought, Mrs Banks. It's *murder*. A murder that's been in the papers and that everybody has read about. Don't you see? People might think, "Two women living together, and one of them is killed – and *perhaps the companion did it*." Don't you see, Mrs Banks? I'm sure that if *I* was looking for someone, I'd – well, I'd think twice before engaging myself – if you understand what I mean. Because one never *knows*! It's been worrying me dreadfully, Mrs Banks; I've been lying awake at night thinking that perhaps I'll never get another job – not of this kind. And what else is there that I can do?'

The question came out with unconscious pathos. Susan felt suddenly stricken. She realized the desperation of this pleasant-spoken commonplace woman who was dependent for existence on the fears and whims of employers. And there was a lot of truth in what Miss Gilchrist had said. You wouldn't, if you could help it, engage a woman to share domestic intimacy who had figured, however innocently, in a murder case.

Susan said: 'But if they find the man who did it –'

'Oh *then*, of course, it will be quite all right. But will they find him? I don't think, myself, the police have the *least idea*. And if he's *not* caught – well, that leaves me as – as not quite the most likely person, but as a person who *could* have done it.'

Susan nodded thoughtfully. It was true that Miss Gilchrist did not benefit from Cora Lansquenet's death – but who was to know that? And besides, there were so many tales – ugly tales – of animosity arising between women who lived together – strange pathological motives for sudden violence. Someone who had not known them might imagine that Cora Lansquenet and Miss Gilchrist had lived on those terms . . .

Susan spoke with her usual decision.

'Don't worry, Miss Gilchrist,' she said, speaking briskly and cheerfully. 'I'm sure I can find you a post amongst my friends. There won't be the least difficulty.'

'I'm afraid,' said Miss Gilchrist, regaining some of her customary manner, 'that I couldn't undertake any really rough work. Just a little plain cooking and housework –'

The telephone rang and Miss Gilchrist jumped.

'Dear me, I wonder who *that* can be.'

'I expect it's my husband,' said Susan, jumping up. 'He said he'd ring me tonight.'

She went to the telephone.

'Yes? – yes, this is Mrs Banks speaking personally . . .' There was a pause and then her voice changed. It became soft and warm. 'Hallo, darling – yes, it's me . . . Oh, quite well . . . Murder by someone unknown . . . the usual thing . . . Only Mr Entwhistle . . . What? . . . it's difficult to say, but I think so . . . Yes, just as we thought . . . Absolutely according to plan . . . I shall sell the stuff. There's nothing *we'd* want . . . Not for a day or two . . . Absolutely frightful . . . Don't fuss. I know what I'm doing . . . Greg, you didn't . . . You were careful to . . . No, it's nothing. Nothing at all. Goodnight, darling.'

She rang off. The nearness of Miss Gilchrist had hampered her a little. Miss Gilchrist could probably hear from the kitchen, where she had tactfully retired, exactly what went on. There were things she had wanted to ask Greg, but she hadn't liked to.

She stood by the telephone, frowning abstractedly. Then suddenly an idea came to her.

'Of course,' she murmured. 'Just the thing.'

Lifting the receiver she asked for Trunk Enquiry.

Some quarter of an hour later a weary voice from the exchange was saying:

'I'm afraid there's no reply.'

'Please go on ringing them.'

Susan spoke autocratically. She listened to the far off buzzing of a telephone bell. Then, suddenly it was interrupted and a man's voice, peevish and slightly indignant, said:

'Yes, yes, what is it?'

'Uncle Timothy?'

'What's that? I can't hear you.'

'Uncle Timothy? I'm Susan Banks.'

'Susan who?'

'Banks. Formerly Abernethie. Your niece Susan.'

'Oh, you're Susan, are you? What's the matter? What are you ringing up for at this time of night?'

'It's quite early still.'

'It isn't. I was in bed.'

'You must go to bed very early. How's Aunt Maude?'

'Is that all you rang up to ask? Your aunt's in a good deal of pain and she can't do a thing. Not a thing. She's helpless. We're in a nice mess, I can tell you. That fool of a doctor says he can't even get a nurse. He wanted to cart Maude off to hospital. I stood out against *that*. He's trying to get hold of someone for us. *I* can't do anything – I daren't even try. There's a fool from the village staying in the house tonight – but she's murmuring about getting back to her husband. Don't know *what* we're going to do.'

'That's what I rang up about. Would you like Miss Gilchrist?'

'Who's she? Never heard of her.'

'Aunt Cora's companion. She's very nice and capable.'

'Can she cook?'

'Yes, she cooks very well, and she could look after Aunt Maude.'

'That's all very well, but when could she come? Here I am, all on my own, with only these idiots of village women popping in and out at odd hours, and it's not good for me. My heart's playing me up.'

'I'll arrange for her to get off to you as soon as possible. The day after tomorrow, perhaps?'

'Well, thanks very much,' said the voice rather grudgingly. 'You're a good girl, Susan – er – thank you.'

Susan rang off and went into the kitchen.

'Would you be willing to go up to Yorkshire and look after my aunt? She fell and broke her ankle and my uncle is quite useless. He's a bit of a pest but Aunt Maude is a very good sort. They have help in from the village, but you could cook and look after Aunt Maude.'

Miss Gilchrist dropped the coffee pot in her agitation.

'Oh, thank you, thank you – that really is kind. I think I can say of myself that I am really good in the sickroom, and I'm sure I can manage your uncle and cook him nice little meals. It's really very kind of you, Mrs Banks, and I *do* appreciate it.'

CHAPTER 11

I

Susan lay in bed and waited for sleep to come. It had been a long day and she was tired. She had been quite sure that she would go to sleep at once. She never had any difficulty in going to sleep. And yet here she lay, hour after hour, wide awake, her mind racing.

She had said she did not mind sleeping in this room, in this bed. This bed where Cora Abernethie –

No, no she must put all that out of her mind. She had always prided herself on having no nerves. Why think of that afternoon less than a week ago? Think ahead – the future. Her future and

Greg's. Those premises in Cardigan Street – just what they wanted. The business on the ground floor and a charming flat upstairs. The room out at the back a laboratory for Greg. For purposes of income tax it would be an excellent set-up. Greg would get calm and well again. There would be no more of those alarming brain-storms. The times when he looked at her without seeming to know who she was. Once or twice she'd been quite frightened . . . And old Mr Cole – he'd hinted – threatened: 'If this happens again . . .' And it might have happened again – it *would* have happened again. If Uncle Richard hadn't died just when he did . . .

Uncle Richard – but really why look at it like that? He'd nothing to live for. Old and tired and ill. His son dead. It was a mercy really. To die in his sleep quietly like that. Quietly . . . in his sleep . . . If only she could sleep. It was so stupid lying awake hour after hour . . . hearing the furniture creak, and the rustling of trees and bushes outside the window and the occasional queer melancholy hoot – an owl, she supposed. How sinister the country was, somehow. So different from the big noisy indifferent town. One felt so safe there – surrounded by people – never alone. Whereas here . . .

Houses where a murder had been committed were sometimes haunted. Perhaps this cottage would come to be known as the haunted cottage. Haunted by the spirit of Cora Lansquenet . . . Aunt Cora. Odd, really, how ever since she had arrived she had felt as though Aunt Cora were quite close to her . . . within reach. All nerves and fancy. Cora Lansquenet was dead, tomorrow she would be buried. There was no one in the cottage except Susan herself and Miss Gilchrist. Then why did she feel that there was someone in this room, someone close beside her . . .

She had lain on this bed when the hatchet fell . . . Lying there trustingly asleep . . . Knowing nothing till the hatchet fell . . . And now she wouldn't let Susan sleep . . .

The furniture creaked again . . . was that a stealthy step? Susan switched on the light. Nothing. Nerves, nothing but nerves. Relax . . . close your eyes . . .

Surely that was a groan – a groan or a faint moan . . . Someone in pain – someone dying . . .

'I mustn't imagine things, I mustn't, I mustn't,' Susan whispered to herself.

Death was the end – there was no existence after death. Under no circumstances could anyone come back. Or was she reliving a scene from the past – a dying woman groaning . . .

There it was again . . . stronger . . . someone groaning in acute pain . . .

But – this was real. Once again Susan switched on the light, sat up in bed and listened. The groans were real groans and she was hearing them through the wall. They came from the room next door.

Susan jumped out of bed, flung on a dressing-gown and crossed to the door. She went out on to the landing, tapped for a moment on Miss Gilchrist's door and then went in. Miss Gilchrist's light was on. She was sitting up in bed. She looked ghastly. Her face was distorted with pain.

'Miss Gilchrist, what's the matter? Are you ill?'

'Yes. I don't know what – I –' she tried to get out of bed, was seized with a fit of vomiting and then collapsed back on the pillows.

She murmured: 'Please – ring up doctor. Must have eaten something . . .'

'I'll get you some bicarbonate. We can get the doctor in the morning if you're no better.'

Miss Gilchrist shook her head.

'No, get the doctor now. I – I feel dreadful.'

'Do you know his number? Or shall I look in the book?'

Miss Gilchrist gave her the number. She was interrupted by another fit of retching.

Susan's call was answered by a sleepy male voice.

'Who? Gilchrist? In Mead's Lane. Yes, I know. I'll be right along.'

He was as good as his word. Ten minutes later Susan heard his car draw up outside and she went to open the door to him.

She explained the case and she took him upstairs. 'I think,' she said, 'she must have eaten something that disagreed with her. But she seems pretty bad.'

The doctor had had the air of one keeping his temper in leash and who has had some experience of being called out unnecessarily on more than one occasion. But as soon as he examined the moaning woman his manner changed. He gave various curt orders to Susan and presently came down and telephoned. Then he joined Susan in the sitting-room.

'I've sent for an ambulance. Must get her into hospital.'

'She's really bad then?'

'Yes. I've given her a shot of morphia to ease the pain. But it looks –' He broke off. 'What's she eaten?'

'We had macaroni *au gratin* for supper and a custard pudding. Coffee afterwards.'

'You have the same things?'

'Yes.'

'And you're all right? No pain or discomfort?'

'No.'

'She's taken nothing else? No tinned fish? Or sausages?'

'No. We had lunch at the King's Arms – after the inquest.'

'Yes, of course. You're Mrs Lansquenet's niece?'

'Yes.'

'That was a nasty business. Hope they catch the man who did it.'

'Yes, indeed.'

The ambulance came. Miss Gilchrist was taken away and the doctor went with her. He told Susan he would ring her up in the morning. When he had left she went upstairs to bed.

This time she fell asleep as soon as her head touched the pillow.

II

The funeral was well attended. Most of the village had turned out. Susan and Mr Entwhistle were the only mourners, but various wreaths had been sent by the other members of the family. Mr Entwhistle asked where Miss Gilchrist was, and Susan explained the circumstances in a hurried whisper. Mr Entwhistle raised his eyebrows.

'Rather an odd occurrence?'

'Oh, she's better this morning. They rang up from the hospital. People do get these bilious turns. Some make more fuss than others.'

Mr Entwhistle said no more. He was returning to London immediately after the funeral.

Susan went back to the cottage. She found some eggs and made herself an omelette. Then she went up to Cora's room and started to sort through the dead woman's things.

She was interrupted by the arrival of the doctor.

The doctor was looking worried. He replied to Susan's inquiry by saying that Miss Gilchrist was much better.

'She'll be out and around in a couple of days,' he said. 'But it was lucky I got called in so promptly. Otherwise – it might have been a near thing.'

Susan stared. 'Was she really so bad?'

'Mrs Banks, will you tell me again exactly what Miss Gilchrist had to eat and drink yesterday. Everything.'

Susan reflected and gave a meticulous account. The doctor shook his head in a dissatisfied manner.

'There must have been something she had and you didn't?'

'I don't think so . . . Cakes, scones, jam, tea – and then supper. No, I can't remember anything.'

The doctor rubbed his nose. He walked up and down the room.

'Was it definitely something she ate? Definitely food poisoning?'

The doctor threw her a sharp glance. Then he seemed to come to a decision.

'It was arsenic,' he said.

'Arsenic?' Susan started. 'You mean somebody gave her arsenic?'

'That's what it looks like.'

'Could she have taken it herself? Deliberately, I mean?'

'Suicide? She says not and she should know. Besides, if she wanted to commit suicide she wouldn't be likely to choose arsenic. There are sleeping pills in this house. She could have taken an overdose of them.'

'Could the arsenic have got into something by accident?'

'That's what I'm wondering. It seems very unlikely, but such things have been known. But if you and she ate the same things –'

Susan nodded. She said, 'It all seems impossible –' then she gave a sudden gasp. 'Why, of course, the wedding cake!'

'What's that? Wedding cake?'

Susan explained. The doctor listened with close attention.

'Odd. And you say she wasn't sure who sent it? Any of it left? Or is the box it came in lying around?'

'I don't know. I'll look.'

They searched together and finally found the white cardboard box with a few crumbs of cake still in it lying on the kitchen dresser. The doctor packed it away with some care.

'I'll take charge of this. Any idea where the wrapping paper it came in might be?'

Here they were not successful and Susan said that it had probably gone into the Ideal boiler.

'You won't be leaving here just yet, Mrs Banks?'

His tone was genial, but it made Susan feel a little uncomfortable.

'No, I have to go through my aunt's things. I shall be here for a few days.'

'Good. You understand the police will probably want to ask some questions. You don't know of anyone who – well, might have had it in for Miss Gilchrist?'

Susan shook her head.

'I don't really know much about her. She was with my aunt for some years – that's all I know.'

'Quite, quite. Always seemed a pleasant unassuming woman – quite ordinary. Not the kind, you'd say, to have enemies or anything melodramatic of that kind. Wedding cake through the post. Sounds like some jealous woman – but who'd be jealous of Miss Gilchrist? Doesn't seem to fit.'

'No.'

'Well, I must be on my way. I don't know what's happening to us in quiet little Lytchett St Mary. First a brutal murder and now attempted poisoning through the post. Odd, the one following the other.'

He went down the path to his car. The cottage felt stuffy and Susan left the door standing open as she went slowly upstairs to resume her task.

Cora Lansquenet had not been a tidy or methodical woman. Her drawers held a miscellaneous assortment of things. There were toilet accessories and letters and old handkerchiefs and paint brushes mixed up together in one drawer. There were a few old letters and bills thrust in amongst a bulging drawer of underclothes. In another drawer under some woollen jumpers was a cardboard box holding two false fringes. There was another drawer full of old photographs and sketching books. Susan lingered over a group taken evidently at some French place many years ago and which showed a younger, thinner Cora clinging to the arm of a tall lanky man with a straggling beard dressed in what seemed to be a velveteen coat and whom Susan took to be the late Pierre Lansquenet.

The photographs interested Susan, but she laid them aside, sorted all the papers she had found into a heap and began to go through them methodically. About a quarter way through she came to a letter. She read it through twice and was still staring at it when a voice speaking behind her caused her to give a cry of alarm.

'And what may you have got hold of there, Susan? Hallo, what's the matter?'

Susan reddened with annoyance. Her cry of alarm had been quite involuntary and she felt ashamed and anxious to explain.

'George? How you startled me!'

Her cousin smiled lazily.

'So it seems.'

'How did you get here?'

'Well, the door downstairs was open, so I walked in. There seemed to be nobody about on the ground floor, so I came up here. If you mean how did I get to this part of the world, I started down this morning to come to the funeral.'

'I didn't see you there?'

'The old bus played me up. The petrol feed seemed choked. I tinkered with it for some time and finally it seemed to clear itself. I was too late for the funeral by then, but I thought I might as well come on down. I knew you were here.'

He paused, and then went on:

'I rang you up, as a matter of fact, and Greg told me you'd come down to take possession, as it were. I thought I might give you a hand.'

Susan said, 'Aren't you needed in the office? Or can you take days off whenever you like?'

'A funeral has always been a recognized excuse for absenteeism. And this funeral is indubitably genuine. Besides, a murder always fascinates people. Anyway, I shan't be going much to the office in future – not now that I'm a man of means. I shall have better things to do.'

He paused and grinned, 'Same as Greg,' he said.

Susan looked at George thoughtfully. She had never seen much of this cousin of hers and when they did meet she had always found him rather difficult to make out.

She asked, 'Why did you really come down here, George?'

'I'm not sure it wasn't to do a little detective work. I've been thinking a good deal about the last funeral we attended. Aunt Cora certainly threw a spanner into the works that day. I've wondered whether it was sheer irresponsibility and aunty *joie de vivre* that prompted her words, or whether she really had something to go upon. What actually is in that letter that you were reading so attentively when I came in?'

Susan said slowly, 'It's a letter that Uncle Richard wrote to Cora after he'd been down here to see her.'

How very black George's eyes were. She'd thought of them as brown but they were black, and there was something curiously impenetrable about black eyes. They concealed the thoughts that lay behind them.

George drawled slowly. 'Anything interesting in it?'

'No, not exactly . . .'

'Can I see?'

She hesitated for a moment, then put the letter into his outstretched hand.

He read it, skimming over the contents in a low monotone.

'*Glad to have seen you again after all these years . . . looking very well . . . had a good journey home and arrived back not too tired . . .*'

His voice changed suddenly, sharpened:

'*Please don't say anything to anyone about what I told you. It may be a mistake. Your loving brother, Richard.*'

He looked up at Susan. 'What does that mean?'

'It might mean anything . . . It might be just about his health. Or it might be some gossip about a mutual friend.'

'Oh yes, it might be a lot of things. It isn't conclusive – but it's suggestive . . . What did he tell Cora? Does anyone know what he told her?'

'Miss Gilchrist might know,' said Susan thoughtfully. 'I think she listened.'

'Oh, yes, the companion help. Where is she, by the way?'

'In hospital, suffering from arsenic poisoning.'

George stared.

'You don't mean it?'

'I do. Someone sent her some poisoned wedding cake.'

George sat down on one of the bedroom chairs and whistled.

'It looks,' he said, 'as though Uncle Richard was not mistaken.'

III

On the following morning Inspector Morton called at the cottage.

He was a quiet middle-aged man with a soft country burr in his voice. His manner was quiet and unhurried, but his eyes were shrewd.

'You realize what this is about, Mrs Banks?' he said. 'Dr Proctor has already told you about Miss Gilchrist. The few crumbs of wedding cake that he took from here have been analysed to show traces of arsenic.'

'So someone deliberately wanted to poison her?'

'That's what it looks like. Miss Gilchrist herself doesn't seem able to help us. She keeps repeating that it's impossible – that nobody would do such a thing. But somebody did. *You* can't throw any light on the matter?'

Susan shook her head.

'I'm simply dumbfounded,' she said. 'Can't you find out anything from the postmark? Or the handwriting?'

'You've forgotten – the wrapping paper was presumably burnt. And there's a little doubt whether it came through the post at all. Young Andrews, the driver of the postal van, doesn't seem able to remember delivering it. He's got a big round, and he can't be sure – but there it is – there's a doubt about it.'

'But – what's the alternative?'

'The alternative, Mrs Banks, is that an old piece of brown paper was used that already had Miss Gilchrist's name and address on it and a cancelled stamp, and that the package was pushed through the letter box or deposited inside the door by hand to create the impression that it had come by post.'

He added dispassionately:

'It's quite a clever idea, you know, to choose wedding cake. Lonely middle-aged women are sentimental about wedding cake, pleased at having been remembered. A box of sweets, or something of that kind *might* have awakened suspicion.'

Susan said slowly:

'Miss Gilchrist speculated a good deal about who could have sent it, but she wasn't at all suspicious – as you say, she was pleased and yes – flattered.'

She added: 'Was there enough poison in it to – kill?'

'That's difficult to say until we get the quantitative analysis. It rather depends on whether Miss Gilchrist ate the whole of the wedge. She seems to think that she didn't. Can you remember?'

'No – no, I'm not sure. She offered me some and I refused and then she ate some and said it was a very good cake, but I don't remember if she finished it or not.'

'I'd like to go upstairs if you don't mind, Mrs Banks.'

'Of course.'

She followed him up to Miss Gilchrist's room. She said apologetically:

'I'm afraid it's in a rather disgusting state. But I didn't have time to do anything about it with my aunt's funeral and everything, and then after Dr Proctor came I thought perhaps I ought to leave it as it was.'

'That was very intelligent of you, Mrs Banks. It's not everyone who would have been so intelligent.'

He went to the bed and slipping his hand under the pillow raised it carefully. A slow smile spread over his face.

'There you are,' he said.

A piece of wedding cake lay on the sheet looking somewhat the worse for wear.

'How extraordinary,' said Susan.

'Oh no, it's not. Perhaps your generation doesn't do it. Young ladies nowadays mayn't set so much store on getting married. But it's an old custom. Put a piece of wedding cake under your pillow and you'll dream of your future husband.'

'But surely Miss Gilchrist –'

'She didn't want to tell us about it because she felt foolish doing such a thing at her age. But I had a notion that's what it might be.' His face sobered. 'And if it hadn't been for an old maid's foolishness, Miss Gilchrist mightn't be alive today.'

'But who could have possibly wanted to kill her?'

His eyes met hers, a curious speculative look in them that made Susan feel uncomfortable.

'You don't know?' he asked.

'No – of course I don't.'

'It seems then as though we shall have to find out,' said Inspector Morton.

CHAPTER 12

Two elderly men sat together in a room whose furnishings were of the most modern kind. There were no curves in the room. Everything was square. Almost the only exception was Hercule Poirot himself who was full of curves. His stomach was pleasantly rounded, his head resembled an egg in shape, and his moustaches curved upwards in a flamboyant flourish.

He was sipping a glass of *sirop* and looking thoughtfully at Mr Goby.

Mr Goby was small and spare and shrunken. He had always been refreshingly nondescript in appearance and he was now so nondescript as practically not to be there at all. He was not looking at Poirot because Mr Goby never looked at anybody.

Such remarks as he was now making seemed to be addressed to the left-hand corner of the chromium-plated fireplace curb.

Mr Goby was famous for the acquiring of information. Very few people knew about him and very few employed his services – but those few were usually extremely rich. They had to be, for Mr Goby was very expensive. His speciality was the acquiring of information quickly. At the flick of Mr Goby's double-jointed thumb, hundreds of patient questioning plodding men and women, old and young, of all apparent stations in life, were despatched to question, and probe, and achieve results.

Mr Goby had now practically retired from business. But he

occasionally 'obliged' a few old patrons. Hercule Poirot was one of these.

'I've got what I could for you,' Mr Goby told the fire curb in a soft confidential whisper. 'I sent the boys out. They do what they can – good lads – good lads all of them, but not what they used to be in the old days. They don't come that way nowadays. Not willing to learn, that's what it is. Think they know everything after they've only been a couple of years on the job. And they work to time. Shocking the way they work to time.'

He shook his head sadly and shifted his gaze to an electric plug socket.

'It's the Government,' he told it. 'And all this education racket. It gives them ideas. They come back and tell us what they think. They *can't* think, most of them, anyway. All they know is things out of books. That's no good in our business. Bring in the answers – that's all that's needed – no thinking.'

Mr Goby flung himself back in his chair and winked at a lampshade.

'Mustn't crab the Government, though! Don't know really what we'd do without it. I can tell you that nowadays you can walk in most anywhere with a notebook and pencil, dressed right, and speaking B.B.C., and ask people all the most intimate details of their daily lives and all their back history, and what they had for dinner on November 23rd because that was a test day for middle-class incomes – or whatever it happens to be (making it a grade above to butter them up!) – ask 'em any mortal thing you can; and nine times out of ten they'll come across pat, and even the tenth time though they may cut up rough, they won't doubt for a minute that you're what you say you are – and that the Government really wants to know – for some completely unfathomable reason! I can tell you, M. Poirot,' said Mr Goby, still talking to the lampshade, 'that it's the best line we've ever had; much better than reading the electric meter or tracing a fault in the telephone – yes, or than calling as nuns, or the Girl Guides or Boy Scouts asking for subscriptions – though we use all those too. Yes, Government snooping is God's gift to investigators and long may it continue!'

Poirot did not speak. Mr Goby had grown a little garrulous

with advancing years, but he would come to the point in his own good time.

'Ar,' said Mr Goby, and took out a very scrubby little notebook. He licked his finger and flicked over the pages. 'Here we are. Mr George Crossfield. We'll take him first. Just the plain facts. You won't want to know how I got them. He's been in Queer Street for quite a while now. Horses, mostly, and gambling – he's not a great one for women. Goes over to France now and then, and Monte too. Spends a lot of time at the Casino. Too downy to cash cheques there, but gets hold of a lot more money than his travelling allowance would account for. I didn't go into that, because it wasn't what you want to know. But he's not scrupulous about evading the law – and being a lawyer he knows how to do it. Some reason to believe he's been using trust funds entrusted to him to invest. Plunging pretty wildly of late – on the Stock Exchange *and* on the gee-gees! Bad judgement and bad luck. Been off his feed badly for three months. Worried, bad-tempered and irritable in the office. *But* since his uncle's death that's all changed. He's like the breakfast eggs (if we had 'em). Sunny side up!

'Now, as to particular information asked for. Statement that he was at Hurst Park races on the day in question almost certainly untrue. Almost invariably places bets with one or other of two bookies on the course. They didn't see him that day. Possible that he left Paddington by train for destination unknown. Taxi-driver who took fare to Paddington made doubtful identification of his photograph. But I wouldn't bank on it. He's a very common type – nothing outstanding about him. No success with porters, etc., at Paddington. Certainly didn't arrive at Cholsey station – which is nearest for Lytchett St Mary. Small station, strangers noticeable. Could have got out at Reading and taken bus. Buses there crowded, frequent and several routes go within a mile or so of Lytchett St Mary as well as the bus service that goes right into the village. He wouldn't take that – not if he meant business. All in all, he's a downy card. Wasn't seen in Lytchett St Mary but he needn't have been. Other ways of approach than through the village. Was in the OUDS at Oxford, by the way. If he went to the cottage that day he mayn't have looked quite like the usual George Crossfield. I'll keep him in my book, shall I? There's a black market angle I'd like to play up.'

'You may keep him in,' said Hercule Poirot.

Mr Goby licked his finger and turned another page of his notebook.

'Mr Michael Shane. He's thought quite a lot of in the profession. Has an even better idea of himself than other people have. Wants to star and wants to star quickly. Fond of money and doing himself well. Very attractive to women. They fall for him right and left. He's partial to them himself – but business comes first, as you might say. He's been running around with Sorrel Dainton who was playing the lead in the last show he was in. He only had a minor part but made quite a hit in it, and Miss Dainton's husband doesn't like him. His wife doesn't know about him and Miss Dainton. Doesn't know much about anything, it seems. Not much of an actress I gather, but easy on the eye. Crazy about her husband. Some rumour of a bust-up likely between them not long ago, but that seems out now. Out since Mr Richard Abernethie's death.'

Mr Goby emphasised the last point by nodding his head at a cushion on the sofa.

'On the day in question, Mr Shane says he was meeting a Mr Rosenheim and a Mr Oscar Lewis to fix up some stage business. He didn't meet them. Sent them a wire to say he was terribly sorry he couldn't make it. What he *did* do was to go to the Emeraldo Car people, who hire out "drive yourself" cars. He hired a car about twelve o'clock and drove away in it. He returned it about six in the evening. According to the speedometer it had been driven just about the right number of miles for what we're after. No confirmation from Lytchett St Mary. No strange car seems to have been observed there that day. Lots of places it could be left unnoticed a mile or so away. And there's even a disused quarry a few hundred yards down the lane from the cottage. Three market towns within walking distance where you can park in side streets, without the police bothering about you. All right, we keep Mr Shane in?'

'Most certainly.'

'Now Mrs Shane.' Mr Goby rubbed his nose and told his left cuff about Mrs Shane. 'She says she was shopping. Just shopping . . .' Mr Goby raised his eyes to the ceiling. 'Women who are shopping – just scatty, that's what they are. And she'd heard she'd come into money the day before. Naturally there'd be no holding her. She has one or two charge accounts but they're overdrawn and they've been pressing her for payment and she didn't put any more on the sheet. It's quite on the cards that she went in here and there and everywhere, trying on clothes, looking at jewellery, pricing this, that, and the other – and as likely as not, not buying anything! She's easy to approach – I'll say that. I had one of my young ladies who's knowledgeable on the theatrical line to do a hook up. Stopped by her table in a restaurant and exclaimed the way they do: "Darling, I haven't seen you since *Way Down Under*. You were *wonderful* in that! Have you seen Hubert lately?" That was the producer and Mrs Shane was a bit of a flop in the play – but that makes it go all the better. They're chatting theatrical stuff at once, and my girl throws the right names about, and then she says, "I believe I caught a glimpse of you at so and so, on so and so," giving the day – and most ladies fall for it and say, "Oh no, I was –" whatever it may be. But not Mrs Shane. Just looks vacant and says, "Oh, I dare say." What can you do with a lady like that?' Mr Goby shook his head severely at the radiator.

'Nothing,' said Hercule Poirot with feeling. 'Do I not have cause to know it? Never shall I forget the killing of Lord Edgware. I was nearly defeated – yes, I, Hercule Poirot – by the extremely simple cunning of a vacant brain. The very simple-minded have often the genius to commit an uncomplicated crime and then leave it alone. Let us hope that our murderer – if there is a murderer in this affair – is intelligent and superior and thoroughly pleased with himself and unable to resist painting the lily. *Enfin* – but continue.'

Once more Mr Goby applied himself to his little book.

'Mr and Mrs Banks – who said they were at home all day. *She* wasn't, anyway! Went round to the garage, got out her car, and drove off in it about 1 o'clock. Destination unknown. Back about five. Can't tell about mileage because she's had it out every day since and it's been nobody's business to check.

'As to Mr Banks, we've dug up something curious. To begin with, I'll mention that on the day in question we don't know *what* he did. He didn't go to work. Seems he'd already asked for a couple of days off on account of the funeral. And since then he's chucked his job – with no consideration for the firm. Nice, well-established pharmacy it is. They're not too keen on Master Banks. Seems he used to get into rather queer excitable states.

'Well, as I say, we don't know what he was doing on the day of Mrs L.'s death. He didn't go with his wife. It *could* be that he stopped in their little flat all day. There's no porter there, and nobody knows whether tenants are in or out. But his back history is interesting. Up till about four months ago – just before he met his wife, he was in a Mental Home. Not certified – just what they call a mental breakdown. Seems he made some slip up in dispensing a medicine. (He was working with a Mayfair firm then.) The woman recovered, and the firm were all over themselves apologizing, and there was no prosecution. After all, these accidental slips do occur, and most decent people are sorry for a poor young chap who's done it – so long as there's no permanent harm done, that is. The firm didn't sack him, but he resigned – said it had shaken his nerve. But afterwards, it seems, he got into a very low state and told the doctor he was obsessed by guilt – that it had all been deliberate – the woman had been overbearing and rude to him when she came into the shop, had complained that her last prescription had been badly made up – and that he had resented this and had deliberately added a near lethal dose of some drug or other. He said, "She had to be punished for daring to speak to me like that!" And then wept and said he was too wicked to live and a lot of things like that. The medicos have a long word for that sort of thing – guilt complex or something – and don't believe it was deliberate at all, just carelessness, but that he wanted to make it important and serious.'

'*Ça se peut*,' said Hercule Poirot.

'Pardon? Anyway, he went into this Sanatorium and they treated him and discharged him as cured, and he met Miss Abernethie as she was then. And he got a job in this respectable but rather obscure little chemist's shop. Told them he'd been out of England for a year and a half, and gave them his former reference from some shop in Eastbourne. Nothing against him in that shop, but a fellow dispenser said he had a very queer temper and was odd in his manner sometimes. There's a story about a customer saying once as a joke, "Wish you'd sell me something to poison my wife, ha ha!" And Banks says to him, very soft and quiet: "I could . . . It would cost you two hundred pounds." The man felt uneasy and laughed it off. *May* have been all a joke, but it doesn't seem to me that Banks is the joking kind.'

'*Mon ami*,' said Hercule Poirot. 'It really amazes me how you get your information! Medical and highly confidential most of it!'

Mr Goby's eyes swivelled right round the room and he murmured, looking expectantly at the door, that there were *ways* . . .

'Now we come to the country department. Mr and Mrs Timothy Abernethie. Very nice place they've got, but sadly needing money spent on it. Very straitened they seem to be, very straitened. Taxation and unfortunate investments. Mr Abernethie enjoys ill health and the emphasis is on the enjoyment. Complains a lot and has everyone running and fetching and carrying. Eats hearty meals, and seems quite strong physically if he likes to make the effort. There's no one in the house after the daily woman goes and no one's allowed into Mr Abernethie's room unless he rings the bell. He was in a very bad temper the morning of the day after the funeral. Swore at Mrs Jones. Ate only a little of his breakfast and said he wouldn't have any lunch – he'd had a bad night. He said the supper she had left out for him was unfit to eat and a good deal more. He was alone in the house and unseen by anybody from 9.30 that morning until the following morning.'

'And Mrs Abernethie?'

'She started off from Enderby by car at the time you mentioned. Arrived on foot at a small local garage in a place called Cathstone and explained her car had broken down a couple of miles away.

'A mechanic drove her out to it, made an investigation and said they'd have to tow it in and it would be a long job – couldn't promise to finish it that day. The lady was very put out, but went to a small inn, arranged to stay the night, and asked for some sandwiches as she said she'd like to see something of the countryside – it's on the edge of the moorland country. She didn't come back to the inn till quite late that evening. My informant said he didn't wonder. It's a sordid little place!'

'And the times?'

'She got the sandwiches at eleven. If she'd walked to the main road, a mile, she could have hitch-hiked into Wallcaster and caught a special South Coast express which stops at Reading West. I won't go into details of buses etcetera. It *could* just have been done if you could make the – er – attack fairly late in the afternoon.'

'I understand the doctor stretched the time limit to possibly 4.30.'

'Mind you,' said Mr Goby, 'I shouldn't say it was likely. She seems to be a nice lady, liked by everybody. She's devoted to her husband, treats him like a child.'

'Yes, yes, the maternal complex.'

'She's strong and hefty, chops the wood and often hauls in great baskets of logs. Pretty good with the inside of a car, too.'

'I was coming to that. What exactly *was* wrong with the car?'

'Do you want the exact details, M. Poirot?'

'Heaven forbid. I have no mechanical knowledge.'

'It was a difficult thing to spot. And also to put right. And it *could* have been done maliciously by someone without very much trouble. By someone who was familiar with the insides of a car.'

'*C'est magnifique!*' said Poirot with bitter enthusiasm. 'All so convenient, all so possible. *Bon dieu*, can we eliminate *nobody*? And Mrs Leo Abernethie?'

'She's a very nice lady, too. Mr Abernethie deceased was very fond of her. She came there to stay about a fortnight before he died.'

'After he had been to Lytchett St Mary to see his sister?'

'No, just before. Her income is a good deal reduced since the war. She gave up her house in England and took a small flat in London. She has a villa in Cyprus and spends part of the year there. She has a young nephew whom she is helping to educate, and there seems to be one or two young artists whom she helps financially from time to time.'

'St Helen of the blameless life,' said Poirot, shutting his eyes. 'And it was quite impossible for her to have left Enderby that day without the servants knowing? Say that is so, I implore you!'

Mr Goby brought his glance across to rest apologetically on Poirot's polished patent leather shoe, the nearest he had come to a direct encounter, and murmured:

'I'm afraid I can't say that, M. Poirot. Mrs Abernethie went to London to fetch some extra clothes and belongings as she had agreed with Mr Entwhistle to stay on and see to things.'

'*Il ne manquait ça!*' said Poirot with strong feeling.

CHAPTER 13

When the card of Inspector Morton of the Berkshire County Police was brought to Hercule Poirot, his eyebrows went up.

'Show him in, Georges, show him in. And bring – what is it that the police prefer?'

'I would suggest beer, sir.'

'How horrible! But how British. Bring beer, then.'

Inspector Morton came straight to the point.

'I had to come to London,' he said. 'And I got hold of your address, M. Poirot. I was interested to see you at the inquest on Thursday.'

'So you saw me there?'

'Yes. I was surprised – and, as I say, interested. You won't remember me but I remember you very well. In that Pangbourne Case.'

'Ah, you were connected with that?'

'Only in a very junior capacity. It's a long time ago but I've never forgotten you.'

'And you recognized me at once the other day?'

'That wasn't difficult, sir.' Inspector Morton repressed a slight smile. 'Your appearance is – rather unusual.'

His gaze took in Poirot's sartorial perfection and rested finally on the curving moustaches.

'You stick out in a country place,' he said.

'It is possible, it is possible,' said Poirot with complacency.

'It interested me *why* you should be there. That sort of crime – robbery – assault – doesn't usually interest you.'

'Was it the usual ordinary brutal type of crime?'

'That's what I've been wondering.'

'You have wondered from the beginning, have you not?'

'Yes, M. Poirot. There were some unusual features. Since then we've worked along the routine lines. Pulled in one or two people for questioning, but everyone has been able to account quite satisfactorily for his time that afternoon. It wasn't what you'd call an "ordinary" crime, M. Poirot – we're quite sure of that. The Chief Constable agrees. It was done by someone who wished to make it appear that way. It could have been the Gilchrist woman, but there doesn't seem to be any motive – and there wasn't any emotional background, Mrs Lansquenet was perhaps a bit mental – or "simple", if you like to put it that way, but it was a household of mistress and dogsbody with no feverish feminine friendship about it. There are dozens of Miss Gilchrists about, and they're not usually the murdering type.'

He paused.

'So it looks as though we'd have to look farther afield. I came to ask if you could help us at all. *Something* must have brought you down there, M. Poirot.'

'Yes, yes, something did. An excellent Daimler car. But not only that.'

'You had – information?'

'Hardly in your sense of the word. Nothing that could be used as evidence.'

'But something that could be – a pointer?'

'Yes.'

'You see, M. Poirot, there have been developments.'

Meticulously, in detail, he told of the poisoned wedge of wedding cake.

Poirot took a deep, hissing breath.

'Ingenious – yes, ingenious . . . I warned Mr Entwhistle to look after Miss Gilchrist. An attack on her was always a possibility. But I must confess that I did *not* expect poison. I anticipated a repetition of the hatchet *motif*. I merely thought that it would be inadvisable for her to walk alone in unfrequented lanes after dark.'

'But *why* did you anticipate an attack on her? I think, M. Poirot, you ought to tell me that.'

Poirot nodded his head slowly.

'Yes, I will tell you. Mr Entwhistle will not tell you, because he is a lawyer and lawyers do not like to speak of suppositions, or inferences made from the character of a dead woman, or from a few irresponsible words. But he will not be averse to *my* telling you – no, he will be relieved. He does not wish to appear foolish or fanciful, but he wants you to know what may – only *may* – be the facts.'

Poirot paused as Georges entered with a tall glass of beer.

'Some refreshment, Inspector. No, no, I insist.'

'Won't you join me?'

'I do not drink the beer. But I will myself have a glass of *sirop de cassis* – the English they do not care for it, I have noticed.'

Inspector Morton looked gratefully at his beer.

Poirot, sipping delicately from his glass of dark purple fluid, said:

'It begins, all this, at a funeral. Or rather, to be exact, *after* the funeral.'

Graphically, with many gestures, he set forth the story as Mr Entwhistle had told it to him, but with such embellishments as his exuberant nature suggested. One almost felt that Hercule Poirot himself had been an eyewitness of the scene.

Inspector Morton had an excellent clear-cut brain. He seized at once on what were, for his purposes, the salient points.

'This Mr Abernethie may have been poisoned?'

'It is a possibility.'

'And the body has been cremated and there is no evidence?'

'Exactly.'

Inspector Morton ruminated.

'Interesting. There's nothing in it for *us*. Nothing, that is, to make Richard Abernethie's death worth investigating. It would be a waste of time.'

'Yes.'

'But there are the *people* – the people who were there – the people who heard Cora Lansquenet say what she did, and one of whom may have thought that she might say it again and with more detail.'

'As she undoubtedly would have. There are, Inspector, as you say, *the people*. And now you see why I was at the inquest, why I interested myself in the case – because it is, always, *people* in whom I interest myself.'

'Then the attack on Miss Gilchrist –'

'Was always indicated. Richard Abernethie had been down to the cottage. He had talked to Cora. He had, perhaps, actually mentioned a *name*. The only person who might possibly have known or overheard something was Miss Gilchrist. After Cora is silenced, the murderer might continue to be anxious. Does the other woman know something – anything? Of course, if the murderer is wise he will let well alone, but murderers, Inspector, are seldom wise. Fortunately for us. They brood, they feel uncertain, they desire to make sure – quite sure. They are pleased with their own cleverness. And so, in the end, they protrude their necks, as you say.'

Inspector Morton smiled faintly.

Poirot went on:

'This attempt to silence Miss Gilchrist, already it is a mistake. For now there are *two* occasions about which you make inquiry. There is the handwriting on the wedding label also. It is a pity the wrapping paper was burnt.'

'Yes, I could have been certain, then, whether it came by post or whether it didn't.'

'You have reason for thinking the latter, you say?'

'It's only what the postman thinks – he's not sure. If the parcel had gone through a village post office, it's ten to one the postmistress would have noticed it, but nowadays the mail is delivered by van from Market Keynes and of course the young chap does quite a round and delivers a lot of things. He thinks it was letters only and no parcel at the cottage – but he isn't sure. As a matter of fact he's having a bit of girl trouble and he can't think about anything else. I've tested his memory and he isn't reliable in any way. If he *did* deliver it, it seems to me odd that the parcel shouldn't have been noticed until after this Mr – whatshisname – Guthrie –'

'Ah, Mr Guthrie.'

Inspector Morton smiled.

'Yes, M. Poirot. We're checking up on him. After all, it would be easy, wouldn't it, to come along with a plausible tale of having been a friend of Mrs Lansquenet's. Mrs Banks wasn't to know if he was or he wasn't. He could have dropped that little parcel, you know. It's easy to make a thing look as though it's been through the post. Lamp black a little smudged, makes quite a good postmark cancellation mark over a stamp.'

He paused and then added:

'And there are other possibilities.'

Poirot nodded.

'You think –?'

'Mr George Crossfield was down in that part of the world – but not until the next day. Meant to attend the funeral, but had a little engine trouble on the way. Know anything about him, M. Poirot?'

'A little. But not as much as I would like to know.'

'Like that, is it? Quite a little bunch interested in the late Mr Abernethie's will, I understand. I hope it doesn't mean going after all of them.'

'I have accumulated a little information. It is at your disposal. Naturally *I* have no authority to ask these people questions. In fact, it would not be wise for me to do so.'

'I shall go slowly myself. You don't want to fluster your bird too soon. But when you do fluster it, you want to fluster it well.'

'A very sound technique. For you then, my friend, the routine – with all the machinery you have at your disposal. It is slow – but sure. For myself –'

'Yes, M. Poirot?'

'For myself, I go North. As I have told you, it is *people* in whom I interest myself. Yes – a little preparatory *camouflage* – and I go North.'

'I intend,' added Hercule Poirot, 'to purchase a country mansion for foreign refugees. I represent U.N.A.R.C.O.'

'And what's U.N.A.R.C.O.?'

'United Nations Aid for Refugee Centre Organization. It sounds well, do you not think?'

Inspector Morton grinned.

CHAPTER 14

Hercule Poirot said to a grim-faced Janet:

'Thank you very much. You have been most kind.'

Janet, her lips still fixed in a sour line, left the room. These foreigners! The questions they asked. Their impertinence! All very well to say that he was a specialist interested in unsuspected heart conditions such as Mr Abernethie must have suffered from. That was very likely true – gone very sudden the master had, and the doctor had been surprised. But what business was it of some foreign doctor coming along and nosing around?

All very well for Mrs Leo to say: 'Please answer Monsieur Pontarlier's questions. He has a good reason for asking.'

Questions. Always questions. Sheets of them sometimes to fill in as best you could – and what did the Government or anyone else want to know about your private affairs for? Asking your age at that census – downright impertinent and she hadn't told them, either! Cut off five years she had. Why not? If she only felt fifty-four, she'd *call* herself fifty-four!

At any rate Monsieur Pontarlier hadn't wanted to know her age. He'd had *some* decency. Just questions about the medicines the master had taken, and where they were kept, and if, perhaps, he might have taken too much of them if he was feeling not quite the thing – or if he'd been forgetful. As though she could remember all that rubbish – the master knew what he was doing! And asking if any of the medicines he took were still in the house. Naturally they'd all been thrown away. Heart condition – and some long word he'd used. Always thinking of something new they were, these doctors. Look at them telling old Rogers he had a disc or some such in his spine. Plain lumbago, that was all that was the matter with him. Her father had been a gardener and *he'd* suffered from lumbago. Doctors!

The self-appointed medical man sighed and went downstairs in search of Lanscombe. He had not got very much out of Janet but he had hardly expected to do so. All he had really wanted to do was to check such information as could unwillingly be extracted from her with that given him by Helen Abernethie and which had been obtained from the same source – but with much less difficulty, since Janet was ready to admit that Mrs Leo had a perfect right to ask such questions and indeed Janet herself had enjoyed dwelling at length on the last few weeks of her master's life. Illness and death were congenial subjects to her.

Yes, Poirot thought, he could have relied on the information that Helen had got for him. He had done so really. But by nature and long habit he trusted nobody until he himself had tried and proved them.

In any case the evidence was slight and unsatisfactory. It boiled down to the fact that Richard Abernethie had been prescribed vitamin oil capsules. That these had been in a large bottle which had been nearly finished at the time of his death. Anybody who had wanted to, could have operated on one or more of those capsules with a hypodermic syringe and could have rearranged the bottle so that the fatal dose would only be taken some weeks after that somebody had left the house. Or someone might have slipped into the house on the day before Richard Abernethie died and have doctored a capsule then – or, which was more likely – have substituted something else for a sleeping tablet in the little bottle that stood beside the bed. Or again he might have quite simply tampered with the food or drink.

Hercule Poirot had made his own experiments. The front door was kept locked, but there was a side door giving on the garden which was not locked until evening. At about quarter-past one, when the gardeners had gone to lunch and when the household was in the dining-room, Poirot had entered the grounds, come to the side door, and mounted the stairs to Richard Abernethie's bedroom without meeting anybody. As a variant he had pushed through a baize door and slipped into the larder. He had heard voices from the kitchen at the end of the passage but no one had seen him.

Yes, it could have been done. But had it been done? There was nothing to indicate that that was so. Not that Poirot was really looking for evidence – he wanted only to satisfy himself as to possibilities. The murder of Richard Abernethie could only be a hypothesis. It was Cora Lansquenet's murder for which evidence was needed. What he wanted was to study the people who had been assembled for the funeral that day, and to form his own conclusions about them. He already had his plan, but first he wanted a few more words with old Lanscombe.

Lanscombe was courteous but distant. Less resentful than Janet, he nevertheless regarded this upstart foreigner as the materialization of the Writing on the Wall. This was What We are Coming to!

He put down the leather with which he was lovingly polishing the Georgian teapot and straightened his back.

'Yes, sir?' he said politely.

Poirot sat down gingerly on a pantry stool.

'Mrs Abernethie tells me that you hoped to reside in the lodge by the north gate when you retired from service here?'

'That is so, sir. Naturally all that is changed now. When the propety is sold –'

Poirot interrupted deftly:

'It might still be possible. There are cottages for the gardeners. The lodge is not needed for the guests or their attendants. It might be possible to make an arrangement of some kind.'

'Well, thank you, sir, for the suggestion. But I hardly think – The majority of the – guests would be foreigners, I presume?'

'Yes, they will be foreigners. Amongst those who fled from Europe to this country are several who are old and infirm. There can be no future for them if they return to their own countries, for these persons, you understand, are those whose relatives there have perished. They cannot earn their living here as an able-bodied man or woman can do. Funds have been raised and are being administered by the organization which I represent to endow various country homes for them. This place is, I think, eminently suitable. The matter is practically settled.'

Lanscombe sighed.

'You'll understand, sir, that it's sad for me to think that this won't be a private dwelling-house any longer. But I know how things are nowadays. None of the family could afford to live here – and I don't think the young ladies and gentlemen would even want to do so. Domestic help is too difficult to obtain these days, and even if obtained is expensive and unsatisfactory. I quite realize that these fine mansions have served their turn.' Lanscombe sighed again. 'If it has to be an – an institution of some kind, I'll be glad to think that it's the kind you're mentioning. We were Spared in This Country, sir, owing to our Navy and Air Force and our brave young men and being fortunate enough to be an island. If Hitler had landed here we'd all have turned out and given him short shrift. My sight isn't good enough for shooting, but I could have used a pitchfork, sir, and I intended to do so if necessary. We've always welcomed the unfortunate in this country, sir, it's been our pride. We shall continue so to do.'

'Thank you, Lanscombe,' said Poirot gently. 'Your master's death must have been a great blow to you.'

'It was, sir. I'd been with the master since he was quite a young man. I've been very fortunate in my life, sir. No one could have had a better master.'

'I have been conversing with my friend and – er – colleague, Dr Larraby. We were wondering if your master could have had any extra worry – any unpleasant interview – on the day before he died? You do not remember if any visitors came to the house that day?'

'I think not, sir. I do not recall any.'

'No one called at all just about that time?'

'The vicar was here to tea the day before. Otherwise some nuns called for a subscription – and a young man came to the back door and wanted to sell Marjorie some brushes and saucepan cleaners. Very persistent he was. Nobody else.'

A worried expression had appeared on Lanscombe's face. Poirot did not press him further. Lanscombe had already unburdened himself to Mr Entwhistle. He would be far less forthcoming with Hercule Poirot.

With Marjorie, on the other hand, Poirot had had instant success. Marjorie had none of the conventions of 'good service'. Marjorie was a first-class cook and the way to her heart lay through her cooking. Poirot had visited her in the kitchen, praised certain dishes with discernment, and Marjorie, realizing that here was someone who knew what he was talking about, hailed him immediately as a fellow spirit. He had no difficulty in finding out exactly what had been served the night before Richard Abernethie had died. Marjorie, indeed, was inclined to view the matter as, 'It was the night I made that chocolate soufflé that Mr Abernethie died. Six eggs I'd saved up for it.

The dairyman he's a friend of mine. Got hold of some cream too. Better not ask how. Enjoyed it, Mr Abernethie did.' The rest of the meal was likewise detailed. What had come out from the dining-room had been finished in the kitchen. Ready as Marjorie was to talk, Poirot had learned nothing of value from her.

He went now to fetch his overcoat and a couple of scarves, and thus padded against the North Country air he went out on the terrace and joined Helen Abernethie, who was clipping some late roses.

'Have you found out anything fresh?' she asked.

'Nothing. But I hardly expected to do so.'

'I know. Ever since Mr Entwhistle told me you were coming, I've been ferreting around, but there's really been nothing.'

She paused and said hopefully:

'Perhaps it *is* all a mare's nest?'

'To be attacked with a hatchet?'

'I wasn't thinking of Cora.'

'But it is of Cora that I think. Why was it necessary for someone to kill her? Mr Entwhistle has told me that on that day, at the moment that she came out suddenly with her *gaffe*, you yourself felt that something was wrong. That is so?'

'Well – yes, but I don't know –'

Poirot swept on.

'How "wrong"? Unexpected? Surprising? Or – what shall we say – uneasy? Sinister?'

'Oh no, not sinister. Just something that wasn't – oh, I don't know. I can't remember and it wasn't important.'

'But why cannot you remember – because something else put it out of your head – something more important?'

'Yes – yes – I think you're right there. It was the mention of murder, I suppose. That swept away everything else.'

'It was, perhaps, the reaction of some particular person to the word "murder"?'

'Perhaps . . . But I don't remember looking at anyone in particular. We were all staring at Cora.'

'It may have been something you heard – something dropped perhaps . . . or broken . . .'

Helen frowned in an effort of remembrance.

'No . . . I don't think so . . .'

'Ah well, some day it will come back. And it may be of no consequence. Now tell me, Madame, of those there, who knew Cora best?'

Helen considered.

'Lanscombe, I suppose. He remembers her from a child. The housemaid, Janet, only came after she had married and gone away.'

'And next to Lanscombe?'

Helen said thoughtfully: 'I suppose – *I* did. Maude hardly knew her at all.'

'Then, taking you as the person who knew her best, why do you think she asked that question as she did?'

Helen smiled.

'It was very characteristic of Cora!'

'What I mean is, was it a *bêtise* pure and simple? Did she just blurt out what was in her mind without thinking? Or was she being malicious – amusing herself by upsetting everyone?'

Helen reflected.

'You can't ever be quite sure about a person, can you? I never have known whether Cora was just ingenuous – or whether she counted, childishly, on making an effect. That's what you mean, isn't it?'

'Yes. I was thinking: Suppose this Mrs Cora says to herself "What fun it would be to ask if Richard was murdered and see how they all look!" That would be like her, yes?'

Helen looked doubtful.

'It might be. She certainly had an impish sense of humour as a child. But what difference does it make?'

'It would underline the point that it is unwise to make jokes about murder,' said Poirot drily.

Helen shivered.

'Poor Cora.'

Poirot changed the subject.

'Mrs Timothy Abernethie stayed the night after the funeral?'

'Yes.'

'Did she talk to you at all about what Cora had said?'

'Yes, she said it was outrageous and just like Cora!'

'She didn't take it seriously?'

'Oh no. No, I'm sure she didn't.'

The second 'no', Poirot thought, had sounded suddenly doubtful. But was not that almost always the case when you went back over something in your mind?

'And you, Madame, did you take it seriously?'

Helen Abernethie, her eyes looking very blue and strangely young under the sideways sweep of crisp grey hair, said thoughtfully:

'Yes, M. Poirot, I think I did.'

'Because of your feeling that something was wrong?'

'Perhaps.'

He waited – but as she said nothing more, he went on:

'There had been an estrangement, lasting many years, between Mrs Lansquenet and her family?'

'Yes. None of us liked her husband and she was offended about it, and so the estrangement grew.'

'And then, suddenly, your brother-in-law went to see her. Why?'

'I don't know – I suppose he knew, or guessed, that he hadn't very long to live and wanted to be reconciled – but I really don't know.'

'He didn't tell you?'

'Tell *me*?'

'Yes. You were here, staying with him, just before he went there. He didn't even mention his intention to you?'

He thought a slight reserve came into her manner.

'He told me that he was going to see his brother Timothy – which he did. He never mentioned Cora at all. Shall we go in? It must be nearly lunch-time.'

She walked beside him carrying the flowers she had picked. As they went in by the side door, Poirot said:

'You are sure, quite sure, that during your visit, Mr Abernethie said nothing to you about any member of the family which might be relevant?'

A faint resentment in her manner, Helen said:

'You are speaking like a policeman.'

'I *was* a policeman – once. I have no status – no right to question you. But you want the truth – or so I have been led to believe?'

They entered the green drawing-room. Helen said with a sigh:

'Richard was disappointed in the younger generation. Old men usually are. He disparaged them in various ways – but there was nothing – *nothing*, do you understand – that could possibly suggest a motive for murder.'

'Ah,' said Poirot. She reached for a Chinese bowl, and began to arrange the roses in it. When they were disposed to her satisfaction she looked round for a place to put it.

'You arrange flowers admirably, Madame,' said Hercule. 'I think that anything you undertook you would manage to do with perfection.'

'Thank you. I am fond of flowers. I think this would look well on that green malachite table.'

There was a bouquet of wax flowers under a glass shade on the malachite table. As she lifted it off, Poirot said casually:

'Did anyone tell Mr Abernethie that his niece Susan's husband had come near to poisoning a customer when making up a prescription? Ah, *pardon*!'

He sprang forward.

The Victorian ornament had slipped from Helen's fingers. Poirot's spring forward was not quick enough. It dropped on the floor and the glass shade broke. Helen gave an expression of annoyance.

'How careless of me. However, the flowers are not damaged. I can get a new glass shade made for it. I'll put it away in the big cupboard under the stairs.'

It was not until Poirot had helped her to lift it on to a shelf in the dark cupboard and had followed her back to the drawing-room that he said:

'It was my fault. I should not have startled you.'

'What was it that you asked me? I have forgotten.'

'Oh, there is no need to repeat my question. Indeed – I have forgotten what it was.'

Helen came up to him. She laid her hand on his arm. 'M. Poirot, is there anyone whose life would really bear close investigation? *Must* people's lives be dragged into this when they have nothing to do with – with –'

'With the death of Cora Lansquenet? Yes. Because one has

to examine *everything*. Oh! it is true enough – it is an old maxim – *everyone has something to hide*. It is true of all of us – it is perhaps true of you, too, Madame. But I say to you, nothing can be ignored. That is why your friend, Mr Entwhistle, he has come to me. For I am not the police. I am discreet and what I learn does not concern me. But I have to *know*. And since in this matter it is not so much *evidence* as *people* – then it is *people* with whom I occupy myself. I need, Madame, to meet everyone who was here on the day of the funeral. And it would be a great convenience – yes, and it would be strategically satisfactory – if I could meet them *here*.'

'I'm afraid,' said Helen slowly, 'that that would be too difficult –'

'Not so difficult as you think. Already I have devised a means. The house, it is sold. So Mr Entwhistle will declare. (*Entendu*, sometimes these things fall through!) He will invite the various members of the family to assemble here and to choose what they will from the furnishings before it is all put up to auction. A suitable week-end can be selected for that purpose.'

He paused and then said:

'You see, it is easy, is it not?'

Helen looked at him. The blue eyes were cold – almost frosty.

'Are you laying a trap for someone, M. Poirot?'

'Alas! I wish I knew enough. No, I have still the open mind.

'There may,' Hercule Poirot added thoughtfully, 'be certain tests . . .'

'Tests? What kind of tests?'

'I have not yet formulated them to myself. And in any case, Madame, it would be better that you should not know them.'

'So that I can be tested too?'

'You, Madame, have been taken behind the scenes. Now there is one thing that is doubtful. The young people will, I think, come readily. But it may be difficult, may it not, to secure the presence here of Mr Timothy Abernethie. I hear that he never leaves home.'

Helen smiled suddenly.

'I believe you may be lucky there, M. Poirot. I heard from Maude yesterday. The workmen are in painting the house and

Timothy is suffering terribly from the smell of the paint. He says that it is seriously affecting his health. I think that he and Maude would both be pleased to come here – perhaps for a week or two. Maude is still not able to get about very well – you know she broke her ankle?'

'I had not heard. How unfortunate.'

'Luckily they have got Cora's companion, Miss Gilchrist. It seems that she has turned out a perfect treasure.'

'What is that?' Poirot turned sharply on Helen. 'Did they ask for Miss Gilchrist to go to them? Who suggested it?'

'I think Susan fixed it up. Susan Banks.'

'Aha,' said Poirot in a curious voice. 'So it was the little Susan who suggested it. She is fond of making the arrangements.'

'Susan struck me as being a very competent girl.'

'Yes. She is competent. Did you hear that Miss Gilchrist had a narrow escape from death with a piece of poisoned wedding cake?'

'No!' Helen looked startled. 'I do remember now that Maude said over the telephone that Miss Gilchrist had just come out of hospital but I'd no idea why she had been in hospital. Poisoned? But, M. Poirot – *why* –'

'Do you really ask that?'

Helen said with sudden vehemence:

'Oh! get them all here! Find out the truth! There mustn't be any more murders.'

'So you will co-operate?'

'Yes – I will co-operate.'

CHAPTER 15

I

'That linoleum does look nice, Mrs Jones. What a hand you have with lino. The teapot's on the kitchen table, so go and help yourself. I'll be there as soon as I've taken up Mr Abernethie's elevenses.'

Miss Gilchrist trotted up the staircase, carrying a daintily set out tray. She tapped on Timothy's door, interpreted a growl from within as an invitation to enter, and tripped briskly in.

'Morning coffee and biscuits, Mr Abernethie. I do hope you're feeling brighter today. Such a lovely day.'

Timothy grunted and said suspiciously:

'Is there skim on that milk?'

'Oh no, Mr Abernethie. I took it off very carefully, and anyway I've brought up the little strainer in case it should form again. Some people like it, you know, they say it's the *cream* – and so it is really.'

'Idiots!' said Timothy. 'What kind of biscuits are those?'

'They're those nice digestive biscuits.'

'Digestive tripe. Ginger-nuts are the only biscuits worth eating.'

'I'm afraid the grocer hadn't got any this week. But these are really very nice. You try them and see.'

'I know what they're like, thank you. Leave those curtains alone, can't you?'

'I thought you might like a little sunshine. It's such a nice sunny day.'

'I want the room kept dark. My head's terrible. It's this paint. I've always been sensitive to paint. It's poisoning me.'

Miss Gilchrist sniffed experimentally and said brightly:

'One really can't smell it much in here. The workmen are over on the other side.'

'You're not sensitive like I am. Must I have *all* the books I'm reading taken out of my reach?'

'I'm so sorry, Mr Abernethie, I didn't know you were reading all of them.'

'Where's my wife? I haven't seen her for over an hour.'

'Mrs Abernethie is resting on the sofa.'

'Tell her to come and rest up here.'

'I'll tell her, Mr Abernethie. But she may have dropped off to sleep. Shall we say in about a quarter of an hour?'

'No, tell her I want her now. Don't monkey about with that rug. It's arranged the way I like it.'

'I'm so sorry. I thought it was slipping off the far side.'

'I like it slipping off. Go and get Maude. I want her.'

Miss Gilchrist departed downstairs and tiptoed into the drawing-room where Maude Abernethie was sitting with her leg up reading a novel.

'I'm so sorry, Mrs Abernethie,' she said apologetically. 'Mr Abernethie is asking for you.'

Maude thrust aside her novel with a guilty expression.

'Oh dear,' she said. 'I'll go at once.'

She reached for her stick.

Timothy burst out as soon as his wife entered the room:

'So there you are at last!'

'I'm so sorry dear, I didn't know you wanted me.'

'That woman you've got into the house will drive me mad. Twittering and fluttering round like a demented hen. Real typical old maid, that's what she is.'

'I'm sorry she annoys you. She tries to be kind, that's all.'

'I don't want anybody kind. I don't want a blasted old maid always chirruping over me. She's so damned arch, too –'

'Just a little, perhaps.'

'Treats me as thought I was a confounded kid! It's maddening.'

'I'm sure it must be. But please, *please*, Timothy, do try not to be rude to her. I'm really very helpless still – and you yourself say she cooks well.'

'Her cooking's all right,' Mr Abernethie admitted grudgingly. 'Yes, she's a decent enough cook. But keep her in the kitchen, that's all I ask. Don't let her come fussing round me.'

'No, dear, of course not. How are you feeling?'

'Not at all well. I think you'd better send for Barton to come and have a look at me. This paint affects my heart. Feel my pulse – the irregular way it's beating.'

Maude felt it without comment.

'Timothy, shall we go to an hotel until the house painting is finished?'

'It would be a great waste of money.'

'Does that matter so much – now?'

'You're just like all women – hopelessly extravagant! Just because we've come into a ridiculously small part of my brother's estate, you think we can go and live indefinitely at the Ritz.'

'I didn't quite say that, dear.'

'I can tell you that the difference Richard's money will make will be hardly appreciable. This bloodsucking Government will see to that. You mark my words, the whole lot will go in taxation.'

Mrs Abernethie shook her head sadly.

'This coffee's cold,' said the invalid, looking with distaste at the cup which he had not as yet tasted. 'Why can't I ever get a cup of really hot coffee?'

'I'll take it down and warm it up.'

In the kitchen Miss Gilchrist was drinking tea and conversing affably, though with slight condescension, with Mrs Jones.

'I'm so anxious to spare Mrs Abernethie all I can,' she said. 'All this running up and down stairs is so painful for her.'

'Waits on him hand and foot, she does,' said Mrs Jones, stirring the sugar in her cup.

'It's very sad his being such an invalid.'

'Not such an invalid either,' Mrs Jones said darkly. 'Suits him very well to lie up and ring bells and have trays brought up and down. But he's well able to get up and go about. Even seen him out in the village, I have, when *she's* been away. Walking as hearty as you please. Anything he *really* needs – like his tobacco or a stamp – he can come and get. And that's why when *she* was off to that funeral and got held up on the way back, and *he* told me I'd got to come in and stay the night again, I refused. "I'm sorry, sir," I said, "but I've got my husband to think of. Going out to oblige in the mornings is all very well, but I've got to be there to see to him when he comes back from work." Nor I wouldn't budge, I wouldn't. Do him good, I thought, to get about the house and look after himself for once. Might make him see what a lot he gets done for him. So I stood firm, I did. He didn't half create.'

Mrs Jones drew a deep breath and took a long satisfying drink of sweet inky tea. 'Ar,' she said.

Though deeply suspicious of Miss Gilchrist, and considering her as a finicky thing and a 'regular fussy old maid', Mrs Jones approved of the lavish way in which Miss Gilchrist dispensed her employer's tea and sugar ration.

She set down the cup and said affably:

'I'll give the kitchen floor a nice scrub down and then I'll be getting along. The potatoes is all ready peeled, dear, you'll find them by the sink.'

Though slightly affronted by the 'dear', Miss Gilchrist was appreciative of the goodwill which had divested an enormous quantity of potatoes of their outer coverings.

Before she could say anything the telephone rang and she hurried out in the hall to answer it. The telephone, in the style of fifty-odd years ago, was situated inconveniently in a draughty passage behind the staircase.

Maude Abernethie appeared at the top of the stairs while Miss Gilchrist was still speaking. The latter looked up and said:

'It's Mrs – Leo – is it? – Abernethie speaking.'

'Tell her I'm just coming.'

Maude descended the stairs slowly and painfully.

Miss Gilchrist murmured, 'I'm so sorry you've had to come down again, Mrs Abernethie. Has Mr Abernethie finished his elevenses? I'll just nip up and get the tray.'

She trotted up the stairs as Mrs Abernethie said into the receiver:

'Helen? This is Maude here.'

The invalid received Miss Gilchrist with a baleful glare. As she picked up the tray he asked fretfully:

'Who's that on the telephone?'

'Mrs Leo Abernethie.'

'Oh? Suppose they'll go on gossiping for about an hour. Women have no sense of time when they get on the phone. Never think of the money they're wasting.'

Miss Gilchrist said brightly that it would be Mrs Leo who had to pay, and Timothy grunted.

'Just pull that curtain aside, will you? No, not that one, the *other* one. I don't want the light slap in my eyes. That's better. No reason because I'm an invalid that I should have to sit in the dark all day.'

He went on:

'And you might look in that bookcase over there for a green – What's the matter *now*? What are you rushing off for?'

'It's the front door, Mr Abernethie.'

'*I* didn't hear anything. You've got that woman downstairs, haven't you? Let her go and answer it.'

'Yes, Mr Abernethie. What was the book you wanted me to find?'

The invalid closed his eyes.

'I can't remember now. You've put it out of my head. You'd better go.'

Miss Gilchrist seized the tray and hurriedly departed. Putting the tray on the pantry table she hurried into the front hall, passing Mrs Abernethie who was still at the telephone.

She returned in a moment to ask in a muted voice:

'I'm so sorry to interrupt. It's a nun. Collecting. The Heart of Mary Fund, I think she said. She has a book. Half a crown or five shillings most people seem to have given.'

Maude Abernethie said:

'Just a moment, Helen,' into the telephone, and to Miss Gilchrist, 'I don't subscribe to Roman Catholics. We have our own Church charities.'

Miss Gilchrist hurried away again.

Maude terminated her conversation after a few minutes with the phrase, 'I'll talk to Timothy about it.'

She replaced the receiver and came into the front hall. Miss Gilchrist was standing quite still by the drawing-room door. She was frowning in a puzzled way and jumped when Maude Abernethie spoke to her.

'There's nothing the matter, is there, Miss Gilchrist?'

'Oh no, Mrs Abernethie, I'm afraid I was just wool gathering. So stupid of me when there's so much to be done.'

Miss Gilchrist resumed her imitation of a busy ant and Maude Abernethie climbed the stairs slowly and painfully to her husband's room.

'That was Helen on the telephone. It seems that the place is definitely sold – some Institution for Foreign Refugees –'

She paused whilst Timothy expressed himself forcibly on the subject of Foreign Refugees, with side issues as to the house in which he had been born and brought up. 'No decent standards left in this country. My old home! I can hardly bear to think of it.'

Maude went on:

'Helen quite appreciates what you – we – will feel about it. She suggests that we might like to come there for a visit before it goes. She was very distressed about your health and the way the painting is affecting it. She thought you might prefer coming to Enderby to going to an hotel. The servants are there still, so you could be looked after comfortably.'

Timothy, whose mouth had been open in outraged protests half-way through this, had closed it again. His eyes had become suddenly shrewd. He now nodded his head approvingly.

'Thoughtful of Helen,' he said. 'Very thoughtful. I don't know, I'm sure, I'll have to think it over . . . There's no doubt that this paint is poisoning me – there's arsenic in paint, I believe. I seem to have heard something of the kind. On the other hand the exertion of moving might be too much for me. It's difficult to know what would be the best.'

'Perhaps you'd prefer an hotel, dear,' said Maude. 'A good hotel is very expensive, but where your health is concerned –'

Timothy interrupted.

'I wish I could make you understand, Maude, that we *are not millionaires*. Why go to an hotel when Helen has very kindly suggested that we should go to Enderby? Not that it's really for her to suggest! The house isn't hers. I don't understand legal subtleties, but I presume it belongs to us equally until it's sold and the proceeds divided. Foreign Refugees! It would have made old Cornelius turn in his grave. Yes,' he sighed, 'I should like to see the old place again before I die.'

Maude played her last card adroitly.

'I understand that Mr Entwhistle has suggested that the members of the family might like to choose certain pieces of furniture or china or something – before the contents are put up for auction.'

Timothy heaved himself briskly upright.

'We must certainly go. There must be a very exact valuation of what is chosen by each person. Those men the girls have married – I wouldn't trust either of them from what I've heard. There might be some sharp practice. Helen is far too amiable. As the head of the family, it is my duty to be present!'

He got up and walked up and down the room with a brisk vigorous tread.

'Yes, it is an excellent plan. Write to Helen and accept. What I am really thinking about is you, my dear. It will be a nice rest and change for you. You have been doing far too much lately. The decorators can get on with the painting while we are away and that Gillespie woman can stay here and look after the house.'

'Gilchrist,' said Maude.

Timothy waved a hand and said that it was all the same.

II

'I can't do it,' said Miss Gilchrist.

Maude looked at her in surprise.

Miss Gilchrist was trembling. Her eyes looked pleadingly into Maude's.

'It's stupid of me, I know . . . But I simply can't. Not stay here all alone in the house. If there was anyone who could come and – and sleep here too?'

She looked hopefully at the other woman, but Maude shook her head. Maude Abernethie knew only too well how difficult it was to get anyone in the neighbourhood to 'live in'.

Miss Gilchrist went on, a kind of desperation in her voice. 'I know you'll think it nervy and foolish – and I wouldn't have dreamed once that I'd ever feel like this. I've never been a nervous woman – or fanciful. But now it all seems different. I'd be terrified – yes, literally terrified – to be all alone here.'

'Of course,' said Maude. 'It's stupid of me. After what happend at Lytchett St Mary.'

'I suppose that's it . . . It's not logical, I know. And I didn't feel it at first. I didn't mind being alone in the cottage after – after it had happened. The feeling's grown up gradually. You'll have no opinion of me at all, Mrs Abernethie, but ever since I've been here I've been feeling it – *frightened*, you know. Not of anything in particular – but just *frightened* . . . It's so silly and I really am ashamed. It's just as though all the time I was expecting something awful to happen . . . Even that nun coming to the door startled me. Oh dear, I *am* in a bad way . . .'

'I suppose it's what they call delayed shock,' said Maude vaguely.

'Is it? I don't know. Oh, dear, I'm so sorry to appear so – so ungrateful, and after all your kindness. What you will think –'

Maude soothed her.

'We must think of some other arrangement,' she said.

CHAPTER 16

George Crossfield paused irresolutely for a moment as he watched a particular feminine back disappear through a doorway. Then he nodded to himself and went in pursuit.

The doorway in question was that of a double-fronted shop – a shop that had gone out of business. The plate-glass windows showed a disconcerting emptiness within. The door was closed, but George rapped on it. A vacuous faced young man with spectacles opened it and stared at George.

'Excuse me,' said George. 'But I think my cousin just came in here.'

The young man drew back and George walked in.

'Hallo, Susan,' he said.

Susan, who was standing on a packing-case and using a foot-rule, turned her head in some surprise.

'Hallo, George. Where did you spring from?'

'I saw your back. I was sure it was yours.'

'How clever of you. I suppose backs are distinctive.'

'Much more so than faces. Add a beard and pads in your cheeks and do a few things to your hair and nobody will know you when you come face to face with them – but beware of the moment when you walk away.'

'I'll remember. Can you remember seven feet five inches until I've got time to write it down.'

'Certainly. What is this, book shelves?'

'No, cubicle space. Eight feet nine – and three seven . . .'

The young man with the spectacles who had been fidgeting from one foot to the other, coughed apologetically.

'Excuse me, Mrs Banks, but if you want to be here for some time –'

'I do, rather,' said Susan. 'If you leave the keys, I'll lock the door and return them to the office when I go past. Will that be all right?'

'Yes, thank you. If it weren't that we're short staffed this morning –'

Susan accepted the apologetic intent of the half-finished sentence and the young man removed himself to the outer world of the street.

'I'm glad we've got rid of him,' said Susan. 'House agents are a bother. They will keep talking just when I want to do sums.'

'Ah,' said George. 'Murder in an empty shop. How exciting it would be for the passers-by to see the dead body of a beautiful young woman displayed behind plate glass. How they would goggle. Like goldfish.'

'There wouldn't be any reason for you to murder me, George.'

'Well, I should get a fourth part of your share of our esteemed uncle's estate. If one were sufficiently fond of money that should be a reason.'

Susan stopped taking measurements and turned to look at him. Her eyes opened a little.

'You look a different person, George. It's really – extraordinary.'

'Different? How different?'

'Like an advertisement. *This is the same man that you saw overleaf, but now he has taken Uppington's Health Salts.*'

She sat down on another packing-case and lit a cigarette.

'You must have wanted your share of old Richard's money pretty badly, George?'

'Nobody could honestly say that money isn't welcome these days.'

George's tone was light.

Susan said: 'You were in a jam, weren't you?'

'Hardly your business, is it, Susan?'

'I was just interested.'

'Are you renting this shop as a place of business?'

'I'm buying the whole house.'

'With possession?'

'Yes. The two upper floors were flats. One's empty and went with the shop. The other, I'm buying the people out.'

'Nice to have money, isn't it, Susan?'

There was a malicious tone in George's voice. But Susan merely took a deep breath and said:

'As far as I'm concerned, it's wonderful. An answer to prayer.'

'Does prayer kill off elderly relatives?'

Susan paid no attention.

'This place is exactly *right*. To begin with, it's a very good piece of period architecture. I can make the living part upstairs something quite unique. There are two lovely moulded ceilings and the rooms are a beautiful shape. This part down here which has already been hacked about I shall have completely modern.'

'What is this? A dress business?'

'No. Beauty culture. Herbal preparations. Face creams!'

'The full racket?'

'The racket as before. It pays. It always pays. What you need to put it over is personality. I can do it.'

George looked at his cousin appreciatively. He admired the slanting planes of her face, the generous mouth, the radiant colouring. Altogether an unusual and vivid face. And he recognized in Susan that odd, indefinable quality, the quality of success.

'Yes,' he said, 'I think you've got what it takes, Susan. You'll get back your outlay on this scheme and you'll get places with it.'

'It's the right neighbourhood, just off a main shopping street *and* you can park a car right in front of the door.'

Again George nodded.

'Yes, Susan, you're going to succeed. Have you had this in mind for a long time?'

'Over a year.'

'Why didn't you put it up to old Richard? He might have staked you.'

'I did put it up to him.'

'And he didn't see his way? I wonder why. I should have thought he'd have recognized the same mettle that he himself was made of.'

Susan did not answer, and into George's mind there leapt a swift bird's eye view of another figure. A thin, nervous, suspicious-eyed young man.

'Where does – what's his name – Greg – come in on all

this?' he asked. 'He'll give up dishing out pills and powders, I take it?'

'Of course. There will be a laboratory built out at the back. We shall have our own formulas for face creams and beauty preparations.'

George suppressed a grin. He wanted to say: 'So baby is to have his play pen,' but he did not say it. As a cousin he did not mind being spiteful, but he had an uneasy sense that Susan's feeling for her husband was a thing to be treated with care. It had all the qualities of a dangerous explosive. He wondered, as he had wondered on the day of the funeral, about that queer fish, Gregory. Something odd about the fellow. So nondescript in appearance – and yet, in some way, not nondescript . . .

He looked again at Susan, calmly and radiantly triumphant.

'You've got the true Abernethie touch,' he said. 'The only one of the family who has. Pity as far as old Richard was concerned that you're a woman. If you'd been a boy, I bet he'd have left you the whole caboodle.'

Susan said slowly: 'Yes, I think he would.'

She paused and then went on:

'He didn't like Greg, you know . . .'

'Ah.' George raised his eyebrows. 'His mistake.'

'Yes.'

'Oh, well. Anyway, things are going well now – all going according to plan.'

As he said the words he was struck by the fact that they seemed particularly applicable to Susan.

The idea made him, just for a moment, a shade uncomfortable.

He didn't really like a woman who was so cold-bloodedly efficient.

Changing the subject he said:

'By the way, did you get a letter from Helen? About Enderby?'

'Yes, I did. This morning. Did you?'

'Yes. What are you going to do about it?'

'Greg and I thought of going up the week-end after next – if that suits everyone else. Helen seemed to want us all together.'

George laughed shrewdly.

'Or somebody might choose a more valuable piece of furniture than somebody else?'

Susan laughed.

'Oh, I suppose there is a proper valuation. But a valuation for probate will be much lower than the things would be in the open market. And besides, I'd quite like to have a few relics of the founder of the family fortunes. Then I think it would be amusing to have one or two really absurd and charming specimens of the Victorian age in this place. Make a kind of *thing* of them! That period's coming in now. There was a green malachite table in the drawing-room. You could build quite a colour scheme around it. And perhaps a case of stuffed humming birds – or one of those crowns made of waxed flowers. Something like that – just as a key-note – can be very effective.'

'I trust your judgement.'

'You'll be there, I suppose?'

'Oh, I shall be there – to see fair play if nothing else.'

Susan laughed.

'What do you bet there will be a grand family row?' she asked.

'Rosamund will probably want your green malachite table for a stage set!'

Susan did not laugh. Instead she frowned.

'Have you seen Rosamund lately?'

'I have not seen beautiful Cousin Rosamund since we all came back third-class from the funeral.'

'I've seen her once or twice ... She – she seemed rather odd –'

'What was the matter with her? Trying to think?'

'No. She seemed – well – upset.'

'Upset about coming into a lot of money and being able to put on some perfectly frightful play in which Michael can make an ass of himself?'

'Oh, that's going ahead and it *does* sound frightful – but all the same, it may be a success. Michael's good, you know. He can put himself across the footlights – or whatever the term is. He's not like Rosamund, who's just beautiful and ham.'

'Poor beautiful ham Rosamund.'

'All the same Rosamund is not quite so dumb as one might

think. She says things that are quite shrewd, sometimes. Things that you wouldn't have imagined she'd even noticed. It's – it's quite disconcerting.'

'Quite like our Aunt Cora –'

'Yes . . .'

A momentary uneasiness descended on them both – conjured up it seemed, by the mention of Cora Lansquenet.

Then George said with a rather elaborate air of unconcern:

'Talking of Cora – what about that companion woman of hers? I rather think something ought to be done about her.'

'Done about her? What do you mean?'

'Well, it's up to the family, so to speak. I mean I've been thinking Cora was our Aunt – and it occurred to me that this woman mayn't find it easy to get another post.'

'That occurred to you, did it?'

'Yes. People are so careful of their skins. I don't say they'd actually think that this Gilchrist female would take a hatchet to them – but at the back of their minds they'd feel that it might be unlucky. People are superstitious.'

'How odd that you should have thought of all that, George? How would you know about things like that?'

George said drily:

'You forget that I'm a lawyer. I see a lot of the queer illogical side of people. What I'm getting at is, that I think we might do something about the woman, give her a small allowance or something, to tide her over, or find some office post for her if she's capable of that sort of thing. I feel rather as though we ought to keep in touch with her.'

'You needn't worry,' said Susan. Her voice was dry and ironic. 'I've seen to things. She's gone to Timothy and Maude.'

George looked startled.

'I say, Susan – is that wise?'

'It was the best thing I could think of – at the moment.'

George looked at her curiously.

'You're very sure of yourself, aren't you, Susan? You know what you're doing and you don't have – regrets.'

Susan said lightly:

'It's a waste of time – having regrets.'

CHAPTER 17

Michael tossed the letter across the table to Rosamund.

'What about it?'

'Oh, we'll go. Don't you think so?'

Michael said slowly:

'It might be as well.'

'There might be some jewellery . . . Of course all the things in the house are quite hideous – stuffed birds and wax flowers – ugh!'

'Yes. Bit of a mausoleum. As a matter of fact I'd like to make a sketch or two – particularly in that drawing-room. The mantel-piece, for instance, and that very odd shaped couch. They'd be just right for *The Baronet's Progress* – if we revive it.'

He got up and looked at his watch.

'That reminds me. I must go round and see Rosenheim. Don't expect me until rather late this evening. I'm dining with Oscar and we're going into the question of taking up that option and how it fits in with the American offer.'

'Darling Oscar. He'll be pleased to see you after all this time. Give him my love.'

Michael looked at her sharply. He no longer smiled and his face had an alert predatory look.

'What do you mean – after all this time? Anyone would think I hadn't seen him for months.'

'Well, you haven't, have you?' murmured Rosamund.

'Yes, I have. We lunched together only a week ago.'

'How funny. He must have forgotten about it. He rang up yesterday and said he hadn't seen you since the first night of *Tilly Looks West*.'

'The old fool must be off his head.'

Michael laughed. Rosamund, her eyes wide and blue, looked at him without emotion.

'You think I'm a fool, don't you, Mick?'

Michael protested.

'Darling, of course I don't.'

'Yes, you do. But I'm not an absolute nitwit. You didn't go near Oscar that day. I know where you did go.'

'Rosamund darling – what do you mean?'

'I mean I know where you really were . . .'

Michael, his attractive face uncertain, stared at his wife. She stared back at him, placid, unruffled.

How very disconcerting, he suddenly thought, a really empty stare could be.

He said rather unsuccessfully:

'I don't know what you're driving at . . .'

'I just meant it's rather silly telling me a lot of lies.'

'Look here, Rosamund –'

He had started to bluster – but he stopped, taken aback as his wife said softly:

'We do want to take up this option and put this play on, don't we?'

'Want to? It's the part I've always dreamed must exist somewhere.'

'Yes – that's what I mean.'

'Just what do you mean?'

'Well – it's worth a good deal, isn't it? But one mustn't take *too* many risks.'

He stared at her and said slowly:

'It's your money – I know that. If you don't want to risk it –'

'It's *our* money, darling.' Rosamund stressed it. 'I think that's rather important.'

'Listen, darling. The part of Eileen – it would bear writing up.'

Rosamund smiled.

'I don't think – really – I want to play it.'

'My dear girl.' Michael was aghast. 'What's come over you?'

'Nothing.'

'Yes, there is, you've been different lately – moody – nervous, what is it?'

'Nothing. I only want you to be – careful, Mick.'

'Careful about what? I'm always careful.'

'No, I don't think you are. You always think you can get away with things and that everyone will believe whatever you want them to. You were stupid about Oscar that day.'

Michael flushed angrily.

'And what about you? You said you were going shopping with Jane. You didn't. Jane's in America, has been for weeks.'

'Yes,' said Rosamund. 'That was stupid, too. I really just went for a walk – in Regent's Park.'

Michael looked at her curiously.

'Regent's Park? You never went for a walk in Regent's Park in your life. What's it all about? Have you got a boyfriend? You may say what you like, Rosamund, you *have* been different lately. Why?'

'I've been – thinking about things. About what to do . . .'

Michael came round the table to her in a satisfying spontaneous rush. His voice held fervour as he cried:

'Darling – you know I love you madly!'

She responded satisfactorily to the embrace, but as they drew apart he was struck again disagreeably by the odd calculation in those beautiful eyes.

'Whatever I'd done, you'd always forgive me, wouldn't you?' he demanded.

'I suppose so,' said Rosamund vaguely. 'That's not the point. You see, it's all different now. We've got to think and plan.'

'Think and plan – what?'

Rosamund, frowning, said:

'Things aren't over when you've done them. It's really a sort of beginning and then one's got to arrange what to do next, and what's important and what is not.'

'Rosamund . . .'

She sat, her face perplexed, her wide gaze on a middle distance in which Michael, apparently, did not feature.

At the third repetition of her name, she started slightly and came out of her reverie.

'What did you say?'

'I asked you what you were thinking about . . .'

'Oh? Oh yes, I was wondering if I'd go down to – what is it? – Lytchett St Mary, and see that Miss Somebody – the one who was with Aunt Cora.'

'But why?'

'Well, she'll be going away soon, won't she? To relatives or someone. I don't think we ought to let her go away until we've asked her.'

'Asked her what?'

'Asked her who killed Aunt Cora.'

Michael stared.

'You mean – you think she *knows*?'

Rosamund said rather absently:

'Oh yes, I *expect* so . . . She lived there, you see.'

'But she'd have told the police.'

'Oh, I don't mean she knows *that* way – I just mean that she's probably quite sure. Because of what Uncle Richard said when he went down there. He did go down there, you know, Susan told me so.'

'But she wouldn't have heard what he said.'

'Oh yes, she would, darling.' Rosamund sounded like someone arguing with an unreasonable child.

'Nonsense, I can hardly see old Richard Abernethie discussing his suspicions of his family before an outsider.'

'Well, of course. She'd have heard it through the door.'

'Eavesdropping, you mean?'

'I expect so – in fact I'm sure. It must be deadly dull shut up, two women in a cottage and nothing ever happening except washing up and the sink and putting the cat out and things like that. Of course she listened and read letters – anyone would.'

Michael looked at her with something faintly approaching dismay.

'Would you?' he demanded bluntly.

'I wouldn't go and be a companion in the country.' Rosamund shuddered. 'I'd rather die.'

'I mean – would you read letters and – and all that?'

Rosamund said calmly:

'If I wanted to know, yes. Everybody does, don't you think so?'

The limpid gaze met his.

'One just wants to know,' said Rosamund. 'One doesn't want to do anything about it. I expect that's how *she* feels – Miss Gilchrist, I mean. But I'm certain she *knows*.'

Michael said in a stifled voice:

'Rosamund, who do you think killed Cora? And old Richard?'

Once again that limpid blue gaze met his.

'Darling – don't be absurd . . . You know as well as I do. But it's much, much better *never* to mention it. So we won't.'

CHAPTER 18

From his seat by the fireplace in the library, Hercule Poirot looked at the assembled company.

His eyes passed thoughtfully over Susan, sitting upright, looking vivid and animated, over her husband, sitting near her, his expression rather vacant and his fingers twisting a loop of string; they went on to George Crossfield, debonair and distinctly pleased with himself, talking about card sharpers on Atlantic cruises to Rosamund, who said mechanically, 'How extraordinary, darling. But why?' in a completely uninterested voice; went on to Michael with his very individual type of haggard good looks and his very apparent charm; to Helen, poised and slightly remote; to Timothy, comfortably settled in the best armchair with an extra cushion at his back; and Maude, sturdy and thick-set, in devoted attendance, and finally to the figure sitting with a tinge of apology just beyond the range of the family circle – the figure of Miss Gilchrist wearing a rather peculiar 'dressy' blouse. Presently, he judged, she would get up, murmur her excuse and leave the family gathering and go up to her room. Miss Gilchrist, he thought, knew her place. She had learned it the hard way.

Hercule Poirot sipped his after-dinner coffee and between half-closed lids made his appraisal.

He had wanted them there – all together, and he had got them. And what, he thought to himself, was he going to do with them now? He felt a sudden weary distaste for going on with the business. Why was that, he wondered? Was it the influence of Helen Abernethie? There was a quality of passive resistance about her that seemed unexpectedly strong. Had she, while apparently graceful and unconcerned, managed to impress her own reluctance upon him? She was averse to this raking up of the details of old Richard's death, he knew that. She wanted it left alone, left to die out into oblivion. Poirot was not surprised by that. What did surprise him was his own disposition to agree with her.

Mr Entwhistle's account of the family had, he realized, been admirable. He had described all these people shrewdly and well.

With the old lawyer's knowledge and appraisal to guide him, Poirot had wanted to see for himself. He had fancied that, meeting these people intimately, he would have a very shrewd idea – not of *how* and *when* – (those were questions with which he did not propose to concern himself. Murder had been possible – that was all he needed to know!) – but of who. For Hercule Poirot had a lifetime of experience behind him, and as a man who deals with pictures can recognize the artist, so Poirot believed he could recognize a likely type of the amateur criminal who will – if his own particular need arises – be prepared to kill.

But it was not to be so easy.

Because he could visualize almost all of these people as a possible – though not a probable – murderer. George might kill – as the cornered rat kills. Susan calmly – efficiently – to further a plan. Gregory because he had that queer morbid streak which discounts and invites, almost craves, punishment. Michael because he was ambitious and had a murderer's cocksure vanity. Rosamund because she was frighteningly simple in outlook. Timothy because he had hated and resented his brother and had craved the power his brother's money would give. Maude because Timothy was her child and where her child was con- cerned she would be ruthless. Even Miss Gilchrist, he thought, might have contemplated murder if it could have restored to her the Willow Tree in its lady-like glory! And Helen? He could not see Helen as committing murder. She was too civilized – too removed from violence. And she and her husband had surely loved Richard Abernethie.

Poirot sighed to himself. There were to be no short cuts to the truth. Instead he would have to adopt a longer, but a reasonably sure method. There would have to be conversation. Much conversation. For in the long run, either through a lie, or through truth, people were bound to give themselves away . . .

He had been introduced by Helen to the gathering, and had set to work to overcome the almost universal annoyance caused by his presence – a foreign stranger! – in this family gathering. He had used his eyes and his ears. He had watched and listened – openly and behind doors! He had noticed affinities, antagonism, the unguarded words that arose as always when property was to be divided. He had engineered adroitly tête-à-têtes, walks upon the terrace, and had made his deductions and observations. He had talked with Miss Gilchrist about the vanished glories of her tea-shop and about the correct composition of brioches and chocolate éclairs and had visited the kitchen garden with her to discuss the proper use of herbs in cooking. He had spent some long half-hours listening to Timothy talking about his own health and about the effect upon it of paint.

Paint? Poirot frowned. Somebody else had said something about paint – Mr Entwhistle?

There had also been discussion of a different kind of painting. Pierre Lansquenet as a painter. Cora Lansquenet's paintings, rapturized over by Miss Gilchrist, dismissed scornfully by Susan. 'Just like picture postcards,' she had said. 'She did them from postcards, too.'

Miss Gilchrist had been quite upset by that and had said sharply that dear Mrs Lansquenet always painted from Nature.

'But I bet she cheated,' said Susan to Poirot when Miss Gilchrist had gone out of the room. 'In fact I know she did, though I won't upset the old pussy by saying so.'

'And how do you know?'

Poirot watched the strong confident line of Susan's chin.

'She will always be sure, this one,' he thought. 'And perhaps sometimes, she will be too sure . . .'

Susan was going on.

'I'll tell you, but don't pass it on to the Gilchrist. One picture is of Polflexan, the cove and lighthouse and the pier – the usual aspect that all amateur artists sit down and sketch. But the pier was blown up in the war, and since Aunt Cora's sketch was done a couple of years ago, it can't very well be from Nature, can it? But the postcards they sell there still show the pier as it used to be. There was one in her bedroom drawer. So Aunt Cora started her "rough sketch" down there, I expect, and then finished it surreptitiously later at home from a postcard! It's funny, isn't it, the way people get caught out?'

'Yes, it is, as you say, funny.' He paused, and then thought that the opening was a good one.

'You do not remember me, Madame,' he said, 'but I remember you. This is not the first time that I have seen you.'

She stared at him. Poirot nodded with great gusto.

'Yes, yes, it is so. I was inside an automobile, well wrapped up and from the window I saw you. You were talking to one of the mechanics in the garage. You do not notice me – it is natural – I am inside the car – an elderly muffled-up foreigner! But *I* noticed you, for you are young and agreeable to look at and you stand there in the sun. So when I arrive here, I say to myself, "Tiens! What a coincidence!"'

'A garage? Where? When was this?'

'Oh, a little time ago – a week – no, more. For the moment,' said Poirot disingenuously and with a full recollection of the King's Arms garage in his mind, 'I cannot remember where. I travel so much all over this country.'

'Looking for a suitable house to buy for your refugees?'

'Yes. There is so much to take into consideration, you see. Price – neighbourhood – suitability for conversion.'

'I suppose you'll have to pull the house about a lot? Lots of horrible partitions.'

'In the bedrooms, yes, certainly. But most of the ground floor rooms we shall not touch.' He paused before going on. 'Does it sadden you, Madame, that this old family mansion of yours should go this way – to strangers?'

'Of course not.' Susan looked amused. 'I think it's an excellent idea. It's an impossible place for anybody to think of living in as it is. And I've nothing to be sentimental about. It's not *my* old home. My mother and father lived in London. We just came here for Christmas sometimes. Actually I've always thought it quite hideous – an almost indecent temple to wealth.'

'The altars are different now. There is the building in, and the concealed lighting and the expensive simplicity. But wealth still has its temples, Madame. I understand – I am not, I hope, indiscreet – that you yourself are planning such an edifice? Everything *de luxe* – and no expense spared.'

Susan laughed.

'Hardly a temple – it's just a place of business.'

'Perhaps the name does not matter . . . But it will cost much money – that is true, is it not?'

'Everything's wickedly expensive nowadays. But the initial outlay will be worth while, I think.'

'Tell me something about these plans of yours. It amazes me

to find a beautiful young woman so practical, so competent. In my young days – a long time ago, I admit – beautiful women thought only of their pleasures, of cosmetics – of *la toilette.*'

'Women still think a great deal about their faces – that's where I come in.'

'Tell me.'

And she had told him. Told him with a wealth of detail and with a great deal of unconscious self-revelation. He appreciated her business acumen, her boldness of planning and her grasp of detail. A good bold planner, sweeping all side issues away. Perhaps a little ruthless as all those who plan boldly must be.

Watching her, he had said:

'Yes, you will succeed. You will go ahead. How fortunate that you are not restricted, as so many are, by poverty. One cannot go far without the capital outlay. To have had these creative ideas and to have been frustrated by lack of means – that would have been unbearable.'

'I couldn't have borne it! But I'd have raised money somehow or other – got someone to back me.'

'Ah! of course. Your uncle, whose house this was, was rich. Even if he had not died, he would, as you express it, have "staked" you.'

'Oh no, he wouldn't. Uncle Richard was a bit of a stick-in-the-mud where women were concerned. If I'd been a man –' A quick flash of anger swept across her face. 'He made me very angry.'

'I see – yes, I see . . .'

'The old shouldn't stand in the way of the young. I – oh, I beg your pardon.'

Hercule Poirot laughed easily and twirled his moustache.

'I am old, yes. But I do not impede youth. There is no one who needs to wait for my death.'

'What a horrid idea.'

'But you are a realist, Madame. Let us admit without more ado that the world is full of the young – or even the middle-aged – who wait, patiently or impatiently, for the death of someone whose decease will give them if not affluence – then opportunity.'

'Opportunity!' Susan said, taking a deep breath. 'That's what one needs.'

Poirot who had been looking beyond her, said gaily:

'And here is your husband come to join our little discussion . . . We talk, Mr Banks, of opportunity. Opportunity the golden – opportunity who must be grasped with both hands. How far in conscience can one go? Let us hear your views?'

But he was not destined to hear the views of Gregory Banks on opportunity or on anything else. In fact he had found it next to impossible to talk to Gregory Banks at all. Banks had a curious fluid quality. Whether by his own wish, or by that of his wife, he seemed to have no liking for tête-à-têtes or quiet discussions. No, 'conversation' with Gregory had failed.

Poirot had talked with Maude Abernethie – also about paint (the smell of) and how fortunate it had been that Timothy had been able to come to Enderby, and how kind it had been of Helen to extend an invitation to Miss Gilchrist also.

'For really she is *most* useful. Timothy so often feels like a snack – and one cannot ask too much of other people's servants but there is a gas ring in a little room off the pantry, so that Miss Gilchrist can warm up Ovaltine or Benger's there without disturbing anybody. And she's so willing about fetching things, she's quite willing to run up and down stairs a dozen times a day. Oh yes, I feel that it was really quite Providential that she should have lost her nerve about staying alone in the house as she did, though I admit it vexed me at the time.'

'Lost her nerve?' Poirot was interested.

He listened whilst Maude gave him an account of Miss Gilchrist's sudden collapse.

'She was frightened, you say? And yet could not exactly say why? That is interesting. Very interesting.'

'I put it down myself to delayed shock.'

'Perhaps.'

'Once during the war, when a bomb dropped about a mile from us, I remember Timothy –'

Poirot abstracted his mind from Timothy.

'Had anything particular happened that day?' he asked.

'On what day?' Maude looked blank.

'The day that Miss Gilchrist was upset.'

'Oh, that – no, I don't think so. It seems to have been coming on ever since she left Lytchett St Mary, or so she said. She didn't seem to mind when she was there.'

And the result, Poirot thought, had been a piece of poisoned wedding cake. Not so very surprising that Miss Gilchrist was frightened after that . . . And even when she had removed herself to the peaceful country round Stansfield Grange, the fear had lingered. More than lingered. Grown. Why grown? Surely attending on an exacting hypochondriac like Timothy must be so exhausting that nervous fears would be likely to be swallowed up in exasperation?

But something in that house had made Miss Gilchrist afraid. What? Did she know herself?

Finding himself alone with Miss Gilchrist for a brief space before dinner, Poirot had sailed into the subject with an exaggerated foreign curiosity.

'Impossible, you comprehend, for me to mention the matter of murder to members of the family. But I am intrigued. Who would not be? A brutal crime – a sensitive artist attacked in a lonely cottage. Terrible for her family. But terrible, also, I imagine, for *you*. Since Mrs Timothy Abernethie gives me to understand that you were there at the time?'

'Yes, I was. And if you'll excuse me, M. Pontarlier, I don't want to talk about it.'

'I understand – oh yes, I completely understand.'

Having said this, Poirot waited. And, as he had thought, Miss Gilchrist immediately *did* begin to talk about it.

He heard nothing from her that he had not heard before, but he played his part with perfect sympathy, uttering little cries of comprehension and listening with an absorbed interest which Miss Gilchrist could not help but enjoy.

Not until she had exhausted the subject of what she herself had felt, and what the doctor had said, and how kind Mr Entwhistle had been, did Poirot proceed cautiously to the next point.

'You were wise, I think, not to remain alone down in that cottage.'

'I couldn't have done it, M. Pontarlier. I really couldn't have done it.'

'No. I understand even that you were afraid to remain alone in the house of Mr Timothy Abernethie whilst they came here?'

Miss Gilchrist looked guilty.

'I'm terribly ashamed about that. So foolish really. It was just a kind of panic I had – really don't know *why*.'

'But of course one knows why. You had just recovered from a dastardly attempt to poison you –'

Miss Gilchrist here sighed and said she simply couldn't understand it. Why should anyone try to poison her?

'But obviously, my dear lady, because this criminal, this assassin, thought that you knew something that might lead to his apprehension by the police.'

'But what could *I* know? Some dreadful tramp, or semi-crazed creature.'

'If it *was* a tramp. It seems to me unlikely –'

'Oh, please, M. Pontarlier –' Miss Gilchrist became suddenly very upset. 'Don't suggest such things. I don't want to believe it.'

'You do not want to believe what?'

'I don't want to believe that it wasn't – I mean – that it was –'

She paused, confused.

'And yet,' said Poirot shrewdly, 'you *do* believe.'

'Oh, I don't. I *don't!*'

'But I think you do. That is why you are frightened . . . You are still frightened, are you not?'

'Oh, no, not since I came here. So many people. And such a nice family atmosphere. Oh, no, everything seems quite all right here.'

'It seems to me – you must excuse my interest – I am an old man, somewhat infirm and a great part of my time is given to idle speculation on matters which interest me – it seems to me that there must have been some definite occurrence at Stansfield Grange which, so to speak, brought your fears to a *head*. Doctors recognize nowadays how much takes place in our subconscious.'

'Yes, yes – I know they say so.'

'And I think your subconscious fears might have been brought to a point by some small concrete happening, something, perhaps, quite extraneous, serving, shall we say, as a focal point.'

Miss Gilchrist seemed to lap this up eagerly.

'I'm sure you are right,' she said.

'Now what, should you think, was this – er – extraneous circumstance?'

Miss Gilchrist pondered a moment, and then said, unexpectedly:

'I think, you know, M. Pontarlier, it was the *nun*.'

Before Poirot could take this up, Susan and her husband came in, closely followed by Helen.

'A nun,' thought Poirot . . . 'Now where, in all this, have I heard something about a nun?'

He resolved to lead the conversation on to nuns some time in the course of the evening.

<hr>

CHAPTER 19

The family had all been polite to M. Pontarlier, the representative of U.N.A.R.C.O. And how right he had been to have chosen to designate himself by initials. Everyone had accepted U.N.A.R.C.O. as a matter of course – had even pretended to know all about it! How averse human beings were ever to admit ignorance! An exception had been Rosamund, who had asked him wonderingly: 'But what *is* it? I never heard of it?' Fortunately no one else had been there at the time. Poirot had explained the organization in such a way that anyone but Rosamund would have felt abashed at having displayed ignorance of such a well-known world-wide institution. Rosamund, however, had only said vaguely, 'Oh! refugees all over *again*. I'm so *tired* of refugees.' Thus voicing the unspoken reaction of many, who were usually too conventional to express themselves so frankly.

M. Pontarlier was, therefore, now accepted – as a nuisance but also as a nonentity. He had become, as it were, a piece of foreign *décor*. The general opinion was that Helen should have avoided having him here this particular week-end, but as he was here they must make the best of it. Fortunately this queer little foreigner did not seem to know much English. Quite often he did not understand what you said to him, and when everyone was speaking more or less at once he seemed completely at sea. He appeared to be interested only in refugees and post-war conditions, and his vocabulary only included those subjects. Ordinary chit-chat appeared to bewilder him. More or less forgotten by all, Hercule Poirot leant back in his chair, sipped his coffee and observed, as a cat may observe the twitterings and comings and goings of a flock of birds. The cat is not ready yet to make its spring.

After twenty-four hours of prowling round the house and examining its contents, the heirs of Richard Abernethie were ready to state their preferences, and, if need be, to fight for them.

The subject of conversation was, first, a certain Spode dinner dessert service off which they had just been eating dessert.

'I don't suppose I have long to live,' said Timothy in a faint melancholy voice. 'And Maude and I have no children. It is hardly worth while our burdening ourselves with useless possessions. But for sentiment's sake I *should* like to have the old dessert service. I remember it in the dear old days. It's out of fashion, of course, and I understand dessert services have very little value nowadays – but there it is. I shall be *quite* content with that – and perhaps the Boule Cabinet in the White Boudoir.'

'You're too late, Uncle,' George spoke with debonair insouciance. 'I asked Helen to mark off the Spode service to me this morning.'

Timothy became purple in the face.

'Mark it off – mark it off? What do you mean? Nothing's been settled yet. And what do *you* want with a dessert service? You're not married.'

'As a matter of fact I collect Spode. And this is really a splendid specimen. But it's quite all right about the Boule Cabinet, Uncle. I wouldn't have that as a gift.'

Timothy waved aside the Boule Cabinet.

'Now look here, young George. You can't go butting in, in this way. I'm an older man than you are – and I'm Richard's only surviving brother. That dessert service is *mine*.'

'Why not take the Dresden service, Uncle? A very fine example and I'm sure just as full of sentimental memories. Anyway, the Spode's mine. First come, first served.'

'Nonsense – nothing of the kind!' Timothy spluttered.

Maude said sharply:

'Please don't upset your uncle, George. It's very bad for him. Naturally he will take the Spode if he wants to! The first choice is *his*, and you young people must come afterwards. He was Richard's brother, as he says, and you are only a nephew.'

'And I can tell you this, young man.' Timothy was seething with fury. 'If Richard had made a proper will, the disposal of the contents of this place would have been entirely in my hands. That's the way the property *should* have been left, and if it wasn't, I can only suspect *undue influence*. Yes – and I repeat it – *undue influence*.'

Timothy glared at his nephew.

'A preposterous will,' he said. 'Preposterous!'

He leant back, placed a hand to his heart, and groaned:

'This is very bad for me. If I could have – a little brandy.'

Miss Gilchrist hurried to get it and returned with the restorative in a small glass.

'Here you are, Mr Abernethie. Please – please don't excite youself. Are you sure you oughtn't to go up to bed?'

'Don't be a fool.' Timothy swallowed the brandy. 'Go to bed? I intend to protect my interests.'

'Really, George, I'm surprised at you,' said Maude. 'What your uncle says is perfectly true. His wishes come first. If he wants the Spode dessert service he shall have it!'

'It's quite hideous anyway,' said Susan.

'Hold your tongue, Susan,' said Timothy.

The thin young man who sat beside Susan raised his head. In a voice that was a little shriller than his ordinary tones, he said:

'Don't speak like that to my wife!'

He half rose from his seat.

Susan said quickly: 'It's all right, Greg. I don't mind.'

'But *I* do.'

Helen said: 'I think it would be graceful on your part, George, to let your uncle have the dessert service.'

Timothy spluttered indignantly: 'There's no "letting" about it!'

But George, with a slight bow to Helen said, 'Your wish is law, Aunt Helen. I abandon my claim.'

'You didn't really want it, anyway, did you?' said Helen.

He cast a sharp glance at her, then grinned:

'The trouble with you, Aunt Helen, is that you're too sharp by half! You see more than you're meant to see. Don't worry, Uncle Timothy, the Spode is yours. Just my idea of fun.'

'Fun, indeed.' Maude Abernethie was indignant. 'Your uncle might have had a heart attack!'

'Don't you believe it,' said George cheerfully. 'Uncle Timothy will probably outlive us all. He's what is known as a creaking gate.'

Timothy leaned forward balefully.

'I don't wonder,' he said, 'that Richard was disappointed in *you*.'

'What's that?' The good humour went out of George's face.

'You came up here after Mortimer died, expecting to step into his shoes – expecting that Richard would make you his heir, didn't you? But my poor brother soon took *your* measure. He knew where the money would go if you had control of it. I'm surprised that he even left you a part of his fortune. He knew where it would go. Horses, gambling, Monte Carlo, foreign casinos. Perhaps worse. He suspected you of not being straight, didn't he?'

George, a white dint appearing each side of his nose, said quietly:

'Hadn't you better be careful of what you are saying?'

'I wasn't well enough to come here for the funeral,' said Timothy slowly, 'but Maude told me what *Cora said*. Cora always was a fool – but there *may* have been something in it! And if so, I know who *I'd* suspect –'

'Timothy!' Maude stood up, solid, calm, a tower of forcefulness. 'You have had a very trying evening. You must consider your health. I can't have you getting ill again. Come up with me. You must take a sedative and go straight to bed. Timothy and I, Helen, will take the Spode dessert service and the Boule Cabinet as mementoes of Richard. There is no objection to that, I hope?'

Her glance swept round the company. Nobody spoke, and she marched out of the room supporting Timothy with a hand under his elbow, waving aside Miss Gilchrist who was hovering half-heartedly by the door.

George broke the silence after they had departed.

'*Femme formidable!*' he said. 'That describes Aunt Maude exactly. I should hate ever to impede her triumphal progress.'

Miss Gilchrist sat down again rather uncomfortably and murmured:

'Mrs Abernethie is always so kind.'

The remark fell rather flat.

Michael Shane laughed suddenly and said: 'You know, I'm enjoying all this! "The Voysey Inheritance" to the life. By the way, Rosamund and I want that malachite table in the drawing-room.'

'Oh, no,' cried Susan. '*I* want that.'

'Here we go again,' said George, raising his eyes to the ceiling.

'Well, we needn't get angry about it,' said Susan. 'The reason I want it is for my new Beauty shop. Just a note of colour – and I shall put a great bouquet of wax flowers on it. It would look wonderful. I can find wax flowers easily enough, but a green malachite table isn't so common.'

'But, darling,' said Rosamund, 'that's just why *we* want it. For the new set. As you say, a note of colour – and so *absolutely* period. And either wax flowers or stuffed humming birds. It will be absolutely *right*.'

'I see what you mean, Rosamund,' said Susan. 'But I don't think you've got as good a case as I have. You could easily have a painted malachite table for the stage – it would look just the same. But for my *salon* I've *got* to have the genuine thing.'

'Now, ladies,' said George. 'What about a sporting decision? Why not toss for it? Or cut the cards? All quite in keeping with the period of the table.'

Susan smiled pleasantly.

'Rosamund and I will talk about it tomorrow,' she said.

She seemed, as usual, quite sure of herself. George looked with some interest from her face to that of Rosamund. Rosamund's face had a vague, rather far-away expression.

'Which one will you back, Aunt Helen?' he asked. 'An even money chance, I'd say. Susan has determination, but Rosamund is so wonderfully single-minded.'

'Or perhaps *not* humming birds,' said Rosamund. 'One of those big Chinese vases would make a lovely lamp, with a gold shade.'

Miss Gilchrist hurried into placating speech.

'This house is full of so many beautiful things,' she said. 'That green table would look wonderful in your new establishment, I'm sure, Mrs Banks. I've never seen one like it. It must be worth a lot of money.'

'It will be deducted from my share of the estate, of course,' said Susan.

'I'm so sorry – I didn't mean –' Miss Gilchrist was covered with confusion.

'It may be deducted from *our* share of the estate,' Michael pointed out. 'With the wax flowers thrown in.'

'They look so right on that table,' Miss Gilchrist murmured. 'Really artistic. Sweetly pretty.'

But nobody was paying any attention to Miss Gilchrist's well-meant trivialities.

Greg said, speaking again in that high nervous voice:

'Susan *wants* that table.'

There was a momentary stir of unease, as though, by his words, Greg had set a different musical key.

Helen said quickly:

'And what do you really want, George? Leaving out the Spode service.'

George grinned and the tension relaxed.

'Rather a shame to bait old Timothy,' he said. 'But he really is quite unbelievable. He's had his own way in everything so long that he's become quite pathological about it.'

'You have to humour an invalid, Mr Crossfield,' said Miss Gilchrist.

'Ruddy old hypochondriac, that's what he is,' said George.

'Of course he is,' Susan agreed. 'I don't believe there's anything whatever the matter with him, do you, Rosamund?'

'What?'

'Anything the matter with Uncle Timothy.'

'No – no, I shouldn't think so.' Rosamund was vague. She apologized. 'I'm sorry. I was thinking about what lighting would be right for the table.'

'You see?' said George. 'A woman of one idea. Your wife's a dangerous woman, Michael. I hope you realize it.'

'I realize it,' said Michael rather grimly.

George went on with every appearance of enjoyment.

'The Battle of the Table! To be fought tomorrow – politely – but with grim determination. We ought all to take sides. I back

Rosamund who looks so sweet and yielding and isn't. Husbands, presumably back their own wives. Miss Gilchrist? On Susan's side, obviously.'

'Oh, really, Mr Crossfield, I wouldn't venture to –'

'Aunt Helen?' George paid no attention to Miss Gilchrist's flutterings. 'You have the casting vote. Oh, er – I forgot. M. Pontarlier?'

'*Pardon?*' Hercule Poirot looked blank.

George considered explanations, but decided against it. The poor old boy hadn't understood a word of what was going on. He said: 'Just a family joke.'

'Yes, yes, I comprehend.' Poirot smiled amiably.

'So yours is the casting vote, Aunt Helen. Whose side are you on?'

Helen smiled.

'Perhaps I want it myself, George.'

She changed the subject deliberately, turning to her foreign guest.

'I'm afraid this is all very dull for you, M. Pontarlier?'

'Not at all, Madame. I consider myself privileged to be admitted to your family life –' he bowed. 'I would like to say – I cannot quite express my meaning – my regret that this house had to pass out of your hands into the hands of strangers. It is without doubt – a great sorrow.'

'No, indeed, we don't regret at all,' Susan assured him.

'You are very amiable, Madame. It will be, let me tell you, perfection here for my elderly sufferers of persecution. What a haven! What peace! I beg you to remember that, when the harsh feelings come to you as assuredly they must. I hear that there was also the question of a school coming here – not a regular school, a convent – run by *religieuses* – by "nuns", I think you say? You would have preferred that, perhaps?'

'Not at all,' said George.

'The Sacred Heart of Mary,' continued Poirot. 'Fortunately, owing to the kindness of an unknown benefactory we were able to make a slightly higher offer.' He addressed Miss Gilchrist directly. 'You do not like nuns, I think?'

Miss Gilchrist flushed and looked embarrassed.

'Oh, really, Mr Pontarlier, you mustn't – I mean, it's nothing *personal.* But I never do see that it's right to shut yourself up from the world in that way – not necessary, I mean, and really almost selfish, though not teaching ones, of course, or the ones that go about amongst the poor – because I'm sure they're thoroughly unselfish women and do a lot of good.'

'I simply can't imagine wanting to be a nun,' said Susan.

'It's very becoming,' said Rosamund. 'You remember – when they revived *The Miracle* last year. Sonia Wells looked absolutely too glamorous for *words*.'

'What beats me,' said George, 'is why it should be pleasing to the Almighty to dress oneself up in medieval dress. For after all, that's all a nun's dress is. Thoroughly cumbersome, unhygienic and impractical.'

'And it makes them look so alike, doesn't it?' said Miss Gilchrist. 'It's silly, you know, but I got quite a turn when I was at Mrs Abernethie's and a nun came to the door, collecting. I got it into my head she was the same as the nun who came to the door on the day of the inquest on poor Mrs Lansquenet at Lytchett St Mary. I felt, you know, almost as though she had been following me round!'

'I thought nuns always collected in couples,' said George. 'Surely a detective story hinged on that point once?'

'There was only one this time,' said Miss Gilchrist. 'Perhaps they've got to economize,' she added vaguely. 'And anyway it couldn't have been the same nun, for the other one was collecting for an organ for St – Barnabas, I think – and this one was for something quite different – something to do with children.'

'But they both had the same type of features?' Hercule Poirot asked. He sounded interested. Miss Gilchrist turned to him.

'I suppose that must be it. The upper lip – almost as though she had a moustache. I think, you know, that *that* is really what alarmed me – being in a rather nervous state at the time, and remembering those stories during the war of nuns who were really men and in the Fifth Column and landed by parachute. Of course it was very foolish of me. I knew that afterwards.'

'A nun would be a good disguise,' said Susan thoughtfully. 'It hides your feet.'

'The truth is,' said George, 'that one very seldom looks properly at anyone. That's why one gets such wildly differing accounts of a person from different witnesses in court. You'd be surprised. A man is often described as tall – short; thin – stout; fair – dark; dressed in a dark – light – suit, and so on. There's usually *one* reliable observer, but one has to make up one's mind who that is.'

'Another queer thing,' said Susan, 'is that you sometimes catch sight of yourself in a mirror unexpectedly and don't know who it is. It just looks vaguely familiar. And you say to yourself, "There's somebody I know quite well . . ." and then suddenly realize it's yourself!'

George said: 'It would be more difficult still if you could really see yourself – and not a mirror image.'

'Why?' asked Rosamund, looking puzzled.

'Because, don't you see, nobody ever sees themselves – *as they appear to other people*. They always see themselves in a *glass* – that is – as a reversed image.'

'But why does that look any different?'

'Oh yes,' said Susan quickly. 'It must. Because people's faces aren't the same both sides. Their eyebrows are different, and their mouths go up one side, and their noses aren't really straight. You can see with a pencil – who's got a pencil?'

Somebody produced a pencil, and they experimented, holding a pencil each side of the nose and laughing to see the ridiculous variation in angle.

The atmosphere now had lightened a good deal. Everybody was in a good humour. They were no longer the heirs of Richard Abernethie gathered together for a division of property. They were a cheerful and normal set of people gathered together for a week-end in the country.

Only Helen Abernethie remained silent and abstracted.

With a sigh, Hercule Poirot rose to his feet and bade his hostess a polite good night.

'And perhaps, Madame, I had better say goodbye. My train departs itself at nine o'clock tomorrow morning. That is very early. So I will thank you now for all your kindness and hospitality. The date of possession – that will be arranged with the good Mr Entwhistle. To suit your convenience, of course.'

'It can be any time you please, M. Pontarlier. I – I have finished all that I came here to do.'

'You will return now to your villa at Cyprus?'

'Yes.' A little smile curved Helen Abernethie's lips.

Poirot said:

'You are glad, yes. You have no regrets?'

'At leaving England? Or leaving here, do you mean?'

'I meant – leaving here?'

'Oh – no. It's no good, is it, to cling on to the past? One must leave that behind one.'

'If one can.' Blinking his eyes innocently Poirot smiled apologetically round on the group of polite faces that surrounded him.

'Sometimes, is it not, the Past will not be left, will not suffer itself to pass into oblivion? It stands at one's elbow – it says, "*I am not done with yet.*"'

Susan gave a rather doubtful laugh. Poirot said:

'But I am serious – yes.'

'You mean,' said Michael, 'that your refugees when they come here will not be able to put their past sufferings completely behind them?'

'I did not mean my Refugees.'

'He meant us, darling,' said Rosamund. 'He means Uncle Richard and Aunt Cora and the hatchet and all that.'

She turned to Poirot.

'Didn't you?'

Poirot looked at her with a blank face. Then he said:

'Why do you think that, Madame?'

'Because you're a detective, aren't you? That's why you're here. N.A.R.C.O., or whatever you call it, is just nonsense, isn't it?'

CHAPTER 20

I

There was a moment of extraordinary tenseness. Poirot felt it, though he himself did not remove his eyes from Rosamund's lovely placid face.

He said with a little bow, 'You have great perspicacity, Madame.'

'Not really,' said Rosamund. 'You were pointed out to me once in a restaurant. I remembered.'

'But you have not mentioned it – until now?'

'I thought it would be more fun not to,' said Rosamund.

Michael said in an imperfectly controlled voice:

'My – dear girl.'

Poirot shifted his gaze then to look at him.

Michael was angry. Angry and something else – apprehensive?

Poirot's eyes went slowly round all the faces. Susan's, angry and watchful; Gregory's dead and shut in; Miss Gilchrist's, foolish, her mouth wide open; George, wary; Helen, dismayed and nervous . . .

All those expressions were normal ones under the circumstances. He wished he could have seen their faces a split second earlier, when the words 'a detective' fell from Rosamund's lips. For now, inevitably, it could not be quite the same . . .

He squared his shoulders and bowed to them. His language and his accent became less foreign.

'Yes,' he said. 'I am a detective.'

George Crossfield said, the white dints showing once more each side of his nose, 'Who sent you here?'

'I was commissioned to inquire into the circumstances of Richard Abernethie's death.'

'By whom?'

'For the moment, that does not concern you. But it would be an advantage, would it not, if you could be assured *beyond any possible doubt* that Richard Abernethie died a natural death?'

'Of course he died a natural death. Who says anything else?'

'Cora Lansquenet said so. And Cora Lansquenet is dead herself.'

A little wave of uneasiness seemed to sigh through the room like an evil breeze.

'She said it here – in this room,' said Susan. 'But I didn't really think –'

'Didn't you, Susan?' George Crossfield turned his sardonic glance upon her. 'Why pretend any more? You won't take M. Pontarlier in?'

'We all thought so really,' said Rosamund. And his name isn't Pontarlier – it's Hercules something.'

'Hercule Poirot – at your service.'

Poirot bowed.

There were no gasps of astonishment or of apprehension. His name seemed to mean nothing at all to them.

They were less alarmed by it than they had been by the single word '*detective*'.

'May I ask what conclusions you have come to?' asked George.

'He won't tell you, darling,' said Rosamund. 'Or if he does tell you, what he says won't be true.'

Alone of all the company she appeared to be amused.

Hercule Poirot looked at her thoughtfully.

II

Hercule Poirot did not sleep well that night. He was perturbed, and he was not quite sure *why* he was perturbed. Elusive snatches of conversation, various glances, odd movements – all seemed fraught with a tantalizing significance in the loneliness of the night. He was on the threshold of sleep, but sleep would not come. Just as he was about to drop off, something flashed into his mind and woke him up again. Paint – Timothy and paint. Oil paint – the smell of oil paint – connected somehow with Mr Entwhistle. Paint and Cora. Cora's paintings – picture postcards . . . Cora was deceitful about her painting . . . No, back to Mr Entwhistle – something Mr Entwhistle had said – or was it Lanscombe? A nun who came to the house on the day that Richard Abernethie died. A nun with a moustache. A nun at Stansfield Grange – and at Lytchett St Mary. Altogether too many nuns! Rosamund looking glamorous as a nun on the stage. Rosamund – saying that he was a detective – and everyone staring at her when she said it. That was the way that they must all have stared at Cora that day when she said, 'But he was murdered, wasn't he?' What was it Helen Abernethie had felt to be 'wrong' on that occasion? Helen Abernethie – leaving the past behind – going to Cyprus . . . Helen dropping the wax flowers with a crash when he had said – *what* was it he had said? He couldn't quite remember . . .

He slept then, and as he slept he dreamed . . .

He dreamed of the green malachite table. On it was the glass-covered stand of wax flowers – only the whole thing had been painted over with thick crimson oil paint. Paint the colour of blood. He could smell the paint, and Timothy was groaning, was saying, 'I'm dying – dying . . . this is the end.' And Maude, standing by, tall and stern, with a large knife in her hand was echoing him, saying, 'Yes, it's the end . . .' The end – a deathbed, with candles and a nun praying. If he could just see the nun's face, he would know . . .

Hercule Poirot woke up – and he did know!

Yes, it *was* the end . . .

Though there was still a long way to go.

He sorted out the various bits of the mosaic.

Mr Entwhistle, the smell of paint, Timothy's house and something that must be in it – or might be in it . . . the wax flowers . . . Helen . . . Broken glass . . .

III

Helen Abernethie, in her room, took some time in going to bed. She was thinking.

Sitting in front of her dressing-table, she stared at herself unseeingly in the glass.

She had been forced into having Hercule Poirot in the house. She had not wanted it. But Mr Entwhistle had made it hard for her to refuse. And now the whole thing had come out into the open. No question any more of letting Richard Abernethie lie quiet in his grave. All started by those few words of Cora's . . .

That day after the funeral . . . How had they all looked, she wondered? How had they looked to Cora? How had she herself looked?

What was it George had said? About seeing oneself?

There was some quotation, too. *To see ourselves as others see us* . . . As others see us.

The eyes that were staring into the glass unseeingly suddenly focused. She was seeing herself – but not really herself – not herself as others saw her – not as Cora had seen her that day.

Her right – no, her left eyebrow was arched a little higher than the right. The mouth? No, the curve of the mouth was symmetrical. If she met herself she would surely not see much difference from this mirror image. Not like Cora.

Cora – the picture came quite clearly . . . Cora, on the day of the funeral, her head tilted sideways – asking her question – looking at Helen . . .

Suddenly Helen raised her hands to her face. She said to herself, '*It doesn't make sense . . . it can't make sense . . .*'

IV

Miss Entwhistle was aroused from a delightful dream in which she was playing Piquet with Queen Mary, by the ringing of the telephone.

She tried to ignore it – but it persisted. Sleepily she raised her head from the pillow and looked at the watch beside her bed. Five minutes to seven – who on earth could be ringing up at that hour? It must be a wrong number.

The irritating ding-dong continued. Miss Entwhistle sighed, snatched up a dressing-gown and marched into the sitting-room.

'This is Kensington 675498,' she said with asperity as she picked up the receiver.

'This is Mrs Abernethie speaking. Mrs *Leo* Abernethie. Can I speak to Mr Entwhistle?'

'Oh, good morning, Mrs Abernethie.' The 'good morning' was not cordial. 'This is Miss Entwhistle. My brother is still asleep, I'm afraid. I was asleep myself.'

'I'm so sorry,' Helen was forced to the apology. 'But it's very important that I should speak to your brother at once.'

'Wouldn't it do later?'

'I'm afraid not.'

'Oh, very well then.'

Miss Entwhistle was tart.

She tapped at her brother's door and went in.

'Those Abernethies again!' she said bitterly.

'Eh! The Aberbethies?'

'Mrs Leo Abernethie. Ringing up before seven in the morning! Really!'

'Mrs Leo, is it? Dear me. How remarkable. Where is my dressing-gown? Ah, thank you.'

Presently he was saying:

'Entwhistle speaking. Is that you, Helen?'

'Yes. I'm terribly sorry to get you out of bed like this. But you did tell me once to ring you up at once if I remembered what it was that struck me as having been wrong somehow on the day of the funeral when Cora electrified us all by suggesting that Richard had been murdered.'

'Ah! You *have* remembered?'

Helen said in a puzzled voice:

'Yes, but it doesn't make sense.'

'You must allow me to be the judge of that. Was it something you noticed about one of the people?'

'Yes.'

'Tell me.'

'It seems absurd.' Helen's voice sounded apologetic. 'But I'm quite sure of it. It came to me when I was looking at myself in the glass last night. Oh . . .'

The little startled half cry was succeeded by a sound that came oddly through the wires – a dull heavy sound that Mr Entwhistle couldn't place at all.

He said urgently:

'Hallo – hallo – are you there? Helen, are you there? . . . Helen . . .'

CHAPTER 21

I

It was not until nearly an hour later that Mr Entwhistle, after a great deal of conversation with supervisors and others, found himself at last speaking to Hercule Poirot.

'Thank heaven!' said Mr Entwhistle with pardonable exasperation. 'The Exchange seems to have had the greatest difficulty in getting the number.'

'That is not surprising. The receiver was off the hook.'

There was a grim quality in Poirot's voice which carried through to the listener.

Mr Entwhistle said sharply:

'Has something happened?'

'Yes. Mrs Leo Abernethie was found by the housemaid about twenty minutes ago lying by the telephone in the study. She was unconscious. A serious concussion.'

'Do you mean she was struck on the head?'

'I think so. It is *just* possible that she fell and struck her head on a marble doorstop, but me I do not think so, and the doctor, he does not think so either.'

'She was telephoning to me at the time. I wondered when we were cut off so suddenly.'

'So it was to you she was telephoning? What did she say?'

'She mentioned to me some time ago that on the occasion when Cora Lansquenet suggested her brother had been murdered, she herself had a feeling of something being wrong – odd – she did not quite know how to put it – unfortunately she could not remember *why* she had that impression.'

'And suddenly, she did remember?'

'Yes.'

'And rang you up to tell you?'

'Yes.'

'*Eh bien.*'

'There's no *eh bien* about it,' said Mr Entwhistle testily. 'She started to tell me, but was interrupted.'

'How much had she said?'

'Nothing pertinent.'

'You will excuse me, *mon ami*, but *I* am the judge of that, not you. What exactly did she say?'

'She reminded me that I had asked her to let me know at once if she remembered what it was that had struck her as peculiar. She said she had remembered – but that it "didn't make sense".'

'I asked her if it was something about one of the people who were there that day, and she said, yes, it was. She said it had come to her when she was looking in the glass –'

'Yes?'

'That was all.'

'She gave no hint as to – which of the people concerned it was?'

'I should hardly fail to let you know if she had told me *that*,' said Mr Entwhistle acidly.

'I apologize, *mon ami*. Of course you would have told me.'

Mr Entwhistle said:

'We shall just have to wait until she recovers consciousness before we know.'

Poirot said gravely:

'That may not be for a very long time. Perhaps never.'

'Is it as bad as that?' Mr Entwhistle's voice shook a little.

'Yes, it is as bad as that.'

'But – that's terrible, Poirot.'

'Yes, it is terrible. And it is why we cannot afford to wait. For it shows that we have to deal with someone who is either completely ruthless or so frightened that it comes to the same thing.'

'But look here, Poirot. What about Helen? I feel worried. Are you sure she will be safe at Enderby?'

'No, she would not be safe. So she is not at Enderby. Already the ambulance has come and is taking her to a nursing home where she will have special nurses and where *no one*, family or otherwise, will be allowed in to see her.'

Mr Entwhistle sighed.

'You relieve my mind! She might have been in danger.'

'She assuredly would have been in danger!'

Mr Entwhistle's voice sounded deeply moved.

'I have a great regard for Helen Abernethie. I always have had. A woman of very exceptional character. She may have had certain – what shall I say? – reticences in her life.'

'Ah, there were reticences?'

'I have always had an idea that such was the case.'

'Hence the villa in Cyprus. Yes, that explains a good deal . . .'

'I don't want you to begin thinking –'

'You cannot stop me thinking. But now, there is a little commission that I have for you. One moment.'

There was a pause, then Poirot's voice spoke again.

'I had to make sure that nobody was listening. All is well. Now here is what I want you to do for me. You must prepare to make a journey.'

'A journey?' Mr Entwhistle sounded faintly dismayed. 'Oh, I see – you want me to come down to Enderby?'

'Not at all. *I* am in charge here. No, you will not have to travel so far. Your journey will not take you very far from London. You will travel to Bury St Edmunds – (*Ma foi!* what names your English towns have!) and there you will hire a car and drive to Forsdyke House. It is a Mental Home. Ask for Dr Penrith and inquire of him particulars about a patient who was recently discharged.'

'What patient? Anyway, surely –'

Poirot broke in:

'The name of the patient is Gregory Banks. Find out for what form of insanity he was being treated.'

'Do you mean that Gregory Banks is insane?'

'Sh! Be careful what you say. And now – I have not yet breakfasted and you, too, I suspect, have not breakfasted?'

'Not yet. I was too anxious –'

'Quite so. Then, I pray you, eat your breakfast, repose yourself. There is a good train to Bury St Edmunds at twelve o'clock. If I have any more news I will telephone you before you start.'

'Be careful of *yourself*, Poirot,' said Mr Entwhistle with some concern.

'Ah that, yes! Me, I do not want to be hit on the head with a marble doorstop. You may be assured that I will take every precaution. And now – for the moment – goodbye.'

Poirot heard the sound of the receiver being replaced at the other end, then he heard a very faint second click – and smiled to himself. Somebody had replaced the receiver on the telephone in the hall.

He went out there. There was no one about. He tiptoed to the cupboard at the back of the stairs and looked inside. At that moment Lanscombe came through the service door carrying a tray with toast and a silver coffee pot. He looked slightly surprised to see Poirot emerge from the cupboard.

'Breakfast is ready in the dining-room, sir,' he said.

Poirot surveyed him thoughtfully.

The old butler looked white and shaken.

'Courage,' said Poirot, clapping him on the shoulder. 'All will yet be well. Would it be too much trouble to serve me a cup of coffee in my bedroom?'

'Certainly, sir. I will send Janet up with it, sir.'

Lanscombe looked disapprovingly at Hercule Poirot's back as the latter climbed the stairs. Poirot was attired in an exotic silk dressing-gown with a pattern of triangles and squares.

'Foreigners!' thought Lanscombe bitterly. 'Foreigners in the house! And Mrs Leo with concussion! I don't know what we're coming to. Nothing's the same since Mr Richard died.'

Hercule Poirot was dressed by the time he received his coffee from Janet. His murmurs of sympathy were well received, since he stressed the shock her discovery must have given her.

'Yes, indeed, sir, what I felt when I opened the door of the study and came in with the Hoover and saw Mrs Leo lying there I shall never forget. There she lay – and I made sure she was dead. She must have been taken faint as she stood at the phone – and fancy her being up at that time in the morning! I've never known her to do such a thing before.'

'Fancy, indeed!' He added casually: 'No one else was up, I suppose?'

'As it happens, sir, Mrs Timothy was up and about. She's a very early riser always – often goes for a walk before breakfast.'

'She is of the generation that rises early,' said Poirot, nodding his head. 'The younger ones, now – *they* do not get up so early?'

'No, indeed, sir, all fast asleep when I brought them their tea – and very late I was, too, what with the shock and getting the doctor to come and having to have a cup first to steady myself.'

She went off and Poirot reflected on what she had said.

Maude Abernethie had been up and about, and the younger generation had been in bed – but that, Poirot reflected, meant nothing at all. Anyone could have heard Helen's door open and close, and have followed her down to listen – and would afterwards have made a point of being fast asleep in bed.

'But if I am right,' thought Poirot, 'and after all, it is natural to me to be right – it is a habit I have! – then there is no need to go into who was here and who was these. First, I must seek a proof where I have deduced the proof may be. And then – I make my little speech. And I sit back and see what happens . . .'

As soon as Janet had left the room, Poirot drained his coffee cup, put on his overcoat and his hat, left his room, ran nimbly down the back stairs and left the house by the side door. He walked briskly the quarter-mile to the post office where he demanded a trunk call. Presently he was once more speaking to Mr Entwhistle.

'Yes, it is I yet again! Pay no attention to the commission with which I entrusted you. C'était une blague! Someone was listening. Now, mon vieux, to the real commission. You must, as I said, take a train. But not to Bury St Edmunds. I want you to proceed to the house of Mr Timothy Abernethie.'

'But Timothy and Maude are at Enderby.'

'Exactly. There is no one in the house but a woman by the name of Jones who has been persuaded by the offer of considerable *largesse* to guard the house whilst they are absent. What I want you to do is to take something out of that house!'

'My dear Poirot! I really can't stoop to burglary!'

'It will not seem like burglary. You will say to the excellent Mrs Jones who knows you, that you have been asked by Mr or Mrs Abernethie to fetch this particular object and take it to London. She will not suspect anything amiss.'

'No, no, probably not. But I don't like it.' Mr Entwhistle sounded most reluctant. 'Why can't you go and get whatever it is yourself?'

'Because, my friend, I should be a stranger of foreign appearance and as such a suspicious character, and Mrs Jones would at once raise the difficulties! With you, she will not.'

'No, no – I see that. But what on earth are Timothy and Maude going to think when they hear about it? I have known them for forty odd years.'

'And you knew Richard Abernethie for that time also! And you knew Cora Lansquenet when she was a little girl!'

In a martyred voice Mr Entwhistle asked:

'You're sure this is really *necessary*, Poirot?'

'The old question they asked in wartime on the posters. *Is your journey really necessary?* I say to you, it *is* necessary. It is vital!'

'And what is this object I've got to get hold of?'

Poirot told him.

'But really, Poirot, I don't see –'

'It is not necessary for *you* to see. *I* am doing the seeing.'

'And what do you want me to do with the damned thing?'

'You will take it to London, to an address in Elm Park Gardens. If you have a pencil, note it down.'

Having done so, Mr Entwhistle said, still in his martyred voice:

'I hope you know what you are doing, Poirot?'

He sounded very doubtful – but Poirot's reply was not doubtful at all.

'Of course I know what I am doing. We are nearing the end.'

Mr Entwhistle sighed:

'If we could only guess what Helen was going to tell me.'

'No need to guess, I *know*.'

'You know? But my dear Poirot –'

'Explanations must wait. But let me assure you of this. *I know what Helen Abernethie saw when she looked in her mirror.*'

II

Breakfast had been an uneasy meal. Neither Rosamund nor Timothy had appeared, but the others were there and had talked in rather subdued tones, and eaten a little less than they normally would have done.

George was the first one to recover his spirits. His temperament was mercurial and optimistic.

'I expect Aunt Helen will be all right,' he said. 'Doctors always like to pull a long face. After all, what's concussion? Often clears up completely in a couple of days.'

'A woman I knew had concussion during the war,' said Miss Gilchrist conversationally. 'A brick or something hit her as she was walking down Tottenham Court Road – it was during fly bomb time – and she never felt *anything* at all. Just went on with what she was doing – and collapsed in a train to Liverpool twelve hours later. And would you believe it, she had no recollection at all of going to the station and catching the train or *anything*. She just couldn't understand it when she woke up in hospital. She was there for nearly three weeks.'

'What I can't make out,' said Susan, 'is what Helen was doing telephoning at that unearthly hour, and who she was telephoning to?'

'Felt ill,' said Maude with decision. 'Probably woke up feeling queer and came down to ring up the doctor. Then had a giddy fit and fell. That's the only thing that makes sense.'

'Bad luck hitting her head on that doorstop,' said Michael. 'If she'd just pitched over on to that thick pile carpet she'd have been all right.'

The door opened and Rosamund came in, frowning.

'I can't find those wax flowers,' she said. 'I mean the ones that were standing on the malachite table the day of Uncle Richard's funeral.' She looked accusingly at Susan. 'You haven't taken them?'

'Of course I haven't! Really, Rosamund, you're not still thinking about malachite tables with poor old Helen carted off to hospital with concussion?'

'I don't see why I shouldn't think about them. If you've got concussion you don't know what's happening and it doesn't matter to you. We can't do anything for Aunt Helen, and Michael and I have got to get back to London by tomorrow lunch-time because we're seeing Jackie Lygo about opening dates for *The Baronet's Progress*. So I'd like to fix up definitely about the table. But I'd like to have a look at those wax flowers again. There's a kind of Chinese vase on the table now – nice – but not nearly so period. I do wonder where they are – perhaps Lanscombe knows.'

Lanscombe had just looked in to see if they had finished breakfast.

'We're all through, Lanscombe,' said George getting up. 'What's happened to our foreign friend?'

'He is having his coffee and toast served upstairs, sir.'

'*Petit déjeuner* for N.A.R.C.O.'

'Lanscombe, do you know where those wax flowers are that used to be on that green table in the drawing-room?' asked Rosamund.

'I understand Mrs Leo had an accident with them, ma'am. She was going to have a new glass shade made, but I don't think she has seen about it yet.'

'Then where is the thing?'

'It would probably be in the cupboard behind the staircase, ma'am. That is where things are usually placed when awaiting repair. Shall I ascertain for you?'

'I'll go and look myself. Come with me, Michael sweetie. It's dark there, and I'm not going in any dark corners by myself after what happened to Aunt Helen.'

Everybody showed a sharp reaction. Maude demanded in her deep voice:

'What *do* you mean, Rosamund?'

'Well, she was coshed by someone, wasn't she?'

Gregory Banks said sharply:

'She was taken suddenly faint and fell.'

Rosamund laughed.

'Did she tell you so? Don't be silly, Greg, of course she was coshed.'

George said sharply:

'You shouldn't say things like that, Rosamund.'

'Nonsense,' said Rosamund. 'She *must* have been. I mean, it all adds up. A detective in the house looking for clues, and Uncle Richard poisoned, and Aunt Cora killed with a hatchet, and Miss Gilchrist given poisoned wedding cake, and now Aunt Helen struck down with a blunt instrument. You'll see, it will go on like that. One after another of us will be killed and the one that's left will be It – the murderer, I mean. But it's not going to be *me* – who's killed, I mean.'

'And why should anyone want to kill you, beautiful Rosamund?' asked George lightly.

Rosamund opened her eyes very wide.

'Oh,' she said. 'Because I know too much, of course.'

'What do you know?' Maude Abernethie and Gregory Banks spoke almost in unison.

Rosamund gave her vacant and angelic smile.

'Wouldn't you all like to know?' she said agreeably. 'Come on, Michael.'

CHAPTER 22

I

At eleven o'clock, Hercule Poirot called an informal meeting in the library. Everyone was there and Poirot looked thoughtfully round the semi-circle of faces.

'Last night,' he said, 'Mrs Shane announced to you that I was a private detective. For myself, I hoped to retain my – *camouflage*, shall we say? – a little longer. But no matter! Today – or at most the day after – I would have told you the truth. Please listen carefully now to what I have to say.

'I am in my own line a celebrated person – I may say a *most* celebrated person. My gifts, in fact, are unequalled!'

George Crossfield grinned and said:

'That's the stuff, M. Pont – no, it's M. Poirot, isn't it? Funny, isn't it, that I've never even heard of you?'

'It is not funny,' said Poirot severely. 'It is lamentable! Alas, there is no proper education nowadays. Apparently one learns nothing but economics – and how to sit Intelligence Tests! But to continue. I have been a friend for many years of Mr Entwhistle's –'

'So *he's* the fly in the ointment!'

'If you like to put it that way, Mr Crossfield! Mr Entwhistle was greatly upset by the death of his old friend, Mr Richard Abernethie. He was particularly perturbed by some words spoken on the day of the funeral by Mr Abernethie's sister, Mrs Lansquenet. Words spoken in this very room.'

'Very silly – and just like Cora,' said Maude. 'Mr Entwhistle should have had more sense than to pay attention to them!'

Poirot went on:

'Mr Entwhistle was even more perturbed after the – the coincidence, shall I say? – of Mrs Lansquenet's death. He wanted one thing only – to be assured that that death *was* a coincidence. In other words he wanted to feel assured that Richard Abernethie had died a natural death. To that end he commissioned me to make the necessary investigations.'

There was a pause.

'I have made them . . .'

Again there was a pause. No one spoke.

Poirot threw back his head.

'*Eh bien*, you will all be delighted to hear that as a result of my investigations – *there is absolutely no reason to believe that Mr Abernethie died anything but a natural death*. There is no reason *at all* to believe that he was murdered!' He smiled. He threw out his hands in a triumphant gesture.

'That is good news, is it not?'

It hardly seemed to be, by the way they took it. They stared at him and in all but the eyes of one person there still seemed to be doubt and suspicion.

The exception was Timothy Abernethie, who was nodding his head in violent agreement.

'Of course Richard wasn't murdered,' he said angrily. 'Never could understand why anybody ever even thought of such a thing for a moment! Just Cora up to her tricks, that was all. Wanting to give you all a scare. Her idea of being funny. Truth is that although she was my own sister, she was always a bit mental, poor girl. Well, Mr whatever your name is, I'm glad you've had the sense to come to the right conclusion, though if you ask me, I call it damned cheek of Entwhistle to go commissioning you to come prying and poking about. And if he thinks he's going to charge the estate with your fee, I can tell you he won't get away with it! Damned cheek, and most uncalled for! Who's Entwhistle to set himself up? If the family's satisfied –'

'But the family wasn't, Uncle Timothy,' said Rosamund.

'Hey – what's that?'

Timothy peered at her under beetling brows of displeasure.

'We weren't satisfied. And what about Aunt Helen this morning?'

Maude said sharply:

'Helen's just the age when you're liable to get a stroke. That's all there is to that.'

'I see,' said Rosamund. 'Another coincidence, you think?'

She looked at Poirot.

'Aren't there rather too many coincidences?'

'Coincidences,' said Hercule Poirot, 'do happen.'

'Nonsense,' said Maude. 'Helen felt ill, came down and rang up the doctor, and then –'

'But she didn't ring up the doctor,' said Rosamund. 'I asked him –'

Susan said sharply:

'Who did she ring up?'

'I don't know,' said Rosamund, a shade of vexation passing over her face. 'But I dare say I can find out,' she added hopefully.

II

Hercule Poirot was sitting in the Victorian summer-house. He drew his large watch from his pocket and laid it on the table in front of him.

He had announced that he was leaving by the twelve o'clock train. There was still half an hour to go. Half an hour for someone to make up their mind and come to him. Perhaps more than one person . . .

The summer-house was clearly visible from most of the windows of the house. Surely, soon, someone would come?

If not, his knowledge of human nature was deficient, and his main premises incorrect.

He waited – and above his head a spider in its web waited for a fly.

It was Miss Gilchrist who came first. She was flustered and upset and rather incoherent.

'Oh, Mr Pontarlier – I can't remember your other name,' she said. 'I had to come and speak to you although I *don't* like doing it – but really I feel I *ought* to. I mean, after what happened to poor Mrs Leo this morning – and I think myself Mrs Shane was *quite right* – and *not* coincidence, and certainly not a *stroke* – as Mrs Timothy suggested, because my own father had a stroke and it was quite a different appearance, and anyway the doctor *said* concussion quite clearly!'

She paused, took breath and looked at Poirot with appealing eyes.

'Yes,' said Poirot gently and encouragingly. 'You want to tell me something?'

'As I say, I don't like doing it – because she's been so kind. She found me the position with Mrs Timothy and everything. She's been really *very* kind. That's why I feel so ungrateful. And even gave me Mrs Lansquenet's musquash jacket which is really *most* handsome and fits beautifully because it never matters if fur is a little on the large side. And when I wanted to return her amethyst brooch she wouldn't hear of it –'

'You are referring,' said Poirot gently, 'to Mrs Banks?'

'Yes, you see –' Miss Gilchrist looked down, twisting her fingers unhappily. She looked up and said with a sudden gulp:

'You see, I *listened*!'

'You mean you happened to overhear a conversation –'

'No.' Miss Gilchrist shook her head with an air of heroic determination. 'I'd rather speak the truth. And it's not so bad telling you because you're not English.'

Hercule Poirot understood her without taking offence.

'You mean that to a foreigner it is natural that people should listen at doors and open letters, or read letters that are left about?'

'Oh, I'd never open anybody else's letters,' said Miss Gilchrist in a shocked tone. 'Not *that*. But I *did* listen that day – the day that Mr Richard Abernethie came down to see his sister. I was curious, you know, about his turning up suddenly after all those years. And I did wonder why – and – and – you see when you haven't much life of your own or very many friends, you do tend to get interested – when you're living *with* anybody, I mean.'

'Most natural,' said Poirot.

'Yes, I do think it was natural . . . Though not, of course, at all *right*. But I did it! And I heard what he said!'

'You heard what Mr Abernethie said to Mrs Lansquenet?'

'Yes. He said something like – "It's no good talking to Timothy. He pooh-poohs everything. Simply won't listen. But I thought I'd like to get it off my chest to you, Cora. We three are the only ones left. And though you've always liked to play the simpleton you've got a lot of common sense. So what would *you* do about it, if you were me?"

'I couldn't quite hear what Mrs Lansquenet said, but I caught the word *police* – and then Mr Abernethie burst out quite loud, and said, "I can't do that. Not when it's a question of *my own niece*." And then I had to run in the kitchen for something boiling over and when I got back Mr Abernethie was saying, "Even if I die an unnatural death I don't want the police called in, if it can possibly be avoided. You understand that, don't you, my dear girl? But don't worry. Now that I *know*, I shall take all possible precautions." And he went on, saying he'd made a new will, and that she, Cora, would be quite all right. And then he said about her having been happy with her husband and how perhaps he'd made a mistake over that in the past.'

Miss Gilchrist stopped.

'Poirot said: 'I see – I see . . .'

'But I never wanted to say – to tell. I didn't think Mrs Lansquenet would have wanted me to . . . But now – after Mrs Leo being attacked this morning – and then you saying so calmly it was coincidence. But, oh, M. Pontarlier, it *wasn't* coincidence!'

Poirot smiled. He said:

'No, it wasn't coincidence . . . Thank you, Miss Gilchrist, for coming to me. It was very necessary that you should.'

III

He had a little difficulty in getting rid of Miss Gilchrist, and it was urgent that he should, for he hoped for further confidences.

His instinct was right. Miss Gilchrist had hardly gone before Gregory Banks, striding across the lawn, came impetuously into the summer-house. His face was pale and there were beads of perspiration on his forehead. His eyes were curiously excited.

'At last!' he said. 'I thought that stupid woman would never go. You're all wrong in what you said this morning. You're wrong about everything. Richard Abernethie *was* killed. *I* killed him.'

Hercule Poirot let his eyes move up and down over the excited young man. He showed no surprise.

'So you killed him, did you? How?'

Gregory Banks smiled.

'It wasn't difficult for *me*. You can surely realize that. There were fifteen or twenty different drugs I could lay my hands on that would do it. The method of administration took rather more thinking out, but I hit on a very ingenious idea in the end. The beauty of it was that *I* didn't need to be anywhere near at the time.'

'Clever,' said Poirot.

'Yes.' Gregory Banks cast his eyes down modestly. He seemed pleased. 'Yes – I *do* think it was ingenious.'

Poirot asked with interest:

'Why did you kill him? For the money that would come to your wife?'

'No. No, of course not.' Greg was suddenly excitedly indignant. 'I'm not a money grubber. I didn't marry Susan for her *money*!'

'Didn't you, Mr Banks?'

'That's what *he* thought,' Greg said with sudden venom. 'Richard Abernethie! He liked Susan, he admired her, he was proud of her as an example of Abernethie blood! But he thought she'd married beneath her – he thought *I* was no good – he despised me! I dare say I hadn't the right accent – I didn't wear my clothes the right way. He was a snob – a filthy snob!'

'I don't think so,' said Poirot mildly. 'From all I have heard, Richard Abernethie was no snob.'

'He was. He was.' The young man spoke with something approaching hysteria. 'He thought nothing of me. He sneered at me – always very polite but underneath I could *see* that he didn't like me!'

'Possibly.'

'People can't treat me like that and get away with it! They've tried it before! A woman who used to come and have her medicines made up. She was rude to me. Do you know what I did?'

'Yes,' said Poirot.

Gregory looked startled.

'So you know that?'

'Yes.'

'She nearly died.' He spoked in a satisfied manner. 'That shows you I'm not the sort of person to be trifled with! Richard Abernethie despised me – and what happened to him? He died.'

'A most successful murder,' said Poirot with grave congratulation.

He added: 'But why come and give yourself away – to me?'

'Because you said you were through with it all! You said he *hadn't* been murdered. I had to show you that you're not as clever as you think you are – and besides – besides –'

'Yes,' said Poirot. 'And besides?'

Greg collapsed suddenly on the bench. His face changed. It took on a sudden ecstatic quality.

'It was wrong – wicked . . . I must be punished . . . I must go back there – to the place of punishment . . . to atone . . . Yes, to *atone*! Repentance! Retribution!'

His face was alight now with a kind of glowing ecstasy. Poirot studied him for a moment or two curiously.

Then he asked:

'How badly do you want to get away from your wife?'

Gregory's face changed.

'Susan? Susan is wonderful – wonderful!'

'Yes. Susan is wonderful. That is a grave burden. Susan loves you devotedly. That is a burden, too?'

Gregory sat looking in front of him. Then he said, rather in the manner of a sulky child:

'Why couldn't she let me alone?'

He sprang up.

'She's coming now – across the lawn. I'll go now. But you'll tell her what I told you? Tell her I've gone to the police station. To confess.'

IV

Susan came in breathlessly.

'Where's Greg? He was here! I saw him.'

'Yes.' Poirot paused a moment – before saying: 'He came to tell me that it was he who poisoned Richard Abernethie . . .'

'What absolute *nonsense*! You didn't believe him, I hope?'

'Why should I not believe him?'

'He wasn't even near this place when Uncle Richard died!'

'Perhaps not. Where was he when Cora Lansquenet died?'

'In London. We both were.'

Hercule Poirot shook his head.

'No, no, that will not do. You, for instance, took out your car that day and were away all the afternoon. I think I know where you went. You went to Lytchett St Mary.'

'I did no such thing!'

Poirot smiled.

'When I met you here, Madame, it was not, as I told you, the first time I had seen you. After the inquest on Mrs Lansquenet you were in the garage of the King's Arms. You talk there to a mechanic and close by you is a car containing an elderly foreign gentleman. You did not notice him, but he noticed you.'

'I don't see what you mean. That was the day of the inquest.'

'Ah, but remember what that mechanic said to you! He asked you if you were a relative of the victim, and you said you were her niece.'

'He was just being a ghoul. They're all ghouls.'

'And his next words were, "Ah, wondered where I'd seen you before." Where did he see you before, Madame? It must have been in Lytchett St Mary, since in his mind his seeing you before was accounted for by your being Mrs Lansquenet's niece. Had he seen you near her cottage? And when? It was a matter, was it not, that demands inquiry. And the result of the inquiry is, that you were there – in Lytchett St Mary – on the afternoon Cora

Lansquenet died. You parked your car in the same quarry where you left it the morning of the inquest. The car was seen and the number was noted. By this time Inspector Morton knows whose car it was.'

Susan stared at him. Her breath came rather fast, but she showed no signs of discomposure.

'You're talking nonsense, M. Poirot. And you're making me forget what I came here to say – I wanted to try and find you alone –'

'To confess to me it was you and not your husband who committed the murder?'

'No, of course not. What kind of a fool do you think I am? And I've already told you that Gregory never left London that day.'

'A fact which you cannot possibly know since you were away yourself. Why did you go down to Lytchett St Mary, Mrs Banks?'

Susan drew a deep breath.

'All right, if you must have it! What Cora said at the funeral worried me. I kept on thinking about it. Finally I decided to run down in the car and see her, and ask her what had put the idea into her head. Greg thought it a silly idea, so I didn't even tell him where I was going. I got there about three o'clock, knocked and rang, but there was no answer, so I thought she must be out or gone away. That's all there is to it. I didn't go round to the back of the cottage. If I had, I might have seen the broken window. I just went back to London without the faintest idea there was anything wrong.'

Poirot's face was non-committal. He said:

'Why does your husband accuse himself of the crime?'

'Because he's –' a word trembled on Susan's tongue and was rejected. Poirot seized on it.

'You were going to say "because he is batty" speaking in jest – but the jest was too near the truth, was it not?'

'Greg's all right. He is. He *is*.'

'I know something of his history,' said Poirot. 'He was for some months in Forsdyke House Mental Home before you met him.'

'He was never certified. He was a voluntary patient.'

'That is true. He is not, I agree, to be classed as insane. But he is, very definitely, unbalanced. He has a punishment complex – has had it, I suspect, since infancy.'

Susan spoke quickly and eagerly:

'You don't understand, M. Poirot. Greg has never had a *chance*. That's why I wanted Uncle Richard's money so badly. Uncle Richard was so matter-of-fact. He couldn't understand. I knew Greg had got to set up for himself. He had got to feel he was *someone* – not just a chemist's assistant, being pushed around. Everything will be different now. He will have his own laboratory. He can work out his own formulas.'

'Yes, yes – you will give him the earth – because you love him. Love him too much for safety or for happiness. But you cannot give to people what they are incapable of receiving. At the end of it all, he will still be something that he does not want to be . . .'

'What's that?'

'*Susan's husband.*'

'How cruel you are! And what nonsense you talk!'

'Where Gregory Banks is concerned you are unscrupulous. You wanted your uncle's money – not for yourself – but for your husband. *How badly did you want it?*'

Angrily, Susan turned and dashed away.

V

'I thought,' said Michael Shane lightly, 'that I'd just come along and say goodbye.'

He smiled, and his smile had a singularly intoxicating quality.

Poirot was aware of the man's vital charm.

He studied Michael Shane for some moments in silence. He felt as though he knew this man least well of all the house party, for Michael Shane only showed the side of himself that he wanted to show.

'Your wife,' said Poirot conversationally, 'is a very unusual woman.'

Michael raised his eyebrows.

'Do you think so? She's a lovely, I agree. But not, or so I've found, conspicuous for brains.'

'She will never try to be too clever,' Poirot agreed. 'But she knows what she wants.' He sighed. 'So few people do.'

'Ah!' Michael's smile broke out again. 'Thinking of the malachite table?'

'Perhaps.' Poirot paused and added: '*And of what was on it.*'

'The wax flowers, you mean?'

'The wax flowers.'

Michael frowned.

'I don't always quite understand you, M. Poirot. However,' the smile was switched on again, 'I'm more thankful than I can say that we're all out of the wood. It's unpleasant, to say the least of it, to go around with the suspicion that somehow or other one of us murdered poor old Uncle Richard.'

'That is how he seemed to you when you met him?' Poirot inquired. 'Poor old Uncle Richard?'

'Of course he was very well preserved and all that –'

'And in full possession of his faculties –'

'Oh yes.'

'And, in fact, quite *shrewd*?'

'I dare say.'

'A shrewd judge of character.'

The smile remained unaltered.

'You can't expect me to agree with *that*, M. Poirot. He didn't approve of *me*.'

'He thought you, perhaps, the unfaithful type?' Poirot suggested.

Michael laughed.

'What an old-fashioned idea!'

'But it is true, isn't it?'

'Now I wonder what you mean by *that*?'

Poirot placed the tips of his fingers together.

'There have been inquiries made, you know,' he murmured.

'By you?'

'Not only by me.'

Michael Shane gave him a quick searching glance. His reactions, Poirot noted, were quick. Michael Shane was no fool.

'You mean – the police are interested?'

'They have never been quite satisfied, you know, to regard the murder of Cora Lansquenet as a casual crime.'

'And they've been making inquiries about me?'

Poirot said primly:

'They are interested in the movements of Mrs Lansquenet's relations on the day that she was killed.'

'That's extremely awkward.' Michael spoke with a charming confidential rueful air.

'Is it, Mr Shane?'

'More so than you can imagine! I told Rosamund, you see, that I was lunching with a certain Oscar Lewis on that day.'

'When, in actual fact, you were not?'

'No. Actually I motored down to see a woman called Sorrel Dainton – quite a well-known actress. I was with her in her last show. Rather awkward, you see – for though it's quite satisfactory as far as the police are concerned, it won't go down very well with Rosamund.'

'Ah!' Poirot looked discreet. 'There has been a little trouble over this friendship of yours?'

'Yes . . . In fact – Rosamund made me promise I wouldn't see her any more.'

'Yes, I can see that may be awkward . . . *Entre nous*, you had an affair with the lady?'

'Oh, just one of those things! It's not as though I cared for the woman at all.'

'But she cares for you?'

'Well, she's been rather tiresome . . . Women do cling so. However, as you say, the police at any rate will be satisfied.'

'You think so?'

'Well, I could hardly be taking a hatchet to Cora if I was dallying with Sorrel miles and miles away. She's got a cottage in Kent.'

'I see – I see – and this Miss Dainton, she will testify for you?'

'She won't like it – but as it's murder, I suppose she'll have to do it.'

'She will do it, perhaps, even if you were *not* dallying with her.'

'What do you mean?' Michael looked suddenly black as thunder.

'The lady is fond of you. When they are fond, women will swear to what is true – and also to what is untrue.'

'Do you mean to say that you don't believe me?'

'It does not matter if *I* believe you or not. It is not *I* you have to satisfy.'

'Who then?'

Poirot smiled.

'Inspector Morton – who has just come out on the terrace through the side door.'

Michael Shane wheeled round sharply.

CHAPTER 23

I

'I heard you were here, M. Poirot,' said Inspector Morton.

The two men were pacing the terrace together.

'I came over with Superintendent Parwell from Matchfield. Dr Larraby rang him up about Mrs Leo Abernethie and he's come over here to make a few inquiries. The doctor wasn't satisfied.'

'And you, my friend,' inquired Poirot, 'where do you come in? You are a long way from your native Berkshire.'

'I wanted to ask a few questions – and the people I wanted to ask them of seemed very conveniently assembled here.' He paused before adding, 'Your doing?'

'Yes, my doing.'

'And as a result Mrs Leo Abernethie gets knocked out.'

'You must not blame me for that. If she had come to *me* . . . But she did not. Instead she rang up her lawyer in London.'

'And was in the process of spilling the beans to him when – Wonk!'

'When – as you say – Wonk!'

'And what had she managed to tell him?'

'Very little. She had only got as far as telling him that she was looking at herself in the glass.'

'Ah! well,' said Inspector Morton philosophically. 'Women will do it.' He looked sharply at Poirot. 'That suggests something to you?'

'Yes, I think I know what it was she was going to tell him.'

'Wonderful guesser, aren't you? You always were. Well, what was it?'

'Excuse me, are you inquiring into the death of Richard Abernethie?'

'Officially, no. Actually, of course, if it has a bearing on the murder of Mrs Lansquenet –'

'It has a bearing on that, yes. But I will ask you, my friend, to give me a few more hours. I shall know by then if what I have imagined – imagined only, you comprehend – is correct. If it *is* –'

'Well, if it is?'

'Then I may be able to place in your hands a piece of concrete evidence.'

'We could certainly do with it,' said Inspector Morton with feeling. He looked askance at Poirot. 'What have you been holding back?'

'Nothing. Absolutely nothing. Since the piece of evidence I have imagined may not in fact exist. I have only deduced its existence from various scraps of conversation. I may,' said Poirot in a completely unconvinced tone, 'be wrong.'

Morton smiled.

'But that doesn't often happen to you?'

'No. Though I will admit – yes, I am forced to admit – that it *has* happened to me.'

'I must say I'm glad to hear it! To be always right must be sometimes monotonous.'

'I do not find it so,' Poirot assured him.

Inspector Morton laughed.

'And you're asking me to hold off with my questioning?'

'No, no, not at all. Proceed as you had planned to do. I suppose you were not actually contemplating an arrest?'

Morton shook his head.

'Much too flimsy for that. We'd have to get a decision from the Public Prosecutor first – and we're a long way from that. No, just statements from certain parties of their movements on the day in question – in one case with a caution, perhaps.'

'I see. Mrs Banks?'

'Smart, aren't you? Yes. She was there that day. Her car was parked in that quarry.'

'She was not seen actually *driving* the car?'

'No.'

The Inspector added, 'It's bad you know, that she's never said a word about being down there that day. She's got to explain that satisfactorily.'

'She is quite skilful at explanations,' said Poirot drily.

'Yes. Clever young lady. Perhaps a thought too clever.'

'It is never wise to be too clever. That is how murderers get caught. Has anything more come up about George Crossfield?'

'Nothing definite. He's a very ordinary type. There are a lot of young men like him going about the country in trains and buses or on bicycles. People find it hard to remember when a week or so has gone by if it was Wednesday or Thursday when they were at a certain place or noticed a certain person.'

He paused and went on: 'We've had one piece of rather curious information – from the Mother Superior of some convent or other. Two of her nuns had been out collecting from door to door. It seems that they went to Mrs Lansquenet's cottage on the day *before* she was murdered, but couldn't make anyone hear when they knocked and rang. That's natural enough – she was up North at the Abernethie funeral and Gilchrist had been given the day off and had gone on an excursion to Bournemouth. The point is that they say *there was someone in the cottage*. They say they heard sighs and groans. I've queried whether it wasn't a day later but the Mother Superior is quite definite that that couldn't be so. It's all entered up in some book. Was there someone searching for something in the cottage that day, who seized the opportunity of both the women being away? And did that somebody not find what he or she was looking for and come back the next day? I don't set much store on the sighs and still less on the groans. Even nuns are suggestible and a cottage where murder has occurred positively *asks* for groans. The point is, was there someone in the cottage who shouldn't have been there? And if so, who was it? All the Abernethie crowd were at the funeral.'

Poirot asked a seemingly irrelevant question:

'These nuns who were collecting in that district, did they return at all at a later date to try again?'

'As a matter of fact they did come again – about a week later. Actually on the day of the inquest, I believe.'

'That fits,' said Hercule Poirot. 'That fits very well.'

Inspector Morton looked at him.

'Why this interest in nuns?'

'They have been forced on my attention whether I will or no. It will not have escaped your attention, Inspector, that the visit of the nuns was the same day that poisoned wedding cake found its way into that cottage.'

'You don't think – Surely that's a ridiculous idea?'

'My ideas are never ridiculous,' said Hercule Poirot severely. 'And now, *mon cher*, I must leave you to your questions and to the inquiries into the attack on Mrs Abernethie. I myself must go in search of the late Richard Abernethie's niece.'

'Now be careful what you go saying to Mrs Banks.'

'I do not mean Mrs Banks. I mean Richard Abernethie's other niece.'

II

Poirot found Rosamund sitting on a bench overlooking a little stream that cascaded down in a waterfall and then flowed through rhododendron thickets. She was staring into the water.

'I do not, I trust, disturb an Ophelia,' said Poirot as he took his seat beside her. 'You are, perhaps, studying the role?'

'I've never played in Shakespeare,' said Rosamund. 'Except once in Rep. I was Jessica in *The Merchant*. A lousy part.'

'Yet not without pathos. "*I am never merry when I hear sweet music.*" What a load she carried, poor Jessica, the daughter of the hated and despised Jew. What doubts of herself she must have had when she brought with her her father's ducats when she ran away to her lover. Jessica with gold was one thing – Jessica without gold might have been another.'

Rosamund turned her head to look at him.

'I thought you'd gone,' she said with a touch of reproach. She glanced down at her wrist-watch. 'It's past twelve o'clock.'

'I have missed my train,' said Poirot.

'Why?'

'You think I missed it for a reason?'

'I suppose so. You're rather precise, aren't you? If you wanted to catch a train, I should think you'd catch it.'

'Your judgement is admirable. Do you know, Madame, I have been sitting in the little summer-house hoping that you would, perhaps, pay me a visit there?'

Rosamund stared at him.

'Why should I? You more or less said goodbye to us all in the library.'

'Quite so. And there was nothing – *you* wanted to say to *me*?'

'No.' Rosamund shook her head. 'I had a lot I wanted to think about. Important things.'

'I see.'

'I don't often do much thinking,' said Rosamund. 'It seems a waste of time. But this *is* important. I think one ought to plan one's life just as one wants it to be.'

'And that is what you are doing?'

'Well, yes . . . I was trying to make a decision about something.'

'About your husband?'

'In a way.'

Poirot waited a moment, then he said:

'Inspector Morton has just arrived here.' He anticipated Rosamund's question by going on: 'He is the police officer in charge of the inquiries about Mrs Lansquenet's death. He has come here to get statements from you all about what you were doing on the day she was murdered.'

'I see. *Alibis*,' said Rosamund cheerfully.

Her beautiful face relaxed into an impish glee.

'That will be hell for Michael,' she said. 'He thinks I don't really know he went off to be with that woman that day.'

'How did you know?'

'It was obvious from the *way* he said he was going to lunch with Oscar. So frightfully casually, you know, and his nose twitching just a tiny bit like it always does when he tells lies.'

'How devoutly thankful I am I am not married to you, Madame!'

'And then, of course, I made sure by ringing up Oscar,' continued Rosamund. 'Men always tell such silly lies.'

'He is not, I fear, a very faithful husband?' Poirot hazarded.

Rosamund, however, did not reject the statement.

'No.'

'But you do not mind?'

'Well, it's rather fun in a way,' said Rosamund. 'I mean having a husband that all the other women want to snatch away from you. I should hate to be married to a man that nobody wanted – like poor Susan. Really Greg is so completely wet!'

Poirot was studying her.

'And suppose someone did succeed – in snatching your husband away from you?'

'They won't,' said Rosamund. 'Not now,' she added.

'You mean –'

'Not now that there's Uncle Richard's money. Michael falls for these creatures in a way – that Sorrel Dainton woman nearly got her hooks into him – wanted him for keeps – but with Michael the show will always come first. He can launch out now in a big way – put his own shows on. Do some production as well as acting. He's ambitious, you know, and he really is good. Not like me. I adore acting – but I'm ham, though I look nice. No, I'm not worried about Michael any more. Because it's my money, you see.'

Her eyes met Poirot's calmly. He thought how strange it was that both Richard Abernethie's nieces should have fallen deeply in love with men who were incapable of returning that love. And yet Rosamund was unusually beautiful and Susan was attractive and full of sex appeal. Susan needed and clung to the illusion that Gregory loved her. Rosamund, clear-sighted, had no illusions at all, but knew what she wanted.

'The point is,' said Rosamund, 'that I've got to make a big decision – about the future. Michael doesn't know yet.' Her face curved into a smile. 'He found out that I wasn't shopping that day and he's madly suspicious about Regent's Park.'

'What is this about Regent's Park?' Poirot looked puzzled.

'I went there, you see, after Harley Street. Just to walk about and think. Naturally Michael thinks that if I went there at all, I went to meet some man!'

Rosamund smiled beatifically and added:

'He didn't like that *at all*!'

'But why should you not go to Regent's Park?' asked Poirot.

'Just to walk there, you mean?'

'Yes. Have you never done it before?'

'Never. Why should I? What is there to go to Regent's Park *for*?'

Poirot looked at her and said:

'For you – nothing.'

He added:

'I think, Madame, that you must cede the green malachite table to your cousin Susan.'

Rosamund's eyes opened very wide.

'Why should I? I *want* it.'

'I know. I know. But you – you will keep your husband. And the poor Susan, she will lose hers.'

'Lose him? Do you mean Greg's going off with someone? I wouldn't have believed it of him. He looks so *wet*.'

'Infidelity is not the only way of losing a husband, Madame.'

'You don't mean –?' Rosamund stared at him. 'You're not thinking that Greg poisoned Uncle Richard and killed Aunt Cora and conked Aunt Helen on the head? That's ridiculous. Even *I* know better than that.'

'Who did, then?'

'George, of course. George is a wrong un, you know, he's mixed up in some sort of currency swindle – I heard about it from some friends of mine who were in Monte. I expect Uncle Richard got to know about it and was just going to cut him out of his will.'

Rosamund added complacently:

'I've always known it was George.'

CHAPTER 24

I

The telegram came about six o'clock that evening.

As specially requested it was delivered by hand, not telephoned, and Hercule Poirot, who had been hovering for some time in the neighbourhood of the front door, was at hand to receive it from Lanscombe as the latter took it from the telegraph boy.

He tore it open with somewhat less than his usual precision. It consisted of three words and a signature.

Poirot gave vent to an enormous sigh of relief.

Then he took a pound note from his pocket and handed it to the dumbfounded boy.

'There are moments,' he said to Lanscombe, 'when economy should be abandoned.'

'Very possibly, sir,' said Lanscombe politely.

'Where is Inspector Morton?' asked Poirot.

'One of the police gentlemen,' Lanscombe spoke with distaste – and indicated subtly that such things as names for police officers were impossible to remember – 'has left. The other is, I believe, in the study.'

'Splendid,' said Poirot. 'I join him immediately.'

He once more clapped Lanscombe on the shoulder and said:

'Courage, we are on the point of arriving!'

Lanscombe looked slightly bewildered since departures, and not arrivals, had been in his mind.

He said:

'You do not, then, propose to leave by the nine-thirty train after all, sir?'

'Do not lose hope,' Poirot told him.

Poirot moved away, then wheeling round, he asked:

'I wonder, can you remember what were the first words Mrs Lansquenet said to you when she arrived here on the day of your master's funeral?'

'I remember very well, sir,' said Lanscombe, his face lighting up. 'Miss Cora – I beg pardon, Mrs Lansquenet – I always think of her as Miss Cora, somehow –'

'Very naturally.'

'She said to me: "Hallo, Lanscombe. It's a long time since you used to bring us out meringues to the huts." All the children used to have a hut of their own – down by the fence in the Park. In summer, when there was going to be a dinner party, I used to take the young ladies and gentlemen – the younger ones, you understand, sir – some meringues. Miss Cora, sir, was always very fond of her food.'

Poirot nodded.

'Yes,' he said, 'that was as I thought. Yes, it was very typical, that.'

He went into the study to find Inspector Morton and without a word handed him the telegram.

Morton read it blankly.

'I don't understand a word of this.'

'The time has come to tell you all.'

Inspector Morton grinned.

'You sound like a young lady in a Victorian melodrama. But it's about time you came across with something. I can't hold out on this set-up much longer. That Banks fellow is still insisting that he poisoned Richard Abernethie and boasting that we can't find out how. What beats me is why there's always somebody who comes forward when there's a murder and yells out that they did it! What do they think there is in it for them? I've never been able to fathom that.'

'In this case, probably shelter from the difficulties of being responsible for oneself – in other words – Forsdyke Sanatorium.'

'More likely to be Broadmoor.'

'That might be equally satisfactory.'

'*Did* he do it, Poirot? The Gilchrist woman came out with the story she'd already told you and it would fit with what Richard Abernethie said about his niece. If her husband did it, it would involve her. Somehow, you know, I can't visualize that girl committing a lot of crimes. But there's nothing she wouldn't do to try and cover *him*.'

'I will tell you all –'

'Yes, yes, tell me all! And for the Lord's sake hurry up and do it!'

II

This time it was in the big drawing-room that Hercule Poirot assembled his audience.

There was amusement rather than tension in the faces that were turned towards him. Menace had materialized in the shape of Inspector Morton and Superintendent Parwell. With the police in charge, questioning, asking for statements, Hercule Poirot, private detective, had receded into something closely resembling a joke.

Timothy was not far from voicing the general feeling when he remarked in an audible *sotto voce* to his wife:

'Damned little mountebank! Entwhistle must be *gaga*! – that's all I can say.'

It looked as though Hercule Poirot would have to work hard to make his proper effect.

He began in a slightly pompous manner.

'For the second time, I announce my departure! This morning I announced it for the twelve o'clock train. This evening I announce it for the nine-thirty – immediately, that is, after dinner. I go because there is nothing more here for me to do.'

'Could have told him that all along.' Timothy's commentary was still in evidence. 'Never was anything for him to do. The cheek of these fellows!'

'I came here originally to solve a riddle. The riddle is solved. Let me, first, go over the various points which were brought to my attention by the excellent Mr Entwhistle.

'First, Mr Richard Abernethie dies suddenly. Secondly, after his funeral, his sister Cora Lansquenet says, "He was murdered, wasn't he?" Thirdly Mrs Lansquenet is killed. The question is, are those three things part of a *sequence*? Let us observe what happens next? Miss Gilchrist, the dead woman's companion, is taken ill after eating a piece of wedding cake which contains arsenic. That, then, is the *next* step in the sequence.

'Now, as I told you this morning, in the course of my inquiries I have come across nothing – nothing at all, to substantiate the belief that Mr Abernethie was poisoned. Equally, I may say, I have found nothing to prove conclusively that he was *not* poisoned. But as we proceed, things become easier. Cora Lansquenet undoubtedly asked that sensational question at the funeral. Everyone agrees upon *that*. And undoubtedly, on the following day, Mrs Lansquenet was murdered – a hatchet being the instrument employed. Now let us examine the fourth happening. The local post van driver is strongly of the belief – though he will not definitely swear to it – that he did not deliver that parcel of wedding cake in the usual way. And if that is so, then the parcel was left by hand and though we cannot exclude a "person unknown" – we must take particular notice of those people who were actually on the spot and in a position to put the parcel where it was subsequently found. Those were: Miss Gilchrist herself, of course; Susan Banks who came down that day for the inquest; Mr Entwhistle (but yes, we must consider Mr Entwhistle; he was present, remember, when Cora made her disquieting remark!) And there were two other people. An old gentleman who represented himself to be a Mr Guthrie, an art critic, and a nun or nuns who called early that morning to collect a subscription.

'Now I decided that I would start on the assumption that the postal van driver's recollection was correct. Therefore the little group of people under suspicion must be very carefully studied. Miss Gilchrist did not benefit in any way by Richard Abernethie's death and in only a very minute degree by Mrs Lansquenet's – in actual fact the death of the latter put her out of employment and left her with the possibility of finding it difficult to get new employment. Also Miss Gilchrist was taken to hospital definitely suffering from arsenic poisoning.

'Susan Banks *did* benefit from Richard Abernethie's death, and in a small degree from Mrs Lansquenet's – though here her motive must almost certainly have been security. She might have very good reason to believe that Miss Gilchrist had overheard a conversation between Cora Lansquenet and her brother which referred to her, and she might therefore decide that Miss Gilchrist must be eliminated. She herself, remember, refused to partake of the wedding cake and also suggested not calling in a doctor until the morning, when Miss Gilchrist was taken ill in the night.

'Mr Entwhistle did *not* benefit by either of the deaths – but he had had considerable control over Mr Abernethie's affairs, and the trust funds, and there might well be some reason why Richard Abernethie should not live too long. But – you will say – if it is Mr Entwhistle who was concerned, why should he come to *me*?

'And to that I will answer – it is not the first time that a murderer has been too sure of himself.

'We now come to what I may call the two outsiders. Mr Guthrie and a nun. If Mr Guthrie is really Mr Guthrie, the art critic, then that clears him. The same applies to the nun, if she is really a nun. The question is, are these people themselves, or are they somebody else?

'And I may say that there seems to be a curious – *motif* – one might call it – of a nun running through this business. A nun comes to the door of Mr Timothy Abernethie's house and Miss Gilchrist believes it is the same nun she has seen at Lytchett St Mary. Also a nun, or nuns, called here the day before Mr Abernethie died . . .'

George Crossfield murmured, 'Three to one, the nun.'

Poirot went on:

'So here we have certain pieces of our pattern – the death of

Mr Abernethie, the murder of Cora Lansquenet, the poisoned wedding cake, the "*motif*" of the "nun".

'I will add some other features of the case that engaged my attention:

'The visit of an art critic, a smell of oil paint, a picture postcard of Polflexan harbour, and finally a bouquet of wax flowers standing on that malachite table where a Chinese vase stands now.

'It was reflecting on these things that led me to the truth – and I am now about to tell you the truth.

'The first part of it I told you this morning. Richard Abernethie died suddenly – but there would have been no reason at all to suspect foul play had it not been for the words uttered by his sister Cora at his funeral. *The whole case for the murder of Richard Abernethie rests upon those words.* As a result of them, you all believed that murder had taken place, and you believed it, not really because of the words themselves but because of *the character of Cora Lansquenet herself.* For Cora Lansquenet had always been famous for speaking the truth at awkward moments. So the case for Richard's murder rested not only upon what Cora had *said* but upon Cora herself.

'And now I come to the question that I suddenly asked myself: '*How well did you all know Cora Lansquenet?*'

He was silent for a moment, and Susan asked sharply, 'What do you mean?'

Poirot went on:

'*Not well at all* – that is the answer! The younger generation had never seen her at all, or if so, only when they were very young children. There were actually only three people present that day who actually *knew* Cora. Lanscombe, the butler, who is old and very blind; Mrs Timothy Abernethie who had only seen her a few times round about the date of her own wedding, and Mrs Leo Abernethie who had known her quite well, but who had not seen her for over twenty years.

'So I said to myself: "Supposing it was *not* Cora Lansquenet who came to the funeral that day?"'

'Do you mean that Aunt Cora – *wasn't* Aunt Cora?' Susan demanded incredulously. 'Do you mean that it wasn't Aunt Cora who was murdered, but someone else?'

'No, no, it was Cora Lansquenet who was murdered. *But it was not Cora Lansquenet* who came the day before to her brother's funeral. The woman who came that day came for one purpose only – to exploit, one may say, the fact that Richard died suddenly. And to create in the minds of his relations that he had been murdered. Which she managed to do most successfully!'

'Nonsense! Why? What was the point of it?' Maude spoke bluffly.

'Why? *To draw attention away from the other murder*. From the murder of Cora Lansquenet herself. For if Cora says that Richard has been murdered and the next day *she herself is killed*, the two deaths are bound to be at least considered as possible cause and effect. But if Cora is murdered and her cottage is broken into, and if the apparent robbery does not convince the police, then they will look – where? Close at home, will they not? Suspicion will tend to fall on the woman who shares the house with her.'

Miss Gilchrist protested in a tone that was almost bright:

'Oh come – really – Mr Pontarlier – you don't suggest I'd commit a murder for an amethyst brooch and a few worthless sketches?'

'No,' said Poirot. 'For a little more than that. There was one of those sketches, Miss Gilchrist, that represented Polflexan harbour and which, as Mrs Banks was clever enough to realize, had been copied from a picture postcard which showed the old pier still in position. But Mrs Lansquenet painted always from life. I remembered then that Mr Entwhistle had mentioned there being *a smell of oil paint* in the cottage when he first got there. You can paint, can't you, Miss Gilchrist? Your father was an artist and you know a good deal about pictures. Supposing that one of the pictures that Cora picked up cheaply at a sale was a valuable picture. Supposing that she herself did not recognize it for what it was, but that you did. You knew she was expecting, very shortly, a visit from an old friend of hers who was a well-known art critic. Then her brother died suddenly – and a plan leaps into your head. Easy to administer a sedative to her in her early cup of tea that will keep her unconscious for the whole of the day of the funeral whilst you yourself are playing her part at Enderby. You know Enderby well from listening to her talk about it. She has talked, as people do when they get on in life, a great deal about her childhood days. Easy for you to start off by a remark to old Lanscombe about meringues and huts which will make him quite sure of your identity in case he was inclined to doubt. Yes, you used your knowledge of Enderby well that day, with allusions to this and that, and recalling memories, None of them suspected you were not Cora. You were wearing her clothes, slightly padded, and since she wore a false front of hair, it was easy for you to assume that. Nobody had seen Cora for twenty years – and in twenty years people change so much that one often hears the remark: "I would never have known her!" But mannerisms are remembered, and Cora had certain very definite mannerisms, all of which you had practised carefully before the glass.

'And it was there, strangely enough, that you made your first mistake. *You forgot that a mirror image is reversed.* When you saw in the glass the perfect reproduction of Cora's birdlike sidewise tilt of the head, you didn't realize that it was actually the *wrong way round*. You saw, let us say, Cora inclining her head to the *right* – but you forgot that actually your own head was inclined to the *left* to produce that effect *in the glass*.

'That was what puzzled and worried Helen Abernethie at the moment when you made your famous insinuation. Something seemed to her "wrong". I realized myself the other night when Rosamund Shane made an unexpected remark what happens on such an occasion. Everybody inevitably looks at the *speaker*. Therefore, when Mrs Leo felt something was "wrong", it must be that something was wrong with *Cora Lansquenet*. The other evening, after talk about mirror images and "seeing oneself" I think Mrs Leo experimented before a looking-glass. Her own face is not particularly asymmetrical. She probably thought of Cora, remembered how Cora used to incline her head to the right, did so, and looked in the glass – when, of course, the image seemed to her "wrong" and she realized, in a flash, just what had been wrong on the day of the funeral. She puzzled it out – either Cora had taken to inclining her head in the opposite direction – most unlikely – or else *Cora had not been Cora*. Neither way seemed to her to make sense. But she was determined to tell Mr Entwhistle of her discovery at once. Someone who was used to getting up early was already about, and followed her down, and fearful of what revelations she might be about to make struck her down with a heavy doorstop.'

Poirot paused and added:

'I may as well tell you now, Miss Gilchrist, that Mrs Abernethie's concussion is not serious. She will soon be able to tell us her own story.'

'I never did anything of the sort,' said Miss Gilchrist. 'The whole thing is a wicked lie.'

'It *was* you that day,' said Michael Shane suddenly. He had been studying Miss Gilchrist's face. 'I ought to have seen it sooner – I felt in a vague kind of way I had seen you before somewhere – but of course one never looks much at –' he stopped.

'No, one doesn't bother to look at a mere companionhelp,' said Miss Gilchrist. Her voice shook a little. 'A drudge, a domestic drudge! Almost a servant! But go on, M. Poirot. Go on with this fantastic piece of nonsense!'

'The suggestion of murder thrown out at the funeral was only the first step, of course,' said Poirot. 'You had more in reserve. At any moment you were prepared to admit to having listened to a conversation between Richard and his sister. What he actually told her, no doubt, was the fact that he had not long to live, and that explains a cryptic phrase in the letter he wrote to her after getting home. The "nun" was another of your suggestions. The nun – or rather nuns – who called at the cottage on the day of the inquest suggested to you a mention of a nun who was "following you round", and you used that when you were anxious to hear what Mrs Timothy was saying to her sister-in-law at Enderby. And also because you wished to accompany her there and find out for yourself just how suspicions were going. Actually to poison *yourself*, badly but not fatally, with arsenic, is a very old device – and I may say that it served to awaken Inspector Morton's suspicions of you.'

'But the picture?' said Rosamund. 'What kind of a picture was it?'

Poirot slowly unfolded a telegram.

'This morning I rang up Mr Entwhistle, a responsible person, to go to Stansfield Grange and, acting on authority from Mr Abernethie himself' (here Poirot gave a hard stare at Timothy) 'to look amongst the pictures in Miss Gilchrist's room and select the one of Polflexan Harbour on pretext of having it reframed as a surprise for Miss Gilchrist. He was to take it back to London and call upon Mr Guthrie whom I had warned by telegram. The hastily painted sketch of Polflexan Harbour was removed and the original picture exposed.'

He held up the telegram and read:

'*Definitely a Vermeer. Guthrie.*'

Suddenly, with electrifying effect, Miss Gilchrist burst into speech.

'I knew it was a Vermeer. I *knew* it! *She* didn't know! Talking about Rembrandts and Italian Primitives and unable to recognize a Vermeer when it was under her nose! Always prating about Art – and really knowing nothing about it! She was a thoroughly stupid woman. Always maundering on about this place – about Enderby, and what they did there as children, and about Richard and Timothy and Laura and all the rest of them. Rolling in money always! Always the best of everything those children had. You don't know how boring it is listening to somebody going on about the same things, hour after hour and day after day. And saying, "Oh, yes, Mrs Lansquenet" and "Really, Mrs Lansquenet?" Pretending to be interested. And really bored – bored – *bored* . . . And nothing to look forward to . . . And then – a Vermeer! I saw in the papers that a Vermeer sold the other day for over five thousand pounds!'

'You killed her – in that brutal way – for five thousand pounds?' Susan's voice was incredulous.

'Five thousand pounds,' said Poirot, 'would have rented and equipped a *tea-shop* . . .'

Miss Gilchrist turned to him.

'At least,' she said. 'You *do* understand. It was the only chance I'd ever get. I *had* to have a capital sum.' Her voice vibrated with the force and obsession of her dream. 'I was going to call it the Palm Tree. And have little camels as menu holders. One can occasionally get quite nice china – export rejects – not that awful white utility stuff. I meant to start it in some nice neighbourhood where nice people would come in. I had thought of Rye . . . Or perhaps Chichester . . . I'm sure I could have made a success of it.' She paused a minute, then added musingly, 'Oak tables – and little basket chairs with striped red and white cushions . . .'

For a few moments, the tea-shop that would never be, seemed more real than the Victorian solidity of the drawing-room at Enderby . . .

It was Inspector Morton who broke the spell.

Miss Gilchrist turned to him quite politely.

'Oh, certainly,' she said. 'At once. I don't want to give any trouble, I'm sure. After all, if I can't have the Palm Tree, nothing really seems to matter very much . . .'

She went out of the room with him and Susan said, her voice still shaken:

'I've never imagined a *ladylike* murderer. It's horrible . . .'

CHAPTER 25

'But I don't understand about the wax flowers,' said Rosamund.

She fixed Poirot with large reproachful blue eyes.

They were at Helen's flat in London. Helen herself was resting on the sofa and Rosamund and Poirot were having tea with her.

'I don't see that *wax flowers* had anything to *do* with it,' said Rosamund. 'Or the malachite table.'

'The malachite table, no. But the wax flowers were Miss Gilchrist's second mistake. She said how nice they looked on the malachite table. And you see, Madame, *she* could not have seen them there. Because they had been broken and put away before she arrived with the Timothy Abernethies. *So she could only have seen them when she was there as Cora Lansquenet.*'

'That *was* stupid of her, wasn't it?' said Rosamund.

Poirot shook a forefinger at her.

'It shows you, Madame, the dangers of *conversations*. It is a profound belief of mine that if you can induce a person to talk to you for long enough, *on any subject whatever*! sooner or later they will give themselves away. Miss Gilchrist did.'

'I shall have to be careful,' said Rosamund thoughtfully.

Then she brightened up.

'Did you know? I'm going to have a baby.'

'Aha! So that is the meaning of Harley Street and Regent's Park?'

'Yes. I was so upset, you know, and so surprised – that I just had to go somewhere and *think*.'

'You said, I remember, that that does not very often happen.'

'Well, it's much easier not to. But this time I had to decide about the future. And I've decided to leave the stage and just be a mother.'

'A role that will suit you admirably. Already I foresee delightful pictures in the *Sketch* and the *Tatler*.'

Rosamund smiled happily.

'Yes, it's wonderful. Do you know, Michael is *delighted*. I didn't really think he would be.'

She paused and added:

'Susan's got the malachite table. I thought, as I was having a baby –'

She left the sentence unfinished.

'Susan's cosmetic business promises well,' said Helen. 'I think she is all set for a big success.'

'Yes, she was born to succeed,' said Poirot. 'She is like her uncle.'

'You mean Richard, I suppose,' said Rosamund. 'Not Timothy?'

'Assuredly not like Timothy,' said Poirot.

They laughed.

'Greg's away somewhere,' said Rosamund. 'Having a rest cure Susan *says*?'

She looked inquiringly at Poirot who said nothing.

'I can't think why he kept on saying he'd killed Uncle Richard,' said Rosamund. 'Do you think it was a form of Exhibitionism?'

Poirot reverted to the previous topic.

'I received a very amiable letter from Mr Timothy Abernethie,' he said. 'He expressed himself as highly satisfied with the services I had rendered the family.'

'I do think Uncle Timothy is quite awful,' said Rosamund.

'I am going to stay with them next week,' said Helen. 'They seem to be getting the gardens into order, but domestic help is still difficult.'

'They miss the awful Gilchrist, I suppose,' said Rosamund. 'But I dare say in the end, she'd have killed Uncle Timothy too. What fun if she had!'

'Murder has always seemed fun to you, Madame.'

'Oh! not really,' said Rosamund vaguely. 'But I *did* think it was George.' She brightened up. 'Perhaps he will do one some day.'

'And that will be fun,' said Poirot sarcastically.

'Yes, won't it?' Rosamund agreed.

She ate another éclair from the plate in front of her.

Poirot turned to Helen.

'And you, Madame, are off to Cyprus?'

'Yes, in a fortnight's time.'

'Then let me wish you a happy journey.'

He bowed over her hand. She came with him to the door, leaving Rosamund dreamily stuffing herself with cream pastries.

Helen said abruptly:

'I should like you to know, M. Poirot, that the legacy Richard left me meant more to me than theirs did to any of the others.'

'As much as that, Madame?'

'Yes. You see – there is a child in Cyprus . . . My husband and I were very devoted – it was a great sorrow to us to have no children. After he died my loneliness was unbelievable. When I was nursing in London at the end of the war, I met someone . . . He was younger than I was and married, though not very happily. We came together for a little while. That was all. He went back to Canada – to his wife and his children. He never knew about – our child. He would not have wanted it. I did. It seemed like a miracle to me – a middle-aged woman with everything behind her. With Richard's money I can educate my so-called nephew, and give him a start in life.' She paused, then added, 'I never told Richard. He was fond of me and I of him – but he would not have understood. You know so much about us all that I thought I would like you to know this about me.'

Once again Poirot bowed over her hand.

He got home to find the armchair on the left of the fire-place occupied.

'Hallo, Poirot,' said Mr Entwhistle. 'I've just come back from the Assizes. They brought in a verdict of Guilty, of course. But I shouldn't be surprised if she ends up in Broadmoor. She's gone definitely over the edge since she's been in prison. Quite happy, you know, and *most* gracious. She spends most her time making the most elaborate plans to run a chain of tea-shops. Her newest establishment is to be the Lilac Bush. She's opening it in Cromer.'

'One wonders if she was always a little mad? But me, I think not.'

'Good Lord, no! Sane as you and I when she planned that murder. Carried it out in cold blood. She's got a good head on her, you know, underneath the fluffy manner.'

Poirot gave a little shiver.

'I am thinking,' he said, 'of some words that Susan Banks said – that she had never imagined a *ladylike* murderer.'

'Why not?' said Mr Entwhistle. 'It takes all sorts.'

They were silent – and Poirot thought of murderers he had known . . .

HICKORY DICKORY DOCK

Hercule Poirot frowned.

'Miss Lemon,' he said.

'Yes, M. Poirot?'

'There are three mistakes in this letter.'

His voice held incredulity. For Miss Lemon, that hideous and efficient woman, never made mistakes. She was never ill, never tired, never upset, never inaccurate. For all practical purposes, that is to say, she was not a woman at all. She was a machine – the perfect secretary. She knew everything, she coped with everything. She ran Hercule Poirot's life for him, so that it, too, functioned like a machine. Order and method had been Hercule Poirot's watchwords from many years ago. With George, his perfect manservant, and Miss Lemon, his perfect secretary, order and method ruled supreme in his life. Now that crumpets were baked square as well as round, he had nothing about which to complain.

And yet, this morning, Miss Lemon had made three mistakes in typing a perfectly simple letter, and moreover, had not even noticed those mistakes. The stars stood still in their courses!

Hercule Poirot held out the offending document. He was not annoyed, he was merely bewildered. This was one of the things that could not happen – but it had happened!

Miss Lemon took the letter. She looked at it. For the first time in his life, Poirot saw her blush; a deep ugly unbecoming flush that dyed her face right up to the roots of her strong grizzled hair.

'Oh, dear,' she said. 'I can't think how – at least I *can*. It's because of my sister.'

'Your sister?'

Another shock. Poirot had never conceived of Miss Lemon's having a sister. Or, for that matter, having a father, mother, or even grandparents. Miss Lemon, somehow, was so completely machine made – a precision instrument so to speak – that to think of her having affections, or anxieties, or family worries, seemed quite ludicrous. It was well known that the whole of Miss Lemon's heart and mind was given, when she was not on duty, to the perfection of a new filing system which was to be patented and bear her name.

'Your sister?' Hercule Poirot repeated, therefore, with an incredulous note in his voice.

Miss Lemon nodded a vigorous assent.

'Yes,' she said, 'I don't think I've ever mentioned her to you. Practically all her life has been spent in Singapore. Her husband was in the rubber business there.'

Hercule Poirot nodded understandingly. It seemed to him appropriate that Miss Lemon's sister should have spent most of her life in Singapore. That was what places like Singapore were for. The sisters of women like Miss Lemon married men in Singapore, so that the Miss Lemons of this world could devote themselves with machine-like efficiency to their employers' affairs (and of course to the invention of filing systems in their moments of relaxation).

'I comprehend,' he said. 'Proceed.'

Miss Lemon proceeded.

'She was left a widow four years ago. No children. I managed to get her fixed up in a very nice little flat at quite a reasonable rent –'

(Of course Miss Lemon *would* manage to do just that almost impossible thing.)

'She is reasonably well off – though money doesn't go as far as it did, but her tastes aren't expensive and she has enough to be quite comfortable if she is careful.'

Miss Lemon paused and then continued:

'But the truth is, of course, she was lonely. She had never lived in England and she'd got no old friends or cronies and of course she had a lot of time on her hands. Anyway, she told me about six months ago that she was thinking of taking up this job.'

'Job?'

'Warden, I think they call it – or matron – of a hostel for students. It was owned by a woman who was partly Greek and she wanted someone to run it for her. Manage the catering and see that things went smoothly. It's an old-fashioned roomy house

– in Hickory Road, if you know where that is.' Poirot did not. 'It used to be a superior neighbourhood once, and the houses are well built. My sister was to have very nice accommodation, bedroom and sitting-room and a tiny bath kitchenette of her own –'

Miss Lemon paused. Poirot made an encouraging noise. So far this did not seem at all like a tale of disaster.

'I wasn't any too sure about it myself, but I saw the force of my sister's arguments. She's never been one to sit with her hands crossed all day long and she's a very practical woman and good at running things – and of course it wasn't as though she were thinking of putting money into it or anything like that. It was purely a salaried position – not a high salary, but she didn't need that, and there was no hard physical work. She's always been fond of young people and good with them, and having lived in the East so long she understands racial differences and people's susceptibilities. Because these students at the hostel are of all nationalities; mostly English, but some of them actually *black*, I believe.'

'Naturally,' said Hercule Poirot.

'Half the nurses in our hospitals seem to be black nowadays,' said Miss Lemon doubtfully, 'and I understand much pleasanter and more attentive than the English ones. But that's neither here nor there. We talked the scheme over and finally my sister moved in. Neither she nor I cared very much for the proprietress, Mrs Nicoletis, a woman of very uncertain temper, sometimes charming and sometimes, I'm sorry to say, quite the reverse – and both cheese-paring and impractical. Still, naturally, if she'd been a thoroughly competent woman, she wouldn't have needed any assistance. My sister is not one to let people's tantrums and vagaries worry her. She can hold her own with anyone and she never stands any nonsense.'

Poirot nodded. He felt a vague resemblance to Miss Lemon showing in this account of Miss Lemon's sister – a Miss Lemon softened as it were by marriage and the climate of Singapore, but a woman with the same hard core of sense.

'So your sister took the job?' he asked.

'Yes, she moved into 26 Hickory Road about six months ago. On the whole, she liked her work there and found it interesting.'

Hercule Poirot listened. So far the adventure of Miss Lemon's sister had been disappointingly tame.

'But for some time now she's been badly worried. Very badly worried.'

'Why?'

'Well, you see, M. Poirot, she doesn't like the things that are going on.'

'There are students there of both sexes?' Poirot inquired delicately.

'Oh no, M. Poirot, I don't mean *that*! One is always prepared for difficulties of *that* kind, one *expects* them! No, you see, things have been disappearing.'

'Disappearing?'

'Yes: And such odd things . . . And all in rather an unnatural way.'

'When you say things have been disappearing, you mean things have been stolen?'

'Yes.'

'Have the police been called in?'

'No. Not yet. My sister hopes that it may not be necessary. She is fond of these young people – of some of them, that is – and she would very much prefer to straighten things out by herself.'

'Yes,' said Poirot thoughtfully. 'I can quite see that. But that does not explain, if I may say so, your own anxiety which I take to be a reflex of your sister's anxiety.'

'I don't like the situation, M. Poirot. I don't like it at all. I cannot help feeling that something is going on which I do not understand. No ordinary explanation seems quite to cover the facts – and I really cannot imagine what other explanation there can be.'

Poirot nodded thoughtfully.

Miss Lemon's Heel of Achilles had always been her imagination. She had none. On questions of fact she was invincible. On questions of surmise, she was lost. Not for her the state of mind of Cortez's men upon the peak of Darien.

'Not ordinary petty thieving? A kleptomaniac, perhaps?'

'I do not think so. I read up the subject,' said the conscientious Miss Lemon, 'in the *Encyclopaedia Britannica* and in a medical work. But I was not convinced.'

Hercule Poirot was silent for a minute and a half.

Did he wish to embroil himself in the troubles of Miss Lemon's sister and the passions and grievances of a polyglot hostel? But it was very annoying and inconvenient to have Miss Lemon making mistakes in typing his letters. He told himself that *if* he were to embroil himself in the matter, that would be the reason. He did not admit to himself that he had been rather bored of late and that the very triviality of the business attracted him.

'"The parsley sinking into the butter on a hot day,"' he murmured to himself.

'Parsley? Butter?' Miss Lemon looked startled.

'A quotation from one of your classics,' he said. 'You are acquainted, no doubt, with the Adventures, to say nothing of the Exploits, of Sherlock Holmes.'

'You mean these Baker Street societies and all that,' said Miss Lemon. 'Grown men being so silly! But there, that's men all over. Like the model railways they go on playing with. I can't say I've ever had time to *read* any of the stories. When I do get time for reading, which isn't very often, I prefer an improving book.'

Hercule Poirot bowed his head gracefully.

'How would it be, Miss Lemon, if you were to invite your sister here for some suitable refreshment – afternoon tea, perhaps? I might be able to be of some slight assistance to her.'

'That's very kind of you, M. Poirot. Really very kind indeed. My sister is always free in the afternoons.'

'Then shall we say tomorrow, if you can arrange it?'

And in due course, the faithful George was instructed to provide a meal of square crumpets richly buttered, symmetrical sandwiches, and other suitable components of a lavish English afternoon tea.

CHAPTER 2

Miss Lemon's sister, whose name was Mrs Hubbard, had a definite resemblance to her sister. She was a good deal yellower of skin, she was plumper, her hair was more frivolously done, and she was less brisk in manner, but the eyes that looked out of a round and amiable countenance were the same shrewd eyes that gleamed through Miss Lemon's pince-nez.

'This is very kind of you, I'm sure, M. Poirot,' she said. '*Very* kind. And such a delicious tea, too. I'm sure I've eaten far more than I should – well, perhaps just *one* more sandwich – tea? Well, just *half* a cup.'

'First,' said Poirot, 'we make the repast – afterwards we get down to business.'

He smiled at her amiably and twirled his moustache, and Mrs Hubbard said:

'You know, you're exactly like I pictured you from Felicity's description.'

After a moment's startled realisation that Felicity was the severe Miss Lemon's Christian name, Poirot replied that he should have expected no less given Miss Lemon's efficiency.

'Of course,' said Mrs Hubbard absently, taking a second sandwich, 'Felicity has never cared for *people*. I do. That's why I'm so worried.'

'Can you explain to me exactly what does worry you?'

'Yes, I can. It would be natural enough for money to be taken – small sums here and there. And if it were jewellery that's quite straightforward too – at least, I don't mean straightforward, quite the opposite – but it would fit in – with kleptomania or dishonesty. But I'll just read you a list of the things that have been taken, that I've put down on paper.'

Mrs Hubbard opened her bag and took out a small notebook.

Evening shoe (one of a new pair)
Bracelet (costume jewellery)
Diamond ring (found in plate of soup)
Powder compact
Lipstick
Stethoscope
Ear-rings
Cigarette lighter
Old flannel trousers
Electric light bulbs
Box of chocolates
Silk scarf (found cut to pieces)

Rucksack (ditto)
Boracic powder
Bath salts
Cookery book

Hercule Poirot drew in a long deep breath.

'Remarkable,' he said, 'and quite – quite fascinating.'

He was entranced. He looked from the severe disapproving face of Miss Lemon to the kindly, distressed face of Mrs Hubbard.

'I congratulate you,' he said warmly to the latter.

She looked startled.

'But why, M. Poirot?'

'I congratulate you on having such a unique and beautiful problem.'

'Well, perhaps it makes sense to you, M. Poirot, but –'

'It does not make sense at all. It reminds me of nothing so much as a round game I was recently persuaded to play by some young friends during the Christmas season. It was called, I understand, the Three Horned Lady. Each person in turn uttered the following phrase, "I went to Paris and bought –" adding some article. The next person repeated that and added a further article and the object of the game was to memorise in their proper order the articles thus enumerated, some of them, I may say, of a most monstrous and ridiculous nature. A piece of soap, a white elephant, a gate-legged table and a Muscovy duck were, I remember, some of the items. The difficulty of memorisation lay, of course, in the totally unrelated nature of the objects – the lack of sequence, so to speak. As in the list you have just shown me. By the time that, say, twelve objects had been mentioned, to enumerate them in their proper order became almost impossible. A failure to do so resulted in a paper horn being handed to the competitor and he or she had to continue the recitation next time in the terms, "I, a one horned lady, went to Paris," etc. After three horns had been acquired, retirement was compulsory, the last left in was the winner.'

'I'm sure you were the winner, M. Poirot,' said Miss Lemon, with the faith of a loyal employee.

Poirot beamed.

'That was, in fact, so,' he said. 'To even the most haphazard assembly of objects one can bring order, and with a little ingenuity, sequence, so to speak. That is: one says to oneself mentally, "With a piece of soap I wash the dirt from a large white marble elephant which stands on a gate-legged table" – and so on.'

Mrs Hubbard said respectfully: 'Perhaps you could do the same thing with the list of things I've given you.'

'Undoubtedly I *could*. A lady with her right shoe on, puts a bracelet on her left arm. She then puts on powder and lipstick and goes down to dinner and drops her ring in the soup, and so on – I could thus commit your list to memory – but that is not what we are seeking. Why was such a haphazard collection of things stolen? Is there any system behind it? Some fixed idea of any kind? We have here primarily a process of analysis. The first thing to do is to study the list of objects very carefully.'

There was a silence whilst Poirot applied himself to study. Mrs Hubbard watched him with the rapt attention of a small boy watching a conjurer, waiting hopefully for a rabbit or at least streams of coloured ribbons to appear. Miss Lemon, unimpressed, withdrew into consideration of the finer points of the system.

When Poirot finally spoke, Mrs Hubbard jumped.

'The first thing that strikes me is this,' said Poirot. 'Of all these things that disappeared, most of them were of small value (some quite negligible) with the exception of two – a stethoscope and a diamond ring. Leaving the stethoscope aside for a moment, I should like to concentrate on the ring. You say a valuable ring – how valuable?'

'Well, I couldn't say exactly, M. Poirot. It was a solitaire diamond, with a cluster of small diamonds top and bottom. It had been Miss Lane's mother's engagement ring, I understand. She was most upset when it was missing, and we were all relieved when it turned up the same evening in Miss Hobhouse's plate of soup. Just a nasty practical joke, we thought.'

'And so it may have been. But I myself consider that its theft and return are significant. If a lipstick, or a powder compact or a book are missing – it is not sufficient to make you call in the police. But a valuable diamond ring is different. There is every chance that the police *will* be called in. So the ring is returned.'

'But why take it if you're going to return it?' said Miss Lemon, frowning.

'Why indeed,' said Poirot. 'But for the moment we will leave the questions. I am engaged now on classifying these thefts, and I am taking the ring first. Who is this Miss Lane from whom it was stolen?'

'Patricia Lane? She's a very nice girl. Going in for a what-do-you-call-it, a diploma in history or archaeology or something.'

'Well off?'

'Oh no. She's got a little money of her own, but she's very careful always. The ring, as I say, belonged to her mother. She has one or two nice bits of jewellery but she doesn't have many new clothes, and she's given up smoking lately.'

'What is she like? Describe her to me in your own words.'

'Well, she's sort of betwixt and between in colouring. Rather washed-out looking. Quiet and ladylike, but not much spirit to her. What you'd call rather a – well, an earnest type of girl.'

'And the ring turned up again in Miss Hobhouse's plate of soup. Who is Miss Hobhouse?'

'Valerie Hobhouse? She's a clever dark girl with rather a sarcastic way of talking. She works in a beauty parlour. Sabrina Fair – I suppose you have heard of it.'

'Are these two girls friendly?'

Mrs Hubbard considered.

'I should say so – yes. They don't have much to do with each other. Patricia gets on well with everybody, I should say, without being particularly popular or anything like that. Valerie Hobhouse has her enemies, her tongue being what it is – but she's got quite a following too, if you know what I mean.'

'I think I know,' said Poirot.

So Patricia Lane was nice but dull, and Valerie Hobhouse had personality. He resumed his study of the list of thefts.

'What is so intriguing is all the different categories represented here. There are the small trifles that would tempt a girl who was both vain and hard-up, the lipstick, the costume jewellery, a powder compact – bath salts – the box of chocolates, perhaps. Then we have the stethoscope, a more likely theft for a man who would know just where to sell it or pawn it. Who did it belong to?'

'It belonged to Mr Bateson – he's a big friendly young man.'

'A medical student?'

'Yes.'

'Was he very angry?'

'He was absolutely livid, M. Poirot. He's got one of those flaring up tempers – say anything at the time, but it's soon over. He's not the sort who'd take kindly to having his things pinched.'

'Does anyone?'

'Well, there's Mr Gopal Ram, one of our Indian students. He smiles at everything. He waves his hand and says material possessions do not matter –'

'Has anything been stolen from him?'

'No.'

'Ah! Who did the flannel trousers belong to?'

'Mr McNabb. Very old they were, and anyone else would say they were done for, but Mr McNabb is very attached to his old clothes and he never throws anything away.'

'So we have come to the things that it would seem were not worth stealing – old flannel trousers, electric light bulbs, boracic powder, bath salts – a cookery book. They may be important, more likely they are not. The boracic was probably removed by error, someone may have removed a dead bulb and intended to replace it, but forgot – the cookery book may have been borrowed and not returned. Some charwoman may have taken away the trousers.'

'We employ two very reliable cleaning women. I'm sure they would neither of them have done such a thing without asking first.'

'You may be right. Then there is the evening shoe, one of a new pair, I understand? Who do they belong to?'

'Sally Finch. She's an American girl studying over here on a Fulbright scholarship.'

'Are you sure that the shoe has not simply been mislaid? I cannot conceive what use one shoe could be to anyone.'

'It wasn't mislaid, M. Poirot. We all had a terrific hunt. You see Miss Finch was going out to a party in what she calls "formal dress" – evening dress to us – and the shoes were really vital – they were her only evening ones.'

'It caused her inconvenience – and annoyance – yes . . . yes, I wonder. Perhaps there is something there . . .'

He was silent for a moment or two and then went on.

'And there are two more items – a rucksack cut to pieces and a silk scarf in the same state. Here we have something that is neither vanity, nor profit – instead we have something that is deliberately vindictive. Who did the rucksack belong to?'

'Nearly all the students have rucksacks – they all hitch-hike a lot, you know. And a great many of the rucksacks are alike – bought at the same place, so it's hard to identify one from the other. But it seems fairly certain that this one belonged to Leonard Bateson or Colin McNabb.'

'And the silk scarf that was also cut about. To whom did that belong?'

'To Valerie Hobhouse. She had it as a Christmas present – it was emerald green and really good quality.'

'Miss Hobhouse . . . I see.'

Poirot closed his eyes. What he perceived mentally was a kaleidoscope, no more, no less. Pieces of cut-up scarves and rucksacks, cookery books, lipsticks, bath salts; names and thumbnail sketches of odd students. Nowhere was there cohesion or form. Unrelated incidents and people whirled round in space. But Poirot knew quite well that somehow and somewhere there must be a pattern . . . The question was where to start . . .

He opened his eyes.

'This is a matter that needs some reflection. A good deal of reflection.'

'Oh, I'm sure it does, M. Poirot,' assented Mrs Hubbard eagerly. 'And I'm sure I didn't want to trouble you –'

'You are not troubling me. I am intrigued. But whilst I am reflecting, we might make a start on the practical side. A start . . . The shoe, the evening shoe . . . yes, we might make a start there. Miss Lemon.'

'Yes, M. Poirot?' Miss Lemon banished filing from her thoughts, sat even more upright, and reached automatically for pad and pencil.

'Mrs Hubbard will obtain for you, perhaps, the remaining shoe. Then go to Baker Street Station, to the lost property department. The loss occurred – when?'

Mrs Hubbard considered.

'Well, I can't remember exactly now, M. Poirot. Perhaps two months ago. I can't get nearer than that. But I could find out from Sally Finch the date of the party.'

'Yes. Well—' He turned once more to Miss Lemon. 'You can be a little vague. You will say you left a shoe in an Inner Circle train – that is the most likely – or you may have left it in some other train. Or possibly a bus. How many buses serve the neighbourhood of Hickory Road?'

'Two only, M. Poirot.'

'Good. If you get no results from Baker Street, try Scotland Yard and say it was left in a taxi.'

'Lambeth,' corrected Miss Lemon efficiently.

Poirot waved a hand.

'You always know these things.'

'But why do you think –' began Mrs Hubbard.

Poirot interrupted her.

'Let us see first what results we get. Then, if they are negative or positive, you and I, Mrs Hubbard, must consult again. You will tell me then those things which it is necessary that I should know.'

'I really think I've told you everything I can.'

'No, no. I disagree. Here we have young people herded together, of varying temperaments, of different sexes. A loves B, but B loves C, and D and E are at daggers drawn because of A perhaps. It is all *that* I need to know. The interplay of human emotions. The quarrels, the jealousies, the friendships, the malice and all uncharitableness.'

'I'm sure,' said Mrs Hubbard uncomfortably, 'I don't know anything about *that* sort of thing. I don't mix at all. I just run the place and see to the catering and all that.'

'But you are interested in people. You have told me so. You like young people. You took this post, not because it was of much interest financially, but because it would bring you in contact with human problems. There will be those of the students that you like and some that you do not like so well, or indeed at all, perhaps. You will tell me – yes, you will tell me! Because you are worried – not about what has been happening – you could go to the police about that –'

'Mrs Nicoletis wouldn't like to have the police in, I assure you.'
Poirot swept on, disregarding the interruption.

'No, you are worried about *someone* – someone who you think may have been responsible or at least mixed up in this. Someone, therefore, that you like.'

'Really, M. Poirot.'

'Yes, really. And I think you are right to be worried. For that silk scarf cut to pieces, it is not nice. And the slashed rucksack, that also is not nice. For the rest it seems childishness – and yet – I am not sure. I am not sure at all!'

CHAPTER 3

Hurrying a little as she went up the steps, Mrs Hubbard inserted her latch key into the door of 26 Hickory Road. Just as the door opened, a big young man with fiery red hair ran up the steps behind her.

'Hallo, Ma,' he said, for in such a fashion did Len Bateson usually address her. He was a friendly soul, with a Cockney accent and mercifully free from any kind of inferiority complex. 'Been out gallivanting?'

'I've been out to tea, Mr Bateson. Don't delay me now, I'm late.'

'I cut up a lovely corpse today,' said Len. 'Smashing!'

'Don't be so horrid, you nasty boy. A lovely corpse, indeed! The idea. You make me feel quite squeamish.'

Len Bateson laughed, and the hall echoed the sound in a great ha ha.

'Nothing to Celia,' he said. 'I went along to the Dispensary. "Come to tell you about a corpse," I said. She went as white as a sheet and I thought she was going to pass out. What do you think of that, Mother Hubbard?'

'I don't wonder at it,' said Mrs Hubbard. 'The idea! Celia probably thought you meant a *real* one.'

'What do you mean – a real one? What do you think our corpses are? Synthetic?'

A thin young man with long untidy hair strolled out of a room on the right, and said in a waspish way:

'Oh, it's only *you*. I thought it was at least a *posse* of strong men. The voice is but the voice of one man, but the volume is as the volume of ten.'

'Hope it doesn't get on your nerves, I'm sure.'

'Not more than usual,' said Nigel Chapman and went back again.

'Our delicate flower,' said Len.

'Now don't you two scrap,' said Mrs Hubbard. 'Good temper, that's what I like, and a bit of give and take.'

The big young man grinned down at her affectionately.

'I don't mind our Nigel, Ma,' he said.

'Oh, Mrs Hubbard, Mrs Nicoletis is in her room and said she would like to see you as soon as you got back.'

Mrs Hubbard sighed and started up the stairs. The tall dark girl who had given the message stood against the wall to let her pass.

Len Bateson, divesting himself of his mackintosh said, 'What's up, Valerie? Complaints of our behaviour to be passed on by Mother Hubbard in due course?'

The girl shrugged her thin elegant shoulders. She came down the stairs and across the hall. 'This place gets more like a madhouse every day,' she said over her shoulder.

She went through the door at the right as she spoke. She moved with that insolent effortless grace that is common to those who have been professional mannequins.

Twenty-six Hickory Road was in reality two houses, 24 and 26 semi-detached. They had been thrown into one on the ground floor so that there was both a communal sitting-room and a large dining-room on the ground floor, as well as two cloak-rooms and a small office towards the back of the house. Two separate staircases led to the floors above which remained detached. The girls occupied bedrooms in the right-hand side of the house, and the men on the other, the original No. 24.

Mrs Hubbard went upstairs loosening the collar of her coat. She sighed as she turned in the direction of Mrs Nicoletis's room.

She tapped on the door and entered.

'In one of her states again, I suppose,' she muttered.

Mrs Nicoletis's sitting-room was kept very hot. The big electric fire had all its bars turned on and the window was tightly shut. Mrs Nicoletis was sitting smoking on a sofa surrounded by a lot of rather dirty silk and velvet sofa cushions. She was a big dark woman, still good-looking, with a bad-tempered mouth and enormous brown eyes.

'Ah! So there you are.' Mrs Nicoletis made it sound like an accusation.

Mrs Hubbard, true to her Lemon blood, was unperturbed.

'Yes,' she said tartly, 'I'm here. I was told you wanted to see me specially.'

'Yes, indeed I do. It is monstrous, no less, monstrous!'

'What's monstrous?'

'These bills! Your accounts!' Mrs Nicoletis produced a sheaf of papers from beneath a cushion in the manner of a successful conjuror. 'What are we feeding these miserable students on? *Foie gras* and quails? Is this the Ritz? Who do they think they are, these students?'

'Young people with a healthy appetite,' said Mrs Hubbard. 'They get a good breakfast and a decent evening meal – plain food but nourishing. It all works out very economically.'

'Economically? Economically? You dare to say that to me? When I am being ruined?'

'You make a very substantial profit, Mrs Nicoletis, out of this place. For students, the rates are on the high side.'

'But am I not always full? Do I ever have a vacancy that is not applied for three times over? Am I not sent students by the British Council, by London University Lodging Board – by the Embassies – by the French Lycée? Are not there always three applications for every vacancy?'

'That's very largely because the meals here are appetising and sufficient. Young people must be properly fed.'

'Bah! These totals are scandalous. It is that Italian cook and her husband. They swindle you over the food.'

'Oh no, they don't, Mrs Nicoletis. I can assure you that no foreigner is going to put anything over on *me*.'

'Then it is you yourself – you who are robbing me.'

Mrs Hubbard remained unperturbed.

'I can't allow you to say things like that,' she said, in the voice an old-fashioned Nanny might have used to a particularly truculent charge. 'It isn't a nice thing to do, and one of these days it will land you in trouble.'

'Ah!' Mrs Nicoletis threw the sheaf of bills dramatically up in the air whence they fluttered to the ground in all directions. Mrs Hubbard bent and picked them up, pursing her lips. 'You enrage me,' shouted her employer.

'I dare say,' said Mrs Hubbard, 'but it's bad for you, you know, getting all worked up. Tempers are bad for the blood pressure.'

'You admit that these totals are higher than those of last week?'

'Of course they are. There's been some very good cut price stuff going at Lampson's Stores. I've taken advantage of it. Next week's totals will be below average.'

Mrs Nicoletis looked sulky.

'You explain everything so plausibly.'

'There.' Mrs Hubbard put the bills in a neat pile on the table. 'Anything else?'

'The American girl, Sally Finch, she talks of leaving – I do not want her to go. She is a Fulbright scholar. She will bring here other Fulbright scholars. She must not leave.'

'What's her reason for leaving?'

Mrs Nicoletis humped monumental shoulders.

'How can I remember? It was not genuine. I could tell *that*. I always know.'

Mrs Hubbard nodded thoughtfully. She was inclined to believe Mrs Nicoletis on that point.

'Sally hasn't said anything to me,' she said.

'But you will talk to her?'

'Yes, of course.'

'And if it is these coloured students, these Indians, these Negresses – then they can all go, you understand? The colour bar, it means everything to these Americans – and for me it is the Americans that matter – as for these coloured ones – scram!'

She made a dramatic gesture.

'Not while I'm in charge,' said Mrs Hubbard coldly. 'And anyway, you're wrong. There's no feeling of that sort here amongst the students, and Sally certainly isn't like that. She and Mr Akibombo have lunch together quite often, and nobody could be blacker than he is.'

'Then it is Communists – you know what the Americans are about Communists. Nigel Chapman now – *he* is a Communist.'

'I doubt it.'

'Yes, yes. You should have heard what he was saying the other evening.'

'Nigel will say anything to annoy people. He is very tiresome that way.'

'You know them all so well. Dear Mrs Hubbard, you are wonderful! I say to myself again and again – what should I do without Mrs Hubbard? I rely on you *utterly*. You are a wonderful, wonderful woman.'

'After the powder, the jam,' said Mrs Hubbard.

'What is that?'

'Don't worry. I'll do what I can.'

She left the room, cutting short a gushing speech of thanks.

Muttering to herself: 'Wasting my time – what a maddening woman she is!' she hurried along the passage and into her own sitting-room.

But there was to be no peace for Mrs Hubbard as yet. A tall figure rose to her feet as Mrs Hubbard entered and said:

'I should be glad to speak to you for a few minutes, please.'

'Of course, Elizabeth.'

Mrs Hubbard was rather surprised. Elizabeth Johnston was a girl from the West Indies who was studying law. She was a hard worker, ambitious, who kept very much to herself. She had always seemed particularly well balanced and competent, and Mrs Hubbard had always regarded her as one of the most satisfactory students in the hostel.

She was perfectly controlled now, but Mrs Hubbard caught the slight tremor in her voice although the dark features were quite impassive.

'Is something the matter?'

'Yes. Will you come with me to my room, please?'

'Just a moment.' Mrs Hubbard threw off her coat and gloves and then followed the girl out of the room and up the next flight of stairs. The girl had a room on the top floor. She opened the door and went across to a table near the window.

'Here are the notes of my work,' she said. 'This represents several months of hard study. You see what has been done?'

Mrs Hubbard caught her breath with a slight gasp.

Ink had been spilled on the table. It had run all over the papers, soaking them through. Mrs Hubbard touched it with her fingertip. It was still wet.

She said, knowing the question to be foolish as she asked it:

'You didn't spill the ink yourself?'

'No. It was done whilst I was out.'

'Mrs Biggs, do you think –'

Mrs Biggs was the cleaning woman who looked after the top-floor bedrooms.

'It was not Mrs Biggs. It was not even my own ink. That is here on the shelf by my bed. It has not been touched. It was done by someone who brought ink here and did it deliberately.'

Mrs Hubbard was shocked.

'What a very wicked – and cruel thing to do.'

'Yes, it is a bad thing.'

The girl spoke quietly, but Mrs Hubbard did not make the mistake of underrating her feelings.

'Well, Elizabeth, I hardly know what to say. I am shocked, badly shocked, and I shall do my utmost to find out who did this wicked malicious thing. You've no ideas yourself as to that?'

The girl replied at once.

'This is green ink, you saw that.'

'Yes, I noticed that.'

'It is not very common, this green ink. I know one person here who uses it. Nigel Chapman.'

'Nigel? Do you think Nigel would do a thing like that?'

'I should not have thought so – no. But he writes his letters and his notes with green ink.'

'I shall have to ask a lot of questions. I'm very sorry, Elizabeth, that such a thing should happen in this house and I can only tell you that I shall do my best to get to the bottom of it.'

'Thank you, Mrs Hubbard. There have been – other things, have there not?'

'Yes – er – yes.'

Mrs Hubbard left the room and started towards the stairs. But she stopped suddenly before proceeding down and instead went along the passage to a door at the end of the corridor. She knocked and the voice of Miss Sally Finch bade her enter.

The room was a pleasant one and Sally Finch herself, a cheerful redhead, was a pleasant person.

She was writing on a pad and looked up with a bulging cheek. She held out an open box of sweets and said indistinctly:

'Candy from home. Have some.'

'Thank you, Sally. Not just now. I'm rather upset.' She paused. 'Have you heard what's happened to Elizabeth Johnston?'

'What's happened to Black Bess?'

The nickname was an affectionate one and had been accepted as such by the girl herself.

Mrs Hubbard described what had happened. Sally showed every sign of sympathetic anger.

'I'll say that's a mean thing to do. I wouldn't believe anyone would do a thing like that to our Bess. Everybody likes her. She's quiet and doesn't get around much, or join in, but I'm sure there's no one who dislikes her.'

'That's what I should have said.'

'Well, it's all of a piece, isn't it, with the other things? That's why –'

'That's why what?' Mrs Hubbard asked as the girl stopped abruptly.

Sally said slowly:

'That's why I'm getting out of here. Did Mrs Nick tell you?'

'Yes. She was very upset about it. Seemed to think you hadn't given her the real reason.'

'Well, I didn't. No point in making her go up in smoke. You know what she's like. But that's the reason, right enough. I just don't like what's going on here. It was odd losing my shoe, and then Valerie's scarf being all cut to bits and Len's rucksack . . . it wasn't so much things being pinched – after all, that may happen any time – it's not nice but it's roughly normal – but this other *isn't*.' She paused for a moment, smiling, and then suddenly grinned. 'Akibombo's scared,' she said. 'He's always very superior and civilised – but there's a good old West African belief in magic very close to the surface.'

'Tchah!' said Mrs Hubbard crossly. 'I've no patience with superstitious nonsense. Just some ordinary human being making a nuisance of themselves. That's all there is to it.'

Sally's mouth curved up in a wide cat-like grin.

'The emphasis,' she said, 'is on *ordinary*. I've a sort of feeling that there's a person in this house who isn't ordinary.'

Mrs Hubbard went on down the stairs. She turned into the students' common-room on the ground floor. There were four people in the room. Valerie Hobhouse, prone on a sofa with her narrow, elegant feet stuck up over the arm of it; Nigel Chapman sitting at a table with a heavy book open in front of him; Patricia Lane leaning against the mantelpiece, and a girl in a mackintosh who had just come in and who was pulling off a woolly cap as Mrs Hubbard entered. She was a stocky, fair girl with brown eyes set wide apart and a mouth that was usually just a little open so that she seemed perpetually startled.

Valerie, removing a cigarette from her mouth, said in a lazy, drawling voice:

'Hallo, Ma, have you administered soothing syrup to the old devil, our revered proprietress?'

Patricia Lane said:

'Has she been on the warpath?'

'And how?' said Valerie and chuckled.

'Something very unpleasant has happened,' said Mrs Hubbard. 'Nigel, I want you to help me.'

'Me, ma'am?' Nigel looked at her and shut his book. His thin, malicious face was suddenly illuminated by a mischievous but surprisingly sweet smile. 'What have I done?'

'Nothing, I hope,' said Mrs Hubbard. 'But ink has been deliberately and maliciously spilt all over Elizabeth Johnston's notes, and it's green ink. You write with green ink, Nigel.'

He stared at her, his smile disappearing.

'Yes, I use green ink.'

'Horrid stuff,' said Patricia. 'I wish you wouldn't, Nigel. I've always told you I think it's horribly affected of you.'

'I like being affected,' said Nigel. 'Lilac ink would be even better, I think. I must try and get some. But are you serious, Mum? About the sabotage, I mean?'

'Yes, I *am* serious. Was it your doing, Nigel?'

'No, of course not. I like annoying people, as you know, but I'd never do a filthy trick like that – and certainly not to Black Bess who minds her own business in a way that's an example to some people I could mention. Where is that ink of mine? I filled my pen yesterday evening, I remember. I usually keep it on the shelf over there.' He sprang up and went across the room. 'You're right. The bottle's nearly empty. It should be practically full.'

The girl in the mackintosh gave a little gasp.

'Oh dear,' she said. 'Oh dear, I don't like it –'

Nigel wheeled at her accusingly.

'Have you got an alibi, Celia?' he said menacingly.

The girl gave a gasp.

'I didn't do it. I really didn't do it. Anyway, I've been at the hospital all day. I couldn't –'

'Now, Nigel,' said Mrs Hubbard. 'Don't tease Celia.'

Patricia Lane said angrily:

'I don't see why Nigel should be suspected. Just because *his* ink was taken –'

Valerie said cattishly:

'That's right, darling, defend your young.'

'But it's so unfair –'

'But really *I* didn't have anything to do with it,' Celia protested earnestly.

'Nobody thinks you did, infant,' said Valerie impatiently. 'All the same, you know,' her eyes met Mrs Hubbard's and exchanged a glance, 'all this is getting beyond a joke. Something will have to be done about it.'

'Something is going to be done,' said Mrs Hubbard grimly.

CHAPTER 4

'Here you are, M. Poirot.'

Miss Lemon laid a small brown paper parcel before Poirot. He removed the paper and looked appraisingly at a well-cut silver evening shoe.

'It was at Baker Street just as you said.'

'That has saved us trouble,' said Poirot. 'Also it confirms my ideas.'

'Quite,' said Miss Lemon, who was sublimely incurious by nature.

She was, however, susceptible to the claims of family affection. She said:

'If it is not troubling you too much, M. Poirot, I received a letter from my sister. There have been some new developments.'

'You permit that I read it?'

She handed it to him and, after reading it, he directed Miss Lemon to get her sister on the telephone. Presently Miss Lemon indicated that the connection had been obtained. Poirot took the receiver.

'Mrs Hubbard?'

'Oh yes, M. Poirot. So kind of you to ring me up so promptly. I was really very –'

Poirot interrupted her.

'Where are you speaking from?'

'Why – from 26 Hickory Road, of course. Oh I see what you mean. I am in my own sitting-room.'

'There is an extension?'

'This is the extension. The main phone is downstairs in the hall.'

'Who is in the house who might listen in?'

'All the students are out at this time of day. The cook is out marketing. Geronimo, her husband, understands very little English. There is a cleaning woman, but she is deaf and I'm quite sure wouldn't bother to listen in.'

'Very good, then. I can speak freely. Do you occasionally have lectures in the evening, or films? Entertainments of some kind?'

'We do have lectures occasionally. Miss Baltrout, the explorer, came not long ago, with her coloured transparencies. And we had an appeal for Far Eastern Missions, though I am afraid that quite a lot of the students went out that night.'

'Ah. Then this evening you will have prevailed on M. Hercule Poirot, the employer of your sister, to come and discourse to your students on the more interesting of his cases.'

'That will be very nice, I'm sure, but do you think –'

'It is not a question of *thinking*. I am sure!'

That evening, students entering the common-room found a notice tacked up on the board which stood just inside the door.

M. Hercule Poirot, the celebrated private detective, has kindly consented to give a talk this evening on the theory and practice

*of successful detection, with an account of certain celebrated
criminal cases.*

Returning students made varied comments on this.

'Who's this private eye?' 'Never heard of him.' 'Oh, I have. There was a man condemned to death for the murder of a charwoman and this detective got him off at the last moment by finding the real person.' 'Sounds crummy to me.' 'I think it might be rather fun.' 'Colin ought to enjoy it. He's mad on criminal psychology.' 'I would not put it precisely like that, but I'll not deny that a man who has been closely acquainted with criminals might be interesting to interrogate.'

Dinner was at seven-thirty and most of the students were already seated when Mrs Hubbard came down from her sitting-room (where sherry had been served to the distinguished guest) followed by a small elderly man with suspiciously black hair and a moustache of ferocious proportions which he twirled continuously.

'These are some of our students, M. Poirot. This is M. Hercule Poirot who is kindly going to talk to us after dinner.'

Salutations were exchanged and Poirot sat down by Mrs Hubbard and busied himself with keeping his moustaches out of the excellent minestrone which was served by a small active Italian manservant from a big tureen.

This was followed by a piping hot dish of spaghetti and meat balls and it was then that a girl sitting on Poirot's right spoke shyly to him.

'Does Mrs Hubbard's sister really work for you?'

Poirot turned to her.

'But yes indeed. Miss Lemon has been my secretary for many years. She is the most efficient woman that ever lived. I am sometimes afraid of her.'

'Oh I see. I wondered –'

'Now what did you wonder, mademoiselle?'

He smiled upon her in paternal fashion, making a mental note as he did so.

'*Pretty, worried, not too quick mentally, frightened . . .*' He said:

'May I know your name and what it is you are studying?'

'Celia Austin. I don't study. I'm a dispenser at St Catherine's Hospital.'

'Ah, that is interesting work?'

'Well, I don't know – perhaps it is.' She sounded rather uncertain.

'And these others? Can you tell me something about them, perhaps? I understood this was a home for foreign students, but these seem mostly to be English.'

'Some of the foreign ones are out. Mr Chandra Lal and Mr Gopal Ram – they're Indians – and Miss Reinjeer who's Dutch – and Mr Achmed Ali who's Egyptian and frightfully political!'

'And those who are here? Tell me about these.'

'Well, sitting on Mrs Hubbard's left is Nigel Chapman. He's studying Medieval History and Italian at London University. Then there's Patricia Lane next to him, with the spectacles. She's taking a diploma in Archaeology. The big red-headed boy is Len Bateson, he's a medical and the dark girl is Valerie Hobhouse, she's in a beauty shop. Next to her is Colin McNabb – he's doing a post-graduate course in Psychiatry.'

There was a faint change in her voice as she described Colin. Poirot glanced keenly at her and saw that the colour had come up in her face.

He said to himself:

'So – she is in love and she cannot easily conceal the fact.'

He noticed that young McNabb never seemed to look at her across the table, being far too much taken up with his conversation with a laughing red-headed girl beside him.

'That's Sally Finch. She's American – over here on a Fulbright. Then there's Genevieve Maricaud. She's doing English, and so is René Halle who sits next to her. The small fair girl is Jean Tomlinson – she's at St Catherine's too. She's a physiotherapist. The black man is Akibombo – he comes from West Africa and he's frightfully nice. Then there's Elizabeth Johnston, she's from Jamaica and she's studying law. Next to us on my right are two Turkish students who came about a week ago. They know hardly any English.'

'Thank you. And do you all get on well together? Or do you have quarrels?'

The lightness of his tone robbed the words of seriousness.

Celia said:

'Oh, we're all too busy really to have fights – although –'

'Although what, Miss Austin?'

'Well – Nigel – next to Mrs Hubbard. He likes stirring people up and making them angry. And Len Bateson *gets* angry. He gets wild with rage sometimes. But he's very sweet really.'

'And Colin McNabb – does he too get annoyed?'

'Oh no. Colin just raises his eyebrows and looks amused.'

'I see. And the young ladies, do you have your quarrels?'

'Oh no, we all get on very well. Genevieve has feelings sometimes. I think French people are inclined to be touchy – oh, I mean – I'm sorry –'

Celia was the picture of confusion.

'Me, I am Belgian,' said Poirot solemnly. He went on quickly, before Celia could recover control of herself: 'What did you mean just now, Miss Austin, when you said that you wondered. You wondered – what?'

She crumbled her bread nervously.

'Oh that – nothing – nothing really – just, there have been some silly practical jokes lately – I thought Mrs Hubbard – But really it was silly of me. I didn't mean anything.'

Poirot did not press her. He turned away to Mrs Hubbard and was presently engaged in a three-cornered conversation with her and with Nigel Chapman, who introduced the controversial challenge that crime was a form of creative art – and that the misfits of society were really the police who only entered that profession because of their secret sadism. Poirot was amused to note that the anxious-looking young woman in spectacles who sat beside him tried desperately to explain away his remarks as fast as he made them. Nigel, however, took absolutely no notice of her.

Mrs Hubbard looked benignly amused.

'All you young people nowadays think of nothing but politics and psychology,' she said. 'When I was a girl we were much more lighthearted. We danced. If you rolled back the carpet in the common-room there's quite a good floor, and you could dance to the wireless, but you never do.'

Celia laughed and said with a tinge of malice:

'But you used to dance, Nigel. I've danced with you myself once, though I don't expect you remember.'

'You've danced with *me*,' said Nigel incredulously. 'Where?'

'At Cambridge – in May Week.'

'Oh, May Week!' Nigel waved away the follies of youth.

'One goes through that adolescent phase. Mercifully it soon passes.'

Nigel was clearly not much more than twenty-five now. Poirot concealed a smile in his moustache.

Patricia Lane said earnestly:

'You see, Mrs Hubbard, there is so much study to be done. With lectures to attend and one's notes to write up, there's really not time for anything but what is really worth while.'

'Well, my dear, one's only young once,' said Mrs Hubbard.

A chocolate pudding succeeded the spaghetti and afterwards they all went into the common-room, and helped themselves to coffee from an urn that stood on a table. Poirot was then invited to begin his discourse. The two Turks politely excused themselves. The rest seated themselves and looked expectant.

Poirot rose to his feet and spoke with his usual aplomb. The sound of his own voice was always pleasant to him, and he spoke for three-quarters of an hour in a light and amusing fashion, recalling those of his experiences that lent themselves to an agreeable exaggeration. If he managed to suggest, in a subtle fashion, that he was, perhaps, something of a mountebank, it was not too obviously contrived.

'And so, you see,' he finished, 'I say to this city gentleman that I am reminded of a soap manufacturer I knew in Liége who poisoned his wife in order to marry a beautiful blonde secretary. I say it very lightly but at once I get a reaction. He presses upon me the stolen money I had just recovered for him. He goes pale and there is fear in his eyes. "I will give this money," I say, "to a deserving charity." "Do anything you like with it," he says. And I say to him then, and I say it very significantly, "It will be advisable, monsieur, to be *very* careful." He nods, speechless, and as I go out, I see that he wipes his forehead. He has had the big fright, and I – I have saved his life. For though he is infatuated with his blonde secretary he will not now try and poison his stupid and disagreeable wife. Prevention, always, is better than cure. We want to prevent murders – not wait until they have been committed.'

He bowed and spread out his hands.

'There, I have wearied you long enough.'

The students clapped him vigorously. Poirot bowed. And then, as he was about to sit down, Colin McNabb took his pipe from between his teeth and observed:

'And now, perhaps, you'll talk about what you're really here for!'

There was a momentary silence and then Patricia said reproachfully, 'Colin.'

'Well, we can guess, can't we?' He looked round scornfully. 'M. Poirot's given us a very amusing little talk, but that's not what he came here for. He's on the job. You don't really think, M. Poirot, that we're not wise to *that*?'

'You speak for yourself, Colin,' said Sally.

'It's true, isn't it?' said Colin.

Again Poirot spread out his hands in a graceful acknowledging gesture.

'I will admit,' he said, 'that my kind hostess has confided to me that certain events have caused her – worry.'

Len Bateson got up, his face heavy and truculent.

'Look here,' he said, 'what's all this? Has this been planted on us?'

'Have you really only just tumbled to *that*, Bateson?' asked Nigel sweetly.

Celia gave a frightened gasp and said: Then I *was* right!'

Mrs Hubbard spoke with decisive authority.

'I asked M. Poirot to give us a talk, but I also wanted to ask his advice about various things that have happened lately. Something's got to be done and it seemed to me that the only other alternative is – the police.'

At once a violent altercation broke out. Genevieve burst into heated French. 'It was a disgrace, shameful, to go to the police!' Other voices chimed in, for or against. In a final lull Leonard Bateson's voice was raised with decision.

'Let's hear what M. Poirot has to say about our trouble.'

Mrs Hubbard said:

'I've given M. Poirot all the facts. If he wants to ask any questions, I'm sure none of you will object.'

Poirot bowed to her.

'Thank you.' With the air of a conjurer he brought out a pair of evening shoes and handed them to Sally Finch.

'Your shoes, mademoiselle?'

'Why – yes – *both* of them? Where did the missing one come from?'

'From the Lost Property Office at Baker Street Station.'

'But what made you think it might be there, M. Poirot?'

'A very simple process of deduction. Someone takes a shoe from your room. Why? Not to wear and not to sell. And since the house will be searched by everyone to try and find it, then the shoe must be got out of the house, or destroyed. But it is not so easy to destroy a shoe. The easiest way is to take it in a bus or train in a parcel in the rush hour and leave it thrust down under a seat. That was my first guess and it proved right – so I knew that I was on safe ground – the shoe was taken, as your poet says, "to annoy, because he knows it teases."'

Valerie gave a short laugh.

'That points to you, Nigel, my love, with an unerring finger.'

Nigel said, smirking a little, 'If the shoe fits, wear it.'

'Nonsense,' said Sally. 'Nigel didn't take my shoe.'

'Of course he didn't,' said Patricia angrily. 'It's the most absurd idea.'

'I don't know about absurd,' said Nigel. 'Actually I didn't do anything of the kind – as no doubt we shall all say.'

It was as though Poirot had been waiting for just those words as an actor waits for his cue. His eyes rested thoughtfully on Len Bateson's flushed face, then they swept inquiringly over the rest of the students.

He said, using his hands in a deliberately foreign gesture:

'My position is delicate. I am a guest here. I have come at the invitation of Mrs Hubbard – to spend a pleasant evening, that is all. And also, of course, to return a very charming pair of shoes to mademoiselle. For anything further –' he paused. 'Monsieur – Bateson? yes, Bateson – has asked me to say what I myself think of this – trouble. But it would be an impertinence for me to speak unless I were invited so to do not by one person alone, but by you all.'

Mr Akibombo was seen to nod his black curled head in vigorous asseveration.

'That is very correct procedure, yes,' he said. 'True democratic proceeding is to put matter to the voting of all present.'

The voice of Sally Finch rose impatiently.

'Oh, shucks,' she said. 'This is a kind of party, all friends together. Let's hear what M. Poirot advises without any more fuss.'

'I couldn't agree with you more, Sally,' said Nigel.

Poirot bowed his head.

'Very well,' he said. 'Since you all ask me this question, I reply that my advice is quite simple. Mrs Hubbard – or Mrs Nicoletis rather – should call in the police *at once*. No time should be lost.'

CHAPTER 5

There was no doubt that Poirot's statement was unexpected. It caused not a ripple of protest or comment, but a sudden and uncomfortable silence.

Under cover of that momentary paralysis, Poirot was taken by Mrs Hubbard up to her own sitting-room, with only a quick polite 'Good night to you all,' to herald his departure.

Mrs Hubbard switched on the light, closed the door, and begged M. Poirot to take the arm-chair by the fireplace. Her nice good-humoured face was puckered with doubt and anxiety. She offered her guest a cigarette, but Poirot refused politely, explaining that he preferred his own. He offered her one, but she refused, saying in an abstracted tone: 'I don't smoke, M. Poirot.'

Then, as she sat down opposite him, she said, after a momentary hesitation:

'I dare say you're right, M. Poirot. Perhaps we *should* get the police in on this – especially after this malicious ink business. But I rather wish you hadn't said so – right out like that.'

'Ah,' said Poirot, as he lit one of his tiny cigarettes and watched the smoke ascend. 'You think I should have dissembled?'

'Well, I suppose it's nice to be fair and above board about things – but it seems to me it might have been better to keep quiet, and just ask an officer to come round and explain things privately to him. What I mean is, whoever's been doing these stupid things – well, that person's warned now.'

'Perhaps, yes.'

'I should say quite certainly,' said Mrs Hubbard, rather sharply. 'No perhaps about it! Even if he's one of the servants or a student who wasn't here this evening, the word will get around. It always does.'

'So true. It always does.'

'And there's Mrs Nicoletis, too. I really don't know what attitude she'll take up. One never does know with her.'

'It will be interesting to find out.'

'Naturally we can't call in the police unless she agrees – oh, who's that now?'

There had been a sharp authoritative tap on the door. It was repeated and almost before Mrs Hubbard had called an irritable 'Come in,' the door opened and Colin McNabb, his pipe clenched firmly between his teeth and a scowl on his face, entered the room.

Removing the pipe, and closing the door behind him, he said:

'You'll excuse me, but I was anxious to just have a word with M. Poirot here.'

'With me?' Poirot turned his head in innocent surprise.

'Ay, with you.' Colin spoke grimly.

He drew up a rather uncomfortable chair and sat squarely on it facing Hercule Poirot.

'You've given us an amusing talk tonight,' he said indulgently. 'And I'll not deny that you're a man who's had a varied and lengthy experience, but if you'll excuse me for saying so, your methods and your ideas are both equally antiquated.'

'Really, Colin,' said Mrs Hubbard, colouring. 'You're extremely rude.'

'I'm not meaning to give offence, but I've got to make things clear. Crime and Punishment, M. Poirot – that's as far as your horizon stretches.'

'They seem to me a natural sequence,' said Poirot.

'You take the narrow view of the Law – and what's more, of the Law at its most old-fashioned. Nowadays, even the Law has to keep itself cognisant of the newest and most up-to-date theories of what *causes* crime. It is the *causes* that are important, M. Poirot.'

'But there,' cried Poirot, 'to speak in your new-fashioned phrase, I could not agree with you more!'

'Then you've got to consider the *cause* of what has been happening in this house – you've got to find out *why* these things have been done.'

'But I am still agreeing with you – yes, that is most important.'

'Because there always is a reason, and it may be, to the person concerned, a very good reason.'

At this point Mrs Hubbard, unable to contain herself, interjected sharply, 'Rubbish.'

'That's where you're wrong,' said Colin, turning slightly towards her. 'You've got to take into account the psychological background.'

'Psychological balderdash,' said Mrs Hubbard. 'I've no patience with all that sort of talk!'

'That's because you know precisely nothing about it,' said Colin, in a gravely rebuking fashion. He returned his gaze to Poirot.

'I'm interested in these subjects. I am at present taking a post-graduate course in psychiatry and psychology. We come across the most involved and astounding cases and what I'm pointing out to you, M. Poirot, is that you can't just dismiss the criminal with a doctrine of original sin, or wilful disregard of the laws of the land. You've got to have an understanding of the root of the trouble if you're ever to effect a cure of the young delinquent. These ideas were not known or thought of in your day and I've no doubt you find them hard to accept –'

'Stealing's stealing,' put in Mrs Hubbard stubbornly.

Colin frowned impatiently.

Poirot said meekly:

'My ideas are doubtless old-fashioned, but I am perfectly prepared to listen to you, Mr McNabb.'

Colin looked agreeably surprised.

'That's very fairly said, M. Poirot. Now I'll try to make this matter clear to you, using very simple terms.'

'Thank you,' said Poirot meekly.

'For convenience's sake, I'll start with the pair of shoes you brought with you tonight and returned to Sally Finch. If you remember, *one* shoe was stolen. Only *one*.'

'I remember being struck by the fact,' said Poirot.

Colin McNabb leaned forward; his dour but handsome features were lit up by eagerness.

'Ah, but you didn't see the *significance* of it. It's one of the prettiest and most satisfying examples anyone could wish to come across. We have here, very definitely, a *Cinderella complex*. You are maybe acquainted with the Cinderella fairy story.'

'Of French origin – *mais oui*.'

'Cinderella, the unpaid drudge, sits by the fire; her sisters, dressed in their finery, go to the Prince's ball. A Fairy Godmother sends Cinderella too, to that ball. At the stroke of midnight, her finery turns back to rags – she escapes hurriedly, leaving behind her *one slipper*. So here we have a mind that compares itself to Cinderella (unconsciously, of course). Here we have frustration, envy, the sense of inferiority. The girl steals a slipper. Why?'

'A girl?'

'But naturally, a girl. That,' said Colin reprovingly, 'should be clear to the meanest intelligence.'

'Really, Colin!' said Mrs Hubbard.

'Pray continue,' said Poirot courteously.

'Probably she herself *does not know why she does it* – but the *inner* wish is clear. She wants to be the Princess, to be identified by the Prince and claimed by him. Another significant fact, the slipper is stolen from an attractive girl *who is going to a ball*.'

Colin's pipe had long since gone out. He waved it now with mounting enthusiasm.

'And now we'll take a few of the other happenings. A magpie acquiring of pretty things – all things associated with attractive femininity. A powder compact, lipsticks, ear-rings, a bracelet, a ring – there is a two-fold significance here. The girl wants to be *noticed*. She wants, even, to be *punished* – as is frequently the case with very young juvenile delinquents. These things are none of them what you could call ordinary criminal thefts. It is not the *value* of these things that is wanted. In just such a way do well-to-do women go into department stores and steal things they could perfectly well afford to pay for.'

'Nonsense,' said Mrs Hubbard belligerently. 'Some people are just plain dishonest, that's all there is to it.'

'Yet a diamond ring of some value was amongst the things stolen,' said Poirot, ignoring Mrs Hubbard's interpolation.

'That was returned.'

'And surely, Mr McNabb, you would not say that a stethoscope is a feminine pretty pretty?'

'That had a deeper significance. Women who feel they are deficient in feminine attraction can find sublimation in the pursuit of a career.'

'And the cookery book?'

'A symbol of home life, husband and family.'

'And boracic powder?'

Colin said irritably:

'My dear M. Poirot. *Nobody* would steal boracic powder! Why should they?'

'This is what I have asked myself. I must admit, M. McNabb, that you seem to have an answer for everything. Explain to me, then, the significance of the disappearance of an old pair of flannel trousers – *your* flannel trousers, I understand.'

For the first time Colin appeared ill at ease. He blushed and cleared his throat.

'I could explain that – but it would be somewhat involved, and perhaps – er well, rather embarrassing.'

'Ah, you spare my blushes.'

Suddenly Poirot leaned forward and tapped the young man on the knee.

'And the ink that is spilt over another student's papers, the silk scarf that is cut and slashed. Do these things cause you no disquietude?'

The complacence and superiority of Colin's manner underwent a sudden and not unlikeable change.

'They do,' he said. 'Believe me, they do. It's serious. She ought to have treatment – *at once*. But *medical* treatment, that's the point. It's not a case for the police. She's all tied up in knots. If I . . .'

Poirot interrupted him.

'You know then who she is?'

'Well, I have a very strong suspicion.'

Poirot murmured with the air of one who is recapitulating:

'A girl who is not outstandingly successful with the other sex. A shy girl. An affectionate girl. A girl whose brain is inclined to be slow in its reactions. A girl who feels frustrated and lonely. A girl . . .'

There was a tap on the door. Poirot broke off. The tap was repeated.

'Come in,' said Mrs Hubbard.

The door opened and Celia Austin came in.

'Ah,' said Poirot, nodding his head. 'Exactly. Miss Celia Austin.'

Celia looked at Colin with agonised eyes.

'I didn't know you were here,' she said breathlessly. 'I came – I came . . .'

She took a deep breath and rushed to Mrs Hubbard.

'Please, please don't send for the police. It's me. I've been taking those things. I don't know why. I can't imagine. I didn't want to. It just – it just came over me.' She whirled round on Colin. 'So now you know what I'm like . . . and I suppose you'll never speak to me again. I know I'm awful . . .'

'Och! not a bit of it,' said Colin. His rich voice was warm and friendly. 'You're just a bit mixed-up, that's all. It's just a kind of illness you've had, from not looking at things clearly. If you'll trust me, Celia, I'll soon be able to put you right.'

'Oh Colin – really?'

Celia looked at him with unconcealed adoration.

'I've been so dreadfully worried.'

He took her hand in a slightly avuncular manner.

'Well, there's no need to worry any more.' Rising to his feet he drew Celia's hand through his arm and looked sternly at Mrs Hubbard.

'I hope now,' he said, 'that there'll be no more foolish talk of calling in the police. Nothing's been stolen of any real worth, and what has been taken Celia will return.'

'I can't return the bracelet and the powder compact,' said Celia anxiously. 'I pushed them down a gutter. But I'll buy new ones.'

'And the stethoscope?' said Poirot. 'Where did you put that?'

Celia flushed.

'I never took any stethoscope. What should I want with a silly old stethoscope?' Her flush deepened. 'And it wasn't me who spilt ink all over Elizabeth's papers. I'd never do a – malicious thing like that.'

'Yet you cut and slashed Miss Hobhouse's scarf, mademoiselle.'

Celia looked uncomfortable. She said rather uncertainly:

'That was different. I mean – Valerie didn't *mind*.'

'And the rucksack?'

'Oh, I didn't cut that up. That was just temper.'

Poirot took out the list he had copied from Mrs Hubbard's little book.

'Tell me,' he said, 'and this time it must be the truth. What are you or are you not responsible for of these happenings?'

Celia glanced down the list and her answer came at once.

'I don't know anything about the rucksack, or the electric light bulbs, or boracic or bath salts, and the ring was just a mistake. When I realised it was valuable I returned it.'

'I see.'

'Because really I didn't mean to be dishonest. It was only –'

'Only what?'

A faintly wary look came into Celia's eyes.

'I don't know – really I don't. I'm all mixed-up.'

Colin cut in in a peremptory manner.

'I'll be thankful if you'll not catechise her. I can promise you that there will be no recurrence of this business. From now on I'll definitely make myself responsible for her.'

'Oh, Colin, you *are* good to me.'

'I'd like you to tell me a great deal about yourself, Celia. Your early home life, for instance. Did your father and mother get on well together?'

'Oh no, it was *awful* – at home –'

'Precisely. And –'

Mrs Hubbard cut in. She spoke with the voice of authority.

'That will do now, both of you. I'm glad, Celia, that you've come and owned up. You've caused a great deal of worry and anxiety, though, and you ought to be ashamed of yourself. But I'll say this. I accept your word that you didn't spill ink deliberately on Elizabeth's notes. I don't believe you'd do a thing like that. Now take yourself off, you and Colin. I've had enough of you both for this evening.'

As the door closed behind them, Mrs Hubbard drew a deep breath.

'Well,' she said. 'What do you think of that?'

There was a twinkle in Hercule Poirot's eye. He said:

'I think – that we have assisted at a love scene – modern style.'

Mrs Hubbard made an ejaculation of disapproval.

'*Autres temps, autres mœurs*,' murmured Poirot. 'In my young days the young men lent the girls books on theosophy or discussed Maeterlinck's "Bluebird". All was sentiment and high ideals. Nowadays it is the maladjusted lives and the complexes which bring a boy and girl together.'

'All such nonsense,' said Mrs Hubbard.

Poirot dissented.

'No, it is not all nonsense. The underlying principles are sound enough – but when one is an earnest young researcher like Colin one sees nothing *but* complexes and the victim's unhappy home life.'

'Celia's father died when she was four years old,' said Mrs Hubbard. 'And she's had a very agreeable childhood with a nice but stupid mother.'

'Ah, but she is wise enough not to say so to the young McNabb! She will say what he wants to hear. She is very much in love.'

'Do you believe all this hooey, M. Poirot?'

'I do not believe that Celia had a Cinderella complex or that she stole things without knowing what she was doing. I think she took the risk of stealing unimportant trifles with the object of attracting the attention of the earnest Colin McNabb – in which object she has been successful. Had she remained a pretty, shy, ordinary girl he might never have looked at her. In my opinion,' said Poirot, 'a girl is entitled to attempt desperate measures to get her man.'

'I shouldn't have thought she had the brains to think it up,' said Mrs Hubbard.

Poirot did not reply. He frowned. Mrs Hubbard went on:

'So the whole thing's been a mare's nest! I really do apologise, M. Poirot, for taking up your time over such a trivial business. Anyway, all's well that ends well.'

'No, no.' Poirot shook his head. 'I do not think we are at the end yet. We have cleared out of the way something rather trivial that was at the front of the picture. But there are things still that are not explained; and me, I have the impression that we have here something serious – really serious.'

'Oh, M. Poirot, do you really think so?'

'It is my impression . . . I wonder, madame, if I could speak to Miss Patricia Lane. I would like to examine the ring that was stolen.'

'Why, of course, M. Poirot. I'll go down and send her up to you. I want to speak to Len Bateson about something.'

Patricia Lane came in shortly afterwards with an inquiring look on her face.

'I am so sorry to disturb you, Miss Lane.'

'Oh, that's all right. I wasn't busy. Mrs Hubbard said you wanted to see my ring.'

She slipped it off her finger and held it out to him.

'It's quite a large diamond really, but of course it's an old-fashioned setting. It was my mother's engagement ring.'

Poirot, who was examining the ring, nodded his head.

'She is alive still, your mother?'

'No. Both my parents are dead.'

'That is sad.'

'Yes. They were both very nice people but somehow I was never quite so close to them as I ought to have been. One regrets that afterwards. My mother wanted a frivolous pretty daughter, a daughter who was fond of clothes and social things. She was very disappointed when I took up archaeology.'

'You have always been of a serious turn of mind?'

'I think so, really. One feels life is so short one ought really to be doing something worth while.'

Poirot looked at her thoughtfully.

Patricia Lane was, he guessed, in her early thirties. Apart from a smear of lipstick, carelessly applied, she wore no make-up. Her mouse-coloured hair was combed back from her face and arranged without artifice. Her quite pleasant blue eyes looked at you seriously through glasses.

'No allure, *bon Dieu*,' said Poirot to himself with feeling. 'And her clothes! What is it they say? Dragged through a hedge backwards? *Ma foi*, that expresses it exactly!'

He was disapproving. He found Patricia's well-bred unaccented tones wearisome to the ear. 'She is intelligent and cultured, this girl,' he said to himself, 'and, alas, every year she will grow more boring! In old age –' His mind darted for a fleeting moment to the memory of Countess Vera Rossakoff. What exotic splendour there, even in decay! These girls of nowadays –

'But that is because I grow old,' said Poirot to himself. 'Even this excellent girl may appear a veritable Venus to some man.' But he doubted that.

Patricia was saying:

'I'm really very shocked about what happened to Bess – to Miss Johnston. Using that green ink seems to me to be a deliberate attempt to make it look as though it was Nigel's doing. But I do assure you, M. Poirot, Nigel would never do a thing like that.'

'Ah.' Poirot looked at her with more interest. She had become flushed and quite eager.

'Nigel's not easy to understand,' she said earnestly. 'You see, he had a very difficult home life as a child.'

'*Mon Dieu*, another of them!'

'I beg your pardon?'

'Nothing. You were saying –'

'About Nigel. His being difficult. He's always had the tendency to go against authority of any kind. He's very clever – brilliant really, but I must admit that he sometimes has a very unfortunate manner. Sneering – you know. And he's much too scornful ever to explain or defend himself. Even if everybody in this place thinks he did that trick with the ink, he won't go out of his way to say he didn't. He'll just say, "Let them think it if they want to." And that attitude is really so utterly foolish.'

'It can be misunderstood, certainly.'

'It's a kind of pride, I think. Because he's been so much misunderstood always.'

'You have known him for many years?'

'No, only for about a year. We met on a tour of the Châteaux of the Loire. He went down with flu which turned to pneumonia and I nursed him through it. He's very delicate and he takes absolutely no care of his own health. In some ways, in spite of his being so independent, he needs looking after like a child. He really needs someone to look after him.'

Poirot sighed. He felt, suddenly, very tired of love . . . First there had been Celia, with the adoring eyes of a spaniel. And now here was Patricia looking like an earnest Madonna. Admittedly there must be love, young people must meet and pair off, but he, Poirot, was mercifully past all that. He rose to his feet.

'Will you permit me, mademoiselle, to retain your ring? It shall be returned to you tomorrow without fail.'

'Certainly, if you like,' said Patricia, rather surprised.

'You are very kind. And please, mademoiselle, be careful.'

'Careful? Careful of what?'

'I wish I knew,' said Hercule Poirot.

He was still worried.

CHAPTER 6

The following day Mrs Hubbard found exasperating in every particular. She had awoken with a considerable sense of relief. The nagging doubt about recent occurrences was at last relieved. A silly girl, behaving in that silly modern fashion (with which Mrs Hubbard had no patience) had been responsible. And from now on, order would reign.

Descending to breakfast in this comfortable assurance, Mrs Hubbard found her newly attained ease menaced. The students chose this particular morning to be particularly trying, each in his or her way.

Mr Chandra Lal who had heard of the sabotage to Elizabeth's papers became excited and voluble. 'Oppression,' he spluttered, 'deliberate oppression of native races. Contempt and prejudice, colour prejudice. It is here well authenticated example.'

'Now, Mr Chandra Lal,' said Mrs Hubbard sharply. 'You've no call to say anything of that kind. Nobody knows who did it or why it was done.'

'Oh but, Mrs Hubbard, I thought Celia had come to you herself and really faced up,' said Jean Tomlinson. 'I thought it splendid of her. We must all be very kind to her.'

'Must you be so revoltingly pi, Jean,' demanded Valerie Hobhouse angrily.

'I think that's a very unkind thing to say.'

'Faced up,' said Nigel, with a shudder. 'Such an utterly revolting term.'

'I don't see why. The Oxford Group use it and –'

'Oh, for Heaven's sake, have we *got* to have the Oxford Group for breakfast?'

'What's all this, Ma? It is Celia who's been pinching those things, do you say? Is that why she's not down to breakfast?'

'I do not understand, please,' said Mr Akibombo.

Nobody enlightened him. They were all too anxious to say their own piece.

'Poor kid,' Len Bateson went on. 'Was she hard-up or something?'

'I'm not really surprised, you know,' said Sally slowly. 'I always had a sort of idea . . .'

'You are saying that it was Celia who spilt ink on my notes?' Elizabeth Johnston looked incredulous. 'That seems to be surprising and hardly credible.'

'Celia did *not* throw ink on your work,' said Mrs Hubbard. 'And I wish you would all stop discussing this. I meant to tell you all quietly later but –'

'But Jean was listening outside the door last night,' said Valerie.

'I was not listening. I just happened to go –'

'Come now, Bess,' said Nigel. 'You know quite well who spilt the ink. I, said bad Nigel, with my little green phial, *I* spilt the ink.'

'He didn't. He's only pretending. Oh, Nigel, how can you be so stupid?'

'I'm being noble and shielding *you*, Pat. Who borrowed my ink yesterday morning? *You* did.'

'I do not understand, please,' said Mr Akibombo.

'You don't want to,' Sally told him. 'I'd keep right out of it if I were you.'

Mr Chandra Lal rose to his feet.

'You ask why is the Mau Mau? You ask why does Egypt resent the Suez Canal?'

'Oh, *hell*!' said Nigel violently, and crashed his cup down on his saucer. 'First the Oxford Group and now politics! At *breakfast*! I'm going.'

He pushed back his chair violently and left the room.

'There's a cold wind. Do take your coat.' Patricia rushed after him.

'Cluck, cluck, cluck,' said Valerie unkindly. 'She'll grow feathers and flap her wings soon.'

The French girl, Genevieve, whose English was as yet not equal to following rapid exchanges of English, had been listening to explanations hissed into her ear by René. She now burst into rapid French, her voice rising to a scream.

'*Comment donc? C'est cette petite qui m'a volé mon compact? Ah, par example! J'irai à la police. Je ne supporterai pas une pareille* . . .'

Colin McNabb had been attempting to make himself heard for some time, but his deep superior drawl had been drowned by the higher pitched voices. Abandoning his superior attitude he now brought down his fist with a heavy crash on the table and startled everyone into silence. The marmalade pot skidded off the table and broke.

'Will you hold your tongues, all of you, and hear me speak. I've never heard more crass ignorance and unkindness! Don't any of you have even a nodding acquaintance with psychology? The girl's not to be blamed, I tell you. She's been going through a severe emotional crisis and she needs treating with the utmost sympathy and care – or she may remain unstable for life. I'm warning you. The utmost care – that's what she needs.'

'But after all,' said Jean, in a clear, priggish voice, 'although I quite agree about being *kind* – we oughtn't to condone that sort of thing, ought we? Stealing, I mean.'

'Stealing,' said Colin. 'This wasn't *stealing*. Och! You make me sick – all of you.'

'Interesting case, is she, Colin?' said Valerie, and grinned at him.

'If you're interested in the workings of the mind, yes.'

'Of course, she didn't take anything of *mine*,' began Jean, 'but I do think –'

'No, she didn't take anything of yours,' said Colin, turning to scowl at her. 'And if you knew in the least what that meant you'd maybe not be too pleased about it.'

'Really, I don't see –'

'Oh, come on, Jean,' said Len Bateson. 'Let's stop nagging and nattering. I'm going to be late and so are you.'

They went out together. 'Tell Celia to buck up,' he said over his shoulder.

'I should like to make formal protest,' said Mr Chandra Lal. 'Boracic powder, very necessary for my eyes which much inflamed by study, was removed.'

'And you'll be late too, Mr Chandra Lal,' said Mrs Hubbard firmly.

'My professor is often unpunctual,' said Mr Chandra Lal gloomily, but moving towards the door. 'Also, he is irritable and unreasonable when I ask many questions of searching nature.'

'*Mais il faut qu'elle me le rende, ce compact,*' said Genevieve.

'You must speak English, Genevieve – you'll never learn English if you go back into French whenever you're excited. And you had Sunday dinner in this week and you haven't paid me for it.'

'Ah, I have not my purse just now. Tonight – *Viens, René, nous serons en retard.*'

'Please,' said Mr Akibombo, looking round him beseechingly. 'I do not understand.'

'Come along, Akibombo,' said Sally. 'I'll tell you about it on the way to the Institute.'

She nodded reassuringly to Mrs Hubbard and steered the bewildered Akibombo out of the room.

'Oh dear,' said Mrs Hubbard, drawing a deep breath. 'Why in the world I ever took this job on!'

Valerie, who was the only person left, grinned in a friendly fashion.

'Don't worry, Ma,' she said. 'It's a good thing it's all come out. Everyone was getting on the jumpy side.'

'I must say I was very surprised.'

'That it turned out to be Celia?'

'Yes. Weren't you?'

Valerie said in a rather absent voice:

'Rather obvious, really, I should have thought.'

'Have you been thinking so all along?'

'Well, one or two things made me wonder. At any rate she's got Colin where she wants him.'

'Yes. I can't help feeling that it's wrong.'

'You can't get a man with a gun,' Valerie laughed. 'But a spot of kleptomania does the trick? Don't worry, Mum. And for God's sake make Celia give Genevieve back her *compact*, otherwise we shall never have *any* peace at meals.'

Mrs Hubbard said with a sigh:

'Nigel has cracked his saucer and the marmalade pot is broken.'

'Hell of a morning, isn't it?' said Valerie. She went out. Mrs Hubbard heard her voice in the hall saying cheerfully:

'Good morning, Celia. The coast's clear. All is known and all is going to be forgiven – by order of Pious Jean. As for Colin, he's been roaring like a lion on your behalf.'

Celia came into the dining-room. Her eyes were reddened with crying.

'Oh, Mrs Hubbard.'

'You're very late, Celia. The coffee's cold and there's not much left to eat.'

'I didn't want to meet the others.'

'So I gather. But you've got to meet them sooner or later.'

'Oh, yes, I know, But I thought – by this evening – it would be easier. And of course I shan't stop here. I'll go at the end of the week.'

Mrs Hubbard frowned.

'I don't think there's any need for that. You must expect a little unpleasantness – that's only fair – but they're generous minded young people on the whole. Of course you'll have to make reparation as far as possible.'

Celia interrupted her eagerly.

'Oh, yes, I've got my cheque book here. That's one of the things I wanted to say to you.' She looked down. She was holding a cheque book and an envelope in her hand. 'I'd written to you in case you weren't about when I got down, to say how sorry I was and I meant to put in a cheque, so that you could square up with people – but my pen ran out of ink.'

'We'll have to make a list.'

'I have – as far as possible. But I don't know whether to try and buy new things or just to give the money.'

'I'll think it over. It's difficult to say off-hand.'

'Oh, but do let me give you a cheque now. I'd feel so much better.'

About to say uncompromisingly 'Really? And why should you be allowed to make yourself feel better?' Mrs Hubbard reflected that since the students were always short of ready cash, the whole affair would be more easily settled that way. It would also placate Genevieve who otherwise might make trouble with Mrs Nicoletis. (There would be trouble enough there anyway).

'All right,' she said. She ran her eye down the list of objects. 'It's difficult to say how much off-hand —'

Celia said eagerly, 'Let me give you a cheque for what you think roughly and then you find out from people and I can take some back or give you more.'

'Very well.' Mrs Hubbard tentatively mentioned a sum which gave, she considered, ample margin, and Celia agreed at once. She opened the cheque book.

'Oh, bother my pen.' She went over to the shelves where odds and ends were kept belonging to various students. 'There doesn't seem to be any ink here except Nigel's awful green. Oh, I'll use that. Nigel won't mind. I must remember to get a new bottle of Quink when I go out.'

She filled the pen and came back and wrote out the cheque. Giving it to Mrs Hubbard, she glanced at her watch.

'I shall be late. I'd better not stop for breakfast.'

'Now, you'd better have something, Celia – even if it's only a bit of bread and butter – no good going out on an empty stomach. Yes, what is it?'

Geronimo, the Italian manservant, had come into the room and was making emphatic gestures with his hands, his wizened, monkey-like face screwed up in a comical grimace.

'The padrona, she just come in. She want to see you.' He added, with a final gesture, 'She plenty mad.'

'I'm coming.'

Mrs Hubbard left the room while Celia hurriedly began hacking a piece off the loaf.

Mrs Nicoletis was walking up and down her room in a fairly good imitation of a tiger at the Zoo near feeding-time.

'What is this I hear?' she burst out. 'You send for the police?

Without a word to me? Who do you think you are? My God, who does the woman think she is?'

'I did not send for the police.'

'You are a liar.'

'Now then, Mrs Nicoletis, you can't talk to me like that.'

'Oh no. Certainly not! It is *I* who am wrong. Not *you*. Always *me*. Everything *you* do is perfect. Police in my respectable hostel.'

'It wouldn't be the first time,' said Mrs Hubbard, recalling various unpleasant incidents. 'There was that West Indian student who was wanted for living on immoral earnings and the notorious young Communist agitator who came here under a false name – and –'

'Ah! You throw that in my teeth? Is it my fault that people come here and lie to me and have forged papers and are wanted to assist the police in murder cases? And you reproach me for what I have suffered!'

'I'm doing nothing of the kind. I only point out that it wouldn't be exactly a novelty to have the police here – I dare say it's inevitable with a mixed lot of students. But the fact is that no one has "called in the police". A private detective with a big reputation happened to dine here as my guest last night. He gave a very interesting talk on criminology to the students.'

'As if there were any need to talk about criminology to our students! They know quite enough already. Enough to steal and destroy and sabotage as they like! And nothing is done about it – nothing!'

'I have done something about it.'

'Yes, you have told this friend of yours all about our most intimate affair. That is a gross breach of confidence.'

'Not at all. I'm responsible for running this place. I'm glad to tell you the matter is now cleared up. One of the students has confessed that she has been responsible for most of these happenings.'

'Dirty little cat,' said Mrs Nicoletis. 'Throw her into the street.'

'She is ready to leave of her own accord and she is making full reparation.'

'What is the good of that? My beautiful Students' Home will

now have a bad name. No one will come.' Mrs Nicoletis sat down on the sofa and burst into tears. 'Nobody thinks of my feelings,' she sobbed. 'It is abominable, the way I am treated. Ignored! Thrust aside! If I were to die tomorrow, who would care?'

Wisely leaving this question unanswered, Mrs Hubbard left the room.

'May the Almighty give me patience,' said Mrs Hubbard to herself, and went down to the kitchen to interview Maria.

Maria was sullen and unco-operative. The word 'police' hovered unspoken in the air.

'It is I who will be accused. I and Geronimo – the *povero*. What justice can you expect in a foreign land? No, I cannot cook the risotto as you suggest – they send the wrong rice. I make you instead the spaghetti.'

'We had spaghetti last night.'

'It does not matter. In my country we eat the spaghetti every day – every single day. The pasta, it is good all the time.'

'Yes, but you're in England now.'

'Very well then, I make the stew. The English stew. You will not like it but I make it – pale – pale – with the onions boiled in much water instead of cooked in the oil – and pale meat on cracked bones.'

Maria spoke so menacingly that Mrs Hubbard felt she was listening to an account of a murder.

'Oh, cook what you like,' she said angrily, and left the kitchen.

By six o'clock that evening, Mrs Hubbard was once more her efficient self again. She had put notes in all the students' rooms asking them to come and see her before dinner, and when the various summonses were obeyed, she explained that Celia had asked her to arrange matters. They were all, she thought, very nice about it. Even Genevieve, softened by a generous estimate of the value of her compact, said cheerfully that all would be *sans rancune* and added with a wise air, 'One knows that these crises of the nerves occur. She is rich, this Celia, she does not need to steal. No, it is a storm in her head. M. McNabb is right there.'

Len Bateson drew Mrs Hubbard aside as she came down when the dinner bell rang.

'I'll wait for Celia out in the hall,' he said, 'and bring her in. So that she sees it's all right.'

'That's very nice of you, Len.'

'That's OK, Ma.'

In due course, as soup was being passed round, Len's voice was heard booming from the hall.

'Come along in, Celia. All friends here.'

Nigel remarked waspishly to his soup plate:

'Done *his* good deed for the day!' but otherwise controlled his tongue and waved a hand of greeting to Celia as she came in with Len's large arm passed round her shoulders.

There was a general outburst of cheerful conversation on various topics and Celia was appealed to by one and the other.

Almost inevitably this manifestation of goodwill died away into a doubtful silence. It was then that Mr Akibombo turned a beaming face towards Celia and, leaning across the table, said:

'They have explained me good now all that I did not understand. You very clever at steal things. Long time nobody know. Very clever.'

At this point Sally Finch, gasping out, 'Akibombo, you'll be the death of me,' had such a severe choke that she had to go out in the hall to recover. And the laughter broke out in a thoroughly natural fashion.

Colin McNabb came in late. He seemed reserved and even more uncommunicative than usual. At the close of the meal and before the others had finished he got up and said in an embarrassed mumble:

'Got to go out and see someone. Like to tell you all first. Celia and I – hope to get married next year when I've done my course.'

The picture of blushing misery, he received the congratulations and jeering cat-calls of his friends and finally escaped, looking terribly sheepish. Celia, on the other hand, was pink and composed.

'Another good man gone west,' sighed Len Bateson.

'I'm so glad, Celia,' said Patricia. 'I hope you'll be very happy.'

'Everything in the garden is now perfect,' said Nigel. 'Tomorrow we'll bring some *chianti* in and drink your health. Why is our dear Jean looking so grave? Do you disapprove of marriage, Jean?'

'Of course not, Nigel.'

'I always think it's so *much* better than free love, don't you? Nicer for the children. Looks better on their passports.'

'But the mother should not be too young,' said Genevieve. 'They tell one that in the physiology classes.'

'Really, dear,' said Nigel, 'you're not suggesting that Celia's below the age of consent or anything like that, are you? She's free, white, and twenty-one.'

'That,' said Mr Chandra Lal, 'is a *most* offensive remark.'

'No, no, Mr Chandra Lal,' said Patricia. 'It's just a – a kind of idiom. It doesn't mean anything.'

'I do not understand,' said Mr Akibombo. 'If a thing does not mean anything, why should it be said?'

Elizabeth Johnston said suddenly, raising her voice a little:

'Things are sometimes said that do not seem to mean anything but they may mean a good deal. No, it is not your American quotation I mean. I am talking of something else.' She looked round the table. 'I am talking of what happened yesterday.'

Valerie said sharply:

'What's up, Bess?'

'Oh, please,' said Celia. 'I think – I really do – that by tomorrow everything will be cleared up. I really mean it. The ink on your papers, and that silly business of the rucksack. And if – if the person owns up, like I've done, then everything will be cleared up.'

She spoke earnestly, with a flushed face, and one or two people looked at her curiously.

Valerie said with a short laugh:

'And we'll all live happy ever afterwards.'

Then they got up and went into the common-room. There was quite a little competition to give Celia her coffee. Then the wireless was turned on, some students left to keep appointments or to work and finally the inhabitants of 24 and 26 Hickory Road got to bed.

It had been, Mrs Hubbard reflected, as she climbed gratefully between the sheets, a long wearying day.

'But thank goodness,' she said to herself. 'It's all over now.'

CHAPTER 7

Miss Lemon was seldom, if ever, unpunctual. Fog, storm, epidemic of flu, transport breakdowns – none of these things seemed to affect that remarkable woman. But this morning Miss Lemon arrived, breathless, at five minutes past ten instead of on the stroke of ten o'clock. She was profusely apologetic and for her, quite ruffled.

'I'm extremely sorry, M. Poirot – really extremely sorry. I was just about to leave the flat when my sister rang up.'

'Ah, she is in good health and spirits, I trust?'

'Well, frankly no.' Poirot looked inquiring. 'In fact, she's very distressed. One of the students has committed suicide.'

Poirot stared at her. He muttered something softly under his breath.

'I beg your pardon, M. Poirot?'

'What is the name of the student?'

'A girl called Celia Austin.'

'How?'

'They think she took morphia.'

'Could it have been an accident?'

'Oh no. She left a note, it seems.'

Poirot said softly, 'It was not this I expected, no, it was not this . . . and yet it is true, I expected *something*.'

He looked up to find Miss Lemon at attention, waiting with pencil poised above her pad. He sighed and shook his head.

'No, I will hand you here this morning's mail. File them, please, and answer what you can. Me, I shall go round to Hickory Road.'

Geronimo let Poirot in, and recognising him as the honoured guest of two nights before, became at once voluble in a sibilant conspiratorial whisper.

'Ah, signor, it is you. We have here the trouble – the big trouble. The little signorina, she is dead in her bed this morning. First the doctor come. He shake his head. Now comes an inspector of the police. He is upstairs with the signora and the padrona. Why should she wish to kill herself, the *poverina*? When last night is so gay and the betrothment is made?'

'Betrothment?'

'*Si, si.* To Mr Colin – you know – big, dark, always smoke the pipe.'

'I know.'

Geronimo opened the door of the common-room and introduced Poirot into it with a redoublement of the conspiratorial manner.

'You stay here, yes? Presently, when the police go, I tell the signora you are here. That is good, yes?'

Poirot said that it was good and Geronimo withdrew. Left to himself, Poirot, who had no scruples of delicacy, made as minute an examination as possible of everything in the room with special attention to everything belonging to the students. His rewards were mediocre. The students kept most of their belongings and personal papers in their bedrooms.

Upstairs, Mrs Hubbard was sitting facing Inspector Sharpe, who was asking questions in a soft apologetic voice. He was a big comfortable looking man with a deceptively mild manner.

'It's very awkward and distressing for you, I know,' he said soothingly. 'But you see, as Dr Coles has already told you, there will have to be an inquest, and we have just to get the picture right, so to speak. Now this girl had been distressed and unhappy lately, you say?'

'Yes.'

'Love affair?'

'Not exactly.' Mrs Hubbard hesitated.

'You'd better tell me, you know,' said Inspector Sharpe, persuasively. 'As I say, we've got to get the picture. There was a reason, or she thought there was, for taking her own life? Any possibility that she might have been pregnant?'

'It wasn't that kind of thing at all. I hesitated, Inspector Sharpe, simply because the child had done some very foolish things and I hoped it wouldn't be necessary to bring them out in the open.'

Inspector Sharpe coughed.

'We have a good deal of discretion, and the coroner is a man of wide experience. But we have to *know*.'

'Yes, of course. I was being foolish. The truth is that for some time past, three months or more, things have been disappearing – small things, I mean – nothing very important.'

'Trinkets, you mean, finery, nylon stockings and all that? Money, too?'

'No money as far as I know.'

'Ah. And this girl was responsible?'

'Yes.'

'You'd caught her at it?'

'Not exactly. The night before last a – er – a friend of mine came to dine. A M. Hercule Poirot – I don't know if you know the name.'

Inspector Sharpe had looked up from his notebook. His eyes had opened rather wide. It happened that he did know that name.

'M. Hercule Poirot?' he said. 'Indeed? Now that's very interesting.'

'He gave us a little talk after dinner and the subject of these thefts came up. He advised me, in front of them all, to go to the police.'

'He did, did he?'

'Afterwards, Celia came along to my room and owned up. She was very distressed.'

'Any question of prosecution?'

'No. She was going to make good the losses, and everyone was very nice to her about it.'

'Had she been hard-up?'

'No. She had an adequately paid job as a dispenser at St Catherine's Hospital and has a little money of her own, I believe. She's rather better off than most of our students.'

'So she'd no need to steal – but did,' said the inspector, writing it down.

'It's kleptomania, I suppose,' said Mrs Hubbard.

'That's the label that's used. I just mean one of the people that don't *need* to take things, but nevertheless *do* take them.'

'I wonder if you're being a little unfair to her. You see, there was a young man.'

'And he ratted on her?'

'Oh no. *Quite* the reverse. He spoke very strongly in her defence and as a matter of fact, last night, after supper, he announced that they'd become engaged.'

Inspector Sharpe's eyebrows mounted his forehead in a surprised fashion.

'And then she goes to bed and takes morphia? That's rather surprising, isn't it?'

'It is. I can't understand it.'

Mrs Hubbard's face was creased with perplexity and distress.

'And yet the facts are clear enough.' Sharpe nodded to the small torn piece of paper that lay on the table between them.

Dear Mrs Hubbard (it ran), *I really am sorry and this is the best thing I can do.*

'It's not signed, but you've no doubt it's her handwriting?'

'No.'

Mrs Hubbard spoke rather uncertainly and frowned as she looked at the torn scrap of paper. Why did she feel so strongly that there was something *wrong* about it –?

'There's one clear fingerprint on it which is definitely hers,' said the inspector. 'The morphia was in a small bottle with the label of St Catherine's Hospital on it and you tell me that she works as a dispenser in St Catherine's. She'd have access to the poison cupboard and that's where she probably got it. Presumably she brought it home with her yesterday with suicide in mind.'

'I really can't believe it. It doesn't seem right somehow. She was so happy last night.'

'Then we must suppose that a reaction set in when she went up to bed. Perhaps there's more in her past than you know about. Perhaps she was afraid of that coming out. You think she was very much in love with this young man – what's his name, by the way?'

'Colin McNabb. He's doing a post-graduate course at St Catherine's.'

'A doctor? And at St Catherine's?'

'Celia was very much in love with him, more, I should say, than he with her. He's a rather self-centred young man.'

'Then that's probably the explanation. She didn't feel worthy of him, or hadn't told him all she ought to tell him. She was quite young, wasn't she?'

'Twenty-three.'

'They're idealistic at that age and they take love affairs hard. Yes, that's it, I'm afraid. Pity.'

He rose to his feet. 'I'm afraid the actual facts will have to come out, but we'll do all we can to gloss things over. Thank you, Mrs Hubbard, I've got all the information I need now. Her mother died two years ago and the only relative you know of is this elderly aunt in Yorkshire – we'll communicate with her.'

He picked up a small torn fragment with Celia's agitated writing on it.

'There's something wrong about that,' said Mrs Hubbard suddenly.

'Wrong? In what way?'

'I don't know – but I feel I ought to know. Oh dear.'

'You're quite sure it's her handwriting?'

'Oh yes. It's not *that*.' Mrs Hubbard pressed her hands to her eyeballs.

'I feel so dreadfully stupid this morning,' she said apologetically.

'It's all been very trying for you, I know,' said the inspector with gentle sympathy. 'I don't think we'll need to trouble you further at the moment, Mrs Hubbard.'

Inspector Sharpe opened the door and immediately fell over Geronimo, who was pressed against the door outside.

'Hallo,' said Inspector Sharpe pleasantly. 'Listening at doors, eh?'

'No, no,' Geronimo answered with an air of virtuous indignation. 'I do not listen – never, never! I am just coming in with message.'

'I *see*. What message?'

Geronimo said sulkily:

'Only that there is gentleman downstairs to see la Signora Hubbard.'

'All right. Go along in, sonny, and tell her.'

He walked past Geronimo down the passage and then, taking a leaf out of the Italian's book, turned sharply, and tiptoed noiselessly back. Might as well know if little monkey-face had been telling the truth.

He arrived in time to hear Geronimo say:

'The gentleman who came to supper the other night, the gentleman with the moustaches, he is downstairs waiting to see you.'

'Eh? What?' Mrs Hubbard sounded abstracted. 'Oh, thank you, Geronimo. I'll be down in a minute or two.'

'Gentleman with the moustaches, eh,' said Sharpe to himself, grinning. 'I bet I know who *that* is.'

He went downstairs and into the common-room.

'Hallo, M. Poirot,' he said. 'It's a long time since we met.'

Poirot rose without visible discomposure from a kneeling position by the bottom shelf near the fireplace.

'Aha,' he said. 'But surely – yes, it is Inspector Sharpe, is it not? But you were not formerly in this division?'

'Transferred two years ago. Remember that business down at Crays Hill?'

'Ah yes. That is a long time ago now. You are still a young man, Inspector –'

'Getting on, getting on.'

'– and I am an old one. Alas!' Poirot sighed.

'But still active, eh, M. Poirot. Active in certain ways, shall we say?'

'Now what do you mean by that?'

'I mean that I'd like to know *why* you came along here the other night to give a talk on criminology to students.'

Poirot smiled.

'But there is such a simple explanation. Mrs Hubbard here is the sister of my much valued secretary, Miss Lemon. So when she asked me –'

'When she asked you to look into what had been going on here, you came along. That's it really, isn't it?'

'You are quite correct.'

'But why? That's what I want to know. What was there in it for you?'

'To interest me, you mean?'

'That's what I mean. Here's a silly kid who's been pinching a few things here and there. Happens all the time. Rather small beer for you, M. Poirot, isn't it?'

Poirot shook his head.

'It is not so simple as that.'

'Why not? What isn't simple about it?'

Poirot sat down on a chair. With a slight frown he dusted the knees of his trousers.

'I wish I knew,' he said simply.

Sharpe frowned.

'I don't understand,' he said.

'No, and I do not understand. The things that were taken –'
He shook his head. 'They did not make a pattern – they did not
make sense. It is like seeing a trail of footprints and they are not
all made by the same feet. There is, quite clearly, the print of
what you have called "a silly kid" – but there is more than that.
Other things happened that were meant to fit in with the pattern
of Celia Austin – but they did *not* fit in. They were meaningless,
apparently purposeless. There was evidence, too, of malice. And
Celia was not malicious.'

'She was a kleptomaniac?'

'I should very much doubt it.'

'Just an ordinary petty thief, then?'

'Not in the way you mean. I give it you as my opinion that all
this pilfering of petty objects was done to attract the attention of
a certain young man.'

'Colin McNabb?'

'Yes. She was desperately in love with Colin McNabb. Colin
never noticed her. Instead of a nice, pretty, well behaved young
girl, she displayed herself as an interesting young criminal. The
result was successful. Colin McNabb immediately fell for her, as
they say, in a big way.'

'He must be a complete fool, then.'

'Not at all. He is a keen psychologist.'

'Oh,' Inspector Sharpe groaned. 'One of *those*! I understand
now.' A faint grin showed on his face. 'Pretty smart of the girl.'

'Surprisingly so.'

Poirot repeated, musingly, 'Yes, surprisingly so.'

Inspector Sharpe looked alert.

'Meaning by that, M. Poirot?'

'That I wondered – I still wonder – if the idea had been
suggested to her by someone else?'

'For what reason?'

'How do I know? Altruism? Some ulterior motive? One is in
the dark.'

'Any idea as to who it might have been who gave her the
tip?'

'No – unless – but no –'

'All the same,' said Sharpe, pondering, 'I don't quite get it. If she's been simply trying this kleptomania business on, *and* it's succeeded, why the hell go and commit suicide?'

'The answer is that she should *not* have committed suicide.'

The two men looked at each other.

Poirot murmured:

'You are quite sure that she did?'

'It's clear as day, M. Poirot. There's no reason to believe otherwise and –'

The door opened and Mrs Hubbard came in. She looked flushed and triumphant. Her chin stuck out aggressively.

'I've got it,' she said triumphantly. 'Good morning, M. Poirot. I've got it, Inspector Sharpe. It came to me quite suddenly. Why that suicide note looked wrong, I mean. Celia couldn't possibly have written it.'

'Why not, Mrs Hubbard?'

'Because it's written in ordinary blue black ink. And Celia filled her pen with green ink – that ink over there,' Mrs Hubbard nodded towards the shelf, 'at breakfast-time yesterday morning.'

Inspector Sharpe, a somewhat different Inspector Sharpe, came back into the room which he had left abruptly after Mrs Hubbard's statement.

'Quite right,' he said. 'I've checked up. The only pen in the girl's room, the one that was by her bed, has green ink in it. Now that green ink –'

Mrs Hubbard held up the nearly empty bottle.

Then she explained, clearly and concisely, the scene at the breakfast table.

'I feel sure,' she ended, 'that the scrap of paper was torn out of the letter she had written to me yesterday – and which I never opened.'

'What did she do with it? Can you remember?'

Mrs Hubbard shook her head.

'I left her alone in here and went to do my housekeeping. She must, I think, have left it lying somewhere in here, and forgotten about it.'

'And somebody found it . . . and opened it . . . somebody –'

He broke off.

'You realise,' he said, 'what this means? I haven't been very happy about this torn bit of paper all along. There was quite a pile of lecture notepaper in her room – much more natural to write a suicide note on one of them. This means that somebody saw the possibility of using the opening phrase of her letter to you – to suggest something very different. To suggest suicide –'

He paused and then said slowly:

'This means –'

'Murder,' said Hercule Poirot.

CHAPTER 8

Though personally deprecating *le five o'clock* as inhibiting the proper appreciation of the supreme meal of the day, dinner, Poirot was now getting quite accustomed to serving it.

The resourceful George had on this occasion produced large cups, a pot of really strong Indian tea and, in addition to the hot and buttery square crumpets, bread and jam and a large square of rich plum cake.

All this for the delectation of Inspector Sharpe, who was leaning back contentedly sipping his third cup of tea.

'You don't mind my coming along like this, M. Poirot? I've got an hour to spare until the time when the students will be getting back. I shall want to question them all – and, frankly, it's not a business I'm looking forward to. You met some of them the other night and I wondered if you could give me any useful dope – on the foreigners, anyway.'

'You think I am a good judge of foreigners? But *mon cher*, there were no Belgians amongst them.'

'No Belg – oh, I see what you mean! You mean that as you're a Belgian, all the other nationalities are as foreign to you as they are to me. But that's not quite true, is it? I mean you probably know more about the Continental types than I do – though not the Indians and the West Africans and that lot.'

'Your best assistance will probably be from Mrs Hubbard. She has been there for some months in intimate association with these young people and she is quite a good judge of human nature.'

'Yes, thoroughly competent woman. I'm relying on her. I shall have to see the proprietress of the place, too. She wasn't there this morning. Owns several of these places, I understand, as well as some of the student clubs. Doesn't seem to be much liked.'

Poirot said nothing for a moment or two, then he asked:

'You have been to St Catherine's?'

'Yes. The chief pharmacist was most helpful. He was much shocked and distressed by the news.'

'What did he say of the girl?'

'She'd worked there for just over a year and was well liked. He described her as rather slow, but very conscientious.' He paused and then added, 'The morphia came from there all right.'

'It did? That is interesting – and rather puzzling.'

'It was morphine tartrate. Kept in the poison cupboard in the Dispensary. Upper shelf – amongst drugs that were not often used. The hypodermic tablets, of course, are what are in general use, and it appears that morphine hydrochloride is more often used than the tartrate. There seems to be a kind of fashion in drugs like everything else. Doctors seem to follow one another in prescribing like a lot of sheep. He didn't say that. It was my own thought. There are some drugs in the upper shelf of that cupboard that were once popular, but haven't been prescribed for years.'

'So the absence of one small dusty phial would not immediately be noticed?'

'That's right. Stock-taking is only done at regular intervals. Nobody remembers any prescription with morphine tartrate in it for a long time. The absence of the bottle wouldn't be noticed until it was wanted – or until they went over stock. The three dispensers all had keys of the poison cupboard and the dangerous drug cupboard. The cupboards are opened as needed, and as on a busy day (which is practically every day) someone is going to the cupboard every few minutes, the cupboard is unlocked and remains unlocked till the end of work.'

'Who has access to it, other than Celia herself?'

'The two other women dispensers, but they have no connection of any kind with Hickory Road. One has been there for four years, the other only came a few weeks ago, was formerly at a hospital in Devon. Good record. Then there are the three senior pharmacists who have all been at St Catherine's for years. Those are the people who have what you might call rightful and normal access to the cupboard. Then there's an old woman who scrubs the floors. She's there between nine and ten in the morning and she could have grabbed a bottle out of the cupboard if the girls were busy at the outpatients' hatches, or attending to the ward baskets, but she's been working for the hospital for years and it seems very unlikely. The lab attendant comes through with stock bottles and he, too, could help himself to a bottle if he watched his opportunity – but none of these suggestions seem at all probable.'

'What outsiders come into the Dispensary?'

'Quite a lot, one way or another. They'd pass through the Dispensary to go to the chief pharmacist's office for instance – or travellers from the big wholesale drug houses would go though it to the manufacturing departments. Then, of course, friends come in occasionally to see one of the dispensers – not a usual thing, but it happens.'

'That is better. Who came in recently to see Celia Austin?'

Sharpe consulted his notebook.

'A girl called Patricia Lane came in on Tuesday of last week. She wanted Celia to come to meet her at the pictures after the Dispensary closed.'

'Patricia Lane,' said Poirot thoughtfully.

'She was only there about five minutes and she did not go near the poison cupboard but remained near the outpatients' windows talking to Celia and another girl. They also remember a coloured girl coming – about two weeks ago – a very superior girl, they said. She was interested in the work and asked questions about it and made notes. Spoke perfect English.'

'That would be Elizabeth Johnston. She was interested, was she?'

'It was a Welfare Clinic afternoon. She was interested in the organisation of such things and also in what was prescribed for such ailments as infant diarrhoea and skin infections.'

Poirot nodded.

'Anyone else?'

'Not that can be remembered.'

'Do doctors come to the Dispensary?'

Sharpe grinned.

'All the time. Officially and unofficially. Sometimes to ask about a particular formula, or to see what is kept in stock.'

'To see what is kept in stock?'

'Yes, I thought of that. Sometimes they ask advice – about a substitute for some preparation that seems to irritate a patient's skin or interfere with digestion unduly. Sometimes a physician just strolls in for a chat – slack moment. A good many of the young chaps come in for Vegenin or aspirin when they've got a hangover – and occasionally, I'd say, for a flirtatious word or two with one of the girls if the opportunity arises. Human nature is always human nature. You see how it is. Pretty hopeless.'

Poirot said, 'And if I recollect rightly, one or more of the students at Hickory Road is attached to St Catherine's – a big, red-haired boy – Bates – Bateman –'

'Leonard Bateson. That's right. And Colin McNabb is doing a post-graduate course there. Then there's a girl, Jean Tomlinson, who works in the physiotherapy department.'

'And all of these have probably been quite often in the Dispensary?'

'Yes, and what's more, nobody remembers when because they're used to seeing them and know them by sight. Jean Tomlinson was by way of being a friend of the senior dispenser –'

'It is not easy,' said Poirot.

'I'll say it's not! You see, anyone who was on the staff could take a look in the poison cupboard, and say, "Why on earth do you have so much Liquor Arsenicalis?" or something like that. "Didn't know anybody used it nowadays." And nobody would think twice about it or remember it.'

Sharpe paused and then said:

'What we are postulating is that someone gave Celia Austin morphia and afterwards put the morphia bottle and the torn-out fragment of letter in her room to make it look like suicide. But why, M. Poirot, why?'

Poirot shook his head. Sharpe went on:

'You hinted this morning that someone might have suggested the kleptomania idea to Celia Austin.'

Poirot moved uneasily.

'That was only a vague idea of mine. It was just that it

seemed doubtful if she would have had the wits to think of it herself.'

'Then who?'

'As far as I know, only three of the students would have been capable of thinking out such an idea. Leonard Bateson would have had the requisite knowledge. He is aware of Colin's enthusiasm for "maladjusted personalities". He might have suggested something of the kind to Celia more or less as a joke and coached her in her part. But I cannot really see him conniving at such a thing for month after month – unless, that is, he had an ulterior motive, or is a very different person from what he appears to be. (That is always a thing one must take into account.) Nigel Chapman has a mischievous and slightly malicious turn of mind. He'd think it good fun, and I should imagine would have no scruples whatever. He is a kind of grown up "*enfant terrible*". The third person I have in mind is a young woman called Valerie Hobhouse. She has brains, is modern in outlook and education, and has probably read enough psychology to judge Colin's probable reaction. If she were fond of Celia, she might think it legitimate fun to make a fool of Colin.'

'Leonard Bateson, Nigel Chapman, Valerie Hobhouse,' said Sharpe, writing down the names. 'Thanks for the tip. I'll remember when I'm questioning them. What about the Indians? One of them is a medical student.'

'His mind is entirely occupied with politics and persecution mania,' said Poirot. 'I don't think he would be interested enough to suggest kleptomania to Celia Austin and I don't think she would have accepted such advice from him.'

'And that's all the help you can give me, M. Poirot?' said Sharpe, rising to his feet and buttoning away his notebook.

'I fear so. But I consider myself personally interested – that is if you do not object, my friend?'

'Not in the least. Why should I?'

'In my own amateurish way I shall do what I can. For me, there is, I think, only one line of action.'

'And that is?'

Poirot sighed.

'*Conversation*, my friend. Conversation and again conversation! All the murderers I have ever come across enjoyed talking. In my opinion the strong silent man seldom commits a crime – and if he does it is simple, violent, and perfectly obvious. But our clever subtle murderer – he is so pleased with himself that sooner or later he says something unfortunate and trips himself up. Talk to these people, *mon cher*, do not confine yourself to simple interrogation. Encourage their views, demand their help, inquire about their hunches – but, *bon dieu!* I do not need to teach you your business. I remember your abilities well enough.'

Sharpe smiled gently.

'Yes,' he said, 'I've always found – well – amiability – a great help.'

The two men smiled at each other in mutual accord. Sharpe rose to depart.

'I suppose every single one of them is a possible murderer,' he said slowly.

'I should think so,' said Poirot nonchalantly. 'Leonard Bateson, for instance, has a temper. He could lose control. Valerie Hobhouse has brains and could plan cleverly. Nigel Chapman is the childish type that lacks proportion. There is a French girl there who might kill if enough money were involved. Patricia Lane is a maternal type and maternal types are always ruthless. The American girl, Sally Finch, is cheerful and gay, but she could play an assumed part better than most. Jean Tomlinson is very full of sweetness and righteousness but we have all known killers who attended Sunday school with sincere devotion. The West Indian girl Elizabeth Johnston has probably the best brains of anyone in the hostel. She has subordinated her emotional life to her brain – that is dangerous. There is a charming young African who might have motives for killing about which we could never guess. We have Colin McNabb, the psychologist. How many psychologists does one know to whom it might be said *Physician, heal thyself*?'

'For heaven's sake, Poirot. You are making my head spin! Is nobody incapable of murder?'

'I have often wondered,' said Hercule Poirot.

CHAPTER 9

Inspector Sharpe sighed, leaned back in his chair and rubbed his forehead with a handkerchief. He had interviewed an indignant and tearful French girl, a supercilious and unco-operative young Frenchman, a stolid and suspicious Dutchman, a voluble and aggressive Egyptian. He had exchanged a few brief remarks with two nervous young Turkish students who did not really understand what he was saying and the same went for a charming young Iraqi. None of these, he was pretty certain, had had anything to do, or could help him in any way with the death of Celia Austin. He had dismissed them one by one with a few reassuring words and was now preparing to do the same to Mr Akibombo.

The young West African looked at him with smiling white teeth and rather childlike, plaintive, eyes.

'I should like to help – yes – please,' he said. 'She is very nice to me, this Miss Celia. She give me once a box of Edinburgh rock – very nice confection which I do not know before. It seems very sad she should be killed. Is it blood feud, perhaps? Or is it perhaps fathers or uncles who come and kill her because they have heard false stories that she do wrong things.'

Inspector Sharpe assured him that none of these things were remotely possible. The young man shook his head sadly.

'Then I do not know why it happened,' he said. 'I do not see why anybody here should want to do harm to her. But you give me piece of her hair and nail clippings,' he continued, 'and I see if I find out by old method. Not scientific, not modern, but very much in use where I come from.'

'Well, thank you, Mr Akibombo, but I don't think that will be necessary. We – er – don't do things that way over here.'

'No, sir, I quite understand. Not modern. Not atomic age. Not done at home now by new policemen – only old men from bush. I am sure all new methods very superior and sure to achieve complete success.' Mr Akibombo bowed politely and removed himself. Inspector Sharpe murmured to himself:

'I sincerely hope we do meet with success – if only to maintain prestige.'

His next interview was with Nigel Chapman, who was inclined to take the conduct of the conversation into his own hands.

'This is an absolutely extraordinary business, isn't it?' he said. 'Mind you, I had an idea that you were barking up the wrong tree when you insisted on suicide. I must say, it's rather gratifying to me to think that the whole thing hinges, really, on her having filled her fountain-pen with my green ink. Just the one thing the murderer couldn't possibly foresee. I suppose you've given due consideration as to what can possibly be the motive for this crime?'

'I'm asking the questions, Mr Chapman,' said Inspector Sharpe drily.

'Oh, of course, of course,' said Nigel, airily, waving a hand. 'I was trying to make a bit of a short-cut of it, that was all. But I suppose we've got to go through with all the red tape as usual. Name, Nigel Chapman. Age, twenty-five. Born, I believe, in Nagasaki – it really seems a most ridiculous place. What my father and mother were doing there at the time I can't imagine. On a world tour, I suppose. However, it doesn't make me necessarily a Japanese, I understand. I'm taking a diploma at London University in Bronze Age and Medieval History. Anything else you want to know?'

'What is your home address, Mr Chapman?'

'No home address, my dear sir. I have a papa, but he and I have quarrelled, and his address is therefore no longer mine. So 26 Hickory Road and Coutts Bank, Leadenhall Street Branch, will always find me, as one says to travelling acquaintances whom you hope you will never meet again.'

Inspector Sharpe displayed no reaction towards Nigel's airy impertinence. He had met Nigels before and shrewdly suspected that Nigel's impertinence masked a natural nervousness of being questioned in connection with murder.

'How well did you know Celia Austin?' he asked.

'That's really quite a difficult question. I knew her very well in the sense of seeing her practically every day, and being on quite cheerful terms with her, but actually I didn't *know* her at all. Of course, I wasn't in the least bit interested in her and I think she probably disapproved of me, if anything.'

'Did she disapprove of you for any particular reason?'

'Well, she didn't like my sense of humour very much. Then, of course, I wasn't one of those brooding, rude young men like Colin McNabb. That kind of rudeness is really the perfect technique for attracting women.'

'When was the last time you saw Celia Austin?'

'At dinner yesterday evening. We'd all given her the big hand, you know. Colin had got up and hemmed and hawed and finally admitted, in a coy and bashful way, that they were engaged. Then we all ragged him a bit, and that was that.'

'Was that at dinner or in the common-room?'

'Oh, at dinner. Afterwards, when we went into the common-room Colin went off somewhere.'

'And the rest of you had coffee in the common-room.'

'If you call the fluid they serve coffee – yes,' said Nigel.

'Did Celia Austin have coffee?'

'Well, I suppose so. I mean, I didn't actually notice her having coffee, but she must have had it.'

'You did not personally hand her her coffee, for instance?'

'How horribly suggestive all this is! When you said that and looked at me in that searching way, d'you know I felt quite certain that I had handed Celia her coffee and had filled it up with strychnine, or whatever it was. Hypnotic suggestion, I suppose, but actually, Mr Sharpe, I didn't go near her – and to be frank, I didn't even notice her drinking coffee, and I can assure you, whether you believe me or not, that I have never had any passion for Celia myself and that the announcement of her engagement to Colin McNabb aroused no feelings of murderous revenge in me.'

'I'm not really suggesting anything of the kind, Mr Chapman,' said Sharpe mildly. 'Unless I'm very much mistaken, there's no particular love angle to this, but somebody wanted Celia Austin out of the way. Why?'

'I simply can't imagine why, Inspector. It's really most intriguing because Celia was really a most harmless kind of girl, if you know what I mean. Slow on the uptake; a bit of a bore; thoroughly nice; and absolutely, I should say, not the kind of girl to get herself murdered.'

'Were you surprised when you found that it was Celia Austin who had been responsible for the various disappearances, thefts, etcetera, in this place?'

'My dear man, you could have knocked me over with a feather! Most uncharacteristic, that's what I thought.'

'You didn't, perhaps, put her up to doing these things?'

Nigel's stare of surprise seemed quite genuine.

'I? Put her up to it? Why should I?'

'Well, that would be rather the question, wouldn't it? Some people have a funny sense of humour.'

'Well, really, I may be dense, but I can't see anything amusing about all this silly pilfering that's been going on.'

'Not your idea of a joke?'

'It never occurred to me it was meant to be funny. Surely, Inspector, the thefts were purely psychological?'

'You definitely consider that Celia Austin was a kleptomaniac?'

'But surely there can't be any other explanation, Inspector?'

'Perhaps you don't know as much about kleptomaniacs as I do, Mr Chapman.'

'Well, I really can't think of any other explanation.'

'You don't think it's possible that someone might have put Miss Austin up to all this as a means of – say – arousing Mr McNabb's interest in her?'

Nigel's eyes glistened with appreciative malice.

'Now that really is a most diverting explanation, Inspector,' he said. 'You know, when I think of it, it's perfectly possible and of course old Colin would swallow it, line, hook and sinker.' Nigel savoured this with much glee for a second or two. Then he shook his head sadly.

'But Celia wouldn't have played,' he said. 'She was soppy about him.'

'You've no theory of your own, Mr Chapman, about the things that have been going on in this house? About, for instance, the spilling of ink over Miss Johnston's papers?'

'If you're thinking I did it, Inspector Sharpe, that's quite untrue. Of course, it looks like me because of the green ink, but if you ask *me*, that was just spite.'

'What was spite?'

'Using my ink. Somebody deliberately used my ink to make it look like me. There's a lot of spite about here, Inspector.'

The Inspector looked at him sharply.

'Now what exactly do you mean by a lot of spite about?'

But Nigel immediately drew back into his shell and became noncommittal.

'I didn't mean anything really – just that when a lot of people are cooped up together, they get rather petty.'

The next person on Inspector Sharpe's list was Leonard Bateson. Len Bateson was even less at his ease than Nigel, though it showed in a different way. He was suspicious and truculent.

'All right!' he burst out, after the first routine inquiries were concluded. '*I* poured out Celia's coffee and gave it to her. So what?'

'You gave her her after-dinner coffee – is that what you're saying, Mr Bateson?'

'Yes. At least I filled the cup up from the urn and put it down beside her and you can believe it or not, but there was no morphia in it.'

'You saw her drink it?'

'No, I didn't actually see her drink it. We were all moving around and I got into an argument with someone just after that. I didn't notice when she drank it. There were other people round her.'

'I see. In fact, what you are saying is that *anybody* could have dropped morphia into her coffee cup?'

'You try and put anything in anyone's cup! Everybody would see you.'

'Not necessarily,' said Sharpe.

Len burst out aggressively:

'What the hell do you think I want to poison the kid for? I've nothing against her.'

'I've not suggested that you did want to poison her.'

'She took the stuff herself. She must have taken it herself. There's no other explanation.'

'We might think so, if it weren't for that faked suicide note.'

'Faked my hat! She wrote it, didn't she?'

'She wrote it as part of a letter, early that morning.'

'Well – she could have torn a bit out and used it as a suicide note.'

'Come now, Mr Bateson. If you wanted to write a suicide

note you'd write one. You wouldn't take a letter you'd written to somebody else and carefully tear out one particular phrase.'

'I might do. People do all sorts of funny things.'

'In that case, where is the rest of the letter?'

'How should I know? That's your business, not mine.'

'I'm making it my business. You'd be well advised, Mr Bateson, to answer my questions civilly.'

'Well, what do you want to know? I didn't kill the girl, and I'd no motive for killing her.'

'You liked her?'

Len said less aggressively:

'I liked her very much. She was a nice kid. A bit dumb, but nice.'

'You believed her when she owned up to having committed the thefts which had been worrying everyone for some time past?'

'Well, I believed her, of course, since she said so. But I must say it seemed odd.'

'You didn't think it was a likely thing for her to do?'

'Well, no. Not really.'

Leonard's truculence had subsided now that he was no longer on the defensive and was giving his mind to a problem which obviously intrigued him.

'She didn't seem to be the type of a kleptomaniac, if you know what I mean,' he said. 'Nor a thief either.'

'And you can't think of any other reason for her having done what she did?'

'Other reason? What other reason could there be?'

'Well, she might have wanted to arouse the interest of Mr Colin McNabb.'

'That's a bit far-fetched, isn't it?'

'But it did arouse his interest.'

'Yes, of course it did. Old Colin's absolutely dead keen on any kind of psychological abnormality.'

'Well, then. If Celia Austin knew that . . .'

Len shook his head.

'You're wrong there. She wouldn't have been capable of thinking a thing like that out. Of planning it, I mean. She hadn't got the knowledge.'

'*You've* got the knowledge, though, haven't you?'

'What do you mean?'

'I mean that, out of a purely kind intention, you might have suggested something of the kind to her.'

Len gave a short laugh.

'Think I'd do a damfool thing like that? You're crazy.'

The Inspector shifted his ground.

'Do you think that Celia Austin spilled the ink over Elizabeth Johnston's papers or do you think someone else did it?'

'Someone else. Celia said she didn't do that and I believe her. Celia never got riled by Bess; not like some other people did.'

'Who got riled by her – and why?'

'She ticked people off, you know.' Len thought about it for a moment or two. 'Anyone who made a rash statement. She'd look across the table and she'd say, in that precise way of hers, "I'm afraid that is not borne out by the facts. It has been well established by statistics that . . ." Something of that kind. Well, it was riling, you know – especially to people who like making rash statements, like Nigel Chapman for instance.'

'Ah yes. Nigel Chapman.'

'And it was green ink, too.'

'So you think it was Nigel who did it?'

'Well, it's possible, at least. He's a spiteful sort of cove, you know, and I think he might have a bit of racial feeling. About the only one of us who has.'

'Can you think of anybody else who Miss Johnston annoyed with her exactitude and her habit of correction?'

'Well, Colin McNabb wasn't too pleased now and again, and she got Jean Tomlinson's goat once or twice.'

Sharpe asked a few more desultory questions but Len Bateson had nothing useful to add. Next Sharpe saw Valerie Hobhouse.

Valerie was cool, elegant, and wary. She displayed much less nervousness than either of the men had done. She had been fond of Celia, she said. Celia was not particularly bright and it was rather pathetic the way she had set her heart on Colin McNabb.

'Do you think she was a kleptomaniac, Miss Hobhouse?'

'Well, I suppose so. I don't really know much about the subject.'

'Do you think anyone had put her up to doing what she did?'

Valerie shrugged her shoulders.

'You mean in order to attract that pompous ass Colin?'

'You're very quick on the point, Miss Hobhouse. Yes, that's what I mean. You didn't suggest it to her yourself, I suppose?'

Valerie looked amused.

'Well, hardly, my dear man, considering that a particularly favourite scarf of mine was cut to ribbons. I'm not so altruistic as that.'

'Do you think anyone else suggested it to her?'

'I should hardly think so. I should say it was just natural on her part.'

'What do you mean by natural?'

'Well, I first had a suspicion that it was Celia when all the fuss happened about Sally's shoe. Celia was jealous of Sally. Sally Finch, I'm talking about. She's far and away the most attractive girl here and Colin paid her a fair amount of attention. So on the night of this party Sally's shoe disappears and she has to go in an old black dress and black shoes. There was Celia looking as smug as a cat that's swallowed cream about it. Mind you, I didn't suspect her of all these petty thievings of bracelets and compacts.'

'Who did you think was responsible for those?'

Valerie shrugged her shoulders.

'Oh, I don't know. One of the cleaning women, I thought.'

'And the slashed rucksack?'

'Was there a slashed rucksack? I'd forgotten. That seems very pointless.'

'You've been here a good long time, haven't you, Miss Hobhouse?'

'Well, yes. I should say I'm probably the oldest inhabitant. That is to say, I've been here two years and a half now.'

'So you probably know more about this hostel than anybody else?'

'I should say so, yes.'

'Have you any ideas of your own about Celia Austin's death? Any idea of the motive that underlay it?'

Valerie shook her head. Her face was serious now.

'No,' she said. 'It was a horrible thing to happen. I can't see anybody who could possibly have wanted Celia to die. She was a nice, harmless child, and she'd just got engaged to be married, and . . .'

'Yes. And?' the Inspector prompted.

'I wondered if that was why,' said Valerie slowly. 'Because she'd got engaged. Because she was going to be happy. But that means, doesn't it, somebody – well – mad.'

She said the word with a little shiver, and Inspector Sharpe looked at her thoughtfully.

'Yes,' he said. 'We can't quite rule out madness.' He went on, 'Have you any theory about the damage done to Elizabeth Johnston's notes and papers?'

'No. That was a spiteful thing, too. I don't believe for a moment that Celia would do a thing like that.'

'Any idea who it could have been?'

'Well . . . Not a reasonable idea.'

'But an unreasonable one?'

'You don't want to hear something that's just a hunch, do you, Inspector?'

'I'd like to hear a hunch very much. I'll accept it as such, and it'll only be between ourselves.'

'Well, I may probably be quite wrong, but I've got a sort of idea that it was Patricia Lane's work.'

'Indeed! Now you do surprise me, Miss Hobhouse. I shouldn't have thought of Patricia Lane. She seems a very well balanced, amiable, young lady.'

'I don't say she did do it. I just had a sort of idea she might have done.'

'For what reason in particular?'

'Well, Patricia disliked Black Bess. Black Bess was always ticking off Patricia's beloved Nigel, putting him right, you know, when he made silly statements in the way he does sometimes.'

'You think it was more likely to have been Patricia Lane than Nigel himself?'

'Oh, yes. I don't think Nigel would bother, and he'd certainly not go using his own pet brand of ink. He's got plenty of brains. But it's just the sort of stupid thing that Patricia would do without thinking that it might involve her precious Nigel as a suspect.'

'Or again, it might be somebody who had a down on Nigel Chapman and wanted to suggest that it was his doing?'

'Yes, that's another possibility.'

'Who dislikes Nigel Chapman?'

'Oh, well, Jean Tomlinson for one. And he and Len Bateson are always scrapping a good deal.'

'Have you any ideas, Miss Hobhouse, how morphia could have been administered to Celia Austin?'

'I've been thinking and thinking. Of course, I suppose the coffee is the most obvious way. We were all milling around in the common-room. Celia's coffee was on a small table near her and she always waited until her coffee was nearly cold before she drank it. I suppose anybody who had sufficient nerve could have dropped a tablet or something into her cup without being seen, but it would be rather a risk to take. I mean, it's the sort of thing that might be noticed quite easily.'

'The morphia,' said Inspector Sharpe, 'was not in tablet form.'

'What was it? Powder?'

'Yes.'

Valerie frowned.

'That would be rather more difficult, wouldn't it?'

'Anything else besides coffee you can think of?'

'She sometimes had a glass of hot milk before she went to bed. I don't think she did that night, though.'

'Can you describe to me exactly what happened that evening in the common-room?'

'Well, as I say, we all sat about, talked; somebody turned the wireless on. Most of the boys, I think, went out. Celia went up to bed fairly early and so did Jean Tomlinson. Sally and I sat on there fairly late. I was writing letters and Sally was mugging over some notes. I rather think I was the last to go up to bed.'

'It was just a usual evening, in fact?'

'Absolutely, Inspector.'

'Thank you, Miss Hobhouse. Will you send Miss Lane to me now?'

Patricia Lane looked worried, but not apprehensive. Questions and answers elicited nothing very new. Asked about the damage to Elizabeth Johnston's papers Patricia said that she had no doubt that Celia had been responsible.

'But she denied it, Miss Lane, very vehemently.'

'Well, of course,' said Patricia. 'She would. I think she was ashamed of having done it. But it fits in, doesn't it, with all the other things?'

'Do you know what I find about this case, Miss Lane? That nothing fits in very well.'

'I suppose,' said Patricia, flushing, 'that you would think it was Nigel who messed up Bess's papers. Because of the ink. That's such absolute *nonsense*. I mean, Nigel wouldn't have used his own ink if he'd done a thing like that. He wouldn't be such a fool. But anyway, he wouldn't do it.'

'He didn't always get on very well with Miss Johnston, did he?'

'Oh, she had an annoying manner sometimes, but he didn't really mind.' Patricia Lane leaned forward earnestly. 'I would like to try and make you understand one or two things, Inspector. About Nigel Chapman, I mean. You see, Nigel is really very much his own worst enemy. I'm the first to admit that he's got a very difficult manner. It prejudices people against him. He's rude and sarcastic and makes fun of people, and so he puts people's backs up and they think the worst of him. But really he's quite different from what he seems. He's one of those shy, rather unhappy people who really want to be liked but who, from a kind of spirit of contradiction, find themselves saying and doing the opposite to what they mean to say and do.'

'Ah,' said Inspector Sharpe. 'Rather unfortunate for them, that.'

'Yes, but they really can't help it, you know. It comes from having had an unfortunate childhood. Nigel had a very unhappy home life. His father was very harsh and severe and never understood him. And his father treated his mother very badly. After she died they had the most terrific quarrel and Nigel flung out of the house, and his father said that he'd never give him a penny and he must get on as well as he could without any help from him. Nigel said he didn't want any help from his father; and wouldn't take it if it was offered. A small amount of money came to him under his mother's will, and he never wrote to his father or went near him again. Of course, I think that was a pity in a way, but there's no doubt that his father is a very unpleasant man. I don't wonder that that's made Nigel bitter and difficult to get on with. Since his mother died, he's never had anyone to care for him and look after him. His health's not been good, though his mind is brilliant. He is handicapped in life and he just can't show himself as he really is.'

Patricia Lane stopped. She was flushed and a little breathless as the result of her long earnest speech. Inspector Sharpe looked at her thoughtfully. He had come across many Patricia Lanes before. 'In love with the chap,' he thought to himself. 'Don't suppose he cares twopence for her, but probably accepts being mothered. Father certainly sounds a cantankerous old cuss, but I dare say the mother was a foolish woman who spoilt her son and by doting on him, widened the breach between him and his father. I've seen enough of that kind of thing.' He wondered if Nigel Chapman had been attracted at all to Celia Austin. It seemed unlikely, but it might be so. 'And if so,' he thought, 'Patricia Lane might have bitterly resented the fact.' Resented it enough to do murder? Surely not – and in any case, the fact that Celia had got engaged to Colin McNabb would surely wash that out as a possible motive for murder. He dismissed Patricia Lane and asked for Jean Tomlinson.

CHAPTER 10

Miss Tomlinson was a severe-looking young woman of twenty-seven, with fair hair, regular features and a rather pursed-up mouth. She sat down and said primly:

'Yes, Inspector? What can I do for you?'

'I wonder if you can help us at all, Miss Tomlinson, about this very tragic matter.'

'It's shocking. Really quite shocking,' said Jean. 'It was bad enough when we thought Celia had committed suicide, but now that it's supposed to be murder . . .' She stopped and shook her head, sadly.

'We are fairly sure that she did not poison herself,' said Sharpe. 'You know where the poison came from?'

Jean nodded.

'I gather it came from St Catherine's Hospital, where she works. But surely that makes it seem more like suicide?'

'It was intended to, no doubt,' said the inspector.

'But who else could possibly have got that poison except Celia?'

'Quite a lot of people,' said Inspector Sharpe, 'if they were determined to do so. Even you, yourself, Miss Tomlinson,' he said, 'might have managed to help yourself to it if you had wished to do so.'

'Really, Inspector Sharpe!' Jean's tones were sharp with indignation.

'Well, you visited the Dispensary fairly often, didn't you, Miss Tomlinson?'

'I went in there to see Mildred Carey, yes. But naturally I would never have dreamed of tampering with the poison cupboard.'

'But you could have done so?'

'I certainly couldn't have done anything of the kind!'

'Oh, come now, Miss Tomlinson. Say that your friend was busy packing up the ward baskets and the other girl was at the outpatients' window. There are frequent times when there are only two dispensers in the front room. You could have wandered casually round the back of the shelves of bottles that run across the middle of the floor. You could have nipped a bottle out of the cupboard and into your pocket, and neither of the two dispensers would have dreamed of what you had done.'

'I resent what you say very much, Inspector Sharpe. It's – it's a – disgraceful accusation.'

'But it's not an accusation, Miss Tomlinson. It's nothing of the kind. You mustn't misunderstand me. You said to me that it wasn't possible for you to do such a thing, and I'm trying to show you that it was *possible*. I'm not suggesting for a moment that you did so. After all,' he added, 'why should you?'

'Quite so. You don't seem to realise, Inspector Sharpe, that I was a friend of Celia's.'

'Quite a lot of people get poisoned by their friends. There's a certain question we have to ask ourselves sometimes. "When is a friend not a friend?"'

'There was no disagreement between me and Celia; nothing of the kind. I liked her very much.'

'Had you any reason to suspect it was she who had been responsible for these thefts in the house?'

'No, indeed. I was never so surprised in my life. I always

thought Celia had high principles. I wouldn't have dreamed of her doing such a thing.'

'Of course,' said Sharpe, watching her carefully, 'kleptomaniacs can't really help themselves, can they?'

Jean Tomlinson's lips pursed themselves together even more closely. Then she opened them and spoke.

'I can't say I can quite subscribe to *that* idea, Inspector Sharpe. I'm old-fashioned in my views and believe that stealing is stealing.'

'You think that Celia stole things because, frankly, she wanted to take them?'

'Certainly I do.'

'Plain dishonest, in fact?'

'I'm afraid so.'

'Ah!' said Inspector Sharpe, shaking his head. 'That's bad.'

'Yes, it's always upsetting when you feel you're disappointed in anyone.'

'There was a question, I understand, of our being called in – the police, I mean.'

'Yes. That would have been the right thing to do in my opinion.'

'Perhaps you think it ought to have been done anyway?'

'I think it would have been the right thing. Yes, I don't think, you know, people ought to be allowed to get away with these things.'

'With calling oneself a kleptomaniac when one is really a thief, do you mean?'

'Well, more or less, yes – that is what I mean.'

'Instead of which everything was ending happily and Miss Austin had wedding bells ahead.'

'Of course, one isn't surprised at anything Colin McNabb does,' said Jean Tomlinson viciously. 'I'm sure he's an atheist and a most disbelieving, mocking, unpleasant young man. He's rude to everybody. It's my opinion that he's a *Communist*!'

'Ah!' said Inspector Sharpe. 'Bad!' He shook his head.

'He backed up Celia, I think, because he hasn't got any proper feeling about property. He probably thinks everyone should help themselves to everything they want.'

'Still, at any rate,' said Inspector Sharpe, 'Miss Austin did own up.'

'After she was found out. Yes,' said Jean sharply.

'Who found her out?'

'That Mr – what-was-his-name . . . Poirot, who came.'

'But why do you think he found her out, Miss Tomlinson? He didn't say so. He just advised calling in the police.'

'He must have shown her that he knew. She obviously knew the game was up and rushed off to confess.'

'What about the ink on Elizabeth Johnston's papers? Did she confess to that?'

'I really don't know. I suppose so.'

'You suppose wrong,' said Sharpe. 'She denied most vehemently that she had anything to do with that.'

'Well, perhaps that may be so. I must say it doesn't seem very likely.'

'You think it is more likely that it was Nigel Chapman?'

'No, I don't think Nigel would do that either. I think it's much more likely to be Mr Akibombo.'

'Really? Why should he do it?'

'Jealousy. All these coloured people are very jealous of each other and very hysterical.'

'That's interesting, Miss Tomlinson. When was the last time you saw Celia Austin?'

'After dinner on Friday night.'

'Who went up to bed first? Did she or did you?'

'I did.'

'You did not go to her room or see her after you'd left the common-room?'

'No.'

'And you've no idea who could have introduced morphia into her coffee – if it was given that way?'

'No idea at all.'

'You never saw morphia lying about the house or in anyone's room?'

'No. No, I don't think so.'

'You don't think so? What do you mean by that, Miss Tomlinson?'

'Well, I just wondered. There was that silly bet, you know.'

'What bet?'

'One – oh, two or three of the boys were arguing –'

'What were they arguing about?'

'Murder, and ways of doing it. Poisoning in particular.'

'Who was concerned in the discussion?'

'Well, I think Colin and Nigel started it, and then Len Bateson chipped in and Patricia was there too –'

'Can you remember, as closely as possible, what was said on that occasion – how the argument went?'

Jean Tomlinson reflected a few moments.

'Well, it started, I think, with a discussion on murdering by poisoning, saying that the difficulty was to get hold of the poison, that the murderer was usually traced by either the sale of the poison or having an opportunity to get it, and Nigel said that wasn't at all necessary. He said that he could think of three distinct ways by which anyone could get hold of poison, and nobody would ever know they had it. Len Bateson said then that he was talking through his hat. Nigel said no he wasn't, and he was quite prepared to prove it. Pat said that of course Nigel was quite right. She said that either Len or Colin could probably help themselves to poison any time they liked from a hospital, and so could Celia, she said. And Nigel said that wasn't what he meant at all. He said it would be noticed if Celia took anything from the Dispensary. Sooner or later they'd look for it and find it gone. And Pat said no, not if she took the bottle and emptied some stuff out and filled it up with something else. Colin laughed then and said there'd be very serious complaints from the patients one of these days, in that case. But Nigel said of course he didn't mean special opportunities. He said that he himself, who hadn't got any particular access, either as a doctor or dispenser, could jolly well get three different kinds of poison by three different methods. Len Bateson said, "All right, then, but what are your methods?" and Nigel said, "I shan't tell you, now, but I'm prepared to bet you that within three weeks I can produce samples of three deadly poisons here," and Len Bateson said he'd bet him a fiver he couldn't do it.'

'Well?' said Inspector Sharpe, when Jean stopped.

'Well, nothing more came of it, I think, for some time and then, one evening in the common-room, Nigel said, "Now then, chaps, look here – I'm as good as my word," and he threw down three things on the table. He had a tube of hyoscine tablets, and a bottle of tincture of digitalin, and a tiny bottle of morphine tartrate.'

The inspector said sharply:

'Morphine tartrate. Any label on it?'

'Yes, it had St Catherine's Hospital on it. I do remember that because, naturally, it caught my eye.'

'And the others?'

'I didn't notice. They were not hospital stores, I should say.'

'What happened next?'

'Well, of course, there was a lot of talk and jawing, and Len Bateson said, "Come now, if you'd done a murder this would be traced to you soon enough," and Nigel said, "Not a bit of it. I'm a layman. I've no connection with any clinic or hospital and nobody will connect me for one moment with these. I didn't buy them over the counter," and Colin McNabb took his pipe out of his teeth and said, "No, you'd certainly not be able to do that. There's no chemist would sell you those three things without a doctor's prescription." Anyway, they argued a bit but in the end Len said he'd pay up. He said, "I can't do it now, because I'm a bit short of cash, but there's no doubt about it; Nigel's proved his point," and then he said, "What are we going to do with the guilty spoils?" Nigel grinned and said we'd better get rid of them before any accidents occurred, so they emptied out the tube and threw the tablets on the fire and emptied out the powder from the morphine tartrate and threw that on the fire too. The tincture of digitalis they poured down the lavatory.'

'And the bottles?'

'I don't know what happened to the bottles ... I should think they probably were just thrown into the waste-paper basket?'

'But the poison itself was destroyed?'

'Yes. I'm sure of that. I saw it.'

'And that was – when?'

'About, oh, just over a fortnight ago, I think.'

'I see. Thank you, Miss Tomlinson.'

Jean lingered, clearly wanting to be told more.

'D'you think it might be important?'

'It might be. One can't tell.'

Inspector Sharpe remained brooding for a few moments. Then he had Nigel Chapman in again.

'I've just had a rather interesting statement from Miss Jean Tomlinson,' he said.

'Ah! Who's dear Jean been poisoning your mind against? Me?'

'She's been talking about poison, and in connection with you, Mr Chapman.'

'Poison and me? What on earth?'

'Do you deny that some weeks ago you had a wager with Mr Bateson about methods of obtaining poison in some way that could not be traced to you?'

'Oh, that!' Nigel was suddenly enlightened. 'Yes, of course! Funny I never thought of that. I don't even remember Jean being there. But you don't think it could have any possible significance, do you?'

'Well, one doesn't know. You admit the fact, then?'

'Oh yes, we were arguing on the subject. Colin and Len were being very superior and high-handed about it so I told them that with a little ingenuity anyone could get hold of a suitable supply of poison – in fact I said I could think of three distinct ways of doing it, and I'd prove my point, I said, by putting them into practice.'

'Which you then proceeded to do?'

'Which I then proceeded to do, Inspector.'

'And what were those three methods, Mr Chapman?'

Nigel put his head a little on one side.

'Aren't you asking me to incriminate myself?' he said. 'Surely you ought to warn me?'

'It hasn't come to warning you yet, Mr Chapman, but, of course, there's no need for you to incriminate yourself, as you put it. In fact you're perfectly entitled to refuse my questions if you like to do so.'

'I don't know that I want to refuse.' Nigel considered for a moment or two, a slight smile playing round his lips.

'Of course,' he said, 'what I did was, no doubt, against the law. You could haul me in for it if you liked. On the other hand, this is a murder case and if it's got any bearing on poor little Celia's death I suppose I ought to tell you.'

'That would certainly be the sensible point of view to take.'

'All right then. I'll talk.'

'What were these three methods?'

'Well.' Nigel leant back in his chair. 'One's always reading in the papers, isn't one, about doctors losing dangerous drugs from a car? People are being warned about it.'

'Yes.'

'Well, it occurred to me that one very simple method would be to go down to the country, follow a GP about on his rounds, when occasion offered – just open the car, look in the doctor's case, and extract what you wanted. You see, in these country districts, the doctor doesn't always take his case into the house. It depends what sort of patient he's going to see.'

'Well?'

'Well, that's all. That's to say that's all for method number one. I had to sleuth three doctors until I found a suitably careless one. When I did, it was simplicity itself. The car was left outside a farmhouse in a rather lonely spot. I opened the door, looked at the case, took out a tube of hyoscine hydrobromide, and that was that.'

'Ah! And method number two?'

'That entailed just a little pumping of dear Celia, as a matter of fact. She was quite unsuspicious. I told you she was a stupid girl, she had no idea what I was doing. I simply talked a bit about the mumbo jumbo Latin of doctors' prescriptions, and asked her to write me out a prescription in the way a doctor writes it, for tincture digitalin. She obliged quite unsuspecting. All I had to do after that was to find a doctor in the classified directory, living in a far off district of London, add his initials or slightly illegible signature. I then took it to a chemist in a busy part of London, who would not be likely to be familiar with that particular doctor's signature, and I received the prescription made up without any difficulty at all. Digitalin is prescribed in quite large quantities for heart cases and I had written out the prescription on hotel notepaper.'

'Very ingenious,' said Inspector Sharpe drily.

'I *am* incriminating myself! I can hear it in your voice.'

'And the third method?'

Nigel did not reply at once. Then he said:

'Look here. What exactly am I letting myself in for?'

'The theft of drugs from an unlocked car is larceny,' said Inspector Sharpe. 'Forging a prescription . . .'

Nigel interrupted him.

'Not exactly forging, is it? I mean, I didn't obtain money by it, and it wasn't exactly an imitation of any doctor's signature. I mean, if I write a prescription and write H R James on it, you can't say I'm forging any particular Dr James's name, can you?' He went on with rather a wry smile. 'You see what I mean? I'm sticking my neck out. If you like to turn nasty over this – well – I'm obviously for it. On the other hand, if . . .'

'Yes, Mr Chapman, on the other hand?'

Nigel said with a sudden passion:

'I don't like murder. It's a beastly, horrible thing. Celia, poor little devil, didn't deserve to be murdered. I want to help. But does it help? I can't see that it does. Telling you my peccadilloes, I mean.'

'The police have a good deal of latitude, Mr Chapman. It's up to them to look upon certain happenings as a light-hearted prank of an irresponsible nature. I accept your assurance that you want to help in the solving of this girl's murder. Now please go on, and tell me about your third method.'

'Well,' said Nigel, 'we're coming fairly near the bone now. It was a bit more risky than the other two, but at the same time it was a great deal more fun. You see, I'd been to visit Celia once or twice in her Dispensary. I knew the lay of the land there . . .'

'So you were able to pinch the bottle out of the cupboard?'

'No, no, nothing as simple as that. That wouldn't have been fair from my point of view. And, incidentally, if it had been a *real* murder – that is, if I had been stealing the poison for the purpose of murder – it would probably be remembered that I had been there. Actually, I hadn't been in Celia's Dispensary for about six months. No, I knew that Celia always went into the back room at eleven-fifteen for what you might call "elevenses", that is, a cup of coffee and a biscuit. The girls went in turn, two at a time. There was a new girl there who had only just come and she certainly wouldn't know me by sight. So what I did was this. I strolled into the Dispensary with a white coat on and a stethoscope round my neck. There was only the new girl there and she was busy at the outpatients' hatch. I strolled in, went along to the poison cupboard, took out a bottle, strolled round the end of the partition, said to the girl, "What strength adrenalin do you keep?" She told me and I nodded, then I asked her if she had a couple of Veganin as I had a terrific hangover. I swallowed them down and strolled out again. She never had the least suspicion that I wasn't somebody's houseman or a medical student. It was child's play. Celia never even knew I'd been there.'

'A stethoscope,' said Inspector Sharpe curiously. 'Where did you get a stethoscope?'

Nigel grinned suddenly.

'It was Len Bateson's,' he said. 'I pinched it.'

'From this house?'

'Yes.'

'So that explains the theft of the stethoscope. That was not Celia's doing.'

'Good lord no! Can't see a kleptomaniac stealing a stethoscope, can you?'

'What did you do with it afterwards?'

'Well, I had to pawn it,' said Nigel apologetically.

'Wasn't that a little hard on Bateson?'

'Very hard on him. But without explaining my methods, which I didn't mean to do, I couldn't tell him about it. However,' added Nigel cheerfully, 'I took him out not long after and gave him a hell of a party one evening.'

'You're a very irresponsible young man,' said Inspector Sharpe.

'You should have seen their faces,' said Nigel, his grin widening, 'when I threw down those three lethal preparations on the table and told them I had managed to pinch them without anybody being wise as to who took them.'

'What you're telling me is,' said the inspector, 'that you had three means of poisoning someone by three different poisons and that in each case the poison could not have been traced to you.'

Nigel nodded.

'That's fair enough,' he said. 'And given the circumstances it's not a very pleasant thing to admit. But the point is, that the poisons were all disposed of at least a fortnight ago or longer.'

'That is what you think, Mr Chapman, but it may not really be so.'

Nigel stared at him.

'What do you mean?'

'You had these things in your possession, how long?'

Nigel considered.

'Well, the tube of hyoscine about ten days, I suppose. The morphine tartrate, about four days. The tincture digitalin I'd only got that very afternoon.'

'And where did you keep these things – the hyoscine hydro-bromide and the morphine tartrate, that is to say?'

'In the drawer of my chest-of-drawers, pushed to the back under my socks.'

'Did anyone know you had it there?'

'No. No, I'm sure they didn't.'

There had been, however, a faint hesitation in his voice which Inspector Sharpe noticed, but for the moment he did not press the point.

'Did you tell anyone what you were doing? Your methods? The way you were going about these things?'

'No. At least – no, I didn't.'

'You said "at least", Mr Chapman.'

'Well, I didn't actually. As a matter of fact, I was going to tell Pat, then I thought she wouldn't approve. She's very strict, Pat is, so I fobbed her off.'

'You didn't tell her about stealing the stuff from the doctor's car, or the prescription, or the morphia from the hospital?'

'Actually, I told her afterwards about the digitalin; that I'd written a prescription and got a bottle from the chemist, and about masquerading as a doctor at the hospital. I'm sorry to say Pat wasn't amused. I didn't tell her about pinching things from a car. I thought she'd go up in smoke.'

'Did you tell her you were going to destroy this stuff after you'd won the bet?'

'Yes. She was all worried and het up about it. Started to insist I took the things back or something like that.'

'That course of action never occurred to you yourself?'

'Good lord no! That would have been fatal; it would have landed me in no end of a row. No, we three just chucked the stuff on the fire and poured it down the loo and that was that. No harm done.'

'You say that, Mr Chapman, but it's quite possible that harm was done.'

'How can it have been, if the stuff was chucked away as I tell you?'

'Has it ever occurred to you, Mr Chapman, that someone might have seen where you put those things, or found them perhaps, and that someone might have emptied morphia out of the bottle and replaced it with something else?'

'Good lord no!' Nigel stared at him. 'I never thought of anything of that kind. I don't believe it.'

'But it's a possibility, Mr Chapman.'

'But nobody could possibly have known.'

'I should say,' said the inspector drily, 'that in a place of this kind a great deal more is known than you yourself might believe possible.'

'Snooping, you mean?'

'Yes.'

'Perhaps you're right there.'

'Which of the students might normally, at any time, be in your room?'

'Well, I share it with Len Bateson. Most of the men here have been in it now and again. Not the girls, of course. The girls aren't supposed to come to the bedroom floors on our side of the house. Propriety. Pure living.'

'They're not supposed to, but they might do so, I suppose?'

'Anyone *might*,' said Nigel. 'In the daytime. The afternoon, for instance, there's nobody about.'

'Does Miss Lane ever come to your room?'

'I hope you don't mean that the way it sounds, Inspector. Pat comes to my room sometimes to replace some socks she's been darning. Nothing more than that.'

Leaning forward, Inspector Sharpe said:

'You do realise, Mr Chapman, that the person who could most easily have taken some of that poison out of the bottle and substituted something else for it, was yourself?'

Nigel looked at him, his face suddenly hard and haggard.

'Yes,' he said. 'I've seen that just a minute and a half ago. I could have done just exactly that. But I'd no reason on earth for putting that girl out of the way, Inspector, and I didn't do it. Still, there it is – I quite realise that you've only got my word for it.'

CHAPTER 11

The story of the bet and the disposal of the poison was confirmed by Len Bateson and by Colin McNabb. Sharpe retained Colin McNabb after the others had gone.

'I don't want to cause you any more pain than I can help, Mr McNabb,' he said. 'I can realise what it means to you for your fiancée to have been poisoned on the very night of your engagement.'

'There'll be no need to go into that aspect of it,' said Colin McNabb, his face immovable. 'You'll not need to concern yourself with my feelings. Just ask me any questions you like which you think may be useful to you.'

'It was your considered opinion that Celia Austin's behaviour had a psychological origin?'

'There's no doubt about it at all,' said Colin McNabb. 'If you'd like me to go into the theory of the thing . . .'

'No, no,' said Inspector Sharpe hastily. 'I'm taking your word for it as a student of psychology.'

'Her childhood had been particularly unfortunate. It had set up an emotional block . . .'

'Quite so, quite so.' Inspector Sharpe was desperately anxious to avoid hearing the story of yet another unhappy childhood. Nigel's had been quite enough.

'You had been attracted to her for some time?'

'I would not say precisely that,' said Colin, considering the matter conscientiously. 'These things sometimes surprise you by the way they dawn upon you suddenly, like. Subconsciously no doubt, I had been attracted, but I was not aware of the fact. Since it was not my intention to marry young, I had no doubt set up a considerable resistance to the idea in my conscious mind.'

'Yes. Just so. Celia Austin was happy in her engagement to you? I mean, she expressed no doubts? Uncertainties? There was nothing she felt she ought to tell you?'

'She made a very full confession of all she'd been doing. There was nothing more in her mind to worry her.'

'And you were planning to get married – when?'

'Not for a considerable time. I'm not in a position at the moment to support a wife.'

'Had Celia any enemies here? Anyone who did not like her?'

'I can hardly believe so. I've given that point of view a great deal of thought, Inspector. Celia was well liked here. I'd say, myself, it was not a personal matter at all which brought about her end.'

'What do you mean by "not a personal matter"?'

'I do not wish to be very precise at the moment. It's only a vague kind of idea I have and I'm not clear about it myself.'

From that position the inspector could not budge him.

The last two students to be interviewed were Sally Finch and Elizabeth Johnston. The inspector took Sally Finch first.

Sally was an attractive girl with a mop of red hair and eyes that were bright and intelligent. After routine inquiries Sally Finch suddenly took the initiative.

'D'you know what I'd like to do, Inspector? I'd like to tell you just what I think. I personally. There's something all wrong about this house, something very wrong indeed. I'm sure of that.'

'You mean you're afraid of something, Miss Finch?' Sally nodded her head.

'Yes, I'm afraid. There's something or someone here who's pretty ruthless. The whole place isn't – well, how shall I put it? – it isn't what it seems. No, no, Inspector, I don't mean Communists. I can see that just trembling on your lips. It's not Communists I mean. Perhaps it isn't even criminal. I don't know. But I'll bet you anything you like that awful old woman knows about it all.'

'What old woman? You don't mean Mrs Hubbard?'

'No. Not Ma Hubbard. She's a dear. I mean old Nicoletis. That old she-wolf.'

'That's interesting, Miss Finch. Can you be more definite? About Mrs Nicoletis, I mean.'

Sally shook her head.

'No. That's just what I can't be. All I can tell you is she gives me the creeps every time I pass her. Something queer is going on here, Inspector.'

'I wish you could be a little more definite.'

'So do I. You'll be thinking I'm fanciful. Well, perhaps I am, but other people feel it too. Akibombo does. He's scared. I believe Black Bess does, too, but she wouldn't let on. And I think, Inspector, that Celia knew something about it.'

'Knew something about what?'

'That's just it. What? But there were things she said. Said that last day. About clearing everything up. She had owned up to *her* part in what was going on, but she sort of hinted that there were other things she knew about and she wanted to get them cleared up too. I think she knew *something*, Inspector, about *someone*. That's the reason I think she was killed.'

'But if it was something as serious as that . . .'

Sally interrupted him.

'I'd say that she had no idea how serious it was. She wasn't bright, you know. She was pretty dumb. She'd got hold of something but she'd no idea that the something she'd got hold of was dangerous. Anyway, that's my hunch for what it's worth.'

'I see. Thank you . . . Now the last time you saw Celia Austin was in the common-room after dinner last night, is that right?'

'That's right. At least, actually, I saw her after that.'

'You saw her after that? Where? In her room?'

'No. When I went up to bed she was going out of the front door just as I came out of the common-room.'

'Going out of the front door? Out of the house, do you mean?'

'Yes.'

'That's rather surprising. Nobody else has suggested that.'

'I dare say they didn't know. She certainly said good night and that she was going up to bed, and if I hadn't seen her I would have assumed that she *had* gone up to bed.'

'Whereas actually she went upstairs, put on some outdoor things and then left the house. Is that right?'

Sally nodded.

'And I think she was going to meet someone.'

'I see. Someone from outside. Or could it have been one of the students?'

'Well, it's my hunch that it would be one of the students. You see, if she wanted to speak to somebody privately, there was nowhere very well she could do it in the house. Someone might have suggested that she should come out and meet them somewhere outside.'

'Have you any idea when she got in again?'

'No idea whatever.'

'Would Geronimo know, the manservant?'

'He'd know if she came in after eleven o'clock because that's the time he bolts and chains the door. Up to that time anyone can get in with their own key.'

'Do you know exactly what time it was when you saw her going out of the house?'

'I'd say it was about – ten. Perhaps a little past ten, but not much.'

'I see. Thank you, Miss Finch, for what you've told me.'

Last of all the inspector talked to Elizabeth Johnston. He was at once impressed with the quiet capability of the girl. She answered his questions with intelligent decision and then waited for him to proceed.

'Celia Austin,' he said, 'protested vehemently that it was not she who damaged your papers, Miss Johnston. Do you believe her?'

'I do not think Celia did that. No.'

'You don't know who did?'

'The obvious answer is Nigel Chapman. But it seems to me a little too obvious. Nigel is intelligent. He would not use his own ink.'

'And if not Nigel, who then?'

'That is more difficult. But I think Celia knew who it was – or at least guessed.'

'Did she tell you so?'

'Not in so many words; but she came to my room on the evening of the day she died, before going down to dinner. She came to tell me that though she was responsible for the thefts she had not sabotaged my work. I told her that I accepted that assurance. I asked her if she knew who had done so.'

'And what did she say?'

'She said' – Elizabeth paused a moment, as though to be sure of the accuracy of what she was about to say – 'she said, "*I can't really be sure, because I don't see why . . . It might have been a mistake or an accident . . . I'm sure whoever did it is very unhappy about it, and would really like to own up.*" Celia went on, "*There are some things I don't understand, like the electric light bulbs the day the police came."'*

Sharpe interrupted.

'What's this about the police and electric light bulbs?'

'I don't know. All Celia said was: "*I* didn't take them out." And then she said: "I wondered if it had anything to do with the passport?" I said, "What passport are you talking about?" And she said: "I think someone might have a forged passport."'

The inspector was silent for a moment or two.

Here at last some vague pattern seemed to be taking shape. A passport . . .

He asked, 'What more did she say?'

'Nothing more. She just said: "Anyway I shall know more about it tomorrow."'

'She said that, did she? *I shall know more about it tomorrow.* That's a very significant remark, Miss Johnston.'

'Yes.'

The inspector was again silent as he reflected.

Something about a passport – and a visit from the police . . . Before coming to Hickory Road, he had carefully looked up the files. A fairly close eye was kept on hostels which housed foreign students. 26 Hickory Road had a good record. Such details as there were, were meagre and unsuggestive. A West African student wanted by the Sheffield police for living on a woman's earnings; the student in question had been at Hickory Road for a few days and had then gone elsewhere, and had in due course been gathered in and since deported. There had been a routine check of all hostels and boarding-houses for a Eurasian 'wanted to assist the police' in the investigation of the murder of a publican's wife near Cambridge. That had been cleared up when the young man in question had walked into the police station at Hull and had given himself up for the crime. There had been an inquiry into a student's distribution of subversive pamphlets. All these occurrences had taken place some time ago and could not possibly have any connection with the death of Celia Austin.

He sighed and looked up to find Elizabeth Johnston's dark intelligent eyes watching him.

On an impulse, he said, 'Tell me, Miss Johnston, have you

ever had a feeling – an impression – of something *wrong* about this place?'

She looked surprised.

'In what way – wrong?'

'I couldn't really say. I'm thinking of something Miss Sally Finch said to me.'

'Oh – Sally Finch!'

There was an intonation in her voice which he found hard to place. He felt interested and went on:

'Miss Finch seemed to me a good observer, both shrewd and practical. She was very insistent on there being something – odd, about this place – though she found it difficult to define just what it was.'

Elizabeth said sharply:

'That is her American way of thought. They are all the same, these Americans, nervous, apprehensive, suspecting every kind of foolish thing! Look at the fools they make of themselves with their witch hunts, their hysterical spy mania, their obsession over Communism. Sally Finch is typical.'

The inspector's interest grew. So Elizabeth disliked Sally Finch. Why? Because Sally was an American? Or did Elizabeth dislike Americans merely because Sally Finch was an American, and had she some reason of her own for disliking the attractive redhead? Perhaps it was just simple female jealousy.

He resolved to try a line of approach that he had sometimes found useful. He said smoothly:

'As you may appreciate, Miss Johnston, in an establishment like this, the level of intelligence varies a great deal. Some people – most people – we just ask for facts. But when we come across someone with a high level of intelligence –'

He paused. The inference was flattering. Would she respond?

After a brief pause, she did.

'I think I understand what you mean, Inspector. The intellectual level here is not, as you say, very high. Nigel Chapman has a certain quickness of intellect, but his mind is shallow. Leonard Bateson is a plodder – no more. Valerie Hobhouse has a good quality of mind, but her outlook is commercial, and she's too lazy to use her brains on anything worth while. What you want is the detachment of a trained mind.'

'Such as yours, Miss Johnston.'

She accepted the tribute without a protest. He realised, with some interest, that behind her modest pleasant manner, here was a young woman who was positively arrogant in her appraisement of her own qualities.

'I'm inclined to agree with your estimate of your fellow students, Miss Hobhouse. Chapman is clever but childish. Valerie Hobhouse has brains but a *blasé* attitude to life. You, as you say, have a trained mind. That's why I'd value your views – the views of a powerful detached intellect.'

For a moment he was afraid he had overdone it, but he need have had no fears.

'There is nothing wrong about this place, Inspector. Pay no attention to Sally Finch. This is a decent well run hostel. I am certain that you will find no trace here of any subversive activities.'

Inspector Sharpe felt a little surprised.

'It wasn't really subversive activities I was thinking about.'

'Oh – I see –' She was a little taken aback. 'I was linking up what Celia said about a passport. But looking at it impartially and weighing up all the evidence, it seems quite certain to me that the reason for Celia's death was what I should express as a private one – some sex complication, perhaps. I'm sure it had nothing to do with what I might call the hostel as a hostel, or anything "going on" here. Nothing, I am sure, is going on. I should be aware of the fact if it were so, my perceptions are very keen.'

'I see. Well, thank you, Miss Johnston. You've been very kind and helpful.'

Elizabeth Johnston went out. Inspector Sharpe sat staring at the closed door and Sergeant Cobb had to speak to him twice before he roused himself.

'Eh?'

'I said that's the lot, sir.'

'Yes, and what have we got? Precious little. But I'll tell you one thing, Cobb. I'm coming back here tomorrow with a search warrant. We'll go away talking pretty now and they'll think it's all over. *But there's something going on in this place.* Tomorrow I'll turn it upside down – not so easy when you don't know what you're looking for, but there's a chance that I'll find something to give me a clue. That's a very interesting girl who just went out. She's got the ego of a Napoleon, and I strongly suspect that she knows something.'

CHAPTER 12

I

Hercule Poirot, at work upon his correspondence, paused in the middle of a sentence that he was dictating. Miss Lemon looked up questioningly.

'Yes, M. Poirot?'

'My mind wanders!' Poirot waved a hand. 'After all, this letter is not important. Be so kind, Miss Lemon, as to get me your sister upon the telephone.'

'Yes, M. Poirot.'

A few moments later Poirot crossed the room and took the receiver from his secretary's hand.

''Allo!' he said.

'Yes, M. Poirot?'

Mrs Hubbard sounded rather breathless.

'I trust, Mrs Hubbard, that I am not disturbing you?'

'I'm past being disturbed,' said Mrs Hubbard.

'There have been agitations, yes?' Poirot asked delicately.

'That's a very nice way of putting it, M. Poirot. That's exactly what they have been. Inspector Sharpe finished questioning all the students yesterday, and then he came back with a search warrant today and I've got Mrs Nicoletis on my hands with raving hysterics.'

Poirot clucked his tongue sympathetically.

Then he said, 'It is just a little question I have to ask. You sent me a list of those things that had disappeared – and other queer happenings – what I have to ask is this, did you write that list in chronological order?'

'You mean?'

'I mean, were the things written down exactly in the order of their disappearance?'

'No, they weren't. I'm sorry – I just put them down as I thought of them. I'm so sorry if I misled you.'

'I should have asked you before,' said Poirot. 'But it did not strike me then as important. I have your list here. One evening shoe, bracelet, diamond ring, powder compact, lipstick, stethoscope, and so on. But you say that was not the order of disappearance?'

'No.'

'Can you remember now, or would it be too difficult for you, what was the proper order?'

'Well, I'm not sure if I could now, M. Poirot. You see it's all some time ago. I should have to think it out. Actually, after I had talked with my sister and knew I was coming to see you, I made a list, and I should say that I put it down in the order of things as I remembered them. I mean, the evening shoe because it was so peculiar; and then the bracelet and the powder compact and the cigarette lighter and the diamond ring because they were all rather important things and looked as though we had a genuine thief at work; and then I remembered the other more unimportant things later and added them. I mean the boracic and the electric light bulbs and the rucksack. They weren't really important and I only really thought of them as a kind of afterthought.'

'I see,' said Poirot. 'Yes, I see . . . Now what I would ask of you, madame, is to sit down now, when you have the leisure, that is . . .'

'I dare say when I've got Mrs Nicoletis to bed with a sedative and calmed down Geronimo and Maria, I shall have a little time. What is it you want me to do?'

'Sit down and try to put down, as nearly as you can, the chronological order in which the various incidents occurred.'

'Certainly, M. Poirot. The rucksack, I believe, was the first, and the electric light bulbs — which I really didn't think had any connection with the other things — and then the bracelet and the compact, no — the evening shoe. But there, you don't want to hear me speculate about it. I'll put them down as best I can.'

'Thank you, madame, I shall be much obliged to you.'

Poirot hung up the phone.

'I am vexed with myself,' he said to Miss Lemon. 'I have departed from the principles of order and method. I should have made quite sure from the start, the exact order in which these thefts occurred.'

'Dear, dear,' said Miss Lemon mechanically. 'Are you going to finish these letters now, M. Poirot?'

But once again Poirot waved her indignantly away.

II

On arrival back at Hickory Road with a search warrant on Saturday morning, Inspector Sharpe had demanded an interview with Mrs Nicoletis, who always came on Saturdays to do accounts with Mrs Hubbard. He had explained what he was about to do.

Mrs Nicoletis protested with vigour.

'But it is an insult, that! My students they will leave – they will all leave. I shall be ruined . . .'

'No, no, madam. I'm sure they will be sensible. After all, this is a case of murder.'

'It is not murder – it is suicide.'

'And I'm sure once I've explained, no one will object . . .'

Mrs Hubbard put in a soothing word.

'I'm sure,' she said, 'everyone will be sensible – except,' she added thoughtfully, 'perhaps Mr Achmed Ali and Mr Chandra Lal.'

'Pah!' said Mrs Nicoletis. 'Who cares about them?'

'Thank you, madam,' said the inspector. 'Then I'll make a start here, in your sitting-room.'

An immediate and violent protest came from Mrs Nicoletis at the suggestion.

'You search where you please,' she said, 'but here, *no*! I refuse.'

'I'm sorry, Mrs Nicoletis, but I have to go through the house from top to bottom.'

'That is right, yes, but not in my room. *I* am above the law.'

'No one's above the law. I'm afraid I shall have to ask you to stand aside.'

'It is an outrage,' Mrs Nicoletis screamed with fury. 'You are officious busybodies. I will write to everyone. I will write to my member of Parliament. I will write to the papers.'

'Write to anyone you please, madam,' said Inspector Sharpe. 'I'm going to search this room.'

He started straight away upon the bureau. A large carton of confectionery, a mass of papers, and a large variety of assorted junk rewarded his search. He moved from there to a cupboard in the corner of the room.

'This is locked. Can I have the key, please?'

'Never!' screamed Mrs Nicoletis. 'Never, never, never shall you have the key! Beast and pig of a policeman, I spit at you. I spit! I spit! I spit!'

'You might just as well give me the key,' said Inspector Sharpe. 'If not, I shall simply prise the door open.'

'I will not give you the key! You will have to tear my clothes off me before you get the key! And that – *that* will be a scandal.'

'Get a chisel, Cobb,' said Inspector Sharpe resignedly.

Mrs Nicoletis uttered a scream of fury. Inspector Sharpe paid no attention. The chisel was brought. Two sharp cracks and the door of the cupboard came open. As it swung forward a large consignment of empty brandy bottles poured out of the cupboard.

'Beast! Pig! Devil!' screamed Mrs Nicoletis.

'Thank you, madam,' said the inspector politely. 'We've finished in here.'

Mrs Hubbard tactfully replaced the bottles while Mrs Nicoletis had hysterics.

One mystery, the mystery of Mrs Nicoletis's tempers, was now cleared up.

III

Poirot's telephone call came through just as Mrs Hubbard was pouring out an appropriate dose of sedative from the private medicine cupboard in her sitting-room. After replacing the receiver she went back to Mrs Nicoletis whom she had left screaming and kicking her heels on the sofa in her own sitting-room.

'Now you drink this,' said Mrs Hubbard. 'And you'll feel better.'

'Gestapo!' said Mrs Nicoletis, who was now quiet but sullen.

'I shouldn't think any more about it if I were you,' said Mrs Hubbard soothingly.

'Gestapo!' said Mrs Nicoletis again. 'Gestapo! That is what they are!'

'They have to do their duty, you know,' said Mrs Hubbard.

'Is it their duty to pry into my private cupboards? I say to them, "That is not for you." I lock it. I put the key down my bosom. If you had not been there as a witness they would have torn my clothes off me without shame.'

'Oh no, I don't think they would have done *that*,' said Mrs Hubbard.

'That is what *you* say! Instead they get a chisel and they force my door. That is structural damage to the house for which *I* shall be responsible.'

'Well, you see, if you wouldn't give them the key . . .'

'Why should I give them the key? It is *my* key. My private key. And this is my private room. My private room and I say to the police, "Keep out" and they do *not* keep out.'

'Well, after all, Mrs Nicoletis, there has been a murder, remember. And after a murder one has to put up with certain things which might not be very pleasant at ordinary times.'

'I spit upon the murder!' said Mrs Nicoletis. 'That little Celia she commits suicide. She has a silly love affair and she takes poison. It is the sort of thing that is always happening. They are so stupid about love, these girls – as though love mattered! One year, two years and it is all finished, the grand passion! The man is the same as any other man! But these silly girls they do not know that. They take the sleeping draught and the disinfectant and they turn on gas taps and then it is too late.'

'Well,' said Mrs Hubbard, turning full circle, as it were, to where the conversation had started, 'I shouldn't worry any more about it all now.'

'That is all very well for *you*. Me, I have to worry. It is not safe for me any longer.'

'Safe?' Mrs Hubbard looked at her, startled.

'It was my private cupboard,' Mrs Nicoletis insisted. 'Nobody knows what was in my private cupboard. I did not want them to know. And now they *do* know. I am very uneasy. They may think – what will they think?'

'Who do you mean by *they*?'

Mrs Nicoletis shrugged her large, handsome shoulders and looked sulky.

'You do not understand,' she said, 'but it makes me uneasy. Very uneasy.'

'You'd better tell me,' said Mrs Hubbard. 'Then perhaps I can help you.'

'Thank goodness I do not sleep here,' said Mrs Nicoletis. 'These locks on the doors here they are all alike; one key fits any other. No, thanks to heaven, I do not sleep here.'

Mrs Hubbard said:

'Mrs Nicoletis, if you are afraid of something, hadn't you better tell me just what it is?'

Mrs Nicoletis gave her a flickering look from her dark eyes and then looked away again.

'You have said it yourself,' she said evasively. 'You have said there has been a murder in this house, so naturally one is uneasy. Who may be next? One does not even know who the murderer is. That is because the police are so stupid, or perhaps they have been bribed.'

'That's all nonsense and you know it,' said Mrs Hubbard. 'But tell me, have you got any cause for real anxiety . . .'

Mrs Nicoletis flew into one of her tempers.

'Ah, *you* do not think I have any cause for anxiety? You know best as usual! You know everything! You are so wonderful; you cater, you manage, you spend money like water on food so that the students are fond of you, and now you want to manage *my* affairs! But that, no! I keep my affairs to myself and nobody shall pry into them, do you hear? No, Mrs What-do-you-call-it Paul Pry.'

'Please yourself,' said Mrs Hubbard, exasperated.

'You are a spy – I always knew it.'

'A spy on what?'

'Nothing,' said Mrs Nicoletis. 'There is nothing here to spy upon. If you think there is it is because you made it up. If lies are told about me I shall know who told them.'

'If you wish me to leave,' said Mrs Hubbard, 'you've only got to say so.'

'No, you are not to leave. I forbid it. Not at this moment. Not when I have all the cares of the police, of murder, of everything else on my hands, I shall not allow you to abandon me.'

'Oh, all right,' said Mrs Hubbard helplessly. 'But really, it's very difficult to know what you do want. Sometimes I don't think you know yourself. You'd better lie down on my bed and have a sleep –'

CHAPTER 13

Hercule Poirot alighted from a taxi at 26 Hickory Road.

The door was opened to him by Geronimo who welcomed him as an old friend. There was a constable standing in the hall and Geronimo drew Poirot into the dining-room and closed the door.

'It is terrible,' he whispered, as he assisted Poirot off with his overcoat. 'We have police there all time! Ask questions, go here, go there, look in cupboards, look in drawers, come into Maria's kitchen even. Maria very angry. She says she like to hit policeman with rolling-pin but I say better not. I say policeman not like being hit by rolling-pins and they make us more embarrassments if Maria do that.'

'You have the good sense,' said Poirot approvingly. 'Is Mrs Hubbard at liberty?'

'I take you upstairs to her.'

'A little moment.' Poirot stopped him. 'Do you remember the day when certain electric light bulbs disappeared?'

'Oh yes, I remember. But that long time ago now. One – two – three months ago.'

'Exactly what electric light bulbs were taken?'

'The one in the hall and I think in the common-room. Someone make joke. Take all the bulbs out.'

'You don't remember the exact date?'

Geronimo struck an attitude as he thought.

'I do not remember,' he said. 'But I think it was on day when policeman come, some time in February –'

'A policeman? What did a policeman come here for?'

'He come here to see Mrs Nicoletis about a student. Very bad student, come from Africa. Not do work. Go to labour exchange, get National Assistance, then have woman and she go out with men for him. Very bad that. Police not like that. All this in Manchester, I think, or Sheffield. So he ran away from there and he come here, but police come after him and they talk to Mrs Hubbard about him. Yes. And she say he not stop here because she no like him and she send him away.'

'I see. They were trying to trace him.'

'Scusi?'

'They were trying to find him?'

'Yes, yes, that is right. They find him and then they put him in prison because he live on woman, and live on woman must not do. This is nice house here. Nothing like that *here*.'

'And that was the day the bulbs were missing?'

'Yes. Because I turn switch and nothing happen. And I go into common-room and no bulb there, and I look in drawer here for spares and I see bulbs have been taken away. So I go down to kitchen and ask Maria if she know where spare bulbs – but she angry because she not like police come and she say spare bulbs not her business, so I bring just candles.'

Poirot digested this story as he followed Geronimo up the stairs to Mrs Hubbard's room.

Poirot was welcomed warmly by Mrs Hubbard, who was looking tired and harassed. She held out, at once, a piece of paper to him.

'I've done my best, M. Poirot, to write down these things in the proper order but I wouldn't like to say that it's a hundred per cent accurate now. You see, it's very difficult when you look back over a period of months to remember just when this, that or the other happened.'

'I am deeply grateful to you, madame. And how is Mrs Nicoletis?'

'I've given her a sedative and I hope she's asleep now. She made a terrible fuss over the search warrant. She refused to open the cupboard in her room and the inspector broke it open and quantities of empty brandy bottles tumbled out.'

'Ah!' said Poirot, making a tactful sound.

'Which really explains quite a lot of things,' said Mrs Hubbard. 'I really can't imagine why I didn't think of that before, having seen as much of drink as I have out in Singapore. But all that, I'm sure, isn't what interests you.'

'Everything interests me,' said Poirot.

He sat down and studied the piece of paper that Mrs Hubbard had handed to him.

'Ah!' he said, after a moment or two. 'I see that now the rucksack heads the list.'

'Yes. It wasn't a very important thing, but I do remember now, definitely, that it happened before the jewellery and those sort of things began to disappear. It was all rather mixed up with some trouble we had about one of the coloured students. He'd left a day or two before this happened and I remember thinking that it might have been a revengeful act on his part before he went. There'd been, well – a little trouble.'

'Ah! Geronimo has recounted to me something like that. You had, I believe, the police here? Is that right?'

'Yes. It seems they had an inquiry from Sheffield or Birmingham or somewhere. It had all been rather a scandal. Immoral earnings and all that sort of thing. He was had up about it in court later. Actually, he'd only stayed here about three or four days. Then I didn't like his behaviour, the way he was carrying on, so I told him that his room was engaged and that he'd have to go. I wasn't really at all surprised when the police called. Of course, I couldn't tell them where he'd gone to, but they got on his track all right.'

'And it was after that that you found the rucksack?'

'Yes, I think so – it's hard to remember. You see, Len Bateson was going off on a hitch-hike and he couldn't find his rucksack anywhere and he created a terrible fuss about it, and everyone did a lot of searching, and at last Geronimo found it shoved behind the boiler all cut to ribbons. Such an odd thing to happen. So curious; and pointless, M. Poirot.'

'Yes,' Poirot agreed. 'Curious and pointless.'

He remained thoughtful for a moment.

'And it was on that same day, the day the police came to inquire about this African student, that some electric bulbs disappeared – or so Geronimo tells me. Was it that day?'

'Well, I can't really remember. Yes, yes, I think you're right, because I remember coming downstairs with the police inspector and going into the common-room with him and there were candles there. We wanted to ask Akibombo whether this other young man had spoken to him at all or told him where he was going to stay.'

'Who else was in the common-room?'

'Oh, I think most of the students had come back by that time. It was in the evening, you know, just about six o'clock. I asked Geronimo about the bulbs and he said they'd been taken out. I asked him why he hadn't replaced them and he said we were right out of electric bulbs. I was rather annoyed as it seemed such a silly pointless joke. I thought of it as a joke, not as stealing, but I was rather surprised that we had no more electric bulbs because we usually keep quite a good supply in stock. Still, I didn't take it seriously, M. Poirot, not at that time.'

'The bulbs and the rucksack,' said Poirot thoughtfully.

'But it still seems to me possible,' said Mrs Hubbard, 'that those two things have no connection with poor little Celia's peccadilloes. You remember she denied very earnestly that she'd ever touched the rucksack at all.'

'Yes, yes, that is true. How soon after this did the thefts begin?'

'Oh dear, M. Poirot, you've no idea how difficult all this is to remember. Let me see – that was March, no, February – the end of February. Yes, yes, I think Genevieve said she'd missed her bracelet about a week after that. Yes, between the 20th and 25th of February.'

'And after that the thefts went on fairly continuously?'

'Yes.'

'And this rucksack was Len Bateson's?'

'Yes.'

'And he was very annoyed about it?'

'Well, you mustn't go by that, M. Poirot,' said Mrs Hubbard, smiling a little. 'Len Bateson is that kind of boy, you know. Warm hearted, generous, kind to a fault, but one of those fiery, outspoken tempers.'

'What was it, this rucksack – something special?'

'Oh no, it was just the ordinary kind.'

'Could you show me one like it?'

'Well, yes, of course. Colin's got one, I think, just like it. So has Nigel – in fact Len's got one again now because he had to go and buy another. The students usually buy them at the shop at the end of the road. It's a very good place for all kinds of camping equipment and hikers' outfits. Shorts, sleeping-bags, all that sort of thing. And very cheap – much cheaper than any of the big stores.'

'If I could just see one of these rucksacks, madame?'

Mrs Hubbard obligingly led him to Colin McNabb's room. Colin himself was not there, but Mrs Hubbard opened the wardrobe, stooped, and picked up a rucksack which she held out to Poirot.

'There you are, M. Poirot. That's exactly like the one that was missing and that we found all cut up.'

'It would take some cutting,' murmured Poirot, as he fingered the rucksack appreciatively. 'One could not snip at this with a little pair of embroidery scissors.'

'Oh no, it wasn't what you'd expect a – well, a girl to do, for instance. There must have been a certain amount of strength involved, I should say. Strength and – well – malice, you know.'

'I know, yes, I know. It is not pleasant. Not pleasant to think about.'

'Then, when later that scarf of Valerie's was found, also slashed to pieces, well, it did look – what shall I say – unbalanced.'

'Ah,' said Poirot. 'But I think there you are wrong, madame. I do not think there is anything unbalanced about this business. I think it has aim and purpose, and shall we say, method?'

'Well, I dare say you know more about these things, M. Poirot, than I do,' said Mrs Hubbard. 'All I can say is, I don't like it. As far as I can judge we've got a very nice lot of students here and it would distress me very much to think that one of them is – well, not what I'd like to think he or she is.'

Poirot had wandered over to the window. He opened it and stepped out on to the old-fashioned balcony.

The room looked out over the back of the house. Below was a small, sooty garden.

'It is more quiet here than at the front, I expect?' he said.

'In a way. But Hickory Road isn't really a noisy road. And facing this way you get all the cats at night. Yowling, you know, and knocking the lids off the dustbins.'

Poirot looked down at four large battered ash-cans and other assorted backyard junk.

'Where is the boiler-house?'

'That's the door to it, down there next to the coal-house.'

'I see.'

He gazed down speculatively.

'Who else has rooms facing this way?'

'Nigel Chapman and Len Bateson have the next room to this.'

'And beyond them?'

'Then it's the next house – and the girls' rooms. First the room Celia had and beyond it Elizabeth Johnston's and then Patricia Lane's. Valerie and Jean Tomlinson look out to the front.'

Poirot nodded and came back into the room.

'He is neat, this young man,' he murmured, looking round him appreciatively.

'Yes. Colin's room is always very tidy. Some of the boys live in a terrible mess,' said Mrs Hubbard. 'You should see Len Bateson's room.' She added indulgently, 'But he is a nice boy, M. Poirot.'

'You say that these rucksacks are bought at the shop at the end of the road?'

'Yes.'

'What is the name of that shop?'

'Now really, M. Poirot, when you ask me like that I can't remember. Mabberley, I think. Or else Kelso. No, I know they don't sound the same kind of name but they're the same sort of name in my mind. Really, of course, because I knew some people once called Kelso and some other ones called Mabberley, and they were very alike.'

'Ah,' said Poirot. 'That is one of the reasons for things that always fascinate me. The unseen link.'

He looked once more out of the window and down into the garden, then took his leave of Mrs Hubbard and left the house.

He walked down Hickory Road until he came to the corner and turned into the main road. He had no difficulty in recognising the shop of Mrs Hubbard's description. It displayed in great profusion picnic baskets, rucksacks, Thermos flasks, sports equipment of all kinds, shorts, bush shirts, topees, tents, swimming suits, bicycle lamps and torches; in fact all possible needs of young and athletic youth. The name above the shop, he noted, was neither Mabberley nor Kelso but Hicks. After a careful study of the goods displayed in the window, Poirot entered and represented himself as desirous of purchasing a rucksack for a hypothetical nephew.

'He makes "*le camping*", you understand,' said Poirot at his most foreign. 'He goes with other students upon the feet and all he needs he takes with him on his back, and the cars and the lorries that pass, they give him a lift.'

The proprietor, who was a small obliging man with sandy hair, replied promptly.

'Ah, hitch-hiking,' he said. 'They all do it nowadays. Must lose the buses and the railways a lot of money, though. Hitch-hike themselves all over Europe some of these young people do. Now it's a rucksack you're wanting sir. Just an ordinary rucksack?'

'I understand so. You have a variety then?'

'Well, we have one or two extra light ones for ladies, but this is the general article we sell. Good, stout, stand a lot of wear, and really very cheap though I say it myself.'

He produced a stout canvas affair which was, as far as Poirot could judge, an exact replica of the one he had been shown in Colin's room. Poirot examined it, asked a few more exotic and unnecessary questions, and ended by paying for it then and there.

'Ah yes, we sell a lot of these,' said the man as he made it up into a parcel.

'A good many students lodge round here, do they not?'

'Yes. This is a neighbourhood with a lot of students.'

'There is one hostel, I believe in Hickory Road?'

'Oh yes, I've sold several to the young gentlemen there. And the young ladies. They usually come here for any equipment they want before they go off. My prices are cheaper than the big stores, and so I tell them. There you are, sir, and I'm sure your nephew will be delighted with the service he gets out of this.'

Poirot thanked him and went out with his parcel.

He had only gone a step or two when a hand fell on his shoulder.

It was Inspector Sharpe.

'Just the man I want to see,' said Sharpe.

'You have accomplished your search of the house?'

'I've searched the house, but I don't know that I've accomplished very much. There's a place along here where you can get a decent sandwich and a cup of coffee. Come along with me if you're not busy. I'd like to talk to you.'

The sandwich bar was almost empty. The two men carried their plates and cups to a small table in a corner.

Here Sharpe recounted the results of his questioning of the students.

'The only person we've got any evidence against is young Chapman,' he said. 'And there we've got too much. Three lots of poison through his hands! But there's no reason to believe he'd any animus against Celia Austin, and I doubt if he'd have been as frank about his activities if he was really guilty.'

'It opens out other possibilities, though.'

'Yes – all that stuff knocking about in a drawer. Silly young ass!'

He went on to Elizabeth Johnston and her account of what Celia had said to her.

'If what she said is true, it's significant.'

'Very significant,' Poirot agreed.

The inspector quoted:

'"I shall know more about it tomorrow."'

'And so – tomorrow never came for that poor girl. Your search of the house – did it accomplish anything?'

'There were one or two things that were – what shall I say? – unexpected, perhaps.'

'Such as?'

'Elizabeth Johnston is a member of the Communist Party. We found her Party card.'

'Yes,' said Poirot, thoughtfully. 'That is interesting.'

'You wouldn't have expected it,' said Inspector Sharpe. 'I didn't until I questioned her yesterday. She's got a lot of personality, that girl.'

'I should think she was a valuable recruit to the Party,' said Hercule Poirot. 'She is a young woman of quite unusual intelligence, I should say.'

'It was interesting to me,' said Inspector Sharpe, 'because she has never paraded those sympathies, apparently. She's kept very quiet about it at Hickory Road. I don't see that it has any significance in connection with the case of Celia Austin, I mean – but it's a thing to bear in mind.'

'What else did you find?'

Inspector Sharpe shrugged his shoulders.

'Miss Patricia Lane, in her drawer, had a handkerchief rather extensively stained with green ink.'

Poirot's eyebrows rose.

'Green ink? Patricia Lane! So it may have been she who took

the ink and spilled it over Elizabeth Johnston's papers and then wiped her hands afterwards. But surely . . .'

'Surely she wouldn't want her dear Nigel to be suspected,' Sharpe finished for him.

'One would not have thought so. Of course, someone else might have put the handkerchief in her drawer.'

'Likely enough.'

'Anything else?'

'Well,' Sharpe reflected for a moment. 'It seems Leonard Bateson's father is in Longwith Vale Mental Hospital, a certified patient. I don't suppose it's of any particular interest, but . . .'

'But Len Bateson's father is insane. Probably without significance, as you say, but it is a fact to be stored away in the memory. It would even be interesting to know what particular form his mania takes.'

'Bateson's a nice young fellow,' said Sharpe, 'but of course his temper is a bit, well, uncontrolled.'

Poirot nodded. Suddenly, vividly, he remembered Celia Austin saying, 'Of course, I wouldn't cut up a rucksack. Anyway that was only temper.' How did she know it was temper? Had she seen Len Bateson hacking at that rucksack? He came back to the present to hear Sharpe say, with a grin:

'. . . and Mr Achmed Ali has some extremely pornographic literature and postcards which explains why *he* went up in the air over the search.'

'There were many protests, no doubt?'

'I should say there were. A French girl practically had hysterics and an Indian, Mr Chandra Lal, threatened to make an international incident of it. There were a few subversive pamphlets amongst *his* belongings – the usual half-baked stuff – and one of the West Africans had some rather fearsome souvenirs and fetishes. Yes, a search warrant certainly shows you the peculiar side of human nature. You heard about Mrs Nicoletis and her private cupboard?'

'Yes, I heard about that.'

Inspector Sharpe grinned.

'Never seen so many empty brandy bottles in my life! And was she mad at us!'

He laughed, and then, abruptly, became serious.

'But we didn't find what we went after,' he said. 'No passports except strictly legitimate ones.'

'You can hardly expect such a thing as a false passport to be left about for you to find, *mon ami*. You never had occasion, did you, to make an official visit to 26 Hickory Road in connection with a passport? Say, in the last six months?'

'No. I'll tell you the only occasions on which we did call round – within the times you mention.'

He detailed them carefully.

Poirot listened with a frown.

'All that, it does not make sense,' he said.

He shook his head.

'Things will only make sense if we begin at the beginning.'

'What do you call the beginning, Poirot?'

'The rucksack, my friend,' said Poirot softly. 'The rucksack. All this began with a rucksack.'

CHAPTER 14

I

Mrs Nicoletis came up the stairs from the basement, where she had just succeeded in thoroughly infuriating both Geronimo and the temperamental Maria.

'Liars and thieves,' said Mrs Nicoletis, in a loud triumphant voice. 'All Italians are liars and thieves!'

Mrs Hubbard, who was just descending the stairs, gave a short vexed sigh.

'It's a pity,' she said, 'to upset them just while they're cooking the supper.'

Mrs Hubbard suppressed the retort that rose to her lips.

'I shall come in as usual on Monday,' said Mrs Nicoletis.

'Yes, Mrs Nicoletis.'

'And please get someone to repair my cupboard door first thing Monday morning. The bill for repairing it will go to the police, do you understand? To the police.'

Mrs Hubbard looked dubious.

'And I want fresh electric light bulbs put in the dark passages – stronger ones. The passages are too dark.'

'You said especially that you wanted low power bulbs in the passages – for economy.'

'That was last week,' snapped Mrs Nicoletis. '*Now* – it is different. Now I look over my shoulder – and I wonder "Who is following me?"'

Was her employer dramatising herself, Mrs Hubbard wondered, or was she really afraid of something or someone? Mrs Nicoletis had such a habit of exaggerating everything that it was always hard to know how much reliance to place on her statements.

Mrs Hubbard said doubtfully:

'Are you sure you ought to go home by yourself? Would you like me to come with you?'

'I shall be safer there than here, I can tell you!'

'But what is it you are afraid of? If I knew, perhaps I could –'

'It is not your business. I tell you nothing. I find it insupportable the way you continually ask me questions.'

'I'm sorry. I'm sure –'

'Now you are offended.' Mrs Nicoletis gave her a beaming smile. 'I am bad tempered and rude – yes. But I have much to worry me. And remember I trust you and rely on you. What I should do without you, dear Mrs Hubbard, I really do not know. See, I kiss my hand to you. Have a pleasant weekend. Good night.'

Mrs Hubbard watched her as she went out through the front door and pulled it to behind her. Relieving her feelings with a rather inadequate 'Well, really!' Mrs Hubbard turned towards the kitchen stairs.

Mrs Nicoletis went down the front steps, out through the gate and turned to the left. Hickory Road was a fairly broad road. The houses in it were set back a little in their gardens. At the end of the road, a few minutes' walk from number 26, was one of London's main thoroughfares, down which buses were roaring. There were traffic lights at the end of the road and a public-house, The Queen's Necklace, at the corner. Mrs Nicoletis walked in the middle of the pavement and from time to time sent a nervous glance over her shoulder, but there was no one in sight. Hickory Road appeared to be unusually deserted this evening. She quickened her steps a little as she drew near

The Queen's Necklace. Taking another hasty glance round she slipped rather guiltily through into the saloon bar.

Sipping the double brandy that she had asked for, her spirits revived. She no longer looked the frightened and uneasy woman that she had a short time previously. Her animosity against the police, however, was not lessened. She murmured under her breath, 'Gestapo! I shall make them pay. Yes, they shall pay!' and finished off her drink. She ordered another and brooded over recent happenings. Unfortunate, extremely unfortunate, that the police should have been so tactless as to discover her secret hoard, and too much to hope that word would not get around amongst the students and the rest of them. Mrs Hubbard would be discreet, perhaps, or again perhaps not, because really, could one trust anyone? These things always did get round. Geronimo knew. He had probably already told his wife, and she would tell the cleaning women and so it would go on until – she started violently as a voice behind her said:

'Why, Mrs Nick, I didn't know this was a haunt of yours?'

'Oh, it's you,' she said. 'I thought . . .'

'Who did you think it was? The big bad wolf? What are you drinking? Have another on me.'

'It is all the worry,' Mrs Nicoletis explained with dignity. 'These policemen searching my house, upsetting everyone. My poor heart. I have to be careful with my heart. I do not care for drink, but really I felt quite faint outside. I thought a little brandy . . .'

'Nothing like brandy. Here you are.'

Mrs Nicoletis left The Queen's Necklace a short while later feeling revived and positively happy. She would not take a bus, she decided. It was such a fine night and the air would be good for her. Yes, definitely, the air would be good for her. She felt not exactly unsteady on her feet but just a little bit uncertain. One brandy less, perhaps, would have been wise, but the air would soon clear her head. After all, why shouldn't a lady have a quiet drink in her own room from time to time? What was there wrong with it? It was not as though she had ever allowed herself to be seen intoxicated. Intoxicated? Of course, she was never intoxicated. And anyway, if they didn't like it; if they ticked her off, she'd soon tell them where they got off! *She* knew a thing or two, didn't she? If she liked to shoot off her mouth! Mrs Nicoletis tossed her head in a bellicose manner and swerved abruptly to avoid a pillar-box which had advanced upon her in a menacing manner. No doubt, her head *was* swimming a little. Perhaps if she just leant against the wall here for a little? If she closed her eyes for a moment or two . . .

II

Police Constable Bott, swinging magnificently down on his beat, was accosted by a timid-looking clerk.

'There's a woman here, Officer. I really – she seems to have been taken ill or something. She's lying in a heap.'

Police Constable Bott bent his energetic steps that way, and stooped over the recumbent form. A strong aroma of brandy confirmed his suspicions.

'Passed out,' he said. 'Drunk. Ah well, don't worry, sir, *we'll* see to it.'

III

Hercule Poirot, having finished his Sunday breakfast, wiped his moustaches carefully free from all traces of his breakfast cup of chocolate and passed into his sitting-room.

Neatly arranged on the table were four rucksacks, each with its bill attached – the result of instructions given to George. Poirot took the rucksack he had purchased the day before from its wrapping, and added it to the others. The result was interesting. The rucksack he had bought from Mr Hicks did not seem inferior in any way that he could see, to the articles purchased by George from various other establishments. But it was very decidedly cheaper.

'Interesting,' said Hercule Poirot.

He stared at the rucksacks.

Then he examined them in detail. Inside and outside, turning them upside down, feeling the seams, the pockets, the handles. Then he rose, went into the bathroom and came back with a small sharp corn-knife. Turning the rucksack he had bought at Mr Hicks's store inside out, he attacked the bottom of it with the knife. Between the inner lining and the bottom there was a heavy piece of corrugated stiffening, rather resembling in appearance corrugated paper. Poirot looked at the dismembered rucksack with a great deal of interest.

Then he proceeded to attack the other rucksacks.

He sat back finally and surveyed the amount of destruction he had just accomplished.

Then he drew the telephone towards him and after a short delay managed to get through to Inspector Sharpe.

'*Ecoutez, mon cher*,' he said. 'I want to know just two things.'

Something in the nature of a guffaw came from Inspector Sharpe.

'*I know two things about the horse,*
And one of them is rather coarse,' he observed.

'I beg your pardon?' said Hercule Poirot, surprised.

'Nothing. Nothing. Just a rhyme I used to know. What are the two things you want to know?'

'You mentioned yesterday certain police inquiries at Hickory Road made during the last three months. Can you tell me the dates of them and also the time of day they were made?'

'Yes – well – that should be easy. It'll be in the files. Just wait and I'll look it up.'

It was not long before the inspector returned to the phone. 'First inquiry as to Indian student disseminating subversive propaganda, 18th December last – 3.30 p.m.'

'That is too long ago.'

'Inquiry *re* Montague Jones, Eurasian, wanted in connection with murder of Mrs Alice Combe of Cambridge – February 24th – 5.30 p.m. Inquiry *re* William Robinson – native West Africa, wanted by Sheffield police – March 6th, 11 a.m.'

'Ah! I thank you.'

'But if you think that either of those cases could have any connection with –'

Poirot interrupted him.

'No, they have no connection. I am interested only in the time of day they were made.'

'What *are* you up to, Poirot?'

'I dissect rucksacks, my friend. It is very interesting.'

Gently he replaced the receiver.

He took from his pocket-book the amended list that Mrs Hubbard had handed him the day before. It ran as follows:

Rucksack (Len Bateson's)
Electric light bulbs
Bracelet (Genevieve's)
Diamond ring (Patricia's)
Powder compact (Genevieve's)
Evening shoe (Sally's)
Lipstick (Elizabeth Johnston's)
Ear-rings (Valerie's)
Stethoscope (Len Bateson's)
Bath salts (?)
Scarf cut in pieces (Valerie's)
Trousers (Colin's)
Cookery book (?)
Boracic (Chandra Lal's)
Costume brooch (Sally's)
Ink spilled on Elizabeth's notes.
(This is the best I can do. It's not absolutely accurate.
L Hubbard.)

Poirot looked at it a long time.

He sighed and murmured to himself, 'Yes . . . decidedly . . . we have to eliminate the things that do not matter . . .'

He had an idea as to who could help him to do that. It was Sunday. Most of the students would probably be at home.

He dialled the number of 26 Hickory Road and asked to speak to Miss Valerie Hobhouse. A thick rather guttural voice seemed rather doubtful as to whether she was up yet, but said it would go and see.

Presently he heard a low husky voice:

'Valerie Hobhouse speaking.'

'It is Hercule Poirot. You remember me?'

'Of course, M. Poirot. What can I do for you?'

'I would like, if I may, to have a short conversation with you?'

'Certainly.'

'I may come round, then, to Hickory Road?'

'Yes. I'll be expecting you. I'll tell Geronimo to bring you up to my room. There's not much privacy here on a Sunday.'

'Thank you, Miss Hobhouse. I am most grateful.'

Geronimo opened the door to Poirot with a flourish, then bending forward he spoke with his usual conspiratorial air.

'I take you up to Miss Valerie very quietly. Hush sh sh.'

Placing a finger on his lips, he led the way upstairs and into a good sized room overlooking Hickory Road. It was furnished with taste and a reasonable amount of luxury as a bed-sitting-room. The divan bed was covered with a worn but beautiful Persian rug, and there was an attractive Queen Anne walnut bureau which Poirot judged hardly likely to be one of the original furnishings of 26 Hickory Road.

Valerie Hobhouse was standing ready to greet him. She looked tired, he thought, and there were dark circles round her eyes.

'*Mais vous êtes très bien ici*,' said Poirot, as he greeted her. 'It is chic. It has an air.'

Valerie smiled.

'I've been here a good time,' she said. 'Two and a half years. Nearly three. I've dug myself in more or less and I've got some of my own things.'

'You are not a student, are you, mademoiselle?'

'Oh no. Purely commercial. I've got a job.'

'In a – cosmetic firm, was it?'

'Yes. I'm one of the buyers for Sabrina Fair – it's a beauty salon. Actually I have a small share in the business. We run a certain amount of side-lines besides beauty treatment. Accessories, that type of thing. Small Parisian novelties. And that's my department.'

'You go over then fairly often to Paris and to the Continent?'

'Oh yes, about once a month, sometimes oftener.'

'You must forgive me,' said Poirot, 'if I seem to be displaying curiosity . . .'

'Why not?' She cut him short. 'In the circumstances in which we find ourselves we must all put up with curiosity. I've answered a good many questions yesterday from Inspector Sharpe. You look as though you would like an upright chair, M. Poirot, rather than a low arm-chair.'

'You display the perspicacity, mademoiselle.' Poirot sat down carefully and squarely in a high-backed chair with arms to it.

Valerie sat down on the divan. She offered him a cigarette and took one herself and lighted it. He studied her with some attention.

She had a nervous, rather haggard elegance that appealed to him more than mere conventional good looks would have done. An intelligent and attractive young woman, he thought. He wondered if her nervousness was the result of the recent inquiry or whether it was a natural component of her manner. He remembered that he had thought much the same about her on the evening when he had come to supper.

'Inspector Sharpe has been making inquiries of you?' he asked.

'Yes, indeed.'

'And you have told him all that you know?'

'Of course.'

'I wonder,' said Poirot, 'if that is true.'

She looked at him with an ironic expression.

'Since you did not hear my answers to Inspector Sharpe you can hardly be a judge,' she said.

'Ah no. It is merely one of my little ideas. I have them, you know – the little ideas. They are here.' He tapped his head.

It could be noticed that Poirot, as he sometimes did, was deliberately playing the mountebank. Valerie, however, did not smile. She looked at him in a straightforward manner. When she spoke it was with a certain abruptness.

'Shall we come to the point, M. Poirot?' she asked. 'I really don't know what you're driving at.'

'But certainly, Miss Hobhouse.'

He took from his pocket a little package.

'You can guess, perhaps, what I have here?'

'I'm not clairvoyant, M. Poirot. I can't see through paper and wrappings.'

'I have here,' said Poirot, 'the ring that was stolen from Miss Patricia Lane.'

'The engagement ring? I mean, her mother's engagement ring? But why should *you* have it?'

'I asked her to lend it to me for a day or two.'

Again Valerie's rather surprised eyebrows mounted her forehead.

'Indeed,' she observed.

'I was interested in the ring,' said Poirot. 'Interested in its disappearance, in its return and in something else about it. So

I asked Miss Lane to lend it to me. She agreed readily. I took it straight away to a jeweller friend of mine.'

'Yes?'

'I asked him to report on the diamond in it. A fairly large stone, if you remember, flanked at either side by a little cluster of small stones. You remember – mademoiselle?'

'I think so. I don't really remember it very well.'

'But you handled it, didn't you? It was in your soup plate.'

'That was how it was returned! Oh yes, I remember that. I nearly swallowed it.' Valerie gave a short laugh.

'As I say, I took the ring to my jeweller friend and I asked him his opinion on the diamond. Do you know what his answer was?'

'How could I?'

'His answer was that the stone was not a diamond. It was merely a zircon. A white zircon.'

'Oh!' She stared at him. Then she went on, her tone a little uncertain. 'D'you mean that – Patricia thought it was a diamond but it was only a zircon or . . .'

Poirot was shaking his head.

'No, I do not mean that. It was the engagement ring, so I understand, of this Patricia Lane's mother. Miss Patricia Lane is a young lady of good family, and her people, I should say, certainly before recent taxation, were in comfortable circumstances. In those circles, mademoiselle, money is spent upon an engagement ring – a *diamond* ring or a ring containing some other precious stone. I am quite certain that the papa of Miss Lane would not have given her mamma anything but a valuable engagement ring.'

'As to that,' said Valerie, 'I couldn't agree with you more. Patricia's father was a small country squire, I believe.'

'Therefore,' said Poirot, 'it would seem that the stone in the ring must have been replaced by another stone later.'

'I suppose,' said Valerie slowly, 'that Pat might have lost the stone out of it, couldn't afford to replace it with a diamond, and had a zircon put in instead.'

'That is possible,' said Hercule Poirot, 'but I do not think it is what happened.'

'Well, M. Poirot, if we're guessing, what *do* you think happened?'

'I think,' said Poirot, 'that the ring was taken by Mademoiselle Celia and that the diamond was deliberately removed and the zircon substituted before the ring was returned.'

Valerie sat up very straight.

'You think that Celia stole that diamond deliberately?'

Poirot shook his head.

'No,' he said. 'I think *you* stole it, mademoiselle.'

Valerie Hobhouse caught her breath sharply:

'Well, really!' she exclaimed. 'That seems to me pretty thick. You've no earthly evidence of any kind.'

'But, yes,' Poirot interrupted her. 'I have evidence. The ring was returned in a plate of soup. Now me, I dined here one evening. I noticed the way the soup was served. It was served from a tureen on the side table. Therefore, if anyone found a ring in their soup plate it could only have been placed there *either* by the person who was serving the soup (in this case Geronimo) or by the person whose soup plate it was. *You!* I do not think it was Geronimo. I think that *you* staged the return of the ring in the soup in that way because it amused you. You have, if I may make the criticism, rather too humorous a sense of the dramatic. To hold up the ring! To exclaim! I think you indulged your sense of humour there, mademoiselle, and did not realise that you betrayed yourself in so doing.'

'Is that all?' Valerie spoke scornfully.

'Oh, no, it is by no means all. You see, when Celia confessed that evening to having been responsible for the thefts here, I noticed several small points. For instance, in speaking of this ring she said, "I didn't realise how valuable it was. As soon as I knew I managed to return it." How did she know, Miss Valerie? Who told her how valuable the ring was? And then again in speaking of the cut scarf, little Miss Celia said something like, "That didn't matter, Valerie didn't mind . . ." Why did you not mind if a good quality silk scarf belonging to you was cut to shreds? I formed the impression then and there that the whole campaign of stealing things, of making herself out to be a kleptomaniac, and so attracting the attention of Colin McNabb, had been thought out for Celia by *someone else*. Someone with far more intelligence than Celia Austin had and with a good working knowledge of psychology. *You* told her the ring was valuable; you took it from her and arranged for its return. In the same way it was at your suggestion that she slashed a scarf of yours to pieces.'

'These are all theories,' said Valerie, 'and rather farfetched theories at that. The inspector has already suggested to me that I put Celia up to doing these tricks.'

'And what did you say to him?'

'I said it was nonsense,' said Valerie.

'And what do you say to me?'

Valerie looked at him searchingly for a moment or two. Then she gave a short laugh, stubbed out her cigarette, leaned back thrusting a cushion behind her back, and said:

'You're quite right. I put her up to it.'

'May I ask you why?'

Valerie said impatiently:

'Oh, sheer foolish good nature. Benevolent interfering. There Celia was, mooning about like a little ghost, yearning over Colin who never looked at her. It all seemed so *silly*. Colin's one of those conceited opinionated young men wrapped up in psychology and complexes and emotional blocks and all the rest of it, and I thought it would be really rather fun to egg him on and make a fool of him. Anyway I hated to see Celia look so miserable, so I got hold of her, gave her a talking-to, explained in outline the whole scheme, and urged her on to it. She was a bit nervous, I think, about it all, but rather thrilled at the same time. Then, of course, one of the first things the little idiot does is to find Pat's ring left in the bathroom and pinch that – a really valuable piece of jewellery about which there'd be a lot of hoo-haa and the police would be called in and the whole thing might take a serious turn. So I grabbed the ring off her, told her I'd return it somehow, and urged her in future to stick to costume jewellery and cosmetics and a little wilful damage to something of mine which wouldn't land her in trouble.'

Poirot drew a deep breath.

'That was exactly what I thought,' he said.

'I wish that I hadn't done it now,' said Valerie sombrely. 'But I really did mean well. That's an atrocious thing to say and just like Jean Tomlinson, but there it is.'

'And now,' said Poirot, 'we come to this business of Patricia's ring. Celia gave it to you. You were to find it somewhere and return it to Patricia. But *before* returning it to Patricia,' he paused. 'What happened?'

He watched her fingers nervously plaiting and unplaiting the end of a fringed scarf that she was wearing round her neck. He went on, in an even more persuasive voice:

'You were hard up, eh, was that it?'

Without looking up at him she gave a short nod of the head.

'I said I'd come clean,' she said and there was bitterness in her voice. 'The trouble with me is, M. Poirot, I'm a gambler. That's one of the things that's born in you and you can't do anything much about it. I belong to a little club in Mayfair – oh, I shan't tell you just where – I don't want to be responsible for getting it raided by the police or anything of that kind. We'll just let it go at the fact that I belong to it. There's roulette there, baccarat, all the rest of it. I've taken a nasty series of losses one after the other. I had this ring of Pat's. I happened to be passing a shop where there was a zircon ring. I thought to myself, "if this diamond was replaced with a white zircon Pat would never know the difference!" You never do look at a ring you know really well. If the diamond seems a bit duller than usual you just think it needs cleaning or something like that. All right, I had an impulse. I fell. I prised out the diamond and sold it. Replaced it with a zircon and that night I pretended to find it in my soup. That was a damn silly thing to do, too, I agree. There! Now you know it all. But honestly, I never meant Celia to be blamed for that.'

'No, no, I understand.' Poirot nodded his head. 'It was just an opportunity that came your way. It seemed easy and you took it. But you made there a great mistake, mademoiselle.'

'I realise that,' said Valerie drily. Then she broke out unhappily:

'But what the hell! Does that matter now? Oh, turn me in if you like. Tell Pat. Tell the inspector. Tell the world! But what *good* is it going to do? How's it going to help us with finding out who killed Celia?'

Poirot rose to his feet.

'One never knows,' he said, 'what may help and what may not. One has to clear out of the way so many things that do not matter and that confuse the issue. It was important for me to know who had inspired the little Celia to play the part she did. I know that now. As to the ring, I suggest that you go yourself to Miss Patricia Lane and that you tell her what you did and express the customary sentiments.'

Valerie made a grimace.

'I dare say that's pretty good advice on the whole,' she said. 'All right, I'll go to Pat and I'll eat humble pie. Pat's a very decent sort. I'll tell her that when I can afford it again I'll replace the diamond. Is that what you want, M. Poirot?'

'It is not what I want, it is what is advisable.'

The door opened suddenly and Mrs Hubbard came in.

She was breathing hard and the expression in her face made Valerie exclaim:

'What's the matter, Mum? What's happened?'

Mrs Hubbard dropped into a chair.

'It's Mrs Nicoletis.'

'Mrs Nick? What about her?'

'Oh, my dear. She's *dead*.'

'Dead?' Valerie's voice came harshly. 'How? When?'

'It seems she was picked up in the street last night – they took her to the police station. They thought she was – was –'

'Drunk? I suppose . . .'

'Yes – she *had* been drinking. But anyway – she died –'

'Poor old Mrs Nick,' said Valerie. There was a tremor in her husky voice.

Poirot said gently:

'You were fond of her, mademoiselle?'

'It's odd in a way – she could be a proper old devil – but yes – I was . . . When I first came here – three years ago, she wasn't nearly as – as temperamental as she became later. She was good company – amusing – warm-hearted. She's changed a lot in the last year –'

Valerie looked at Mrs Hubbard.

'I suppose that's because she'd taken to drinking on the quiet – they found a lot of bottles and things in her room, didn't they?'

'Yes,' Mrs Hubbard hesitated, then burst out: 'I do blame myself – letting her go off home alone last night – she was afraid of something, you know.'

'Afraid?'

Poirot and Valerie said it in unison.

Mrs Hubbard nodded unhappily. Her mild round face was troubled.

'Yes. She kept saying she wasn't safe. I asked her to tell me what she was afraid of – and she snubbed me. And one never knew with her, of course, how much was exaggeration. But now – I wonder –'

Valerie said:

'You don't think that she – that she, too – that she was –'

She broke off with a look of horror in her eyes.

Poirot asked:

'What did they say was the cause of death?'

Mrs Hubbard said unhappily:

'They – they didn't say. There's to be an inquest – on Tuesday –'

CHAPTER 15

In a quiet room at New Scotland Yard, four men were sitting round a table.

Presiding over the conference was Superintendent Wilding of the Narcotics squad. Next to him was Sergeant Bell, a young man of great energy and optimism who looked rather like an eager greyhound. Leaning back in his chair, quiet and alert, was Inspector Sharpe. The fourth man was Hercule Poirot. On the table was a rucksack.

Superintendent Wilding stroked his chin thoughtfully.

'It's an interesting idea, M. Poirot,' he said cautiously. 'Yes, it's an interesting idea.'

'It is, as I say, simply an idea,' said Poirot.

Wilding nodded.

'We've outlined the general position,' he said. 'Smuggling goes on all the time, of course, in one form or another. We clear up one lot of operators, and after a due interval things start again somewhere else. Speaking for my own branch, there's been a good lot of the stuff coming into this country in the last year and a half. Heroin mostly – a fair amount of coke. There are various depots dotted here and there on the Continent. The French police have got a lead or two as to how it comes into France – they're less certain how it goes out again.'

'Would I be right in saying,' Poirot asked, 'that your problem could be divided roughly under three heads. There is the problem of distribution, there is the problem of how the consignments enter the country, and there is the problem of who really runs the business and takes the main profits?'

'Roughly I'd say that's quite right. We know a fair amount about the small distributors and how the stuff is distributed. Some of the distributors we pull in, some we leave alone hoping that they may lead us to the big fish. It's distributed in a lot of different ways, night-clubs, pubs, drug stores, an odd doctor or so, fashionable women's dressmakers and hairdressers. It is handed over on racecourses, and in antique dealers', sometimes in a crowded multiple store. But I needn't tell you all this. It's not that side of it that's important. We can keep pace with all that fairly well. And we've got certain very shrewd suspicions as to what I've called the big fish. One or two very respectable wealthy gentlemen against whom there's never a breath of suspicion. Very careful they are; they never handle the stuff themselves, and the little fry don't even know who they are. But every now and again, one of them makes a slip – and then – we get him.'

'That is all very much as I supposed. The line in which I am interested is the third line – how do the consignments come into the country?'

'Ah. We're an island. The most usual way is the good old-fashioned way of the sea. Running a cargo. Quiet landing somewhere on the east coast, or a little cove down south, by a motor-boat that's slipped quietly across the Channel. That succeeds for a bit but sooner or later we get a line on the particular fellow who owns the boat and once he's under suspicion his opportunity's gone. Once or twice lately the stuff's come in on one of the air liners. There's big money offered, and occasionally one of the stewards or one of the crew proves to be only too human. And then there are the commercial importers. Respectable firms that import grand pianos, or what have you! They have quite a good run for a bit, but we usually get wise to them in the end.'

'You would agree that it is one of the chief difficulties when you are running an illicit trade – the entry from abroad into this country?'

'Decidedly. And I'll say more. For some time now, we've been worried. More stuff is coming in than we can keep pace with.'

'And what about other things, such as gems?'

Sergeant Bell spoke.

'There's a good deal of it going on, sir. Illicit diamonds and other stones are coming out of South Africa and Australia, some from the Far East. They're coming into this country in a steady stream, and we don't know how. The other day a young woman, an ordinary tourist, in France, was asked by a casual acquaintance if she'd take a pair of shoes across the Channel. Not new ones, nothing dutiable, just some shoes someone had left behind. She agreed quite unsuspiciously. We happened to be on to that. The heels of the shoes turned out to be hollow and packed with uncut diamonds.'

Superintendent Wilding said:

'But look here, M. Poirot, what is it you're on the track of, dope or smuggled gems?'

'Either. Anything, in fact, of high value and small bulk. There is an opening, it seems to me, for what you might call a freight service, conveying goods such as I have described to and fro across the Channel. Stolen jewellery, the stones removed from their settings, could be taken out of England, illicit stones and drugs brought in. It could be a small independent agency, unconnected with distribution, that carried stuff on a commission basis. And the profits might be high.'

'I'll say you're right there! You can pack ten or twenty thousand pounds' worth of heroin in a very small space and the same goes for uncut stones of high quality.'

'You see,' said Poirot, 'the weakness of the smuggler is always the human element. Sooner or later you suspect a *person*, an air line steward, a yachting enthusiast with a small cabin cruiser, the woman who travels to and fro to France too often, the importer who seems to be making more money than is reasonable, the man who lives well without visible means of support. But if the stuff is brought into this country by an innocent person, and what is more, *by a different person each time*, then the difficulties of spotting the cargoes are enormously increased.'

Wilding pushed a finger towards the rucksack. 'And that's your suggestion?'

'Yes. Who is the person who is least vulnerable to suspicion these days? The student. The earnest, hard-working student. Badly off, travelling about with no more luggage than what he can carry on his back. Hitch-hiking his way across Europe. If one particular student were to bring the stuff in all the time, no doubt you'd get wise to him or her, but the whole essence of the arrangement is that the carriers are innocent and that there are a lot of them.'

Wilding rubbed his jaw.

'Just how exactly do you think it's managed, M. Poirot?' he asked.

Hercule Poirot shrugged his shoulders.

'As to that it is my guess only. No doubt I am wrong in many details, but I should say that it worked roughly like this: First, a line of rucksacks is placed on the market. They are of the ordinary, conventional type, just like any other rucksack, well and strongly made and suitable for their purpose. When I say "just like any other rucksack" that is not so. The lining at the base is slightly different. As you see, it is quite easily removable and is of a thickness and composition to allow for rouleaux of gems or powder concealed in the corrugations. You would never suspect it unless you were looking for it. Pure heroin or pure cocaine would take up very little room.'

'Too true,' said Wilding. 'Why,' he measured with rapid fingers, 'you could bring in stuff worth five or six thousand pounds each time without anyone being the wiser.'

'Exactly,' said Hercule Poirot. '*Alors!* The rucksacks are made, put on the market, are on sale – probably in more than one shop. The proprietor of the shop may be in the racket or he may not. It may be that he has just been sold a cheap line which he finds profitable, since his prices will compare favourably with that charged by other camping outfit sellers. There is, of course, a definite organisation in the background; a carefully kept list of students at the medical schools, at London University and at other places. Someone who is himself a student, or posing as a student, is probably at the head of the racket. Students go abroad. At some point in the return journey a duplicate rucksack is exchanged. The student returns to England; customs investigations will be perfunctory. The student arrives back at his or her hostel, unpacks, and the empty rucksack is tossed into a cupboard or into a corner of the room. At this point there will be again an exchange of rucksacks or possibly the false bottom will be neatly extracted and an innocent one replace it.'

'And you think that's what happened at Hickory Road?'

Poirot nodded.

'That is my suspicion. Yes.'

'But what put you on to it, M. Poirot – assuming you're right, that is?'

'A rucksack was cut to pieces,' said Poirot. 'Why? Since the reason is not plain, one has to imagine a reason. There is something queer about the rucksacks that come to Hickory Road. They are too cheap. There have been a series of peculiar happenings at Hickory Road, but the girl responsible for them swore that the destruction of the rucksack was *not* her doing. Since she has confessed to the other things why should she deny that, unless she was speaking the truth? So there must be another reason for the destruction of the rucksack – and to destroy a rucksack, I may say, is not an easy thing. It was hard work and someone must have been pretty desperate to undertake it. I got my clue when I found that roughly – (only roughly, alas, because people's memories after a period of some months are not too certain) but roughly – that that rucksack was destroyed at about the date when a police officer called to see the person in charge of the hostel. The actual reason that the police officer called had to do with quite another matter, but I will put it to you like this: You are someone concerned in this smuggling racket. You go home to the house that evening and you are informed that the police have called and are at the moment upstairs with Mrs Hubbard. Immediately you assume that the police are on to the smuggling racket, that they have come to make an investigation; and let us say that at that moment *there is in the house a rucksack* just brought back from abroad containing – or which has recently contained – contraband. Now, if the police have a line on what has been going on, they will have come to Hickory Road for the express purpose of examining the rucksacks of the students. You dare not walk out of the house with the rucksack in question because, for all you know, somebody may have been left outside by the police to watch the house with just that object in view, and a rucksack is not an easy thing to conceal or disguise. The only thing you can think of is to rip up the rucksack, and cram the pieces away among the junk in the boiler-house. If there is dope or gems on the premises, they can be concealed in bath salts as a temporary measure. But even an empty rucksack, if it had held dope, might yield traces of heroin or cocaine on close examination or analysis. So the rucksack must be destroyed. You agree that that is possible?'

'It is an idea, as I said before,' said Superintendent Wilding.

'It also seems possible that a small incident not hitherto regarded as important may be connected with the rucksack. According to the Italian servant, Geronimo, on the day, or one of the days, when the police called, the light in the hall had gone. He went to look for a bulb to replace it; found the spare bulbs, too, were missing. He was quite sure that a day or two previously there had been spare bulbs in the drawer. It seems to me a possibility – this is far-fetched and I would not say that I am sure of it, you understand, it is a mere possibility – that there was someone with a guilty conscience who had been mixed up with a smuggling racket before and who feared that his face might be known to the police if they saw him in a bright light. So he quietly removed the bulb from the hall light and took away the new ones so that it should not be replaced. As a result the hall was illuminated by a candle only. This, as I say, is merely a supposition.'

'It's an ingenious idea,' said Wilding.

'It's possible, sir,' said Sergeant Bell eagerly. 'The more I think of it the more possible I think it is.'

'But if so,' went on Wilding, 'there's more to it than just Hickory Road?'

Poirot nodded.

'Oh yes. The organisation must cover a wide range of students' clubs and so on.'

'You have to find a connecting link between them,' said Wilding.

Inspector Sharpe spoke for the first time.

'There is such a link, sir,' he said, 'or there was. A woman who ran several student clubs and organisations. A woman who was right on the spot at Hickory Road. Mrs Nicoletis.'

Wilding flicked a quick glance at Poirot.

'Yes,' said Poirot. 'Mrs Nicoletis fits the bill. She had a financial interest in all these places though she didn't run them herself. Her method was to get someone of unimpeachable integrity and antecedents to run the place. My friend Mrs Hubbard is such a person. The financial backing was supplied by Mrs Nicoletis – but there again I suspect her of being only a figurehead.'

'H'm,' said Wilding. 'I think it would be interesting to know a little more about Mrs Nicoletis.'

Sharpe nodded.

'We're investigating her,' he said. 'Her background and where she came from. It has to be done carefully. We don't want to alarm our birds too soon. We're looking into her financial background, too. My word, that woman was a tartar if ever there was one.'

He described his experiences of Mrs Nicoletis when confronted with a search warrant.

'Brandy bottles, eh?' said Wilding. 'So she drank? Well, that ought to make it easier. What's happened to her? Hooked it –'

'No sir. She's dead.'

'Dead?' Wilding raised his eyebrows. 'Monkey business, do you mean?'

'We think so – yes. We'll know for certain after the autopsy. I think myself she'd begun to crack. Maybe she didn't bargain for murder.'

'You're talking about the Celia Austin case. Did the girl know something?'

'She knew something,' said Poirot, 'but if I may so put it, I do not think she knew what it was she knew!'

'You mean she knew something but didn't appreciate the implications of it?'

'Yes. Just that. She was not a clever girl. She would be quite likely to fail to grasp an inference. But having seen something, or heard something, she may have mentioned the fact quite unsuspiciously.'

'You've no idea what she saw or heard, M. Poirot?'

'I make guesses,' said Poirot. 'I cannot do more. There has been mention of a passport. Did someone in the house have a false passport allowing them to go to and fro to the Continent under another name? Would the revelation of that fact be a serious danger to that person? Did she see the rucksack being tampered with or did she, perhaps, one day see someone removing the false bottom from the rucksack without realising what it was that that person was doing? Did she perhaps see the person who removed the light bulbs? And mention the fact to him or her, not realising that it was of any importance? Ah, *mon dieu!*' said Hercule Poirot with irritation. 'Guesses! guesses! guesses! One must *know* more. Always one must know more!'

'Well,' said Sharpe, 'we can make a start on Mrs Nicoletis's antecedents. Something may come up.'

'She was put out of the way because they thought she might talk? Would she have talked?'

'She'd been drinking secretly for some time . . . and that means her nerves were shot to pieces,' said Sharpe. 'She might have broken down and spilled the whole thing. Turned Queen's Evidence.'

'She didn't really run the racket, I suppose?'

Poirot shook his head.

'I should not think so, no. She was out in the open, you see. She knew what was going on, of course, but I should not say she was the brains behind it. No.'

'Any idea who is the brains behind it?'

'I could make a guess – I might be wrong. Yes – I *might* be wrong!'

CHAPTER 16

I

'Hickory, dickory, dock,' said Nigel, 'the mouse ran up the clock. The police said "Boo", I wonder who, will eventually stand in the Dock?'

He added:

'To tell or not to tell? *That* is the question!'

He poured himself out a fresh cup of coffee and brought it back to the breakfast table.

'Tell what?' asked Len Bateson.

'Anything one knows,' said Nigel, with an airy wave of the hand.

Jean Tomlinson said disapprovingly:

'But of course! If we have any information that may be of use, of course we must tell the police. That would be only right.'

'And there speaks our bonnie Jean,' said Nigel.

'*Moi je n'aime pas les flics,*' said René, offering his contribution to the discussion.

'Tell what?' Leonard Bateson said again.

'The things we know,' said Nigel. 'About each other, I mean,' he said helpfully. His glance swept round the breakfast-table with a malicious gleam.

'After all,' he said cheerfully, 'we all *do* know lots of things about each other, don't we? I mean, one's bound to, living in the same house.'

'But who is to decide what is important or not? There are many things no business of the police at all,' said Mr Achmed Ali. He spoke hotly, with an injured remembrance of the inspector's sharp remarks about his collection of postcards.

'I hear,' said Nigel, turning towards Mr Akibombo, 'that they found some very interesting things in *your* room.'

Owing to his colour, Mr Akibombo was not able to blush, but his eyelids blinked in a discomfited manner.

'Very much superstition in my country,' he said. 'My grandfather give me things to bring here. I keep out of feeling of piety and respect. I, myself, am modern and scientific; not believe in voodoo, but owing to imperfect command of language I find very difficult to explain to policeman.'

'Even dear little Jean has her secrets, I expect,' said Nigel, turning his gaze back to Miss Tomlinson.

Jean said hotly that she wasn't going to be insulted.

'I shall leave this place and go to the YWCA,' she said.

'Come now, Jean,' said Nigel. 'Give us another chance.'

'Oh, cut it out, Nigel!' said Valerie wearily. 'The police have to snoop, I suppose, under the circumstances.'

Colin McNabb cleared his throat, preparatory to making a remark.

'In my opinion,' he said judicially, 'the present position ought to be made clear to us. What exactly was the cause of Mrs Nick's death?'

'We'll hear at the inquest, I suppose,' said Valerie, impatiently.

'I very much doubt it,' said Colin. 'In my opinion they'll adjourn the inquest.'

'I suppose it was her heart, wasn't it?' said Patricia. 'She fell down in the street.'

'Drunk and incapable,' said Len Bateson. 'That's how she got taken to the police station.'

'So she *did* drink,' said Jean. 'You know, I always thought so. When the police searched the house they found cupboards full of empty brandy bottles in her room, I believe,' she added.

'Trust our Jean to know all the dirt,' said Nigel approvingly.

'Well, that does explain why she was sometimes so odd in her manner,' said Patricia.

Colin cleared his throat again.

'Ahem!' he said. 'I happened to observe her going into The Queen's Necklace on Saturday evening, when I was on my way home.'

'That's where she got tanked up, I suppose,' said Nigel.

'I suppose she just died of drink, then?' said Jean.

Len Bateson shook his head.

'Cerebral haemorrhage? I rather doubt it.'

'For goodness' sake, you don't think *she* was murdered too, do you?' said Jean.

'I bet she was,' said Sally Finch. 'Nothing would surprise me less.'

'Please,' said Mr Akibombo. 'It is thought someone killed her? Is that right?'

He looked from face to face.

'We've no reason to suppose anything of the sort yet,' said Colin.

'But who would want to kill her?' demanded Genevieve. 'Had she much money to leave? If she was rich it is possible, I suppose.'

'She was a maddening woman, my dear,' said Nigel. 'I'm sure everybody wanted to kill her. I often did,' he added, helping himself happily to marmalade.

II

'Please, Miss Sally, may I ask you a question? It is after what was said at breakfast. I have been thinking very much.'

'Well, I shouldn't think too much if I were you, Akibombo,' said Sally. 'It isn't healthy.'

Sally and Akibombo were partaking of an open-air lunch in Regent's Park. Summer was officially supposed to have come and the restaurant was open.

'All this morning,' said Akibombo mournfully, 'I have been much disturbed. I cannot answer my professor's questions good at all. He is not pleased at me. He says to me that I copy large bits out of books and do not think for myself. But I am here to acquire wisdom from much books and it seems to me that they say better in the books than the way I put it, because I have not good command of the English. And besides, this morning I find it very hard to think at all except of what goes on at Hickory Road and difficulties there.'

'I'll say you're right about that,' said Sally. 'I just couldn't concentrate myself this morning.'

'So that is why I ask you please to tell me certain things, because as I say, I have been thinking very much.'

'Well, let's hear what you've been thinking about, then.'

'Well, it is this borr – ass – sic.'

'Borr-ass-ic? Oh, boracic! Yes. What about it?'

'Well, I do not understand very well. It is an acid, they say? An acid like sulphuric acid?'

'Not like sulphuric acid, no,' said Sally.

'It is not something for laboratory experiment only?'

'I shouldn't imagine they ever did any experiments in laboratories with it. It's something quite mild and harmless.'

'You mean, even you could put it in your *eyes*?'

'That's right. That's just what one does use it for.'

'Ah, that explains that then. Mr Chandra Lal, he have little white bottle with white powder, and he puts powder in hot water and bathes his eyes with it. He keeps it in bathroom and then it is not there one day and he is very angry. That would be the bor-ac-ic, yes?'

'What *is* all this about boracic?'

'I tell you by and by. Please not now. I think some more.'

'Well, don't go sticking your neck out,' said Sally. 'I don't want yours to be the next corpse, Akibombo.'

III

'Valerie, do you think you could give me some advice?'

'Of course I could give you advice, Jean, though I don't know why anyone ever wants advice. They never take it.'

'It's really a matter of conscience,' said Jean.

'Then I'm the last person you ought to ask. I haven't got any conscience, to speak of.'

'Oh, Valerie, don't say things like that!'

'Well, it's quite true,' said Valerie. She stubbed out a cigarette as she spoke. 'I smuggle clothes in from Paris and tell the most frightful lies about their faces to the hideous women who come to the *salon*. I even travel on buses without paying my fare when I'm hard up. But come on, tell me. What's it all about?'

'It's what Nigel said at breakfast. If one knows something about someone else, do you think one ought to tell?'

'What an idiotic question! You can't put a thing like that in general terms. What is it you want to tell, or don't want to tell?'

'It's about a passport.'

'A passport?' Valerie sat up, surprised. 'Whose passport?'

'Nigel's. He's got a false passport.'

'Nigel?' Valerie sounded disbelieving. 'I don't believe it. It seems most improbable.'

'But he has. And you know, Valerie, I believe there's some question – I think I heard the police saying that Celia had said something about a passport. Supposing she'd found out about it and he killed her?'

'Sounds very melodramatic,' said Valerie. 'But frankly, I don't believe a word of it. What is this story about a passport?'

'I saw it.'

'How did you see it?'

'Well, it was absolutely an accident,' said Jean. 'I was looking for something in my despatch case a week or two ago, and by mistake I must have looked in Nigel's attaché-case instead. They were both on the shelf in the common-room.'

Valerie laughed rather disagreeably.

'Tell that to the marines!' she said. 'What were you really doing? Snooping?'

'No, of course not!' Jean sounded justly indignant. 'The one thing I'd never do is to look among anybody's private papers. I'm not that sort of person. It was just that I was feeling rather absent minded, so I opened the case and I was just sorting through it . . .'

'Look here, Jean, you can't get away with that. Nigel's attaché-case is a good deal larger than yours and it's an entirely different colour. While you're admitting things you might just as well admit that you *are* that sort of person. All right. You found a chance to go through some of Nigel's things and you took it.'

Jean rose.

'Of course, Valerie, if you're going to be so unpleasant and so very unfair and unkind, I shall . . .'

'Oh, come back, child!' said Valerie. 'Get on with it. I'm getting interested now. I want to know.'

'Well, there was this passport,' said Jean. 'It was down at the bottom and it had a name on it. Stanford or Stanley or some name like that, and I thought, "How odd that Nigel should have somebody else's passport here." I opened it and the photograph inside was Nigel! So don't you see, he must be leading a double life? What I wonder is, ought I to tell the police? Do you think it's my duty?'

Valerie laughed.

'Bad luck, Jean,' she said. 'As a matter of fact, I believe there's quite a simple explanation. Pat told me. Nigel came into some money, or something, on condition that he changed his name. He did it perfectly properly by deed poll or whatever it is, but that's all it is. I believe his original name *was* Stanfield or Stanley, or something like that.'

'Oh!' Jean looked thoroughly chagrined.

'Ask Pat about it if you don't believe me,' said Valerie.

'Oh – no – well, if it's as you say, I must have made a mistake.'

'Better luck next time,' said Valerie.

'I don't know what you mean, Valerie.'

'You'd like to get your knife into Nigel, wouldn't you? And get him in wrong with the police?'

Jean drew herself up.

'You may not believe me, Valerie,' she said, 'but all I wanted to do was my duty.'

She left the room.

'Oh, hell!' said Valerie.

There was a tap at the door and Sally entered.

'What's the matter, Valerie? You're looking a bit down in the mouth.'

'It's that disgusting Jean. She really is *too* awful! You don't think, do you, that there's the remotest chance it was Jean that bumped off poor Celia? I should rejoice madly if I ever saw Jean in the dock.'

'I'm with you there,' said Sally. 'But I don't think it's particularly likely. I don't think Jean would ever stick her neck out enough to murder anybody.'

'What do you think about Mrs Nick?'

'I just don't know what to think. I suppose we shall hear soon.'

'I'd say ten to one she was bumped off, too,' said Valerie.

'But why? What's going on here?' said Sally.

'I wish I knew. Sally, do you ever find yourself looking at people?'

'What do you mean, Val, looking at people?'

'Well, looking and wondering, "Is it *you*?" I've got a feeling, Sally, that there's someone here who's mad. *Really* mad. Bad mad, I mean – not just thinking they're a cucumber.'

'That may well be,' said Sally. She shivered.

'Ouch!' she said. 'Somebody's walking over my grave.'

IV

'Nigel I've got something I *must* tell you.'

'Well, what is it, Pat?' Nigel was burrowing frantically in his chest of drawers. 'What the hell did I do with those notes of mine I can't imagine. I shoved them in here, I thought.'

'Oh, Nigel, don't scrabble like that! You leave everything in such a frightful mess and I've just tidied it.'

'Well, what the hell, I've got to find my notes, haven't I?'

'Nigel, you *must* listen!'

'OK, Pat, don't look so desperate. What is it?'

'It's something I've got to confess.'

'Not murder, I hope?' said Nigel, with his usual flippancy.

'No, of course not!'

'Good. Well, what lesser sin?'

'It was one day when I mended your socks and I brought them along here to your room and was putting them away in your drawer . . .'

'Yes?'

'And the bottle of morphia was there. The one you told me about, that you got from the hospital.'

'Yes, and you made such a fuss about it!'

'But, Nigel, it was there in your drawer among your socks, where *anybody* could have found it.'

'Why should they? Nobody else goes rooting about among my socks except you.'

'Well, it seemed to me dreadful to leave it about like that, and I know you'd said you were going to get rid of it after you'd won your bet, but in the meantime there it was, still there.'

'Of course. I hadn't got the third thing yet.'

'Well, I thought it was very wrong, and so I took the bottle out of the drawer and I emptied the poison out of it, and I replaced it with some ordinary bicarbonate of soda. It looked almost exactly the same.'

Nigel paused in his scramble for his lost notes.

'Good lord!' he said. 'Did you really? You mean that when I was swearing to Len and old Colin that the stuff was morphine sulphate or tartrate or whatever it was, it was merely bicarbonate of soda all the time?'

'Yes. You see . . .'

Nigel interrupted her. He was frowning.

'I'm not sure, you know, that that doesn't invalidate the bet. Of course, *I'd* no idea –'

'But Nigel, it was really *dangerous* keeping it there.'

'Oh lord, Pat, must you always fuss so? What did you do with the actual stuff?'

'I put it in the soda bic bottle and I hid it at the back of my handkerchief drawer.'

Nigel looked at her in mild surprise.

'Really, Pat, your logical thought processes beggar description! What was the point?'

'I felt it was safer there.'

'My dear girl, either the morphia should have been under lock and key, or if it wasn't, it couldn't really matter whether it was among my socks or your handkerchiefs.'

'Well, it did matter. For one thing, I have a room to myself and you share yours.'

'Why, you don't think poor old Len was going to pinch the morphia off me, do you?'

'I wasn't going to tell you about it, ever, but I must now. Because, you see, it's *gone*.'

'You mean the police have swiped it?'

'No. It disappeared before that.'

'Do you mean . . . ?' Nigel gazed at her in consternation. 'Let's get this straight. There's a bottle labelled "Soda Bic", containing morphine sulphate, which is knocking about the place somewhere, and at any time someone may take a heaping teaspoonful of it if they've got a pain in their middle? Good God, Pat! You *have* done it! Why the hell didn't you throw the stuff away if you were so upset about it?'

'Because I thought it was valuable and ought to go back to the hospital instead of being just thrown away. As soon as you'd won your bet, I meant to give it to Celia and ask her to put it back.'

'You're sure you *didn't* give it to her?'

'No, of course not. You mean I gave it to her, and she took it and it *was* suicide, and it was all my fault?'

'Calm down. When did it disappear?'

'I don't know exactly. I looked for it the day before Celia died. I couldn't find it, but I just thought I'd perhaps put it somewhere else.'

'It was gone the day *before* she died?'

'I suppose,' said Patricia, her face white, 'that I've been very stupid.'

'That's putting it mildly,' said Nigel. 'To what lengths can a muddled mind and an active conscience go!'

'Nigel. D'you think I ought to tell the police?'

'Oh, hell!' said Nigel. 'I suppose so, yes. And it's going to be all my fault.'

'Oh, no, Nigel darling, it's me. I –'

'I pinched the damned stuff in the first place,' said Nigel. 'It all seemed to be a very amusing stunt at the time. But now – I can already hear the vitriolic remarks from the bench.'

'I *am* sorry. When I took it I really meant it for –'

'You meant it for the best. *I* know! Look here, Pat, I simply can't believe the stuff has disappeared. You've forgotten just where you put it. You do mislay things sometimes, you know.'

'Yes, but –'

She hesitated, a shade of doubt appearing on her frowning face.

Nigel rose briskly.

'Let's go along to your room and have a thorough search.'

V

'Nigel, those are my *underclothes*.'

'Really, Pat, you can't go all prudish on me at this stage. Down among the panties is just where you would hide a bottle, now, isn't it?'

'Yes, but I'm sure I –'

'We can't be sure of anything until we've looked everywhere. And I'm jolly well going to do it.'

There was a perfunctory tap on the door and Sally Finch entered. Her eyes widened with surprise. Pat, clasping a handful of Nigel's socks, was sitting on the bed, and Nigel, the bureau drawers all pulled out, was burrowing like an excited terrier into a heap of pullovers whilst about him were strewn panties, brassières, stockings, and other component parts of female attire.

'For land's sake,' said Sally, 'what goes on?'

'Looking for bicarbonate,' said Nigel briefly.

'Bicarbonate? Why?'

'I've got a pain,' said Nigel, grinning. 'A pain in my tum-tum-tum – and nothing but bicarbonate will assuage it.'

'I've got some somewhere, I believe.'

'No good, Sally, it's got to be Pat's. Hers is the only brand that will ease my particular ailment.'

'You're crazy,' said Sally. 'What's he up to, Pat?'

Patricia shook her head miserably.

'*You* haven't seen my soda bic, have you, Sally?' she asked. 'Just a little in the bottom of the bottle?'

'No.' Sally looked at her curiously. Then she frowned. 'Let me see. Somebody around here – no, I can't remember – Have you got a stamp, Pat? I want to mail a letter and I've run out.'

'In the drawer there.'

Sally opened the shallow drawer of the writing-table, took out a book of stamps, extracted one, affixed it to the letter she held in her hand, dropped the stamp book back in the drawer, and put twopence-halfpenny on the desk.

'Thanks. Shall I mail this letter of yours at the same time?'

'Yes – no – no, I think I'll wait.'

Sally nodded and left the room.

Pat dropped the socks she had been holding, and twisted her fingers nervously together.

'Nigel?'

'Yes?' Nigel had transferred his attention to the wardrobe and was looking in the pockets of a coat.

'There's something else I've got to confess.'

'Good lord, Pat, what else have you been doing?'

'I'm afraid you'll be angry.'

'I'm past being angry. I'm just plain scared. If Celia was poisoned with the stuff that I pinched, I shall probably go to prison for years and years, even if they don't hang me.'

'It's nothing to do with that. It's about your father.'

'*What*?' Nigel spun round, an expression of incredulous astonishment on his face.

'You do know he's very ill, don't you?'

'I don't care how ill he is.'

'It said so on the wireless last night. "Sir Arthur Stanley, the famous research chemist, is lying in a very critical condition."'

'So nice to be a VIP. All the world gets the news when you're ill.'

'Nigel, if he's dying, you ought to be reconciled to him.'

'Like hell I will!'

'But if he's dying.'

'He's the same swine dying as he was when he was in the pink of condition!'

'You mustn't be like that, Nigel. So bitter and unforgiving.'

'Listen, Pat – I told you once: he killed my mother.'

'I know you said so, and I know you adored her. But I do think, Nigel, that you sometimes *exaggerate*. Lots of husbands are unkind and unfeeling and their wives resent it and it makes them very unhappy. But to say your father killed your mother is an extravagant statement and isn't really true.'

'You know so much about it, don't you?'

'I know that some day you'll regret not having made it up with your father before he died. That's why—' Pat paused and braced herself. 'That's why I – I've written to your father – telling him –'

'You've written to him? Is that the letter Sally wanted to post?' He strode over to the writing-table. '*I* see.'

He picked up the letter lying addressed and stamped, and with quick, nervous fingers, he tore it into small pieces and threw it into the waste-paper basket.

'That's that! And don't you dare do anything of that kind again.'

'Really, Nigel, you are absolutely childish. You can tear the letter up, but you can't stop me writing another, and I shall.'

'You're so incurably sentimental. Did it ever occur to you that when I said my father killed my mother, I was stating just a plain unvarnished *fact*. My mother died of an overdose of medinal. Took it by mistake, they said at the inquest. *But she didn't take it by mistake*. It was given to her, deliberately, by my father. He wanted to marry another woman, you see, and my mother wouldn't give him a divorce. It's a plain sordid murder story. What would you have done in my place? Denounced him to the police? My mother wouldn't have wanted that . . . So I did the only thing I could do – told the swine I knew – and cleared out – for ever. I even changed my name.'

'Nigel – I'm sorry . . . I never dreamed . . .'

'Well, you know now . . . The respected and famous Arthur Stanley with his researches and antibiotics. Flourishing like the green bay tree! But his fancy piece didn't marry him after all. She sheered off. I think she guessed what he'd done –'

'Nigel dear, how awful – I am sorry . . .'

'All right. We won't talk of it again. Let's get back to this blasted bicarbonate business. Now think back carefully to exactly what you did with the stuff. Put your head in your hands and *think*, Pat.'

VI

Genevieve entered the common-room in a state of great excitement. She spoke to the assembled students in a low thrilled voice.

'I am sure now, but absolutely sure I know who killed the little Celia.'

'Who was it, Genevieve?' demanded René. 'What has arrived to make you so positive?'

Genevieve looked cautiously round to make sure the door of the common-room was closed. She lowered her voice.

'It is Nigel Chapman.'

'Nigel Chapman, but why?'

'Listen. I pass along the corridor to go down the stairs just now and I hear voices in Patricia's room. It is Nigel who speaks.'

'Nigel? In Patricia's room?' Jean spoke in a disapproving voice. But Genevieve swept on.

'And he is saying to her that his father killed his mother, and that, *pour ça*, he has changed his name. So it is clear, is it not? His father was a convicted murderer, and Nigel he has the hereditary taint . . .'

'It is possible,' said Mr Chandra Lal, dwelling pleasurably on the possibility. 'It is certainly possible. He is so violent, Nigel, so unbalanced. No self-control. You agree?' He turned condescendingly to Akibombo, who nodded an enthusiastic black woolly head and showed his white teeth in a pleased smile.

'I've always felt very strongly,' said Jean, 'that Nigel has *no* moral sense . . . A thoroughly *degenerate* character.'

'It is sex murder, yes,' said Mr Achmed Ali. 'He sleeps with this girl, then he kills her. Because she is a nice girl, respectable, she will expect marriage . . .'

'Rot,' said Leonard Bateson explosively.

'What did you say?'

'I said ROT!' roared Len.

CHAPTER 17

I

Seated in a room at the police station, Nigel looked nervously into the stern eyes of Inspector Sharpe. Stammering slightly, he had just brought his narrative to a close.

'You realise, Mr Chapman, that what you have just told us is very serious? Very serious indeed.'

'Of course I realise it. I wouldn't have come here to tell you about it unless I'd felt that it was urgent.'

'And you say Miss Lane can't remember exactly when she last saw this bicarbonate bottle containing morphine?'

'She's got herself all muddled up. The more she tries to think the more uncertain she gets. She said I flustered her. She's trying to think it out while I came round to you.'

'We'd better go round to Hickory Road right away.'

As the inspector spoke the telephone on the table rang, and the constable who had been taking notes of Nigel's story stretched out his hand and lifted the receiver.

'It's Miss Lane now,' he said, as he listened. 'Wanting to speak to Mr Chapman.'

Nigel leaned across the table and took the receiver from him.

'Pat? Nigel here.'

The girl's voice came, breathless, eager, the words tumbling over each other.

'Nigel. *I think I've got it!* I mean, I think I know now who must have taken – you know – taken it from my handkerchief drawer, I mean – you see, there's only one person who –'

The voice broke off.

'Pat. Hallo? Are you there? Who was it?'

'I can't tell you now. Later. You'll be coming round?'

The receiver was near enough for the constable and the inspector to have heard the conversation clearly, and the latter nodded in answer to Nigel's questioning look.

'Tell her "at once",' he said.

'We're coming round at once,' said Nigel. 'On our way this minute.'

'Oh! Good. I'll be in my room.'

'So long, Pat.'

Hardly a word was spoken during the brief ride to Hickory Road. Sharpe wondered to himself whether this was a break at last. Would Patricia Lane have any definite evidence to offer, or would it be pure surmise on her part? Clearly she had remembered *something* that had seemed to her important. He supposed that she had been telephoning from the hall, and that therefore she had had to be guarded in her language. At this time in the evening so many people would have been passing through.

Nigel opened the front door at 26 Hickory Road with his key and they passed inside. Through the open door of the common-room, Sharpe could see the rumpled red head of Leonard Bateson bent over some books.

Nigel led the way upstairs and along the passage to Pat's room. He gave a short tap on the door and entered.

'Hallo, Pat. Here we –'

His voice stopped, dying away in a long choking gasp. He stood motionless. Over his shoulder, Sharpe saw also what there was to see.

Patricia Lane lay slumped on the floor.

The inspector pushed Nigel gently aside. He went forward and knelt down by the girl's huddled body. He raised her head, felt for the pulse, then delicately let the head resume its former position. He rose to his feet, his face grim and set.

'No?' said Nigel, his voice high and unnatural. 'No. No. *No.*'

'Yes, Mr Chapman. She's dead.'

'No, *no*. Not Pat! Dear stupid Pat. How –'

'With this.'

It was a simple, quickly improvised weapon. A marble paper-weight slipped into a woollen sock.

'Struck on the back of the head. A very efficacious weapon. If it's any consolation to you, Mr Chapman, I don't think she even knew what happened to her.'

Nigel sat down shakily on the bed. He said:

'That's one of *my* socks . . . She was going to mend it . . . Oh, God, she was going to mend it . . .'

Suddenly he began to cry. He cried like a child – with abandon and without self-consciousness.

Sharpe was continuing his reconstruction.

'It was someone she knew quite well. Someone who picked up a sock and just slipped the paperweight into it. Do you recognise the paperweight, Mr Chapman?'

He rolled the sock back so as to display it.

Nigel, still weeping, looked.

'Pat always had it on her desk. A Lion of Lucerne.'

He buried his face in his hands.

'Pat – oh, Pat! What shall I do without you!'

Suddenly he sat upright, flinging back his untidy fair hair.

'I'll kill whoever did this! I'll kill him! Murdering swine!'

'Gently, Mr Chapman. Yes, yes, I know how you feel. A brutal piece of work.'

'Pat never harmed anybody . . .'

Speaking soothingly, Inspector Sharpe got him out of the room. Then he went back himself into the bedroom. He stooped over the dead girl. Very gently he detached something from between her fingers.

II

Geronimo, perspiration running down his forehead, turned frightened dark eyes from one face to the other.

'I see nothing. I hear nothing, I tell you. I do not know anything *at all.* I am with Maria in kitchen. I put the minestrone on, I grate the cheese –'

Sharpe interrupted the catalogue.

'Nobody's accusing you. We just want to get some times quite clear. Who was in and out of the house the last hour?'

'I do not know. How should I know?'

'But you can see very clearly from the kitchen window who goes in and out, can't you?'

'Perhaps, yes.'

'Then just tell us.'

'They come in and out all the time at this hour of the day.'

'Who was in the house from six o'clock until six thirty-five when we arrived?'

'Everybody except Mr Nigel and Mrs Hubbard and Miss Hobhouse.'

'When did they go out?'

'Mrs Hubbard she go out before tea-time, she has not come back yet.'

'Go on.'

'Mr Nigel goes out about half an hour ago, just before six – look very upset. He come back with you just now –'

'That's right, yes.'

'Miss Valerie, she goes out just at six o'clock. Time signal, pip, pip, pip. Dressed for cocktails, very smart. She still out.'

'And everybody else is here?'

'Yes, sir. All here.'

Sharpe looked down at his notebook. The time of Patricia's call was noted there. Eight minutes past six, exactly.

'Everybody else was here, in the house? Nobody came back during that time?'

'Only Miss Sally. She been down to pillar-box with letter and come back in –'

'Do you know what time she came in?'

Geronimo frowned.

'She came back while the news was going on.'

'*After* six, then?'

'Yes, sir.'

'What part of the news was it?'

'I don't remember, sir. But before the sport. Because when sport come we switch off.'

Sharpe smiled grimly. It was a wide field. Only Nigel Chapman, Valerie Hobhouse and Mrs Hubbard could be excluded. It would mean long and exhaustive questioning. Who had been in the common-room, who had left it? And when? Who would vouch for who? Add to that, that many of the students, especially the Asiatic and African ones, were constitutionally vague about times, and the task was no enviable one.

But it would have to be done.

III

In Mrs Hubbard's room the atmosphere was unhappy. Mrs Hubbard herself, still in her outdoor things, her nice round face strained and anxious, sat on the sofa. Sharpe and Sergeant Cobb sat at a small table.

'I think she telephoned from in here,' said Sharpe. 'Around

about six-eight several people left or entered the common-room, or so they say – and nobody saw or noticed or heard the hall telephone being used. Of course, their times aren't reliable, half these people never seem to look at a clock. But I think that anyway she'd come in here if she wanted to telephone the police station. You were out, Mrs Hubbard, but I don't suppose you lock your door?'

Mrs Hubbard shook her head.

'Mrs Nicoletis always did, but I never do –'

'Well then, Patricia Lane comes in here to telephone, all agog with what's she's remembered. Then, whilst she was talking, the door opened and somebody looked in or came in. Patricia stalled and hung up. Was that because she recognised the intruder as the person whose name she was just about to say? Or was it just a general precaution? Might be either. I incline myself to the first supposition.'

Mrs Hubbard nodded emphatically.

'Whoever it was may have followed her here, perhaps listening outside the door. Then came in to stop Pat from going on.'

'And then –'

Sharpe's face darkened. 'That person went back to Patricia's room with her, talking quite normally and easily. Perhaps Patricia taxed her with removing the bicarbonate, and perhaps the other gave a plausible explanation.'

Mrs Hubbard said sharply:

'Why do you say "*her*"?'

'Funny thing – a pronoun! When we found the body, Nigel Chapman said, "I'll kill whoever did this. I'll kill *him*." "*Him*," you notice. Nigel Chapman clearly believed the murder was done by a *man*. It may be because he associated the idea of violence with a man. It may be that he's got some particular suspicion pointing to a man, to some particular man. If the latter, we must find out his reasons for thinking so. But speaking for myself, I plump for a woman.'

'Why?'

'Just this. Somebody went into Patricia's room with her – someone with whom she felt quite at home. That points to another girl. The men don't go to the girls' bedroom floors unless it's for some special reason. That's right, isn't it, Mrs Hubbard?'

'Yes. It's not exactly a hard and fast rule, but it's fairly generally observed.'

'The other side of the house is cut off from this side, except on the ground floor. Taking it that the conversation earlier between Nigel and Pat was overheard, it would in all probability be a woman who overheard it.'

'Yes, I see what you mean. And some of the girls seem to spend half their time here listening at keyholes.'

She flushed and added apologetically:

'That's rather too harsh. Actually, although these houses are solidly built, they've been cut up and partitioned, and all the new work is flimsy as anything, like paper. You can't help hearing through it. Jean, I must admit, does do a good deal of snooping. She's the type. And of course, when Genevieve heard Nigel telling Pat his father had murdered his mother, she stopped and listened for all she was worth.'

The inspector nodded. He had listened to the evidence of Sally Finch and Jean Tomlinson and Genevieve. He said:

'Who occupies the rooms on either side of Patricia's?'

'Genevieve's is beyond it – but that's a good original wall. Elizabeth Johnston's is on the other side, nearer the stairs. That's only a partition wall.'

'That narrows it down a bit,' said the inspector.

'The French girl heard the *end* of the conversation. Sally Finch was present earlier on *before* she went out to post her letter. But the fact that those two girls *were* there automatically excludes anybody else having been able to snoop, except for a very short period. Always with the exception of Elizabeth Johnston, who could have heard everything through the partition wall if she'd been in her bedroom, but it seems to be fairly clear that she was already in the common-room when Sally Finch went out to the post.'

'She did not remain in the common-room all the time?'

'No, she went upstairs again at some period to fetch a book she had forgotten. As usual, nobody can say *when.*'

'It might have been any of them,' said Mrs Hubbard help-lessly.

'As far as their statements go, yes – but we've got a little extra evidence.'

He took a small folded paper packet out of his pocket.

'What's that?' demanded Mrs Hubbard.

Sharpe smiled.

'A couple of hairs – I took them from between Patricia Lane's fingers.'

'You mean that –'

There was a tap on the door.

'Come in,' said the inspector.

The door opened to admit Mr Akibombo. He was smiling broadly, all over his black face.

'Please,' he said.

Inspector Sharpe said impatiently:

'Yes, Mr – er – um, what is it?'

'I think, please, I have a statement to make. Of first-class importance to elucidation of sad and tragic occurrence.'

CHAPTER 18

'Now, Mr Akibombo,' said Inspector Sharpe, resignedly, 'let's hear, please, what all this is about.'

Mr Akibombo had been provided with a chair. He sat facing the others who were all looking at him with keen attention.

'Thank you. I begin now?'

'Yes, please.'

'Well, it is, you see, that sometimes I have the disquieting sensations in my stomach.'

'Oh.'

'Sick to my stomach. That is what Miss Sally calls it. But I am not, you see, actually *sick*. I do not, that is, vomit.'

Inspector Sharpe restrained himself with difficulty while these medical details were elaborated.

'Yes, yes,' he said. 'Very sorry, I'm sure. But you want to tell us –'

'It is, perhaps, unaccustomed food. I feel very full *here*.' Mr Akibombo indicated exactly where. 'I think myself, not enough meat, and too much what you call cardohydrates.'

'Carbohydrates,' the inspector corrected him mechanically. 'But I don't see –'

'Sometimes I take small pill, soda mint; and sometimes stomach powder. It does not matter very much what it is – so that a great pouf comes and much air – like this.' Mr Akibombo gave a most realistic and gigantic belch. 'After that,' he smiled seraphically, 'I feel much better, much better.'

The inspector's face was becoming a congested purple. Mrs Hubbard said authoritatively:

'We understand all about *that*. Now get on to the next part.'

'Yes. Certainly. Well, as I say, this happens to me early last week – I do not remember exactly which day. Very good macaroni and I eat a lot, and afterwards feel very bad. I try to do work for my professor but difficult to think with fullness here.' (Again Akibombo indicated the spot.) 'It is after supper in the common-room and only Elizabeth there and I say to her, "Have you bicarbonate or stomach powder, I have finished mine." And she says, "No. But," she says, "I saw some in Pat's drawer when I was putting back a handkerchief I borrowed from her. I will get it for you," she says. "Pat will not mind." So she goes upstairs and comes back with soda bicarbonate bottle. Very little left, at bottom of bottle, almost empty. I thank her and go with it to the bathroom, and I put nearly all of it about a teaspoonful in water and stir it up and drink it.'

'A *teaspoonful*? A teaspoonful! My God!'

The inspector gazed at him fascinated. Sergeant Cobb leaned forward with an astonished face. Mrs Hubbard said obscurely:

'Rasputin!'

'You swallowed a teaspoonful of *morphia*?'

'Naturally, I think it is bicarbonate.'

'Yes, yes, what I can't understand is why you're sitting here now!'

'And then, afterwards, I was ill, but really ill. Not just the fullness. Pain, bad pain in my stomach.'

'I can't make out why you're not dead!'

'Rasputin,' said Mrs Hubbard. 'They used to give him poison again and again, lots of it, and it didn't kill him!'

Mr Akibombo was continuing.

'So then, next day, when I am better, I take the bottle and the tiny bit of powder that is left in it to a chemist and I say please tell me what is this I have taken that has made me feel so bad?'

'Yes?'

'And he says come back later, and when I do, he says, "No wonder! This is not the bicarbonate. It is the borasseek. The acid borasseek. You can put it in the eyes, yes, but if you swallow a teaspoonful it makes you ill."'

'Boracic?' The Inspector stared at him stupefied. 'But how did boracic get into that bottle? What happened to the morphia?' He groaned. 'Of all the haywire cases!'

'And I have been thinking, please,' went on Akibombo.

'You have been thinking,' Sharpe said. 'And what have you been thinking?'

'I have been thinking of Miss Celia and how she died and that someone, after she was dead, must have come into her room and left there the empty morphia bottle and the little piece of paper that say she killed herself –'

Akibombo paused and the inspector nodded.

'And so I say – who could have done that? And I think if it is one of the girls it will be easy, but if a man not so easy, because he would have to go downstairs in our house and up the other stairs and someone might wake up and hear him or see him. So I think again, and I say, suppose it is someone in our house, but in the next room to Miss Celia's – only she is in this house, you understand? Outside his window is a balcony and outside hers is a balcony too, and she will sleep with her window open because that is hygienic practice. So if he is big and strong and athletic he could jump across.'

'The room next to Celia's in the other house,' said Mrs Hubbard, 'Let me see, that's Nigel's and – and . . .'

'Len Bateson's,' said the inspector. His finger touched the folded paper in his hand. 'Len Bateson.'

'He is very nice, yes, said Mr Akibombo sadly. 'And to me most pleasant, but psychologically one does not know what goes on below top surface. That is so, is it not? That is modern theory. Mr Chandra Lal very angry when his boracic for the eyes disappears and later, when I ask, he says he has been told that it was taken by Len Bateson . . .'

'The morphia was taken from Nigel's drawer and boracic was substituted for it, and when Patricia Lane came along and substituted soda bicarbonate for what she thought was morphia but which was really boracic powder . . . Yes . . . I see . . .'

'I have helped you, yes?' Mr Akibombo asked politely.

'Yes, indeed, we're most grateful to you. Don't – er – repeat any of this.'

'No, sir. I will be most careful.'

Mr Akibombo bowed politely to all and left the room.

'Len Bateson,' said Mrs Hubbard, in a distressed voice. 'Oh! *No*.'

Sharpe looked at her.

'You don't want it to be Len Bateson?'

'I've got fond of that boy. He's got a temper, I know, but he's always seemed so *nice*.'

'That's been said about a lot of criminals,' said Sharpe.

Gently he unfolded his little paper packet. Mrs Hubbard obeyed his gesture and leaned forward to look.

On the white paper were two red short curly hairs . . .

'Oh! dear,' said Mrs Hubbard.

'Yes,' said Sharpe reflectively. 'In my experience a murderer usually makes at least *one* mistake.'

CHAPTER 19

I

'But it is beautiful, my friend,' said Hercule Poirot with admiration. 'So clear – so beautifully clear.'

'You sound as if you were talking about soup,' grumbled the inspector. 'It may be Consommé to you – but to me there's a good deal of thick Mock Turtle about it still.'

'Not now. Everything fits in in its appointed place.'

'Even these?'

As he had done to Mrs Hubbard, Inspector Sharpe produced his exhibit of two red hairs.

Poirot's answer was almost in the same words as Sharpe had used.

'Ah – yes,' he said. 'What do you call it on the radio? The one deliberate mistake.'

The eyes of the two men met.

'No one,' said Hercule Poirot, 'is as clever as they think they are.'

Inspector Sharpe was greatly tempted to say:

'Not even Hercule Poirot?' but he restrained himself.

'For the other, my friend, it is all fixed?'

'Yes, the balloon goes up tomorrow.'

'You go yourself?'

'No. I'm scheduled to appear at 26 Hickory Road. Cobb will be in charge.'

'We will wish him good luck.'

Gravely, Hercule Poirot raised his glass. It contained crème de menthe.

Inspector Sharpe raised his whisky glass.

'Here's hoping,' he said.

II

'They do think up things, these places,' said Sergeant Cobb.

He was looking with grudging admiration at the display window of SABRINA FAIR. Framed and enclosed in an expensive illustration of the glassmaker's art – the 'glassy green translucent wave' – Sabrina was displayed, recumbent, clad in brief and exquisite panties and happily surrounded with every variety of deliciously packaged cosmetics. Besides the panties she wore various examples of barbaric costume jewellery.

Detective-Constable McCrae gave a snort of deep disapproval.

'Blasphemy, I call it. Sabrina Fair, that's Milton, that is.'

'Well, Milton isn't the Bible, my lad.'

'You'll not deny that Paradise Lost is about Adam and Eve and the garden of Eden and all the devils of hell and if that's not religion, what is?'

Sergeant Cobb did not enter on these controversial matters. He marched boldly into the establishment, the dour constable at his heels. In the shell pink interior of Sabrina Fair the sergeant and his satellite looked as out of place as the traditional bull in a china shop.

An exquisite creature in delicate salmon pink swam up to them, her feet hardly seeming to touch the floor.

Sergeant Cobb said, 'Good morning, madam,' and produced his credentials. The lovely creature withdrew in a flutter. An equally lovely but slightly older creature appeared. She in turn gave way to a superb and resplendent duchess whose blue grey hair and smooth cheeks set age and wrinkles at nought. Appraising steel grey eyes met the steady gaze of Sergeant Cobb.

'This is most unusual,' said the duchess severely. 'Please come this way.'

She led him through a square salon with a centre table where magazines and periodicals were heaped carelessly. All round the walls were curtained recesses where glimpses could be obtained of recumbent women supine under the ministrant hands of pink robed priestesses.

The duchess led the police officers into a small business-like apartment with a big roll top desk, severe chairs, and no softening of the harsh northern light.

'I am Mrs Lucas, the proprietress of this establishment,' she said. 'My partner, Miss Hobhouse, is not here today.'

'No, madam,' said Sergeant Cobb, to whom this was no news.

'This search warrant of yours seems to be most high-handed,' said Mrs Lucas. 'This is Miss Hobhouse's private office. I sincerely hope that it will not be necessary for you to – er – upset our clients in any way.'

'I don't think you need to worry unduly on that score,' said Cobb. 'What we're after isn't likely to be in the public rooms.'

He waited politely until she unwillingly withdrew. Then he looked round Valerie Hobhouse's office. The narrow window gave a view of the back premises of the other Mayfair firms. The walls were panelled in pale grey and there were two good Persian rugs on the floor. His eyes went from the small wall safe to the big desk.

'Won't be in the safe,' said Cobb. 'Too obvious.'

A quarter of an hour later, the safe and the drawers of the desk had yielded up their secrets.

'Looks like it's maybe a mare's nest,' said McCrae, who was by nature both gloomy and disapproving.

'We're only beginning,' said Cobb.

Having emptied the drawers of their contents and arranged the latter neatly in piles, he now proceeded to take the drawers out and turn them upside down.

He uttered an ejaculation of pleasure.

'Here we are, my lad,' he said.

Fastened to the underneath side of the bottom drawer with adhesive tape were a half-dozen small dark blue books with gilt lettering.

'Passports,' said Sergeant Cobb. 'Issued by Her Majesty's Secretary of State for Foreign Affairs, God bless his trusting heart.'

McCrae bent over with interest as Cobb opened the passports and compared the affixed photographs.

'Hardly think it was the same woman, would you?' said McCrae.

The passports were those of Mrs da Silva, Miss Irene French, Mrs Olga Kohn, Miss Nina Le Mesurier, Mrs Gladys Thomas, and Miss Moira O'Neele. They represented a dark young woman whose age varied between twenty-five and forty.

'It's the different hair-do every time that does it,' said Cobb. 'Pompadour, curls, straight cut, page boy bob, etc. She's done something to her nose for Olga Kohn, plumpers in her cheeks for Mrs Thomas. Here are two more – foreign passports – Madame Mahmoudi, Algerian. Sheila Donovan, Eire. I'll say she's got bank accounts in all these different names.'

'Bit complicated, isn't that?'

'It has to be complicated, my lad. Inland Revenue always snooping round asking embarrassing questions. It's not so difficult to make money by smuggling goods – but it's hell and all to account for money when you've got it! I bet this little gambling club in Mayfair was started by the lady for just that reason. Winning money by gambling is about the only thing an income tax inspector can't check up on. A good part of the loot, I should say, is cached around in Algerian and French banks and in Eire. The whole thing's a thoroughly well thought out business-like set up. And then, one day, she must have had one of these fake passports lying about at Hickory Road and that poor little devil Celia saw it.'

CHAPTER 20

'It was a clever idea of Miss Hobhouse's,' said Inspector Sharpe. His voice was indulgent, almost fatherly.

He shuffled the passports from one hand to the other like a man dealing cards.

'Complicated thing, finance,' he said. 'We've had a busy time haring round from one bank to the other. She covered her tracks well – her financial tracks, I mean. I'd say that in a couple of years' time she could have cleared out, gone abroad and lived happily ever after, as they say, on ill-gotten gains. It wasn't a big show – illicit diamonds, sapphires, etc., coming in – stolen stuff going out – and narcotics on the side, as you might say. Thoroughly well organised. She went abroad under her own and under different names, but never too often, and the actual smuggling was always done, unknowingly, by someone else. She had agents abroad who saw to the exchange of rucksacks at the right moment. Yes, it was a clever idea. And we've got M. Poirot here to thank for putting us on to it. It was smart of her, too, to suggest that psychological stealing stunt to poor little Miss Austin. You were wise to that almost at once, weren't you, M. Poirot?'

Poirot smiled in a deprecating manner and Mrs Hubbard looked admiringly at him. The conversation was strictly off the record in Mrs Hubbard's sitting-room.

'Greed was her undoing,' said Poirot. 'She was tempted by that fine diamond in Patricia Lane's ring. It was foolish of her because it suggested at once that she was used to handling precious stones – that business of prising the diamond out and replacing it with a zircon. Yes, that certainly gave me ideas about Valerie Hobhouse. She was clever, though, when I taxed her with inspiring Celia, she admitted it and explained it in a thoroughly sympathetic way.'

'But murder!' said Mrs Hubbard. 'Cold-blooded murder. I can't really believe it even now.'

Inspector Sharpe looked gloomy.

'We aren't in a position to charge her with the murder of Celia Austin yet,' he said. 'We've got her cold on the smuggling, of course. No difficulties about that. But the murder charge is more tricky. The public prosecutor doesn't see his way. There's motive, of course, and opportunity. She probably knew all about the bet and Nigel's possession of morphia, but there's no real evidence, and there are the two other deaths to take into account. She could have poisoned Mrs Nicoletis all right – but on the other hand, she definitely did not kill Patricia Lane. Actually she's about the only person who's completely in the clear. Geronimo says positively that she left the house at six o'clock. He sticks to that. I don't know whether she bribed him –'

'No,' said Poirot, shaking his head. 'She did not bribe him.'

'And we've the evidence of the chemist at the corner of the road. He knows her quite well and he sticks to it that she came in at five minutes past six and bought face powder and aspirin and used the telephone. She left his shop at quarter-past six and took a taxi from the rank outside.'

Poirot sat up in his chair.

'But that,' he said, 'is magnificent! It is just what we want!'

'What on earth do you mean?'

'I mean that she actually telephoned from the box at the chemist's shop.'

Inspector Sharpe looked at him in an exasperated fashion.

'Now, see here, M. Poirot. Let's take the known facts. At eight minutes past six, Patricia Lane is alive and telephoning to the police station from this room. You agree to that?'

'I do not think she was telephoning from this room.'

'Well then, from the hall downstairs.'

'Not from the hall either.'

Inspector Sharpe sighed.

'I suppose you don't deny that a call *was* put through to the police station? You don't think that I and my sergeant and Police Constable Nye and Nigel Chapman were the victims of mass hallucination?'

'Assuredly not. A call was put through to you. I should say at a guess that it was put through from the public call-box at the chemist's on the corner.'

Inspector Sharpe's jaw dropped for a moment.

'You mean that *Valerie Hobhouse* put through that call? That she pretended to speak as Patricia Lane, and that Patricia Lane was *already dead*.'

'That is what I mean, yes.'

The inspector was silent for a moment, then he brought down his fist with a crash on the table.

'I don't believe it. The voice – I heard it myself –'

'You heard it, yes. A girl's voice, breathless, agitated. But you didn't know Patricia Lane's voice well enough to say definitely that it *was* her voice.'

'*I* didn't, perhaps. But it was Nigel Chapman who actually took the call. You can't tell me that Nigel Chapman could be deceived. It isn't so easy to disguise a voice over the telephone, or to counterfeit somebody else's voice. Nigel Chapman would have known if it wasn't Pat's voice speaking.'

'Yes,' said Poirot. '*Nigel Chapman would have known*. Nigel Chapman knew quite well that it *wasn't* Patricia. Who should know better than he, since he had killed her with a blow on the back of the head only a short while before.'

It was a moment or two before the inspector recovered his voice.

'Nigel Chapman? Nigel Chapman? But when we found her dead – he cried – cried like a child.'

'I dare say,' said Poirot. 'I think he was as fond of that girl as he could be of anybody – but that wouldn't save her – not if she represented a menace to his interests. All along, Nigel Chapman has stood out as the obvious probability. Who had morphia in his possession? Nigel Chapman. Who had the shallow brilliant intellect to plan and the audacity to carry out fraud and murder? Nigel Chapman. Who do we know to be both ruthless and vain? Nigel Chapman. He has all the hallmarks of the killer; the overweening vanity, the spitefulness, the growing recklessness that led him to draw attention to himself in every conceivable way – using the green ink in a stupendous double bluff, and finally overreaching himself by the silly deliberate mistake of putting Len Bateson's hairs in Patricia's fingers, oblivious of the fact that as Patricia was struck down from behind, she could not possibly have grasped her assailant by the hair. They are like that, these murderers, carried away by their own egotism, by their admiration of their own cleverness, relying on their charm – for he *has* charm, this Nigel – he has all the charm of a spoiled child who has never grown up, who never will grow up – who sees only one thing, himself, and what he wants!'

'But why, M. Poirot? Why murder? Celia Austin, perhaps, but why Patricia Lane?'

'That,' said Poirot, 'we have got to find out.'

CHAPTER 21

'I haven't seen you for a long time,' said old Mr Endicott to Hercule Poirot. He peered at the other keenly. 'It's very nice of you to drop in.'

'Not really,' said Hercule Poirot. 'I want something.'

'Well, as you know, I'm deeply in your debt. You cleared up that nasty Abernethy business for me.'

'I am surprised really to find you here. I thought you had retired.'

The old lawyer smiled grimly. His firm was a most respectable and old-established one.

'I came in specially today to see a very old client. I still attend to the affairs of one or two old friends.'

'Sir Arthur Stanley was an old friend and client, was he not?'

'Yes. We've undertaken all his legal work since he was quite a young man. A very brilliant man, Poirot – quite an exceptional brain.'

'His death was announced on the six o'clock news yesterday, I believe.'

'Yes. The funeral's on Friday. He's been ailing some time. A malignant growth, I understand.'

'Lady Stanley died some years ago?'

'Two and a half years ago, roughly.'

The keen eyes below the bushy brows looked sharply at Poirot.

'How did she die?'

The lawyer replied promptly.

'Overdose of sleeping stuff. Medinal as far as I remember.'

'There was an inquest?'

'Yes. The verdict was that she took it accidentally.'

'Did she?'

Mr Endicott was silent for a moment.

'I won't insult you,' he said. 'I've no doubt you've got a

good reason for asking. Medinal's a rather dangerous drug, I understand, because there's not a big margin between an effective dose and a lethal one. If the patient gets drowsy and forgets she's taken a dose and takes another – well, it can have a fatal result.'

Poirot nodded.

'Is that what she did?'

'Presumably. There was no suggestion of suicide, or suicidal tendencies.'

'And no suggestion of – anything else?'

Again that keen glance was shot at him.

'Her husband gave evidence.'

'And what did he say?'

'He made it clear that she did sometimes get confused after taking her nightly dose and ask for another.'

'Was he lying?'

'Really, Poirot, what an outrageous question. Why should you suppose for a minute that I should know?'

Poirot smiled. The attempt at bluster did not deceive him.

'I suggest, my friend, that you know very well. But for the moment I will not embarrass you by asking you what you know. Instead I will ask you for an opinion. The opinion of one man about another. Was Arthur Stanley the kind of man who would do away with his wife if he wanted to marry another woman?'

Mr Endicott jumped as though he had been stung by a wasp.

'Preposterous,' he said angrily. 'Quite preposterous. And there was no other woman. Stanley was devoted to his wife.'

'Yes,' said Poirot. 'I thought so. And now – I will come to the purpose of my call upon you. You are the solicitors who drew up Arthur Stanley's will. You are, perhaps, his executor.'

'That is so.'

'Arthur Stanley had a son. The son quarrelled with his father at the time of his mother's death. Quarrelled with him and left home. He even went so far as to change his name.'

'That I did not know. What's he calling himself?'

'We shall come to that. Before we do I am going to make an assumption. If I am right, perhaps you will admit the fact. I think that Arthur Stanley left a sealed letter with you, a letter to be opened under certain circumstances or after his death.'

'Really, Poirot! In the Middle Ages you would certainly have been burnt at the stake. How you can possibly know the things you do!'

'I am right then? I think there was an alternative in the letter. Its contents were either to be destroyed – or you were to take a certain course of action.'

He paused.

'*Bon dieu!*' said Poirot with alarm. 'You have not already destroyed –'

He broke off in relief as Mr Endicott slowly shook his head in negation.

'We never act in haste,' he said reprovingly. 'I have to make full inquiries – to satisfy myself absolutely –'

He paused. 'This matter,' he said severely, 'is highly confidential. Even to you, Poirot –' He shook his head.

'And if I show you good cause why you should speak.'

'That is up to you. I cannot conceive how you can possibly know anything at all that is relevant to the matter we are discussing.'

'I do not *know* – so I have to guess. If I guess correctly –'

'Highly unlikely,' said Mr Endicott, with a wave of his hand.

Poirot drew a deep breath.

'Very well then. It is in my mind that your instructions are as follows. In the event of Sir Arthur's death, you are to trace his son Nigel, to ascertain where he is living and how he is living and particularly whether he is or has been engaged in any criminal activity whatsoever.'

This time Mr Endicott's impregnable legal calm was really shattered. He uttered an exclamation such as few had ever heard from his lips.

'Since you appear to be in full possession of the facts,' he said, 'I'll tell you anything you want to know. I gather you've come across young Nigel in the course of your professional activities. What's the young devil been up to?'

'I think the story goes as follows. After he had left home he changed his name, telling anyone who was interested that he had to do so as a condition of a legacy. He then fell in with some people who were running a smuggling racket – drugs and jewels. I think it was due to him that the racket assumed its final form – an exceedingly clever one involving the using of innocent *bona fide* students. The whole thing was operated by two people, Nigel Chapman, as he now called himself, and a young woman called Valerie Hobhouse who, I think, originally introduced him to the smuggling trade. It was a small private concern and they worked it on a commission basis – but it was immensely profitable. The goods had to be of small bulk, but thousands of pounds worth of gems and narcotics occupy a very small space. Everything went well until one of those unforeseen chances occurred. A police officer came one day to a students' hostel to make inquiries in connection with a murder near Cambridge. I think you know the reason why that particular piece of information should cause Nigel to panic. He thought the police were after *him*. He removed certain electric light bulbs so that the light should be dim and he also, in a panic, took a certain rucksack out into the back yard, hacked it to pieces and threw it behind the boiler since he feared traces of narcotic might be found in its false bottom.

'His panic was quite unfounded – the police had merely come to ask questions about a certain Eurasian student – but one of the girls living in the hostel had happened to look out of her window and had seen him destroying the rucksack. That did not immediately sign her death warrant. Instead, a clever scheme was thought up by which she herself was induced to commit certain foolish actions which would place her in a very invidious position. But they carried that scheme too far. I was called in. I advised going to the police. The girl lost her head and confessed. She confessed, that is, to the things that she had done. But she went, I think, to Nigel, and urged him to confess also to the rucksack business and to spilling ink over a fellow student's work. Neither Nigel nor his accomplice could consider attention being called to the rucksack – their whole plan of campaign would be ruined. Moreover Celia, the girl in question, had another dangerous piece of knowledge which she revealed, as it happened, the night I dined there. She knew who Nigel really was.'

'But surely –' Mr Endicott frowned.

'Nigel had moved from one world to another. Any former friends he met might know that he now called himself Chapman, but they knew nothing of what he was doing. In the hostel nobody knew that his real name was Stanley – but Celia suddenly revealed that she knew him in both capacities. She also knew that Valerie

Hobhouse, on one occasion at least, had travelled abroad on a false passport. She knew too much. The next evening she went out to meet him by appointment somewhere. He gave her a drink of coffee and in it was morphia. She died in her sleep with everything arranged to look like suicide.'

Mr Endicott stirred. An expression of deep distress crossed his face. He murmured something under his breath.

'But that was not the end,' said Poirot. 'The woman who owned the chain of hostels and students' clubs died soon after in suspicious circumstances and then, finally, there came the last most cruel and heartless crime. Patricia Lane, a girl who was devoted to Nigel and of whom he himself was really fond, meddled unwittingly in his affairs, and moreover insisted that he should be reconciled to his father before the latter died. He told her a string of lies, but he realised that her obstinacy might urge her actually to write a second letter after the first was destroyed. I think, my friend, that you can tell me why, from his point of view, that would have been such a fatal thing to happen.'

Mr Endicott rose. He went across the room to a safe, unlocked it, and came back with a long envelope in his hand. It had a broken red seal on the back of it. He drew out two enclosures and laid them before Poirot.

Dear Endicott,

You will open this after I am dead. I wish you to trace my son Nigel and find out if he has been guilty of any criminal actions whatsoever.

The facts I am about to tell you are known to me only. Nigel has always been profoundly unsatisfactory in his character. He has twice been guilty of forging my name to a cheque. On each occasion I acknowledged the signature as mine, but warned him that I would not do so again. On the third occasion it was his mother's name he forged. She charged him with it. He begged her to keep silent. She refused. She and I had discussed him, and she made it clear she was going to tell me. It was then, in handing her her evening sleeping mixture, he administered an overdose. Before it took effect, however, she had come to my room and told me all about matters. When, the next morning, she was found dead, I knew who had done it.

I accused Nigel and told him that I intended to make a clean breast of all the facts to the police. He pleaded desperately with me. What would you have done, Endicott? I have no illusions about my son, I know him for what he is, one of those dangerous misfits who have neither conscience nor pity. I had no cause to save him. But it was the thought of my beloved wife that swayed me. Would she wish me to execute justice? I thought that I knew the answer – she would have wanted her son saved from the scaffold. She would have shrunk, as I shrank, from the dragging down of our name. But there was another consideration. I firmly believe that once a killer, always a killer. There might be, in the future, other victims. I made a bargain with my son, and whether I did right or wrong, I do not know. He was to write out a confession of his crime which I should keep. He was to leave my house and never return, but make a new life for himself. I would give him a second chance. Money belonging to his mother would come to him automatically. He had had a good education. He had every chance of making good.

But – if he were convicted of any criminal activity whatsoever the confession he had left with me should go to the police. I safeguarded myself by explaining that my own death would not solve the problem.

You are my oldest friend. I am placing a burden on your shoulders, but I ask it in the name of a dead woman who was also your friend. Find Nigel. If his record is clean, destroy this letter and the enclosed confession. If not – then justice must be done.

Your affectionate friend,
Arthur Stanley

'Ah!' Poirot breathed a long sigh.
He unfolded the enclosure.

I hereby confess that I murdered my mother by giving her an overdose of medinal on November 18, 195—
Nigel Stanley

CHAPTER 22

'You quite understand your position, Miss Hobhouse. I have already warned you –'

Valerie Hobhouse cut him short.

'I know what I'm doing. You've warned me what I say will be used in evidence. I'm prepared for that. You've got me on the smuggling charge. I haven't got a hope. That means a long term of imprisonment. This other means that I'll be charged as an accessory to murder.'

'Your being willing to make a statement may help you, but I can't make any promise or hold out any inducement.'

'I don't know that I care. Just as well end it all as languish in prison for years. I want to make a statement. I may be what you call an accessory, but I'm not a killer. I never intended murder or wanted it. I'm not such a fool. What I do want is that there should be a clear case against Nigel . . .

'Celia knew far too much, but I could have dealt with that somehow. Nigel didn't give me time. He got her to come out and meet him, told her that he was going to own up to the rucksack and the ink business and then slipped her the morphia in a cup of coffee. He'd got hold of her letter to Mrs Hubbard earlier on and had torn out a useful "suicide" phrase. He put that and the empty morphia phial (which he had retrieved after pretending to throw it away) by her bed. I see now that he'd been contemplating murder for quite a little time. Then he came and told me what he'd done. For my own sake I had to stand in with him.

'The same thing must have happened with Mrs Nick. He'd found out that she drank, that she was getting unreliable – he managed to meet her somewhere on her way home, and poisoned her drink. He denied it to me – but I know that that's what he did. Then came Pat. He came up to my room and told me what had happened. He told me what I'd got to do – so that both he and I would have an unbreakable alibi. I was in the net by then, there was no way out . . . I suppose, if you hadn't caught me, I'd have got away abroad somewhere, and made a new life for myself. But you did catch me . . . And now I only care about one thing – to make sure that that cruel smiling devil gets hanged.'

Inspector Sharpe drew a deep breath. All this was eminently satisfactory, it was an unbelievable piece of luck; but he was puzzled.

The constable licked his pencil.

'I'm not sure that I quite understand,' began Sharpe.

She cut him short.

'You don't need to understand. I've got my reasons.'

Hercule Poirot spoke very gently.

'Mrs Nicoletis?' he asked.

He heard the sharp intake of her breath.

'She was – your mother, was she not?'

'Yes,' said Valerie Hobhouse. 'She was my mother . . .'

CHAPTER 23

I

'I do not understand,' said Mr Akibombo plaintively.

He looked anxiously from one red head to the other.

Sally Finch and Len Bateson were conducting a conversation which Mr Akibombo found hard to follow.

'Do you think,' asked Sally, 'that Nigel meant *me* to be suspected, or *you*?'

'Either, I should say,' replied Len. 'I believe he actually took the hairs from *my* brush.'

'I do not understand, please,' said Mr Akibombo. 'Was it then Mr Nigel who jumped the balcony?'

'Nigel can jump like a cat. I couldn't have jumped across that space. I'm far too heavy.'

'I want to apologise very deeply and humbly for wholly unjustifiable suspicions.'

'That's all right,' said Len.

'Actually, you helped a lot,' said Sally. 'All your thinking – about the boracic.'

Mr Akibombo brightened up.

'One ought to have realised all along,' said Len, 'that Nigel was a thoroughly maladjusted type and –'

'Oh, for heaven's sake – you sound just like Colin. Frankly, Nigel always gave me the creeps – and at last I see why. Do you realise, Len, that if poor Sir Arthur Stanley hadn't been sentimental and had turned Nigel straight over to the police, three other people would be alive today? It's a solemn thought.'

'Still, one can understand what he felt about it –'

'Please, Miss Sally.'

'Yes, Akibombo?'

'If you meet my professor at University party tonight will you tell him, please, that I have done some good thinking? My professor he says often that I have a muddled thought process.'

'I'll tell him,' said Sally.

Len Bateson was looking the picture of gloom.

'In a week's time you'll be back in America,' he said.

There was a momentary silence.

'I shall come back,' said Sally. 'Or you might come and do a course over there.'

'What's the use?'

'Akibombo,' said Sally, 'would you like, one day, to be best man at a wedding?'

'What is best man, please?'

'The bridegroom, Len here for instance, gives you a ring to keep for him, and he and you go to church very smartly dressed and at the right moment he asks you for the ring and you give it to him, and he puts it on my finger, and the organ plays the wedding march and everybody cries. And there we are.'

'You mean that you and Mr Len are to be married?'

'That's the idea.'

'*Sally!*'

'Unles, of course, Len doesn't care for the idea.'

'*Sally!* But you don't know – about my father –'

'So what? Of course I know. So your father's nuts. All right, so are lots of people's fathers.'

'It isn't a hereditary type of mania. I can assure you of that, Sally. If you only knew how desperately unhappy I've been about you.'

'I did just have a tiny suspicion.'

'In Africa,' said Mr Akibombo, 'in old days, before atomic age and scientific thought had come, marriage customs very curious and interesting. I tell you –'

'You'd better not,' said Sally. 'I have an idea they might make both Len and me blush, and when you've got red hair it's very noticeable when you blush.'

II

Hercule Poirot signed the last of the letters that Miss Lemon had laid before him.

'*Très bien*,' he said gravely. 'Not a single mistake.'

Miss Lemon looked slightly affronted.

'I don't often make mistakes, I hope,' she said.

'Not often. But it has happened. How is your sister, by the way?'

'She is thinking of going on a cruise, M. Poirot. To the northern capitals.'

'Ah,' said Hercule Poirot.

He wondered if – possibly – on a cruise –?

Not that he himself would undertake a sea voyage – not for any inducement . . .

The clock behind him struck one.

'The clock struck one,
The mouse ran down
Hickory, dickory, dock,'

declared Hercule Poirot.

'I beg your pardon, M. Poirot?'

'Nothing,' said Hercule Poirot.

CAT AMONG THE PIGEONS

For Stella and Larry Kirwan

CONTENTS

SUMMER TERM

I

It was the opening day of the summer term at Meadowbank school. The late afternoon sun shone down on the broad gravel sweep in front of the house. The front door was flung hospitably wide, and just within it, admirably suited to its Georgian proportions, stood Miss Vansittart, every hair in place, wearing an impeccably cut coat and skirt.

Some parents who knew no better had taken her for the great Miss Bulstrode herself, not knowing that it was Miss Bulstrode's custom to retire to a kind of holy of holies to which only a selected and privileged few were taken.

To one side of Miss Vansittart, operating on a slightly different plane, was Miss Chadwick, comfortable, knowledgeable, and so much a part of Meadowbank that it would have been impossible to imagine Meadowbank without her. It had never been without her. Miss Bulstrode and Miss Chadwick had started Meadowbank school together. Miss Chadwick wore pince-nez, stooped, was dowdily dressed, amiably vague in speech, and happened to be a brilliant mathematician.

Various welcoming words and phrases, uttered graciously by Miss Vansittart, floated through the house.

'How do you do, Mrs Arnold? Well, Lydia, did you enjoy your Hellenic cruise? What a wonderful opportunity! Did you get some good photographs?

'Yes, Lady Garnett, Miss Bulstrode had your letter about the Art Classes and everything's been arranged.

'How are you, Mrs Bird? . . . Well? I don't think Miss Bulstrode will have time *today* to discuss the point. Miss Rowan is somewhere about if you'd like to talk to her about it?

'We've moved your bedroom, Pamela. You're in the far wing by the apple tree . . .

'Yes, indeed, Lady Violet, the weather has been terrible so far this spring. Is this your youngest? What is your name? Hector? What a nice aeroplane you have, Hector.

'*Très heureuse de vous voir, Madame. Ah, je regrette, ce ne serait pas possible, cette après-midi. Mademoiselle Bulstrode est tellement occupée.*

'Good afternoon, Professor. Have you been digging up some more interesting things?'

II

In a small room on the first floor, Ann Shapland, Miss Bulstrode's secretary, was typing with speed and efficiency. Ann was a nice-looking young woman of thirty-five, with hair that fitted her like a black satin cap. She could be attractive when she wanted to be but life had taught her that efficiency and competence often paid better results and avoided painful complications. At the moment she was concentrating on being everything that a secretary to the headmistress of a famous girls' school should be.

From time to time, as she inserted a fresh sheet in her machine, she looked out of the window and registered interest in the arrivals.

'Goodness!' said Ann to herself, awed, 'I didn't know there were so many chauffeurs left in England!'

Then she smiled in spite of herself, as a majestic Rolls moved away and a very small Austin of battered age drove up. A harassed-looking father emerged from it with a daughter who looked far calmer than he did.

As he paused uncertainly, Miss Vansittart emerged from the house and took charge.

'Major Hargreaves? And this is Alison? Do come into the house. I'd like you to see Alison's room for yourself. I –'

Ann grinned and began to type again.

'Good old Vansittart, the glorified understudy,' she said to herself. 'She can copy all the Bulstrode's tricks. In fact she's word perfect!'

An enormous and almost incredibly opulent Cadillac, painted in two tones, raspberry fool and azure blue, swept (with difficulty owing to its length) into the drive and drew up behind Major the Hon. Alistair Hargreaves' ancient Austin.

The chauffeur sprang to open the door, an immense bearded, dark-skinned man, wearing a flowing aba, stepped out, a Parisian fashion plate followed and then a slim dark girl.

That's probably Princess Whatshername herself, thought Ann. Can't imagine her in school uniform, but I suppose the miracle will be apparent tomorrow . . .

Both Miss Vansittart and Miss Chadwick appeared on this occasion.

'They'll be taken to the Presence,' decided Ann.

Then she thought that, strangely enough, one didn't quite like making jokes about Miss Bulstrode. Miss Bulstrode was Someone.

'So you'd better mind your P.s and Q.s, my girl,' she said to herself, 'and finish these letters without making any mistakes.'

Not that Ann was in the habit of making mistakes. She could take her pick of secretarial posts. She had been P.A. to the chief executive of an oil company, private secretary to Sir Mervyn Todhunter, renowned alike for his erudition, his irritability and the illegibility of his handwriting. She numbered two Cabinet Ministers and an important Civil Servant among her employers. But on the whole, her work had always lain amongst men. She wondered how she was going to like being, as she put it herself, completely submerged in women. Well – it was all experience! And there was always Dennis! Faithful Dennis returning from Malaya, from Burma, from various parts of the world, always the same, devoted, asking her once again to marry him. Dear Dennis! But it would be very dull to be married to Dennis.

She would miss the company of men in the near future. All these schoolmistressy characters – not a man about the place, except a gardener of about eighty.

But here Ann got a surprise. Looking out of the window, she saw there was a man clipping the hedge just beyond the drive – clearly a gardener but a long way from eighty. Young, dark, good-looking. Ann wondered about him – there had been some talk of getting extra labour – but this was no yokel. Oh well, nowadays people did every kind of job. Some young man trying to get together some money for some project or other, or indeed just to keep body and soul together. But he was cutting the hedge in a very expert manner. Presumably he was a real gardener after all!

'He looks,' said Ann to herself, 'he looks as though he *might* be amusing . . .'

Only one more letter to do, she was pleased to note, and then she might stroll round the garden . . .

III

Upstairs, Miss Johnson, the matron, was busy allotting rooms, welcoming newcomers, and greeting old pupils.

She was pleased it was term time again. She never knew quite what to do with herself in the holidays. She had two married sisters with whom she stayed in turn, but they were naturally more interested in their own doings and families than in Meadowbank. Miss Johnson, though dutifully fond of her sisters, was really only interested in Meadowbank.

Yes, it was nice that term had started –

'Miss Johnson?'

'Yes, Pamela.'

'I say, Miss Johnson. I think something's broken in my case. It's oozed all over things. I *think* it's hair oil.'

'Chut, chut!' said Miss Johnson, hurrying to help.

IV

On the grass sweep of lawn beyond the gravelled drive, Mademoiselle Blanche, the new French mistress, was walking. She looked with appreciative eyes at the powerful young man clipping the hedge.

'*Assez bien,*' thought Mademoiselle Blanche.

Mademoiselle Blanche was slender and mouselike and not very noticeable, but she herself noticed everything.

Her eyes went to the procession of cars sweeping up to the front door. She assessed them in terms of money. This Meadowbank was certainly *formidable*! She summed up mentally the profits that Miss Bulstrode must be making.

Yes, indeed! *Formidable*!

V

Miss Rich, who taught English and Geography, advanced towards the house at a rapid pace, stumbling a little now and then because, as usual, she forgot to look where she was going. Her hair, also as usual, had escaped from its bun. She had an eager ugly face.

She was saying to herself:

'To be back again! To be *here* . . . It seems years . . .' She fell over a rake, and the young gardener put out an arm and said:

'Steady, miss.'

Eileen Rich said 'Thank you,' without looking at him.

VI

Miss Rowan and Miss Blake, the two junior mistresses, were strolling towards the Sports Pavilion. Miss Rowan was thin and dark and intense, Miss Blake was plump and fair. They were discussing with animation their recent adventures in Florence: the pictures they had seen, the sculpture, the fruit blossom, and the attentions (hoped to be dishonourable) of two young Italian gentlemen.

'Of course one knows,' said Miss Blake, 'how Italians go on.'

'Uninhibited,' said Miss Rowan, who had studied Psychology as well as Economics. 'Thoroughly healthy, one feels. No repressions.'

'But Guiseppe was quite impressed when he found I taught at Meadowbank,' said Miss Blake. 'He became much more respectful at once. He has a cousin who wants to come here, but Miss Bulstrode was not sure she had a vacancy.'

'Meadowbank is a school that really counts,' said Miss Rowan, happily. 'Really, the new Sports Pavilion looks most impressive. I never thought it would be ready in time.'

'Miss Bulstrode said it had to be,' said Miss Blake in the tone of one who has said the last word.

'Oh,' she added in a startled kind of way.

The door of the Sports Pavilion had opened abruptly, and a bony young woman with ginger-coloured hair emerged. She gave them a sharp unfriendly stare and moved rapidly away.

'That must be the new Games Mistress,' said Miss Blake. 'How uncouth!'

'*Not* a very pleasant addition to the staff,' said Miss Rowan. 'Miss Jones was always so friendly and sociable.'

'She absolutely glared at us,' said Miss Blake resentfully.

They both felt quite ruffled.

VII

Miss Bulstrode's sitting-room had windows looking out in two directions, one over the drive and lawn beyond, and another towards a bank of rhododendrons behind the house. It was quite an impressive room, and Miss Bulstrode was rather more than quite an impressive woman. She was tall, and rather noble looking, with well-dressed grey hair, grey eyes with plenty of humour in them, and a firm mouth. The success of her school (and Meadowbank was one of the most successful schools in England) was entirely due to the personality of its Headmistress. It was a very expensive school, but that was not really the point. It could be put better by saying that though you paid through the nose, you got what you paid for.

Your daughter was educated in the way you wished, and also in the way Miss Bulstrode wished, and the result of the two together seemed to give satisfaction. Owing to the high fees, Miss Bulstrode was able to employ a full staff. There was nothing mass produced about the school, but if it was individualistic, it also had discipline. Discipline without regimentation, was Miss Bulstrode's motto. Discipline, she held, was reassuring to the young, it gave them a feeling of security; regimentation gave rise to irritation. Her pupils were a varied lot. They included several foreigners of good family, often foreign royalty. There were also English girls of good family or of wealth, who wanted a training in culture and the arts, with a general knowledge of life and social facility who would be turned out agreeable, well groomed and able to take part in intelligent discussion on any subject. There were girls who wanted to work hard and pass entrance examinations, and eventually take degrees and who, to do so, needed only good teaching and special attention. There were girls who had reacted unfavourably to school life of the conventional type. But Miss Bulstrode had her rules, she did not accept morons, or juvenile delinquents, and she preferred to accept girls whose parents she liked, and girls in whom she herself saw a prospect of development. The ages of her pupils varied within wide limits. There were girls who would have been labelled in the past as 'finished', and there were girls little more than children, some of them with parents abroad, and for whom Miss Bulstrode had a scheme of interesting holidays. The last and final court of appeal was Miss Bulstrode's own approval.

She was standing now by the chimneypiece listening to Mrs Gerald Hope's slightly whining voice. With great foresight, she had not suggested that Mrs Hope should sit down.

'Henrietta, you see, is very highly strung. Very highly strung indeed. Our doctor says –'

Miss Bulstrode nodded, with gentle reassurance, refraining from the caustic phrase she sometimes was tempted to utter.

'Don't you know, you idiot, that that is what every fool of a woman says about her child?'

She spoke with firm sympathy.

'You need have no anxiety, Mrs Hope. Miss Rowan, a member of our staff, is a fully trained psychologist. You'll be surprised, I'm sure, at the change you'll find in Henrietta' (Who's a nice intelligent child, and far too good for you) 'after a term or two here.'

'Oh I know. You did wonders with the Lambeth child – absolutely wonders! So I am quite happy. And I – oh yes, I forgot. We're going to the South of France in six weeks' time. I thought I'd take Henrietta. It would make a little break for her.'

'I'm afraid that's quite impossible,' said Miss Bulstrode, briskly and with a charming smile, as though she were granting a request instead of refusing one.

'Oh! but –' Mrs Hope's weak petulant face wavered, showed temper. 'Really, I must insist. After all, she's *my* child.'

'Exactly. But it's *my* school,' said Miss Bulstrode.

'Surely I can take the child away from a school any time I like?'

'Oh yes,' said Miss Bulstrode. 'You can. Of course you can. But then, *I* wouldn't have her back.'

Mrs Hope was in a real temper now.

'Considering the size of the fees I pay here –'

'Exactly,' said Miss Bulstrode. 'You wanted my school for your daughter, didn't you? But it's take it as it is, or leave it.

Like that very charming Balenciaga model you are wearing. It is Balenciaga, isn't it? It is so delightful to meet a woman with real clothes sense.'

Her hand enveloped Mrs Hope's, shook it, and imperceptibly guided her towards the door.

'Don't worry at all. Ah, here is Henrietta waiting for you.' (She looked with approval at Henrietta, a nice well-balanced intelligent child if ever there was one, and who deserved a better mother.) 'Margaret, take Henrietta Hope to Miss Johnson.'

Miss Bulstrode retired into her sitting-room and a few moments later was talking French.

'But certainly, Excellence, your niece can study modern ball-room dancing. Most important socially. And languages, also, are most necessary.'

The next arrivals were prefaced by such a gust of expensive perfume as almost to knock Miss Bulstrode backwards.

'Must pour a whole bottle of the stuff over herself every day,' Miss Bulstrode noted mentally, as she greeted the exquisitely dressed dark-skinned woman.

'*Enchantée, Madame.*'

Madame giggled very prettily.

The big bearded man in Oriental dress took Miss Bulstrode's hand, bowed over it, and said in very good English, 'I have the honour to bring to you the Princess Shaista.'

Miss Bulstrode knew all about her new pupil who had just come from a school in Switzerland, but was a little hazy as to who it was escorting her. Not the Emir himself, she decided, probably the Minister, or Chargé d'Affaires. As usual when in doubt, she used that useful title *Excellence*, and assured him that Princess Shaista would have the best of care.

Shaista was smiling politely. She was also fashionably dressed and perfumed. Her age, Miss Bulstrode knew, was fifteen, but like many Eastern and Mediterranean girls, she looked older – quite mature. Miss Bulstrode spoke to her about her projected studies and was relieved to find that she answered promptly in excellent English and without giggling. In fact, her manners compared favourably with the awkward ones of many English school girls of fifteen. Miss Bulstrode had often thought that it might be an excellent plan to send English girls abroad to the Near Eastern countries to learn courtesy and manners there. More compliments were uttered on both sides and then the room was empty again though still filled with such heavy perfume that Miss Bulstrode opened both windows to their full extent to let some of it out.

The next comers were Mrs Upjohn and her daughter Julia.

Mrs Upjohn was an agreeable young woman in the late thirties with sandy hair, freckles and an unbecoming hat which was clearly a concession to the seriousness of the occasion, since she was obviously the type of young woman who usually went hatless.

Julia was a plain freckled child, with an intelligent forehead, and an air of good humour.

The preliminaries were quickly gone through and Julia was despatched via Margaret to Miss Johnson, saying cheerfully as she went, 'So long, Mum. *Do* be careful lighting that gas heater now that I'm not there to do it.'

Miss Bulstrode turned smilingly to Mrs Upjohn, but did not ask her to sit. It was possible that, despite Julia's appearance of cheerful common-sense, her mother, too, might want to explain that her daughter was highly strung.

'Is there anything special you want to tell me about Julia?' she asked.

Mrs Upjohn replied cheerfully:

'Oh no, I don't think so. Julia's a very ordinary sort of child. Quite healthy and all that. I think she's got reasonably good brains, too, but I daresay mothers usually think that about their children, don't they?'

'Mothers,' said Miss Bulstrode grimly, 'vary!'

'It's wonderful for her to be able to come here,' said Mrs Upjohn. 'My aunt's paying for it, really, or helping. I couldn't afford it myself. But I'm awfully pleased about it. And so is Julia.' She moved to the window as she said enviously, 'How lovely your garden is. And so tidy. You must have lots of real gardeners.'

'We had three,' said Miss Bulstrode, 'but just now we're short-handed except for local labour.'

'Of course the trouble nowadays,' said Mrs Upjohn, 'is that what one calls a gardener usually isn't a gardener, just a milkman who wants to do something in his spare time, or an old man of eighty. I sometimes think – Why!' exclaimed Mrs Upjohn, still gazing out of the window – 'how extraordinary!'

Miss Bulstrode paid less attention to this sudden exclamation than she should have done. For at that moment she herself had glanced casually out of the other window which gave on to the rhododendron shrubbery, and had perceived a highly unwelcome sight, none other than Lady Veronica Carlton-Sandways, weaving her way along the path, her large black velvet hat on one side, muttering to herself and clearly in a state of advanced intoxication.

Lady Veronica was not an unknown hazard. She was a charming woman, deeply attached to her twin daughters, and very delightful when she was, as they put it, *herself* – but unfortunately at unpredictable intervals, she was not herself. Her husband, Major Carlton-Sandways, coped fairly well. A cousin lived with them, who was usually at hand to keep an eye on Lady Veronica and head her off if necessary. On Sports Day, with both Major Carlton-Sandways and the cousin in close attendance, Lady Veronica arrived completely sober and beautifully dressed and was a pattern of what a mother should be.

But there were times when Lady Veronica gave her well-wishers the slip, tanked herself up and made a bee-line for her daughters to assure them of her maternal love. The twins had arrived by train early today, but no one had expected Lady Veronica.

Mrs Upjohn was still talking. But Miss Bulstrode was not listening. She was reviewing various courses of action, for she recognized that Lady Veronica was fast approaching the truculent stage. But suddenly, an answer to prayer, Miss Chadwick appeared at a brisk trot, slightly out of breath. Faithful Chaddy, thought Miss Bulstrode. Always to be relied upon, whether it was a severed artery or an intoxicated parent.

'Disgraceful,' said Lady Veronica to her loudly. 'Tried to keep me away – didn't want me to come down here – I fooled Edith all right. Went to have my rest – got out car – gave silly old Edith slip . . . regular old maid . . . no man would ever look at her twice . . . Had a row with police on the way . . . said I was unfit to drive car . . . nonshense . . . Going to tell Miss Bulstrode I'm taking the girls home – want 'em home, mother love. Wonderful thing, mother love –'

'Splendid, Lady Veronica,' said Miss Chadwick. 'We're so

pleased you've come. I particularly want you to see the new Sports Pavilion. You'll love it.'

Adroitly she turned Lady Veronica's unsteady footsteps in the opposite direction, leading her away from the house.

'I expect we'll find your girls there,' she said brightly. 'Such a nice Sports Pavilion, new lockers, and a drying room for the swim suits –' their voices trailed away.

Miss Bulstrode watched. Once Lady Veronica tried to break away and return to the house, but Miss Chadwick was a match for her. They disappeared round the corner of the rhododendrons, headed for the distant loneliness of the new Sports Pavilion.

Miss Bulstrode heaved a sigh of relief. Excellent Chaddy. So reliable! Not modern. Not brainy – apart from mathematics – but always a present help in time of trouble.

She turned with a sigh and a sense of guilt to Mrs Upjohn who had been talking happily for some time . . .

'. . . though, of course,' she was saying, 'never real cloak and dagger stuff. Not dropping by parachute, or sabotage, or being a courier. I shouldn't have been brave enough. It was mostly dull stuff. Office work. And plotting. Plotting things on a map, I mean – not the story telling kind of plotting. But of course it was exciting sometimes and it was often quite funny, as I just said – all the secret agents followed each other round and round Geneva, all knowing each other by sight, and often ending up in the same bar. I wasn't married then, of course. It was all great fun.'

She stopped abruptly with an apologetic and friendly smile.

'I'm sorry I've been talking so much. Taking up your time. When you've got such lots of people to see.'

She held out a hand, said goodbye and departed.

Miss Bulstrode stood frowning for a moment. Some instinct warned her that she had missed something that might be important.

She brushed the feeling aside. This was the opening day of summer term, and she had many more parents to see. Never had her school been more popular, more assured of success. Meadowbank was at its zenith.

There was nothing to tell her that within a few weeks Meadowbank would be plunged into a sea of trouble; that disorder, confusion and murder would reign there, that already certain events had been set in motion . . .

CHAPTER I
REVOLUTION IN RAMAT

About two months earlier than the first day of the summer term at Meadowbank, certain events had taken place which were to have unexpected repercussions in that celebrated girls' school.

In the Palace of Ramat, two young men sat smoking and considering the immediate future. One young man was dark, with a smooth olive face and large melancholy eyes. He was Prince Ali Yusuf, Hereditary Sheikh of Ramat, which, though small, was one of the richest states in the Middle East. The other young man was sandy haired and freckled and more or less penniless, except for the handsome salary he drew as private pilot to His Highness Prince Ali Yusuf. In spite of this difference in status, they were on terms of perfect equality. They had been at the same public school and had been friends then and ever since.

'They shot at us, Bob,' said Prince Ali almost incredulously.

'They shot at us all right,' said Bob Rawlinson.

'And they meant it. They meant to bring us down.'

'The bastards meant it all right,' said Bob grimly.

Ali considered for a moment.

'It would hardly be worth while trying again?'

'We mightn't be so lucky this time. The truth is, Ali, we've left things too late. You should have got out two weeks ago. I told you so.'

'One doesn't like to run away,' said the ruler of Ramat.

'I see your point. But remember what Shakespeare or one of these poetical fellows said about those who run away living to fight another day.'

'To think,' said the young Prince with feeling, 'of the money that has gone into making this a Welfare State. Hospitals, schools, a Health Service –'

Bob Rawlinson interrupted the catalogue.

'Couldn't the Embassy do something?'

Ali Yusuf flushed angrily.

'Take refuge in your Embassy? That, never. The extremists would probably storm the place – they wouldn't respect diplomatic immunity. Besides, if I did that, it really would be the end! Already the chief accusation against me is of being pro-Western.' He sighed. 'It is so difficult to understand.' He sounded wistful, younger than his twenty-five years. 'My grandfather was a cruel man, a real tyrant. He had hundreds of slaves and treated them ruthlessly. In his tribal wars, he killed his enemies unmercifully and executed them horribly. The mere whisper of his name made everyone turn pale. And yet – *he* is a legend still! Admired! Respected! The great Achmed Abdullah! And I? What have I done? Built hospitals and schools, welfare, housing . . . all the things people are said to want. Don't they want them? Would they prefer a reign of terror like my grandfather's?'

'I expect so,' said Bob Rawlinson. 'Seems a bit unfair, but there it is.'

'But why, Bob? *Why?*'

Bob Rawlinson sighed, wriggled and endeavoured to explain what he felt. He had to struggle with his own inarticulateness.

'Well,' he said. 'He put up a show – I suppose that's it really. He was – sort of – dramatic, if you know what I mean.'

He looked at his friend who was definitely not dramatic. A nice quiet decent chap, sincere and perplexed, that was what Ali was, and Bob liked him for it. He was neither picturesque nor violent, but whilst in England people who are picturesque and violent cause embarrassment and are not much liked, in the Middle East, Bob was fairly sure, it was different.

'But democracy –' began Ali.

'Oh, democracy –' Bob waved his pipe. 'That's a word that means different things everywhere. One thing's certain. It never means what the Greeks originally meant by it. I bet you anything you like that if they boot you out of here, some spouting hot air merchant will take over, yelling his own praises, building himself up into God Almighty, and stringing up, or cutting off the heads of anyone who dares to disagree with him in any way. And, mark you, he'll *say* it's a Democratic Government – of the people and for the people. I expect the people will like it too. Exciting for them. Lots of bloodshed.'

'But we are not savages! We are civilized nowadays.'

'There are different kinds of civilization . . .' said Bob vaguely. 'Besides – I rather think we've all got a bit of savage in us – if we can think up a good excuse for letting it rip.'

'Perhaps you are right,' said Ali sombrely.

'The thing people don't seem to want anywhere, nowadays,' said Bob, 'is anyone who's got a bit of common sense. I've never been a brainy chap – well, you know that well enough, Ali – but I often think that that's what the world really needs – just a bit of common sense.' He laid aside his pipe and sat in his chair. 'But never mind all that. The thing is how we're going to get you out of here. Is there anybody in the Army you can really trust?'

Slowly, Prince Ali Yusuf shook his head.

'A fortnight ago, I should have said "Yes." But now, I do not know . . . cannot be *sure* –'

Bob nodded. 'That's the hell of it. As for this palace of yours, it gives me the creeps.'

Ali acquiesced without emotion.

'Yes, there are spies everywhere in palaces . . . They hear everything – they – know everything.'

'Even down in the hangars –' Bob broke off. 'Old Achmed's all right. He's got a kind of sixth sense. Found one of the mechanics trying to tamper with the plane – one of the men we'd have sworn was absolutely trustworthy. Look here, Ali, if we're going to have a shot at getting you away, it will have to be soon.'

'I know – I know. I think – I am quite certain now – that if I stay I shall be killed.'

He spoke without emotion, or any kind of panic: with a mild detached interest.

'We'll stand a good chance of being killed anyway,' Bob warned him. 'We'll have to fly out north, you know. They can't intercept us that way. But it means going over the mountains – and at this time of year –'

He shrugged his shoulders. 'You've got to understand. It's damned risky.'

Ali Yusuf looked distressed.

'If anything happened to you, Bob –'

'Don't worry about me, Ali. That's not what I meant. I'm not important. And anyway, I'm the sort of chap that's sure to get killed sooner or later. I'm always doing crazy things. No – it's you – I don't want to persuade you one way or the other. If a portion of the Army *is* loyal –'

'I don't like the idea of running away,' said Ali simply. 'But I do not in the least want to be a martyr, and be cut to pieces by a mob.'

He was silent for a moment or two.

'Very well then,' he said at last with a sigh. 'We will make the attempt. When?'

Bob shrugged his shoulders.

'Sooner the better. We've got to get you to the airstrip in some natural way . . . How about saying you're going to inspect the new road construction out at Al Jasar? Sudden whim. Go this afternoon. Then, as your car passes the airstrip, stop there – I'll have the bus all ready and tuned up. The idea will be to go up to inspect the road construction from the air, see? We take off and *go*! We can't take any baggage, of course. It's got to be all quite impromptu.'

'There is nothing I wish to take with me – except one thing –'

He smiled, and suddenly the smile altered his face and made a different person of him. He was no longer the modern conscientious Westernized young man – the smile held all the racial guile and craft which had enabled a long line of his ancestors to survive.

'You are my friend, Bob, you shall see.'

His hand went inside his shirt and fumbled. Then he held out a little chamois leather bag.

'This?' Bob frowned and looked puzzled.

Ali took it from him, untied the neck, and poured the contents on the table.

Bob held his breath for a moment and then expelled it in a soft whistle.

'Good lord. Are they *real*?'

Ali looked amused.

'Of course they are real. Most of them belonged to my father. He acquired new ones every year. I, too. They have come from many places, bought for our family by men we can trust – from London, from Calcutta, from South Africa. It is a tradition of our family. To have these in case of need.' He added in a matter of fact voice: 'They are worth, at today's prices, about three quarters of a million.'

'Three quarters of a million pounds.' Bob let out a whistle, picked up the stones, let them run through his fingers. 'It's fantastic. Like a fairy tale. It does things to you.'

'Yes.' The dark young man nodded. Again that age-long weary look was on his face. 'Men are not the same when it comes to jewels. There is always a trail of violence to follow such things. Deaths, bloodshed, murder. And women are the worst. For with women it will not only be the value. It is something to do with the jewels themselves. Beautiful jewels drive women mad. They want to own them. To wear them round their throats, on their bosoms. I would not trust any woman with these. But I shall trust you.'

'Me?' Bob stared.

'Yes. I do not want these stones to fall into the hands of my enemies. I do not know when the rising against me will take place. It may be planned for today. I may not live to reach the airstrip this afternoon. Take the stones and do the best you can.'

'But look here – I don't understand. What am I to do with them?'

'Arrange somehow to get them out of the country.'

Ali stared placidly at his perturbed friend.

'You mean, you want *me* to carry them instead of you?'

'You can put it that way. But I think, really, you will be able to think of some better plan to get them to Europe.'

'But look here, Ali, I haven't the first idea how to set about such a thing.'

Ali leaned back in his chair. He was smiling in a quietly amused manner.

'You have common sense. And you are honest. And I remember, from the days when you were my fag, that you could always think up some ingenious idea . . . I will give you the name and address of a man who deals with such matters for me – that is – in case I should not survive. Do not look so worried, Bob. Do the best you can. That is all I ask. I shall not blame you if you fail. It is as Allah wills. For me, it is simple. I do not want those stones taken from my dead body. For the rest –' he shrugged his shoulders. 'It is as I have said. All will go as Allah wills.'

'You're nuts!'

'No. I am a fatalist, that is all.'

'But look here, Ali. You said just now I was honest. But three quarters of a million . . . Don't you think that might sap any man's honesty?'

Ali Yusuf looked at his friend with affection.

'Strangely enough,' he said, 'I have no doubt on that score.'

CHAPTER 2

THE WOMAN ON THE BALCONY

I

As Bob Rawlinson walked along the echoing marble corridors of the Palace, he had never felt so unhappy in his life. The knowledge that he was carrying three quarters of a million pounds in his trousers pocket caused him acute misery. He felt as though every Palace official he encountered must know the fact. He felt even that the knowledge of his precious burden must show in his face. He would have been relieved to learn that his freckled countenance bore exactly its usual expression of cheerful good nature.

The sentries outside presented arms with a clash. Bob walked down the main crowded street of Ramat, his mind still dazed. Where was he going? What was he planning to do? He had no idea. And time was short.

The main street was like most main streets in the Middle East. It was a mixture of squalor and magnificence. Banks reared their vast newly built magnificence. Innumerable small shops presented a collection of cheap plastic goods. Babies' bootees and cheap cigarette lighters were displayed in unlikely juxtaposition. There were sewing machines, and spare parts for cars. Pharmacies displayed flyblown proprietary medicines, and large notices of penicillin in every form and antibiotics galore. In very few of the shops was there anything that you could normally want to buy, except possibly the latest Swiss watches, hundreds of which were displayed crowded into a tiny window. The assortment was so great that even there one would have shrunk from purchase, dazzled by sheer mass.

Bob, still walking in a kind of stupor, jostled by figures in native or European dress, pulled himself together and asked himself again where the hell he was going?

He turned into a native café and ordered lemon tea. As he sipped it, he began, slowly, to come to. The atmosphere of the café was soothing. At a table opposite him an elderly Arab was peacefully clicking through a string of amber beads. Behind him two men played tric trac. It was a good place to sit and think.

And he'd got to think. Jewels worth three quarters of a million had been handed to him, and it was up to him to devise some plan of getting them out of the country. No time to lose either. At any minute the balloon might go up . . .

Ali was crazy, of course. Tossing three quarters of a million light-heartedly to a friend in that way. And then sitting back quietly himself and leaving everything to Allah. Bob had not got that recourse. Bob's God expected his servants to decide on and perform their own actions to the best of the ability their God had given them.

What the hell was he going to do with those damned stones?

He thought of the Embassy. No, he couldn't involve the Embassy. The Embassy would almost certainly refuse to be involved.

What he needed was some person, some perfectly ordinary person who was leaving the country in some perfectly ordinary way. A business man, or a tourist would be best. Someone with no political connections whose baggage would, at most, be subjected to a superficial search or more probably no search at all. There was, of course, the other end to be considered . . . Sensation at London Airport. Attempt to smuggle in jewels worth three quarters of a million. And so on and so on. One would have to risk that –

Somebody ordinary – a *bona fide* traveller. And suddenly Bob kicked himself for a fool. Joan, of course. His sister Joan Sutcliffe. Joan had been out here for two months with her daughter Jennifer who after a bad bout of pneumonia had been ordered sunshine and a dry climate. They were going back by 'long sea' in four or five days' time.

Joan was the ideal person. What was it Ali had said about women and jewels? Bob smiled to himself. Good old Joan! *She* wouldn't lose her head over jewels. Trust her to keep her feet on the earth. Yes – he could trust Joan.

Wait a minute, though . . . could he trust Joan? Her honesty, yes. But her discretion? Regretfully Bob shook his head. Joan would talk, would not be able to help talking. Even worse. She would hint. 'I'm taking home something very important, I mustn't say a word to *anyone*. It's really rather exciting . . .'

Joan had never been able to keep a thing to herself though she was always very incensed if one told her so. Joan, then, mustn't know what she was taking. It would be safer for her that way. He'd make the stones up into a parcel, an innocent-looking parcel. Tell her some story. A present for someone? A commission? He'd think of something . . .

Bob glanced at his watch and rose to his feet. Time was getting on.

He strode along the street oblivious of the midday heat. Everything seemed so normal. There was nothing to show on the surface. Only in the Palace was one conscious of the banked-down fires, of the spying, the whispers. The Army – it all depended on the Army. Who was loyal? Who was disloyal? A coup d'état would certainly be attempted. Would it succeed or fail?

Bob frowned as he turned into Ramat's leading hotel. It was modestly called the Ritz Savoy and had a grand modernistic façade. It had opened with a flourish three years ago with a Swiss manager, a Viennese chef, and an Italian *Maître d'hôtel*. Everything had been wonderful. The Viennese chef had gone first, then the Swiss manager. Now the Italian head waiter had gone too. The food was still ambitious, but bad, the service abominable, and a good deal of the expensive plumbing had gone wrong.

The clerk behind the desk knew Bob well and beamed at him.

'Good morning, Squadron Leader. You want your sister? She has gone on a picnic with the little girl –'

'A picnic?' Bob was taken aback – of all the silly times to go for a picnic.

'With Mr and Mrs Hurst from the Oil Company,' said the clerk informatively. Everyone always knew everything. 'They have gone to the Kalat Diwa dam.'

Bob swore under his breath. Joan wouldn't be home for hours.

'I'll go up to her room,' he said and held out his hand for the key which the clerk gave him.

He unlocked the door and went in. The room, a large double-bedded one, was in its usual confusion. Joan Sutcliffe was not a tidy woman. Golf clubs lay across a chair, tennis racquets had been flung on the bed. Clothing lay about, the table was littered with rolls of film, postcards, paper-backed books and an assortment of native curios from the South, mostly made in Birmingham and Japan.

Bob looked round him, at the suitcases and the zip bags. He was faced with a problem. He wouldn't be able to see Joan before flying Ali out. There wouldn't be time to get to the dam and back. He could parcel up the stuff and leave it with a note – but almost immediately he shook his head. He knew quite well that he was nearly always followed. He'd probably been followed from the Palace to the café and from the café here. He hadn't spotted anyone – but he knew that they were good at the job. There was nothing suspicious in his coming to the hotel to see his sister – but if he left a parcel and a note, the note would be read and the parcel opened.

Time . . . time . . . He'd no *time* . . .

Three quarters of a million in precious stones in his trousers pocket.

He looked round the room . . .

Then, with a grin, he fished out from his pocket the little tool kit he always carried. His niece Jennifer had some plasticine, he noted, that would help.

He worked quickly and skilfully. Once he looked up, suspicious, his eyes going to the open window. No, there was no balcony outside this room. It was just his nerves that made him feel that someone was watching him.

He finished his task and nodded in approval. Nobody would notice what he had done – he felt sure of that. Neither Joan nor anyone else. Certainly not Jennifer, a self-centred child, who never saw or noticed anything outside herself.

He swept up all evidences of his toil and put them into his pocket . . . Then he hesitated, looking round.

He drew Mrs Sutcliffe's writing pad towards him and sat frowning –

He must leave a note for Joan –

But what could he say? It must be something that Joan would understand – but which would mean nothing to anyone who read the note.

And really that was impossible! In the kind of thriller that Bob liked reading to fill up his spare moments, you left a kind of cryptogram which was always successfully puzzled out by someone. But he couldn't even begin to think of a cryptogram – and in any case Joan was the sort of common-sense person who would need the i's dotted and the t's crossed before she noticed anything at all –

Then his brow cleared. There was another way of doing it – divert attention away from Joan – leave an ordinary everyday note. Then leave a message with someone else to be given to Joan in England. He wrote rapidly –

Dear Joan – Dropped in to ask if you'd care to play a round of golf this evening but if you've been up at the dam, you'll probably be dead to the world. What about tomorrow? Five o'clock at the Club.
Yours, Bob.

A casual sort of a message to leave for a sister that he might never see again – but in some ways the more casual the better. Joan mustn't be involved in any funny business, mustn't even know that there was any funny business. Joan could not dissimulate. Her protection would be the fact that she clearly knew nothing.

And the note would accomplish a dual purpose. It would seem that he, Bob, had no plan for departure himself.

He thought for a minute or two, then he crossed to the telephone and gave the number of the British Embassy. Presently he was connected with Edmundson, the third secretary, a friend of his.

'John? Bob Rawlinson here. Can you meet me somewhere when you get off? . . . Make it a bit earlier than that? . . . You've got to, old boy. It's important. Well, actually, it's a girl . . .' He gave an embarrassed cough. 'She's wonderful, quite wonderful. Out of this world. Only it's a bit tricky.'

Edmundson's voice, sounding slightly stuffed-shirt and disapproving, said, 'Really, Bob, you and your girls. All right,

2 o'clock do you?' and rang off. Bob heard the little echoing click as whoever had been listening in, replaced the receiver.

Good old Edmundson. Since all the telephones in Ramat had been tapped, Bob and John Edmundson had worked out a little code of their own. A wonderful girl who was 'out of this world' meant something urgent and important.

Edmundson would pick him up in his car outside the new Merchants Bank at 2 o'clock and he'd tell Edmundson of the hiding place. Tell him that Joan didn't know about it but that, if anything happened to him, it was important. Going by the long sea route Joan and Jennifer wouldn't be back in England for six weeks. By that time the revolution would almost certainly have happened and either been successful or have been put down. Ali Yusuf might be in Europe, or he and Bob might both be dead. He would tell Edmundson enough, but not too much.

Bob took a last look around the room. It looked exactly the same, peaceful, untidy, domestic. The only thing added was his harmless note to Joan. He propped it up on the table and went out. There was no one in the long corridor.

II

The woman in the room next to that occupied by Joan Sutcliffe stepped back from the balcony. There was a mirror in her hand.

She had gone out on the balcony originally to examine more closely a single hair that had had the audacity to spring up on her chin. She dealt with it with tweezers, then subjected her face to a minute scrutiny in the clear sunlight.

It was then, as she relaxed, that she saw something else. The angle at which she was holding her mirror was such that it reflected the mirror of the hanging wardrobe in the room next to hers and in that mirror she saw a man doing something very curious.

So curious and unexpected that she stood there motionless, watching. He could not see her from where he sat at the table, and she could only see him by means of the double reflection.

If he had turned his head behind him, he might have caught sight of her mirror in the wardrobe mirror, but he was too absorbed in what he was doing to look behind him . . .

Once, it was true, he did look up suddenly towards the window, but since there was nothing to see there, he lowered his head again.

The woman watched him while he finished what he was doing. After a moment's pause he wrote a note which he propped up on the table. Then he moved out of her line of vision but she could just hear enough to realize that he was making a telephone call. She couldn't catch what was said, but it sounded light-hearted – casual. Then she heard the door close.

The woman waited a few minutes. Then she opened her door. At the far end of the passage an Arab was flicking idly with a feather duster. He turned the corner out of sight.

The woman slipped quickly to the door of the next room. It was locked, but she had expected that. The hairpin she had with her and the blade of a small knife did the job quickly and expertly.

She went in, pushing the door to behind her. She picked up the note. The flap had only been stuck down lightly and opened easily. She read the note, frowning. There was no explanation there.

She sealed it up, put it back, and walked across the room.

There, with her hand outstretched, she was disturbed by voices through the window from the terrace below.

One was a voice that she knew to be the occupier of the room in which she was standing. A decided didactic voice, fully assured of itself.

She darted to the window.

Below on the terrace, Joan Sutcliffe, accompanied by her daughter Jennifer, a pale solid child of fifteen, was telling the world and a tall unhappy looking Englishman from the British Consulate just what she thought of the arrangements he had come to make.

'But it's absurd! I never *heard* such nonsense. Everything's perfectly quiet here and everyone quite pleasant. I think it's all a lot of panicky fuss.'

'We hope so, Mrs Sutcliffe, we certainly hope so. But H.E. feels that the responsibility is such –'

Mrs Sutcliffe cut him short. She did not propose to consider the responsibility of ambassadors.

'We've a lot of baggage, you know. We were going home by

long sea – next Wednesday. The sea voyage will be good for Jennifer. The doctor said so. I really must absolutely decline to alter all my arrangements and be flown to England in this silly flurry.'

The unhappy looking man said encouragingly that Mrs Sutcliffe and her daughter could be flown, not to England, but to Aden and catch their boat there.

'With our baggage?'

'Yes, yes, that can be arranged. I've got a car waiting – a station wagon. We can load everything right away.'

'Oh well.' Mrs Sutcliffe capitulated. 'I suppose we'd better pack.'

'At once, if you don't mind.'

The woman in the bedroom drew back hurriedly. She took a quick glance at the address on a luggage label on one of the suitcases. Then she slipped quickly out of the room and back into her own just as Mrs Sutcliffe turned the corner of the corridor.

The clerk from the office was running after her.

'Your brother, the Squadron Leader, has been here, Mrs Sutcliffe. He went up to your room. But I think that he has left again. You must just have missed him.'

'How tiresome,' said Mrs Sutcliffe. 'Thank you,' she said to the clerk and went on to Jennifer, 'I suppose Bob's fussing too. I can't see any sign of disturbance *myself* in the streets. This door's unlocked. How careless these people are.'

'Perhaps it was Uncle Bob,' said Jennifer.

'I wish I hadn't missed him . . . Oh, there's a note.' She tore it open.

'At any rate *Bob* isn't fussing,' she said triumphantly. 'He obviously doesn't know a thing about all this. Diplomatic wind up, that's all it is. How I hate trying to pack in the heat of the day. This room's like an oven. Come on, Jennifer, get your things out of the chest of drawers and the wardrobe. We must just shove everything in anyhow. We can repack later.'

'I've never been in a revolution,' said Jennifer thoughtfully.

'I don't expect you'll be in one this time,' said her mother sharply. 'It will be just as I say. Nothing will happen.'

Jennifer looked disappointed.

CHAPTER 3

INTRODUCING MR ROBINSON

I

It was some six weeks later that a young man tapped discreetly on the door of a room in Bloomsbury and was told to come in.

It was a small room. Behind a desk sat a fat middle-aged man slumped in a chair. He was wearing a crumpled suit, the front of which was smothered in cigar ash. The windows were closed and the atmosphere was almost unbearable.

'Well?' said the fat man testily, and speaking with half-closed eyes. 'What is it now, eh?'

It was said of Colonel Pikeaway that his eyes were always just closing in sleep, or just opening after sleep. It was also said that his name was not Pikeaway and that he was not a colonel. But some people will say anything!

'Edmundson, from the F.O., is here sir.'

'Oh,' said Colonel Pikeaway.

He blinked, appeared to be going to sleep again and muttered:

'Third secretary at our Embassy in Ramat at the time of the Revolution. Right?'

'That's right, sir.'

'I suppose, then, I'd better see him,' said Colonel Pikeaway without any marked relish. He pulled himself into a more upright position and brushed off a little of the ash from his paunch.

Mr Edmundson was a tall fair young man, very correctly dressed with manners to match, and a general air of quiet disapproval.

'Colonel Pikeaway? I'm John Edmundson. They said you – er – might want to see me.'

'Did they? Well, they should know,' said Colonel Pikeaway. 'Siddown,' he added.

His eyes began to close again, but before they did so, he spoke:

'You were in Ramat at the time of the Revolution?'

'Yes, I was. A nasty business.'

'I suppose it would be. You were a friend of Bob Rawlinson's, weren't you?'

'I know him fairly well, yes.'

'Wrong tense,' said Colonel Pikeaway. 'He's dead.'

'Yes, sir, I know. But I wasn't sure –' he paused.

'You don't have to take pains to be discreet here,' said Colonel Pikeaway. 'We know everything here. Or if we don't, we pretend we do. Rawlinson flew Ali Yusuf out of Ramat on the day of the Revolution. Plane hasn't been heard of since. Could have landed in some inaccessible place, or could have crashed. Wreckage of a plane has been found in the Arolez mountains. Two bodies. News will be released to the Press tomorrow. Right?'

Edmundson admitted that it was quite right.

'We know all about things here,' said Colonel Pikeaway. 'That's what we're for. Plane flew into the mountain. Could have been weather conditions. Some reason to believe it was sabotage. Delayed action bomb. We haven't got the full reports yet. The plane crashed in a pretty inaccessible place. There was a reward offered for finding it, but these things take a long time to filter through. Then we had to fly out experts to make an examination. All the red tape, of course. Applications to a foreign government, permission from ministers, palm greasing – to say nothing of the local peasantry appropriating anything that might come in useful.'

He paused and looked at Edmundson.

'Very sad, the whole thing,' said Edmundson. 'Prince Ali Yusuf would have made an enlightened ruler, with democratic principles.'

'That's what probably did the poor chap in,' said Colonel Pikeaway. 'But we can't waste time in telling sad stories of the deaths of kings. We've been asked to make certain – inquiries. By interested parties. Parties, that is, to whom Her Majesty's Government is well disposed.' He looked hard at the other. 'Know what I mean?'

'Well, I have heard something.' Edmundson spoke reluctantly.

'You've heard perhaps, that nothing of value was found on the bodies, or amongst the wreckage, or as far as is known, had been pinched by the locals. Though as to that, you can never tell with peasants. They can clam up as well as the Foreign Office itself. And what else have you heard?'

'Nothing else.'

'You haven't heard that perhaps something of value *ought* to have been found? What did they send you to me for?'

'They said you might want to ask me certain questions,' said Edmundson primly.

'If I ask you questions I shall expect answers,' Colonel Pikeaway pointed out.

'Naturally.'

'Doesn't seem natural to you, son. Did Bob Rawlinson say anything to you before he flew out of Ramat? He was in Ali's confidence if anyone was. Come now, let's have it. Did he say anything?'

'As to what, sir?'

Colonel Pikeaway stared hard at him and scratched his ear.

'Oh, all right,' he grumbled. 'Hush up this and don't say that. Overdo it in my opinion! If you don't know what I'm talking about, you don't know, and there it is.'

'I think there was something –' Edmundson spoke cautiously and with reluctance. 'Something important that Bob might have wanted to tell me.'

'Ah,' said Colonel Pikeaway, with the air of a man who has at last pulled the cork out of a bottle. 'Interesting. Let's have what you know.'

'It's very little, sir. Bob and I had a kind of simple code. We'd cottoned on to the fact that all the telephones in Ramat were being tapped. Bob was in the way of hearing things at the Palace, and I sometimes had a bit of useful information to pass on to him. So if one of us rang the other up and mentioned a girl or girls, in a certain way, using the term "out of this world" for her, it meant something was up!'

'Important information of some kind or other?'

'Yes. Bob rang me up using those terms the day the whole show started. I was to meet him at our usual rendezvous – outside one of the banks. But rioting broke out in that particular quarter and the police closed the road. I couldn't make contact with Bob or he with me. He flew Ali out the same afternoon.'

'I see,' said Pikeaway. 'No idea where he was telephoning from?'

'No. It might have been anywhere.'

'Pity.' He paused and then threw out casually:

'Do you know Mrs Sutcliffe?'

'You mean Bob Rawlinson's sister? I met her out there, of course. She was there with a schoolgirl daughter. I don't know her well.'

'Were she and Bob Rawlinson very close?'

Edmundson considered.

'No, I shouldn't say so. She was a good deal older than he was, and rather much of the elder sister. And he didn't much like his brother-in-law – always referred to him as a pompous ass.'

'So he is! One of our prominent industrialists – and how pompous can they get! So you don't think it likely that Bob Rawlinson would have confided an important secret to his sister?'

'It's difficult to say – but no, I shouldn't think so.'

'I shouldn't either,' said Colonel Pikeaway.

He sighed. 'Well, there we are, Mrs Sutcliffe and her daughter are on their way home by the long sea route. Dock at Tilbury on the *Eastern Queen* tomorrow.'

He was silent for a moment or two, whilst his eyes made a thoughtful survey of the young man opposite him. Then, as though having come to a decision, he held out his hand and spoke briskly.

'Very good of you to come.'

'I'm only sorry I've been of such little use. You're sure there's nothing I can do?'

'No. No. I'm afraid not.'

John Edmundson went out.

The discreet young man came back.

'Thought I might have sent him to Tilbury to break the news to the sister,' said Pikeaway. 'Friend of her brother's – all that. But I decided against it. Inelastic type. That's the F.O. training. Not an opportunist. I'll send round what's his name.'

'Derek?'

'That's right,' Colonel Pikeaway nodded approval. 'Getting to know what I mean quite well, ain't you?'

'I try my best, sir.'

'Trying's not enough. You have to succeed. Send me along Ronnie first. I've got an assignment for him.'

II

Colonel Pikeaway was apparently just going off to sleep again when the young man called Ronnie entered the room. He was tall, dark, muscular, and had a gay and rather impertinent manner.

Colonel Pikeaway looked at him for a moment or two and then grinned.

'How'd you like to penetrate into a girls' school?' he asked.

'A girls' school?' The young man lifted his eyebrows. 'That will be something new! What are they up to? Making bombs in the chemistry class?'

'Nothing of that kind. Very superior high-class school. Meadowbank.'

'Meadowbank!' the young man whistled. 'I can't believe it!'

'Hold your impertinent tongue and listen to me. Princess Shaista, first cousin and only near relative of the late Prince Ali Yusuf of Ramat, goes there this next term. She's been at school in Switzerland up to now.'

'What do I do? Abduct her?'

'Certainly not. I think it possible she may become a focus of interest in the near future. I want you to keep an eye on developments. I'll have to leave it vague. I don't know what or who may turn up, but if any of our more unlikeable friends seem to be interested, report it . . . A watching brief, that's what you've got.'

The young man nodded.

'And how do I get in to watch? Shall I be the drawing master?'

'The visiting staff is all female.' Colonel Pikeaway looked at him in a considering manner. 'I think I'll have to make you a gardener.'

'A gardener?'

'Yes. I'm right in thinking you know something about gardening?'

'Yes, indeed. I ran a column on *Your Garden* in the *Sunday Mail* for a year in my younger days.'

'Tush!' said Colonel Pikeaway. 'That's nothing! I could do a column on gardening myself without knowing a thing about it – just crib from a few luridly illustrated Nurseryman's catalogues and a Gardening Encyclopedia. I know all the patter. "*Why not break away from tradition and sound a really tropical note in your border this year? Lovely Amabellis Gossiporia, and some of the wonderful new Chinese hybrids of Sinensis Maka foolia. Try the rich blushing beauty of a clump of Sinistra Hopaless, not very hardy but they should be all right against a west wall.*"' He broke off and grinned. 'Nothing to it! The fools buy the things and early frost sets in and kills them and they wish they'd stuck to wallflowers and forget-me-nots! No, my boy, I mean the real stuff. Spit on your hands and use the spade, be well acquainted with the compost heap, mulch diligently, use the Dutch hoe and every other kind of hoe, trench really deep for your sweet peas – and all the rest of the beastly business. Can you do it?'

'All these things I have done from my youth upwards!'

'Of course you have. I know your mother. Well, that's settled.'

'Is there a job going as a gardener at Meadowbank?'

'Sure to be,' said Colonel Pikeaway. 'Every garden in England is short staffed. I'll write you some nice testimonials. You'll see, they'll simply jump at you. No time to waste, summer term begins on the 29th.'

'I garden and I keep my eyes open, is that right?'

'That's it, and if any oversexed teenagers make passes at you, Heaven help you if you respond. I don't want you thrown out on your ear too soon.'

He drew a sheet of paper towards him. 'What do you fancy as a name?'

'Adam would seem appropriate.'

'Last name?'

'How about Eden?'

'I'm not sure I like the way your mind is running. Adam Goodman will do very nicely. Go and work out your past history with Jenson and then get cracking.' He looked at his watch. 'I've no more time for you. I don't want to keep Mr Robinson waiting. He ought to be here by now.'

Adam (to give him his new name) stopped as he was moving to the door.

'Mr Robinson?' he asked curiously. 'Is *he* coming?'

'I said so.' A buzzer went on the desk. 'There he is now. Always punctual, Mr Robinson.'

'Tell me,' said Adam curiously. 'Who is he really? What's his real name?'

'His name,' said Colonel Pikeaway, 'is Mr Robinson. That's all I know, and that's all anybody knows.'

III

The man who came into the room did not look as though his name was, or could ever have been, Robinson. It might have been Demetrius, or Isaacstein, or Perenna – though not one or the other in particular. He was not definitely Jewish, nor definitely Greek nor Portuguese nor Spanish, nor South American. What did seem highly unlikely was that he was an Englishman called Robinson. He was fat and well dressed, with a yellow face, melancholy dark eyes, a broad forehead, and a generous mouth that displayed rather over-large very white teeth. His hands were well shaped and beautifully kept. His voice was English with no trace of accent.

He and Colonel Pikeaway greeted each other rather in the manner of two reigning monarchs. Politenesses were exchanged.

Then, as Mr Robinson accepted a cigar, Colonel Pikeaway said:

'It is very good of you to offer to help us.'

Mr Robinson lit his cigar, savoured it appreciatively, and finally spoke.

'My dear fellow. I just thought – I hear things, you know. I know a lot of people, and they tell me things. I don't know why.'

Colonel Pikeaway did not comment on the reason why.

He said:

'I gather you've heard that Prince Ali Yusuf's plane has been found?'

'Wednesday of last week,' said Mr Robinson. 'Young Rawlinson was the pilot. A tricky flight. But the crash wasn't due to an error on Rawlinson's part. The plane had been tampered with – by a certain Achmed – senior mechanic. Completely trustworthy – or so Rawlinson thought. But he wasn't. He's got a very lucrative job with the new *régime* now.'

'So it was sabotage! We didn't know that for sure. It's a sad story.'

'Yes. That poor young man – Ali Yusuf, I mean – was ill

equipped to cope with corruption and treachery. His public school education was unwise – or at least that is my view. But we do not concern ourselves with him now, do we? He is yesterday's news. Nothing is so dead as a dead king. We are concerned, you in your way, I in mine, with what dead kings leave behind them.'

'Which is?'

Mr Robinson shrugged his shoulders.

'A substantial bank balance in Geneva, a modest balance in London, considerable assets in his own country now taken over by the glorious new *régime* (and a little bad feeling as to how the spoils have been divided, or so I hear!), and finally a small personal item.'

'Small?'

'These things are relative. Anyway, small in bulk. Handy to carry upon the person.'

'They weren't on Ali Yusuf's person, as far as we know.'

'No. Because he had handed them over to young Rawlinson.'

'Are you sure of that?' asked Pikeaway sharply.

'Well, one is never sure,' said Mr Robinson apologetically. 'In a palace there is so much gossip. It cannot *all* be true. But there was a very strong rumour to that effect.'

'They weren't on young Rawlinson's person, either –'

'In that case,' said Mr Robinson, 'it seems as though they must have been got out of the country by some other means.'

'What other means? Have you any idea?'

'Rawlinson went to a café in the town after he had received the jewels. He was not seen to speak to anyone or approach anyone whilst he was there. Then he went to the Ritz Savoy Hotel where his sister was staying. He went up to her room and was there for about 20 minutes. She herself was out. He then left the hotel and went to the Merchants Bank in Victory Square where he cashed a cheque. When he came out of the bank a disturbance was beginning. Students rioting about something. It was some time before the square was cleared. Rawlinson then went straight to the airstrip where, in company with Sergeant Achmed, he went over the plane.

'Ali Yusuf drove out to see the new road construction, stopped his car at the airstrip, joined Rawlinson and expressed a desire to take a short flight and see the dam and the new highway construction from the air. They took off and did not return.'

'And your deductions from that?'

'My dear fellow, the same as yours. Why did Bob Rawlinson spend twenty minutes in his sister's room when she was out and he had been told that she was not likely to return until evening? He left her a note that would have taken him at most three minutes to scribble. What did he do for the rest of the time?'

'You are suggesting that he concealed the jewels in some appropriate place amongst his sister's belongings?'

'It seems indicated, does it not? Mrs Sutcliffe was evacuated that same day with other British subjects. She was flown to Aden with her daughter. She arrives at Tilbury, I believe, tomorrow.'

Pikeaway nodded.

'Look after her,' said Mr Robinson.

'We're going to look after her,' said Pikeaway. 'That's all arranged.'

'If she has the jewels, she will be in danger.' He closed his eyes. 'I so much dislike violence.'

'You think there is likely to be violence?'

'There are people interested. Various undesirable people – if you understand me.'

'I understand you,' said Pikeaway grimly.

'And they will, of course, double cross each other.'

Mr Robinson shook his head. 'So confusing.'

Colonel Pikeaway asked delicately: 'Have you yourself any – er – special interest in the matter?'

'I represent a certain group of interests,' said Mr Robinson. His voice was faintly reproachful. 'Some of the stones in question were supplied by my syndicate to his late highness – at a very fair and reasonable price. The group of people I represent who were interested in the recovery of the stones, would, I may venture to say, have had the approval of the late owner. I shouldn't like to say more. These matters are so delicate.'

'But you are definitely on the side of the angels,' Colonel Pikeaway smiled.

'Ah, angels! Angels – yes.' He paused. 'Do you happen to know who occupied the rooms in the hotel on either side of the room occupied by Mrs Sutcliffe and her daughter?'

Colonel Pikeaway looked vague.

'Let me see now – I believe I do. On the left hand side was Señora Angelica de Toredo – a Spanish – er – dancer appearing at the local cabaret. Perhaps not strictly Spanish and perhaps not a very good dancer. But popular with the clientèle. On the other side was one of a group of school-teachers, I understand –'

Mr Robinson beamed approvingly.

'You are always the same. I come to tell you things, but nearly always you know them already.'

'No no.' Colonel Pikeaway made a polite disclaimer.

'Between us,' said Mr Robinson, 'we know a good deal.'

Their eyes met.

'I hope,' Mr Robinson said rising, 'that we know enough –'

CHAPTER 4

RETURN OF A TRAVELLER

I

'Really!' said Mrs Sutcliffe, in an annoyed voice, as she looked out of her hotel window, 'I don't see why it always has to rain when one comes back to England. It makes it all seem so depressing.'

'I think it's lovely to be back,' said Jennifer. 'Hearing everyone talk English in the streets! And we'll be able to have a really good tea presently. Bread and butter and jam and proper cakes.'

'I wish you weren't so insular, darling,' said Mrs Sutcliffe. 'What's the good of my taking you abroad all the way to the Persian Gulf if you're going to say you'd rather have stayed at home?'

'I don't mind going abroad for a month or two,' said Jennifer. 'All I said was I'm glad to be back.'

'Now do get out of the way, dear, and let me make sure that they've brought up all the luggage. Really, I do feel – I've felt ever since the war that people have got very dishonest nowadays. I'm sure if I hadn't kept an eye on things that man would have gone off with my green zip bag at Tilbury. And there was another man hanging about near the luggage. I saw him afterwards on the train. I believe, you know, that these sneak thieves meet the boats and if the people are flustered or seasick they go off with some of the suitcases.'

'Oh, you're always thinking things like that, Mother,' said Jennifer. 'You think everybody you meet is dishonest.'

'Most of them are,' said Mrs Sutcliffe grimly.

'Not English people,' said the loyal Jennifer.

'That's worse,' said her mother. 'One doesn't expect anything else from Arabs and foreigners, but in England one's off guard and that makes it easier for dishonest people. Now do let me count. That's the big green suitcase and the black one, and the two small brown and the zip bag and the golf clubs and the racquets and the hold-all and the canvas suitcase – and where's the green bag? Oh, there it is. And that local tin we bought to put the extra things in – yes, one, two, three, four, five, six – yes, that's all right. All fourteen things are here.'

'Can't we have some tea now?' said Jennifer.

'Tea? It's only three o'clock.'

'I'm awfully hungry.'

'All right, all right. Can you go down by yourself and order it? I really feel I must have a rest, and then I'll just unpack the things we'll need for tonight. It's too bad your father couldn't have met us. Why he had to have an important directors' meeting in Newcastle-on-Tyne today I simply cannot imagine. You'd think his wife and daughter would come first. Especially as he hasn't seen us for three months. Are you sure you can manage by yourself?'

'Good gracious, Mummy,' said Jennifer, 'what age do you think I am? Can I have some money, please? I haven't got any English money.'

She accepted the ten shilling note her mother handed to her, and went out scornfully.

The telephone rang by the bed. Mrs Sutcliffe went to it and picked up the receiver.

'Hallo . . . Yes . . . Yes, Mrs Sutcliffe speaking . . .'

There was a knock at the door. Mrs Sutcliffe said, 'Just one moment' to the receiver, laid it down and went over to the door. A young man in dark blue overalls was standing there with a small kit of tools.

'Electrician,' he said briskly. 'The lights in this suite aren't satisfactory. I've been sent up to see to them.'

'Oh – all right . . .'

She drew back. The electrician entered.

'Bathroom?'

'Through there – beyond the other bedroom.'

She went back to the telephone.

'I'm so sorry . . . What were you saying?'

'My name is Derek O'Connor. Perhaps I might come up to your suite, Mrs Sutcliffe. It's about your brother.'

'Bob? Is there – news of him?'

'I'm afraid so – yes.'

'Oh . . . Oh, I see . . . Yes, come up. It's on the third floor, 310.'

She sat down on the bed. She already knew what the news must be.

Presently there was a knock on the door and she opened it to admit a young man who shook hands in a suitably subdued manner.

'Are you from the Foreign Office?'

'My name's Derek O'Connor. My chief sent me round as there didn't seem to be anybody else who could break it to you.'

'Please tell me,' said Mrs Sutcliffe. 'He's been killed. Is that it?'

'Yes, that's it, Mrs Sutcliffe. He was flying Prince Ali Yusuf out from Ramat and they crashed in the mountains.'

'Why haven't I heard – why didn't someone wireless it to the boat?'

'There was no definite news until a few days ago. It was known that the plane was missing, that was all. But under the circumstances there might still have been hope. But now the wreck of the plane has been found . . . I am sure you will be glad to know that death was instantaneous.'

'The Prince was killed as well?'

'Yes.'

'I'm not at all surprised,' said Mrs Sutcliffe. Her voice shook a little but she was in full command of herself. 'I knew Bob would die young. He was always reckless, you know – always flying new planes, trying new stunts. I've hardly seen anything of him for the last four years. Oh well, one can't change people, can one?'

'No,' said her visitor, 'I'm afraid not.'

'Henry always said he'd smash himself up sooner or later,' said Mrs Sutcliffe. She seemed to derive a kind of melancholy satisfaction from the accuracy of her husband's prophecy. A tear rolled down her cheek and she looked for her handkerchief. 'It's been a shock,' she said.

'I know – I'm awfully sorry.'

'Bob couldn't run away, of course,' said Mrs Sutcliffe. 'I mean, he'd taken on the job of being the Prince's pilot. I wouldn't have wanted him to throw in his hand. And he was a good flier too. I'm sure if he ran into a mountain it wasn't his fault.'

'No,' said O'Connor, 'it certainly wasn't his fault. The only hope of getting the Prince out was to fly in no matter what conditions. It was a dangerous flight to undertake and it went wrong.'

Mrs Sutcliffe nodded.

'I quite understand,' she said. 'Thank you for coming to tell me.'

'There's something more,' said O'Connor, 'something I've got to ask you. Did your brother entrust anything to you to take back to England?'

'Entrust something to me?' said Mrs Sutcliffe. 'What do you mean?'

'Did he give you any – package – any small parcel to bring back and deliver to anyone in England?'

She shook her head wonderingly. 'No. Why should you think he did?'

'There was a rather important package which we think your brother may have given to someone to bring home. He called on you at your hotel that day – the day of the Revolution, I mean.'

'I know. He left a note. But there was nothing in that – just some silly thing about playing tennis or golf the next day. I suppose when he wrote that note, he couldn't have known that he'd have to fly the Prince out that very afternoon.'

'That was all it said?'

'The note? Yes.'

'Have you kept it, Mrs Sutcliffe?'

'Kept the note he left? No, of course I haven't. It was quite trivial. I tore it up and threw it away. Why should I keep it?'

'No reason,' said O'Connor. 'I just wondered.'

'Wondered what?' said Mrs Sutcliffe crossly.

'Whether there might have been some – other message concealed in it. After all –' he smiled, '– There is such a thing as invisible ink, you know.'

'Invisible ink!' said Mrs Sutcliffe, with a great deal of distaste, 'do you mean the sort of thing they use in spy stories?'

'Well, I'm afraid I do mean just that,' said O'Connor, rather apologetically.

'How idiotic,' said Mrs Sutcliffe. 'I'm sure Bob would never use anything like invisible ink. Why should he? He was a dear matter-of-fact sensible person.' A tear dripped down her cheek again. 'Oh dear, where *is* my bag? I must have a handkerchief. Perhaps I left it in the other room.'

'I'll get it for you,' said O'Connor.

He went through the communicating door and stopped as a young man in overalls who was bending over a suitcase straightened up to face him, looking rather startled.

'Electrician,' said the young man hurriedly. 'Something wrong with the lights here.'

O'Connor flicked a switch.

'They seem all right to me,' he said pleasantly.

'Must have given me the wrong room number,' said the electrician.

He gathered up his tool bag and slipped out quickly through the door to the corridor.

O'Connor frowned, picked up Mrs Sutcliffe's bag from the dressing-table and took it back to her.

'Excuse me,' he said, and picked up the telephone receiver. 'Room 310 here. Have you just sent up an electrician to see to the light in this suite? Yes . . . Yes, I'll hang on.'

He waited.

'No? No, I thought you hadn't. No, there's nothing wrong.'

He replaced the receiver and turned to Mrs Sutcliffe.

'There's nothing wrong with any of the lights here,' he said. 'And the office didn't send up an electrician.'

'Then what was that man doing? Was he a thief?'

'He may have been.'

Mrs Sutcliffe looked hurriedly in her bag. 'He hasn't taken anything out of my bag. The money is all right.'

'Are you sure, Mrs Sutcliffe, absolutely *sure* that your brother didn't give you anything to take home, to pack among your belongings?'

'I'm absolutely sure,' said Mrs Sutcliffe.

'Or your daughter – you have a daughter, haven't you?'

'Yes. She's downstairs having tea.'

'Could your brother have given anything to her?'

'No, I'm sure he couldn't.'

'There's another possibility,' said O'Connor. 'He might have hidden something in your baggage among your belongings that day when he was waiting for you in your room.'

'But why should Bob do such a thing? It sounds absolutely absurd.'

'It's not quite so absurd as it sounds. It seems possible that Prince Ali Yusuf gave your brother something to keep for him and that your brother thought it would be safer among your possessions than if he kept it himself.'

'Sounds very unlikely to me,' said Mrs Sutcliffe.

'I wonder now, would you mind if we searched?'

'Searched through my luggage, do you mean? Unpack?' Mrs Sutcliffe's voice rose with a wail on that word.

'I know,' said O'Connor. 'It's a terrible thing to ask you. But it might be very important. I could help you, you know,' he said persuasively. 'I often used to pack for my mother. She said I was quite a good packer.'

He exerted all the charm which was one of his assets to Colonel Pikeaway.

'Oh well,' said Mrs Sutcliffe, yielding, 'I suppose – If you say so – if, I mean, it's really important –'

'It might be very important,' said Derek O'Connor. 'Well, now,' he smiled at her. 'Suppose we begin.'

II

Three quarters of an hour later Jennifer returned from her tea. She looked round the room and gave a gasp of surprise.

'Mummy, what *have* you been doing?'

'We've been unpacking,' said Mrs Sutcliffe crossly. 'Now we're packing things up again. This is Mr O'Connor. My daughter Jennifer.'

'But why are you packing and unpacking?'

'Don't ask me why,' snapped her mother. 'There seems to be some idea that your Uncle Bob put something in my luggage to bring home. He didn't give you anything, I suppose, Jennifer?'

'Uncle Bob give me anything to bring back? No. Have you been unpacking my things too?'

'We've unpacked everything,' said Derek O'Connor cheerfully, 'and we haven't found a thing and now we're packing them up again. I think you ought to have a drink of tea or something, Mrs Sutcliffe. Can I order you something? A brandy and soda perhaps?' He went to the telephone.

'I wouldn't mind a good cup of tea,' said Mrs Sutcliffe.

'I had a smashing tea,' said Jennifer. 'Bread and butter and sandwiches and cake and then the waiter brought me more sandwiches because I asked him if he'd mind and he said he didn't. It was lovely.'

O'Connor ordered the tea, then he finished packing up Mrs Sutcliffe's belongings again with a neatness and a dexterity which forced her unwilling admiration.

'Your mother seems to have trained you to pack very well,' she said.

'Oh, I've all sorts of handy accomplishments,' said O'Connor smiling.

His mother was long since dead, and his skill in packing and unpacking had been acquired solely in the service of Colonel Pikeaway.

'There's just one thing more, Mrs Sutcliffe. I'd like you to be very careful of yourself.'

'Careful of myself? In what way?'

'Well,' O'Connor left it vague. 'Revolutions are tricky things. There are a lot of ramifications. Are you staying in London long?'

'We're going down to the country tomorrow. My husband will be driving us down.'

'That's all right then. But – don't take any chances. If anything in the least out of the ordinary happens, ring 999 straight away.'

'Ooh!' said Jennifer, in high delight. 'Dial 999. I've always wanted to.'

'Don't be silly, Jennifer,' said her mother.

III

Extract from account in a local paper.

> *A man appeared before the Magistrate's court yesterday charged with breaking into the residence of Mr Henry Sutcliffe with intent to steal. Mrs Sutcliffe's bedroom was ransacked and left in wild confusion whilst the members of the family were at Church on Sunday morning. The kitchen staff who were preparing the mid-day meal, heard nothing. Police arrested the man as he was making his escape from the house. Something had evidently alarmed him and he had fled without taking anything.*
>
> *Giving his name as Andrew Ball of no fixed abode, he pleaded guilty. He said he had been out of work and was looking for money. Mrs Sutcliffe's jewellery, apart from a few pieces which she was wearing, is kept at her bank.*

'I told you to have the lock of that drawing-room french window seen to,' had been the comment of Mr Sutcliffe in the family circle.

'My dear Henry,' said Mrs Sutcliffe, 'you don't seem to realize that I have been abroad for the last three months. And anyway, I'm sure I've read somewhere that if burglars *want* to get in they always can.'

She added wistfully, as she glanced again at the local paper:

'How beautifully grand "kitchen staff" sounds. So different from what it really is, old Mrs Ellis who is quite deaf and can hardly stand up and that half-witted daughter of the Bardwells who comes in to help on Sunday mornings.'

'What I don't see,' said Jennifer, 'is how the police found out the house was being burgled and got here in time to catch him?'

'It seems extraordinary that he didn't take anything,' commented her mother.

'Are you quite sure about that, Joan?' demanded her husband. 'You were a little doubtful at first.'

Mrs Sutcliffe gave an exasperated sigh.

'It's impossible to tell about a thing like that straight away. The mess in my bedroom – things thrown about everywhere, drawers pulled out and overturned. I had to look through everything before I could be sure – though now I come to think of it, I don't remember seeing my best Jacqmar scarf.'

'I'm sorry, Mummy. That was me. It blew overboard in the Mediterranean. I'd borrowed it. I meant to tell you but I forgot.'

'Really, Jennifer, how often have I asked you not to borrow things without telling me first?'

'Can I have some more pudding?' said Jennifer, creating a diversion.

'I suppose so. Really, Mrs Ellis has a wonderfully light hand. It makes it worth while having to shout at her so much. I do hope, though, that they won't think you too greedy at school. Meadowbank isn't quite an ordinary school, remember.'

'I don't know that I really want to go to Meadowbank,' said Jennifer. 'I knew a girl whose cousin had been there, and she said it was awful. They spent all their time telling you how to get in and out of Rolls-Royces, and how to behave if you went to lunch with the Queen.'

'That will do, Jennifer,' said Mrs Sutcliffe. 'You don't appreciate how extremely fortunate you are in being admitted to Meadowbank. Miss Bulstrode doesn't take every girl, I can tell you. It's entirely owing to your father's important position and the influence of your Aunt Rosamond. You are exceedingly lucky. And if,' added Mrs Sutcliffe, 'you are ever asked to lunch with the Queen, it will be a good thing for you to know how to behave.'

'Oh well,' said Jennifer. 'I expect the Queen often has to have people to lunch who don't know how to behave – African chiefs and jockeys and sheikhs.'

'African chiefs have the most polished manners,' said her father, who had recently returned from a short business trip to Ghana.

'So do Arab sheikhs,' said Mrs Sutcliffe. 'Really courtly.'

'D'you remember that sheikh's feast we went to,' said Jennifer. 'And how he picked out the sheep's eye and gave it to you, and Uncle Bob nudged you not to make a fuss and to eat it? I mean, if a sheikh did that with roast lamb at Buckingham Palace, it would give the Queen a bit of a jolt, wouldn't it?'

'That will do, Jennifer,' said her mother and closed the subject.

IV

When Andrew Ball of no fixed abode had been sentenced to three months for breaking and entering, Derek O'Connor, who had been occupying a modest position at the back of the Magistrate's Court, put through a call to a Museum number.

'Not a thing on the fellow when we picked him up,' he said. 'We gave him plenty of time too.'

'Who was he? Anyone we know?'

'One of the Gecko lot, I think. Small time. They hire him out for this sort of thing. Not much brain but he's said to be thorough.'

'And he took his sentence like a lamb?' At the other end of the line Colonel Pikeaway grinned as he spoke.

'Yes. Perfect picture of a stupid fellow lapsed from the straight and narrow path. You'd never connect him with any big time stuff. That's his value, of course.'

'And he didn't find anything,' mused Colonel Pikeaway. 'And *you* didn't find anything. It rather looks, doesn't it, as though there isn't anything to find? Our idea that Rawlinson planted these things on his sister seems to have been wrong.'

'Other people appear to have the same idea.'

'It's a bit obvious really . . . Maybe we are meant to take the bait.'

'Could be. Any other possibilities?'

'Plenty of them. The stuff may still be in Ramat. Hidden somewhere in the Ritz Savoy Hotel, maybe. Or Rawlinson passed it to someone on his way to the airstrip. Or there may be something in that hint of Mr Robinson's. A woman may have got hold of it. Or it could be that Mrs Sutcliffe had it all the time unbeknownst to herself, and flung it overboard in the Red Sea with something she had no further use for.'

'And that,' he added thoughtfully, 'might be all for the best.'

'Oh, come now, it's worth a lot of money, sir.'

'Human life is worth a lot, too,' said Colonel Pikeaway.

CHAPTER 5

LETTERS FROM MEADOWBANK SCHOOL

Letter from Julia Upjohn to her mother:

Dear Mummy,

I've settled in now and am liking it very much. There's a girl who is new this term too called Jennifer and she and I rather do things together. We're both awfully keen on tennis. She's rather good. She has a really smashing serve when it comes off, but it doesn't usually. She says her racquet's got warped from being out in the Persian Gulf. It's very hot out there. She was in all that Revolution that happened. I said wasn't it very exciting, but she said no, they didn't see anything at all. They were taken away to the Embassy or something and missed it.

Miss Bulstrode is rather a lamb, but she's pretty frightening too – or can be. She goes easy on you when you're new. Behind her back everyone calls her The Bull or Bully. We're taught English literature by Miss Rich, who's terrific. When she gets in a real state her hair comes down. She's got a queer but rather exciting face and when she reads bits of Shakespeare it all seems different and real. She went on at us the other day about Iago, and what he felt – and a lot about jealousy and how it ate into you and you suffered until you went quite mad wanting to hurt the person you loved. It gave us all the shivers – except Jennifer, because nothing upsets her. Miss Rich teaches us Geography, too. I always thought it was such a dull subject, but it isn't with Miss Rich. This morning she told us all about the spice trade and why they had to have spices because of things going bad so easily.

I'm starting Art with Miss Laurie. She comes twice a week and takes us up to London to see picture galleries as well. We do French with Mademoiselle Blanche. She doesn't keep order very well. Jennifer says French people can't. She doesn't get cross, though, only bored. She says 'Enfin, vous m'ennuiez, mes enfants!' Miss

Springer is awful. She does gym and P.T. She's got ginger hair and smells when she's hot. Then there's Miss Chadwick (Chaddy) – she's been here since the school started. She teaches mathematics and is rather fussy, but quite nice. And there's Miss Vansittart who teaches History and German. She's a sort of Miss Bulstrode with the pep left out.

There are a lot of foreign girls here, two Italians and some Germans, and a rather jolly Swede (she's a Princess or something) and a girl who's half Turkish and half Persian and who says she would have been married to Prince Ali Yusuf who got killed in that aeroplane crash, but Jennifer says that isn't true, that Shaista only says so because she was a kind of cousin, and you're supposed to marry a cousin. But Jennifer says he wasn't going to. He liked someone else. Jennifer knows a lot of things but she won't usually tell them.

I suppose you'll be starting on your trip soon. Don't *leave your passport behind you like you did last time!!! And take your first aid kit in case you have an accident.*

Love from Julia

Letter from Jennifer Sutcliffe to her mother:

Dear Mummy,

It really isn't bad here. I'm enjoying it more than I expected to do. The weather has been very fine. We had to write a composition yesterday on 'Can a good quality be carried to excess?' I couldn't think of anything to say. Next week it will be 'Contrast the characters of Juliet and Desdemona.' That seems silly too. Do you think I could have a new tennis racquet? I know you had mine restrung last Autumn – but it feels all wrong. Perhaps it's got warped. I'd rather like to learn Greek. Can I? I love languages. Some of us are going to London to see the ballet next week. It's Swan Lake. *The food here is jolly good. Yesterday we had chicken for lunch, and we had lovely home made cakes for tea.*

I can't think of any more news – have you had any more burglaries?

Your loving daughter,
Jennifer

Letter from Margaret Gore-West, Senior Prefect, to her mother:

Dear Mummy,

There is very little news. I am doing German with Miss Vansittart this term. There is a rumour that Miss Bulstrode is going to retire and that Miss Vansittart will succeed her but they've been saying that for over a year now, and I'm sure it isn't true. I asked Miss Chadwick (of course I wouldn't dare ask Miss Bulstrode!) and she was quite sharp about it. Said certainly not and don't listen to gossip. We went to the ballet on Tuesday. Swan Lake. *Too dreamy for words!*

Princess Ingrid is rather fun. Very blue eyes, but she wears braces on her teeth. There are two new German girls. They speak English quite well.

Miss Rich is back and looking quite well. We did miss her last term. The new Games Mistress is called Miss Springer. She's terribly bossy and nobody likes her much. She coaches you in tennis very well, though. One of the new girls, Jennifer Sutcliffe, is going to be really good, I think. Her backhand's a bit weak. Her great friend is a girl called Julia. We call them the Jays!

You won't forget about taking me out on the 20th, will you? Sports Day is June 19th.

Your Loving
Margaret

Letter from Ann Shapland to Dennis Rathbone:

Dear Dennis,

I shan't get any time off until the third week of term. I should like to dine with you then very much. It would have to be Saturday or Sunday. I'll let you know.

I find it rather fun working in a school. But thank God I'm not a schoolmistress! I'd go raving mad.

Yours ever,
Ann

Letter from Miss Johnson to her sister:

Dear Edith,

Everything much the same as usual here. The summer term is always nice. The garden is looking beautiful and we've got a new gardener to help old Briggs – young and strong! Rather good looking, too, which is a pity. Girls are so silly.

Miss Bulstrode hasn't said anything more about retiring, so I hope she's got over the idea. Miss Vansittart wouldn't be at all the same thing. I really don't believe I would stay on.

Give my love to Dick and to the children, and remember me to Oliver and Kate when you see them.

Elspeth

Letter from Mademoiselle Angèle Blanche to René Dupont, Post Restante, Bordeaux.

Dear René,

All is well here, though I cannot say that I amuse myself. The girls are neither respectful nor well behaved. I think it better, however, not to complain to Miss Bulstrode. One has to be on one's guard when dealing with that one!

There is nothing interesting at present to tell you.

Mouche

Letter from Miss Vansittart to a friend:

Dear Gloria,

The summer term has started smoothly. A very satisfactory set of new girls. The foreigners are settling down well. Our little Princess (the Middle East one, not the Scandinavian) is inclined to lack application, but I suppose one has to expect that. She has very charming manners.

The new Games Mistress, Miss Springer, is not a success. The girls dislike her and she is far too high-handed with them. After all, this is not an ordinary school. We don't stand or fall by P.T.! She is also very inquisitive, and asks far too many personal questions. That sort of thing can be very trying, and is so ill bred. Mademoiselle Blanche, the new French Mistress, is quite amiable but not up to the standard of Mademoiselle Depuy.

We had a near escape on the first day of term. Lady Veronica Carlton-Sandways turned up completely intoxicated!! But for Miss Chadwick spotting it and heading her off, we might have had a most unpleasant incident. The twins are such nice girls, too.

Miss Bulstrode has not said anything definite yet about the future – *but from her manner, I think her mind is definitely made up. Meadowbank is a really fine achievement, and I shall be proud to carry on its traditions.*

Give my love to Marjorie when you see her.

Yours ever,

Eleanor

Letter to Colonel Pikeaway, sent through the usual channels:

Talk about sending a man into danger! I'm the only able-bodied male in an establishment of, roughly, some hundred and ninety females.

Her Highness arrived in style. Cadillac of squashed strawberry and pastel blue, with Wog Notable in native dress, fashion-plate-from-Paris wife, and junior edition of same (H.R.H.).

Hardly recognized her the next day in her school uniform. There will be no difficulty in establishing friendly relations with her. She has already seen to that. Was asking me the names of various flowers in a sweet innocent way, when a female Gorgon with freckles, red hair, and a voice like a corncrake bore down upon her and removed her from my vicinity. She didn't want to go. I'd always understood these Oriental girls were brought up modestly behind the veil. This one must have had a little worldly experience during her schooldays in Switzerland, I think.

The Gorgon, alias Miss Springer, the Games Mistress, came back to give me a raspberry. Garden staff were not *to talk to the pupils, etc. My turn to express innocent surprise. 'Sorry, Miss. The young lady was asking what these here delphiniums was. Suppose they don't have them in the parts she comes from.' The Gorgon was easily pacified, in the end she almost simpered. Less success with Miss Bulstrode's secretary. One of these coat and skirt country girls. French mistress is more cooperative. Demure and mousy to look at, but not such a mouse really. Also have made friends with three pleasant gigglers, Christian names, Pamela, Lois and Mary, surnames unknown, but of aristocratic lineage. A sharp old war-horse called Miss Chadwick keeps a wary eye on me, so I'm careful not to blot my copybook.*

My boss, old Briggs, is a crusty kind of character whose chief subject of conversation is what things used to be in the good old days, when he was, I suspect, the fourth of a staff of five. He grumbles about most things and people, but has a wholesome respect for Miss Bulstrode herself. So have I. She had a few words, very pleasant, with me, but I had a horrid feeling she was seeing right through me and knowing all about me.

No sign, so far, of anything sinister – but I live in hope.

CHAPTER 6
EARLY DAYS

I

In the Mistresses' Common Room news was being exchanged. Foreign travel, plays seen, Art Exhibitions visited. Snapshots were handed round. The menace of coloured transparencies was in the offing. All the enthusiasts wanted to show their own pictures, but to get out of being forced to see other people's.

Presently conversation became less personal. The new Sports Pavilion was both criticized and admired. It was admitted to be a fine building, but naturally everybody would have liked to improve its design in one way or another.

The new girls were then briefly passed in review, and, on the whole, the verdict was favourable.

A little pleasant conversation was made to the two new members of the staff. Had Mademoiselle Blanche been in England before? What part of France did she come from?

Mademoiselle Blanche replied politely but with reserve.

Miss Springer was more forthcoming.

She spoke with emphasis and decision. It might almost have been said that she was giving a lecture. Subject: The excellence of Miss Springer. How much she had been appreciated as a colleague. How headmistresses had accepted her advice with gratitude and had re-organized their schedules accordingly.

Miss Springer was not sensitive. A restlessness in her audience was not noticed by her. It remained for Miss Johnson to ask in her mild tones:

'All the same, I expect your ideas haven't always been accepted in the way they – er – should have been.'

'One must be prepared for ingratitude,' said Miss Springer.

Her voice, already loud, became louder. 'The trouble is, people are so cowardly – won't face facts. They often prefer not to see what's under their noses all the time. I'm not like that. I go straight to the point. More than once I've unearthed a nasty scandal – brought it into the open. I've a good nose – once I'm on the trail, I don't leave it – not till I've pinned down my quarry.' She gave a loud jolly laugh. 'In my opinion, no one should teach in a school whose life isn't an open book. If anyone's got anything to hide, one can soon tell. Oh! you'd be surprised if I told you some of the things I've found out about people. Things that nobody else had dreamed of.'

'You enjoyed that experience, yes?' said Mademoiselle Blanche.

'Of course not. Just doing my duty. But I wasn't backed up. Shameful laxness. So I resigned – as a protest.'

She looked round and gave her jolly sporting laugh again.

'Hope nobody here has anything to hide,' she said gaily.

Nobody was amused. But Miss Springer was not the kind of woman to notice that.

II

'Can I speak to you, Miss Bulstrode?'

Miss Bulstrode laid her pen aside and looked up into the flushed face of the matron, Miss Johnson.

'Yes, Miss Johnson.'

'It's that girl Shaista – the Egyptian girl or whatever she is.'

'Yes?'

'It's her – er – underclothing.'

Miss Bulstrode's eyebrows rose in patient surprise.

'Her – well – her bust bodice.'

'What is wrong with her brassière?'

'Well – it isn't an ordinary kind – I mean it doesn't hold her in, exactly. It – er – well it pushes her up – really quite unnecessarily.'

Miss Bulstrode bit her lip to keep back a smile, as so often when in colloquy with Miss Johnson.

'Perhaps I'd better come and look at it,' she said gravely.

A kind of inquest was then held with the offending contraption held up to display by Miss Johnson, whilst Shaista looked on with lively interest.

'It's this sort of wire and – er – boning arrangement,' said Miss Johnson with disapprobation.

Shaista burst into animated explanation.

'But you see my breasts they are not very big – not nearly big enough. I do not look enough like a woman. And it is very important for a girl – to show she is a woman and not a boy.'

'Plenty of time for that. You're only fifteen,' said Miss Johnson.

'Fifteen – that *is* a woman! And I look like a woman, do I not?'

She appealed to Miss Bulstrode who nodded gravely.

'Only my breasts, they are poor. So I want to make them look not so poor. You understand?'

'I understand perfectly,' said Miss Bulstrode. 'And I quite see your point of view. But in this school, you see, you are amongst girls who are, for the most part, English, and English girls are not very often women at the age of fifteen. I like my girls to use make-up discreetly and to wear clothes suitable to their stage of growth. I suggest that you wear your brassière when you are dressed for a party or for going to London, but not every day here. We do a good deal of sports and games here and for that your body needs to be free to move easily.'

'It is too much – all this running and jumping,' said Shaista sulkily, 'and the P.T. I do not like Miss Springer – she always says, "Faster, faster, do not slack." I get tired.'

'That will do, Shaista,' said Miss Bulstrode, her voice becoming authoritative. 'Your family has sent you here to learn English ways. All this exercise will be very good for your complexion, *and* for developing your bust.'

Dismissing Shaista, she smiled at the agitated Miss Johnson.

'It's quite true,' she said. 'The girl is fully mature. She might easily be over twenty by the look of her. And that is what she feels like. You can't expect her to feel the same age as Julia Upjohn, for instance. Intellectually Julia is far ahead of Shaista. Physically, she could quite well wear a liberty bodice still.'

'I wish they were all like Julia Upjohn,' said Miss Johnson.

'I don't,' said Miss Bulstrode briskly. 'A schoolful of girls all alike would be very dull.'

Dull, she thought, as she went back to her marking of Scripture essays. That word had been repeating itself in her brain for some time now. *Dull* . . .

If there was one thing her school was not, it was dull. During her career as its headmistress, she herself had never felt dull. There had been difficulties to combat, unforeseen crises, irritations with parents, with children: domestic upheavals. She had met and dealt with incipient disasters and turned them into triumphs. It had all been stimulating, exciting, supremely worth while. And even now, though she had made up her mind to it, she did not want to go.

She was physically in excellent health, almost as tough as when she and Chaddy (faithful Chaddy!) had started the great enterprise with a mere handful of children and backing from a banker of unusual foresight. Chaddy's academic distinctions had been better than hers, but it was she who had had the vision to plan and make of the school a place of such distinction that it was known all over Europe. She had never been afraid to experiment, whereas Chaddy had been content to teach soundly but unexcitingly what she knew. Chaddy's supreme achievement had always been to be *there*, at hand, the faithful buffer, quick to render assistance when assistance was needed. As on the opening day of term with Lady Veronica. It was on her solidity, Miss Bulstrode reflected, that an exciting edifice had been built.

Well, from the material point of view, both women had done very well out of it. If they retired now, they would both have a good assured income for the rest of their lives. Miss Bulstrode wondered if Chaddy would want to retire when she herself did? Probably not. Probably, to her, the school was home. She would continue, faithful and reliable, to buttress up Miss Bulstrode's successor.

Because Miss Bulstrode had made up her mind – a successor there must be. Firstly associated with herself in joint rule and then to rule alone. To know when to go – that was one of the great necessities of life. To go before one's powers began to fail, one's sure grip to loosen, before one felt the faint staleness, the unwillingness to envisage continuing effort.

Miss Bulstrode finished marking the essays and noted that the Upjohn child had an original mind. Jennifer Sutcliffe had a complete lack of imagination, but showed an unusually sound grasp of facts. Mary Vyse, of course, was scholarship class – a wonderful retentive memory. But what a dull girl! Dull – that word again. Miss Bulstrode dismissed it from her mind and rang for her secretary.

She began to dictate letters.

Dear Lady Valence. Jane has had some trouble with her ears. I enclose the doctor's report – etc.

Dear Baron Von Eisenger. We can certainly arrange for Hedwig to go to the Opera on the occasion of Hellstern's taking the role of Isolda –

An hour passed swiftly. Miss Bulstrode seldom paused for a word. Ann Shapland's pencil raced over the pad.

A very good secretary, Miss Bulstrode thought to herself. Better than Vera Lorrimer. Tiresome girl, Vera. Throwing up her post so suddenly. A nervous breakdown, she had said. Something to do with a man, Miss Bulstrode thought resignedly. It was usually a man.

'That's the lot,' said Miss Bulstrode, as she dictated the last word. She heaved a sigh of relief.

'So many dull things to be done,' she remarked. 'Writing letters to parents is like feeding dogs. Pop some soothing platitude into every waiting mouth.'

Ann laughed. Miss Bulstrode looked at her appraisingly.

'What made you take up secretarial work?'

'I don't quite know. I had no special bent for anything in particular, and it's the sort of thing almost everybody drifts into.'

'You don't find it monotonous?'

'I suppose I've been lucky. I've had a lot of different jobs. I was with Sir Mervyn Todhunter, the archaeologist, for a year, then I was with Sir Andrew Peters in Shell. I was secretary to Monica Lord, the actress, for a while – that really was hectic!' She smiled in remembrance.

'There's a lot of that nowadays amongst you girls,' said Miss Bulstrode. 'All this chopping and changing.' She sounded disapproving.

'Actually, I can't do anything for very long. I've got an invalid mother. She's rather – well – difficult from time to time. And then I have to go back home and take charge.'

'I see.'

'But all the same, I'm afraid I should chop and change anyway.

I haven't got the gift for continuity. I find chopping and changing far less dull.'

'Dull . . .' murmured Miss Bulstrode, struck again by the fatal word.

Ann looked at her in surprise.

'Don't mind me,' said Miss Bulstrode. 'It's just that sometimes one particular word seems to crop up all the time. How would you have liked to be a schoolmistress?' she asked, with some curiosity.

'I'm afraid I should hate it,' said Ann frankly.

'Why?'

'I'd find it terribly dull – Oh, I am sorry.'

She stopped in dismay.

'Teaching isn't in the least dull,' said Miss Bulstrode with spirit. 'It can be the most exciting thing in the world. I shall miss it terribly when I retire.'

. 'But surely –' Ann stared at her. 'Are you thinking of retiring?'

'It's decided – yes. Oh, I shan't go for another year – or even two years.'

'But – why?'

'Because I've given my best to the school – and had the best from it. I don't want second best.'

'The school will carry on?'

'Oh yes. I have a good successor.'

'Miss Vansittart, I suppose?'

'So you fix on her automatically?' Miss Bulstrode looked at her sharply, 'That's interesting –'

'I'm afraid I hadn't really thought about it. I've just overheard the staff talking. I should think she'll carry on very well – exactly in your tradition. And she's very striking looking, handsome and with quite a presence. I imagine that's important, isn't it?'

'Yes, it is. Yes, I'm sure Eleanor Vansittart is the right person.'

'She'll carry on where you leave off,' said Ann gathering up her things.

But do I want that? thought Miss Bulstrode to herself as Ann went out. Carry on where I leave off? That's just what Eleanor *will* do! No new experiments, nothing revolutionary. That wasn't the way I made Meadowbank what it is. I took chances. I upset lots of people. I bullied and cajoled, and refused to follow the pattern of other schools. Isn't that what I want to follow on here now? Someone to pour new life into the school. Some dynamic personality . . . like – yes – Eileen Rich.

But Eileen wasn't old enough, hadn't enough experience. She was stimulating, though, she could teach. She had ideas. She would never be dull – Nonsense, she must get that word out of her mind. Eleanor Vansittart was not dull . . .

She looked up as Miss Chadwick came in.

'Oh, Chaddy,' she said. 'I *am* pleased to see you!'

Miss Chadwick looked a little surprised.

'Why? Is anything the matter?'

'I'm the matter. I don't know my own mind.'

'That's very unlike you, Honoria.'

'Yes, isn't it? How's the term going, Chaddy?'

'Quite all right, I think.' Miss Chadwick sounded a little unsure.

Miss Bulstrode pounced.

'Now then. Don't hedge. What's wrong?'

'Nothing. Really, Honoria, nothing at all. It's just –' Miss Chadwick wrinkled up her forehead and looked rather like a perplexed Boxer dog – 'Oh, a feeling. But really it's nothing that I can put a finger on. The new girls seem a pleasant lot. I don't care for Mademoiselle Blanche very much. But then I didn't like Geneviève Depuy, either. *Sly.*'

Miss Bulstrode did not pay very much attention to this criticism. Chaddy always accused the French mistresses of being sly.

'She's not a good teacher,' said Miss Bulstrode. 'Surprising really. Her testimonials were so good.'

'The French never can teach. No discipline,' said Miss Chadwick. 'And really Miss Springer is a little too much of a good thing! Leaps about so. Springer by nature as well as by name . . .'

'She's good at her job.'

'Oh yes, first class.'

'New staff is always upsetting,' said Miss Bulstrode.

'Yes,' agreed Miss Chadwick eagerly. 'I'm sure it's nothing more than that. By the way, that new gardener is quite young.

So unusual nowadays. No gardeners seem to be young. A pity he's so good-looking. We shall have to keep a sharp eye open.'

The two ladies nodded their heads in agreement. They knew, none better, the havoc caused by a good-looking young man to the hearts of adolescent girls.

CHAPTER 7

STRAWS IN THE WIND

I

'Not too bad, boy,' said old Briggs grudgingly, 'not too bad.'

He was expressing approval of his new assistant's performance in digging a strip of ground. It wouldn't do, thought Briggs, to let the young fellow get above himself.

'Mind you,' he went on, 'you don't want to rush at things. Take it steady, that's what I say. Steady is what does it.'

The young man understood that his performance had compared rather too favourably with Briggs's own tempo of work.

'Now, along this here,' continued Briggs, 'we'll put some nice asters out. *She* don't like asters – but I pay no attention. Females has their whims, but if you don't pay no attention, ten to one they never notice. Though I will say *She* is the noticing kind on the whole. You'd think she 'ad enough to bother her head about, running a place like this.'

Adam understood that '*She*' who figured so largely in Briggs's conversation referred to Miss Bulstrode.

'And who was it I saw you talking to just now?' went on Briggs suspiciously, 'when you went along to the potting shed for them bamboos?'

'Oh, that was just one of the young ladies,' said Adam.

'Ah. One of them two Eye-ties, wasn't it? Now you be careful, my boy. Don't you get mixed up with no Eye-ties, I know what I'm talkin' about. I knew Eye-ties, I did, in the first war and if I'd known then what I know now I'd have been more careful. See?'

'Wasn't no harm in it,' said Adam, putting on a sulky manner. 'Just passed the time of day with me, she did, and asked the names of one or two things.'

'Ah,' said Briggs, 'but you be careful. It's not your place to talk to any of the young ladies. *She* wouldn't like it.'

'I wasn't doing no harm and I didn't say anything I shouldn't.'

'I don't say you did, boy. But I say a lot o' young females penned up together here with not so much as a drawing master to take their minds off things – well, you'd better be careful. That's all. Ah, here comes the Old Bitch now. Wanting something difficult, I'll be bound.'

Miss Bulstrode was approaching with a rapid step. 'Good morning, Briggs,' she said. 'Good morning – er –'

'Adam, miss.'

'Ah yes, Adam. Well, you seem to have got that piece dug very satisfactorily. The wire netting's coming down by the far tennis court, Briggs. You'd better attend to that.'

'All right, ma'am, all right. It'll be seen to.'

'What are you putting in front here?'

'Well ma'am, I had thought –'

'*Not* asters,' said Miss Bulstrode, without giving him time to finish 'Pom Pom dahlias,' and she departed briskly.

'Coming along – giving orders,' said Briggs. 'Not that she isn't a sharp one. She soon notices if you haven't done work properly. And remember what I've said and be careful, boy. About Eye-ties and the others.'

'If she's any fault to find with me, I'll soon know what I can do,' said Adam sulkily. 'Plenty o' jobs going.'

'Ah. That's like you young men all over nowadays. Won't take a word from anybody. All I say is, mind your step.'

Adam continued to look sulky, but bent to his work once more.

Miss Bulstrode walked back along the path towards the school. She was frowning a little.

Miss Vansittart was coming in the opposite direction.

'What a hot afternoon,' said Miss Vansittart.

'Yes, it's very sultry and oppressive.' Again Miss Bulstrode frowned. 'Have you noticed that young man – the young gardener?'

'No, not particularly.'

'He seems to me – well – an odd type,' said Miss Bulstrode thoughtfully. 'Not the usual kind around here.'

'Perhaps he's just come down from Oxford and wants to make a little money.'

'He's good-looking. The girls notice him.'

'The usual problem.'

Miss Bulstrode smiled. 'To combine freedom for the girls *and* strict supervision – is that what you mean, Eleanor?'

'Yes.'

'We manage,' said Miss Bulstrode.

'Yes, indeed. You've never had a scandal at Meadowbank, have you?'

'We've come near it once or twice,' said Miss Bulstrode. She laughed. 'Never a dull moment in running a school.' She went on, 'Do you ever find life dull here, Eleanor?'

'No indeed,' said Miss Vansittart. 'I find the work here most stimulating and satisfying. You must feel very proud and happy, Honoria, at the great success you have achieved.'

'I think I made a good job of things,' said Miss Bulstrode thoughtfully. 'Nothing, of course, is ever quite as one first imagined it . . .

'Tell me, Eleanor,' she said suddenly, 'if you were running this place instead of me, what changes would you make? Don't mind saying. I shall be interested to hear.'

'I don't think I should want to make any changes,' said Eleanor Vansittart. 'It seems to me the spirit of the place and the whole organization is well-nigh perfect.'

'You'd carry on on the same lines, you mean?'

'Yes, indeed. I don't think they could be bettered.'

Miss Bulstrode was silent for a moment. She was thinking to herself: I wonder if she said that in order to please me. One never knows with people. However close to them you may have been for years. Surely, she can't really mean that. Anybody with any creative feeling at all *must* want to make changes. It's true, though, that it mightn't have seemed tactful to say so . . . And tact *is* very important. It's important with parents, it's important with the girls, it's important with the staff. Eleanor certainly has tact.

Aloud, she said, 'There must always be adjustments, though, mustn't there? I mean with changing ideas and conditions of life generally.'

'Oh, that, yes,' said Miss Vansittart. 'One has, as they say, to go with the times. But it's *your* school, Honoria, you've made it what it is and your traditions are the essence of it. I think tradition is very important, don't you?'

Miss Bulstrode did not answer. She was hovering on the brink of irrevocable words. The offer of a partnership hung in the air. Miss Vansittart, though seeming unaware in her well-bred way, must be conscious of the fact that it was there. Miss Bulstrode did not know really what was holding her back. Why did she so dislike to commit herself? Probably, she admitted ruefully, because she hated the idea of giving up control. Secretly, of course, she wanted to stay, she wanted to go on running her school. But surely nobody could be a worthier successor than Eleanor? So dependable, so reliable. Of course, as far as that went, so was dear Chaddy – reliable as they came. And yet you could never envisage Chaddy as headmistress of an outstanding school.

'What *do* I want?' said Miss Bulstrode to herself. 'How tiresome I am being! Really, indecision has never been one of my faults up to now.'

A bell sounded in the distance.

'My German class,' said Miss Vansittart. 'I must go in.' She moved at a rapid but dignified step towards the school buildings. Following her more slowly, Miss Bulstrode almost collided with Eileen Rich, hurrying from a side path.

'Oh, I'm so sorry, Miss Bulstrode. I didn't see you.' Her hair, as usual, was escaping from its untidy bun. Miss Bulstrode noted anew the ugly but interesting bones of her face, a strange, eager, compelling young woman.

'You've got a class?'

'Yes. English –'

'You enjoy teaching, don't you?' said Miss Bulstrode.

'I love it. It's the most fascinating thing in the world.'

'Why?'

Eileen Rich stopped dead. She ran a hand through her hair. She frowned with the effort of thought.

'How interesting. I don't know that I've really *thought* about it. Why *does* one like teaching? Is it because it makes one feel grand and important? No, no . . . it's not as bad as that. No, it's more like fishing, I think. You don't know what catch you're going to get, what you're going to drag up from the sea. It's the quality of the *response*. It's so exciting when it comes. It doesn't very often, of course.'

Miss Bulstrode nodded in agreement. She had been right! This girl had something!

'I expect you'll run a school of your own some day,' she said.

'Oh, I hope so,' said Eileen Rich. 'I do hope so. That's what I'd like above anything.'

'You've got ideas already, haven't you, as to how a school should be run?'

'Everyone has ideas, I suppose,' said Eileen Rich. 'I daresay a great many of them are fantastic and they'd go utterly wrong. That would be a risk, of course. But one would have to try them out. I would have to learn by experience . . . The awful thing is that one can't go by other people's experience, can one?'

'Not really,' said Miss Bulstrode. 'In life one has to make one's own mistakes.'

'That's all right in life,' said Eileen Rich. 'In life you can pick yourself up and start again.' Her hands, hanging at her sides, clenched themselves into fists. Her expression was grim. Then suddenly it relaxed into humour. 'But if a school's gone to pieces, you can't very well pick that up and start again, can you?'

'If *you* ran a school like Meadowbank,' said Miss Bulstrode, 'would you make changes – experiment?'

Eileen Rich looked embarrassed. 'That's – that's an awfully hard thing to say,' she said.

'You mean you would,' said Miss Bulstrode. 'Don't mind speaking your mind, child.'

'One would always want, I suppose, to use one's own ideas,' said Eileen Rich. 'I don't say they'd work. They mightn't.'

'But it would be worth taking a risk?'

'It's always worth taking a risk, isn't it?' said Eileen Rich. 'I mean if you feel strongly enough about anything.'

'You don't object to leading a dangerous life. I see . . .' said Miss Bulstrode.

'I think I've always led a dangerous life.' A shadow passed over the girl's face. 'I must go. They'll be waiting.' She hurried off.

Miss Bulstrode stood looking after her. She was still standing there lost in thought when Miss Chadwick came hurrying to find her.

'Oh! there you are. We've been looking everywhere for you. Professor Anderson has just rung up. He wants to know if he can take Meroe this next weekend. He knows it's against the rules so soon but he's going off quite suddenly to – somewhere that sounds like Azure Basin.'

'Azerbaijan,' said Miss Bulstrode automatically, her mind still on her own thoughts.

'Not enough experience,' she murmured to herself. 'That's the risk. What did you say, Chaddy?'

Miss Chadwick repeated the message.

'I told Miss Shapland to say that we'd ring him back, and sent her to find you.'

'Say it will be quite all right,' said Miss Bulstrode. 'I recognize that this is an exceptional occasion.'

Miss Chadwick looked at her keenly.

'You're worrying, Honoria.'

'Yes, I am. I don't really know my own mind. That's unusual for me – and it upsets me . . . I know what I'd like to do – but I feel that to hand over to someone without the necessary experience wouldn't be fair to the school.'

'I wish you'd give up this idea of retirement. You belong here. Meadowbank needs you.'

'Meadowbank means a lot to you, Chaddy, doesn't it?'

'There's no school like it anywhere in England,' said Miss Chadwick. 'We can be proud of ourselves, you and I, for having started it.'

Miss Bulstrode put an affectionate arm round her shoulders. 'We can indeed, Chaddy. As for you, you're the comfort of my life. There's nothing about Meadowbank you don't know. You care for it as much as I do. And that's saying a lot, my dear.'

Miss Chadwick flushed with pleasure. It was so seldom that Honoria Bulstrode broke through her reserve.

II

'I simply can't play with the beastly thing. It's no good.'

Jennifer flung her racquet down in despair.

'Oh, Jennifer, what a fuss you make.'

'It's the balance,' Jennifer picked it up again and waggled it experimentally. 'It doesn't balance right.'

'It's much better than my old thing,' Julia compared her racquet. 'Mine's like a sponge. Listen to the sound of it.' She twanged. 'We meant to have it restrung, but Mummy forgot.'

'I'd rather have it than mine, all the same.' Jennifer took it and tried a swish or two with it.

'Well, I'd rather have *yours*. I could really hit something then. I'll swap, if you will.'

'All right then, swap.'

The two girls peeled off the small pieces of adhesive plaster on which their names were written, and re-affixed them, each to the other's racquet.

'I'm not going to swap back again,' said Julia warningly. 'So it's no use saying you don't like my old sponge.'

III

Adam whistled cheerfully as he tacked up the wire netting round the tennis court. The door of the Sports Pavilion opened and Mademoiselle Blanche, the little mousy French Mistress, looked out. She seemed startled at the sight of Adam. She hesitated for a moment and then went back inside.

'Wonder what she's been up to,' said Adam to himself. It would not have occurred to him that Mademoiselle Blanche had been up to anything, if it had not been for her manner. She had a guilty look which immediately roused surmise in his mind. Presently she came out again, closing the door behind her, and paused to speak as she passed him.

'Ah, you repair the netting, I see.'

'Yes, miss.'

'They are very fine courts here, and the swimming pool and the pavilion too. Oh! *le sport*! You think a lot in England of *le sport*, do you not?'

'Well, I suppose we do, miss.'

'Do you play tennis yourself?' Her eyes appraised him in a definitely feminine way and with a faint invitation in her glance. Adam wondered once more about her. It struck him that Mademoiselle Blanche was a somewhat unsuitable French Mistress for Meadowbank.

'No,' he said untruthfully, 'I don't play tennis. Haven't got the time.'

'You play cricket, then?'

'Oh well, I played cricket as a boy. Most chaps do.'

'I have not had much time to look around,' said Angèle Blanche. 'Not until today and it was so fine I thought I would like to examine the Sports Pavilion. I wish to write home to my friends in France who keep a school.'

Again Adam wondered a little. It seemed a lot of unnecessary explanation. It was almost as though Mademoiselle Blanche wished to excuse her presence out here at the Sports Pavilion. But why should she? She had a perfect right to go anywhere in the school grounds that she pleased. There was certainly no need to apologize for it to a gardener's assistant. It raised queries again in his mind. What had this young woman been doing in the Sports Pavilion?

He looked thoughtfully at Mademoiselle Blanche. It would be a good thing perhaps to know a little more about her. Subtly, deliberately, his manner changed. It was still respectful but not quite so respectful. He permitted his eyes to tell her that she was an attractive-looking young woman.

'You must find it a bit dull sometimes working in a girls' school, miss,' he said.

'It does not amuse me very much, no.'

'Still,' said Adam, 'I suppose you get your times off, don't you?'

There was a slight pause. It was as though she were debating with herself. Then, he felt it was with slight regret, the distance between them was deliberately widened.

'Oh yes,' she said, 'I have adequate time off. The conditions of employment here are excellent.' She gave him a little nod of the head. 'Good morning.' She walked off towards the house.

'You've been up to something,' said Adam to himself, 'in the Sports Pavilion.'

He waited till she was out of sight, then he left his work, went across to the Sports Pavilion and looked inside. But nothing that he could see was out of place. 'All the same,' he said to himself, 'she was up to something.'

As he came out again, he was confronted unexpectedly by Ann Shapland.

'Do you know where Miss Bulstrode is?' she asked.

'I think she's gone back to the house, miss. She was talking to Briggs just now.'

Ann was frowning.

'What are you doing in the Sports Pavilion?'

Adam was slightly taken aback. Nasty suspicious mind *she's* got, he thought. He said, with a faint insolence in his voice:

'Thought I'd like to take a look at it. No harm in looking, is there?'

'Oughtn't you to be getting on with your work?'

'I've just about finished nailing the wire round the tennis court.' He turned, looking up at the building behind him. 'This is new, isn't it? Must have cost a packet. The best of everything the young ladies here get, don't they?'

'They pay for it,' said Ann dryly.

'Pay through the nose, so I've heard,' agreed Adam.

He felt a desire he hardly understood himself, to wound or annoy this girl. She was so cool always, so self-sufficient. He would really enjoy seeing her angry.

But Ann did not give him that satisfaction. She merely said:

'You'd better finish tacking up the netting,' and went back towards the house. Half-way there, she slackened speed and looked back. Adam was busy at the tennis wire. She looked from him to the Sports Pavilion in a puzzled manner.

CHAPTER 8

MURDER

I

On night duty in Hurst St Cyprian Police Station, Sergeant Green yawned. The telephone rang and he picked up the receiver. A moment later his manner had changed completely. He began scribbling rapidly on a pad.

'Yes? Meadowbank? Yes – and the name? Spell it, please. S-P-R-I-N-G-for greengage?-E-R. Springer. Yes. Yes, please see that nothing is disturbed. Someone'll be with you very shortly.'

Rapidly and methodically he then proceeded to put into motion the various procedures indicated.

'Meadowbank?' said Detective Inspector Kelsey when his turn came. 'That's the girls' school, isn't it? Who is it who's been murdered?'

'Death of a Games Mistress,' said Kelsey, thoughtfully. 'Sounds like the title of a thriller on a railway bookstall.'

'Who's likely to have done her in, d'you think?' said the Sergeant. 'Seems unnatural.'

'Even Games Mistresses may have their love lives,' said Detective Inspector Kelsey. 'Where did they say the body was found?'

'In the Sports Pavilion. I suppose that's a fancy name for the gymnasium.'

'Could be,' said Kelsey. 'Death of a Games Mistress in the Gymnasium. Sounds a highly athletic crime, doesn't it? Did you say she was shot?'

'Yes.'

'They find the pistol?'

'No.'

'Interesting,' said Detective Inspector Kelsey, and having assembled his retinue, he departed to carry out his duties.

II

The front door at Meadowbank was open, with light streaming from it, and here Inspector Kelsey was received by Miss Bulstrode herself. He knew her by sight, as indeed most people in the neighbourhood did. Even in this moment of confusion and uncertainty, Miss Bulstrode remained eminently herself, in command of the situation and in command of her subordinates.

'Detective Inspector Kelsey, madam,' said the Inspector.

'What would you like to do first, Inspector Kelsey? Do you wish to go out to the Sports Pavilion or do you want to hear full details?'

'The doctor is with me,' said Kelsey. 'If you will show him and two of my men to where the body is, I should like a few words with you.'

'Certainly. Come into my sitting-room. Miss Rowan, will you show the doctor and the others the way?' She added, 'One of my staff is out there seeing that nothing is disturbed.'

'Thank you, madam.'

Kelsey followed Miss Bulstrode into her sitting-room. 'Who found the body?'

'The matron, Miss Johnson. One of the girls had earache and Miss Johnson was up attending to her. As she did so, she noticed the curtains were not pulled properly and going to pull them she observed that there was a light on in the Sports Pavilion which there should not have been at 1 a.m.,' finished Miss Bulstrode dryly.

'Quite so,' said Kelsey. 'Where is Miss Johnson now?'

'She is here if you want to see her?'

'Presently. Will you go on, madam.'

'Miss Johnson went and woke up another member of my staff, Miss Chadwick. They decided to go out and investigate. As they were leaving by the side door they heard the sound of a shot, whereupon they ran as quickly as they could towards the Sports Pavilion. On arrival there –'

The Inspector broke in. 'Thank you, Miss Bulstrode. If, as you say, Miss Johnson is available, I will hear the next part from her. But first, perhaps, you will tell me something about the murdered woman.'

'Her name is Grace Springer.'

'She has been with you long?'

'No. She came to me this term. My former Games Mistress left to take up a post in Australia.'

'And what did you know about this Miss Springer?'

'Her testimonials were excellent,' said Miss Bulstrode.

'You didn't know her personally before that?'

'No.'

'Have you any idea at all, even the vaguest, of what might have precipitated this tragedy? Was she unhappy? Any unfortunate entanglements?'

Miss Bulstrode shook her head. 'Nothing that I know of. I may say,' she went on, 'that it seems to me most unlikely. She was not that kind of a woman.'

'You'd be surprised,' said Inspector Kelsey darkly.

'Would you like me to fetch Miss Johnson now?'

'If you please. When I've heard her story I'll go out to the gym – or the – what d'you call it – Sports Pavilion?'

'It is a newly built addition to the school this year,' said Miss Bulstrode. 'It is built adjacent to the swimming pool and it comprises a squash court and other features. The racquets, lacrosse and hockey sticks are kept there, and there is a drying room for swim suits.'

'Was there any reason why Miss Springer should be in the Sports Pavilion at night?'

'None whatever,' said Miss Bulstrode unequivocally.

'Very well, Miss Bulstrode. I'll talk to Miss Johnson now.'

Miss Bulstrode left the room and returned bringing the matron with her. Miss Johnson had had a sizeable dollop of brandy administered to her to pull her together after her discovery of the body. The result was a slightly added loquacity.

'This is Detective Inspector Kelsey,' said Miss Bulstrode. 'Pull yourself together, Elspeth, and tell him exactly what happened.'

'It's dreadful,' said Miss Johnson, 'it's really dreadful. Such a thing has never happened before in all my experience. Never! I couldn't have believed it, I really couldn't've believed it. Miss Springer too!'

Inspector Kelsey was a perceptive man. He was always willing to deviate from the course of routine if a remark struck him as unusual or worth following up.

'It seems to you, does it,' he said, 'very strange that it was Miss Springer who was murdered?'

'Well yes, it does, Inspector. She was so – well, so tough, you know. So hearty. Like the sort of woman one could imagine taking on a burglar single-handed – or two burglars.'

'Burglars? H'm,' said Inspector Kelsey. 'Was there anything to steal in the Sports Pavilion?'

'Well, no, really I can't see what there can have been. Swim suits of course, sports paraphernalia.'

'The sort of thing a sneak-thief might have taken,' agreed Kelsey. 'Hardly worth breaking in for, I should have thought. Was it broken into, by the way?'

'Well, really, I never thought to look,' said Miss Johnson. 'I mean, the door was open when we got there and –'

'It had not been broken into,' said Miss Bulstrode.

'I see,' said Kelsey. 'A key was used.' He looked at Miss Johnson. 'Was Miss Springer well liked?' he asked.

'Well, really, I couldn't say. I mean, after all, she's dead.'

'So, you didn't like her,' said Kelsey perceptively, ignoring Miss Johnson's finer feelings.

'I don't think anyone could have liked her very much,' said Miss Johnson. 'She had a very positive manner, you know. Never minded contradicting people flatly. She was very efficient and took her work very seriously I should say, wouldn't you, Miss Bulstrode?'

'Certainly,' said Miss Bulstrode.

Kelsey returned from the by-path he had been pursuing. 'Now, Miss Johnson, let's hear just what happened.'

'Jane, one of our pupils, had earache. She woke up with a rather bad attack of it and came to me. I got some remedies and when I'd got her back to bed, I saw the window curtains were flapping and thought perhaps it would be better for once if her window was not opened at night as it was blowing rather in that direction. Of course the girls always sleep with their windows open. We have difficulties sometimes with the foreigners, but I always insist that –'

'That really doesn't matter now,' said Miss Bulstrode. 'Our general rules of hygiene would not interest Inspector Kelsey.'

'No, no, of course not,' said Miss Johnson. 'Well, as I say I went to shut the window and what was my surprise to see a light in the Sports Pavilion. It was quite distinct, I couldn't mistake it. It seemed to be moving about.'

'You mean it was not the electric light turned on but the light of a torch or flashlight?'

'Yes, yes, that's what it must have been. I thought at once "Dear me, what's anyone doing out there at this time of night?" Of course I didn't think of burglars. That would have been a very fanciful idea, as you said just now.'

'What did you think of?' asked Kelsey.

Miss Johnson shot a glance at Miss Bulstrode and back again.

'Well, really, I don't know that I had any ideas in particular. I mean, well – well really, I mean I couldn't think –'

Miss Bulstrode broke in. 'I should imagine that Miss Johnson had the idea that one of our pupils might have gone out there to keep an assignation with someone,' she said. 'Is that right, Elspeth?'

Miss Johnson gasped. 'Well, yes, the idea did come into my head just for the moment. One of our Italian girls, perhaps. Foreigners are so much more precocious than English girls.'

'Don't be so insular,' said Miss Bulstrode. 'We've had plenty of English girls trying to make unsuitable assignations. It was a very natural thought to have occurred to you and probably the one that would have occurred to me.'

'Go on,' said Inspector Kelsey.

'So I thought the best thing,' went on Miss Johnson, 'was to go to Miss Chadwick and ask her to come out with me and see what was going on.'

'Why Miss Chadwick?' asked Kelsey. 'Any particular reason for selecting that particular mistress?'

'Well, I didn't want to disturb Miss Bulstrode,' said Miss Johnson, 'and I'm afraid it's rather a habit of ours always to go to Miss Chadwick if we don't want to disturb Miss Bulstrode. You see, Miss Chadwick's been here a very long time and has had so much experience.'

'Anyway,' said Kelsey, 'you went to Miss Chadwick and woke her up. Is that right?'

'Yes. She agreed with me that we must go out there immediately. We didn't wait to dress or anything, just put on pullovers and coats and went out by the side door. And it was then, just as we were standing on the path, that we heard a shot from the Sports Pavilion. So we ran along the path as fast as we could. Rather stupidly we hadn't taken a torch with us and it was hard to see where we were going. We stumbled once or twice but we got there quite quickly. The door was open. We switched on the light and –'

Kelsey interrupted. 'There was no light then when you got there. Not a torch or any other light?'

'No. The place was in darkness. We switched on the light and there she was. She –'

'That's all right,' said Inspector Kelsey kindly, 'you needn't describe anything. I shall be going out there now and I shall see for myself. You didn't meet anyone on your way there?'

'No.'

'Or hear anybody running away?'

'No. We didn't hear anything.'

'Did anybody else hear the shot in the school building?' asked Kelsey looking at Miss Bulstrode.

She shook her head. 'No. Not that I know of. Nobody has said that they heard it. The Sports Pavilion is some distance away and I rather doubt if the shot would be noticeable.'

'Perhaps from one of the rooms on the side of the house giving on the Sports Pavilion?'

'Hardly, I think, unless one were listening for such a thing. I'm sure it wouldn't be loud enough to wake anybody up.'

'Well, thank you,' said Inspector Kelsey. 'I'll be going out to the Sports Pavilion now.'

'I will come with you,' said Miss Bulstrode.

'Do you want me to come too?' asked Miss Johnson. 'I will if you like. I mean it's no good shirking things, is it? I always feel that one must face whatever comes and –'

'Thank you,' said Inspector Kelsey, 'there's no need, Miss Johnson. I wouldn't think of putting you to any further strain.'

'So awful,' said Miss Johnson, 'it makes it worse to feel I didn't like her very much. In fact, we had a disagreement only last night in the Common Room. I stuck to it that too much P.T. was bad for some girls – the more delicate girls. Miss Springer said nonsense, that they were just the ones who needed it. Toned them up and made new women of them, she said. I said to her that really she didn't know everything though she might think she did. After all I have been professionally trained and I know a great deal more about delicacy and illness than Miss Springer does – did, though I've no doubt that Miss Springer knows everything about parallel bars and vaulting horses and coaching tennis. But, oh dear, now I think of what's happened, I wish I hadn't said quite what I did. I suppose one always feels like that afterwards when something dreadful has occurred. I really do blame myself.'

'Now sit down there, dear,' said Miss Bulstrode, settling her on the sofa. 'You just sit down and rest and pay no attention to any little disputes you may have had. Life would be very dull if we agreed with each other on every subject.'

Miss Johnson sat down shaking her head, then yawned. Miss Bulstrode followed Kelsey into the hall.

'I gave her rather a lot of brandy,' she said, apologetically. 'It's made her a little voluble. But not confused, do you think?'

'No,' said Kelsey. 'She gave quite a clear account of what happened.'

Miss Bulstrode led the way to the side door.

'Is this the way Miss Johnson and Miss Chadwick went out?'

'Yes. You see it leads straight on to the path through the rhododendrons there which comes out at the Sports Pavilion.'

The Inspector had a powerful torch and he and Miss Bulstrode soon reached the building where the lights were now glaring.

'Fine bit of building,' said Kelsey, looking at it.

'It cost us a pretty penny,' said Miss Bulstrode, 'but we can afford it,' she added serenely.

The open door led into a fair-sized room. There were lockers there with the names of the various girls on them. At the end of the room there was a stand for tennis racquets and one for lacrosse sticks. The door at the side led off to showers and changing cubicles. Kelsey paused before going in. Two of his men had been busy. A photographer had just finished his job and another man who was busy testing for fingerprints looked up and said,

'You can walk straight across the floor, sir. You'll be all right. We haven't finished down this end yet.'

Kelsey walked forward to where the police surgeon was kneeling by the body. The latter looked up as Kelsey approached.

'She was shot from about four feet away,' he said. 'Bullet penetrated the heart. Death must have been pretty well instantaneous.'

'Yes. How long ago?'

'Say an hour or thereabouts.'

Kelsey nodded. He strolled round to look at the tall figure of Miss Chadwick where she stood grimly, like a watchdog, against one wall. About fifty-five, he judged, good forehead, obstinate mouth, untidy grey hair, no trace of hysteria. The kind of woman, he thought, who could be depended upon in a crisis though she might be overlooked in ordinary everyday life.

'Miss Chadwick?' he said.

'Yes.'

'You came out with Miss Johnson and discovered the body?'

'Yes. She was just as she is now. She was dead.'

'And the time?'

'I looked at my watch when Miss Johnson roused me. It was ten minutes to one.'

Kelsey nodded. That agreed with the time that Miss Johnson had given him. He looked down thoughtfully at the dead woman. Her bright red hair was cut short. She had a freckled face, with a chin which jutted out strongly, and a spare, athletic figure. She was wearing a tweed skirt and a heavy, dark pullover. She had brogues on her feet with no stockings.

'Any sign of the weapon?' asked Kelsey.

One of his men shook his head. 'No sign at all, sir.'

'What about the torch?'

'There's a torch there in the corner.'

'Any prints on it?'

'Yes. The dead woman's.'

'So she's the one who had the torch,' said Kelsey thoughtfully. 'She came out here with a torch – why?' He asked it partly of himself, partly of his men, partly of Miss Bulstrode and Miss Chadwick. Finally he seemed to concentrate on the latter. 'Any ideas?'

Miss Chadwick shook her head. 'No idea at all. I suppose she might have left something here – forgotten it this afternoon or evening – and come out to fetch it. But it seems rather unlikely in the middle of the night.'

'It must have been something very important if she did,' said Kelsey.

He looked round him. Nothing seemed disturbed except the stand of racquets at the end. That seemed to have been pulled violently forward. Several of the racquets were lying about on the floor.

'Of course,' said Miss Chadwick, 'she could have seen a light here, like Miss Johnson did later, and have come out to investigate. That seems the most likely thing to me.'

'I think you're right,' said Kelsey. 'There's just one small matter. Would she have come out here alone?'

'Yes.' Miss Chadwick answered without hesitation.

'Miss Johnson,' Kelsey reminded her, 'came and woke you up.'

'I know,' said Miss Chadwick, 'and that's what I should have done if I'd seen the light. I would have woken up Miss Bulstrode or Miss Vansittart or somebody. But Miss Springer wouldn't. She would have been quite confident – indeed would have preferred to tackle an intruder on her own.'

'Another point,' said the Inspector. 'You came out through the side door with Miss Johnson. Was the side door unlocked?'

'Yes, it was.'

'Presumably left unlocked by Miss Springer?'

'That seems the natural conclusion,' said Miss Chadwick.

'So we assume,' said Kelsey, 'that Miss Springer saw a light out here in the gymnasium – Sports Pavilion – whatever you call it – that she came out to investigate and that whoever was here shot her.' He wheeled round on Miss Bulstrode as she stood motionless in the doorway. 'Does that seem right to you?' he asked.

'It doesn't seem right at all,' said Miss Bulstrode. 'I grant you the first part. We'll say Miss Springer saw a light out here and that she went out to investigate by herself. That's perfectly probable. But that the person she disturbed here should shoot her – that seems to me all wrong. If anyone was here who had no business to be here they would be more likely to run away, or to try to run away. Why should someone come to this place at this hour of night with a pistol? It's ridiculous, that's what it is. Ridiculous! There's nothing here worth stealing, certainly nothing for which it would be worth while doing murder.'

'You think it more likely that Miss Springer disturbed a rendezvous of some kind?'

'That's the natural and most probable explanation,' said Miss Bulstrode. 'But it doesn't explain the fact of murder, does it? Girls in my school don't carry pistols about with them and any young man they might be meeting seems very unlikely to have a pistol either.'

Kelsey agreed. 'He'd have had a flick knife at most,' he said. 'There's an alternative,' he went on. 'Say Miss Springer came out here to meet a man –'

Miss Chadwick giggled suddenly. 'Oh no,' she said, 'not Miss Springer.'

'I do not mean necessarily an amorous assignment,' said the Inspector dryly. 'I'm suggesting that the murder was deliberate, that someone intended to murder Miss Springer, that they arranged to meet her here and shot her.'

CHAPTER 9
CAT AMONG THE PIGEONS

I

Letter from Jennifer Sutcliffe to her mother:

> *Dear Mummy,*
> *We had a murder last night. Miss Springer, the gym mistress. It happened in the middle of the night and the police came and this morning they're asking everybody questions.*
> *Miss Chadwick told us not to talk to anybody about it but I thought you'd like to know.*
> *With love,*
> *Jennifer*

II

Meadowbank was an establishment of sufficient importance to merit the personal attention of the Chief Constable. While routine investigation was going on Miss Bulstrode had not been inactive. She rang up a Press magnate and the Home Secretary, both personal friends of hers. As a result of those manoeuvres, very little had appeared about the event in the papers. A games mistress had been found dead in the school gymnasium. She had been shot, whether by accident or not was as yet not determined. Most of the notices of the event had an almost apologetic note in them, as though it were thoroughly tactless of any games mistress to get herself shot in such circumstances.

Ann Shapland had a busy day taking down letters to parents. Miss Bulstrode did not waste time in telling her pupils to keep quiet about the event. She knew that it would be a waste of time. More or less lurid reports would be sure to be penned to anxious parents and guardians. She intended her own balanced and reasonable account of the tragedy to reach them at the same time.

Later that afternoon she sat in conclave with Mr Stone, the Chief Constable, and Inspector Kelsey. The police were perfectly amenable to having the Press play the thing down as much as possible. It enabled them to pursue their inquiries quietly and without interference.

'I'm very sorry about this, Miss Bulstrode, very sorry indeed,' said the Chief Constable. 'I suppose it's – well – a bad thing for you.'

'Murder's a bad thing for any school, yes,' said Miss Bulstrode. 'It's no good dwelling on that now, though. We shall weather it, no doubt, as we have weathered other storms. All I do hope is that the matter will be cleared up *quickly*.'

'Don't see why it shouldn't, eh?' said Stone. He looked at Kelsey.

Kelsey said, 'It may help when we get her background.'

'D'you really think so?' asked Miss Bulstrode dryly.

'Somebody may have had it in for her,' Kelsey suggested.

Miss Bulstrode did not reply.

'You think it's tied up with this place?' asked the Chief Constable.

'Inspector Kelsey does really,' said Miss Bulstrode. 'He's only trying to save my feelings, I think.'

'I think it does tie up with Meadowbank,' said the Inspector slowly. 'After all, Miss Springer had her times off like all the other members of the staff. She could have arranged a meeting with anyone if she had wanted to do so at any spot she chose. Why choose the gymnasium here in the middle of the night?'

'You have no objection to a search being made of the school premises, Miss Bulstrode?' asked the Chief Constable.

'None at all. You're looking for the pistol or revolver or whatever it is, I suppose?'

'Yes. It was a small pistol of foreign make.'

'Foreign,' said Miss Bulstrode thoughtfully.

'To your knowledge, do any of your staff or any of the pupils have such a thing as a pistol in their possession?'

'Certainly not to my knowledge,' said Miss Bulstrode. 'I am fairly certain that none of the pupils have. Their possessions are unpacked for them when they arrive and such a thing would have been seen and noted, and would, I may say, have aroused considerable comment. But please, Inspector Kelsey, do exactly as you like in that respect. I see your men have been searching the grounds today.'

The Inspector nodded. 'Yes.'

He went on: 'I should also like interviews with the other members of your staff. One or other of them may have heard some remark made by Miss Springer that will give us a clue. Or may have observed some oddity of behaviour on her part.'

He paused, then went on, 'The same thing might apply to the pupils.'

Miss Bulstrode said: 'I had formed the plan of making a short address to the girls this evening after prayers. I would ask that if any of them has any knowledge that might possibly bear upon Miss Springer's death that they should come and tell me of it.'

'Very sound idea,' said the Chief Constable.

'But you must remember this,' said Miss Bulstrode, 'one or other of the girls may wish to make herself important by exaggerating some incident or even by inventing one. Girls do very odd things: but I expect you are used to dealing with that form of exhibitionism.'

'I've come across it,' said Inspector Kelsey. 'Now,' he added, 'please give me a list of your staff, also the servants.'

III

'I've looked through all the lockers in the Pavilion, sir.'

'And you didn't find anything?' said Kelsey.

'No, sir, nothing of importance. Funny things in some of them, but nothing in our line.'

'None of them were locked, were they?'

'No, sir, they can lock. There were keys in them, but none of them were locked.'

Kelsey looked round the bare floor thoughtfully. The tennis and lacrosse sticks had been replaced tidily on their stands.

'Oh well,' he said, 'I'm going up to the house now to have a talk with the staff.'

'You don't think it was an inside job, sir?'

'It could have been,' said Kelsey. 'Nobody's got an alibi except those two mistresses, Chadwick and Johnson and the child Jane that had the earache. Theoretically, everyone else was in bed and asleep, but there's no one to vouch for that. The girls all have separate rooms and naturally the staff do. Any one of them, including Miss Bulstrode herself, could have come out and met Springer here, or could have followed her here. Then, after she'd been shot, whoever it was could dodge back quietly through the bushes to the side door, and be nicely back in bed again when the alarm was given. It's motive that's difficult. Yes,' said Kelsey, 'it's motive. Unless there's something going on here that we don't know anything about, there doesn't seem to *be* any motive.'

He stepped out of the Pavilion and made his way slowly back to the house. Although it was past working hours, old Briggs, the gardener, was putting in a little work on a flower bed and he straightened up as the Inspector passed.

'You work late hours,' said Kelsey, smiling.

'Ah,' said Briggs. 'Young 'uns don't know what gardening is. Come on at eight and knock off at five – that's what they think it is. You've got to study your weather, some days you might as well not be out in the garden at all, and there's other days as you can work from seven in the morning until eight at night. That is if you love the place and have pride in the look of it.'

'You ought to be proud of this one,' said Kelsey. 'I've never seen any place better kept these days.'

'These days is right,' said Briggs. 'But I'm lucky I am. I've got a strong young fellow to work for me. A couple of boys, too, but they're not much good. Most of these boys and young men won't come and do this sort of work. All for going into factories, they are, or white collars and working in an office. Don't like to get their hands soiled with a bit of honest earth. But I'm lucky, as I say. I've got a good man working for me as come and offered himself.'

'Recently?' said Inspector Kelsey.

'Beginning of the term,' said Briggs. 'Adam, his name is. Adam Goodman.'

'I don't think I've seen him about,' said Kelsey.

'Asked for the day off today, he did,' said Briggs. 'I give it him. Didn't seem to be much doing today with you people tramping all over the place.'

'Somebody should have told me about him,' said Kelsey sharply.

'What do you mean, told you about him?'

'He's not on my list,' said the Inspector. 'Of people employed here, I mean.'

'Oh, well, you can see him tomorrow, mister,' said Briggs. 'Not that he can tell you anything, I don't suppose.'

'You never know,' said the Inspector.

A strong young man who had offered himself at the beginning of the term? It seemed to Kelsey that here was the first thing that he had come across which might be a little out of the ordinary.

IV

The girls filed into the hall for prayers that evening as usual, and afterwards Miss Bulstrode arrested their departure by raising her hand.

'I have something to say to you all. Miss Springer, as you know, was shot last night in the Sports Pavilion. If any of you has heard or seen anything in the past week – anything that has puzzled you relating to Miss Springer, anything Miss Springer may have said or someone else may have said of her that strikes you as at all significant, I should like to know it. You can come to me in my sitting-room any time this evening.'

'Oh,' Julia Upjohn sighed, as the girls filed out, 'how I wish we *did* know something! But we don't, do we, Jennifer?'

'No,' said Jennifer, 'of course we don't.'

'Miss Springer always seemed so very ordinary,' said Julia sadly, 'much too ordinary to get killed in a mysterious way.'

'I don't suppose it was so mysterious,' said Jennifer. 'Just a burglar.'

'Stealing our tennis racquets, I suppose,' said Julia with sarcasm.

'Perhaps someone was blackmailing her,' suggested one of the other girls hopefully.

'What about?' said Jennifer.

But nobody could think of any reason for blackmailing Miss Springer.

V

Inspector Kelsey started his interviewing of the staff with Miss Vansittart. A handsome woman, he thought, summing her up. Possibly forty or a little over; tall, well-built, grey hair tastefully arranged. She had dignity and composure, with a certain sense, he thought, of her own importance. She reminded him a little of Miss Bulstrode herself: she was the schoolmistress type all right. All the same, he reflected, Miss Bulstrode had something that Miss Vansittart had not. Miss Bulstrode had a quality of unexpectedness. He did not feel that Miss Vansittart would ever be unexpected.

Question and answer followed routine. In effect, Miss Vansittart had seen nothing, had noticed nothing, had heard nothing. Miss Springer had been excellent at her job. Yes, her manner had perhaps been a trifle brusque, but not, she thought, unduly so. She had not perhaps had a very attractive personality but that was really not a necessity in a Games Mistress. It was better, in fact, *not* to have mistresses who had attractive personalities. It did not do to let the girls get emotional about the mistresses. Miss Vansittart, having contributed nothing of value, made her exit.

'See no evil, hear no evil, think no evil. Same like the monkeys,' observed Sergeant Percy Bond, who was assisting Inspector Kelsey in his task.

Kelsey grinned. 'That's about right, Percy,' he said.

'There's something about schoolmistresses that gives me the hump,' said Sergeant Bond. 'Had a terror of them ever since I was a kid. Knew one that was a holy terror. So upstage and la-di-da you never knew what she was trying to teach you.'

The next mistress to appear was Eileen Rich. Ugly as sin was Inspector Kelsey's first reaction. Then he qualified it; she had a certain attraction. He started his routine questions, but the answers were not quite so routine as he had expected. After saying No, she had not heard or noticed anything special that anyone else had said about Miss Springer or that Miss Springer herself had said, Eileen Rich's next answer was not what he anticipated. He had asked:

'There was no one as far as you know who had a personal grudge against her?'

'Oh no,' said Eileen Rich quickly. 'One couldn't have. I think that was her tragedy, you know. That she wasn't a person one could ever hate.'

'Now just what do you mean by that, Miss Rich?'

'I mean she wasn't a person one could ever have wanted to destroy. Everything she did and was, was on the surface. She annoyed people. They often had sharp words with her, but it didn't mean anything. Not anything deep. I'm sure she wasn't killed for *herself*, if you know what I mean.'

'I'm not quite sure that I do, Miss Rich.'

'I mean if you had something like a bank robbery, she might quite easily be the cashier that gets shot, but it would be as a cashier, not as Grace Springer. Nobody would love her or hate her enough to want to do away with her. I think she probably felt that without thinking about it, and that's what made her so officious. About finding fault, you know, and enforcing rules and finding out what people were doing that they shouldn't be doing, and showing them up.'

'Snooping?' asked Kelsey.

'No, not exactly snooping.' Eileen Rich considered. 'She wouldn't tiptoe round on sneakers or anything of that kind. But if she found something going on that she didn't understand she'd be quite determined to get to the bottom of it. And she *would* get to the bottom of it.'

'I see.' He paused a moment. 'You didn't like her yourself much, did you, Miss Rich?'

'I don't think I ever thought about her. She was just the Games Mistress. Oh! What a horrible thing that is to say about anybody! Just this – just that! But that's how *she* felt about her job. It was a job that she took pride in doing well. She didn't find it fun. She wasn't keen when she found a girl who might be really good at tennis, or really fine at some form of athletics. She didn't rejoice in it or triumph.'

Kelsey looked at her curiously. An odd young woman, this, he thought.

'You seem to have your ideas on most things, Miss Rich,' he said.

'Yes. Yes, I suppose I do.'

'How long have you been at Meadowbank?'

'Just over a year and a half.'

'There's never been any trouble before?'

'At Meadowbank?' She sounded startled.

'Yes.'

'Oh no. Everything's been quite all right until this term.'

Kelsey pounced.

'What's been wrong this term? You don't mean the murder, do you? You mean something else –'

'I don't –' she stopped – 'Yes, perhaps I do – but it's all very nebulous.'

'Go on.'

'Miss Bulstrode's not been happy lately,' said Eileen slowly. 'That's one thing. You wouldn't know it. I don't think anybody else has even noticed it. But I have. And she's not the only one who's unhappy. But that isn't what you mean, is it? That's just people's feelings. The kind of things you get when you're cooped up together and think about one thing too much. You meant, was there anything that didn't seem right just this term. That's it, isn't it?'

'Yes,' said Kelsey, looking at her curiously, 'yes, that's it. Well, what about it?'

'I think there *is* something wrong here,' said Eileen Rich slowly. 'It's as though there were someone among us who didn't belong.' She looked at him, smiled, almost laughed and said, 'Cat among the pigeons, that's the sort of feeling. We're the pigeons, all of us, and the cat's amongst us. But we can't *see* the cat.'

'That's very vague, Miss Rich.'

'Yes, isn't it? It sounds quite idiotic. I can hear that myself. What I really mean, I suppose, is that there has been something, some little thing that I've noticed but I don't know what I've noticed.'

'About anyone in particular?'

'No, I told you, that's just it. I don't know who it is. The only way I can sum it up is to say that there's *someone* here, who's – somehow – wrong! There's someone here – I don't know who – who makes me uncomfortable. Not when I'm looking at her but when she's looking at me because it's when she's looking at me that it shows, whatever it is. Oh, I'm getting more incoherent than ever. And anyway, it's only a feeling. It's not what you want. It isn't evidence.'

'No,' said Kelsey, 'it isn't evidence. Not yet. But it's interesting, and if your feeling gets any more definite, Miss Rich, I'd be glad to hear about it.'

She nodded. 'Yes,' she said, 'because it's serious, isn't it? I mean, someone's been killed – we don't know why – and the killer may be miles away, or, on the other hand, the killer may be here in the school. And if so that pistol or revolver or whatever it is, must be here too. That's not a very nice thought, is it?'

She went out with a slight nod. Sergeant Bond said,

'Crackers – or don't you think so?'

'No,' said Kelsey, 'I don't think she's crackers. I think she's what's called a sensitive. You know, like the people who know when there's a cat in the room long before they see it. If she'd been born in an African tribe she might have been a witch doctor.'

'They go round smelling out evil, don't they?' said Sergeant Bond.

'That's right, Percy,' said Kelsey. 'And that's exactly what I'm trying to do myself. Nobody's come across with any concrete facts so I've got to go about smelling out things. We'll have the French woman next.'

CHAPTER 10

FANTASTIC STORY

Mademoiselle Angèle Blanche was thirty-five at a guess. No make-up, dark brown hair arranged neatly but unbecomingly. A severe coat and skirt.

It was Mademoiselle Blanche's first term at Meadowbank, she explained. She was not sure that she wished to remain for a further term.

'It is not nice to be in a school where murders take place,' she said disapprovingly.

Also, there did not seem to be burglar alarms anywhere in the house – that was dangerous.

'There's nothing of any great value, Mademoiselle Blanche, to attract burglars.'

Mademoiselle Blanche shrugged her shoulders.

'How does one know? These girls who come here, some of them have very rich fathers. They may have something with them of great value. A burglar knows about that, perhaps, and he comes here because he thinks this is an easy place to steal it.'

'If a girl had something of value with her it wouldn't be in the gymnasium.'

'How do you know?' said Mademoiselle. 'They have lockers there, do they not, the girls?'

'Only to keep their sports kit in, and things of that kind.'

'Ah yes, that is what is supposed. But a girl could hide anything in the toe of a gym shoe, or wrapped up in an old pullover or in a scarf.'

'What sort of thing, Mademoiselle Blanche?'

But Mademoiselle Blanche had no idea what sort of thing.

'Even the most indulgent fathers don't give their daughters diamond necklaces to take to school,' the Inspector said.

Again Mademoiselle Blanche shrugged her shoulders.

'Perhaps it is something of a different kind of value – a scarab, say, or something that a collector would give a lot of money for. One of the girls has a father who is an archaeologist.'

Kelsey smiled. 'I don't really think that's likely, you know, Mademoiselle Blanche.'

She shrugged her shoulders. 'Oh well, I only make the suggestion.'

'Have you taught in any other English schools, Mademoiselle Blanche?'

'One in the north of England some time ago. Mostly I have taught in Switzerland and in France. Also in Germany. I think I will come to England to improve my English. I have a friend here. She went sick and she told me I could take her position here as Miss Bulstrode would be glad to find somebody quickly. So I came. But I do not like it very much. As I tell you, I do not think I shall stay.'

'Why don't you like it?' Kelsey persisted.

'I do not like places where there are shootings,' said Mademoiselle Blanche. 'And the children, they are not respectful.'

'They are not quite children, are they?'

'Some of them behave like babies, some of them might be

twenty-five. There are all kinds here. They have much freedom. I prefer an establishment with more routine.'

'Did you know Miss Springer well?'

'I knew her practically not at all. She had bad manners and I conversed with her as little as possible. She was all bones and freckles and a loud ugly voice. She was like caricatures of Englishwomen. She was rude to me often and I did not like it.'

'What was she rude to you about?'

'She did not like me coming to her Sports Pavilion. That seems to be how she feels about it – or felt about it, I mean – that it was *her* Sports Pavilion! I go there one day because I am interested. I have not been in it before and it is a new building. It is very well arranged and planned and I am just looking round. Then Miss Springer she comes and says "What are you doing here? This is no business of yours to be in here." She says that to me – *me*, a mistress in the school! What does she think I am, a pupil?'

'Yes, yes, very irritating, I'm sure,' said Kelsey, soothingly.

'The manners of a pig, that is what she had. And then she calls out "Do not go away with the key in your hand." She upset me. When I pull the door open the key fell out and I pick it up. I forget to put it back, because she has offended me. And then she shouts after me as though she thinks I was meaning to steal it. *Her* key, I suppose, as well as *her* Sports Pavilion.'

'That seems a little odd, doesn't it?' said Kelsey. 'That she should feel like that about the gymnasium, I mean. As though it were her private property, as though she were afraid of people finding something she had hidden there.' He made the faint feeler tentatively, but Angèle Blanche merely laughed.

'Hide something there – what could you hide in a place like that? Do you think she hides her love letters there? I am sure she has never had a love letter written to her! The other mistresses, they are at least polite. Miss Chadwick, she is old-fashioned and she fusses. Miss Vansittart, she is very nice, *grande dame*, sympathetic. Miss Rich, she is a little crazy I think, but friendly. And the younger mistresses are quite pleasant.'

Angèle Blanche was dismissed after a few more unimportant questions.

'Touchy,' said Bond. 'All the French are touchy.'

'All the same, it's interesting,' said Kelsey. 'Miss Springer didn't like people prowling about *her* gymnasium – Sports Pavilion – I don't know what to call the thing. Now *why*?'

'Perhaps she thought the Frenchwoman was spying on her,' suggested Bond.

'Well, but *why* should she think so? I mean, ought it to have mattered to her that Angèle Blanche should spy on her unless there was something she was afraid of Angèle Blanche finding out?

'Who have we got left?' he added.

'The two junior mistresses, Miss Blake and Miss Rowan, and Miss Bulstrode's secretary.'

Miss Blake was young and earnest with a round good-natured face. She taught Botany and Physics. She had nothing much to say that could help. She had seen very little of Miss Springer and had no idea of what could have led to her death.

Miss Rowan, as befitted one who held a degree in psychology, had views to express. It was highly probable, she said, that Miss Springer had committed suicide.

Inspector Kelsey raised his eyebrows.

'Why should she? Was she unhappy in any way?'

'She was aggressive,' said Miss Rowan, leaning forward and peering eagerly through her thick lenses. 'Very aggressive. I consider that significant. It was a defence mechanism, to conceal a feeling of inferiority.'

'Everything I've heard so far,' said Inspector Kelsey, 'points to her being very sure of herself.'

'*Too* sure of herself,' said Miss Rowan darkly. 'And several of the things she said bear out my assumption.'

'Such as?'

'She hinted at people being "not what they seemed". She mentioned that at the last school where she was employed, she had "unmasked" someone. The Headmistress, however, had been prejudiced, and refused to listen to what she had found out. Several of the other mistresses, too, had been what she called "against her".

'You see what that means, Inspector?' Miss Rowan nearly fell off her chair as she leaned forward excitedly. Strands of lank dark hair fell forward across her face. 'The beginnings of a persecution complex.'

Inspector Kelsey said politely that Miss Rowan might be correct in her assumptions, but that he couldn't accept the theory of suicide, unless Miss Rowan could explain how Miss Springer had managed to shoot herself from a distance of at least four feet away, and had also been able to make the pistol disappear into thin air afterwards.

Miss Rowan retorted acidly that the police were well known to be prejudiced against psychology.

She then gave place to Ann Shapland.

'Well, Miss Shapland,' said Inspector Kelsey, eyeing her neat and businesslike appearance with favour, 'what light can you throw upon this matter?'

'Absolutely none, I'm afraid. I've got my own sitting-room, and I don't see much of the staff. The whole thing's unbelievable.'

'In what way unbelievable?'

'Well, first that Miss Springer should get shot at all. Say somebody broke into the gymnasium and she went out to see who it was. That's all right, I suppose, but who'd want to break into the gymnasium?'

'Boys, perhaps, some young locals who wanted to help themselves to equipment of some kind or another, or who did it for a lark.'

'If that's so, I can't help feeling that what Miss Springer would have said was: "Now then, what are you doing here? Be off with you," and they'd have gone off.'

'Did it ever seem to you that Miss Springer adopted any particular attitude about the Sports Pavilion?'

Ann Shapland looked puzzled. 'Attitude?'

'I mean did she regard it as her special province and dislike other people going there?'

'Not that I know of. Why should she? It was just part of the school buildings.'

'You didn't notice anything yourself? You didn't find that if you went there she resented your presence – anything of that kind?'

Ann Shapland shook her head. 'I haven't been out there myself more than a couple of times. I haven't the time. I've gone out there once or twice with a message for one of the girls from Miss Bulstrode. That's all.'

'You didn't know that Miss Springer had objected to Mademoiselle Blanche being out there?'

'No, I didn't hear anything about that. Oh yes, I believe I did. Mademoiselle Blanche was rather cross about something one day, but then she is a little bit touchy, you know. There was something about her going into the drawing class one day and resenting something the drawing mistress said to her. Of course she hasn't really very much to do – Mademoiselle Blanche, I mean. She only teaches one subject – French, and she has a lot of time on her hands. I think –' she hesitated, 'I think she is perhaps rather an inquisitive person.'

'Do you think it likely that when she went into the Sports Pavilion she was poking about in any of the lockers?'

'The girls' lockers? Well, I wouldn't put it past her. She might amuse herself that way.'

'Does Miss Springer herself have a locker out there?'

'Yes, of course.'

'If Mademoiselle Blanche was caught poking about in Miss Springer's locker, then I can imagine that Miss Springer *would* be annoyed?'

'She certainly would!'

'You don't know anything about Miss Springer's private life?'

'I don't think anyone did,' said Ann. 'Did she have one, I wonder?'

'And there's nothing else – nothing connected with the Sports Pavilion, for instance, that you haven't told me?'

'Well –' Ann hesitated.

'Yes, Miss Shapland, let's have it.'

'It's nothing really,' said Ann slowly. 'But one of the gardeners – not Briggs, the young one. I saw him come out of the Sports Pavilion one day, and he had no business to be in there at all. Of course it was probably just curiosity on his part – or perhaps an excuse to slack off a bit from work – he was supposed to be nailing down the wire on the tennis court. I don't suppose really there's anything in it.'

'Still, you remembered it,' Kelsey pointed out. 'Now why?'

'I think –' she frowned. 'Yes, because his manner was a little odd. Defiant. And – he sneered at all the money that was spent here on the girls.'

'That sort of attitude . . . I see.'

'I don't suppose there's really anything in it.'

'Probably not – but I'll make a note of it, all the same.'

'Round and round the mulberry bush,' said Bond when Ann Shapland had gone. 'Same thing over and over again! For goodness' sake let's hope we get something out of the servants.'

But they got very little out of the servants.

'It's no use asking me anything, young man,' said Mrs Gibbons, the cook. 'For one thing I can't hear what you say, and for another I don't know a thing. I went to sleep last night and I slept unusually heavy. Never heard anything of all the excitement there was. Nobody woke me up and told me anything about it.' She sounded injured. 'It wasn't until this morning I heard.'

Kelsey shouted a few questions and got a few answers that told him nothing.

Miss Springer had come new this term, and she wasn't as much liked as Miss Jones who'd held the post before her. Miss Shapland was new, too, but she was a nice young lady, Mademoiselle Blanche was like all the Frenchies – thought the other mistresses were against her and let the young ladies treat her something shocking in class. 'Not a one for crying, though,' Mrs Gibbons admitted. 'Some schools I've been in the French mistresses used to cry something awful!'

Most of the domestic staff were dailies. There was only one other maid who slept in the house, and she proved equally uninformative, though able to hear what was said to her. She couldn't say, she was sure. She didn't know nothing. Miss Springer was a bit sharp in her manner. She didn't know nothing about the Sports Pavilion nor what was kept there, and she'd never seen nothing like a pistol nowhere.

This negative spate of information was interrupted by Miss Bulstrode. 'One of the girls would like to speak to you, Inspector Kelsey,' she said.

Kelsey looked up sharply. 'Indeed? She knows something?'

'As to that I'm rather doubtful,' said Miss Bulstrode, 'but you had better talk to her yourself. She is one of our foreign girls. Princess Shaista – niece of the Emir Ibrahim. She is inclined to think, perhaps, that she is of rather more importance than she is. You understand?'

Kelsey nodded comprehendingly. Then Miss Bulstrode went out and a slight dark girl of middle height came in.

She looked at them, almond eyed and demure.

'You are the police?'

'Yes,' said Kelsey smiling, 'we are the police. Will you sit down and tell me what you know about Miss Springer?'

'Yes, I will tell you.'

She sat down, leaned forward, and lowered her voice dramatically.

'There have been people watching this place. Oh, they do not show themselves clearly, but they are there!'

She nodded her head significantly.

Inspector Kelsey thought that he understood what Miss Bulstrode had meant. This girl was dramatizing herself – and enjoying it.

'And why should they be watching the school?'

'Because of *me*! They want to kidnap me.'

Whatever Kelsey had expected, it was not this. His eyebrows rose.

'Why should they want to kidnap you?'

'To hold me to ransom, of course. Then they would make my relations pay much money.'

'Er – well – perhaps,' said Kelsey dubiously. 'But – er – supposing this is so, what has it got to do with the death of Miss Springer?'

'She must have found out about them,' said Shaista. 'Perhaps she told them she had found out something. Perhaps she threatened them. Then perhaps they promised to pay her money if she would say nothing. And she believed them. So she goes out to the Sports Pavilion where they say they will pay her the money, and then they shoot her.'

'But surely Miss Springer would never have accepted blackmail money?'

'Do you think it is such fun to be a school teacher – to be a teacher of gymnastics?' Shaista was scornful. 'Do you not think it would be nice instead to have money, to travel, to do what you want? Especially someone like Miss Springer who is not beautiful, at whom men do not even look! Do you not think that money would attract her more than it would attract other people?'

'Well – er –' said Inspector Kelsey, 'I don't know quite what to say.' He had not had this point of view presented to him before.

'This is just – er – your own idea?' he said. 'Miss Springer never said anything to you?'

'Miss Springer never said anything except "Stretch and bend", and "Faster", and "Don't slack",' said Shaista with resentment.

'Yes – quite so. Well, don't you think you may have imagined all this about kidnapping?'

Shaista was immediately much annoyed.

'You do not understand *at all*! My cousin was Prince Ali Yusuf of Ramat. He was killed in a revolution, or at least in fleeing from a revolution. It was understood that when I grew up I should marry him. So you see I am an important person. It may be perhaps the Communists who come here. Perhaps it is not to kidnap. Perhaps they intend to assassinate me.'

Inspector Kelsey looked still more incredulous.

'That's rather far fetched, isn't it?'

'You think such things could not happen? I say they can. They are very very wicked, the Communists! Everybody knows that.'

As he still looked dubious, she went on:

'Perhaps they think I know where the jewels are!'

'What jewels?'

'My cousin had jewels. So had his father. My family always has a hoard of jewels. For emergencies, you comprehend.'

She made it sound very matter of fact.

Kelsey stared at her.

'But what has all this got to do with you – or with Miss Springer?'

'But I already tell you! They think, perhaps, I know where the jewels are. So they will take me prisoner and force me to speak.'

'*Do* you know where the jewels are?'

'No, of course I do not know. They disappeared in the Revolution. Perhaps the wicked Communists take them. But again, perhaps not.'

'Who do they belong to?'

'Now my cousin is dead, they belong to me. No men in his family any more. His aunt, my mother, is dead. He would want them to belong to me. If he were not dead, I marry him.'

'That was the arrangement?'

'I have to marry him. He is my cousin, you see.'

'And you would have got the jewels when you married him?'

'No, I would have had new jewels. From Cartier in Paris. These others would still be kept for emergencies.'

Inspector Kelsey blinked, letting this Oriental insurance scheme for emergencies sink into his consciousness.

Shaista was racing on with great animation.

'I think that is what happens. Somebody gets the jewels out of Ramat. Perhaps good person, perhaps bad. Good person would bring them to me, would say: "These are yours," and I should reward him.'

She nodded her head regally, playing the part.

Quite a little actress, thought the Inspector.

'But if it was a bad person, he would keep the jewels and sell them. Or he would come to me and say: "What will you give me as a reward if I bring them to you?" And if it worth while, he brings – but if not, then not!'

'But in actual fact, nobody has said anything at all to you?'

'No,' admitted Shaista.

Inspector Kelsey made up his mind.

'I think, you know,' he said pleasantly, 'that you're really talking a lot of nonsense.'

Shaista flashed a furious glance at him.

'I tell you what I know, that is all,' she said sulkily.

'Yes – well, it's very kind of you, and I'll bear it in mind.'

He got up and opened the door for her to go out.

'The Arabian Nights aren't in it,' he said, as he returned to the table. 'Kidnapping and fabulous jewels! What next?'

CHAPTER 11

CONFERENCE

When Inspector Kelsey returned to the station, the sergeant on duty said:

'We've got Adam Goodman here, waiting, sir.'

'Adam Goodman? Oh yes. The gardener.'

A young man had risen respectfully to his feet. He was tall, dark and good-looking. He wore stained corduroy trousers loosely held up by an aged belt, and an open-necked shirt of very bright blue.

'You wanted to see me, I hear.'

His voice was rough, and as that of so many young men of today, slightly truculent.

Kelsey said merely:

'Yes, come into my room.'

'I don't know anything about the murder,' said Adam Goodman sulkily. 'It's nothing to do with me. I was at home and in bed last night.'

Kelsey merely nodded noncommittally.

He sat down at his desk, and motioned to the young man to take the chair opposite. A young policeman in plain clothes had followed the two men in unobtrusively and sat down a little distance away.

'Now then,' said Kelsey. 'You're Goodman –' he looked at a note on his desk – 'Adam Goodman.'

'That's right, sir. But first, I'd like to show you this.'

Adam's manner had changed. There was no truculence or sulkiness in it now. It was quiet and deferential. He took something from his pocket and passed it across the desk. Inspector Kelsey's eyebrows rose very slightly as he studied it. Then he raised his head.

'I shan't need you, Barbar,' he said.

The discreet young policeman got up and went out. He managed not to look surprised, but he was.

'Ah,' said Kelsey. He looked across at Adam with speculative interest. 'So that's who you are? And what the hell, I'd like to know, are you –'

'Doing in a girls' school?' the young man finished for him. His voice was still deferential, but he grinned in spite of himself. 'It's certainly the first time I've had an assignment of that kind. Don't I look like a gardener?'

'Not around these parts. Gardeners are usually rather ancient. Do you know anything about gardening?'

'Quite a lot. I've got one of these gardening mothers. England's speciality. She's seen to it that I'm a worthy assistant to her.'

'And what exactly is going on at Meadowbank – to bring you on the scene?'

'We don't know, actually, that there's anything going on at Meadowbank. My assignment is in the nature of a watching brief. Or was – until last night. Murder of a Games Mistress. Not quite in the school's curriculum.'

'It could happen,' said Inspector Kelsey. He sighed. 'Anything could happen – anywhere. I've learnt that. But I'll admit that it's a little off the beaten track. What's behind all this?'

Adam told him. Kelsey listened with interest.

'I did that girl an injustice,' he remarked – 'But you'll admit it sounds too fantastic to be true. Jewels worth between half a million and a million pounds? Who do you say they belong to?'

'That's a very pretty question. To answer it, you'd have to have a gaggle of international lawyers on the job – and they'd probably disagree. You could argue the case a lot of ways. They belonged, three months ago, to His Highness Prince Ali Yusuf of Ramat. But now? If they'd turned up in Ramat they'd have been the property of the present Government, they'd have made sure of that. Ali Yusuf may have willed them to someone. A lot would then depend on where the will was executed and whether it could be proved. They may belong to his family. But the real essence of the matter is, that if you or I happened to pick them up in the street and put them in our pockets, they would for all practical purposes belong to us. That is, I doubt if any legal machine exists that could get them away from us. They could try, of course, but the intricacies of international law are quite incredible . . .'

'You mean that, practically speaking, it's findings are keepings?' asked Inspector Kelsey. He shook his head disapprovingly. 'That's not very nice,' he said primly.

'No,' said Adam firmly. 'It's not very nice. There's more than one lot after them, too. None of them scrupulous. Word's got around, you see. It may be a rumour, it may be true, but the story is that they were got out of Ramat just before the bust up. There are a dozen different tales of *how*.'

'But why Meadowbank? Because of little Princess Butter-won't-melt-in-my-mouth?'

'Princess Shaista, first cousin of Ali Yusuf. Yes. Someone may try and deliver the goods to her or communicate with her. There are some questionable characters from our point of view hanging about the neighbourhood. A Mrs Kolinsky, for instance, staying at the Grand Hotel. Quite a prominent member of what one might describe as International Riff Raff Ltd. Nothing in *your* line, always strictly within the law, all perfectly respectable, but a grand picker-up of useful information. Then there's a woman who was out in Ramat dancing in cabaret there. She's reported to have been working for a certain foreign government. Where she is now we don't know, we don't even know what she looks like, but there's a rumour that she *might* be in this part of the world. Looks, doesn't it, as though it were all centring round Meadowbank? And last night, Miss Springer gets herself killed.'

Kelsey nodded thoughtfully.

'Proper mix up,' he observed. He struggled a moment with his feelings. 'You see this sort of thing on the telly . . . far fetched – that's what you think . . . can't really happen. And it doesn't – not in the normal course of events.'

'Secret agents, robbery, violence, murder, double crossing,' agreed Adam. 'All preposterous – but that side of life exists.'

'But not at Meadowbank!'

The words were wrung from Inspector Kelsey.

'I perceive your point,' said Adam. 'Lese-majesty.'

There was a silence, and then Inspector Kelsey asked:

'What do *you* think happened last night?'

Adam took his time, then he said slowly:

'Springer was in the Sports Pavilion – in the middle of the night. Why? We've got to start there. It's no good asking ourselves who killed her until we've made up our minds why she was there, in the Sports Pavilion at that time of night. We can say that in spite of her blameless and athletic life she wasn't sleeping well, and got up and looked out of her window and saw a light in the Sports Pavilion – her window does look out that way?'

Kelsey nodded.

'Being a tough and fearless young woman, she went out to investigate. She disturbed someone there who was – doing what? We don't know. But it was someone desperate enough to shoot her dead.'

Again Kelsey nodded.

'That's the way we've been looking at it,' he said. 'But your last point had me worried all along. You don't shoot to kill – and come prepared to do so, unless –'

'Unless you're after something big? Agreed! Well, that's the case of what we might call Innocent Springer – shot down in the performance of duty. But there's another possibility. Springer, as a result of private information, gets a job at Meadowbank or is detailed for it by her bosses – because of her qualification – She waits until a suitable night, then slips out to the Sports Pavilion (again our stumbling-block of a question – *why*?) – Somebody is following her – or waiting for her – someone who carries a pistol and is prepared to use it . . . But again – why? What for? In fact, what the devil is there about the Sports Pavilion? It's not the sort of place that one can imagine hiding anything.'

'There wasn't anything hidden there, I can tell you that. We went through it with a tooth comb – the girls' lockers, Miss Springer's ditto. Sports equipment of various kinds, all normal and accounted for. *And* a brand new building! There wasn't anything there in the nature of jewellery.'

'Whatever it was it could have been removed, of course. By the murderer,' said Adam. 'The other possibility is that the Sports Pavilion was simply used as a rendezvous – by Miss Springer or by someone else. It's quite a handy place for that. A reasonable distance from the house. Not too far. And if anyone was noticed going out there, a simple answer would be that whoever it was thought they had seen a light, etc., etc. Let's say that Miss Springer went out to meet someone – there was a disagreement and she got shot. Or, a variation, Miss Springer noticed someone leaving the house, followed that someone, intruded upon something she wasn't meant to see or hear.'

'I never met her alive,' said Kelsey, 'but from the way everyone speaks of her, I get the impression that she might have been a nosey woman.'

'I think that's really the most probable explanation,' agreed Adam. 'Curiosity killed the cat. Yes, I think that's the way the Sports Pavilion comes into it.'

'But if it was a rendezvous, then –' Kelsey paused.

Adam nodded vigorously.

'Yes. It looks as though there is someone in the school who merits our very close attention. Cat among the pigeons, in fact.'

'Cat among the pigeons,' said Kelsey, struck by the phrase.

'Miss Rich, one of the mistresses, said something like that today.'

He reflected a moment or two.

'There were three newcomers to the staff this term,' he said. 'Shapland, the secretary. Blanche, the French Mistress, and, of course, Miss Springer herself. She's dead and out of it. If there is a cat among the pigeons, it would seem that one of the other two would be the most likely bet.' He looked towards Adam. 'Any ideas, as between the two of them?'

Adam considered.

'I caught Mademoiselle Blanche coming out of the Sports Pavilion one day. She had a guilty look. As though she'd been doing something she ought not to have done. All the same, on the whole – I think I'd plump for the other. For Shapland. She's a cool customer and she's got brains. I'd go into her antecedents rather carefully if I were you. What the devil are you laughing for?'

Kelsey was grinning.

'*She* was suspicious of *you*,' he said. 'Caught *you* coming out of the Sports Pavilion – and thought there was something odd about your manner!'

'Well, I'm damned!' Adam was indignant. 'The cheek of her!'

Inspector Kelsey resumed his authoritative manner.

'The point is,' he said, 'that we think a lot of Meadowbank round these parts. It's a fine school. And Miss Bulstrode's a fine woman. The sooner we can get to the bottom of all this, the better for the school. We want to clear things up and give Meadowbank a clean bill of health.'

He paused, looking thoughtfully at Adam.

'I think,' he said, 'we'll have to tell Miss Bulstrode who you are. She'll keep her mouth shut – don't fear for that.'

Adam considered for a moment. Then he nodded his head.

'Yes,' he said. 'Under the circumstances, I think it's more or less inevitable.'

CHAPTER 12

NEW LAMPS FOR OLD

I

Miss Bulstrode had another faculty which demonstrated her superiority over most other women. She could listen.

She listened in silence to both Inspector Kelsey and Adam. She did not so much as raise an eyebrow. Then she uttered one word.

'Remarkable.'

It's you who are remarkable, thought Adam, but he did not say so aloud.

'Well,' said Miss Bulstrode, coming as was habitual to her straight to the point. 'What do you want me to do?'

Inspector Kelsey cleared his throat.

'It's like this,' he said. 'We felt that you ought to be fully informed – for the sake of the school.'

Miss Bulstrode nodded.

'Naturally,' she said, 'the school is my first concern. It has to be. I am responsible for the care and safety of my pupils – and in a lesser degree for that of my staff. And I would like to add now that if there can be as little publicity as possible about Miss Springer's death – the better it will be for me. This is a purely selfish point of view – though I think my school is important in itself – not only to me. And I quite realize that if full publicity is necessary for you, then you will have to go ahead. But is it?'

'No,' said Inspector Kelsey. 'In this case I should say the less publicity the better. The inquest will be adjourned and we'll let it get about that we think it was a local affair. Young thugs – or juvenile delinquents, as we have to call them nowadays – out with guns amongst them, trigger happy. It's usually flick knives, but some of these boys do get hold of guns. Miss Springer surprised them. They shot her. That's what I should like to let it go at – then we can get to work quiet-like. Not more than can be helped in the Press. But of course, Meadowbank's famous. It's news. And murder at Meadowbank will be hot news.'

'I think I can help you there,' said Miss Bulstrode crisply, 'I am not without influence in high places.' She smiled and reeled off a few names. These included the Home Secretary, two Press barons, a bishop and the Minister of Education. 'I'll do what I can.' She looked at Adam. 'You agree?'

Adam spoke quickly.

'Yes, indeed. We always like things nice and quiet.'

'Are you continuing to be my gardener?' inquired Miss Bulstrode.

'If you don't object. It puts me right where I want to be. And I can keep an eye on things.'

This time Miss Bulstrode's eyebrows did rise.

'I hope you're not expecting any more murders?'

'No, no.'

'I'm glad of that. I doubt if any school could survive two murders in one term.'

She turned to Kelsey.

'Have you people finished with the Sports Pavilion? It's awkward if we can't use it.'

'We've finished with it. Clean as a whistle – from our point of view, I mean. For whatever reason the murder was committed – there's nothing there now to help us. It's just a Sports Pavilion with the usual equipment.'

'Nothing in the girls' lockers?'

Inspector Kelsey smiled.

'Well – this and that – copy of a book – French – called *Candide* – with – er – illustrations. Expensive book.'

'Ah,' said Miss Bulstrode. 'So that's where she keeps it! Giselle d'Aubray, I suppose?'

Kelsey's respect for Miss Bulstrode rose.

'You don't miss much, M'am,' he said.

'She won't come to harm with *Candide*,' said Miss Bulstrode. 'It's a classic. Some forms of pornography I do confiscate. Now I come back to my first question. You have relieved my mind about the publicity connected with the school. Can the school help you in any way? Can *I* help you?'

'I don't think so, at the moment. The only thing I can ask is, has anything caused you uneasiness this term? Any incident? Or any person?'

Miss Bulstrode was silent for a moment or two. Then she said slowly:

'The answer, literally, is: I don't know.'

Adam said quickly:

'You've got a feeling that something's wrong?'

'Yes – just that. It's not definite. I can't put my finger on any person, or any incident – unless –'

She was silent for a moment, then she said:

'I feel – I felt at the time – that I'd missed something that I ought not to have missed. Let me explain.'

She recited briefly the little incident of Mrs Upjohn and the distressing and unexpected arrival of Lady Veronica.

Adam was interested.

'Let me get this clear, Miss Bulstrode. Mrs Upjohn, looking out of the window, this front window that gives on the drive, recognized someone. There's nothing in that. You have over a hundred pupils and nothing is more likely than for Mrs Upjohn to see some parent or relation that she knew. But you are definitely of the opinion that she was *astonished* to recognize that person – in fact, that it was someone whom she would *not* have expected to see at Meadowbank?'

'Yes, that was exactly the impression I got.'

'And then through the window looking in the opposite direction you saw one of the pupils' mothers, in a state of intoxication, and that completely distracted your mind from what Mrs Upjohn was saying?'

Miss Bulstrode nodded.

'She was talking for some minutes?'

'Yes.'

'And when your attention did return to her, she was speaking of espionage, of Intelligence work she had done in the war before she married?'

'Yes.'

'It might tie up,' said Adam thoughtfully. 'Someone she had known in her war days. A parent or relation of one of your pupils, or it could have been a member of your teaching staff.'

'Hardly a member of my staff,' objected Miss Bulstrode.

'It's possible.'

'We'd better get in touch with Mrs Upjohn,' said Kelsey. 'As soon as possible. You have her address, Miss Bulstrode?'

'Of course. But I believe she is abroad at the moment. Wait – I will find out.'

She pressed her desk buzzer twice, then went impatiently to the door and called to a girl who was passing.

'Find Julia Upjohn for me, will you, Paula?'

'Yes, Miss Bulstrode.'

'I'd better go before the girl comes,' Adam said. 'It wouldn't be natural for me to assist in the inquiries the Inspector is making. Ostensibly he's called me in here to get the low down on me. Having satisfied himself that he's got nothing on me for the moment, he now tells me to take myself off.'

'Take yourself off and remember I've got my eye on you!' growled Kelsey with a grin.

'By the way,' said Adam, addressing Miss Bulstrode as he paused by the door, 'will it be all right with you if I slightly abuse my position here? If I get, shall we say, a little too friendly with some members of your staff?'

'With which members of my staff?'

'Well – Mademoiselle Blanche, for instance.'

'Mademoiselle Blanche? You think that she –?'

'I think she's rather bored here.'

'Ah!' Miss Bulstrode looked rather grim. 'Perhaps you're right. Anyone else?'

'I shall have a good try all round,' said Adam cheerfully. 'If you should find that some of your girls are being rather silly, and slipping off to assignations in the garden, please believe that my intentions are strictly sleuthial – if there is such a word.'

'You think the girls are likely to know something?'

'Everybody always knows something,' said Adam, 'even if it's something they don't know they know.'

'You may be right.'

There was a knock on the door, and Miss Bulstrode called – 'Come in.'

Julia Upjohn appeared, very much out of breath.

'Come in, Julia.'

Inspector Kelsey growled.

'You can go now, Goodman. Take yourself off and get on with your work.'

'I've told you I don't know a thing about anything,' said Adam sulkily. He went out, muttering 'Blooming Gestapo.'

'I'm sorry I'm so out of breath, Miss Bulstrode,' apologized Julia. 'I've run all the way from the tennis courts.'

'That's quite all right. I just wanted to ask you your mother's address – that is, where can I get in touch with her?'

'Oh! You'll have to write to Aunt Isabel. Mother's abroad.'

'I have your aunt's address. But I need to get in touch with your mother personally.'

'I don't see how you can,' said Julia, frowning. 'Mother's gone to Anatolia on a bus.'

'On a *bus*?' said Miss Bulstrode, taken aback.

Julia nodded vigorously.

'She likes that sort of thing,' she explained. 'And of course it's frightfully cheap. A bit uncomfortable, but Mummy doesn't mind that. Roughly, I should think she'd fetch up in Van in about three weeks or so.'

'I see – yes. Tell me, Julia, did your mother ever mention to you seeing someone here whom she'd known in her war service days?'

'No, Miss Bulstrode, I don't think so. No, I'm sure she didn't.'

'Your mother did Intelligence work, didn't she?'

'Oh, yes. Mummy seems to have loved it. Not that it sounds really exciting to me. She never blew up anything. Or got caught by the Gestapo. Or had her toe nails pulled out. Or anything like that. She worked in Switzerland, I think – or was it Portugal?'

Julia added apologetically: 'One gets rather bored with all that old war stuff; and I'm afraid I don't always listen properly.'

'Well, thank you, Julia. That's all.'

'Really!' said Miss Bulstrode, when Julia had departed. 'Gone to Anatolia on a bus! The child said it exactly as though she were saying her mother had taken a 73 bus to Marshall and Snelgrove's.'

II

Jennifer walked away from the tennis courts rather moodily, swishing her racquet. The amount of double faults she had served this morning depressed her. Not, of course, that you could get a hard serve with this racquet, anyway. But she seemed to have lost control of her service lately. Her backhand, however, had definitely improved. Springer's coaching had been helpful. In many ways it was a pity that Springer was dead.

Jennifer took tennis very seriously. It was one of the things she thought about.

'Excuse me –'

Jennifer looked up, startled. A well-dressed woman with golden hair, carrying a long flat parcel, was standing a few feet away from her on the path. Jennifer wondered why on earth she hadn't seen the woman coming along towards her before. It did not occur to her that the woman might have been hidden behind a tree or in the rhododendron bushes and just stepped out of them. Such an idea would not have occurred to Jennifer, since why should a woman hide behind rhododendron bushes and suddenly step out of them?

Speaking with a slightly American accent the woman said, 'I wonder if you could tell me where I could find a girl called' – she consulted a piece of paper – 'Jennifer Sutcliffe.'

Jennifer was surprised.

'I'm Jennifer Sutcliffe.'

'Why! How ridiculous! That *is* a coincidence. That in a big school like this I should be looking for one girl and I should happen upon the girl herself to ask. And they say things like that don't happen.'

'I suppose they do happen sometimes,' said Jennifer, uninterested.

'I was coming down to lunch today with some friends down here,' went on the woman, 'and at a cocktail party yesterday I happened to mention I was coming, and your aunt – or was it your godmother? – I've got such a terrible memory. She told me her name and I've forgotten that too. But anyway, she said could I possibly call here and leave a new tennis racquet for you. She said you had been asking for one.'

Jennifer's face lit up. It seemed like a miracle, nothing less.

'It must have been my godmother, Mrs Campbell. I call her Aunt Gina. It wouldn't have been Aunt Rosamond. She never gives me anything but a mingy ten shillings at Christmas.'

'Yes, I remember now. That *was* the name. Campbell.'

The parcel was held out. Jennifer took it eagerly. It was quite loosely wrapped. Jennifer uttered an exclamation of pleasure as the racquet emerged from its coverings.

'Oh, it's smashing!' she exclaimed. 'A really *good* one. I've been longing for a new racquet – you can't play decently if you haven't got a decent racquet.'

'Why I guess that's so.'

'Thank you very much for bringing it,' said Jennifer gratefully.

'It was really no trouble. Only I confess I felt a little shy. Schools always make me feel shy. So many girls. Oh, by the way, I was asked to bring back your old racquet with me.'

She picked up the racquet Jennifer had dropped.

'Your aunt – no – godmother – said she would have it restrung. It needs it badly, doesn't it?'

'I don't think that it's really worth while,' said Jennifer, but without paying much attention.

She was still experimenting with the swing and balance of her new treasure.

'But an extra racquet is always useful,' said her new friend. 'Oh dear,' she glanced at her watch. 'It is much later than I thought. I must run.'

'Have you – do you want a taxi? I could telephone –'

'No, thank you, dear. My car is right by the gate. I left it there so that I shouldn't have to turn in a narrow space. Goodbye. So pleased to have met you. I hope you enjoy the racquet.'

She literally ran along the path towards the gate. Jennifer called after her once more. 'Thank you *very* much.'

Then, gloating, she went in search of Julia.

'Look,' she flourished the racquet dramatically.

'I say! Where did you get that?'

'My godmother sent it to me. Aunt Gina. She's not my aunt, but I call her that. She's frightfully rich. I expect Mummy told her about me grumbling about my racquet. It *is* smashing, isn't it? I *must* remember to write and thank her.'

'I should hope so!' said Julia virtuously.

'Well, you know how one does forget things sometimes. Even things you really mean to do. Look, Shaista,' she added as the latter girl came towards them. 'I've got a new racquet. Isn't it a beauty?'

'It must have been very expensive,' said Shaista, scanning it respectfully. 'I wish I could play tennis well.'

'You always run into the ball.'

'I never seem to know where the ball is going to come,' said Shaista vaguely. 'Before I go home, I must have some really good shorts made in London. Or a tennis dress like the American champion Ruth Allen wears. I think that is very smart. Perhaps I will have both,' she smiled in pleasurable anticipation.

'Shaista never thinks of anything except things to wear,' said Julia scornfully as the two friends passed on. 'Do you think *we* shall ever be like that?'

'I suppose so,' said Jennifer gloomily. 'It will be an awful bore.'

They entered the Sports Pavilion, now officially vacated by the police, and Jennifer put her racquet carefully into her press.

'Isn't it lovely?' she said, stroking it affectionately.

'What have you done with the old one?'

'Oh, she took it.'

'Who?'

'The woman who brought this. She'd met Aunt Gina at a cocktail party, and Aunt Gina asked her to bring me this as she was coming down here today, and Aunt Gina said to bring up my old one and she'd have it restrung.'

'Oh, I see . . .' But Julia was frowning.

'What did Bully want with you?' asked Jennifer.

'Bully? Oh, nothing really. Just Mummy's address. But she hasn't got one because she's on a bus. In Turkey somewhere. Jennifer – look here. Your racquet didn't *need* restringing.'

'Oh, it did, Julia. It was like a sponge.'

'I know. But it's *my* racquet really. I mean, we exchanged. It was *my* racquet that needed restringing. Yours, the one I've got now, *was* restrung. You said yourself your mother had had it restrung before you went abroad.'

'Yes, that's true.' Jennifer looked a little startled. 'Oh well, I suppose this woman – whoever she was – I ought to have asked her name, but I was so entranced – just saw that it needed restringing.'

'But you said that *she* said that it was your *Aunt Gina* who had said it needed restringing. And your Aunt Gina couldn't have thought it needed restringing if it didn't.'

'Oh, well –' Jennifer looked impatient. 'I suppose – I suppose –'

'You suppose what?'

'Perhaps Aunt Gina just thought that *if* I wanted a new racquet, it was because the old one wanted restringing. Anyway what does it matter?'

'I suppose it doesn't matter,' said Julia slowly. 'But I do think it's odd, Jennifer. It's like – like new lamps for old. Aladdin, you know.'

Jennifer giggled.

'Fancy rubbing my old racquet – your old racquet, I mean, and having a genie appear! If you rubbed a lamp and a genie did appear, what would you ask him for, Julia?'

'Lots of things,' breathed Julia ecstatically. 'A tape recorder, and an Alsatian – or perhaps a Great Dane, and a hundred thousand pounds, and a black satin party frock, and oh! lots of other things . . . What would you?'

'I don't really know,' said Jennifer. 'Now I've got this smashing new racquet, I don't really want anything else.'

CHAPTER 13

CATASTROPHE

I

The third weekend after the opening of term followed the usual plan. It was the first weekend on which parents were allowed to take pupils out. As a result Meadowbank was left almost deserted.

On this particular Sunday there would only be twenty girls left at the school itself for the midday meal. Some of the staff had weekend leave, returning late Sunday night or early Monday morning. On this particular occasion Miss Bulstrode herself was proposing to be absent for the weekend. This was unusual since it was not her habit to leave the school during term time. But she had her reasons. She was going to stay with the Duchess of Welsham at Welsington Abbey. The duchess had made a special point of it and had added that Henry Banks would be there. Henry Banks was the Chairman of the Governors. He was an important industrialist and he had been one of the original backers of the school. The invitation was therefore almost in the nature of a command. Not that Miss Bulstrode would have allowed herself to be commanded if she had not wished to do so. But as it happened, she welcomed the invitation gladly. She was by no means indifferent to duchesses and the Duchess of Welsham was an influential duchess, whose own daughters had been sent to Meadowbank. She was also particularly glad to have the opportunity of talking to Henry Banks on the subject of the school's future and also to put forward her own account of the recent tragic occurrence.

Owing to the influential connections at Meadowbank the murder of Miss Springer had been played down very tactfully in the Press. It had become a sad fatality rather than a mysterious murder. The impression was given, though not said, that possibly some young thugs had broken into the Sports Pavilion and that Miss Springer's death had been more accident than design. It was reported vaguely that several young men had been asked to come to the police station and 'assist the police'. Miss Bulstrode herself was anxious to mitigate any unpleasant impression that might have been given to these two influential patrons of the school. She knew that they wanted to discuss the veiled hint that she had thrown out of her coming retirement. Both the duchess and Henry Banks were anxious to persuade her to remain on. Now was the time, Miss Bulstrode felt, to push the claims of Eleanor Vansittart, to point out what a splendid person she was, and how well fitted to carry on the traditions of Meadowbank.

On Saturday morning Miss Bulstrode was just finishing off her correspondence with Ann Shapland when the telephone rang. Ann answered it.

'It's the Emir Ibrahim, Miss Bulstrode. He's arrived at Claridge's and would like to take Shaista out tomorrow.'

Miss Bulstrode took the receiver from her and had a brief conversation with the Emir's equerry. Shaista would be ready any time from eleven-thirty onwards on Sunday morning, she said. The girl must be back at the school by eight p.m.

She rang off and said:

'I wish Orientals sometimes gave you a little more warning. It has been arranged for Shaista to go out with Giselle d'Aubray tomorrow. Now that will have to be cancelled. Have we finished all the letters?'

'Yes, Miss Bulstrode.'

'Good, then I can go off with a clear conscience. Type them and send them off, and then you, too, are free for the weekend. I shan't want you until lunch time on Monday.'

'Thank you, Miss Bulstrode.'

'Enjoy yourself, my dear.'

'I'm going to,' said Ann.

'Young man?'

'Well – yes.' Ann coloured a little. 'Nothing serious, though.'

'Then there ought to be. If you're going to marry, don't leave it too late.'

'Oh this is only an old friend. Nothing exciting.'

'Excitement,' said Miss Bulstrode warningly, 'isn't always a good foundation for married life. Send Miss Chadwick to me, will you?'

Miss Chadwick bustled in.

'The Emir Ibrahim, Shaista's uncle, is taking her out tomorrow Chaddy. If he comes himself, tell him she is making good progress.'

'She's not very bright,' said Miss Chadwick.

'She's immature intellectually,' agreed Miss Bulstrode. 'But she has a remarkably mature mind in other ways. Sometimes, when you talk to her, she might be a woman of twenty-five. I suppose it's because of the sophisticated life she's led. Paris, Teheran, Cairo, Istanbul and all the rest of it. In this country we're inclined to keep our children too young. We account it a merit when we say: "She's still quite a child." It isn't a merit. It's a grave handicap in life.'

'I don't know that I quite agree with you there, dear,' said Miss Chadwick. 'I'll go now and tell Shaista about her uncle. You go away for your weekend and don't worry about anything.'

'Oh! I shan't,' said Miss Bulstrode. 'It's a good opportunity, really, for leaving Eleanor Vansittart in charge and seeing how she shapes. With you and her in charge nothing's likely to go wrong.'

'I hope not, indeed. I'll go and find Shaista.'

Shaista looked surprised and not at all pleased to hear that her uncle had arrived in London.

'He wants to take me out tomorrow?' she grumbled. 'But Miss Chadwick, it is all arranged that I go out with Giselle d'Aubray and her mother.'

'I'm afraid you'll have to do that another time.'

'But I would much rather go out with Giselle,' said Shaista crossly. 'My uncle is not at all amusing. He eats and then he grunts and it is all very dull.'

'You mustn't talk like that. It is impolite,' said Miss Chadwick. 'Your uncle is only in England for a week, I understand, and naturally he wants to see you.'

'Perhaps he has arranged a new marriage for me,' said Shaista, her face brightening. 'If so, that would be fun.'

'If that is so, he will no doubt tell you so. But you are too young to get married yet awhile. You must first finish your education.'

'Education is very boring,' said Shaista.

II

Sunday morning dawned bright and serene – Miss Shapland had departed soon after Miss Bulstrode on Saturday. Miss Johnson, Miss Rich and Miss Blake left on Sunday morning.

Miss Vansittart, Miss Chadwick, Miss Rowan and Mademoiselle Blanche were left in charge.

'I hope all the girls won't talk too much,' said Miss Chadwick dubiously. 'About poor Miss Springer I mean.'

'Let us hope,' said Eleanor Vansittart, 'that the whole affair will soon be forgotten.' She added: 'If any parents talk to *me* about it, I shall discourage them. It will be best, I think, to take quite a firm line.'

The girls went to church at 10 o'clock accompanied by Miss Vansittart and Miss Chadwick. Four girls who were Roman Catholics were escorted by Angèle Blanche to a rival religious establishment. Then, about half past eleven, the cars began to roll into the drive. Miss Vansittart, graceful, poised and dignified, stood in the hall. She greeted mothers smilingly, produced their offspring and adroitly turned aside any unwanted references to the recent tragedy.

'Terrible,' she said, 'yes, quite terrible, but, you do understand, *we don't talk about it here.* All these young minds – such a pity for them to dwell on it.'

Chaddy was also on the spot greeting old friends among the parents, discussing plans for the holidays and speaking affectionately of the various daughters.

'I do think Aunt Isabel might have come and taken *me* out,' said Julia who with Jennifer was standing with her nose pressed against the window of one of the classrooms, watching the comings and goings on the drive outside.

'Mummy's going to take me out next weekend,' said Jennifer. 'Daddy's got some important people coming down this weekend so she couldn't come today.'

'There goes Shaista,' said Julia, 'all togged up for London. Oo-ee! Just look at the heels on her shoes. I bet old Johnson doesn't like those shoes.'

A liveried chauffeur was opening the door of a large Cadillac. Shaista climbed in and was driven away.

'You can come out with me next weekend, if you like,' said Jennifer. 'I told Mummy I'd got a friend I wanted to bring.'

'I'd love to,' said Julia. 'Look at Vansittart doing her stuff.'

'Terribly gracious, isn't she?' said Jennifer.

'I don't know why,' said Julia, 'but somehow it makes me want to laugh. It's a sort of copy of Miss Bulstrode, isn't it? Quite a good copy, but it's rather like Joyce Grenfell or someone doing an imitation.'

'There's Pam's mother,' said Jennifer. 'She's brought the little boys. How they can all get into that tiny Morris Minor I don't know.'

'They're going to have a picnic,' said Julia. 'Look at all the baskets.'

'What are you going to do this afternoon?' asked Jennifer. 'I don't think I need write to Mummy this week, do you, if I'm going to see her next week?'

'You are slack about writing letters, Jennifer.'

'I never can think of anything to say,' said Jennifer.

'I can,' said Julia, 'I can think of lots to say.' She added mournfully, 'But there isn't really anyone much to write to at present.'

'What about your mother?'

'I told you she's gone to Anatolia in a bus. You can't write letters to people who go to Anatolia in buses. At least you can't write to them all the time.'

'Where do you write to when you do write?'

'Oh, consulates here and there. She left me a list. Stamboul is the first and then Ankara and then some funny name.' She added, 'I wonder why Bully wanted to get in touch with Mummy so badly? She seemed quite upset when I said where she'd gone.'

'It can't be about you,' said Jennifer. 'You haven't done anything awful, have you?'

'Not that I know of,' said Julia. 'Perhaps she wanted to tell her about Springer.'

'Why should she?' said Jennifer. 'I should think she'd be jolly glad that there's at least one mother who *doesn't* know about Springer.'

'You mean mothers might think that their daughters were going to get murdered too?'

'I don't think my mother's quite as bad as that,' said Jennifer. 'But she did get in quite a flap about it.'

'If you ask me,' said Julia, in a meditative manner, 'I think there's a lot that they haven't told us about Springer.'

'What sort of things?'

'Well, funny things seem to be happening. Like your new tennis racquet.'

'Oh, I meant to tell you,' said Jennifer, 'I wrote and thanked Aunt Gina and this morning I got a letter from her saying she was very glad I'd got a new racquet but that she never sent it to me.'

'I told you that racquet business was peculiar,' said Julia triumphantly, 'and you had a burglary, too, at your home, didn't you?'

'Yes, but they didn't take anything.'

'That makes it even more interesting,' said Julia. 'I think,' she added thoughtfully, 'that we shall probably have a second murder soon.'

'Oh really, Julia, why should we have a second murder?'

'Well, there's usually a second murder in books,' said Julia. 'What I think is, Jennifer, that you'll have to be frightfully careful that it isn't *you* who gets murdered.'

'Me?' said Jennifer, surprised. 'Why should anyone murder me?'

'Because somehow you're mixed up in it all,' said Julia. She added thoughtfully, 'We must try and get a bit more out of your mother next week, Jennifer. Perhaps somebody gave her some secret papers out in Ramat.'

'What sort of secret papers?'

'Oh, how should I know,' said Julia. 'Plans or formulas for a new atomic bomb. That sort of thing.'

Jennifer looked unconvinced.

III

Miss Vansittart and Miss Chadwick were in the Common Room when Miss Rowan entered and said:

'Where is Shaista? I can't find her anywhere. The Emir's car has just arrived to call for her.'

'What?' Chaddy looked up surprised. 'There must be some mistake. The Emir's car came for her about three quarters of an hour ago. I saw her get into it and drive off myself. She was one of the first to go.'

Eleanor Vansittart shrugged her shoulders. 'I suppose a car must have been ordered twice over, or something,' she said.

She went out herself and spoke to the chauffeur. 'There must be some mistake,' she said. 'The young lady has already left for London three quarters of an hour ago.'

The chauffeur seemed surprised. 'I suppose there must be some mistake, if you say so, madam,' he said. 'I was definitely given instructions to call at Meadowbank for the young lady.'

'I suppose there's bound to be a muddle sometimes,' said Miss Vansittart.

The chauffeur seemed unperturbed and unsurprised. 'Happens all the time,' he said. 'Telephone messages taken, written down, forgotten. All that sort of thing. But we pride ourselves in our firm that we *don't* make mistakes. Of course, if I may say so, you never know with these Oriental gentlemen. They've sometimes got quite a big entourage with them, and orders get given twice and even three times over. I expect that's what must have happened in this instance.' He turned his large car with some adroitness and drove away.

Miss Vansittart looked a little doubtful for a moment or two, but she decided there was nothing to worry about and began to look forward with satisfaction to a peaceful afternoon.

After luncheon the few girls who remained wrote letters or wandered about the grounds. A certain amount of tennis was played and the swimming pool was well patronized. Miss Vansittart took her fountain pen and her writing pad to the shade of the cedar tree. When the telephone rang at half past four it was Miss Chadwick who answered it.

'Meadowbank School?' The voice of a well-bred young Englishman spoke. 'Oh, is Miss Bulstrode there?'

'Miss Bulstrode's not here today. This is Miss Chadwick speaking.'

'Oh, it's about one of your pupils. I am speaking from Claridge's, the Emir Ibrahim's suite.'

'Oh yes? You mean about Shaista?'

'Yes. The Emir is rather annoyed at not having got a message of any kind.'

'A message? Why should he get a message?'

'Well, to say that Shaista couldn't come, or wasn't coming.'

'Wasn't coming! Do you mean to say she hasn't arrived?'

'No, no, she's certainly not arrived. Did she leave Meadowbank then?'

'Yes. A car came for her this morning – oh, about half past eleven I should think, and she drove off.'

'That's extraordinary because there's no sign of her here . . . I'd better ring up the firm that supplies the Emir's cars.'

'Oh dear,' said Miss Chadwick, 'I do hope there hasn't been an accident.'

'Oh, don't let's assume the worst,' said the young man cheerfully. 'I think you'd have heard, you know, if there'd been an accident. Or we would. I shouldn't worry if I were you.'

But Miss Chadwick did worry.

'It seems to me very odd,' she said.

'I suppose –' the young man hesitated.

'Yes?' said Miss Chadwick.

'Well, it's not quite the sort of thing I want to suggest to the Emir, but just between you and me there's no – er – well, no boy friend hanging about, is there?'

'Certainly not,' said Miss Chadwick with dignity.

'No, no, well I didn't think there would be, but, well one never knows with girls, does one? You'd be surprised at some of the things I've run into.'

'I can assure you,' said Miss Chadwick with dignity, 'that anything of that kind is quite impossible.'

But was it impossible? Did one ever know with girls?

She replaced the receiver and rather unwillingly went in search of Miss Vansittart. There was no reason to believe that Miss Vansittart would be any better able to deal with the situation than she herself but she felt the need of consulting with someone. Miss Vansittart said at once,

'The second car?'

They looked at each other.

'Do you think,' said Chaddy slowly, 'that we ought to report this to the police?'

'Not to the *police*,' said Eleanor Vansittart in a shocked voice.

'She did say, you know,' said Chaddy, 'that somebody might try to kidnap her.'

'Kidnap her? Nonsense!' said Miss Vansittart sharply.

'You don't think –' Miss Chadwick was persistent.

'Miss Bulstrode left me in charge here,' said Eleanor Vansittart, 'and I shall certainly not sanction anything of the kind. We don't want any more trouble here with the police.'

Miss Chadwick looked at her without affection. She thought Miss Vansittart was being short-sighted and foolish. She went back into the house and put through a call to the Duchess of Welsham's house. Unfortunately everyone was out.

CHAPTER 14

MISS CHADWICK LIES AWAKE

I

Miss Chadwick was restless. She turned to and fro in her bed counting sheep, and employing other time-honoured methods of invoking sleep. In vain.

At eight o'clock, when Shaista had not returned, and there had been no news of her, Miss Chadwick had taken matters into her own hands and rung up Inspector Kelsey. She was relieved to find that he did not take the matter too seriously. She could leave it all to him, he assured her. It would be an easy matter to check up on a possible accident. After that, he would get in touch with London. Everything would be done that was necessary. Perhaps the girl herself was playing truant. He advised Miss Chadwick to say as little as possible at the school. Let it be thought that Shaista was staying the night with her uncle at Claridge's.

'The last thing you want, or that Miss Bulstrode would want, is any more publicity,' said Kelsey. 'It's most unlikely that the girl has been kidnapped. So don't worry, Miss Chadwick. Leave it all to us.'

But Miss Chadwick did worry.

Lying in bed, sleepless, her mind went from possible kidnapping back to murder.

Murder at Meadowbank. It was terrible! Unbelievable! *Meadowbank*. Miss Chadwick loved Meadowbank. She loved it, perhaps, even more than Miss Bulstrode did, though in a somewhat different way. It had been such a risky, gallant enterprise. Following Miss Bulstrode faithfully into the hazardous undertaking, she had endured panic more than once. Supposing the whole thing should fail. They hadn't really had much capital. If they did not succeed – if their backing was withdrawn – Miss Chadwick had an anxious mind and could always tabulate innumerable ifs. Miss Bulstrode had enjoyed the adventure, the hazard of it all, but Chaddy had not. Sometimes, in an agony of apprehension, she had pleaded for Meadowbank to be run on more conventional lines. It would be *safer*, she urged. But Miss Bulstrode had been uninterested in safety. She had her vision of what a school should be and she had pursued it unafraid. And she had been justified in her audacity. But oh, the relief to Chaddy when success was a *fait accompli*. When Meadowbank was established, safely established, as a great English institution. It was then that her love for Meadowbank had flowed most fully. Doubts, fears, anxieties, all slipped from her. Peace and prosperity had come. She basked in the prosperity of Meadowbank like a purring tabby cat.

She had been quite upset when Miss Bulstrode had first begun to talk of retirement. Retire *now* – when everything was set fair? What madness! Miss Bulstrode talked of travel, of all the things in the world to see. Chaddy was unimpressed. Nothing, anywhere, could be half as good as Meadowbank! It had seemed to her that nothing could affect the well-being of Meadowbank – But now – Murder!

Such an ugly violent word – coming in from the outside world like an ill-mannered storm wind. Murder – a word associated by Miss Chadwick only with delinquent boys with flick knives, or evil-minded doctors poisoning their wives. But murder here – at a school – and not any school – at Meadowbank. Incredible.

Really, Miss Springer – poor Miss Springer, naturally it wasn't her *fault* – but, illogically, Chaddy felt that it must have been her fault in some way. She didn't know the traditions of Meadowbank. A tactless woman. She must in some way have invited murder. Miss Chadwick rolled over, turned her pillow, said 'I mustn't go on thinking of it all. Perhaps I had better get up and take some aspirin. I'll just try counting to fifty . . .'

Before she had got to fifty, her mind was off again on the same track. Worrying. Would all this – and perhaps kidnapping too – get into the papers? Would parents, reading, hasten to take their daughters away . . .

Oh dear, she *must* calm down and go to sleep. What time was it? She switched on her light and looked at her watch – Just after a quarter to one. Just about the time that poor Miss Springer . . . No, she would *not* think of it any more. And, how stupid of Miss Springer to have gone off by herself like that without waking up somebody else.

'Oh dear,' said Miss Chadwick. 'I'll have to take some aspirin.'

She got out of bed and went over to the washstand. She took two aspirins with a drink of water. On her way back, she pulled aside the curtain of the window and peered out. She did so to reassure herself more than for any other reason. She wanted to feel that of course there would never again be a light in the Sports Pavilion in the middle of the night.

But there was.

In a minute Chaddy had leapt to action. She thrust her feet into stout shoes, pulled on a thick coat, picked up her electric torch and rushed out of her room and down the stairs. She had blamed Miss Springer for not obtaining support before going out to investigate, but it never occurred to her to do so. She was only eager to get out to the Pavilion and find out who the intruder was. She did pause to pick up a weapon – not perhaps a very good one, but a weapon of kinds, and then she was out of the side door and following quickly along the path through the shrubbery. She was out of breath, but completely resolute. Only when she got at last to the door, did she slacken up and take care to move softly. The door was slightly ajar. She pushed it further open and looked in . . .

II

At about the time when Miss Chadwick was rising from bed in search of aspirin, Ann Shapland, looking very attractive in a black dance frock, was sitting at a table in Le Nid Sauvage eating Supreme of Chicken and smiling at the young man opposite her. Dear Dennis, thought Ann to herself, always so exactly the same. It is what I simply couldn't bear if I married him. He *is* rather a pet, all the same. Aloud she remarked:

'What fun this is, Dennis. Such a glorious *change*.'

'How is the new job?' said Dennis.

'Well, actually, I'm rather enjoying it.'

'Doesn't seem to me quite your sort of thing.'

Ann laughed. 'I'd be hard put to it to say what is my sort of thing. I like variety, Dennis.'

'I never can see why you gave up your job with old Sir Mervyn Todhunter.'

'Well, chiefly because of Sir Mervyn Todhunter. The attention he bestowed on me was beginning to annoy his wife. And it's part of my policy never to annoy wives. They can do you a lot of harm, you know.'

'Jealous cats,' said Dennis.

'Oh no, not really,' said Ann. 'I'm rather on the wives' side. Anyway I liked Lady Todhunter much better than old Mervyn. Why are you surprised at my present job?'

'Oh, a school. You're not scholastically minded at all, I should have said.'

'I'd hate to *teach* in a school. I'd hate to be penned up. Herded with a lot of women. But the work as the secretary of a school like Meadowbank is rather fun. It really is a unique place, you know. And Miss Bulstrode's unique. She's really something, I can tell you. Her steel-grey eye goes through you and sees your innermost secrets. And she keeps you on your toes. I'd hate to make a mistake in any letters I'd taken down for her. Oh yes, she's certainly something.'

'I wish you'd get tired of all these jobs,' said Dennis. 'It's quite time, you know, Ann, that you stopped all this racketing about with jobs here and jobs there and – and settled down.'

'You are sweet, Dennis,' said Ann in a noncommittal manner.

'We could have quite fun, you know,' said Dennis.

'I daresay,' said Ann, 'but I'm not ready yet. And anyway, you know, there's my mamma.'

'Yes, I was – going to talk to you about that.'

'About my mamma? What were you going to say?'

'Well, Ann, you know I think you're wonderful. The way you get an interesting job and then you chuck it all up and go home to her.'

'Well, I have to now and again when she gets a really bad attack.'

'I know. As I say, I think it's wonderful of you. But all the same there are places, you know, very good places nowadays where – where people like your mother are well looked after and all that sort of thing. Not really loony bins.'

'And which cost the earth,' said Ann.

'No, no, not necessarily. Why, even under the Health Scheme –'

A bitter note crept into Ann's voice. 'Yes, I daresay it will come to that one day. But in the meantime I've got a nice old pussy who lives with Mother and who can cope normally. Mother is quite reasonable most of the time – And when she – isn't, I come back and lend a hand.'

'She's – she isn't – she's never –?'

'Are you going to say violent, Dennis? You've got an extraordinarily lurid imagination. No. My dear mamma is *never* violent. She just gets fuddled. She forgets where she is and who she is and wants to go for long walks, and then as like as not she'll jump into a train or a bus and take off somewhere and – well, it's all very difficult, you see. Sometimes it's too much for one person to cope with. But she's quite happy, even when she *is* fuddled. And sometimes quite funny about it. I remember her saying: "Ann, darling, it really is very embarrassing. I knew I was going to Tibet and there I was sitting in that hotel in Dover with no idea how to get there. Then I thought why was I going to Tibet? And I thought I'd better come home. Then I couldn't remember how long ago it was when I left home. It makes it very embarrassing, dear, when you can't quite remember things." Mummy was really very funny over it all, you know. I mean she quite sees the humorous side herself.'

'I've never actually met her,' Dennis began.

'I don't encourage people to meet her,' said Ann. 'That's the one thing I think you *can* do for your people. Protect them from – well, curiosity and pity.'

'It's not curiosity, Ann.'

'No, I don't think it would be that with you. But it would be pity. I don't want that.'

'I can see what you mean.'

'But if you think I mind giving up jobs from time to time and going home for an indefinite period, I don't,' said Ann. 'I never meant to get embroiled in anything too deeply. Not even when I took my first post after my secretarial training. I thought the thing was to get really good at the job. Then if you're really good you can pick and choose your posts. You see different places and you see different kinds of life. At the moment I'm seeing school life. The best school in England seen from within! I shall stay there, I expect, about a year and a half.'

'You never really get caught up in things, do you, Ann?'

'No,' said Ann thoughtfully, 'I don't think I do. I think I'm one of those people who is a born observer. More like a commentator on the radio.'

'You're so detached,' said Dennis gloomily. 'You don't really care about anything or anyone.'

'I expect I shall some day,' said Ann encouragingly.

'I do understand more or less how you're thinking and feeling.'

'I doubt it,' said Ann.

'Anyway, I don't think you'll last a year. You'll get fed up with all those women,' said Dennis.

'There's a very good-looking gardener,' said Ann. She laughed when she saw Dennis's expression. 'Cheer up, I'm only trying to make you jealous.'

'What's this about one of the mistresses having been killed?'

'Oh, that.' Ann's face became serious and thoughtful.

'That's odd, Dennis. Very odd indeed. It was the Games Mistress. You know the type. I-am-a-plain-Games Mistress. I think there's a lot more behind it than has come out yet.'

'Well, don't you get mixed up in anything unpleasant.'

'That's easy to say. I've never had any chance at displaying my talents as a sleuth. I think I *might* be rather good at it.'

'Now, Ann.'

'Darling, I'm not going to trail dangerous criminals. I'm just going to – well, make a few logical deductions. Why and who. And what for? That sort of thing. I've come across one piece of information that's rather interesting.'

'Ann!'

'Don't look so agonized. Only it doesn't seem to link up with anything,' said Ann thoughtfully. 'Up to a point it all fits in very well. And then, suddenly, it doesn't.' She added cheerfully, 'Perhaps there'll be a second murder, and that will clarify things a little.'

It was at exactly that moment that Miss Chadwick pushed open the Sports Pavilion door.

CHAPTER 15

MURDER REPEATS ITSELF

'Come along,' said Inspector Kelsey, entering the room with a grim face. 'There's been another.'

'Another what?' Adam looked up sharply.

'Another murder,' said Inspector Kelsey. He led the way out of the room and Adam followed him. They had been sitting in the latter's room drinking beer and discussing various probabilities when Kelsey had been summoned to the telephone.

'Who is it?' demanded Adam, as he followed Inspector Kelsey down the stairs.

'Another mistress – Miss Vansittart.'

'Where?'

'In the Sports Pavilion.'

'The Sports Pavilion again,' said Adam. 'What is there about this Sports Pavilion?'

'*You'd* better give it the once-over this time,' said Inspector Kelsey. 'Perhaps your technique of searching may be more successful than ours has been. There must be *something* about that Sports Pavilion or why should everyone get killed there?'

He and Adam got into his car. 'I expect the doctor will be there ahead of us. He hasn't so far to go.'

It was, Kelsey thought, like a bad dream repeating itself as he entered the brilliantly lighted Sports Pavilion. There, once again, was a body with the doctor kneeling beside it. Once again the doctor rose from his knees and got up.

'Killed about half an hour ago,' he said. 'Forty minutes at most.'

'Who found her?' said Kelsey.

One of his men spoke up. 'Miss Chadwick.'

'That's the old one, isn't it?'

'Yes. She saw a light, came out here, and found her dead. She stumbled back to the house and more or less went into hysterics. It was the matron who telephoned, Miss Johnson.'

'Right,' said Kelsey. 'How was she killed? Shot again?'

The doctor shook his head. 'No. Slugged on the back of the head, this time. Might have been a cosh or a sandbag. Something of that kind.'

A golf club with a steel head was lying near the door. It was the only thing that looked remotely disorderly in the place.

'What about that?' said Kelsey, pointing. 'Could she have been hit with that?'

The doctor shook his head. 'Impossible. There's no mark on her. No, it was definitely a heavy rubber cosh or a sandbag, something of that sort.'

'Something – professional?'

'Probably, yes. Whoever it was, didn't mean to make any noise this time. Came up behind her and slugged her on the back of the head. She fell forward and probably never knew what hit her.'

'What was she doing?'

'She was probably kneeling down,' said the doctor. 'Kneeling in front of this locker.'

The Inspector went up to the locker and looked at it. 'That's the girl's name on it, I presume,' he said. 'Shaista – let me see, that's the – that's the Egyptian girl, isn't it? Her Highness Princess

Shaista.' He turned to Adam. 'It seems to tie in, doesn't it? Wait a minute – that's the girl they reported this evening as missing?'

'That's right, sir,' said the Sergeant. 'A car called for her here, supposed to have been sent by her uncle who's staying at Claridge's in London. She got into it and drove off.'

'No reports come in?'

'Not as yet, sir. Got a network out. And the Yard is on it.'

'A nice simple way of kidnapping anyone,' said Adam. 'No struggle, no cries. All you've got to know is that the girl's expecting a car to fetch her and all you've got to do is to look like a high-class chauffeur and arrive there before the other car does. The girl will step in without a second thought and you can drive off without her suspecting in the least what's happening to her.'

'No abandoned car found anywhere?' asked Kelsey.

'We've had no news of one,' said the Sergeant. 'The Yard's on it now as I said,' he added, 'and the Special Branch.'

'May mean a bit of a political schemozzle,' said the Inspector. 'I don't suppose for a minute they'll be able to take her out of the country.'

'What do they want to kidnap her for anyway?' asked the doctor.

'Goodness knows,' said Kelsey gloomily. 'She told me she was afraid of being kidnapped and I'm ashamed to say I thought she was just showing off.'

'I thought so, too, when you told me about it,' said Adam.

'The trouble is we don't know enough,' said Kelsey. 'There are far too many loose ends.' He looked around. 'Well, there doesn't seem to be anything more that I can do here. Get on with the usual stuff – photographs, fingerprints, etc. I'd better go along to the house.'

At the house he was received by Miss Johnson. She was shaken but preserved her self-control.

'It's terrible, Inspector,' she said. 'Two of our mistresses killed. Poor Miss Chadwick's in a dreadful state.'

'I'd like to see her as soon as I can.'

'The doctor gave her something and she's much calmer now. Shall I take you to her?'

'Yes, in a minute or two. First of all, just tell me what you can about the last time you saw Miss Vansittart.'

'I haven't seen her at all today,' said Miss Johnson. 'I've been away all day. I arrived back here just before eleven and went straight up to my room. I went to bed.'

'You didn't happen to look out of your window towards the Sports Pavilion?'

'No. No, I never thought of it. I'd spent the day with my sister whom I hadn't seen for some time and my mind was full of home news. I took a bath and went to bed and read a book, and I turned off the light and went to sleep. The next thing I knew was when Miss Chadwick burst in, looking as white as a sheet and shaking all over.'

'Was Miss Vansittart absent today?'

'No, she was here. She was in charge. Miss Bulstrode's away.'

'Who else was here, of the mistresses, I mean?'

Miss Johnson considered a moment. 'Miss Vansittart, Miss Chadwick, the French mistress, Mademoiselle Blanche, Miss Rowan.'

'I see. Well, I think you'd better take me to Miss Chadwick now.'

Miss Chadwick was sitting in a chair in her room. Although the night was a warm one the electric fire had been turned on and a rug was wrapped round her knees. She turned a ghastly face towards Inspector Kelsey.

'She's dead – she *is* dead? There's no chance that – that she might come round?'

Kelsey shook his head slowly.

'It's so awful,' said Miss Chadwick, 'with Miss Bulstrode away.' She burst into tears. 'This will ruin the school,' she said. 'This will ruin Meadowbank. I can't bear it – I really can't bear it.'

Kelsey sat down beside her. 'I know,' he said sympathetically, 'I know. It's been a terrible shock to you, but I want you to be brave, Miss Chadwick, and tell me all you know. The sooner we can find out who did it, the less trouble and publicity there will be.'

'Yes, yes, I can see that. You see, I – I went to bed early because I thought it would be nice for once to have a nice long night. But I couldn't go to sleep. I was worrying.'

'Worrying about the school?'

'Yes. And about Shaista being missing. And then I began thinking of Miss Springer and whether – whether her murder would affect the parents, and whether perhaps they wouldn't send their girls back here next term. I was so terribly upset for Miss Bulstrode. I mean, she's *made* this place. It's been such a fine achievement.'

'I know. Now go on telling me – you were worried, and you couldn't sleep?'

'No, I counted sheep and everything. And then I got up and took some aspirin and when I'd taken it I just happened to draw back the curtains from the window. I don't quite know why. I suppose because I'd been thinking about Miss Springer. Then you see, I saw . . . I saw a light there.'

'What kind of a light?'

'Well, a sort of dancing light. I mean – I think it must have been a torch. It was just like the light that Miss Johnson and I saw before.'

'It was just the same, was it?'

'Yes. Yes, I think so. Perhaps a little feebler, but I don't know.'

'Yes. And then?'

'And then,' said Miss Chadwick, her voice suddenly becoming more resonant, 'I was determined that *this* time I would see who it was out there and what they were doing. So I got up and pulled on my coat and my shoes, and I rushed out of the house.'

'You didn't think of calling anyone else?'

'No. No, I didn't. You see I was in such a hurry to get there, I was so afraid the person – whoever it was – would go away.'

'Yes. Go on, Miss Chadwick.'

'So I went as fast as I could. I went up to the door and just before I got there I went on tiptoe so that – so that I should be able to look in and nobody would hear me coming. I got there. The door was not shut – just ajar and I pushed it very slightly open. I looked round it and – and there she was. Fallen forward on her face, *dead* . . .'

She began to shake all over.

'Yes, yes, Miss Chadwick, it's all right. By the way, there was a golf club out there. Did you take it out? Or did Miss Vansittart?'

'A golf club?' said Miss Chadwick vaguely. 'I can't remember – Oh, yes, I think I picked it up in the hall. I took it out with me in case – well, in case I should have to use it. When I saw Eleanor I suppose I just dropped it. Then I got back to the house somehow and I found Miss Johnson – Oh! I can't bear it. I can't bear it – this will be the end of Meadowbank –'

Miss Chadwick's voice rose hysterically. Miss Johnson came forward.

'To discover two murders is too much of a strain for anyone,' said Miss Johnson. 'Certainly for anyone her age. You don't want to ask her any more, do you?'

Inspector Kelsey shook his head.

As he was going downstairs, he noticed a pile of old-fashioned sandbags with buckets in an alcove. Dating from the war, perhaps, but the uneasy thought occurred to him that it needn't have been a professional with a cosh who had slugged Miss Vansittart. Someone in the building, someone who hadn't wished to risk the sound of a shot a second time, and who, very likely, had disposed of the incriminating pistol after the last murder, could have helped themselves to an innocent-looking but lethal weapon – and possibly even replaced it tidily afterwards!

CHAPTER 16

RIDDLE OF THE SPORTS PAVILION

I

'*My head is bloody but unbowed*,' said Adam to himself.

He was looking at Miss Bulstrode. He had never, he thought, admired a woman more. She sat, cool and unmoved, with her lifework falling in ruins about her.

From time to time telephone calls came through announcing that yet another pupil was being removed.

Finally Miss Bulstrode had taken her decision. Excusing herself to the police officers, she summoned Ann Shapland, and dictated a brief statement. The school would be closed until the end of term. Parents who found it inconvenient to have their children home, were welcome to leave them in her care and their education would be continued.

'You've got the list of parents' names and addresses? And their telephone numbers?'

'Yes, Miss Bulstrode.'

'Then start on the telephone. After that see a typed notice goes to everyone.'

'Yes, Miss Bulstrode.'

On her way out, Ann Shapland paused near the door.

She flushed and her words came with a rush.

'Excuse me, Miss Bulstrode. It's not my business – but isn't it a pity to – to be premature? I mean – after the first panic, when people have had time to think – surely they won't want to take the girls away. They'll be sensible and think better of it.'

Miss Bulstrode looked at her keenly.

'You think I'm accepting defeat too easily?'

Ann flushed.

'I know – you think it's cheek. But – but, well then, yes, I do.'

'You're a fighter, child, I'm glad to see. But you're quite wrong. I'm not accepting defeat. I'm going on my knowledge of human nature. Urge people to take their children away, force it on them – and they won't want to nearly so much. They'll think up reasons for letting them remain. Or at the worst they'll decide to let them come back next term – if there is a next term,' she added grimly.

She looked at Inspector Kelsey.

'That's up to you,' she said. 'Clear these murders up – catch whoever is responsible for them – and we'll be all right.'

Inspector Kelsey looked unhappy. He said: 'We're doing our best.'

Ann Shapland went out.

'Competent girl,' said Miss Bulstrode. 'And loyal.'

This was in the nature of a parenthesis. She pressed her attack.

'Have you absolutely *no* idea of who killed two of my mistresses in the Sports Pavilion? You ought to, by this time. And this kidnapping on top of everything else. I blame myself there. The girl talked about someone wanting to kidnap her. I thought, God forgive me, she was making herself important. I see now that there must have been something behind it. Someone must have hinted, or warned – one doesn't know which –' She broke off, resuming: 'You've no news of any kind?'

'Not yet. But I don't think you need worry too much about that. It's been passed to the C.I.D. The Special Branch is on to it, too. They ought to find her within twenty-four hours, thirty-six at most. There are advantages in this being an island. All the ports, airports, etc., are alerted. And the police in every district are keeping a lookout. It's actually easy enough to kidnap anyone – it's keeping them hidden that's the problem. Oh, we'll find her.'

'I hope you'll find her alive,' said Miss Bulstrode grimly. 'We seem to be up against someone who isn't too scrupulous about human life.'

'They wouldn't have troubled to kidnap her if they'd meant to do away with her,' said Adam. 'They could have done that here easily enough.'

He felt that the last words were unfortunate. Miss Bulstrode gave him a look.

'So it seems,' she said dryly.

The telephone rang. Miss Bulstrode took up the receiver.

'Yes?'

She motioned to Inspector Kelsey.

'It's for you.'

Adam and Miss Bulstrode watched him as he took the call. He grunted, jotted down a note or two, said finally: 'I see. Alderton Priors. That's Wallshire. Yes, we'll cooperate. Yes, Super. I'll carry on here, then.'

He put down the receiver and stayed a moment lost in thought. Then he looked up.

'His Excellency got a ransom note this morning. Typed on a new Corona. Postmark Portsmouth. Bet that's a blind.'

'Where and how?' asked Adam.

'Crossroads two miles north of Alderton Priors. That's a bit of bare moorland. Envelope containing money to be put under stone behind A.A. box there at 2 a.m. tomorrow morning.'

'How much?'

'Twenty thousand.' He shook his head. 'Sounds amateurish to me.'

'What are you going to do?' asked Miss Bulstrode.

Inspector Kelsey looked at her. He was a different man. Official reticence hung about him like a cloak.

'The responsibility isn't mine, madam,' he said. 'We have our methods.'

'I hope they're successful,' said Miss Bulstrode.

'Ought to be easy,' said Adam.

'Amateurish?' said Miss Bulstrode, catching at a word they had used. 'I wonder . . .'

Then she said sharply:

'What about my staff? What remains of it, that is to say? Do I trust them, or don't I?'

As Inspector Kelsey hesitated, she said,

'You're afraid that if you tell me who is *not* cleared, I should show it in my manner to them. You're wrong. I shouldn't.'

'I don't think you would,' said Kelsey. 'But I can't afford to take any chances. It doesn't look, on the face of it, as though any of your staff *can* be the person we're looking for. That is, not so far as we've been able to check up on them. We've paid special attention to those who are new this term – that is Mademoiselle Blanche, Miss Springer and your secretary, Miss Shapland. Miss Shapland's past is completely corroborated. She's the daughter of a retired general, she has held the posts she says she did and her former employers vouch for her. In addition she has an alibi for last night. When Miss Vansittart was killed, Miss Shapland was with a Mr Dennis Rathbone at a night club. They're both well known there, and Mr Rathbone has an excellent character. Mademoiselle Blanche's antecedents have also been checked. She has taught at a school in the north of England and at two schools in Germany, and has been given an excellent character. She is said to be a first-class teacher.'

'Not by our standards,' sniffed Miss Bulstrode.

'Her French background has also been checked. As regards Miss Springer, things are not quite so conclusive. She did her training where she says, but there have been gaps since in her periods of employment which are not fully accounted for.

'Since, however, she was killed,' added the Inspector, 'that seems to exonerate her.'

'I agree,' said Miss Bulstrode dryly, 'that both Miss Springer and Miss Vansittart are *hors de combat* as suspects. Let us talk sense. Is Mademoiselle Blanche, in spite of her blameless background, still a suspect merely because she is still alive?'

'She *could* have done both murders. She was here, in the building, last night,' said Kelsey. 'She *says* she went to bed early and slept and heard nothing until the alarm was given. There's no evidence to the contrary. We've got nothing against her. But Miss Chadwick says definitely that she's sly.'

Miss Bulstrode waved that aside impatiently.

'Miss Chadwick always finds the French Mistresses sly. She's got a thing about them.' She looked at Adam. 'What do *you* think?'

'I think she pries,' said Adam slowly. 'It may be just natural inquisitiveness. It may be something more. I can't make up my mind. She doesn't *look* to me like a killer, but how does one know?'

'That's just it,' said Kelsey. 'There *is* a killer here, a ruthless killer who has killed twice – but it's very hard to believe that it's one of the staff. Miss Johnson was with her sister last night at Limeston on Sea, and anyway she's been with you seven years. Miss Chadwick's been with you since you started. Both of them, anyway, are clear of Miss Springer's death. Miss Rich has been with you over a year and was staying last night at the Alton Grange Hotel, twenty miles away, Miss Blake was with friends at Littleport, Miss Rowan has been with you for a year and has a good background. As for your servants, frankly I can't see any of them as murderers. They're all local, too . . .'

Miss Bulstrode nodded pleasantly.

'I quite agree with your reasoning. It doesn't leave much, does it? So –' She paused and fixed an accusing eye on Adam. 'It looks really – as though it must be *you*.'

His mouth opened in astonishment.

'On the spot,' she mused. 'Free to come and go . . . Good story to account for your presence here. Background OK but you *could* be a double crosser, you know.'

Adam recovered himself.

'Really, Miss Bulstrode,' he said admiringly, 'I take off my hat to you. You think of *everything*!'

II

'Good gracious!' cried Mrs Sutcliffe at the breakfast table. 'Henry!'

She had just unfolded her newspaper.

The width of the table was between her and her husband since her weekend guests had not yet put in an appearance for the meal.

Mr Sutcliffe, who had opened his paper to the financial page, and was absorbed in the unforeseen movements of certain shares, did not reply.

'*Henry!*'

The clarion call reached him. He raised a startled face.

'What's the matter, Joan?'

'The matter? Another murder! At Meadowbank! At Jennifer's school.'

'What? Here, let *me* see!'

Disregarding his wife's remark that it would be in his paper, too, Mr Sutcliffe leant across the table and snatched the sheet from his wife's grasp.

'Miss Eleanor Vansittart . . . Sports Pavilion . . . same spot where Miss Springer, the Games Mistress . . . hm . . . hm . . .'

'I can't believe it!' Mrs Sutcliffe was wailing. 'Meadowbank. Such an exclusive school. Royalty there and everything . . .'

Mr Sutcliffe crumpled up the paper and threw it down on the table.

'Only one thing to be done,' he said. 'You get over there right away and take Jennifer out of it.'

'You mean take her away – altogether?'

'That's what I mean.'

'You don't think that would be a little too drastic? After Rosamond being so good about it and managing to get her in?'

'You won't be the only one taking your daughter away! Plenty of vacancies soon at your precious Meadowbank.'

'Oh, Henry, do you think so?'

'Yes, I do. Something badly wrong there. Take Jennifer away today.'

'Yes – of course – I suppose you're right. What shall we do with her?'

'Send her to a secondary modern somewhere handy. They don't have murders there.'

'Oh, Henry, but they *do*. Don't you remember? There was a boy who shot the science master at one. It was in last week's *News of the World*.'

'I don't know what England's coming to,' said Mr Sutcliffe.

Disgusted, he threw his napkin on the table and strode from the room.

III

Adam was alone in the Sports Pavilion . . . His deft fingers were turning over the contents of the lockers. It was unlikely that he would find anything where the police had failed but after all, one could never be sure. As Kelsey had said every department's technique varied a little.

What was there that linked this expensive modern building with sudden and violent death? The idea of a rendezvous was out. No one would choose to keep a rendezvous a second time in the same place where murder had occurred. It came back to it, then, that there was something here that someone was looking for. Hardly a *cache* of jewels. That seemed ruled out. There could be no secret hiding place, false drawers, spring catches, etc. And the contents of the lockers were pitifully simple. They had their secrets, but they were the secrets of school life. Photographs of pin up heroes, packets of cigarettes, an occasional unsuitable cheap paperback. Especially he returned to Shaista's locker. It was while bending over that that Miss Vansittart had been killed. What had Miss Vansittart expected to find there? Had she found it? Had her killer taken it from her dead hand and then slipped out of the building in the nick of time to miss being discovered by Miss Chadwick?

In that case it was no good looking. Whatever it was, was gone.

The sound of footsteps outside aroused him from his thoughts. He was on his feet and lighting a cigarette in the middle of the floor when Julia Upjohn appeared in the doorway, hesitating a little.

'Anything you want, miss?' asked Adam.

'I wondered if I could have my tennis racquet.'

'Don't see why not,' said Adam. 'Police constable left me here,' he explained mendaciously. 'Had to drop back to the station for something. Told me to stop here while he was away.'

'To see if he came back, I suppose,' said Julia.

'The police constable?'

'No. I mean, the murderer. They do, don't they? Come back to the scene of the crime. They have to! It's a compulsion.'

'You may be right,' said Adam. He looked up at the serried rows of racquets in their presses. 'Whereabouts is yours?'

'Under U,' said Julia. 'Right at the far end. We have our names on them,' she explained, pointing out the adhesive tape as he handed the racquet to her.

'Seen some service,' said Adam. 'But been a good racquet once.'

'Can I have Jennifer Sutcliffe's too?' asked Julia.

'New,' said Adam appreciatively, as he handed it to her.

'Brand new,' said Julia. 'Her aunt sent it to her only the other day.'

'Lucky girl.'

'She ought to have a good racquet. She's very good at tennis. Her backhand's come on like anything this term.' She looked round. 'Don't you think he *will* come back?'

Adam was a moment or two getting it.

'Oh. The murderer? No, I don't think it's really likely. Bit risky, wouldn't it be?'

'You don't think murderers feel they *have* to?'

'Not unless they've left something behind.'

'You mean a clue? I'd like to find a clue. Have the police found one?'

'They wouldn't tell me.'

'No. I suppose they wouldn't . . . Are you interested in crime?'

She looked at him inquiringly. He returned her glance. There was, as yet, nothing of the woman in her. She must be of much the same age as Shaista, but her eyes held nothing but interested inquiry.

'Well – I suppose – up to a point – we all are.'

Julia nodded in agreement.

'Yes. I think so, too . . . I can think of all sorts of solutions – but most of them are very far fetched. It's rather fun, though.'

'You weren't fond of Miss Vansittart?'

'I never really thought about her. She was all right. A bit like the Bull – Miss Bulstrode – but not really like her. More like an understudy in a theatre. I didn't mean it was fun she was dead. I'm sorry about that.'

She walked out holding the two racquets.

Adam remained looking round the Pavilion.

'What the hell could there ever have been here?' he muttered to himself.

IV

'Good lord,' said Jennifer, allowing Julia's forehand drive to pass her. 'There's Mummy.'

The two girls turned to stare at the agitated figure of Mrs Sutcliffe, shepherded by Miss Rich, rapidly arriving and gesticulating as she did so.

'More fuss, I suppose,' said Jennifer resignedly. 'It's the murder. You *are* lucky, Julia, that your mother's safely on a bus in the Caucasus.'

'There's still Aunt Isabel.'

'Aunts don't mind in the same way.'

'Hallo, Mummy,' she added, as Mrs Sutcliffe arrived.

'You must come and pack your things, Jennifer. I'm taking you back with me.'

'Back home?'

'Yes.'

'But – you don't mean altogether? Not for good?'

'Yes. I do.'

'But you can't – really. My tennis has come on like anything. I've got a very good chance of winning the singles and Julia and I *might* win the doubles, though I don't think it's very likely.'

'You're coming home with me today.'

'Why?'

'Don't ask questions.'

'I suppose it's because of Miss Springer and Miss Vansittart being murdered. But no one's murdered any of the girls. I'm sure they wouldn't want to. And Sports Day is in three weeks' time. I *think* I shall win the Long Jump and I've a good chance for the Hurdling.'

'Don't argue with me, Jennifer. You're coming back with me today. Your father insists.'

'But, Mummy –'

Arguing persistently Jennifer moved towards the house by her mother's side.

Suddenly she broke away and ran back to the tennis court.

'Goodbye, Julia. Mummy seems to have got the wind up thoroughly. Daddy, too, apparently. Sickening, isn't it? Goodbye, I'll write to you.'

'I'll write to you, too, and tell you all that happens.'

'I hope they don't kill Chaddy next. I'd rather it was Mademoiselle Blanche, wouldn't you?'

'Yes. She's the one we could spare best. I say, did you notice how black Miss Rich was looking?'

'She hasn't said a word. She's furious at Mummy coming and taking me away.'

'Perhaps she'll stop her. She's very forceful, isn't she? Not like anyone else.'

'She reminds me of someone,' said Jennifer.

'I don't think she's a bit like anybody. She always seems to be quite different.'

'Oh yes. She is different. I meant in appearance. But the person I knew was quite fat.'

'I can't imagine Miss Rich being fat.'

'Jennifer . . .' called Mrs Sutcliffe.

'I do think parents are trying,' said Jennifer crossly. 'Fuss, fuss, fuss. They never stop. I do think you're lucky to –'

'I know. You said that before. But just at the moment, let me tell you, I wish Mummy were a good deal nearer, and *not* on a bus in Anatolia.'

'*Jennifer . . .*'

'Coming . . .'

Julia walked slowly in the direction of the Sports Pavilion. Her steps grew slower and slower and finally she stopped altogether. She stood, frowning, lost in thought.

The luncheon bell sounded, but she hardly heard it. She stared down at the racquet she was holding, moved a step or two along the path, then wheeled round and marched determinedly towards the house. She went in by the front door, which was not allowed, and thereby avoided meeting any of the other girls. The hall was empty. She ran up the stairs to her small bedroom, looked round her hurriedly, then lifting the mattress on her bed, shoved the racquet flat beneath it. Then, rapidly smoothing her hair, she walked demurely downstairs to the dining-room.

CHAPTER 17
ALADDIN'S CAVE

I

The girls went up to bed that night more quietly than usual. For one thing their numbers were much depleted. At least thirty of them had gone home. The others reacted according to their several dispositions. Excitement, trepidation, a certain amount of giggling that was purely nervous in origin and there were some again who were merely quiet and thoughtful.

Julia Upjohn went up quietly amongst the first wave. She went into her room and closed the door. She stood there listening to the whispers, giggles, footsteps and goodnights. Then silence closed down – or a near silence. Faint voices echoed in the distance, and footsteps went to and fro to the bathroom.

There was no lock on the door. Julia pulled a chair against it, with the top of the chair wedged under the handle. That would give her warning if anyone should come in. But no one was likely to come in. It was strictly forbidden for the girls to go into each other's rooms, and the only mistress who did so was Miss Johnson, if one of the girls was ill or out of sorts.

Julia went to her bed, lifted up the mattress and groped under it. She brought out the tennis racquet and stood a moment holding it. She had decided to examine it now, and not later. A light in her room showing under the door might attract attention when all lights were supposed to be off. Now was the time when a light was normal for undressing and for reading in bed until half past ten if you wanted to do so.

She stood staring down at the racquet. How could there be anything hidden in a tennis racquet?

'But there must be,' said Julia to herself. 'There *must*. The burglary at Jennifer's home, the woman who came with that silly story about a new racquet . . .'

Only Jennifer would have believed that, thought Julia scornfully.

No, it was 'new lamps for old' and that meant, like in Aladdin, that there was *something* about this particular tennis racquet. Jennifer and Julia had never mentioned to anyone that they had swopped racquets – or at least, she herself never had.

So really then, *this* was the racquet that everyone was looking for in the Sports Pavilion. And it was up to her to find out *why*! She examined it carefully. There was nothing unusual about it to look at. It was a good quality racquet, somewhat the worse for wear, but restrung and eminently usable. Jennifer had complained of the balance.

The only place you could possibly conceal anything in a tennis racquet was in the handle. You could, she supposed, hollow out the handle to make a hiding place. It sounded a little far fetched but it was possible. And if the handle had been tampered with, that probably *would* upset the balance.

There was a round of leather with lettering on it, the lettering almost worn away. That of course was only stuck on. If one removed that? Julia sat down at her dressing table and attacked it with a penknife and presently managed to pull the leather off. Inside was a round of thin wood. It didn't look quite right. There was a join all round it. Julia dug in her penknife. The blade snapped. Nail scissors were more effective. She succeeded at last in prising it out. A mottled red and blue substance now showed. Julia poked it and enlightenment came to her. *Plasticine!* But surely handles of tennis racquets didn't normally contain plasticine? She grasped the nail scissors firmly and began to dig out lumps of plasticine. The stuff was encasing something. Something that felt like buttons or pebbles.

She attacked the plasticine vigorously.

Something rolled out on the table – then another something. Presently there was quite a heap.

Julia leaned back and gasped.

She stared and stared and stared . . .

Liquid fire, red and green and deep blue and dazzling white . . .

In that moment, Julia grew up. She was no longer a child. She became a woman. A woman looking at jewels . . .

All sorts of fantastic snatches of thought raced through her brain. Aladdin's cave . . . Marguerite and her casket of jewels . . . (They had been taken to Covent Garden to hear Faust last week) . . . Fatal stones . . . the Hope diamond . . . Romance . . . herself in a black velvet gown with a flashing necklace round her throat . . .

She sat and gloated and dreamed . . . She held the stones in her fingers and let them fall through in a rivulet of fire, a flashing stream of wonder and delight.

And then something, some slight sound perhaps, recalled her to herself.

She sat thinking, trying to use her common sense, deciding what she ought to do. That faint sound had alarmed her. She swept up the stones, took them to the washstand and thrust them into her sponge bag and rammed her sponge and nail brush down on top of them. Then she went back to the tennis racquet, forced the plasticine back inside it, replaced the wooden top and tried to gum down the leather on top again. It curled upwards, but she managed to deal with that by applying adhesive plaster the wrong way up in thin strips and then pressing the leather on to it.

It was done. The racquet looked and felt just as before, its weight hardly altered in feel. She looked at it and then cast it down carelessly on a chair.

She looked at her bed, neatly turned down and waiting. But she did not undress. Instead she sat listening. Was that a footstep outside?

Suddenly and unexpectedly she knew fear. Two people had been killed. If anyone knew what she had found, *she* would be killed.

There was a fairly heavy oak chest of drawers in the room. She managed to drag it in front of the door, wishing that it was the custom at Meadowbank to have keys in the locks. She went to the window, pulled up the top sash and bolted it. There was no tree growing near the window and no creepers. She doubted if it was possible for anyone to come in that way but she was not going to take any chances.

She looked at her small clock. Half past ten. She drew a deep breath and turned out the light. No one must notice anything unusual. She pulled back the curtain a little from the window. There was a full moon and she could see the door clearly. Then she sat down on the edge of the bed. In her hand she held the stoutest shoe she possessed.

'If anyone tries to come in,' Julia said to herself, 'I'll rap on the wall here as hard as I can. Mary King is next door and that will wake her up. *And* I'll scream – at the top of my voice. And then, if lots of people come, I'll say I had a nightmare. Anyone might have a nightmare after all the things that have been going on here.'

She sat there and time passed. Then she heard it – a soft step along the passage. She heard it stop outside her door. A long pause and then she saw the handle slowly turning.

Should she scream? Not yet.

The door was pushed – just a crack, but the chest of drawers held it. That must have puzzled the person outside.

Another pause, and then there was a knock, a very gentle little knock, on the door.

Julia held her breath. A pause, and then the knock came again – but still soft and muted.

'I'm asleep,' said Julia to herself. 'I don't hear *anything*.'

Who would come and knock on her door in the middle of the night? If it was someone who had a right to knock, they'd call out, rattle the handle, make a noise. But this person couldn't afford to make a noise . . .

For a long time Julia sat there. The knock was not repeated, the handle stayed immovable. But Julia sat tense and alert.

She sat like that for a long time. She never knew herself how long it was before sleep overcame her. The school bell finally awoke her, lying in a cramped and uncomfortable heap on the edge of the bed.

II

After breakfast, the girls went upstairs and made their beds, then went down to prayers in the big hall and finally dispersed to various classrooms.

It was during that last exercise, when girls were hurrying in different directions, that Julia went into one classroom, out by a further door, joined a group hurrying round the house, dived behind a rhododendron, made a series of further strategic dives and arrived finally near the wall of the grounds where a lime tree had thick growth almost down to the ground. Julia climbed the tree with ease, she had climbed trees all her life. Completely hidden in the leafy branches, she sat, glancing from time to time at her watch. She was fairly sure she would not be missed for some time. Things were disorganized, two teachers were missing, and more than half the girls had gone home. That meant that all classes would have been reorganized, so nobody would be likely to observe the absence of Julia Upjohn until lunch time and by then –

Julia looked at her watch again, scrambled easily down the tree to the level of the wall, straddled it and dropped neatly on the other side. A hundred yards away was a bus stop where a bus ought to arrive in a few minutes. It duly did so, and Julia hailed and boarded it, having by now abstracted a felt hat from inside her cotton frock and clapped it on her slightly dishevelled hair. She got out at the station and took a train to London.

In her room, propped up on the washstand, she had left a note addressed to Miss Bulstrode.

Dear Miss Bulstrode,
   I have not been kidnapped or run away, so don't worry. I will come back as soon as I can.
   Yours very sincerely,
   Julia Upjohn

III

At 228 Whitehouse Mansions, George, Hercule Poirot's immaculate valet and manservant, opened the door and contemplated with some surprise a schoolgirl with a rather dirty face.

'Can I see M. Hercule Poirot, please?'

George took just a shade longer than usual to reply. He found the caller unexpected.

'Mr Poirot does not see anyone without an appointment,' he said.

'I'm afraid I haven't time to wait for that. I really must see him now. It is very urgent. It's about some murders and a robbery and things like that.'

'I will ascertain,' said George, 'if Mr Poirot will see you.'

He left her in the hall and withdrew to consult his master.

'A young lady, sir, who wishes to see you urgently.'

'I daresay,' said Hercule Poirot. 'But things do not arrange themselves as easily as that.'

'That is what I told her, sir.'

'What kind of a young lady?'

'Well, sir, she's more of a little girl.'

'A little girl? A young lady? Which do you mean, Georges? They are really not the same.'

'I'm afraid you did not quite get my meaning sir. She is, I should say, a little girl – of school age, that is to say. But though her frock is dirty and indeed torn, she is essentially a young lady.'

'A social term. I see.'

'And she wishes to see you about some murders and a robbery.'

Poirot's eyebrows went up.

'*Some* murders, and *a robbery*. Original. Show the little girl – the young lady – in.'

Julia came into the room with only the slightest trace of diffidence. She spoke politely and quite naturally.

'How do you do, M. Poirot. I am Julia Upjohn. I think you know a great friend of Mummy's. Mrs Summerhayes. We stayed with her last summer and she talked about you a lot.'

'Mrs Summerhayes . . .' Poirot's mind went back to a village that climbed a hill and to a house on top of that hill. He recalled a charming freckled face, a sofa with broken springs, a large quantity of dogs, and other things both agreeable and disagreeable.

'Maureen Summerhayes,' he said. 'Ah yes.'

'I call her Aunt Maureen, but she isn't really an aunt at all. She told us how wonderful you'd been and saved a man who was in prison for murder, and when I couldn't think of what to do and who to go to, I thought of you.'

'I am honoured,' said Poirot gravely.

He brought forward a chair for her.

'Now tell me,' he said. 'Georges, my servant, told me you

wanted to consult me about a robbery and some murders – more than one murder, then?'

'Yes,' said Julia. 'Miss Springer and Miss Vansittart. And of course there's the kidnapping, too – but I don't think that's really my business.'

'You bewilder me,' said Poirot. 'Where have all these exciting happenings taken place?'

'At my school – Meadowbank.'

'Meadowbank,' exclaimed Poirot. 'Ah.' He stretched out his hand to where the newspapers lay neatly folded beside him. He unfolded one and glanced over the front page, nodding his head.

'I begin to comprehend,' he said. 'Now tell me, Julia, tell me everything from the beginning.'

Julia told him. It was quite a long story and a comprehensive one – but she told it clearly – with an occasional break as she went back over something she had forgotten.

She brought her story up to the moment when she had examined the tennis racquet in her bedroom last night.

'You see, I thought it was just like Aladdin – new lamps for old – and there must be something about that tennis racquet.'

'And there was?'

'Yes.'

Without any false modesty, Julia pulled up her skirt, rolled up her knicker leg nearly to her thigh and exposed what looked like a grey poultice attached by adhesive plaster to the upper part of her leg.

She tore off the strips of plaster, uttering an anguished 'Ouch' as she did so, and freed the poultice which Poirot now perceived to be a packet enclosed in a portion of grey plastic sponge bag. Julia unwrapped it and without warning poured a heap of glittering stones on the table.

'*Nom d'un nom d'un nom!*' ejaculated Poirot in an awe-inspired whisper.

He picked them up, letting them run through his fingers.

'*Nom d'un nom d'un nom!* But they are *real*. Genuine.'

Julia nodded.

'I think they must be. People wouldn't kill other people for them otherwise, would they? But I can understand people killing for *these*!'

And suddenly, as had happened last night, a woman looked out of the child's eyes.

Poirot looked keenly at her and nodded.

'Yes – you understand – you feel the spell. They cannot be to you just pretty coloured playthings – more is the pity.'

'They're *jewels*!' said Julia, in tones of ecstasy.

'And you found them, you say, in this tennis racquet?'

Julia finished her recital.

'And you have now told me everything?'

'I think so. I may, perhaps, have exaggerated a little here and there. I do exaggerate sometimes. Now Jennifer, my great friend, she's the other way round. She can make the most exciting things sound dull.' She looked again at the shining heap. 'M. Poirot, who do they really belong to?'

'It is probably very difficult to say. But they do not belong to either you or to me. We have to decide now what to do next.'

Julia looked at him in an expectant fashion.

'You leave yourself in my hands? Good.'

Hercule Poirot closed his eyes.

Suddenly he opened them and became brisk.

'It seems that this is an occasion when I cannot, as I prefer, remain in my chair. There must be order and method, but in what you tell me, there is no order and method. That is because we have here many threads. But they all converge and meet at one place, Meadowbank. Different people, with different aims, and representing different interests – all converge at Meadowbank. So, I, too, go to Meadowbank. And as for you – where is your mother?'

'Mummy's gone in a bus to Anatolia.'

'Ah, your mother has gone in a bus to Anatolia. *Il ne manquait que ça!* I perceive well that she might be a friend of Mrs Summerhayes! Tell me, did you enjoy your visit with Mrs Summerhayes?'

'Oh yes, it was great fun. She's got some lovely dogs.'

'The dogs, yes, I well remember.'

'They come in and out through all the windows – like in a pantomime.'

'You are so right! And the food? Did you enjoy the food?'

'Well, it was a bit peculiar sometimes,' Julia admitted.

'Peculiar, yes, indeed.'

'But Aunt Maureen makes smashing omelettes.'

'She makes smashing omelettes.' Poirot's voice was happy. He sighed.

'Then Hercule Poirot has not lived in vain,' he said. 'It was *I* who taught your Aunt Maureen to make an omelette.' He picked up the telephone receiver.

'We will now reassure your good schoolmistress as to your safety and announce my arrival with you at Meadowbank.'

'She knows I'm all right. I left a note saying I hadn't been kidnapped.'

'Nevertheless, she will welcome further reassurance.'

In due course he was connected, and was informed that Miss Bulstrode was on the line.

'Ah, Miss Bulstrode? My name is Hercule Poirot. I have with me here your pupil Julia Upjohn. I propose to motor down with her immediately, and for the information of the police officer in charge of the case, a certain packet of some value has been safely deposited in the bank.'

He rang off and looked at Julia.

'You would like a *sirop*?' he suggested.

'Golden syrup?' Julia looked doubtful.

'No, a syrup of fruit juice. Blackcurrant, raspberry, *groseille* – that is, red currant?'

Julia settled for red currant.

'But the jewels aren't in the bank,' she pointed out.

'They will be in a very short time,' said Poirot. 'But for the benefit of anyone who listens in at Meadowbank, or who overhears, or who is told, it is as well to think they are already there and no longer in your possession. To obtain jewels from a bank requires time and organization. And I should very much dislike anything to happen to you, my child. I will admit that I have formed a high opinion of your courage and your resource.'

Julia looked pleased but embarrassed.

CHAPTER 18

CONSULTATION

I

Hercule Poirot had prepared himself to beat down an insular prejudice that a headmistress might have against aged foreigners with pointed patent leather shoes and large moustaches. But he was agreeably surprised. Miss Bulstrode greeted him with cosmopolitan aplomb. She also, to his gratification, knew all about him.

'It was kind of you, M. Poirot,' she said, 'to ring up so promptly and allay our anxiety. All the more so because that anxiety had hardly begun. You weren't missed at lunch, Julia, you know,' she added, turning to the girl. 'So many girls were fetched away this morning, and there were so many gaps at table, that half the school could have been missing, I think, without any apprehension being aroused. These are unusual circumstances,' she said, turning back to Poirot. 'I assure you we would not be so slack normally. When I received your telephone call,' she went on, 'I went to Julia's room and found the note she had left.'

'I didn't want you to think I'd been kidnapped, Miss Bulstrode,' said Julia.

'I appreciate that, but I think, Julia, that you might have told me what you were planning to do.'

'I thought I'd better not,' said Julia, and added unexpectedly, '*Les oreilles ennemies nous écoutent.*'

'Mademoiselle Blanche doesn't seem to have done much to improve your accent yet,' said Miss Bulstrode, briskly. 'But I'm not scolding you, Julia.' She looked from Julia to Poirot. 'Now, if you please, I want to hear exactly what has happened.'

'You permit?' said Hercule Poirot. He stepped across the room, opened the door and looked out. He made an exaggerated gesture of shutting it. He returned beaming.

'We are alone,' he said mysteriously. 'We can proceed.'

Miss Bulstrode looked at him, then she looked at the door, then she looked at Poirot again. Her eyebrows rose. He returned her gaze steadily. Very slowly Miss Bulstrode inclined her head.

Then, resuming her brisk manner, she said, 'Now then, Julia, let's hear all about this.'

Julia plunged into her recital. The exchange of tennis racquets, the mysterious woman. And finally her discovery of what the racquet contained. Miss Bulstrode turned to Poirot. He nodded his head gently.

'Mademoiselle Julia has stated everything correctly,' he said. 'I took charge of what she brought me. It is safely lodged in a bank. I think therefore that you need anticipate no further developments of an unpleasant nature here.'

'I see,' said Miss Bulstrode. 'Yes, I see . . .' She was quiet for a moment or two and then she said, 'You think it wise for Julia to remain here? Or would it be better for her to go to her aunt in London?'

'Oh please,' said Julia, 'do let me stay here.'

'You're happy here then?' said Miss Bulstrode.

'I love it,' said Julia. 'And besides, there have been such exciting things going on.'

'That is *not* a normal feature of Meadowbank,' said Miss Bulstrode, dryly.

'I think that Julia will be in no danger here now,' said Hercule Poirot. He looked again towards the door.

'I think I understand,' said Miss Bulstrode.

'But for all that,' said Poirot, 'there should be discretion. Do you understand discretion, I wonder?' he added, looking at Julia.

'M. Poirot means,' said Miss Bulstrode, 'that he would like you to hold your tongue about what you found. Not talk about it to the other girls. Can you hold your tongue?'

'Yes,' said Julia.

'It is a very good story to tell to your friends,' said Poirot. 'Of what you found in a tennis racquet in the dead of night. But there are important reasons why it would be advisable that that story should not be told.'

'I understand,' said Julia.

'Can I trust you, Julia?' said Miss Bulstrode.

'You can trust me,' said Julia. 'Cross my heart.'

Miss Bulstrode smiled. 'I hope your mother will be home before long,' she said.

'Mummy? Oh, I do hope so.'

'I understand from Inspector Kelsey,' said Miss Bulstrode, 'that every effort is being made to get in touch with her. Unfortunately,' she added, 'Anatolian buses are liable to unexpected delays and do not always run to schedule.'

'I can tell Mummy, can't I?' said Julia.

'Of course. Well, Julia, that's all settled. You'd better run along now.'

Julia departed. She closed the door after her. Miss Bulstrode looked very hard at Poirot.

'I have understood you correctly, I think,' she said. 'Just now, you made a great parade of closing that door. Actually – you deliberately left it slightly open.'

Poirot nodded.

'So that what we said could be overheard?'

'Yes – if there was anyone who wanted to overhear. It was a precaution of safety for the child – the news must get round that what she found is safely in a bank, and not in her possession.'

Miss Bulstrode looked at him for a moment – then she pursed her lips grimly together.

'There's got to be an end to all this,' she said.

II

'The idea is,' said the Chief Constable, 'that we try to pool our ideas and information. We are very glad to have you with us, M. Poirot,' he added. 'Inspector Kelsey remembers you well.'

'It's a great many years ago,' said Inspector Kelsey. 'Chief Inspector Warrender was in charge of the case. I was a fairly raw sergeant, knowing my place.'

'The gentleman called, for convenience's sake by us – Mr Adam Goodman, is not known to you, M. Poirot, but I believe you do know his – his – er – chief. Special Branch,' he added.

'Colonel Pikeaway?' said Hercule Poirot thoughtfully.

'Ah, yes it is some time since I have seen him. Is he still as sleepy as ever?' he asked Adam.

Adam laughed. 'I see you know him all right, M. Poirot. I've never seen him wide awake. When I do, I'll know that for once he isn't paying attention to what goes on.'

'You have something there, my friend. It is well observed.'

'Now,' said the Chief Constable, 'let's get down to things. I shan't push myself forward or urge my own opinions. I'm here to listen to what the men who are actually working on the case know and think. There are a great many sides to all this, and one thing perhaps I ought to mention first of all. I'm saying this as a result of representations that have been made to me from – er – various quarters high up.' He looked at Poirot. 'Let's say,' he said, 'that a little girl – a schoolgirl – came to you with a pretty tale of something she'd found in the hollowed-out handle of a tennis racquet. Very exciting for her. A collection, shall we say, of coloured stones, paste, good imitation – something of that kind – or even semi-precious stones which often look as attractive as the other kind. Anyway let's say something that a child would be excited to find. She might even have exaggerated ideas of its value. That's quite possible, don't you think?' He looked very hard at Hercule Poirot.

'It seems to me eminently possible,' said Hercule Poirot.

'Good,' said the Chief Constable. 'Since the person who brought these – er – coloured stones into the country did so quite unknowingly and innocently, we don't want any question of illicit smuggling to arise.

'Then there is the question of our foreign policy,' he went on. 'Things, I am led to understand, are rather – delicate just at present. When it comes to large interests in oil, mineral deposits, all that sort of thing, we have to deal with whatever government's in power. We don't want any awkward questions to arise. You can't keep murder out of the Press, and murder hasn't been kept out of the Press. But there's been no mention of anything like jewels in connection with it. For the present, at any rate, there needn't be.'

'I agree,' said Poirot. 'One must always consider international complications.'

'Exactly,' said the Chief Constable. 'I think I'm right in saying that the late ruler of Ramat was regarded as a friend of this country, and that the powers that be would like his wishes in respect of any property of his that *might* be in this country to be carried out. What that amounts to, I gather, nobody knows at present. If the new Government of Ramat is claiming certain property which they allege belongs to them, it will be much better if we know nothing about such property being in this country. A plain refusal would be tactless.'

'One does not give plain refusals in diplomacy,' said Hercule Poirot. 'One says instead that such a matter shall receive the utmost attention but that at the moment nothing definite is known about any little – nest egg, say – that the late ruler of Ramat may have possessed. It may be still in Ramat, it may be in the keeping of a faithful friend of the late Prince Ali Yusuf, it may have been taken out of the country by half a dozen people, it may be hidden somewhere in the city of Ramat itself.' He shrugged his shoulders. 'One simply does not know.'

The Chief Constable heaved a sigh. 'Thank you,' he said. 'That's just what I mean.' He went on, 'M. Poirot, you have friends in very high quarters in this country. They put much trust in you. Unofficially they would like to leave a certain article in your hands if you do not object.'

'I do not object,' said Poirot. 'Let us leave it at that. We have more serious things to consider, have we not?' He looked round at them. 'Or perhaps you do not think so? But after all, what is three quarters of a million or some such sum in comparison with human life?'

'You're right, M. Poirot,' said the Chief Constable.

'You're right every time,' said Inspector Kelsey. 'What we want is a murderer. We shall be glad to have your opinion, M. Poirot,' he added, 'because it's largely a question of guess and guess again and your guess is as good as the next man's and sometimes better. The whole thing's like a snarl of tangled wool.'

'That is excellently put,' said Poirot, 'one has to take up that snarl of wool and pull out the one colour that we seek, the colour of a murderer. Is that right?'

'That's right.'

'Then tell me, if it is not too tedious for you to indulge in repetition, all that is known so far.'

He settled down to listen.

He listened to Inspector Kelsey, and he listened to Adam Goodman. He listened to the brief summing up of the Chief Constable. Then he leaned back, closed his eyes, and slowly nodded his head.

'Two murders,' he said, 'committed in the same place and

roughly under the same conditions. One kidnapping. The kidnapping of a girl who might be the central figure of the plot. Let us ascertain first *why* she was kidnapped.'

'I can tell you what she said herself,' said Kelsey.

He did so, and Poirot listened.

'It does not make sense,' he complained.

'That's what I thought at the time. As a matter of fact I thought she was just making herself important . . .'

'But the fact remains that she *was* kidnapped. Why?'

'There have been ransom demands,' said Kelsey slowly, 'but –' he paused.

'But they have been, you think, phoney? They have been sent merely to bolster up the kidnapping theory?'

'That's right. The appointments made weren't kept.'

'Shaista, then, was kidnapped for some other reason. What reason?'

'So that she could be made to tell where the – er – valuables were hidden?' suggested Adam doubtfully.

Poirot shook his head.

'She did not know where they were hidden,' he pointed out. 'That at least, is clear. No, there must be something . . .'

His voice tailed off. He was silent, frowning, for a moment or two. Then he sat up, and asked a question.

'Her knees,' he said. 'Did you ever notice her knees?'

Adam stared at him in astonishment.

'No,' he said. 'Why should I?'

'There are many reasons why a man notices a girl's knees,' said Poirot severely. 'Unfortunately, you did not.'

'Was there something odd about her knees? A scar? Something of that kind? I wouldn't know. They all wear stockings most of the time, and their skirts are just below knee length.'

'In the swimming pool, perhaps?' suggested Poirot hopefully.

'Never saw her go in,' said Adam. 'Too chilly for her, I expect. She was used to a warm climate. What are you getting at? A scar? Something of that kind?'

'No, no, that is not it at all. Ah well, a pity.'

He turned to the Chief Constable.

'With your permission, I will communicate with my old friend, the Préfet, at Geneva. I think he may be able to help us.'

'About something that happened when she was at school there?'

'It is possible, yes. You do permit? Good. It is just a little idea of mine.' He paused and went on: 'By the way, there has been nothing in the papers about the kidnapping?'

'The Emir Ibrahim was most insistent.'

'But I did notice a little remark in a gossip column. About a certain foreign young lady who had departed from school very suddenly. A budding romance, the columnist suggested? To be nipped in the bud if possible!'

'That was my idea,' said Adam. 'It seemed a good line to take.'

'Admirable. So now we pass from kidnapping to something more serious. Murder. Two murders at Meadowbank.'

CHAPTER 19
CONSULTATION CONTINUED

I

'Two murders at Meadowbank,' repeated Poirot thoughtfully.

'We've given you the facts,' said Kelsey. 'If you've any ideas –'

'Why the Sports Pavilion?' said Poirot. 'That was your question, wasn't it?' he said to Adam. 'Well, now we have the answer. Because in the Sports Pavilion there was a tennis racquet containing a fortune in jewels. Someone knew about that racquet. Who was it? It could have been Miss Springer herself. She was, so you all say, rather peculiar about that Sports Pavilion. Disliked people coming there – unauthorized people, that is to say. She seemed to be suspicious of their motives. Particularly was that so in the case of Mademoiselle Blanche.'

'Mademoiselle Blanche,' said Kelsey thoughtfully.

Hercule Poirot again spoke to Adam.

'You yourself considered Mademoiselle Blanche's manner odd where it concerned the Sports Pavilion?'

'She explained,' said Adam. 'She explained too much. I should never have questioned her right to be there if she had not taken so much trouble to explain it away.'

Poirot nodded.

'Exactly. That certainly gives one to think. But all we *know* is that Miss Springer was killed in the Sports Pavilion at one o'clock in the morning when she had no business to be there.'

He turned to Kelsey.

'Where was Miss Springer before she came to Meadowbank?'

'We don't know,' said the Inspector. 'She left her last place of employment,' he mentioned a famous school, 'last summer. Where she has been since we do not know.' He added dryly: 'There was no occasion to ask the question until she was dead. She has no near relatives, nor, apparently, any close friends.'

'She *could* have been in Ramat, then,' said Poirot thoughtfully.

'I believe there was a party of school teachers out there at the time of the trouble,' said Adam.

'Let us say, then, that she was there, that in some way she learned about the tennis racquet. Let us assume that after waiting a short time to familiarize herself with the routine at Meadowbank she went out one night to the Sports Pavilion. She got hold of the racquet and was about to remove the jewels from their hiding place when –' he paused – 'when *someone* interrupted her. Someone who had been watching her? Following her that evening? Whoever it was had a pistol – and shot her – but had no time to prise out the jewels, or to take the racquet away, because people were approaching the Sports Pavilion who had heard the shot.'

He stopped.

'You think that's what happened?' asked the Chief Constable.

'I do not know,' said Poirot. 'It is one possibility. The other is that that person with the pistol was there *first*, and was surprised by Miss Springer. Someone whom Miss Springer was already suspicious of. She was, you have told me, that kind of woman. A noser out of secrets.'

'And the other woman?' asked Adam.

Poirot looked at him. Then, slowly, he shifted his gaze to the other two men.

'*You* do not know,' he said. 'And *I* do not know. It could have been someone from outside –?'

His voice half asked a question.

Kelsey shook his head.

'I think not. We have sifted the neighbourhood very carefully. Especially, of course, in the case of strangers. There was a Madam Kolinsky staying nearby – known to Adam here. But she could not have been concerned in either murder.'

'Then it comes back to Meadowbank. And there is only one method to arrive at the truth – elimination.'

Kelsey sighed.

'Yes,' he said. 'That's what it amounts to. For the first murder, it's a fairly open field. Almost anybody could have killed Miss Springer. The exceptions are Miss Johnson and Miss Chadwick – and a child who had the earache. But the second murder narrows things down. Miss Rich, Miss Blake and Miss Shapland are out of it. Miss Rich was staying at the Alton Grange Hotel, twenty miles away, Miss Blake was at Littleport on Sea, Miss Shapland was in London at a night club, the Nid Sauvage, with Mr Dennis Rathbone.'

'And Miss Bulstrode was also away, I understand?'

Adam grinned. The Inspector and the Chief Constable looked shocked.

'Miss Bulstrode,' said the Inspector severely, 'was staying with the Duchess of Welsham.'

'That eliminates Miss Bulstrode then,' said Poirot gravely. 'And leaves us – what?'

'Two members of the domestic staff who sleep in, Mrs Gibbons and a girl called Doris Hogg. I can't consider either of them seriously. That leaves Miss Rowan and Mademoiselle Blanche.'

'And the pupils, of course.'

Kelsey looked startled.

'Surely you don't suspect them?'

'Frankly, no. But one must be exact.'

Kelsey paid no attention to exactitude. He plodded on.

'Miss Rowan has been here over a year. She has a good record. We know nothing against her.'

'So we come, then, to Mademoiselle Blanche. It is there that the journey ends.'

There was a silence.

'There's no evidence,' said Kelsey. 'Her credentials seem genuine enough.'

'They would have to be,' said Poirot.

'She snooped,' said Adam. 'But snooping isn't evidence of murder.'

'Wait a minute,' said Kelsey, 'there was something about a key. In our first interview with her – I'll look it up – something about the key of the Pavilion falling out of the door and she picked it up and forgot to replace it – walked out with it and Springer bawled her out.'

'Whoever wanted to go out there at night and look for the racquet would have had to have a key to get in with,' said Poirot. 'For that, it would have been necessary to take an impression of the key.'

'Surely,' said Adam, 'in that case she would never have mentioned the key incident to you.'

'That doesn't follow,' said Kelsey. 'Springer might have talked about the key incident. If so, she might think it better to mention it in a casual fashion.'

'It is a point to be remembered,' said Poirot.

'It doesn't take us very far,' said Kelsey.

He looked gloomily at Poirot.

'There would seem,' said Poirot, '(that is, if I have been informed correctly), one possibility. Julia Upjohn's mother, I understand, recognized someone here on the first day of term. Someone whom she was surprised to see. From the context, it would seem likely that that someone was connected with foreign espionage. If Mrs Upjohn definitely points out Mademoiselle as the person she recognized, then I think we could proceed with some assurance.'

'Easier said than done,' said Kelsey. 'We've been trying to get in contact with Mrs Upjohn, but the whole thing's a headache! When the child said a bus, I thought she meant a proper coach tour, running to schedule, and a party all booked together. But that's not it at all. Seems she's just taking local buses to any place she happens to fancy! She's not done it through Cook's or a recognized travel agency. She's all on her own, wandering about. What can you do with a woman like that? She might be anywhere. There's a lot of Anatolia!'

'It makes it difficult, yes,' said Poirot.

'Plenty of nice coach tours,' said the Inspector in an injured voice. 'All made easy for you – where you stop and what you see, and all-in fares so that you know exactly where you are.'

'But clearly, that kind of travel does not appeal to Mrs Upjohn.'

'And in the meantime, here *we* are,' went on Kelsey. 'Stuck! That Frenchwoman can walk out any moment she chooses. We've nothing on which we could hold her.'

Poirot shook his head.

'She will not do that.'

'You can't be sure.'

'I am sure. If you have committed murder, you do not want to do anything out of character, that may draw attention to you. Mademoiselle Blanche will remain here quietly until the end of the term.'

'I hope you're right.'

'I am sure I am right. And remember, the person whom Mrs Upjohn saw, *does not know that Mrs Upjohn saw her.* The surprise when it comes will be complete.'

Kelsey sighed.

'If that's all we've got to go on –'

'There are other things. Conversation, for instance.'

'Conversation?'

'It is very valuable, conversation. Sooner or later, if one has something to hide, one says too much.'

'Gives oneself away?' The Chief Constable sounded sceptical.

'It is not quite so simple as that. One is guarded about the thing one is trying to hide. But often one says too much about other things. And there are other uses for conversation. There are the innocent people who know things, but are unaware of the importance of what they know. And that reminds me –'

He rose to his feet.

'Excuse me, I pray. I must go and demand of Miss Bulstrode if there is someone here who can draw.'

'Draw?'

'Draw.'

'Well,' said Adam, as Poirot went out. 'First girls' knees, and now draughtsmanship! What next, I wonder?'

II

Miss Bulstrode answered Poirot's questions without evincing any surprise.

'Miss Laurie is our visiting Drawing Mistress,' she said briskly. 'But she isn't here today. What do you want her to draw for you?' she added in a kindly manner as though to a child.

'Faces,' said Poirot.

'Miss Rich is good at sketching people. She's clever at getting a likeness.'

'That is exactly what I need.'

Miss Bulstrode, he noted with approval, asked him no questions as to his reasons. She merely left the room and returned with Miss Rich.

After introductions, Poirot said: 'You can sketch people? Quickly? With a pencil?'

Eileen Rich nodded.

'I often do. For amusement.'

'Good. Please, then, sketch for me the late Miss Springer.'

'That's difficult. I knew her for such a short time. I'll try.' She screwed up her eyes, then began to draw rapidly.

'*Bien*,' said Poirot, taking it from her. 'And now, if you please, Miss Bulstrode, Miss Rowan, Mademoiselle Blanche and – yes – the gardener Adam.'

Eileen Rich looked at him doubtfully, then set to work. He looked at the result, and nodded appreciatively.

'You are good – you are very good. So few strokes – and yet the likeness is there. Now I will ask you to do something more difficult. Give, for example, to Miss Bulstrode a different hair arrangement. Change the shape of her eyebrows.'

Eileen stared at him as though she thought he was mad.

'No,' said Poirot. 'I am not mad. I make an experiment, that is all. Please do as I ask.'

In a moment or two she said: 'Here you are.'

'Excellent. Now do the same for Mademoiselle Blanche and Miss Rowan.'

When she had finished he lined up the three sketches.

'Now I will show you something,' he said. 'Miss Bulstrode, in spite of the changes you have made is still unmistakably Miss

Bulstrode. But look at the other two. Because their features are negative, and since they have not Miss Bulstrode's personality, they appear almost different people, do they not?'

'I see what you mean,' said Eileen Rich.

She looked at him as he carefully folded the sketches away.

'What are you going to do with them?' she asked.

'Use them,' said Poirot.

CHAPTER 20

CONVERSATION

'Well – I don't know what to say,' said Mrs Sutcliffe. 'Really I don't know what to say –'

She looked with definite distaste at Hercule Poirot.

'Henry, of course,' she said, 'is not at home.'

The meaning of this pronouncement was slightly obscure, but Hercule Poirot thought that he knew what was in her mind. Henry, she was feeling, would be able to deal with this sort of thing. Henry had so many international dealings. He was always flying to the Middle East and to Ghana and to South America and to Geneva, and even occasionally, but not so often, to Paris.

'The whole thing,' said Mrs Sutcliffe, 'has been *most* distressing. I was so glad to have Jennifer safely at home with me. Though, I must say,' she added, with a trace of vexation, 'Jennifer has really been most tiresome. After having made a great fuss about going to Meadowbank and being quite sure she wouldn't like it there, and saying it was a snobby kind of school and not the kind she wanted to go to, *now* she sulks all day long because I've taken her away. It's really too bad.'

'It is undeniably a very good school,' said Hercule Poirot. 'Many people say the best school in England.'

'It *was*, I daresay,' said Mrs Sutcliffe.

'And will be again,' said Hercule Poirot.

'You think so?' Mrs Sutcliffe looked at him doubtfully. His sympathetic manner was gradually piercing her defences. There is nothing that eases the burden of a mother's life more than to be permitted to unburden herself of the difficulties, rebuffs and frustrations which she has in dealing with her offspring. Loyalty so often compels silent endurance. But to a foreigner like Hercule Poirot Mrs Sutcliffe felt that this loyalty was not applicable. It was not like talking to the mother of another daughter.

'Meadowbank,' said Hercule Poirot, 'is just passing through an unfortunate phase.'

It was the best thing he could think of to say at the moment. He felt its inadequacy and Mrs Sutcliffe pounced upon the inadequacy immediately.

'Rather more than unfortunate!' she said. 'Two murders! And a girl kidnapped. You can't send your daughter to a school where the mistresses are being murdered all the time.'

It seemed a highly reasonable point of view.

'If the murders,' said Poirot, 'turn out to be the work of one person and that person is apprehended, that makes a difference, does it not?'

'Well – I suppose so. Yes,' said Mrs Sutcliffe doubtfully. 'I mean – you mean – oh, I see, you mean like Jack the Ripper or that other man – who was it? Something to do with Devonshire. Cream? Neil Cream. Who went about killing an unfortunate type of woman. I suppose this murderer just goes about killing schoolmistresses! If once you've got him safely in prison, and hanged too, I hope, because you're only allowed one murder, aren't you? – like a dog with a bite – what was I saying? Oh yes, if he's safely caught, well, then I suppose it *would* be different. Of course there can't be many people like that, can there?'

'One certainly hopes not,' said Hercule Poirot.

'But then there's this kidnapping too,' pointed out Mrs Sutcliffe. 'You don't want to send your daughter to a school where she may be kidnapped, either, do you?'

'Assuredly not, madame. I see how clearly you have thought out the whole thing. You are so right in all you say.'

Mrs Sutcliffe looked faintly pleased. Nobody had said anything like that to her for some time. Henry had merely said things like 'What did you want to send her to Meadowbank for anyway?' and Jennifer had sulked and refused to answer.

'I *have* thought about it,' she said. 'A great deal.'

'Then I should not let kidnapping worry you, madame. *Entre nous*, if I may speak in confidence, about Princess Shaista – It is not exactly a kidnapping – one suspects a romance –'

'You mean the naughty girl just ran away to marry some-body?'

'My lips are sealed,' said Hercule Poirot. 'You comprehend it is not desired that there should be any scandal. This is in confidence *entre nous*. I know you will say nothing.'

'Of course not,' said Mrs Sutcliffe virtuously. She looked down at the letter that Poirot had brought with him from the Chief Constable. 'I don't quite understand who you are, M. – er – Poirot. Are you what they call in books – a private eye?'

'I am a consultant,' said Hercule Poirot loftily.

This flavour of Harley Street encouraged Mrs Sutcliffe a great deal.

'What do you want to talk to Jennifer about?' she demanded.

'Just to get her impressions of things,' said Poirot. 'She is observant – yes?'

'I'm afraid I wouldn't say that,' said Mrs Sutcliffe. 'She's not what I call a noticing kind of child at all. I mean, she is always so matter of fact.'

'It is better than making up things that have never happened at all,' said Poirot.

'Oh, Jennifer wouldn't do *that* sort of thing,' said Mrs Sutcliffe, with certainty. She got up, went to the window and called 'Jennifer.'

'I wish,' she said, to Poirot, as she came back again, 'that you'd try and get it into Jennifer's head that her father and I are only doing our best for her.'

Jennifer came into the room with a sulky face and looked with deep suspicion at Hercule Poirot.

'How do you do?' said Poirot. 'I am a very old friend of Julia Upjohn. She came to London to find me.'

'Julia went to London?' said Jennifer, slightly surprised. 'Why?'

'To ask my advice,' said Hercule Poirot.

Jennifer looked unbelieving.

'I was able to give it to her,' said Poirot. 'She is now back at Meadowbank,' he added.

'So her Aunt Isabel didn't *take* her away,' said Jennifer, shooting an irritated look at her mother.

Poirot looked at Mrs Sutcliffe and for some reason, perhaps because she had been in the middle of counting the laundry when Poirot arrived and perhaps because of some unexplained compulsion, she got up and left the room.

'It's a bit hard,' said Jennifer, 'to be out of all that's going on there. All this fuss! I told Mummy it was silly. After all, none of the *pupils* have been killed.'

'Have you any ideas of your own about the murders?' asked Poirot.

Jennifer shook her head. 'Someone who's batty?' she offered. She added thoughtfully, 'I suppose Miss Bulstrode will have to get some new mistresses now.'

'It seems possible, yes,' said Poirot. He went on, 'I am interested, Mademoiselle Jennifer, in the woman who came and offered you a new racquet for your old one. Do you remember?'

'I should think I do remember,' said Jennifer. 'I've never found out to this day who really sent it. It wasn't Aunt Gina at all.'

'What did this woman look like?' said Poirot.

'The one who brought the racquet?' Jennifer half closed her eyes as though thinking. 'Well, I don't know. She had on a sort of fussy dress with a little cape, I think. Blue, and a floppy sort of hat.'

'Yes?' said Poirot. 'I meant perhaps not so much her clothes as her face.'

'A good deal of make-up, I think,' said Jennifer vaguely. 'A bit too much for the country, I mean, and fair hair. I think she was an American.'

'Had you ever seen her before?' asked Poirot.

'Oh no,' said Jennifer. 'I don't think she lived down there. She said she'd come down for a luncheon party or a cocktail party or something.'

Poirot looked at her thoughtfully. He was interested in Jennifer's complete acceptance of everything that was said to her. He said gently,

'But she might not have been speaking the truth?'

'Oh,' said Jennifer. 'No, I suppose not.'

'You're quite sure you hadn't seen her before? She could not have been, for instance, one of the girls dressed up? Or one of the mistresses?'

'Dressed up?' Jennifer looked puzzled.

Poirot laid before her the sketch Eileen Rich had done for him of Mademoiselle Blanche.

'This was not the woman, was it?'

Jennifer looked at it doubtfully.

'It's a little like her – but I don't think it's her.'

Poirot nodded thoughtfully.

There was no sign that Jennifer recognized that this was actually a sketch of Mademoiselle Blanche.

'You see,' said Jennifer, 'I didn't really look at her much. She was an American and a stranger, and then she told me about the racquet –'

After that, it was clear, Jennifer would have had eyes for nothing but her new possession.

'I see,' said Poirot. He went on, 'Did you ever see at Meadow-bank anyone that you'd seen out in Ramat?'

'In Ramat?' Jennifer thought. 'Oh no – at least – I don't think so.'

Poirot pounced on the slight expression of doubt. 'But you are not *sure*, Mademoiselle Jennifer.'

'Well,' Jennifer scratched her forehead with a worried expression, 'I mean, you're always seeing people who look like somebody else. You can't quite remember who it is they look like. Sometimes you see people that you *have* met but you don't remember who they are. And they say to you "You don't remember me," and then that's awfully awkward because really you don't. I mean, you sort of know their face but you can't remember their names or where you saw them.'

'That is very true,' said Poirot. 'Yes, that is very true. One often has that experience.' He paused a moment then he went on, prodding gently, 'Princess Shaista, for instance, you probably recognized *her* when you saw her because you must have seen her in Ramat.'

'Oh, was she in Ramat?'

'Very likely,' said Poirot. 'After all she is a relation of the ruling house. You might have seen her there?'

'I don't think I did,' said Jennifer frowning. 'Anyway, she wouldn't go about with her face showing there, would she? I mean, they all wear veils and things like that. Though they take them off in Paris and Cairo, I believe. And in London, of course,' she added.

'Anyway, you had no feeling of having seen anyone at Meadowbank whom you had seen before?'

'No, I'm sure I hadn't. Of course most people do look rather alike and you might have seen them anywhere. It's only when somebody's got an odd sort of face like Miss Rich, that you notice it.'

'Did you think you'd seen Miss Rich somewhere before?'

'I hadn't really. It must have been someone like her. But it was someone much fatter than she was.'

'Someone much fatter,' said Poirot thoughtfully.

'You couldn't imagine Miss Rich being fat,' said Jennifer with a giggle. 'She's so frightfully thin and nobbly. And anyway Miss Rich couldn't have been in Ramat because she was away ill last term.'

'And the other girls?' said Poirot, 'had you seen any of the girls before?'

'Only the ones I knew already,' said Jennifer. 'I did know one or two of them. After all, you know, I was only there three weeks and I really don't know half of the people there even by sight. I wouldn't know most of them if I met them tomorrow.'

'You should notice things more,' said Poirot severely.

'One can't notice everything,' protested Jennifer. She went on: 'If Meadowbank is carrying on I would like to go back. See if you can do anything with Mummy. Though really,' she added, 'I think it's Daddy who's the stumbling-block. It's awful here in the country. I get *no* opportunity to improve my tennis.'

'I assure you I will do what I can,' said Poirot.

CHAPTER 21

GATHERING THREADS

I

'I want to talk to you, Eileen,' said Miss Bulstrode.

Eileen Rich followed Miss Bulstrode into the latter's sitting-room. Meadowbank was strangely quiet. About twenty-five pupils were still there. Pupils whose parents had found it either difficult or unwelcome to fetch them. The panic-stricken rush had, as Miss Bulstrode had hoped, been checked by her own tactics. There was a general feeling that by next term everything would have been cleared up. It was much wiser of Miss Bulstrode, they felt, to close the school.

None of the staff had left. Miss Johnson fretted with too much time on her hands. A day in which there was too little to do did not in the least suit her. Miss Chadwick, looking old and miserable, wandered round in a kind of coma of misery. She was far harder hit to all appearance than Miss Bulstrode. Miss Bulstrode, indeed, managed apparently without difficulty to be completely herself, unperturbed, and with no sign of strain or collapse. The two younger mistresses were not averse to the extra leisure. They bathed in the swimming pool, wrote long letters to friends and relations and sent for cruise literature to study and compare. Ann Shapland had a good deal of time on her hands and did not appear to resent the fact. She spent a good deal of that time in the garden and devoted herself to gardening with quite unexpected efficiency. That she preferred to be instructed in the work by Adam rather than by old Briggs was perhaps a not unnatural phenomenon.

'Yes, Miss Bulstrode?' said Eileen Rich.

'I've been wanting to talk to you,' said Miss Bulstrode. 'Whether this school can continue or not I do not know. What people will feel is always fairly incalculable because they will all feel differently. But the result will be that whoever feels most strongly will end by converting all the rest. So either Meadowbank is finished –'

'No,' said Eileen Rich, interrupting, 'not finished.' She almost stamped her foot and her hair immediately began coming down. 'You mustn't let it be stopped,' she said. 'It would be a sin – a crime.'

'You speak very strongly,' said Miss Bulstrode.

'I feel strongly. There are so many things that really don't seem worth while a bit, but Meadowbank does seem worth while. It seemed worth while to me the first moment I came here.'

'You're a fighter,' said Miss Bulstrode. 'I like fighters, and I assure you that I don't intend to give in tamely. In a way I'm going to enjoy the fight. You know, when everything's too easy and things go too well one gets – I don't know the exact word I mean – complacent? Bored? A kind of hybrid of the two. But I'm not bored now and I'm not complacent and I'm going to fight with every ounce of strength I've got, and with every penny I've got, too. Now what I want to say to you is this: If Meadowbank continues, will you come in on a partnership basis?'

'Me?' Eileen Rich stared at her. 'Me?'

'Yes, my dear,' said Miss Bulstrode. 'You.'

'I couldn't,' said Eileen Rich. 'I don't know enough. I'm too young. Why, I haven't got the experience, the knowledge that you'd want.'

'You must leave it to me to know what I want,' said Miss Bulstrode. 'Mind you, this isn't, at the present moment of talking, a good offer. You'd probably do better for yourself elsewhere. But I want to tell you this, and you've got to believe me. I had already decided before Miss Vansittart's unfortunate death, that you were the person I wanted to carry on this school.'

'You thought so then?' Eileen Rich stared at her. 'But I thought – we all thought – that Miss Vansittart . . .'

'There was no arrangement made with Miss Vansittart,' said Miss Bulstrode. 'I had her in mind, I will confess. I've had her in mind for the last two years. But something's always held me back from saying anything definite to her about it. I daresay everyone assumed that she'd be my successor. She may have thought so herself. I myself thought so until very recently. And then I decided that she was not what I wanted.'

'But she was so suitable in every way,' said Eileen Rich. 'She would have carried out things in exactly your ways, in exactly your ideas.'

'Yes,' said Miss Bulstrode, 'and that's just what would have been wrong. You can't hold on to the past. A certain amount of tradition is good but never too much. A school is for the children of *today*. It's not for the children of fifty years ago or even of thirty years ago. There are some schools in which tradition is more important than others, but Meadowbank is not one of those. It's not a school with a long tradition behind it. It's a creation, if I may say it, of one woman. Myself. I've tried certain ideas and carried them out to the best of my ability, though occasionally I've had to modify them when they haven't produced the results I'd expected. It's not been a conventional school, but it has not prided itself on being an unconventional school either. It's a school that tries to make the best of both worlds: the past and the future, but the real stress is on the present. That's how it's going to go on, how it ought to go on. Run by someone with ideas – ideas of the present day. Keeping what is wise from the past, looking forward towards the future. You're very much the age I was when I started here but you've got what I no longer can have. You'll find it written in the Bible. *Their old men dream dreams and their young men have visions*. We don't need dreams here, we need vision. I believe you to have vision and that's why I decided that you were the person and not Eleanor Vansittart.'

'It would have been wonderful,' said Eileen Rich. 'Wonderful. The thing I should have liked above all.'

Miss Bulstrode was faintly surprised by the tense, although she did not show it. Instead she agreed promptly.

'Yes,' she said, 'it would have been wonderful. But it isn't wonderful now? Well, I suppose I understand that.'

'No, no, I don't mean that at all,' said Eileen Rich. 'Not at all. I – I can't go into details very well, but if you had – if you had asked me, spoken to me like this a week or a fortnight ago, I should have said at once that I couldn't, that it would have been quite impossible. The only reason why it – why it might be possible now is because – well, because it *is* a case of fighting – of taking on things. May I – may I think it over, Miss Bulstrode? I don't know what to say now.'

'Of course,' said Miss Bulstrode. She was still surprised. One never really knew, she thought, about anybody.

II

'There goes Rich with her hair coming down again,' said Ann Shapland as she straightened herself up from a flower bed. 'If she can't control it I can't think why she doesn't get it cut off. She's got a good-shaped head and she would look better.'

'You ought to tell her so,' said Adam.

'We're not on those terms,' said Ann Shapland. She went on, 'D'you think this place will be able to carry on?'

'That's a very doubtful question,' said Adam, 'and who am I to judge?'

'You could tell as well as another I should think,' said Ann

Shapland. 'It might, you know. The old Bull, as the girls call her, has got what it takes. A hypnotizing effect on parents to begin with. How long is it since the beginning of term – only a month? It seems like a year. I shall be glad when it comes to an end.'

'Will you come back if the school goes on?'

'No,' said Ann with emphasis, 'no indeed. I've had enough of schools to last me for a lifetime. I'm not cut out for being cooped up with a lot of women anyway. And, frankly, I don't like murder. It's the sort of thing that's fun to read about in the paper or to read yourself to sleep with in the way of a nice book. But the real thing isn't so good. I think,' added Ann thoughtfully, 'that when I leave here at the end of the term I shall marry Dennis and settle down.'

'Dennis?' said Adam. 'That's the one you mentioned to me, wasn't it? As far as I remember his work takes him to Burma and Malaya and Singapore and Japan and places like that. It won't be exactly settling down, will it, if you marry him?'

Ann laughed suddenly. 'No, no, I suppose it won't. Not in the physical, geographical sense.'

'I think you can do better than Dennis,' said Adam.

'Are you making me an offer?' said Ann.

'Certainly not,' said Adam. 'You're an ambitious girl, you wouldn't like to marry a humble jobbing gardener.'

'I was wondering about marrying into the C.I.D.,' said Ann.

'I'm not in the C.I.D.,' said Adam.

'No, no, of course not,' said Ann. 'Let's preserve the niceties of speech. You're not in the C.I.D. Shaista wasn't kidnapped, everything in the garden's lovely. It is rather,' she added, looking round. 'All the same,' she said after a moment or two, 'I don't understand in the least about Shaista turning up in Geneva or whatever the story is. How did she get there? All you people must be very slack to allow her to be taken out of this country.'

'My lips are sealed,' said Adam.

'I don't think you know the first thing about it,' said Ann.

'I will admit,' said Adam, 'that we have to thank Monsieur Hercule Poirot for having had a bright idea.'

'What, the funny little man who brought Julia back and came to see Miss Bulstrode?'

'Yes. He calls himself,' said Adam, 'a consultant detective.'

'I think he's pretty much of a has-been,' said Ann.

'I don't understand what he's up to at all,' said Adam. 'He even went to see my mother – or some friend of his did.'

'Your mother?' said Ann. 'Why?'

'I've no idea. He seems to have a kind of morbid interest in mothers. He went to see Jennifer's mother too.'

'Did he go and see Miss Rich's mother, and Chaddy's?'

'I gather Miss Rich hasn't got a mother,' said Adam. 'Otherwise, no doubt, he would have gone to see her.'

'Miss Chadwick's got a mother in Cheltenham, she told me,' said Ann, 'but she's about eighty-odd, I believe. Poor Miss Chadwick, she looks about eighty herself. She's coming to talk to us now.'

Adam looked up. 'Yes,' he said, 'she's aged a lot in the last week.'

'Because she really loves the school,' said Ann. 'It's her whole life. She can't bear to see it go downhill.'

Miss Chadwick indeed looked ten years older than she had done on the day of the opening term. Her step had lost its brisk efficiency. She no longer trotted about, happy and bustling. She came up to them now, her steps dragging a little.

'Will you please come to Miss Bulstrode,' she said to Adam. 'She has some instruction about the garden.'

'I'll have to clean up a bit first,' said Adam. He laid down his tools and moved off in the direction of the potting shed.

Ann and Miss Chadwick walked together towards the house.

'It does seem quiet, doesn't it,' said Ann, looking round. 'Like an empty house at the theatre,' she added thoughtfully, 'with people spaced out by the box office as tactfully as possible to make them look like an audience.'

'It's dreadful,' said Miss Chadwick, 'dreadful! Dreadful to think that Meadowbank has come to *this*. I can't get over it. I can't sleep at night. Everything in ruins. All the years of work, of building up something really fine.'

'It may get all right again,' said Ann cheerfully. 'People have got very short memories, you know.'

'Not as short as all that,' said Miss Chadwick grimly.

Ann did not answer. In her heart she rather agreed with Miss Chadwick.

III

Mademoiselle Blanche came out of the classroom where she had been teaching French literature.

She glanced at her watch. Yes, there would be plenty of time for what she intended to do. With so few pupils there was always plenty of time these days.

She went upstairs to her room and put on her hat. She was not one of those who went about hatless. She studied her appearance in the mirror with satisfaction. Not a personality to be noticed! Well, there could be advantages in that! She smiled to herself. It had made it easy for her to use her sister's testimonials. Even the passport photograph had gone unchallenged. It would have been a thousand pities to waste those excellent credentials when Angèle had died. Angèle had really enjoyed teaching. For herself, it was unutterable boredom. But the pay was excellent. Far above what she herself had ever been able to earn. And besides, things had turned out unbelievably well. The future was going to be very different. Oh yes, very different. The drab Mademoiselle Blanche would be transformed. She saw it all in her mind's eye. The Riviera. Herself smartly dressed, suitably made up. All one needed in this world was money. Oh yes, things were going to be very pleasant indeed. It was worth having come to this detestable English school.

She picked up her handbag, went out of her room and along the corridor. Her eyes dropped to the kneeling woman who was busy there. A new daily help. A police spy, of course. How simple they were – to think that one would not know!

A contemptuous smile on her lips, she went out of the house and down the drive to the front gate. The bus stop was almost opposite. She stood at it, waiting. The bus should be here in a moment or two.

There were very few people about in this quiet country road. A car, with a man bending over the open bonnet. A bicycle leaning against a hedge. A man also waiting for the bus.

One or other of the three would, no doubt, follow her. It would be skilfully done, not obviously. She was quite alive to the fact, and it did not worry her. Her 'shadow' was welcome to see where she went and what she did.

The bus came. She got in. A quarter of an hour later, she got out in the main square of the town. She did not trouble to look behind her. She crossed to where the shop windows of a fairly large departmental store showed their display of new model gowns. Poor stuff, for provincial tastes, she thought, with a curling lip. But she stood looking at them as though much attracted.

Presently she went inside, made one or two trivial purchases, then went up to the first floor and entered the Ladies Rest Room. There was a writing table there, some easy chairs, and a telephone box. She went into the box, put the necessary coins in, dialled the number she wanted, waiting to hear if the right voice answered.

She nodded in approval, pressed button A and spoke.

'This is the Maison Blanche. You understand me, the Maison *Blanche*? I have to speak of an account that is owed. You have until tomorrow evening. Tomorrow evening. To pay into the account of the Maison Blanche at the Credit Nationale in London, Ledbury St branch the sum that I tell you.'

She named the sum.

'If that money is not paid in, then it will be necessary for me to report in the proper quarters what I observed on the night of the 12th. The reference – pay – attention – is to Miss Springer. You have a little over twenty-four hours.'

She hung up and emerged into the rest room. A woman had just come in from outside. Another customer of the shop, perhaps, or again perhaps not. But if the latter, it was too late for anything to be overheard.

Mademoiselle Blanche freshened herself up in the adjoining cloak room, then she went and tried on a couple of blouses, but did not buy them; she went out into the street again, smiling to herself. She looked into a bookshop, and then caught a bus back to Meadowbank.

She was still smiling to herself as she walked up the drive. She had arranged matters very well. The sum she had demanded had not been too large – not impossible to raise at short notice. And it would do very well to go on with. Because, of course, in the future, there would be further demands . . .

Yes, a very pretty little source of income this was going to be. She had no qualms of conscience. She did not consider it in any way her duty to report what she knew and had seen to the police.

That Springer had been a detestable woman, rude, *mal élevée*. Prying into what was no business of hers. Ah, well, she had got her deserts.

Mademoiselle Blanche stayed for a while by the swimming pool. She watched Eileen Rich diving. Then Ann Shapland, too, climbed up and dived – very well, too. There was laughing and squeals from the girls.

A bell rang, and Mademoiselle Blanche went in to take her junior class. They were inattentive and tiresome, but Mademoiselle Blanche hardly noticed. She would soon have done with teaching for ever.

She went up to her room to tidy herself for supper. Vaguely, without really noticing, she saw that, contrary to her usual practice, she had thrown her garden coat across a chair in the corner instead of hanging it up as usual.

She leaned forward, studying her face in the glass. She applied powder, lipstick –

The movement was so quick that it took her completely by surprise. Noiseless! Professional. The coat on the chair seemed to gather itself together, drop to the ground and in an instant behind Mademoiselle Blanche a hand with a sandbag rose and, as she opened her lips to scream, fell, dully, on the back of her neck.

CHAPTER 22

INCIDENT IN ANATOLIA

Mrs Upjohn was sitting by the side of the road overlooking a deep ravine. She was talking partly in French and partly with gestures to a large and solid-looking Turkish woman who was telling her with as much detail as possible under these difficulties of communications all about her last miscarriage. Nine children she had had, she explained. Eight of them boys, and five miscarriages. She seemed as pleased at the miscarriages as she did at the births.

'And you?' she poked Mrs Upjohn amiably in the ribs. '*Combien? – garçons? – filles? – combien?*' She held up her hands ready to indicate on the fingers.

'*Une fille,*' said Mrs Upjohn.

'*Et garçons?*'

Seeing that she was about to fall in the Turkish woman's estimation, Mrs Upjohn in a surge of nationalism proceeded to perjure herself. She held up five fingers of her right hand.

'*Cinq,*' she said.

'*Cinq garçons? Très bien!*'

The Turkish woman nodded with approbation and respect. She added that if only her cousin who spoke French really fluently was here they could understand each other a great deal better. She then resumed the story of her last miscarriage.

The other passengers were sprawled about near them, eating odd bits of food from the baskets they carried with them. The bus, looking slightly the worse for wear, was drawn up against an overhanging rock, and the driver and another man were busy inside the bonnet. Mrs Upjohn had lost complete count of time. Floods had blocked two of the roads, *détours* had been necessary and they had once been stuck for seven hours until the river they were fording subsided. Ankara lay in the not impossible future and that was all she knew. She listened to her friend's eager and incoherent conversation, trying to gauge when to nod admiringly, when to shake her head in sympathy.

A voice cut into her thoughts, a voice highly incongruous with her present surroundings.

'Mrs Upjohn, I believe,' said the voice.

Mrs Upjohn looked up. A little way away a car had driven up. The man standing opposite her had undoubtedly alighted from it. His face was unmistakably British, as was his voice. He was impeccably dressed in a grey flannel suit.

'Good heavens,' said Mrs Upjohn. 'Dr Livingstone?'

'It must seem rather like that,' said the stranger pleasantly. 'My name's Atkinson. I'm from the Consulate in Ankara. We've been trying to get in touch with you for two or three days, but the roads have been cut.'

'You wanted to get in touch with me? Why?' Suddenly Mrs Upjohn rose to her feet. All traces of the gay traveller had disappeared. She was all mother, every inch of her. 'Julia?' she said sharply. 'Has something happened to Julia?'

'No, no,' Mr Atkinson reassured her. 'Julia's quite all right. It's not that at all. There's been a spot of trouble at Meadowbank and we want to get you home there as soon as possible. I'll drive you back to Ankara, and you can get on a plane in about an hour's time.'

Mrs Upjohn opened her mouth and then shut it again. Then she rose and said, 'You'll have to get my bag off the top of that bus. It's the dark one.' She turned, shook hands with her Turkish companion, said: 'I'm sorry, I have to go home now,' waved to the rest of the bus load with the utmost friendliness, called out a Turkish farewell greeting which was part of her small stock of Turkish, and prepared to follow Mr Atkinson immediately without asking any further questions. It occurred to him as it had occurred to many other people that Mrs Upjohn was a very sensible woman.

CHAPTER 23

SHOWDOWN

I

In one of the smaller classrooms Miss Bulstrode looked at the assembled people. All the members of her staff were there: Miss Chadwick, Miss Johnson, Miss Rich and the two younger mistresses. Ann Shapland sat with her pad and pencil in case Miss Bulstrode wanted her to take notes. Beside Miss Bulstrode sat Inspector Kelsey and beyond him, Hercule Poirot. Adam Goodman sat in a no-man's-land of his own halfway between the staff and what he called to himself the executive body. Miss Bulstrode rose and spoke in her practised, decisive voice.

'I feel it is due to you all,' she said, 'as members of my staff, and interested in the fortunes of the school, to know exactly to what point this inquiry has progressed. I have been informed by Inspector Kelsey of several facts. M. Hercule Poirot who has international connections, has obtained valuable assistance from Switzerland and will report himself on that particular matter. We have not yet come to the end of the inquiry, I am sorry to say, but certain minor matters have been cleared up and I thought it would be a relief to you all to know how matters stand at the present moment.' Miss Bulstrode looked towards Inspector Kelsey, and he rose.

'Officially,' he said, 'I am not in a position to disclose all that I know. I can only reassure you to the extent of saying that we are making progress and we are beginning to have a good idea who is responsible for the three crimes that have been committed on the premises. Beyond that I will not go. My friend, M. Hercule Poirot, who is not bound by official secrecy and is at perfect liberty to give you his own ideas, will disclose to you certain information which he himself has been influential in procuring. I am sure you are all loyal to Meadowbank and to Miss Bulstrode and will keep to yourselves various matters upon which M. Poirot is going to touch and which are not of any public interest. The less gossip or speculation about them the better, so I will ask you to keep the facts that you will learn here today to yourselves. Is that understood?'

'Of course,' said Miss Chadwick, speaking first and with emphasis. 'Of course we're all loyal to Meadowbank, I should hope.'

'Naturally,' said Miss Johnson.

'Oh yes,' said the two younger mistresses.

'I agree,' said Eileen Rich.

'Then perhaps, M. Poirot?'

Hercule Poirot rose to his feet, beamed on his audience and carefully twisted his moustaches. The two younger mistresses had a sudden desire to giggle, and looked away from each other pursing their lips together.

'It has been a difficult and anxious time for you all,' he said. 'I want you to know first that I do appreciate that. It has naturally been worst of all for Miss Bulstrode herself, but you have all suffered. You have suffered first the loss of three of your colleagues, one of whom has been here for a considerable period of time. I refer to Miss Vansittart. Miss Springer and Mademoiselle Blanche were, of course, newcomers, but I do not doubt that their deaths were a great shock to you and a distressing happening. You must also have suffered a good deal of apprehension yourselves, for it must have seemed as though there were a kind of vendetta aimed against the mistresses of Meadowbank school. That I can assure you, and Inspector Kelsey will assure you also, is not so. Meadowbank by a fortuitous series of chances became the centre for the attentions of various undesirable interests. There has been, shall we say, a cat among the pigeons. There have been three murders here and also a kidnapping. I will deal first with the kidnapping, for all through this business the difficulty has been to clear out of the way extraneous matters which, though criminal in themselves, obscure the most important thread – the thread of a ruthless and determined killer in your midst.'

He took from his pocket a photograph.

'First, I will pass round this photograph.'

Kelsey took it, handed it to Miss Bulstrode and she in turn handed it to the staff. It was returned to Poirot. He looked at their faces, which were quite blank.

'I ask you, all of you, do you recognize the girl in that photograph?'

One and all they shook their heads.

'You should do so,' said Poirot. 'Since that is a photograph obtained by me from Geneva of Princess Shaista.'

'But it's not Shaista at all,' cried Miss Chadwick.

'Exactly,' said Poirot. 'The threads of all this business start in Ramat where, as you know, a revolutionary *coup d'état* took place about three months ago. The ruler, Prince Ali Yusuf, managed to escape, flown out by his own private pilot. Their plane, however, crashed in the mountains north of Ramat and was not discovered until later in the year. A certain article of great value, which was always carried on Prince Ali's person, was missing. It was not found in the wreck and there were rumours that it had been brought to this country. Several groups of people were anxious to get hold of this very valuable article. One of their leads to it was Prince Ali Yusuf's only remaining relation, his first cousin, a girl who was then at a school in Switzerland. It seemed likely that if the precious article had been safely got out of Ramat it would be brought to Princess Shaista or to her relatives and guardians. Certain agents were detailed to keep an eye on her uncle, the Emir Ibrahim, and others to keep an eye on the Princess herself. It was known that she was due to come to this school, Meadowbank, this term. Therefore it would have been only natural that someone should be detailed to obtain employment here and to keep a close watch on anyone who approached the Princess, her letters, and any telephone messages. But an even simpler and more efficacious idea was evolved, that of kidnapping Shaista and sending one of their own number to the school as Princess

Shaista herself. This could be done successfully since the Emir Ibrahim was in Egypt and did not propose to visit England until late summer. Miss Bulstrode herself had not seen the girl and all arrangements that she had made concerning her reception had been made with the Embassy in London.

'The plan was simple in the extreme. The real Shaista left Switzerland accompanied by a representative from the Embassy in London. Or so it was supposed. Actually, the Embassy in London was informed that a representative from the Swiss school would accompany the girl to London. The real Shaista was taken to a very pleasant chalet in Switzerland where she has been ever since, and an entirely different girl arrived in London, was met there by a representative of the Embassy and subsequently brought to this school. This substitute, of course, was necessarily much older than the real Shaista. But that would hardly attract attention since Eastern girls noticeably look much more mature than their age. A young French actress who specializes in playing schoolgirl parts was the agent chosen.

'I did ask,' said Hercule Poirot, in a thoughtful voice, 'as to whether anyone had noticed Shaista's knees. Knees are a very good indication of age. The knees of a woman of twenty-three or twenty-four can never really be mistaken for the knees of a girl of fourteen or fifteen. Nobody, alas, had noticed her knees.

'The plan was hardly as successful as had been hoped. Nobody attempted to get in touch with Shaista, no letters or telephone calls of significance arrived for her and as time went on an added anxiety arose. The Emir Ibrahim might arrive in England ahead of schedule. He was not a man who announced his plans ahead. He was in the habit, I understand, of saying one evening, "Tomorrow I go to London" and thereupon to go.

'The false Shaista, then, was aware that at any moment some- one who knew the real Shaista might arrive. Especially was this so after the murder and therefore she began to prepare the way for a kidnapping by talking about it to Inspector Kelsey. Of course, the actual kidnapping was nothing of the kind. As soon as she learned that her uncle was coming to take her out the following morning, she sent a brief message by telephone, and half an hour earlier than the genuine car, a showy car with false C.D. plates on it arrived and Shaista was officially "kidnapped". Actually, of course, she was set down by the car in the first large town where she at once resumed her own personality. An amateurish ransom note was sent just to keep up the fiction.'

Hercule Poirot paused, then said, 'It was, as you can see, merely the trick of the conjurer. Misdirection. You focus the eyes on the kidnapping *here* and it does not occur to anyone that the kidnapping *really* occurred three weeks earlier in Switzerland.'

What Poirot really meant, but was too polite to say, was that it had not occurred to anyone but himself!

'We pass now,' he said, 'to something far more serious than kidnapping – murder.

'The false Shaista could, of course, have killed Miss Springer but she could not have killed Miss Vansittart or Mademoiselle Blanche, and would have had no motive to kill anybody, nor was such a thing required of her. Her role was simply to receive a valuable packet if, as seemed likely, it should be brought to her: or, alternatively, to receive news of it.

'Let us go back now to Ramat where all this started. It was widely rumoured in Ramat that Prince Ali Yusuf had given this valuable packet to Bob Rawlinson, his private pilot, and that Bob Rawlinson had arranged for its despatch to England. On the day in question Rawlinson went to Ramat's principal hotel where his sister, Mrs Sutcliffe, and her daughter Jennifer were staying. Mrs Sutcliffe and Jennifer were out, but Bob Rawlinson went up to their room where he remained for at least twenty minutes. That is rather a long time under the circumstances. He might of course have been writing a long letter to his sister. But that was not so. He merely left a short note which he could have scribbled in a couple of minutes.

'It was a very fair inference then, inferred by several separate parties, that during his time in her room he had placed this object amongst his sister's effects and that she had brought it back to England. Now we come to what I may call the dividing of two separate threads. One set of interests – (or possibly more than one set) – assumed that Mrs Sutcliffe had brought this article back to England and in consequence her house in the country was ransacked and a thorough search made. This showed that whoever was searching *did not know where exactly the article was hidden*. Only that it was probably *somewhere* in Mrs Sutcliffe's possession.

'But somebody else knew very definitely exactly where that article was, and I think that by now it will do no harm for me to tell you where, in fact, Bob Rawlinson did conceal it. He concealed it in the handle of a tennis racquet, hollowing out the handle and afterwards piecing it together again so skilfully that it was difficult to see what had been done.

'The tennis racquet belonged, not to his sister, but to her daughter Jennifer. Someone who knew exactly where the cache was, went out to the Sports Pavilion one night, having previously taken an impression of the key and got a key cut. At that time of night everyone should have been in bed and asleep. But that was not so. Miss Springer saw the light of a torch in the Sports Pavilion from the house, and went out to investigate. She was a tough hefty young woman and had no doubts of her own ability to cope with anything she might find. The person in question was probably sorting through the tennis racquets to find the right one. Discovered and recognized by Miss Springer, there was no hesitation . . . The searcher was a killer, and shot Miss Springer dead. Afterwards, however, the killer had to act fast. The shot had been heard, people were approaching. At all costs the killer must get out of the Sports Pavilion unseen. The racquet must be left where it was for the moment . . .

'Within a few days another method was tried. A strange woman with a faked American accent waylaid Jennifer Sutcliffe as she was coming from the tennis courts, and told her a plausible story about a relative of hers having sent her down a new tennis racquet. Jennifer unsuspiciously accepted this story and gladly exchanged the racquet she was carrying for the new, expensive one the stranger had brought. But a circumstance had arisen which the woman with the American accent knew nothing about. That was that a few days previously Jennifer Sutcliffe and Julia Upjohn had exchanged racquets so that what the strange woman took away with her was in actual fact Julia Upjohn's old racquet, though the identifying tape on it bore Jennifer's name.

'We come now to the second tragedy. Miss Vansittart for some unknown reason, but possibly connected with the kidnapping of Shaista which had taken place that afternoon, took a torch and went out to the Sports Pavilion after everybody had gone to bed. Somebody who had followed her there struck her down with a cosh or a sandbag, as she was stooping down by Shaista's locker. Again the crime was discovered almost immediately. Miss Chadwick saw a light in the Sports Pavilion and hurried out there.

'The police once more took charge at the Sports Pavilion, and again the killer was debarred from searching and examining the tennis racquets there. But by now, Julia Upjohn, an intelligent child, had thought things over and had come to the logical conclusion that the racquet she possessed and which had originally belonged to Jennifer, was in some way important. She investigated on her own behalf, found that she was correct in her surmise, and brought the contents of the racquet to me.

'These are now,' said Hercule Poirot, 'in safe custody and need concern us here no longer.' He paused and then went on, 'It remains to consider the third tragedy.

'What Mademoiselle Blanche knew or suspected we shall never know. She may have seen someone leaving the house on the night of Miss Springer's murder. Whatever it was that she knew or suspected, she knew the identity of the murderer. And she kept that knowledge to herself. She planned to obtain money in return for her silence.

'There is nothing,' said Hercule Poirot, with feeling, 'more dangerous than levying blackmail on a person who has killed perhaps twice already. Mademoiselle Blanche may have taken her own precautions but whatever they were, they were inadequate. She made an appointment with the murderer and she was killed.'

He paused again.

'So there,' he said, looking round at them, 'you have the account of this whole affair.'

They were all staring at him. Their faces, which at first had reflected interest, surprise, excitement, seemed now frozen into a uniform calm. It was as though they were terrified to display any emotion. Hercule Poirot nodded at them.

'Yes,' he said, 'I know how you feel. It has come, has it not, very near home? That is why, you see, I and Inspector Kelsey and Mr Adam Goodman have been making the inquiries. We have to know, you see, if there is still a cat among the pigeons! You understand what I mean? Is there still someone here who is masquerading under false colours?'

There was a slight ripple passing through those who listened to him, a brief almost furtive sidelong glance as though they wished to look at each other, but did not dare do so.

'I am happy to reassure you,' said Poirot. 'All of you here at this moment *are exactly who you say you are*. Miss Chadwick, for instance, is Miss Chadwick – that is certainly not open to doubt, she has been here as long as Meadowbank itself! Miss Johnson, too, is unmistakably Miss Johnson. Miss Rich is Miss Rich. Miss Shapland is Miss Shapland. Miss Rowan and Miss Blake are Miss Rowan and Miss Blake. To go further,' said Poirot, turning his head, 'Adam Goodman who works here in the garden, is, if not precisely Adam Goodman, at any rate the person whose name is on his credentials. So then, where are we? We must seek not for someone masquerading as someone else, but for someone who is, in his or her proper identity, a murderer.'

The room was very still now. There was menace in the air.

Poirot went on.

'We want, primarily, *someone who was in Ramat three months ago*. Knowledge that the prize was concealed in the tennis racquet could only have been acquired in one way. Someone must have *seen* it put there by Bob Rawlinson. It is as simple as that. Who then, of all of you present here, was in Ramat three months ago? Miss Chadwick was here, Miss Johnson was here.' His eyes went on to the two junior Mistresses. 'Miss Rowan and Miss Blake were here.'

His finger went out pointing.

'But Miss Rich – Miss Rich was not here last term, was she?'

'I – no. I was ill.' She spoke hurriedly. 'I was away for a term.'

'That is the thing we did not know,' said Hercule Poirot, 'until a few days ago somebody mentioned it casually. When questioned by the police originally, you merely said that you had been at Meadowbank for a year and a half. That in itself is true enough. But you were absent last term. You could have been in Ramat – I think you were in Ramat. Be careful. It can be verified, you know, from your passport.'

There was a moment's silence, then Eileen Rich looked up.

'Yes,' she said quietly. 'I was in Ramat. Why not?'

'Why did you go to Ramat, Miss Rich?'

'You already know. I had been ill. I was advised to take a rest – to go abroad. I wrote to Miss Bulstrode and explained that I must take a term off. She quite understood.'

'That is so,' said Miss Bulstrode. 'A doctor's certificate was enclosed which said that it would be unwise for Miss Rich to resume her duties until the following term.'

'So – you went to Ramat?' said Hercule Poirot.

'Why shouldn't I go to Ramat?' said Eileen Rich. Her voice trembled slightly. 'There are cheap fares offered to school-teachers. I wanted a rest. I wanted sunshine. I went out to Ramat. I spent two months there. *Why not? Why not, I say?*'

'You have never mentioned that you were at Ramat at the time of the Revolution.'

'Why should I? What has it got to do with anyone here? I haven't killed anyone, I tell you. I haven't killed anyone.'

'You were recognized, you know,' said Hercule Poirot. 'Not recognized definitely, but indefinitely. The child Jennifer was very vague. She said she thought she'd seen you in Ramat but concluded it couldn't be you because, she said, the person she had seen was *fat*, not thin.' He leaned forward, his eyes boring into Eileen Rich's face.

'What have you to say, Miss Rich?'

She wheeled round. 'I know what you're trying to make out!' she cried. 'You're trying to make out that it wasn't a secret agent or anything of that kind who did these murders. That it was someone who just *happened* to be there, someone who *happened* to see this treasure hidden in a tennis racquet. Someone who realized that the child was coming to Meadowbank and that she'd have an opportunity to take for herself this hidden thing. But I tell you it isn't *true*!'

'I think that is what happened. Yes,' said Poirot. 'Someone saw the jewels being hidden and forgot all other duties or interests in the determination to possess them!'

'It isn't true, I tell you. I saw nothing –'

'Inspector Kelsey.' Poirot turned his head.

Inspector Kelsey nodded – went to the door, opened it, and Mrs Upjohn walked into the room.

II

'How do you do, Miss Bulstrode,' said Mrs Upjohn, looking rather embarrassed. 'I'm sorry I'm looking rather untidy, but I was somewhere near Ankara yesterday and I've just flown home. I'm in a terrible mess and I really haven't had time to clean myself up or do *anything*.'

'That does not matter,' said Hercule Poirot. 'We want to ask you something.'

'Mrs Upjohn,' said Kelsey, 'when you came here to bring your daughter to the school and you were in Miss Bulstrode's sitting-room, you looked out of the window – the window which gives on the front drive – and you uttered an exclamation as though you recognized someone you saw there. That is so, is it not?'

Mrs Upjohn stared at him. 'When I was in Miss Bulstrode's sitting-room? I looked – oh, yes, of *course*! Yes, I did see some-one.'

'Someone you were surprised to see?'

'Well, I was rather . . . You see, it had all been such years ago.'

'You mean the days when you were working in Intelligence towards the end of the war?'

'Yes. It was about fifteen years ago. Of course, she looked much older, but I recognized her at once. And I wondered what on earth she could be doing *here*.'

'Mrs Upjohn, will you look round this room and tell me if you see that person here now?'

'Yes, of course,' said Mrs Upjohn. 'I saw her as soon as I came in. That's her.'

She stretched out a pointing finger. Inspector Kelsey was quick and so was Adam, but they were not quick enough. Ann Shapland had sprung to her feet. In her hand was a small wicked-looking automatic and it pointed straight at Mrs Upjohn. Miss Bulstrode, quicker than the two men, moved sharply forward, but swifter still was Miss Chadwick. It was not Mrs Upjohn that she was trying to shield, it was the woman who was standing between Ann Shapland and Mrs Upjohn.

'No, you shan't,' cried Chaddy, and flung herself on Miss Bulstrode just as the small automatic went off.

Miss Chadwick staggered, then slowly crumpled down. Miss Johnson ran to her. Adam and Kelsey had got hold of Ann Shapland now. She was struggling like a wild cat, but they wrested the small automatic from her.

Mrs Upjohn said breathlessly:

'They said then that she was a killer. Although she was so young. One of the most dangerous agents they had. Angelica was her code name.'

'You lying bitch!' Ann Shapland fairly spat out the words.

Hercule Poirot said:

'She does not lie. You are dangerous. You have always led a dangerous life. Up to now, you have never been suspected in your own identity. All the jobs you have taken in your own name have been perfectly genuine jobs, efficiently performed – but they have all been jobs with a purpose, and that purpose has been the gaining of information. You have worked with an Oil Company, with an archaeologist whose work took him to a certain part of the globe, with an actress whose protector was an eminent politician. Ever since you were seventeen you have worked as an agent – though for many different masters. Your services have been for hire and have been highly paid. You have played a dual role. Most of your assignments have been carried out in your own name, but there were certain jobs for which you assumed different identities. Those were the times when ostensibly you had to go home and be with your mother.

'But I strongly suspect, Miss Shapland, that the elderly woman I visited who lives in a small village with a nurse-companion to look after her, an elderly woman who is genuinely a mental patient with a confused mind, is not your mother at all. She has been your excuse for retiring from employment and from the circle of your friends. The three months this winter that you spent with your "mother" who had one of her "bad turns" covers the time when you went out to Ramat. Not as Ann Shapland but as Angelica de Toredo, a Spanish, or near-Spanish cabaret dancer. You occupied the room in the hotel next to that of Mrs Sutcliffe and somehow you managed to see Bob Rawlinson conceal the jewels in the racquet. You had no opportunity of taking the racquet then for there was the sudden evacuation of all British people, but you had read the labels on their luggage and it was easy to find out something about them. To obtain a secretarial post here was not difficult. I have made some inquiries. You paid a substantial sum to Miss Bulstrode's former secretary to vacate her post on the plea of a "breakdown". And you had quite a plausible story. You had been commissioned to write a series of articles on a famous girls' school "from within".

'It all seemed quite easy, did it not? If a child's racquet was missing, what of it? Simpler still, you would go out at night to the Sports Pavilion, and abstract the jewels. But you had not reckoned with Miss Springer. Perhaps she had already seen you examining the racquets. Perhaps she just happened to wake that night. She followed you out there and you shot her. Later, Mademoiselle Blanche tried to blackmail you, and you killed her. It comes natural to you, does it not, to kill?'

He stopped. In a monotonous official voice, Inspector Kelsey cautioned his prisoner.

She did not listen. Turning towards Hercule Poirot, she burst out in a low-pitched flood of invective that startled everyone in the room.

'Whew!' said Adam, as Kelsey took her away. 'And I thought she was a nice girl!'

Miss Johnson had been kneeling by Miss Chadwick.

'I'm afraid she's badly hurt,' she said. 'She'd better not be moved until the doctor comes.'

CHAPTER 24

POIROT EXPLAINS

I

Mrs Upjohn, wandering through the corridors of Meadowbank School, forgot the exciting scene she had just been through. She was for the moment merely a mother seeking her young. She found her in a deserted classroom. Julia was bending over a desk, her tongue protruding slightly, absorbed in the agonies of composition.

She looked up and stared. Then flung herself across the room and hugged her mother.

'Mummy!'

Then, with the self-consciousness of her age, ashamed of her unrestrained emotion, she detached herself and spoke in a carefully casual tone – indeed almost accusingly.

'Aren't you back rather *soon*, Mummy?'

'I flew back,' said Mrs Upjohn, almost apologetically, 'from Ankara.'

'Oh,' said Julia. 'Well – I'm glad you're back.'

'Yes,' said Mrs Upjohn, 'I am very glad too.'

They looked at each other, embarrassed. 'What are you doing?' said Mrs Upjohn, advancing a little closer.

'I'm writing a composition for Miss Rich,' said Julia. 'She really does set the most exciting subjects.'

'What's this one?' said Mrs Upjohn. She bent over.

The subject was written at the top of the page. Some nine or ten lines of writing in Julia's uneven and sprawling hand-writing came below. 'Contrast the Attitudes of Macbeth and Lady Macbeth to Murder' read Mrs Upjohn.

'Well,' she said doubtfully, 'you can't say that the subject isn't topical!'

She read the start of her daughter's essay. 'Macbeth,' Julia had written, 'liked the idea of murder and had been thinking of it a lot, but he needed a push to get him started. Once he'd got started he enjoyed murdering people and had no more qualms or fears. Lady Macbeth was just greedy and ambitious. She thought she didn't mind what she did to get what she wanted. But once she'd done it she found she didn't like it after all.'

'Your language isn't very elegant,' said Mrs Upjohn. 'I think you'll have to polish it up a bit, but you've certainly got something there.'

II

Inspector Kelsey was speaking in a slightly complaining tone.

'It's all very well for you, Poirot,' he said. 'You can say and do a lot of things we can't: and I'll admit the whole thing was well stage managed. Got her off her guard, made her think we were after Rich, and then, Mrs Upjohn's sudden appearance made her lose her head. Thank the lord she kept that automatic after shooting Springer. If the bullet corresponds –'

'It will, *mon ami*, it will,' said Poirot.

'Then we've got her cold for the murder of Springer. And I gather Miss Chadwick's in a bad way. But look here, Poirot, I still can't see how she can possibly have killed Miss Vansittart. It's physically impossible. She's got a cast iron alibi – unless young Rathbone and the whole staff of the Nid Sauvage are in it with her.'

Poirot shook his head. 'Oh, no,' he said. 'Her alibi is perfectly good. She killed Miss Springer and Mademoiselle Blanche. But Miss Vansittart –' he hesitated for a moment, his eyes going to where Miss Bulstrode sat listening to them. 'Miss Vansittart was killed by Miss Chadwick.'

'Miss Chadwick?' exclaimed Miss Bulstrode and Kelsey together.

Poirot nodded. 'I am sure of it.'

'But – why?'

'I think,' said Poirot, 'Miss Chadwick loved Meadowbank too much . . .' His eyes went across to Miss Bulstrode.

'I see . . .' said Miss Bulstrode. 'Yes, yes, I see . . . I ought to have known.' She paused. 'You mean that she –?'

'I mean,' said Poirot, 'that she started here with you, that all along she has regarded Meadowbank as a joint venture between you both.'

'Which in one sense it was,' said Miss Bulstrode.

'Quite so,' said Poirot. 'But that was merely the financial aspect. When you began to talk of retiring she regarded herself as the person who would take over.'

'But she's far too old,' objected Miss Bulstrode.

'Yes,' said Poirot, 'she is too old and she is not suited to be a headmistress. But she herself did not think so. She thought that when you went she would be headmistress of Meadowbank as a matter of course. And then she found that was not so. That you were considering someone else, that you had fastened upon Eleanor Vansittart. And she loved Meadowbank. She loved the school and she did not like Eleanor Vansittart. I think in the end she hated her.'

'She might have done,' said Miss Bulstrode. 'Yes, Eleanor Vansittart was – how shall I put it? – she was always very complacent, very superior about everything. That would be hard to bear if you were jealous. That's what you mean, isn't it? Chaddy was jealous.'

'Yes,' said Poirot. 'She was jealous of Meadowbank and jealous of Eleanor Vansittart. She couldn't bear the thought of the school and Miss Vansittart together. And then perhaps something in your manner led her to think that you were weakening?'

'I did weaken,' said Miss Bulstrode. 'But I didn't weaken in the way that perhaps Chaddy thought I would weaken. Actually I thought of someone younger still than Miss Vansittart – I thought it over and then I said No, she's too young . . . Chaddy was with me then, I remember.'

'And she thought,' said Poirot, 'that you were referring to Miss Vansittart. That you were saying Miss Vansittart was too young. She thoroughly agreed. She thought that experience and wisdom such as she had got were far more important things. But then, after all, you returned to your original decision. You chose Eleanor Vansittart as the right person and left her in charge of the school that weekend. This is what I think happened. On that Sunday night Miss Chadwick was restless, she got up and she saw the light in the squash court. She went out there exactly as she says she went. There is only one thing different in her story from what she said. It wasn't a golf club she took with her. She picked up one of the sandbags from the pile in the hall. She went out there all ready to deal with a burglar, with someone who for a second time had broken into the Sports Pavilion. She had the sandbag ready in her hand to defend herself if attacked. And what did she find? She found Eleanor Vansittart kneeling down looking in a locker, and she thought, it may be – (for I am good,' said Hercule Poirot in a parenthesis, '– at putting myself into other people's minds –) she thought *if* I were a marauder, a burglar, I would come up behind her and strike her down. And as the thought came into her mind, only half conscious of what she was doing, she raised the sandbag and struck. And there was Eleanor Vansittart dead, out of her way. She was appalled then, I think, at what she had done. It has preyed on her ever since – for she is not a natural killer, Miss Chadwick. She was driven, as some are driven, by jealousy and by obsession. The obsession of love for Meadowbank. Now that Eleanor Vansittart was dead she was quite sure that she would succeed you at Meadowbank. So she didn't confess. She told her story to the police exactly as it had occurred but for the one vital fact, that it was *she* who had struck the blow. But when she was asked about the golf club which presumably Miss Vansittart took with her being nervous after all that had occurred, Miss Chadwick said quickly that she had taken it out there. She didn't want you to think even for a moment that she had handled the sandbag.'

'Why did Ann Shapland also choose a sandbag to kill Mademoiselle Blanche?' asked Miss Bulstrode.

'For one thing, she could not risk a pistol shot in the school building, and for another she is a very clever young woman. She wanted to tie up this third murder with the second one, for which she had an alibi.'

'I don't really understand what Eleanor Vansittart was doing herself in the Sports Pavilion,' said Miss Bulstrode.

'I think one could make a guess. She was probably far more concerned over the disappearance of Shaista than she allowed to appear on the surface. She was as upset as Miss Chadwick was. In a way it was worse for her, because she had been left by you in charge – and the kidnapping had happened whilst she was responsible. Moreover she had pooh-poohed it as long as possible through an unwillingness to face unpleasant facts squarely.'

'So there was weakness behind the *façade*,' mused Miss Bulstrode. 'I sometimes suspected it.'

'She, too, I think, was unable to sleep. And I think she went out quietly to the Sports Pavilion to make an examination of Shaista's locker in case there might be some clue there to the girl's disappearance.'

'You seem to have explanations for everything, Mr Poirot.'

'That's his speciality,' said Inspector Kelsey with slight malice.

'And what was the point of getting Eileen Rich to sketch various members of my staff?'

'I wanted to test the child Jennifer's ability to recognize a face. I soon satisfied myself that Jennifer was so entirely preoccupied by her own affairs, that she gave outsiders at most a cursory glance, taking in only the external details of their appearance. She did not recognize a sketch of Mademoiselle Blanche with a different hairdo. Still less, then, would she have recognized

Ann Shapland who, as your secretary, she seldom saw at close quarters.'

'You think that the woman with the racquet was Ann Shapland herself.'

'Yes. It has been a one woman job all through. You remember that day, you rang for her to take a message to Julia but in the end, as the buzzer went unanswered, sent a girl to find Julia. Ann was accustomed to quick disguise. A fair wig, differently pencilled eyebrows, a "fussy" dress and hat. She need only be absent from her typewriter for about twenty minutes. I saw from Miss Rich's clever sketches how easy it is for a woman to alter her appearance by purely external matters.'

'Miss Rich – I wonder –' Miss Bulstrode looked thoughtful.

Poirot gave Inspector Kelsey a look and the Inspector said he must be getting along.

'Miss Rich?' said Miss Bulstrode again.

'Send for her,' said Poirot. 'It is the best way.'

Eileen Rich appeared. She was white faced and slightly defiant.

'You want to know,' she said to Miss Bulstrode, 'what I was doing in Ramat?'

'I think I have an idea,' said Miss Bulstrode.

'Just so,' said Poirot. 'Children nowadays know all the facts of life – but their eyes often retain innocence.'

He added that he, too, must be getting along, and slipped out.

'That was it, wasn't it?' said Miss Bulstrode. Her voice was brisk and businesslike. 'Jennifer merely described it as fat. She didn't realize it was a pregnant woman she had seen.'

'Yes,' said Eileen Rich. 'That was it. I was going to have a child. I didn't want to give up my job here. I carried on all right through the autumn, but after that, it was beginning to show. I got a doctor's certificate that I wasn't fit to carry on, and I pleaded illness. I went abroad to a remote spot where I thought I wasn't likely to meet anyone who knew me. I came back to this country and the child was born – dead. I came back this term and I hoped that no one would ever know . . . But you understand now, don't you, why I said I should have had to refuse your offer of a partnership if you'd made it? Only now, with the school in such a disaster, I thought that, after all, I might be able to accept.'

She paused and said in a matter of fact voice,

'Would you like me to leave now? Or wait until the end of term?'

'You'll stay till the end of the term,' said Miss Bulstrode, 'and if there is a new term here, which I still hope, you'll come back.'

'Come back?' said Eileen Rich. 'Do you mean you still want me?'

'Of course I want you,' said Miss Bulstrode. 'You haven't murdered anyone, have you? – not gone mad over jewels and planned to kill to get them? I'll tell you what you've done. You've probably denied your instincts too long. There was a man, you fell in love with him, you had a child. I suppose you couldn't marry.'

'There was never any question of marriage,' said Eileen Rich. 'I knew that. He isn't to blame.'

'Very well, then,' said Miss Bulstrode. 'You had a love affair and a child. You wanted to have that child?'

'Yes,' said Eileen Rich. 'Yes, I wanted to have it.'

'So that's that,' said Miss Bulstrode. 'Now I'm going to tell you something. I believe that in spite of this love affair, your real vocation in life is teaching. I think your profession means more to you than any normal woman's life with a husband and children would mean.'

'Oh yes,' said Eileen Rich. 'I'm sure of that. I've known that all along. That's what I really want to do – that's the real passion of my life.'

'Then don't be a fool,' said Miss Bulstrode. 'I'm making you a very good offer. If, that is, things come right. We'll spend two or three years together putting Meadowbank back on the map. You'll have different ideas as to how that should be done from the ideas that I have. I'll listen to your ideas. Maybe I'll even give in to some of them. You want things to be different, I suppose, at Meadowbank?'

'I do in some ways, yes,' said Eileen Rich. 'I won't pretend. I want more emphasis on getting girls that really matter.'

'Ah,' said Miss Bulstrode, 'I see. It's the snob element that you don't like, is that it?'

'Yes,' said Eileen, 'it seems to me to spoil things.'

'What you don't realize,' said Miss Bulstrode, 'is that to get the kind of girl you want you've *got* to have that snob element. It's quite a small element really, you know. A few foreign royalties, a few great names and everybody, all the silly parents all over this country and other countries want their girls to come to Meadowbank. Fall over themselves to get their girl admitted to Meadowbank. What's the result? An enormous waiting list, and I look at the girls and I see the girls and I choose! You get your pick, do you see? I choose my girls. I choose them very carefully, some for character, some for brains, some for pure academic intellect. Some because I think they haven't had a chance but are capable of being made something of that's worth while. You're young, Eileen. You're full of ideals – it's the teaching that matters to you and the ethical side of it. Your vision's quite right. It's the girls that matter, but if you want to make a success of anything, you know, you've got to be a good tradesman as well. Ideas are like everything else. They've got to be marketed. We'll have to do some pretty slick work in future to get Meadowbank going again. I'll have to get my hooks into a few people, former pupils, bully them, plead with them, get them to send their daughters here. And then the others will come. You let me be up to my tricks, and then you shall have your way. Meadowbank will go on and it'll be a fine school.'

'It'll be the finest school in England,' said Eileen Rich enthusiastically.

'Good,' said Miss Bulstrode, '– and Eileen, I should go and get your hair properly cut and shaped. You don't seem able to manage that bun. And now,' she said, her voice changing, 'I must go to Chaddy.'

She went in and came up to the bed. Miss Chadwick was lying very still and white. The blood had all gone from her face and she looked drained of life. A policeman with a notebook sat nearby and Miss Johnson sat on the other side of the bed. She looked at Miss Bulstrode and shook her head gently.

'Hallo, Chaddy,' said Miss Bulstrode. She took up the limp hand in hers. Miss Chadwick's eyes opened.

'I want to tell you,' she said, 'Eleanor – it was – it was me.'

'Yes, dear, I know,' said Miss Bulstrode.

'Jealous,' said Chaddy. 'I wanted –'

'I know,' said Miss Bulstrode.

Tears rolled very slowly down Miss Chadwick's cheeks. 'It's so awful . . . I didn't mean – I don't know how I came to do such a thing!'

'Don't think about it any more,' said Miss Bulstrode.

'But I can't – you'll never – I'll never forgive myself –'

'Listen, dear,' she said. 'You saved my life, you know. My life and the life of that nice woman, Mrs Upjohn. That counts for something, doesn't it?'

'I only wish,' said Miss Chadwick, 'I could have given *my* life for you both. That would have made it all right . . .'

Miss Bulstrode looked at her with great pity. Miss Chadwick took a great breath, smiled, then, moving her head very slightly to one side, she died . . .

'You *did* give your life, my dear,' said Miss Bulstrode softly. 'I hope you realize that – now.'

CHAPTER 25

LEGACY

I

'A Mr Robinson has called to see you, sir.'

'Ah!' said Hercule Poirot. He stretched out his hand and picked up a letter from the desk in front of him. He looked down on it thoughtfully.

He said: 'Show him in, Georges.'

The letter was only a few lines,

> *Dear Poirot,*
>
> *A Mr Robinson may call upon you in the near future. You may already know something about him. Quite a prominent figure in certain circles. There is a demand for such men in our modern world . . . I believe, if I may so put it, that he is, in this particular matter, on the side of the angels. This is just a recommendation, if you should be in doubt. Of course, and I underline this, we have* no *idea as to the matter on which he wishes to consult you . . .*

Ha ha! and likewise ho ho!
Yours ever,
Ephraim Pikeaway

Poirot laid down the letter and rose as Mr Robinson came into the room. He bowed, shook hands, indicated a chair.

Mr Robinson sat, pulled out a handkerchief and wiped his large yellow face. He observed that it was a warm day.

'You have not, I hope, walked here in this heat?'

Poirot looked horrified at the idea. By a natural association of ideas, his fingers went to his moustache. He was reassured. There was no limpness.

Mr Robinson looked equally horrified.

'No, no, indeed. I came in my Rolls. But these traffic blocks . . . One sits for half an hour sometimes.'

Poirot nodded sympathetically.

There was a pause – the pause that ensues on part one of conversation before entering upon part two.

'I was interested to hear – of course one hears so many things – most of them quite untrue – that you had been concerning yourself with the affairs of a girls' school.'

'Ah,' said Poirot. 'That!'

He leaned back in his chair.

'Meadowbank,' said Mr Robinson thoughtfully. 'Quite one of the premier schools of England.'

'It is a fine school.'

'Is? Or was?'

'I hope the former.'

'I hope so, too,' said Mr Robinson. 'I fear it may be touch and go. Ah well, one must do what one can. A little financial backing to tide over a certain inevitable period of depression. A few carefully chosen new pupils. I am not without influence in European circles.'

'I, too, have applied persuasion in certain quarters. If, as you say, we can tide things over. Mercifully, memories are short.'

'That is what one hopes. But one must admit that events have taken place there that might well shake the nerves of fond mammas – and papas also. The Games Mistress, the French Mistress, and yet another mistress – all murdered.'

'As you say.'

'I hear,' said Mr Robinson, '(one hears so many things), that the unfortunate young woman responsible has suffered from a phobia about schoolmistresses since her youth. An unhappy childhood at school. Psychiatrists will make a good deal of this. They will try at least for a verdict of diminished responsibility, as they call it nowadays.'

'That line would seem to be the best choice,' said Poirot. 'You will pardon me for saying that I hope it will not succeed.'

'I agree with you entirely. A most cold-blooded killer. But they will make much of her excellent character, her work as secretary to various well-known people, her war record – quite distinguished, I believe – counter espionage –'

He let the last words out with a certain significance – a hint of a question in his voice.

'She was very good, I believe,' he said more briskly. 'So young – but quite brilliant, of great use – to both sides. That was her métier – she should have stuck to it. But I can understand the temptation – to play a lone hand, and gain a big prize.' He added softly, 'A very big prize.'

Poirot nodded.

Mr Robinson leaned forward.

'Where are they, M. Poirot?'

'I think you know where they are.'

'Well, frankly, yes. Banks are such useful institutions are they not?'

Poirot smiled.

'We needn't beat about the bush really, need we, my dear fellow? What are you going to do about them?'

'I have been waiting.'

'Waiting for what?'

'Shall we say – for suggestions?'

'Yes – I see.'

'You understand they do not belong to me. I would like to hand them over to the person they do belong to. But that, if I appraise the position correctly, is not so simple.'

'Governments are in such a difficult position,' said Mr Robinson. 'Vulnerable, so to speak. What with oil, and steel, and uranium, and cobalt and all the rest of it, foreign relations are a matter of the utmost delicacy. The great thing is to be able to say that Her Majesty's Government, etc., etc., has absolutely *no* information on the subject.'

'But I cannot keep this important deposit at my bank indefinitely.'

'Exactly. That is why I have come to propose that you should hand it over to me.'

'Ah,' said Poirot. 'Why?'

'I can give you some excellent reasons. These jewels – mercifully we are not official, we can call things by their right names – were unquestionably the personal property of the late Prince Ali Yusuf.'

'I understand that is so.'

'His Highness handed them over to Squadron Leader Robert Rawlinson with certain instructions. They were to be got out of Ramat, and they were to be delivered to *me*.'

'Have you proof of that?'

'Certainly.'

Mr Robinson drew a long envelope from his pocket. Out of it he took several papers. He laid them before Poirot on the desk.

Poirot bent over them and studied them carefully.

'It seems to be as you say.'

'Well, then?'

'Do you mind if I ask a question?'

'Not at all.'

'What do you, personally, get out of this?'

Mr Robinson looked surprised.

'My dear fellow. Money, of course. Quite a lot of money.'

Poirot looked at him thoughtfully.

'It is a very old trade,' said Mr Robinson. 'And a lucrative one. There are quite a lot of us, a network all over the globe. We are, how shall I put it, the Arrangers behind the scenes. For kings, for presidents, for politicians, for all those, in fact, upon whom the fierce light beats, as a poet has put it. We work in with one another and remember this: we keep faith. Our profits are large but we are honest. Our services are costly – but we do render service.'

'I see,' said Poirot. '*Eh bien!* I agree to what you ask.'

'I can assure you that that decision will please everyone.' Mr

Robinson's eyes just rested for a moment on Colonel Pikeaway's letter where it lay at Poirot's right hand.

'But just one little moment. I am human. I have curiosity. What are you going to do with these jewels?'

Mr Robinson looked at him. Then his large yellow face creased into a smile. He leaned forward.

'I shall tell you.'

He told him.

II

Children were playing up and down the street. Their raucous cries filled the air. Mr Robinson, alighting ponderously from his Rolls, was cannoned into by one of them.

Mr Robinson put the child aside with a not unkindly hand and peered up at the number on the house.

No. 15. This was right. He pushed open the gate and went up the three steps to the front door. Neat white curtains at the windows, he noted, and a well-polished brass knocker. An insignificant little house in an insignificant street in an insignificant part of London, but it was well kept. It had self-respect.

The door opened. A girl of about twenty-five, pleasant looking, with a kind of fair, chocolate box prettiness, welcomed him with a smile.

'Mr Robinson? Come in.'

She took him into the small sitting-room. A television set, cretonnes of a Jacobean pattern, a cottage piano against the wall. She had on a dark skirt and a grey pullover.

'You'll have some tea? I've got the kettle on.'

'Thank you, but no. I never drink tea. And I can only stay a short time. I have only come to bring you what I wrote to you about.'

'From Ali?'

'Yes.'

'There isn't – there couldn't be – any hope? I mean – it's really true – that he was killed? There couldn't be any mistake?'

'I'm afraid there was no mistake,' said Mr Robinson gently.

'No – no, I suppose not. Anyway, I never expected – When he went back there I didn't think really I'd ever see him again. I don't mean I thought he was going to be killed or that there would be a

Revolution. I just mean – well, you know – he'd have to carry on, do his stuff – what was expected of him. Marry one of his own people – all that.'

Mr Robinson drew out a package and laid it down on the table.

'Open it, please.'

Her fingers fumbled a little as she tore the wrappings off and then unfolded the final covering . . .

She drew her breath in sharply.

Red, blue, green, white, all sparkling with fire, with life, turning the dim little room into Aladdin's cave . . .

Mr Robinson watched her. He had seen so many women look at jewels . . .

She said at last in a breathless voice,

'Are they – they can't be – *real*?'

'They are real.'

'But they must be worth – they must be worth –'

Her imagination failed.

Mr Robinson nodded.

'If you wish to dispose of them, you can probably get at least half a million pounds for them.'

'No – no, it's not possible.'

Suddenly she scooped them up in her hands and re-wrapped them with shaking fingers.

'I'm scared,' she said. 'They frighten me. What am I to do with them?'

The door burst open. A small boy rushed in.

'Mum, I got a smashing tank off Billy. He –'

He stopped, staring at Mr Robinson.

An olive skinned, dark boy.

His mother said,

'Go in the kitchen, Allen, your tea's all ready. Milk and biscuits and there's a bit of gingerbread.'

'Oh good.' He departed noisily.

'You call him Allen?' said Mr Robinson.

She flushed.

'It was the nearest name to Ali. I couldn't call him Ali – too difficult for him and the neighbours and all.'

She went on, her face clouding over again.

'What am I to do?'

'First, have you got your marriage certificate? I have to be sure you're the person you say you are.'

She stared a moment, then went over to a small desk. From one of the drawers she brought out an envelope, extracted a paper from it and brought it to him.

'Hm ... yes ... Register of Edmonstow ... Ali Yusuf, student ... Alice Calder, spinster ... Yes, all in order.'

'Oh it's legal all right – as far as it goes. And no one ever tumbled to who he was. There's so many of these foreign Moslem students, you see. We knew it didn't mean anything really. He was a Moslem and he could have more than one wife, and he knew he'd have to go back and do just that. We talked about it. But Allen was on the way, you see, and he said this would make it all right for him – we were married all right in this country and Allen would be legitimate. It was the best he could do for me. He really did love me, you know. He really did.'

'Yes,' said Mr Robinson. 'I am sure he did.'

He went on briskly.

'Now, supposing that you put yourself in my hands. I will see to the selling of these stones. And I will give you the address of a lawyer, a really good and reliable solicitor. He will advise you, I expect, to put most of the money in a trust fund. And there will be other things, education for your son, and a new way of life for you. You'll want social education and guidance. You're going to be a very rich woman and all the sharks and the confidence tricksters and the rest of them will be after you. Your life's not going to be easy except in the purely material sense. Rich people don't have an easy time in life, I can tell you – I've seen too many of them to have that illusion. But you've got character. I think you'll come through. And that boy of yours may be a happier man than his father ever was.'

He paused. 'You agree?'

'Yes. Take them.' She pushed them towards him, then said suddenly: 'That schoolgirl – the one who found them – I'd like her to have one of them – which – what colour do you think she'd like?'

Mr Robinson reflected. 'An emerald, I think – green for mystery. A good idea of yours. She will find that very thrilling.'

He rose to his feet.

'I shall charge you for my services, you know,' said Mr Robinson. 'And my charges are pretty high. But I shan't cheat you.'

She gave him a level glance.

'No, I don't think you will. And I need someone who knows about business, because I don't.'

'You seem a very sensible woman if I may say so. Now then, I'm to take these? You don't want to keep – just one – say?'

He watched her with curiosity, the sudden flicker of excitement, the hungry covetous eyes – and then the flicker died.

'No,' said Alice. 'I won't keep – even one.' She flushed. 'Oh I daresay that seems daft to you – not to keep just one big ruby or an emerald – just as a keepsake. But you see, he and I – he was a Moslem but he let me read bits now and again out of the Bible. And we read that bit – about a woman whose price was above rubies. And so – I won't have any jewels. I'd rather not . . .'

'A most unusual woman,' said Mr Robinson to himself as he walked down the path and into his waiting Rolls.

He repeated to himself,

'A most unusual woman . . .'

THE CLOCKS

To my old friend Mario
with happy memories of delicious food
at the Caprice.

The afternoon of the 9th of September was exactly like any other afternoon. None of those who were to be concerned in the events of that day could lay claim to having had a premonition of disaster. (With the exception, that is, of Mrs Packer of 47, Wilbraham Crescent, who specialized in premonitions, and who always described at great length afterwards the peculiar forebodings and tremors that had beset her. But Mrs Packer at No. 47, was so far away from No. 19, and so little concerned with the happenings there, that it seemed unnecessary for her to have had a premonition at all.)

At the Cavendish Secretarial and Typewriting Bureau, Principal, Miss K. Martindale, September 9th had been a dull day, a day of routine. The telephone rang, typewriters clicked, the pressure of business was average, neither above nor below its usual volume. None of it was particularly interesting. Up till 2.35, September 9th might have been a day like any other day.

At 2.35 Miss Martindale's buzzer went, and Edna Brent in the outer office answered it in her usual breathy and slightly nasal voice, as she manoeuvred a toffee along the line of her jaw.

'Yes, Miss Martindale?'

'Now, Edna – that is *not* the way I've told you to speak when answering the telephone. Enunciate *clearly*, and keep your breath *behind* your tone.'

'Sorry, Miss Martindale.'

'That's better. You can do it when you try. Send Sheila Webb in to me.'

'She's not back from lunch yet, Miss Martindale.'

'Ah.' Miss Martindale's eye consulted the clock on her desk. 2.36. Exactly six minutes late. Sheila Webb had been getting slack lately. 'Send her in when she comes.'

'Yes, Miss Martindale.'

Edna restored the toffee to the centre of her tongue and, sucking pleasurably, resumed her typing of *Naked Love* by Armand Levine. Its painstaking eroticism left her uninterested – as indeed it did most of Mr Levine's readers, in spite of his efforts. He was a notable example of the fact that nothing can be duller than dull pornography. In spite of lurid jackets and provocative titles, his sales went down every year, and his last typing bill had already been sent in three times.

The door opened and Sheila Webb came in, slightly out of breath.

'Sandy Cat's asking for you,' said Edna.

Sheila Webb made a face.

'Just my luck – on the one day I'm late back!'

She smoothed down her hair, picked up pad and pencil, and knocked at the Principal's door.

Miss Martindale looked up from her desk. She was a woman of forty-odd, bristling with efficiency. Her pompadour of pale reddish hair and her Christian name of Katherine had led to her nickname of Sandy Cat.

'You're late back, Miss Webb.'

'Sorry, Miss Martindale. There was a terrific bus jam.'

'There is always a terrific bus jam at this time of day. You should allow for it.' She referred to a note on her pad. 'A Miss Pebmarsh rang up. She wants a stenographer at three o'clock. She asked for you particularly. Have you worked for her before?'

'I can't remember doing so, Miss Martindale. Not lately anyway.'

'The address is 19, Wilbraham Crescent.' She paused questioningly, but Sheila Webb shook her head.

'I can't remember going there.'

Miss Martindale glanced at the clock.

'Three o'clock. You can manage that easily. Have you any other appointments this afternoon? Ah, yes,' her eye ran down the appointment book at her elbow. 'Professor Purdy at the Curlew Hotel. Five o'clock. You ought to be back before then. If not, I can send Janet.'

She gave a nod of dismissal, and Sheila went back to the outer office.

'Anything interesting, Sheila?'

'Just another of those dull days. Some old pussy up at Wilbraham Crescent. And at five Professor Purdy – all those awful archaeological names! How I wish something exciting could sometimes happen.'

Miss Martindale's door opened.

'I see I have a memo here, Sheila. If Miss Pebmarsh is not back when you arrive, you are to go in, the door will not be latched. Go in and go into the room on the right of the hall and wait. Can you remember that or shall I write it down?'

'I can remember it, Miss Martindale.'

Miss Martindale went back into her sanctum.

Edna Brent fished under her chair and brought up, secretly, a rather flashy shoe and a stiletto heel that had become detached from it.

'However am I going to get home?' she moaned.

'Oh, do stop fussing – we'll think of something,' said one of the other girls, and resumed her typing.

Edna sighed and put in a fresh sheet of paper:

'Desire had him in its grasp. With frenzied fingers he tore the fragile chiffon from her breasts and forced her down on the soap.'

'Damn,' said Edna and reached for the eraser.

Sheila picked up her handbag and went out.

Wilbraham Crescent was a fantasy executed by a Victorian builder in the 1880's. It was a half-moon of double houses and gardens set back to back. This conceit was a source of considerable difficulty to persons unacquainted with the locality. Those who arrived on the outer side were unable to find the lower numbers and those who hit the inner side first were baffled as to the whereabouts of the higher numbers. The houses were neat, prim, artistically balconied and eminently respectable. Modernization had as yet barely touched them – on the outside, that is to say. Kitchens and bathrooms were the first to feel the wind of change.

There was nothing unusual about No. 19. It had neat curtains and a well-polished brass front-door handle. There were standard rose trees each side of the path leading to the front door.

Sheila Webb opened the front gate, walked up to the front

door and rang the bell. There was no response and after waiting a minute or two, she did as she had been directed, and turned the handle. The door opened and she walked in. The door on the right of the small hall was ajar. She tapped on it, waited, and then walked in. It was an ordinary quite pleasant sitting-room, a little over-furnished for modern tastes. The only thing at all remarkable about it was the profusion of clocks – a grandfather clock ticking in the corner, a Dresden china clock on the mantelpiece, a silver carriage clock on the desk, a small fancy gilt clock on a whatnot near the fireplace and on a table by the window, a faded leather travelling clock, with ROSEMARY in worn gilt letters across the corner.

Sheila Webb looked at the clock on the desk with some surprise. It showed the time to be a little after ten minutes past four. Her gaze shifted to the chimney piece. The clock there said the same.

Sheila started violently as there was a whir and a click above her head, and from a wooden carved clock on the wall a cuckoo sprang out through his little door and announced loudly and definitely: *Cuckoo, Cuckoo, Cuckoo!* The harsh note seemed almost menacing. The cuckoo disappeared again with a snap of his door.

Sheila Webb gave a half-smile and walked round the end of the sofa. Then she stopped short, pulling up with a jerk.

Sprawled on the floor was the body of a man. His eyes were half open and sightless. There was a dark moist patch on the front of his dark grey suit. Almost mechanically Sheila bent down. She touched his cheek – cold – his hand, the same . . . touched the wet patch and drew her hand away sharply, staring at it in horror.

At that moment she heard the click of a gate outside, her head turned mechanically to the window. Through it she saw a woman's figure hurrying up the path. Sheila swallowed mechanically – her throat was dry. She stood rooted to the spot, unable to move, to cry out . . . staring in front of her.

The door opened and a tall elderly woman entered, carrying a shopping bag. She had wavy grey hair pulled back from her forehead, and her eyes were a wide and beautiful blue. Their gaze passed unseeingly over Sheila.

Sheila uttered a faint sound, no more than a croak. The wide blue eyes came to her and the woman spoke sharply:

'Is somebody there?'

'I – it's –' The girl broke off as the woman came swiftly towards her round the back of the sofa.

And then she screamed.

'Don't – don't . . . you'll tread on it – him . . . *And he's dead . . .*'

CHAPTER 1
COLIN LAMB'S NARRATIVE

I

To use police terms: at 2.59 p.m. on September 9th, I was proceeding along Wilbraham Crescent in a westerly direction. It was my first introduction to Wilbraham Crescent, and frankly Wilbraham Crescent had me baffled.

I had been following a hunch with a persistence becoming more dogged day by day as the hunch seemed less and less likely to pay off. I'm like that.

The number I wanted was 61, and could I find it? No, I could not. Having studiously followed the numbers from 1 to 35, Wilbraham Crescent then appeared to end. A thoroughfare uncompromisingly labelled Albany Road barred my way. I turned back. On the north side there were no houses, only a wall. Behind the wall, blocks of modern flats soared upwards, the entrance of them being obviously in another road. No help there.

I looked up at the numbers I was passing. 24, 23, 22, 21. Diana Lodge (presumably 20, with an orange cat on the gate post washing its face), 19 –

The door of 19 opened and a girl came out of it and down the path with what seemed to be the speed of a bomb. The likeness to a bomb was intensified by the screaming that accompanied her progress. It was high and thin and singularly inhuman. Through the gate the girl came and collided with me with a force that nearly knocked me off the pavement. She did not only collide. She clutched – a frenzied desperate clutching.

'Steady,' I said, as I recovered my balance. I shook her slightly. 'Steady now.'

The girl steadied. She still clutched, but she stopped screaming. Instead she gasped – deep sobbing gasps.

I can't say that I reacted to the situation with any brilliance. I asked her if anything was the matter. Recognizing that my question was singularly feeble I amended it.

'What's the matter?'

The girl took a deep breath.

'In *there!*' she gestured behind her.

'Yes?'

'There's a man on the floor . . . dead . . . She was going to step on him.'

'Who was? Why?'

'I think – because she's blind. And there's blood on him.' She looked down and loosened one of her clutching hands. 'And on me. There's blood on *me*.'

'So there is,' I said. I looked at the stains on my coat sleeve. 'And on me as well now,' I pointed out, I sighed and considered the situation. 'You'd better take me in and show me,' I said.

But she began to shake violently.

'I can't – I *can't* . . . I won't go in there again.'

'Perhaps you're right.' I looked round. There seemed nowhere very suitable to deposit a half-fainting girl. I lowered her gently to the pavement and sat her with her back against the iron railings.

'You stay there,' I said, 'until I come back. I shan't be long. You'll be all right. Lean forward and put your head between your knees if you feel queer.'

'I – I think I'm all right now.'

She was a little doubtful about it, but I didn't want to parley. I gave her a reassuring pat on the shoulder and strode off briskly up the path. I went in through the door, hesitated a moment in the hallway, looked into the door on the left, found an empty dining-room, crossed the hall and entered the sitting-room opposite.

The first thing I saw was an elderly woman with grey hair sitting in a chair. She turned her head sharply as I entered and said:

'Who's that?'

I realized at once that the woman was blind. Her eyes which looked directly towards me were focused on a spot behind my left ear.

I spoke abruptly and to the point.

'A young woman rushed out into the street saying there was a dead man in here.'

I felt a sense of absurdity as I said the words. It did not seem possible that there should be a dead man in this tidy room with this calm woman sitting in her chair with her hands folded.

But her answer came at once.

'Behind the sofa,' she said.

I moved round the angle of the sofa. I saw it then – the outflung arms – the glazed eyes – the congealing patch of blood.

'How did this happen?' I asked abruptly.

'I don't know.'

'But – surely. Who is he?'

'I have no idea.'

'We must get the police.' I looked round. 'Where's the telephone?'

'I have not got a telephone.'

I concentrated upon her more closely.

'You live here? This is your house?'

'Yes.'

'Can you tell me what happened?'

'Certainly. I came in from shopping –' I noted the shopping bag flung on a chair near the door. 'I came in here. I realized at once there was someone in the room. One does very easily when one is blind. I asked who was there. There was no answer – only the sound of someone breathing rather quickly. I went towards the sound – and then whoever it was cried out – something about someone being dead and that I was going to tread on him. And then whoever it was rushed past me out of the room screaming.'

I nodded. Their stories clicked.

'And what did you do?'

'I felt my way very carefully until my foot touched an obstacle.'

'And then?'

'I knelt down. I touched something – a man's hand. It was cold – there was no pulse . . . I got up and came over here and sat down – to wait. Someone was bound to come in due course. The young woman, whoever she was, would give the alarm. I thought I had better not leave the house.'

I was impressed with the calm of this woman. She had not screamed, or stumbled panic-stricken from the house. She had sat down calmly to wait. It was the sensible thing to do, but it must have taken some doing.

Her voice inquired:

'Who exactly are you?'

'My name is Colin Lamb. I happened to be passing by.'

'Where is the young woman?'

'I left her propped up by the gate. She's suffering from shock. Where is the nearest telephone?'

'There is a call-box about fifty yards down the road just before you come to the corner.'

'Of course. I remember passing it. I'll go and ring the police. Will you –' I hesitated.

I didn't know whether to say 'Will you remain here?' or to make it 'Will you be all right?'

She relieved me from my choice.

'You had better bring the girl into the house,' she said decisively.

'I don't know that she will come,' I said doubtfully.

'Not into this room, naturally. Put her in the dining-room the other side of the hall. Tell her I am making some tea.'

She rose and came towards me.

'But – can you manage –'

A faint grim smile showed for a moment on her face.

'My dear young man. I have made meals for myself in my own kitchen ever since I came to live in this house – fourteen years ago. To be blind is not necessarily to be helpless.'

'I'm sorry. It was stupid of me. Perhaps I ought to know your name?'

'Millicent Pebmarsh – Miss.'

I went out and down the path. The girl looked up at me and began to struggle to her feet.

'I – I think I'm more or less all right now.'

I helped her up, saying cheerfully:

'Good.'

'There – there was a dead man in there, wasn't there?'

I agreed promptly.

'Certainly there was. I'm just going down to the telephone box to report it to the police. I should wait in the house if I were you.' I raised my voice to cover her quick protest. 'Go into the dining-room – on the left as you go in. Miss Pebmarsh is making a cup of tea for you.'

'So that was Miss Pebmarsh? And she's blind?'

'Yes. It's been a shock to her, too, of course, but she's being very sensible. Come on, I'll take you in. A cup of tea will do you good whilst you are waiting for the police to come.'

I put an arm round her shoulders and urged her up the path. I settled her comfortably by the dining-room table, and hurried off again to telephone.

II

An unemotional voice said, 'Crowdean Police Station.'

'Can I speak to Detective Inspector Hardcastle?'

The voice said cautiously:

'I don't know whether he is here. Who is speaking?'

'Tell him it's Colin Lamb.'

'Just a moment, please.'

I waited. Then Dick Hardcastle's voice spoke.

'Colin? I didn't expect you yet awhile. Where are you?'

'Crowdean. I'm actually in Wilbraham Crescent. There's a man lying dead on the floor of Number 19, stabbed I should think. He's been dead approximately half an hour or so.'

'Who found him. You?'

'No, I was an innocent passer-by. Suddenly a girl came flying out of the house like a bat out of hell. Nearly knocked me down. She said there was a dead man on the floor and a blind woman was trampling on him.'

'You're not having me on, are you?' Dick's voice asked suspiciously.

'It does sound fantastic, I admit. But the facts seem to be as stated. The blind woman is Miss Millicent Pebmarsh who owns the house.'

'And was she trampling on the dead man?'

'Not in the sense you mean it. It seems that being blind she just didn't know he was there.'

'I'll set the machinery in motion. Wait for me there. What have you done with the girl?'

'Miss Pebmarsh is making her a cup of tea.'

Dick's comment was that it all sounded very cosy.

CHAPTER 2

At 19, Wilbraham Crescent the machinery of the Law was in possession. There was a police surgeon, a police photographer, fingerprint men. They moved efficiently, each occupied with his own routine.

Finally came Detective Inspector Hardcastle, a tall, poker-faced man with expressive eyebrows, godlike, to see that all he had put in motion was being done, and done properly. He took a final look at the body, exchanged a few brief words with the police surgeon and then crossed to the dining-room where three people sat over empty tea-cups. Miss Pebmarsh, Colin Lamb and a tall girl with brown curling hair and wide, frightened eyes. 'Quite pretty,' the inspector noted, parenthetically as it were.

He introduced himself to Miss Pebmarsh.

'Detective Inspector Hardcastle.'

He knew a little about Miss Pebmarsh, though their paths had never crossed professionally. But he had seen her about, and he was aware that she was an ex-school teacher, and that she had a job connected with the teaching of Braille at the Aaronberg Institute for handicapped children. It seemed wildly unlikely that a man should be found murdered in her neat, austere house – but the unlikely happened more often than one would be disposed to believe.

'This is a terrible thing to have happened, Miss Pebmarsh,' he said. 'I'm afraid it must have been a great shock to you. I'll need to get a clear statement of exactly what occurred from you all. I understand that it was Miss –' he glanced quickly at the note-book the constable had handed him, 'Sheila Webb who actually discovered the body. If you'll allow me to use your kitchen, Miss Pebmarsh, I'll take Miss Webb in there where we can be quiet.'

He opened the connecting door from the dining-room to the kitchen and waited until the girl had passed through. A young plain-clothes detective was already established in the kitchen, writing unobtrusively at a Formica-topped small table.

'This chair looks comfortable,' said Hardcastle, pulling forward a modernized version of a Windsor chair.

Sheila Webb sat down nervously, staring at him with large frightened eyes.

Hardcastle very nearly said: 'I shan't eat you, my dear,' but repressed himself, and said instead:

'There's nothing to worry about. We just want to get a clear picture. Now your name is Sheila Webb – and your address?'

'14, Palmerstone Road – beyond the gasworks.'

'Yes, of course. And you are employed, I suppose?'

'Yes. I'm a shorthand typist – I work at Miss Martindale's Secretarial Bureau.'

'The Cavendish Secretarial and Typewriting Bureau – that's its full name, isn't it?'

'That's right.'

'And how long have you been working there?'

'About a year. Well, ten months actually.'

'I see. Now just tell me in your own words how you came to be at 19, Wilbraham Crescent today.'

'Well, it was this way.' Sheila Webb was speaking now with more confidence. 'This Miss Pebmarsh rang up the Bureau and asked for a stenographer to be here at three o'clock. So when I came back from lunch Miss Martindale told me to go.'

'That was just routine, was it? I mean – you were the next on the list – or however you arrange these things?'

'Not exactly. Miss Pebmarsh had asked for me specially.'

'Miss Pebmarsh had asked for you specially.' Hardcastle's eyebrows registered this point. 'I see . . . Because you had worked for her before?'

'But I hadn't,' said Sheila quickly.

'You hadn't? You're quite sure of that?'

'Oh, yes, I'm positive. I mean, she's not the sort of person one would forget. That's what seems so odd.'

'Quite. Well, we won't go into that just now. You reached here when?'

'It must have been just before three o'clock, because the cuckoo clock –' she stopped abruptly. Her eyes widened. 'How queer. How very queer. I never really noticed at the time.'

'What didn't you notice, Miss Webb?'

'Why – the clocks.'

'What about the clocks?'

'The cuckoo clock struck three all right, but all the others were about an hour fast. How very odd!'

'Certainly very odd,' agreed the inspector. 'Now when did you first notice the body?'

'Not till I went round behind the sofa. And there it – he – was. It was awful, yes awful . . .'

'Awful, I agree. Now did you recognize the man? Was it anyone you had seen before?'

'Oh *no*.'

'You're quite sure of that? He might have looked rather different from the way he usually looked, you know. Think carefully. You're quite sure he was someone you'd never seen before?'

'Quite sure.'

'Right. That's that. And what did you do?'

'What did I *do*?'

'Yes.'

'Why – nothing . . . nothing at all. I couldn't.'

'I see. You didn't touch him at all?'

'Yes – yes I did. To see if – I mean – just to see – But he was – quite cold – and – and I got blood on my hand. It was horrible – thick and sticky.'

She began to shake.

'There, there,' said Hardcastle in an avuncular fashion. 'It's all over now, you know. Forget about the blood. Go on to the next thing. What happened next?'

'I don't know . . . Oh, yes, she came home.'

'Miss Pebmarsh, you mean?'

'Yes. Only I didn't think about her being Miss Pebmarsh then. She just came in with a *shopping* basket.' Her tone underlined the shopping basket as something incongruous and irrelevant.

'And what did you say?'

'I don't think I said anything . . . I tried to, but I couldn't. I felt all choked up *here*.' She indicated her throat.

The inspector nodded.

'And then – and then – she said: "Who's there?" and she came round the back of the sofa and I thought – I thought she was going to – to tread on *It*. And I screamed . . . And once I began I couldn't stop screaming, and somehow I got out of the room and through the front door –'

'Like a bat out of hell,' the inspector remembered Colin's description.

Sheila Webb looked at him out of miserable frightened eyes and said rather unexpectedly:

'I'm sorry.'

'Nothing to be sorry about. You've told your story very well. There's no need to think about it any more now. Oh, just one point, why were you in that room at all?'

'Why?' She looked puzzled.

'Yes. You'd arrived here, possibly a few minutes early, and you'd pushed the bell, I suppose. But if nobody answered, why did you come in?'

'Oh that. Because she told me to.'

'Who told you to?'

'Miss Pebmarsh did.'

'But I thought you hadn't spoken to her at all.'

'No, I hadn't. It was Miss Martindale she said it to – that I was to come in and wait in the sitting-room on the right of the hall.'

Hardcastle said: 'Indeed' thoughtfully.

Sheila Webb asked timidly:

'Is – is that all?'

'I think so. I'd like you to wait here about ten minutes longer, perhaps, in case something arises I might want to ask you about. After that, I'll send you home in a police car. What about your family – you have a family?'

'My father and mother are dead. I live with an aunt.'

'And her name is?'

'Mrs Lawton.'

The inspector rose and held out his hand.

'Thank you very much, Miss Webb,' he said. 'Try and get a good night's rest tonight. You'll need it after what you've been through.'

She smiled at him timidly as she went through the door into the dining-room.

'Look after Miss Webb, Colin,' the inspector said. 'Now, Miss Pebmarsh, can I trouble you to come in here?'

Hardcastle had half held out a hand to guide Miss Pebmarsh, but she walked resolutely past him, verified a chair against the wall with a touch of her fingertips, drew it out a foot and sat down.

Hardcastle closed the door. Before he could speak, Millicent Pebmarsh said abruptly:

'Who's that young man?'

'His name is Colin Lamb.'

'So he informed me. But who is he? Why did he come here?' Hardcastle looked at her in faint surprise.

'He happened to be walking down the street when Miss Webb rushed out of this house screaming murder. After coming in and satisfying himself as to what had occurred he rang us up, and was asked to come back here and wait.'

'You spoke to him as Colin.'

'You are very observant, Miss Pebmarsh – (observant? hardly the word. And yet none other fitted) – Colin Lamb is a friend of mine, though it is some time since I have seen him.' He added: 'He's a marine biologist.'

'Oh! I see.'

'Now, Miss Pebmarsh, I shall be glad if you can tell me anything about this rather surprising affair.'

'Willingly. But there is very little to tell.'

'You have resided here for some time, I believe?'

'Since 1950. I am – was – a schoolmistress by profession. When I was told nothing could be done about my failing eyesight and that I should shortly go blind, I applied myself to become a specialist in Braille and various techniques for helping the blind. I have a job here at the Aaronberg Institute for Blind and Handicapped children.'

'Thank you. Now as to the events of this afternoon. Were you expecting a visitor?'

'No.'

'I will read you a description of the dead man to see if it suggests to you anyone in particular. Height five feet nine to ten, age approximately sixty, dark hair going grey, brown eyes, clean shaven, thin face, firm jaw. Well nourished but not fat. Dark grey suit, well-kept hands. Might be a bank clerk, an accountant, a lawyer, or a professional man of some kind. Does that suggest to you anyone that you know?'

Millicent Pebmarsh considered carefully before replying.

'I can't say that it does. Of course it's a very generalized description. It would fit quite a number of people. It might be someone I have seen or met on some occasion, but certainly not anyone I know well.'

'You have not received any letter lately from anyone proposing to call upon you?'

'Definitely not.'

'Very good. Now, you rang up the Cavendish Secretarial Bureau and asked for the services of a stenographer and –'

She interrupted him.

'Excuse me. I did nothing of the kind.'

'You did *not* ring up the Cavendish Secretarial Bureau and ask –' Hardcastle stared.

'I don't have a telephone in the house.'

'There is a call-box at the end of the street,' Inspector Hardcastle pointed out.

'Yes, of course. But I can only assure you, Inspector Hardcastle, that I had no need for a stenographer and did not – repeat *not* – ring up this Cavendish place with any such request.'

'You did not ask for Miss Sheila Webb particularly?'

'I have never heard that name before.'

Hardcastle stared at her, astonished.

'You left the front door unlocked,' he pointed out.

'I frequently do so in the daytime.'

'Anybody might walk in.'

'Anybody seems to have done so in this case,' said Miss Pebmarsh drily.

'Miss Pebmarsh, this man according to the medical evidence died roughly between 1.30 and 2.45. Where were you yourself then?'

Miss Pebmarsh reflected.

'At 1.30 I must either have left or been preparing to leave the house. I had some shopping to do.'

'Can you tell me exactly where you went?'

'Let me see. I went to the post office, the one in Albany Road, posted a parcel, got some stamps, then I did some household shopping, yes and I got some patent fasteners and safety pins at the drapers, Field and Wren. Then I returned here. I can tell you exactly what the time was. My cuckoo clock cuckooed three times as I came to the gate. I can hear it from the road.'

'And what about your other clocks?'

'I beg your pardon?'

'Your other clocks seem all to be just over an hour fast.'

'Fast? You mean the grandfather clock in the corner?'

'Not that only – all the other clocks in the sitting-room are the same.'

'I don't understand what you mean by the "other clocks". There are no other clocks in the sitting-room.'

CHAPTER 3

Hardcastle stared.

'Oh come, Miss Pebmarsh. What about that beautiful Dresden china clock on the mantelpiece? And a small French clock – ormolu. And a silver carriage clock, and – oh yes, the clock with "Rosemary" across the corner.'

It was Miss Pebmarsh's turn to stare.

'Either you or I must be mad, Inspector. I assure you I have no Dresden china clock, no – what did you say – clock with "Rosemary" across it – no French ormolu clock and – what was the other one?'

'Silver carriage clock,' said Hardcastle mechanically.

'Not that either. If you don't believe me, you can ask the woman who comes to clean for me. Her name is Mrs Curtin.'

Detective Inspector Hardcastle was taken aback. There was a positive assurance, a briskness in Miss Pebmarsh's tone that carried conviction. He took a moment or two turning over things in his mind. Then he rose to his feet.

'I wonder, Miss Pebmarsh, if you would mind accompanying me into the next room?'

'Certainly. Frankly, I would like to see those clocks myself.'

'See?' Hardcastle was quick to query the word.

'Examine would be a better word,' said Miss Pebmarsh, 'but

even blind people, Inspector, use conventional modes of speech that do not exactly apply to their own powers. When I say I would like to *see* those clocks, I mean I would like to examine and *feel* them with my own fingers.'

Followed by Miss Pebmarsh, Hardcastle went out of the kitchen, crossed the small hall and into the sitting-room. The fingerprint man looked up at him.

'I've about finished in here, sir,' he said. 'You can touch anything you like.'

Hardcastle nodded and picked up the small travelling clock with 'Rosemary' written across the corner. He put it into Miss Pebmarsh's hands. She felt it over carefully.

'It seems an ordinary travelling clock,' she said, 'the leather folding kind. It is not mine, Inspector Hardcastle, and it was not in this room, I am fairly sure I can say, when I left the house at half past one.'

'Thank you.'

The inspector took it back from her. Carefully he lifted the small Dresden clock from the mantelpiece.

'Be careful of this,' he said, as he put it into her hands, 'it's breakable.'

Millicent Pebmarsh felt the small china clock with delicate probing fingertips. Then she shook her head. 'It must be a charming clock,' she said, 'but it's not mine. Where was it, do you say?'

'On the right hand side of the mantelpiece.'

'There should be one of a pair of china candlesticks there,' said Miss Pebmarsh.

'Yes,' said Hardcastle, 'there is a candlestick there, but it's been pushed to the end.'

'You say there was still another clock?'

'Two more.'

Hardcastle took back the Dresden china clock and gave her the small French gilt ormolu one. She felt it over rapidly, then handed it back to him.

'No. That is not mine either.'

He handed her the silver one and that, too, she returned.

'The only clocks ordinarily in this room are a grandfather clock there in that corner by the window –'

'Quite right.'

'– and a cuckoo on the wall near the door.'

Hardcastle found it difficult to know exactly what to say next. He looked searchingly at the woman in front of him with the additional security of knowing that she could not return his survey. There was a slight frown as of perplexity on her forehead. She said sharply:

'I can't understand it. I simply can't understand it.'

She stretched out one hand, with the easy knowledge of where she was in the room, and sat down. Hardcastle looked at the fingerprint man who was standing by the door.

'You've been over these clocks?' he asked.

'I've been over everything, sir. No dabs on the gilt clock, but there wouldn't be. The surface wouldn't take it. The same goes for the china one. But there are no dabs on the leather travelling clock or the silver one and that is a bit unlikely if things were normal – there ought to be dabs. By the way, none of them are wound up and they are all set to the same time – thirteen minutes past four.'

'What about the rest of the room?'

'There are about three or four different sets of prints in the room, all women's, I should say. The contents of the pockets are on the table.'

By an indication of his head he drew attention to a small pile of things on a table. Hardcastle went over and looked at them. There was a notecase containing seven pounds ten, a little loose change, a silk pocket handkerchief, unmarked, a small box of digestive pills and a printed card. Hardcastle bent to look at it.

Mr R. H. Curry,
Metropolis and Provincial Insurance Co. Ltd
7, Denvers Street,
London, W2.

Hardcastle came back to the sofa where Miss Pebmarsh sat.

'Were you by any chance expecting someone from an insurance company to call upon you?'

'Insurance company? No, certainly not.'

'The Metropolis and Provincial Insurance Company,' said Hardcastle.

Miss Pebmarsh shook her head. 'I've never heard of it,' she said.

'You were not contemplating taking out insurance of any kind?'

'No, I was not. I am insured against fire and burglary with the Jove Insurance Company which has a branch here. I carry no personal insurance. I have no family or near relations so I see no point in insuring my life.'

'I see,' said Hardcastle. 'Does the name of Curry mean anything to you? Mr R. H. Curry?' He was watching her closely. He saw no reaction in her face.

'Curry,' she repeated the name, then shook her head. 'It's not a very usual name, is it? No, I don't think I've heard the name or known anyone of that name. Is that the name of the man who is dead?'

'It would seem possible,' said Hardcastle.

Miss Pebmarsh hesitated a moment. Then she said:

'Do you want me to – to – touch –'

He was quick to understand her.

'Would you, Miss Pebmarsh? If it's not asking too much of you, that is? I'm not very knowledgeable in these matters, but your fingers will probably tell you more accurately what a person looks like than you would know by description.'

'Exactly,' said Miss Pebmarsh. 'I agree it is not a very pleasant thing to have to do but I am quite willing to do it if you think it might be a help to you.'

'Thank you,' said Hardcastle. 'If you will let me guide you –'

He took her round the sofa, indicated to her to kneel down, then gently guided her hands to the dead man's face. She was very calm, displaying no emotion. Her fingers traced the hair, the ears, lingering a moment behind the left ear, the line of the nose, mouth and chin. Then she shook her head and got up.

'I have a clear idea what he would look like,' she said, 'but I am quite sure that it is no one I have seen or known.'

The fingerprint man had packed up his kit and gone out of the room. He stuck his head back in.

'They've come for him,' he said, indicating the body. 'All right to take him away?'

'Right,' said Inspector Hardcastle. 'Just come and sit over here, will you, Miss Pebmarsh?'

He established her in a corner chair. Two men came into the room. The removal of the late Mr Curry was rapid and professional. Hardcastle went out to the gate and then returned to the sitting-room. He sat down near Miss Pebmarsh.

'This is an extraordinary business, Miss Pebmarsh,' he said. 'I'd like to run over the main points with you and see if I've got it right. Correct me if I am wrong. You expected no visitors today, you've made no inquiries re insurance of any kind and you have received no letter from anyone stating that a representative of an insurance company was going to call upon you today. Is that correct?'

'Quite correct.'

'You did *not* need the services of a shorthand typist or stenographer and you did *not* ring up the Cavendish Bureau or request that one should be here at three o'clock.'

'That again is correct.'

'When you left the house at approximately 1.30, there were in this room only two clocks, the cuckoo clock and the grandfather clock. No others.'

About to reply, Miss Pebmarsh checked herself.

'If I am to be absolutely accurate, I could not swear to that statement. Not having my sight I would not notice the absence or presence of anything not usually in the room. That is to say, the last time I can be sure of the contents of this room was when I dusted it early this morning. Everything then was in its place. I usually do this room myself as cleaning women are apt to be careless with ornaments.'

'Did you leave the house at all this morning?'

'Yes. I went at ten o'clock as usual to the Aaronberg Institute. I have classes there until twelve-fifteen. I returned here at about quarter to one, made myself some scrambled eggs in the kitchen and a cup of tea and went out again, as I have said, at half past one. I ate my meal in the kitchen, by the way, and did not come into this room.'

'I see,' said Hardcastle. 'So while you can say definitely that at ten o'clock this morning there were no superfluous clocks here, they *could* possibly have been introduced some time during the morning.'

'As to that you would have to ask my cleaning woman, Mrs Curtin. She comes here about ten and usually leaves about twelve o'clock. She lives at 17, Dipper Street.'

'Thank you, Miss Pebmarsh. Now we are left with these following facts and this is where I want you to give me any ideas or suggestions that occur to you. At some time during today four clocks were brought here. The hands of these four clocks were set at thirteen minutes past four. Now does that time suggest anything to you?'

'Thirteen minutes past four.' Miss Pebmarsh shook her head. 'Nothing at all.'

'Now we pass from the clocks to the dead man. It seems unlikely that he would have been let in by your cleaning woman and left in the house by her unless you had told her you were expecting him, but that we can learn from her. He came here presumably to see you for some reason, either a business one or a private one. Between one-thirty and two-forty-five he was stabbed and killed. If he came here by appointment, you say you know nothing of it. Presumably he was connected with insurance – but there again you cannot help us. The door was unlocked so he could have come in and sat down to wait for you – but why?'

'The whole thing's daft,' said Miss Pebmarsh impatiently. 'So you think that this – what's-his-name Curry – brought those clocks with him?'

'There's no sign of a container anywhere,' said Hardcastle. 'He could hardly have brought four clocks in his pockets. Now Miss Pebmarsh, think very carefully. Is there any association in your mind, any suggestion you could possibly make about anything to do with clocks, or if not with clocks, say with *time*. 4.13. Thirteen minutes past four?'

She shook her head.

'I've been trying to say to myself that it is the work of a lunatic or that somebody came to the wrong house. But even that doesn't really explain anything. No, Inspector, I can't help you.'

A young constable looked in. Hardcastle went to join him in

the hall and from there went down to the gate. He spoke for a few minutes to the men.

'You can take the young lady home now,' he said, '14 Palmerston Road is the address.'

He went back and into the dining-room. Through the open door to the kitchen he could hear Miss Pebmarsh busy at the sink. He stood in the doorway.

'I shall want to take those clocks, Miss Pebmarsh. I'll leave you a receipt for them.'

'That will be quite all right, Inspector – they don't belong to me –'

Hardcastle turned to Sheila Webb.

'You can go home now, Miss Webb. The police car will take you.'

Sheila and Colin rose.

'Just see her into the car, will you, Colin?' said Hardcastle as he pulled a chair to the table and started to scribble a receipt.

Colin and Sheila went out and started down the path. Sheila paused suddenly.

'My gloves – I left them –'

'I'll get them.'

'No – I know just where I put them. I don't mind *now* – now that they've taken *it* away.'

She ran back and rejoined him a moment or two later.

'I'm sorry I was so silly – before.'

'Anybody would have been,' said Colin.

Hardcastle joined them as Sheila entered the car. Then, as it drove away, he turned to the young constable.

'I want those clocks in the sitting-room packed up carefully – all except the cuckoo clock on the wall and the big grandfather clock.'

He gave a few more directions and then turned to his friend.

'I'm going places. Want to come?'

'Suits me,' said Colin.

CHAPTER 4

COLIN LAMB'S NARRATIVE

'Where do we go?' I asked Dick Hardcastle.

He spoke to the driver.

'Cavendish Secretarial Bureau. It's on Palace Street, up towards the Esplanade on the right.'

'Yes, sir.'

The car drew away. There was quite a little crowd by now, staring with fascinated interest. The orange cat was still sitting on the gate post of Diana Lodge next door. He was no longer washing his face but was sitting up very straight, lashing his tail slightly, and gazing over the heads of the crowd with that complete disdain for the human race that is the special prerogative of cats and camels.

'The Secretarial Bureau, and then the cleaning woman, in that order,' said Hardcastle, 'because the time is getting on.' He glanced at his watch. 'After four o'clock.' He paused before adding, 'Rather an attractive girl?'

'Quite,' I said.

He cast an amused look in my direction.

'But she told a very remarkable story. The sooner it's checked up on, the better.'

'You don't think that she –'

He cut me short.

'I'm always interested in people who find bodies.'

'But that girl was half mad with fright! If you had heard the way she was screaming . . .'

He gave me another of his quizzical looks and repeated that she was a very attractive girl.

'And how did you come to be wandering about in Wilbraham Crescent, Colin? Admiring our genteel Victorian architecture? Or had you a purpose?'

'I had a purpose. I was looking for Number 61 – and I couldn't find it. Possibly it doesn't exist?'

'It exists all right. The numbers go up to – 88, I think.'

'But look here, Dick, when I came to Number 28, Wilbraham Crescent just petered out.'

'It's always puzzling to strangers. If you'd turned to the right up Albany Road and then turned to the right again you'd have found yourself in the other half of Wilbraham Crescent. It's built back to back, you see. The gardens back on each other.'

'I see,' I said, when he had explained this peculiar geography at length. 'Like those Squares and Gardens in London. Onslow Square, isn't it? Or Cadogan. You start down one side of a square, and then it suddenly becomes a Place or Gardens. Even taxis are frequently baffled. Anyway, there *is* a 61. Any idea who lives there?'

'61? Let me see . . . Yes, that would be Bland the builder.'

'Oh dear,' I said. 'That's bad.'

'You don't want a builder?'

'No. I don't fancy a builder at all. Unless – perhaps he's only just come here recently – just started up?'

'Bland was born here, I think. He's certainly a local man – been in business for years.'

'Very disappointing.'

'He's a very bad builder,' said Hardcastle encouragingly. 'Uses pretty poor materials. Puts up the kind of houses that look more or less all right until you live in them, then everything falls down or goes wrong. Sails fairly near the wind sometimes. Sharp practice – but just manages to get away with it.'

'It's no good tempting me, Dick. The man I want would almost certainly be a pillar of rectitude.'

'Bland came into a lot of money about a year ago – or rather his wife did. She's a Canadian, came over here in the war and met Bland. Her family didn't want her to marry him, and more or less cut her off when she did. Then last year a great-uncle died, his only son had been killed in an air crash and what with war casualties and one thing and another, Mrs Bland was the only one left of the family. So he left his money to her. Just saved Bland from going bankrupt, I believe.'

'You seem to know a lot about Mr Bland.'

'Oh that – well, you see, the Inland Revenue are always interested when a man suddenly gets rich overnight. They wonder if he's been doing a little fiddling and salting away – so they check up. They checked and it was all O.K.'

'In any case,' I said, 'I'm not interested in a man who has

suddenly got rich. It's not the kind of set-up that I'm looking for.'

'No? You've had that, haven't you?'

I nodded.

'And finished with it? Or – not finished with it?'

'It's something of a story,' I said evasively. 'Are we dining
together tonight as planned – or will this business put paid
to that?'

'No, that will be all right. At the moment the first thing to do
is set the machinery in motion. We want to find out all about Mr
Curry. In all probability once we know just who he is and what
he does, we'll have a pretty good idea as to who wanted him out
of the way.' He looked out of the window. 'Here we are.'

The Cavendish Secretarial and Typewriting Bureau was situated in the main shopping street, called rather grandly Palace
Street. It had been adapted, like many other of the establishments
there, from a Victorian house. To the right of it a similar house
displayed the legend Edwin Glen, Artist Photographer. Specialist,
Children's Photographs, Wedding Groups, etc. In support of
this statement the window was filled with enlargements of all
sizes and ages of children, from babies to six-year-olds. These
presumably were to lure in fond mammas. A few couples were
also represented. Bashful looking young men with smiling girls.
On the other side of the Cavendish Secretarial Bureau were the
offices of an old-established and old-fashioned coal merchant.
Beyond that again the original old-fashioned houses had been
pulled down and a glittering three-storey building proclaimed
itself as the Orient Café and Restaurant.

Hardcastle and I walked up the four steps, passed through the
open front door and obeying the legend on a door on the right
which said 'Please Enter,' entered. It was a good-sized room,
and three young women were typing with assiduity. Two of
them continued to type, paying no attention to the entrance
of strangers. The third one who was typing at a table with a
telephone, directly opposite the door, stopped and looked at us
inquiringly. She appeared to be sucking a sweet of some kind.
Having arranged it in a convenient position in her mouth, she
inquired in faintly adenoidal tones:

'Can I help you?'

'Miss Martindale?' said Hardcastle.

'I think she's engaged at the moment on the telephone –' At that moment there was a click and the girl picked up the telephone receiver and fiddled with a switch, and said: 'Two gentlemen to see you, Miss Martindale.' She looked at us and asked, 'Can I have your names, please?'

'Hardcastle,' said Dick.

'A Mr Hardcastle, Miss Martindale.' She replaced the receiver and rose. 'This way, please,' she said, going to a door which bore the name MISS MARTINDALE on a brass plate. She opened the door, flattened herself against it to let us pass, said, 'Mr Hardcastle,' and shut the door behind us.

Miss Martindale looked up at us from a large desk behind which she was sitting. She was an efficient-looking woman of about fifty with a pompadour of pale red hair and an alert glance.

She looked from one to the other of us.

'Mr Hardcastle?'

Dick took out one of his official cards and handed it to her. I effaced myself by taking an upright chair near the door.

Miss Martindale's sandy eyebrows rose in surprise and a certain amount of displeasure.

'Detective Inspector Hardcastle? What can I do for you, Inspector?'

'I have come to you to ask for a little information, Miss Martindale. I think you may be able to help me.'

From his tone of voice, I judged that Dick was going to play it in a roundabout way, exerting charm. I was rather doubtful myself whether Miss Martindale would be amenable to charm. She was of the type that the French label so aptly a *femme formidable*.

I was studying the general layout. On the walls above Miss Martindale's desk was hung a collection of signed photographs. I recognized one as that of Mrs Ariadne Oliver, detective writer, with whom I was slightly acquainted. *Sincerely yours, Ariadne Oliver*, was written across it in a bold black hand. *Yours gratefully, Garry Gregson* adorned another photograph of a thriller writer who had died about sixteen years ago. *Yours ever, Miriam* adorned the photograph of Miriam Hogg, a woman writer who specialized in romance. Sex was represented by a photograph of a timid-looking balding man, signed in tiny writing, *Gratefully,*

Armand Levine. There was a sameness about these trophies. The men mostly held pipes and wore tweeds, the women looked earnest and tended to fade into furs.

Whilst I was using my eyes, Hardcastle was proceeding with his questions.

'I believe you employ a girl called Sheila Webb?'

'That is correct. I am afraid she is not here at present – at least –'

She touched a buzzer and spoke to the outer office.

'Edna, has Sheila Webb come back?'

'No, Miss Martindale, not yet.'

Miss Martindale switched off.

'She went out on an assignment earlier this afternoon,' she explained. 'I thought she might have been back by now. It is possible she has gone on to the Curlew Hotel at the end of the Esplanade where she had an appointment at five o'clock.'

'I see,' said Hardcastle. 'Can you tell me something about Miss Sheila Webb?'

'I can't tell you very much,' said Miss Martindale. 'She has been here for – let me see, yes, I should say close on a year now. Her work has proved quite satisfactory.'

'Do you know where she worked before she came to you?'

'I dare say I could find out for you if you specially want the information, Inspector Hardcastle. Her references will be filed somewhere. As far as I can remember off-hand, she was formerly employed in London and had quite a good reference from her employers there. I think, but I am not sure, that it was some business firm – estate agents possibly, that she worked for.'

'You say she is good at her job?'

'Fully adequate,' said Miss Martindale, who was clearly not one to be lavish with praise.

'Not first-class?'

'No, I should not say that. She has good average speed and is tolerably well educated. She is a careful and accurate typist.'

'Do you know her personally, apart from your official relations?'

'No. She lives, I believe, with an aunt.' Here Miss Martindale got slightly restive. 'May I ask, Inspector Hardcastle, *why* you are asking all these questions? Has the girl got herself into trouble in any way?'

'I would not quite say that, Miss Martindale. Do you know a Miss Millicent Pebmarsh?'

'Pebmarsh,' said Miss Martindale, wrinkling her sandy brows. 'Now when – oh, of course. It was to Miss Pebmarsh's house that Sheila went this afternoon. The appointment was for three o'clock.'

'How was that appointment made, Miss Martindale?'

'By telephone. Miss Pebmarsh rang up and said she wanted the services of a shorthand typist and would I send her Miss Webb.'

'She asked for Sheila Webb particularly?'

'Yes.'

'What time was this call put through?'

Miss Martindale reflected for a moment.

'It came through to me direct. That would mean that it was in the lunch hour. As near as possible I would say that it was about ten minutes to two. Before two o'clock at all events. Ah yes, I see I made a note on my pad. It was 1.49 precisely.'

'It was Miss Pebmarsh herself who spoke to you?'

Miss Martindale looked a little surprised.

'I presume so.'

'But you didn't recognize her voice? You don't know her personally?'

'No. I don't know her. She said that she was Miss Millicent Pebmarsh, gave me her address, a number in Wilbraham Crescent. Then, as I say, she asked for Sheila Webb, if she was free, to come to her at three o'clock.'

It was a clear, definite statement. I thought that Miss Martindale would make an excellent witness.

'If you would kindly tell me what all this is about?' said Miss Martindale with slight impatience.

'Well, you see, Miss Martindale, Miss Pebmarsh herself denies making any such call.'

Miss Martindale stared.

'Indeed! How extraordinary.'

'You, on the other hand, say such a call *was* made, but you cannot say definitely that it was Miss Pebmarsh who made that call.'

'No, of course I can't say definitely. I don't know the woman. But really, I can't see the point of doing such a thing. Was it a hoax of some kind?'

'Rather more than that,' said Hardcastle. 'Did this Miss Pebmarsh – or whoever it was – give any reason for wanting Miss Sheila Webb particularly?'

Miss Martindale reflected a moment.

'I think she said that Sheila Webb had done work for her before.'

'And is that in fact so?'

'Sheila said she had no recollection of having done anything for Miss Pebmarsh. But that is not quite conclusive, Inspector. After all, the girls go out so often to different people at different places that they would be unlikely to remember if it had taken place some months ago. Sheila wasn't very definite on the point. She only said that she couldn't remember having been there. But really, Inspector, even if this was a hoax, I cannot see where your interest comes in?'

'I am just coming to that. When Miss Webb arrived at 19, Wilbraham Crescent she walked into the house and into the sitting-room. She has told me that those were the directions given her. You agree?'

'Quite right,' said Miss Martindale. 'Miss Pebmarsh said that she might be a little late in getting home and that Sheila was to go in and wait.'

'When Miss Webb went into the sitting-room,' continued Hardcastle, 'she found a dead man lying on the floor.'

Miss Martindale stared at him. For a moment she could hardly find her voice.

'Did you say a *dead man*, Inspector?'

'A murdered man,' said Hardcastle. 'Stabbed, actually.'

'Dear, dear,' said Miss Martindale. 'The girl must have been very upset.'

It seemed the kind of understatement characteristic of Miss Martindale.

'Does the name of Curry mean anything to you, Miss Martindale? Mr R. H. Curry?'

'I don't think so, no.'

'From the Metropolis and Provincial Insurance Company?'

Miss Martindale continued to shake her head.

'You see my dilemma,' said the inspector. 'You say Miss Pebmarsh telephoned you and asked for Sheila Webb to go to her house at three o'clock. Miss Pebmarsh denies doing any such thing. Sheila Webb gets there. She finds a dead man there.' He waited hopefully.

Miss Martindale looked at him blankly.

'It all seems to me wildly improbable,' she said disapprovingly.

Dick Hardcastle sighed and got up.

'Nice place you've got here,' he said politely. 'You've been in business some time, haven't you?'

'Fifteen years. We have done extremely well. Starting in quite a small way, we have extended the business until we have almost more than we can cope with. I now employ eight girls, and they are kept busy all the time.'

'You do a good deal of literary work, I see.' Hardcastle was looking up at the photographs on the wall.

'Yes, to start with I specialized in authors. I had been secretary to the well-known thriller writer, Mr Garry Gregson, for many years. In fact, it was with a legacy from him that I started this Bureau. I knew a good many of his fellow authors and they recommended me. My specialized knowledge of authors' requirements came in very useful. I offer a very helpful service in the way of necessary research – dates and quotations, inquiries as to legal points and police procedure, and details of poison schedules. All that sort of thing. Then foreign names and addresses and restaurants for people who set their novels in foreign places. In old days the public didn't really mind so much about accuracy, but nowadays readers take it upon themselves to write to authors on every possible occasion, pointing out flaws.'

Miss Martindale paused. Hardcastle said politely: 'I'm sure you have every cause to congratulate yourself.'

He moved towards the door. I opened it ahead of him.

In the outer office, the three girls were preparing to leave. Lids had been placed on typewriters. The receptionist, Edna, was standing forlornly, holding in one hand a stiletto heel and in the other a shoe from which it had been torn.

'I've only had them a month,' she was wailing. 'And they were quite expensive. It's that beastly grating – the one at the corner by the cake shop quite near here. I caught my heel in it and off it came. I couldn't walk, had to take both shoes off and come back here with a couple of buns, and how I'll ever get home or get on to the bus I really don't know –'

At that moment our presence was noted and Edna hastily concealed the offending shoe with an apprehensive glance towards Miss Martindale whom I appreciated was not the sort of woman to approve of stiletto heels. She herself was wearing sensible flat-heeled leather shoes.

'Thank you, Miss Martindale,' said Hardcastle. 'I'm sorry to have taken up so much of your time. If anything should occur to you –'

'Naturally,' said Miss Martindale, cutting him short rather brusquely.

As we got into the car, I said:

'So Sheila Webb's story, in spite of your suspicions, turns out to have been quite true.'

'All right, all right,' said Dick. 'You win.'

CHAPTER 5

'Mom!' said Ernie Curtin, desisting for a moment from his occupation of running a small metal model up and down the window pane, accompanying it with a semi-zooming, semi-moaning noise intended to reproduce a rocket ship going through outer space on its way to Venus, 'Mom, what d'you think?'

Mrs Curtin, a stern-faced woman who was busy washing up crockery in the sink, made no response.

'Mom, there's a police car drawn up outside our house.'

'Don't you tell no more of yer lies, Ernie,' said Mrs Curtin as she banged cups and saucers down on the draining board. 'You know what I've said to you about that before.'

'I never,' said Ernie virtuously. 'And it's a police car right enough, and there's two men gettin' out.'

Mrs Curtin wheeled round on her offspring.

'What've you been doing *now*?' she demanded. 'Bringing us into disgrace, that's what it is!'

'Course I ain't,' said Ernie. 'I 'aven't done nothin'.'

'It's going with that Alf,' said Mrs Curtin. 'Him and his gang. Gangs indeed! I've told you, and yer father's told you, that gangs isn't respectable. In the end there's trouble. First it'll be the juvenile court and then you'll be sent to a remand home as likely as not. And I won't have it, d'you hear?'

'They're comin' up to the front door,' Ernie announced.

Mrs Curtin abandoned the sink and joined her offspring at the window.

'Well,' she muttered.

At that moment the knocker was sounded. Wiping her hands quickly on the tea-towel, Mrs Curtin went out into the passage and opened the door. She looked with defiance and doubt at the two men on her doorstep.

'Mrs Curtin?' said the taller of the two, pleasantly.

'That's right,' said Mrs Curtin.

'May I come in a moment? I'm Detective Inspector Hardcastle.'

Mrs Curtin drew back rather unwillingly. She threw open a door and motioned the inspector inside. It was a very neat, clean little room and gave the impression of seldom being entered, which impression was entirely correct.

Ernie, drawn by curiosity, came down the passage from the kitchen and sidled inside the door.

'Your son?' said Detective Inspector Hardcastle.

'Yes,' said Mrs Curtin, and added belligerently, 'he's a good boy, no matter what you say.'

'I'm sure he is,' said Detective Inspector Hardcastle, politely.

Some of the defiance in Mrs Curtin's face relaxed.

'I've come to ask you a few questions about 19, Wilbraham Crescent. You work there, I understand.'

'Never said I didn't,' said Mrs Curtin, unable yet to shake off her previous mood.

'For a Miss Millicent Pebmarsh.'

'Yes, I work for Miss Pebmarsh. A very nice lady.'

'Blind,' said Detective Inspector Hardcastle.

'Yes, poor soul. But you'd never know it. Wonderful the way she can put her hand on anything and find her way about. Goes out in the street, too, and over the crossings. She's not one to make a fuss about things, not like some people I know.'

'You work there in the mornings?'

'That's right. I come about half past nine to ten, and leave at twelve o'clock or when I'm finished.' Then sharply, 'You're not saying as anything 'as been *stolen*, are you?'

'Quite the reverse,' said the inspector, thinking of four clocks. Mrs Curtin looked at him uncomprehendingly.

'What's the trouble?' she asked.

'A man was found dead in the sitting-room at 19, Wilbraham Crescent this afternoon.'

Mrs Curtin stared. Ernie Curtin wriggled in ecstasy, opened his mouth to say 'Coo', thought it unwise to draw attention to his presence, and shut it again.

'Dead?' said Mrs Curtin unbelievingly. And with even more unbelief, 'In the *sitting-room*?'

'Yes. He'd been stabbed.'

'You mean it's *murder*?'

'Yes, murder.'

'Oo murdered 'im?' demanded Mrs Curtin.

'I'm afraid we haven't got quite so far as that yet,' said Inspector Hardcastle. 'We thought perhaps you may be able to help us.'

'I don't know anything about murder,' said Mrs Curtin positively.

'No, but there are one or two points that have arisen. This morning, for instance, did any man call at the house?'

'Not that I can remember. Not today. What sort of man was he?'

'An elderly man about sixty, respectably dressed in a dark suit. He may have represented himself as an insurance agent.'

'I wouldn't have let him in,' said Mrs Curtin. 'No insurance agents and nobody selling vacuum cleaners or editions of the Encyclopaedia Britannica. Nothing of that sort. Miss Pebmarsh doesn't hold with selling at the door and neither do I.'

'The man's name, according to a card that was on him, was Mr Curry. Have you ever heard that name?'

'Curry? Curry?' Mrs Curtin shook her head. 'Sounds Indian to me,' she said, suspiciously.

'Oh, no,' said Inspector Hardcastle, 'he wasn't an Indian.'

'Who found him – Miss Pebmarsh?'

'A young lady, a shorthand typist, had arrived because, owing to a misunderstanding, she thought she'd been sent for to do some work for Miss Pebmarsh. It was she who discovered the body. Miss Pebmarsh returned almost at the same moment.'

Mrs Curtin uttered a deep sigh.

'What a to-do,' she said, 'what a to-do!'

'We may ask you at some time,' said Inspector Hardcastle, 'to look at this man's body and tell us if he is a man you have ever seen in Wilbraham Crescent or calling at the house before. Miss Pebmarsh is quite positive he has never been there. Now there are various small points I would like to know. Can you recall off-hand how many clocks there are in the sitting-room?'

Mrs Curtin did not even pause.

'There's that big clock in the corner, grandfather they call it, and there's the cuckoo clock on the wall. It springs out and says "cuckoo". Doesn't half make you jump sometimes.' She added hastily, 'I didn't touch neither of them. I never do. Miss Pebmarsh likes to wind them herself.'

'There's nothing wrong with them,' the inspector assured her. 'You're sure these were the only two clocks in the room this morning?'

'Of course. What others should there be?'

'There was not, for instance, a small square silver clock, what they call a carriage clock, or a little gilt clock – on the mantelpiece that was, or a china clock with flowers on it – or a leather clock with the name Rosemary written across the corner?'

'Of course there wasn't. No such thing.'

'You would have noticed them if they had been there?'

'Of course I should.'

'Each of these four clocks represented a time about an hour later than the cuckoo clock and the grandfather clock.'

'Must have been foreign,' said Mrs Curtin. 'Me and my old man went on a coach trip to Switzerland and Italy once and it was a whole hour further on there. Must be something to do with this Common Market. I don't hold with the Common Market and nor does Mr Curtin. England's good enough for me.'

Inspector Hardcastle declined to be drawn into politics.

'Can you tell me exactly when you left Miss Pebmarsh's house this morning?'

'Quarter past twelve, near as nothing,' said Mrs Curtin.

'Was Miss Pebmarsh in the house then?'

'No, she hadn't come back. She usually comes back some time between twelve and half past, but it varies.'

'And she had left the house – when?'

'Before I got there. Ten o'clock's my time.'

'Well, thank you, Mrs Curtin.'

'Seems queer about these clocks,' said Mrs Curtin. 'Perhaps Miss Pebmarsh had been to a sale. Antiques, were they? They sound like it by what you say.'

'Does Miss Pebmarsh often go to sales?'

'Got a roll of hair carpet about four months ago at a sale. Quite good condition. Very cheap, she told me. Got some velour curtains too. They needed cutting down, but they were really as good as new.'

'But she doesn't usually buy bric-à-brac or things like pictures or china or that kind of thing at sales?'

Mrs Curtin shook her head.

'Not that I've ever known her, but of course, there's no saying in sales, is there? I mean, you get carried away. When you get home you say to yourself "whatever did I want with that?" Bought six pots of jam once. When I thought about it I could have made it cheaper myself. Cups and saucers, too. Them I could have got better in the market on a Wednesday.'

She shook her head darkly. Feeling that he had no more to learn for the moment, Inspector Hardcastle departed. Ernie then made his contribution to the subject that had been under discussion.

'Murder! Coo!' said Ernie.

Momentarily the conquest of outer space was displaced in his mind by a present-day subject of really thrilling appeal.

'Miss Pebmarsh couldn't have done 'im in, could she?' he suggested yearningly.

'Don't talk so silly,' said his mother. A thought crossed her mind. 'I wonder if I ought to have told him –'

'Told him what, Mom?'

'Never you mind,' said Mrs Curtin. 'It was nothing, really.'

CHAPTER 6

COLIN LAMB'S NARRATIVE

I

When we had put ourselves outside two good underdone steaks, washed down with draught beer, Dick Hardcastle gave a sigh of comfortable repletion, announced that he felt better and said:

'To hell with dead insurance agents, fancy clocks and screaming girls! Let's hear about you, Colin. I thought you'd finished with this part of the world. And here you are wandering about the back streets of Crowdean. No scope for a marine biologist at Crowdean, I can assure you.'

'Don't you sneer at marine biology, Dick. It's a very useful subject. The mere mention of it so bores people and they're so afraid you're going to talk about it, that you never have to explain yourself further.'

'No chance of giving yourself away, eh?'

'You forget,' I said coldly, 'that I *am* a marine biologist. I took a degree in it at Cambridge. Not a very good degree, but a degree. It's a very interesting subject, and one day I'm going back to it.'

'I know what you've been working on, of course,' said Hardcastle. 'And congratulations to you. Larkin's trial comes on next month, doesn't it?'

'Yes.'

'Amazing the way he managed to carry on passing stuff out for so long. You'd think somebody would have suspected.'

'They didn't, you know. When you've got it into your head that a fellow is a thoroughly good chap, it doesn't occur to you that he mightn't be.'

'He must have been clever,' Dick commented.

I shook my head.

'No, I don't think he was, really. I think he just did as he was told. He had access to very important documents. He walked out with them, they were photographed and returned to him, and they were back again where they belonged the same day. Good organization there. He made a habit of lunching at different places every day. We think that he hung up his overcoat where there was always an overcoat exactly like it – though the man who wore the other overcoat wasn't always the same man. The overcoats were switched, but the man who switched them never spoke to Larkin, and Larkin never spoke to him. We'd like to know a good deal more about the mechanics of it. It was all very well planned with perfect timing. Somebody had brains.'

'And that's why you're still hanging round the Naval Station at Portlebury?'

'Yes, we know the Naval end of it and we know the London end. We know just when and where Larkin got his pay and how. But there's a gap. In between the two there's a very pretty little bit of organization. That's the part we'd like to know more about, because that's the part where the brains are. *Somewhere* there's a very good headquarters, with excellent planning, which leaves a trail that is confused not once but probably seven or eight times.'

'What did Larkin do it for?' asked Hardcastle, curiously. 'Political idealist? Boosting his ego? Or plain money?'

'He was no idealist,' I said. 'Just money, I'd say.'

'Couldn't you have got on to him sooner that way? He spent the money, didn't he? He didn't salt it away.'

'Oh, no, he splashed it about all right. Actually, we got on to him a little sooner than we're admitting.'

Hardcastle nodded his head understandingly.

'I see. You tumbled and then you used him for a bit. Is that it?'

'More or less. He had passed out some quite valuable information before we got on to him, so we let him pass out more information, also apparently valuable. In the Service I belong to, we have to resign ourselves to looking fools now and again.'

'I don't think I'd care for your job, Colin,' said Hardcastle thoughtfully.

'It's not the exciting job that people think it is,' I said. 'As a matter of fact, it's usually remarkably tedious. But there's something beyond that. Nowadays one gets to feeling that nothing really *is* secret. We know Their secrets and They know our secrets. Our agents are often Their agents, too, and Their agents are very often our agents. And in the end who is double-crossing who becomes a kind of nightmare! Sometimes I think that everybody knows everybody else's secrets and that they enter into a kind of conspiracy to pretend that they don't.'

'I see what you mean,' Dick said thoughtfully.

Then he looked at me curiously.

'I can see why you should still be hanging around Portlebury. But Crowdean's a good ten miles from Portlebury.'

'What I'm really after,' I said, 'are Crescents.'

'Crescents?' Hardcastle looked puzzled.

'Yes. Or alternatively, moons. New moons, rising moons and so on. I started my quest in Portlebury itself. There's a pub there called The Crescent Moon. I wasted a long time over that. It sounded ideal. Then there's The Moon and Stars. The Rising Moon, The Jolly Sickle, The Cross and the Crescent – that was in a little place called Seamede. Nothing doing. Then I abandoned moons and started on Crescents. Several Crescents in Portlebury. Lansbury Crescent, Aldridge Crescent, Livermead Crescent, Victoria Crescent.'

I caught sight of Dick's bewildered face and began to laugh.

'Don't look so much at sea, Dick. I had something tangible to start me off.'

I took out my wallet, extracted a sheet of paper and passed it over to him. It was a single sheet of hotel writing paper on which a rough sketch had been drawn.

'A chap called Hanbury had this in his wallet. Hanbury did a lot of work in the Larkin case. He was good – very good. He was run over by a hit and run car in London. Nobody got its number. I don't know what this means, but it's something that Hanbury jotted down, or copied, because he thought it was important. Some idea that he had? Or something that he'd seen or heard? Something to do with a moon or crescent, the number 61 and the initial M. I took over after his death. I don't know what I'm looking for yet, but I'm pretty sure there's something to find. I don't know what 61 means. I don't know what M means. I've been working in a radius from Portlebury outwards. Three weeks of unremitting and unrewarding toil. Crowdean is on my route. That's all there is to it. Frankly, Dick, I didn't expect very much of Crowdean. There's only one Crescent here. That's Wilbraham Crescent. I was going to have a walk along Wilbraham Crescent and see what I thought of Number 61 before asking you if you'd got any dope that could help me. That's what I was doing this afternoon – but I couldn't find Number 61.'

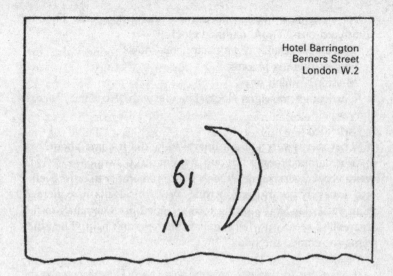

Hotel Barrington
Berners Street
London W.2

'As I told you, 61 is occupied by a local builder.'

'And that's not what I'm after. Have they got a foreign help of any kind?'

'Could be. A good many people do nowadays. If so, she'll be registered. I'll look it up for you by tomorrow.'

'Thanks, Dick.'

'I'll be making routine inquiries tomorrow at the two houses on either side of 19. Whether they saw anyone come to the house, et cetera. I might include the houses directly *behind* 19, the ones whose gardens adjoin it. I rather think that 61 is almost directly behind 19. I could take you along with me if you liked.'

I closed with the offer greedily.

'I'll be your Sergeant Lamb and take shorthand notes.'

We agreed that I should come to the police station at nine thirty the following morning.

II

I arrived the next morning promptly at the agreed hour and found my friend literally fuming with rage.

When he had dismissed an unhappy subordinate, I inquired delicately what had happened.

For a moment Hardcastle seemed unable to speak. Then he spluttered out: 'Those damned clocks!'

'The clocks again? What's happened now?'

'One of them is missing.'

'Missing? Which one?'

'The leather travelling clock. The one with "Rosemary" across the corner.'

I whistled.

'That seems very extraordinary. How did it come about?'

'The damned fools – I'm one of them really, I suppose –' (Dick was a very honest man) '– One's got to remember to cross every t and dot every i or things go wrong. Well, the clocks were there all right yesterday in the sitting-room. I got Miss Pebmarsh to feel them all to see if they felt familiar. She couldn't help. Then they came to remove the body.'

'Yes?'

'I went out to the gate to supervise, then I came back to the house, spoke to Miss Pebmarsh who was in the kitchen, and said I must take the clocks away and would give her a receipt for them.'

'I remember. I heard you.'

'Then I told the girl I'd send her home in one of our cars, and I asked you to see her into it.'

'Yes.'

'I gave Miss Pebmarsh the receipt though she said it wasn't necessary since the clocks weren't hers. Then I joined you. I told Edwards I wanted the clocks in the sitting-room packed up carefully and brought here. All of them except the cuckoo clock and, of course, the grandfather. And that's where I went wrong. I should have said, quite definitely, *four* clocks. Edwards says he went in at once and did as I told him. He insists there were only three clocks other than the two fixtures.'

'That doesn't give much time,' I said. 'It means –'

'The Pebmarsh woman could have done it. She could have picked up the clock after I left the room and gone straight to the kitchen with it.'

'True enough. But why?'

'We've got a lot to learn. Is there anybody else? Could the girl have done it?'

I reflected. 'I don't think so. I –' I stopped, remembering something.

'So she did,' said Hardcastle. 'Go on. When was it?'

'We were just going out to the police car,' I said unhappily. 'She'd left her gloves behind. I said, "I'll get them for you" and she said, "Oh, I know just where I must have dropped them. I don't mind going into that room now that the body's gone." and she ran back into the house. But she was only gone a minute –'

'Did she have her gloves on, or in her hand when she rejoined you?'

I hesitated. 'Yes – yes, I think she did.'

'Obviously she didn't,' said Hardcastle, 'or you wouldn't have hesitated.'

'She probably stuffed them in her bag.'

'The trouble is,' said Hardcastle in an accusing manner, 'you've fallen for that girl.'

'Don't be idiotic,' I defended myself vigorously. 'I saw her for the first time yesterday afternoon, and it wasn't exactly what you'd call a romantic introduction.'

'I'm not so sure of that,' said Hardcastle. 'It isn't every day that young men have girls falling into their arms screaming for help in the approved Victorian fashion. Makes a man feel a hero and a gallant protector. Only you've got to stop protecting her. That's all. So far as you know, that girl may be up to the neck in this murder business.'

'Are you saying that this slip of a girl stuck a knife into a man, hid it somewhere so carefully that none of your sleuths could find it, then deliberately rushed out of the house and did a screaming act all over me?'

'You'd be surprised at what I've seen in my time,' said Hardcastle darkly.

'Don't you realize,' I demanded, indignantly, 'that my life has been full of beautiful spies of every nationality? All of them with vital statistics that would make an American private eye forget all about the shot of rye in his collar drawer. I'm immune to all female allurements.'

'Everybody meets his Waterloo in the end,' said Hardcastle. 'It all depends on the type. Sheila Webb seems to be your type.'

'Anyway, I can't see why you're so set on fastening it on her.'

Hardcastle sighed.

'I'm not fastening it on her – but I've got to start somewhere. The body was found in Pebmarsh's house. That involves her. The body was found by the Webb girl – I don't need to tell you how often the first person to find a dead body is the same as the person who last saw him alive. Until more facts turn up, those two remain in the picture.'

'When I went into that room at just after three o'clock, the body had been dead at least half an hour, probably longer. How about that?'

'Sheila Webb had her lunch hour from 1.30 to 2.30.'

I looked at him in exasperation.

'What have you found out about Curry?'

Hardcastle said with unexpected bitterness: 'Nothing!'

'What do you mean – nothing?'

'Just that he doesn't exist – there's no such person.'

'What do the Metropolis Insurance Company say?'

'They've nothing to say either, because there's no such thing. The Metropolis and Provincial Insurance Company doesn't exist. As far as Mr Curry from Denvers Street goes, there's no Mr Curry, no Denvers Street, Number 7 or any other number.'

'Interesting,' I said. 'You mean he just had some bogus cards printed with a bogus name, address and insurance company?'

'Presumably.'

'What is the big idea, do you think?'

Hardcastle shrugged his shoulders.

'At the moment it's guesswork. Perhaps he collected bogus premiums. Perhaps it was a way of introducing himself into houses and working some confidence trick. He may have been a swindler or a confidence trickster or a picker-up of unconsidered trifles or a private inquiry agent. We just don't know.'

'But you'll find out.'

'Oh, yes, we'll know in the end. We sent up his fingerprints to see if he's got a record of any kind. If he has it'll be a big step on the way. If he hasn't, it'll be rather more difficult.'

'A private dick,' I said thoughtfully. 'I rather like that. It opens up – possibilities.'

'Possibilities are all we've got so far.'

'When's the inquest?'

'Day after tomorrow. Purely formal and an adjournment.'

'What's the medical evidence?'

'Oh, stabbed with a sharp instrument. Something like a kitchen vegetable-knife.'

'That rather lets out Miss Pebmarsh, doesn't it?' I said thoughtfully. 'A blind woman would hardly be able to stab a man. She really *is* blind, I suppose?'

'Oh, yes, she's blind. We checked up. And she's exactly what she says she is. She was a teacher of mathematics in a North Country school – lost her sight about sixteen years ago – took up training in Braille, etc., and finally got a post with the Aaronberg Institute here.'

'She could be mental, I suppose?'

'With a fixation on clocks and insurance agents?'

'It really is all too fantastic for words.' I couldn't help speaking with some enthusiasm. 'Like Ariadne Oliver in her worst moments, or the late Garry Gregson at the top of his form –'

'Go on – enjoy yourself. *You're* not the wretched D.I. in charge. *You* haven't got to satisfy a superintendent or a chief constable and all the rest of it.'

'Oh well! Perhaps we'll get something useful out of the neighbours.'

'I doubt it,' said Hardcastle bitterly. 'If that man was stabbed in the front garden and two masked men carried him into the house – nobody would have looked out of the window or seen anything. This isn't a village, worse luck. Wilbraham Crescent is a genteel residential road. By one o'clock, daily women who might have seen something have gone home. There's not even a pram being wheeled along –'

'No elderly invalid who sits all day by the window?'

'That's what we want – but that's not what we've got.'

'What about numbers 18 and 20?'

'18 is occupied by Mr Waterhouse, Managing Clerk to Gainsford and Swettenham, Solicitors, and his sister who spends her spare time managing him. All I know about 20 is that the woman who lives there keeps about twenty cats. I don't like cats –'

I told him that a policeman's life was a hard one, and we started off.

CHAPTER 7

Mr Waterhouse, hovering uncertainly on the steps of 18, Wilbraham Crescent, looked back nervously at his sister.

'You're quite sure you'll be all right?' said Mr Waterhouse.

Miss Waterhouse snorted with some indignation.

'I really don't know what you mean, James.'

Mr Waterhouse looked apologetic. He had to look apologetic so often that it was practically his prevailing cast of countenance.

'Well, I just meant, my dear, considering what happened next door yesterday . . .'

Mr Waterhouse was prepared for departure to the solicitors' office where he worked. He was a neat, grey-haired man with slightly stooping shoulders and a face that was also grey rather than pink, though not in the least unhealthy looking.

Miss Waterhouse was tall, angular, and the kind of woman with no nonsense about her who is extremely intolerant of nonsense in others.

'Is there any reason, James, because someone was murdered in the next door house that I shall be murdered today?'

'Well, Edith,' said Mr Waterhouse, 'it depends so much, does it not, by whom the murder was committed?'

'You think, in fact, that there's someone going up and down Wilbraham Crescent selecting a victim from every house? Really, James, that is almost blasphemous.'

'Blasphemous, Edith?' said Mr Waterhouse in lively surprise. Such an aspect of his remark would never have occurred to him.

'Reminiscent of the Passover,' said Miss Waterhouse. 'Which, let me remind you, is Holy Writ.'

'That is a little far-fetched I think, Edith,' said Mr Waterhouse.

'I should like to see anyone coming here, trying to murder *me*,' said Miss Waterhouse with spirit.

Her brother reflected to himself that it did seem highly unlikely. If he himself had been choosing a victim he would not have chosen his sister. If anyone were to attempt such a thing it was far more likely that the attacker would be knocked out by a poker or a lead doorstop and delivered over to the police in a bleeding and humiliated condition.

'I just meant,' he said, the apologetic air deepening, 'that there are – well – clearly undesirable characters about.'

'We don't know very much about what did happen yet,' said Miss Waterhouse. 'All sorts of rumours are going about. Mrs Head had some extraordinary stories this morning.'

'I expect so, I expect so,' said Mr Waterhouse. He looked at his watch. He had no real desire to hear the stories brought in by their loquacious daily help. His sister never lost time in debunking these lurid flights of fancy, but nevertheless enjoyed them.

'Some people are saying,' said Miss Waterhouse, 'that this man was the treasurer or a trustee of the Aaronberg Institute and that there is something wrong in the accounts, and that he came to Miss Pebmarsh to inquire about it.'

'And that Miss Pebmarsh murdered him?' Mr Waterhouse looked mildly amused. 'A blind woman? Surely –'

'Slipped a piece of wire round his neck and strangled him,' said Miss Waterhouse. 'He wouldn't be on his guard, you see. Who would be with anyone blind? Not that I believe it myself,' she added. 'I'm sure Miss Pebmarsh is a person of excellent character. If I do not see eye to eye with her on various subjects, that is not because I impute anything of a criminal nature to her. I merely think that her views are bigoted and extravagant. After all, there *are* other things besides education. All these new peculiar looking grammar schools, practically built of glass. You might think they were meant to grow cucumbers in, or tomatoes. I'm sure very prejudicial to children in the summer months. Mrs Head herself told me that her Susan didn't like their new classrooms. Said it was impossible to attend to your lessons because with all those windows you couldn't help looking out of them all the time.'

'Dear, dear,' said Mr Waterhouse, looking at his watch again. 'Well, well, I'm going to be very late, I'm afraid. Goodbye, my dear. Look after yourself. Better keep the door on the chain perhaps?'

Miss Waterhouse snorted again. Having shut the door behind her brother she was about to retire upstairs when she paused thoughtfully, went to her golf bag, removed a niblick, and placed it in a strategic position near the front door. 'There,' said Miss

Waterhouse, with some satisfaction. Of course James talked nonsense. Still it was always as well to be prepared. The way they let mental cases out of nursing homes nowadays, urging them to lead a normal life, was in her view fraught with danger to all sorts of innocent people.

Miss Waterhouse was in her bedroom when Mrs Head came bustling up the stairs. Mrs Head was small and round and very like a rubber ball – she enjoyed practically everything that happened.

'A couple of gentlemen want to see you,' said Mrs Head with avidity. 'Leastways,' she added, 'they aren't really gentlemen – it's the police.'

She shoved forward a card. Miss Waterhouse took it.

'Detective Inspector Hardcastle,' she read. 'Did you show them into the drawing-room?'

'No. I put 'em in the dinin'-room. I'd cleared away breakfast and I thought that that would be more proper a place. I mean, they're only the police after all.'

Miss Waterhouse did not quite follow this reasoning. However she said, 'I'll come down.'

'I expect they'll want to ask you about Miss Pebmarsh,' said Mrs Head. 'Want to know whether you've noticed anything funny in her manner. They say these manias come on very sudden sometimes and there's very little to show beforehand. But there's usually *something*, some way of speaking, you know. You can tell by their eyes, they say. But then that wouldn't hold with a blind woman, would it? Ah –' she shook her head.

Miss Waterhouse marched downstairs and entered the dining-room with a certain amount of pleasurable curiosity masked by her usual air of belligerence.

'Detective Inspector Hardcastle?'

'Good morning, Miss Waterhouse.' Hardcastle had risen. He had with him a tall, dark young man whom Miss Waterhouse did not bother to greet. She paid no attention to a faint murmur of 'Sergeant Lamb'.

'I hope I have not called at too early an hour,' said Hardcastle, 'but I imagine you know what it is about. You've heard what happened next door yesterday.'

'Murder in one's next door neighbour's house does not usually go unnoticed,' said Miss Waterhouse. 'I even had to turn away one or two reporters who came here asking if I had observed anything.'

'You turned them away?'

'Naturally.'

'You were quite right,' said Hardcastle. 'Of course they like to worm their way in anywhere but I'm sure you are quite capable of dealing with anything of *that* kind.'

Miss Waterhouse allowed herself to show a faintly pleasurable reaction to this compliment.

'I hope you won't mind us asking you the same kind of questions,' said Hardcastle, 'but if you did see anything at all that could be of interest to us, I can assure you we should be only too grateful. You were here in the house at the time, I gather?'

'I don't know when the murder was committed,' said Miss Waterhouse.

'We think between half past one and half past two.'

'I was here then, yes, certainly.'

'And your brother?'

'He does not come home to lunch. Who exactly was murdered? It doesn't seem to say in the short account there was in the local morning paper.'

'We don't yet know who he was,' said Hardcastle.

'A stranger?'

'So it seems.'

'You don't mean he was a stranger to Miss Pebmarsh also?'

'Miss Pebmarsh assures us that she was not expecting this particular guest and that she has no idea who he was.'

'She can't be sure of that,' said Miss Waterhouse. 'She can't see.'

'We gave her a very careful description.'

'What kind of man was he?'

Hardcastle took a rough print from an envelope and handed it to her.

'This is the man,' he said. 'Have you any idea who he can be?'

Miss Waterhouse looked at the print. 'No. No . . . I'm certain I've never seen him before. Dear me. He looks quite a respectable man.'

'He was a most respectable-looking man,' said the inspector. 'He looks like a lawyer or a business man of some kind.'

'Indeed. This photograph is not at all distressing. He just looks as though he might be asleep.'

Hardcastle did not tell her that of the various police photographs of the corpse this one had been selected as the least disturbing to the eye.

'Death can be a peaceful business,' he said. 'I don't think this particular man had any idea that it was coming to him when it did.'

'What does Miss Pebmarsh say about it all?' demanded Miss Waterhouse.

'She is quite at a loss.'

'Extraordinary,' commented Miss Waterhouse.

'Now, can you help us in any way, Miss Waterhouse? If you cast your mind back to yesterday, were you looking out of the window at all, or did you happen to be in your garden, say any time between half past twelve and three o'clock?'

Miss Waterhouse reflected.

'Yes, I *was* in the garden . . . Now let me see. It must have been before one o'clock. I came in about ten to one from the garden, washed my hands and sat down to lunch.'

'Did you see Miss Pebmarsh enter or leave the house?'

'I think she came in – I heard the gate squeak – yes, some time after half past twelve.'

'You didn't speak to her?'

'Oh no. It was just the squeak of the gate made me look up. It is her usual time for returning. She finishes her classes then, I believe. She teaches at the Disabled Children as probably you know.'

'According to her own statement, Miss Pebmarsh went out again about half past one. Would you agree to that?'

'Well, I couldn't tell you the exact time but – yes, I do remember her passing the gate.'

'I beg your pardon, Miss Waterhouse, you said "passing the gate".'

'Certainly. I was in my sitting-room. That gives on the street, whereas the dining-room, where we are sitting now, gives as you can see, on the back garden. But I took my coffee into the sitting-room after lunch and I was sitting with it in a chair near the window. I was reading *The Times*, and I think it was when I was turning the sheet that I noticed Miss Pebmarsh passing the front gate. Is there anything extraordinary about that, Inspector?'

'Not extraordinary, no,' said the inspector, smiling. 'Only I understood that Miss Pebmarsh was going out to do a little shopping and to the post office, and I had an idea that the nearest way to the shops and the post office would be to go the other way along the crescent.'

'Depends on which shops you are going to,' said Miss Waterhouse. 'Of course the shops *are* nearer that way, and there's a post office in Albany Road –'

'But perhaps Miss Pebmarsh usually passed your gate about that time?'

'Well, really, I don't know what time Miss Pebmarsh usually went out, or in which direction. I'm not really given to watching my neighbours in any way, Inspector. I'm a busy woman and have far too much to do with my own affairs. Some people I know spend their entire time looking out of the window and noticing who passes and who calls on whom. That is more a habit of invalids or of people who've got nothing better to do than to speculate and gossip about their neighbours' affairs.'

Miss Waterhouse spoke with such acerbity that the inspector felt sure that she had some one particular person in mind. He said hastily, 'Quite so. Quite so.' He added, 'Since Miss Pebmarsh passed your front gate, she might have been going to telephone, might she not? That is where the public telephone box is situated?'

'Yes. It's opposite Number 15.'

'The important question I have to ask you, Miss Waterhouse, is if you saw the arrival of this man – the mystery man as I'm afraid the morning papers have called him.'

Miss Waterhouse shook her head. 'No, I didn't see him or any other caller.'

'What were you doing between half past one and three o'clock?'

'I spent about half an hour doing the crossword in *The Times*, or as much of it as I could, then I went out to the kitchen and washed up the lunch. Let me see. I wrote a couple of letters, made some cheques out for bills, then I went upstairs and sorted out some things I wanted to take to the cleaners. I think it was from my bedroom that I noticed a certain amount of commotion next door. I distinctly heard someone screaming, so naturally I went to the window. There was a young man and a girl at the gate. He seemed to be embracing her.'

Sergeant Lamb shifted his feet but Miss Waterhouse was not looking at him and clearly had no idea that he had been that particular young man in question.

'I could only see the back of the young man's head. He seemed to be arguing with the girl. Finally he sat her down against the gate post. An extraordinary thing to do. And he strode off and went into the house.'

'You had not seen Miss Pebmarsh return to the house a short time before?'

Miss Waterhouse shook her head. 'No. I don't really think I had looked out the window at all until I heard this extraordinary screaming. However, I didn't pay much attention to all this. Young girls and men are always doing such extraordinary things – screaming, pushing each other, giggling or making some kind of noise – that I had no idea it was anything serious. Not until some cars drove up with policemen did I realize anything out of the ordinary had occurred.'

'What did you do then?'

'Well, naturally I went out of the house, stood on the steps and then I walked round to the back garden. I wondered what had happened but there didn't seem to be anything much to see from that side. When I got back again there was quite a little crowd gathering. Somebody told me there'd been a murder in the house. It seemed to me most extraordinary. *Most* extraordinary!' said Miss Waterhouse with a great deal of disapproval.

'There is nothing else you can think of? That you can tell us?'

'Really, I'm afraid not.'

'Has anybody recently written to you suggesting insurance, or has anybody called upon you or proposed calling upon you?'

'No. Nothing of the kind. Both James and I have taken out insurance policies with the Mutual Help Assurance Society. Of course one is always getting letters which are really circulars or advertisements of some kind but I don't recall anything of that kind recently.'

'No letters signed by anybody called Curry?'

'Curry? No, certainly not.'

'And the name of Curry means nothing to you in any way?'

'No. Should it?'

Hardcastle smiled. 'No. I really don't think it should,' he said. 'It just happens to be the name that the man who was murdered was calling himself by.'

'It wasn't his real name?'

'We have some reason to think that it was not his real name.'

'A swindler of some kind, eh?' said Miss Waterhouse.

'We can't say that till we have evidence to prove it.'

'Of course not, of course not. You've got to be careful. I know that,' said Miss Waterhouse. 'Not like some of the people around here. They'd say anything. I wonder some aren't had up for libel all the time.'

'Slander,' corrected Sergeant Lamb, speaking for the first time.

Miss Waterhouse looked at him in some surprise, as though not aware before that he had an entity of his own and was anything other than a necessary appendage to Inspector Hardcastle.

'I'm sorry I can't help you, I really am,' said Miss Waterhouse.

'I'm sorry too,' said Hardcastle. 'A person of your intelligence and judgement with a faculty of observation would have been a very useful witness to have.'

'I wish I *had* seen something,' said Miss Waterhouse.

For a moment her tone was as wistful as a young girl's.

'Your brother, Mr James Waterhouse?'

'James wouldn't know anything,' said Miss Waterhouse scornfully. 'He never does. And anyway he was at Gainsford and Swettenhams in the High Street. Oh no, James wouldn't be able to help you. As I say, he doesn't come back to lunch.'

'Where does he lunch usually?'

'He usually has sandwiches and coffee at the Three Feathers. A very nice respectable house. They specialize in quick lunches for professional people.'

'Thank you, Miss Waterhouse. Well, we mustn't keep you any longer.'

He rose and went out into the hall. Miss Waterhouse accompanied them. Colin Lamb picked up the golf club by the door.

'Nice club, this,' he said. 'Plenty of weight in the head.' He weighed it up and down in his hand. 'I see you are prepared, Miss Waterhouse, for any eventualities.'

Miss Waterhouse was slightly taken aback.

'Really,' she said, 'I can't imagine how that club came to be there.'

She snatched it from him and replaced it in the golf bag.

'A very wise precaution to take,' said Hardcastle.

Miss Waterhouse opened the door and let them out.

'Well,' said Colin Lamb, with a sigh, 'we didn't get much out of her, in spite of you buttering her up so nicely all the time. Is that your invariable method?'

'It gets good results sometimes with a person of her type. The tough kind always respond to flattery.'

'She was purring like a cat that has been offered a saucer of cream in the end,' said Colin. 'Unfortunately, it didn't disclose anything of interest.'

'No?' said Hardcastle.

Colin looked at him quickly. 'What's on your mind?'

'A very slight and possibly unimportant point. Miss Pebmarsh went out to the post office and the shops but she turned *left* instead of *right*, and that telephone call, according to Miss Martindale, was put through about ten minutes to two.'

Colin looked at him curiously.

'You still think that in spite of her denial she might have made it? She was very positive.'

'Yes,' said Hardcastle. 'She was very positive.'

His tone was non-committal.

'But if she did make it, why?'

'Oh, it's all *why*,' said Hardcastle impatiently. 'Why, why? *Why* all this rigmarole? If Miss Pebmarsh made that call, why did she want to get the girl there? If it was someone else, why did they want to involve Miss Pebmarsh? We don't know anything yet. If that Martindale woman had known Miss Pebmarsh personally, she'd have known whether it was her voice or not, or at any rate whether it was reasonably like Miss Pebmarsh's. Oh well, we haven't got much from Number 18. Let's see whether Number 20 will do us any better.'

CHAPTER 8

In addition to its number, 20, Wilbraham Crescent had a name. It was called Diana Lodge. The gates had obstacles against intruders by being heavily wired on the inside. Rather melancholy speckled laurels, imperfectly trimmed, also interfered with the efforts of anyone to enter through the gate.

'If ever a house could have been called The Laurels, this one could,' remarked Colin Lamb. 'Why call it Diana Lodge, I wonder?'

He looked round him appraisingly. Diana Lodge did not run to neatness or to flower-beds. Tangled and overgrown shrubbery was its most salient point together with a strong catty smell of ammonia. The house seemed in a rather tumbledown condition with gutters that could do with repairing. The only sign of any recent kind of attention being paid to it was a freshly painted front door whose colour of bright azure blue made the general unkempt appearance of the rest of the house and garden even more noticeable. There was no electric bell but a kind of handle that was clearly meant to be pulled. The inspector pulled it and a faint sound of remote jangling was heard inside.

'It sounds,' said Colin, 'like the Moated Grange.'

They waited for a moment or two, then sounds were heard from inside. Rather curious sounds. A kind of high crooning, half singing, half speaking.

'What the devil –' began Hardcastle.

The singer or crooner appeared to be approaching the front door and words began to be discernible.

'No, sweet-sweetie. In there, my love. Mindems tailems Shah-Shah-Mimi. Cleo – Cleopatra. Ah de doodlums. Ah lou-lou.'

Doors were heard to shut. Finally the front door opened. Facing them was a lady in a pale moss-green, rather rubbed, velvet tea gown. Her hair, in flaxen grey wisps, was twirled elaborately in a kind of coiffure of some thirty years back. Round her neck she was wearing a necklet of orange fur. Inspector Hardcastle said dubiously:

'Mrs Hemming?'

'I am Mrs Hemming. Gently, Sunbeam, gently doodleums.'

It was then that the inspector perceived that the orange fur was really a cat. It was not the only cat. Three other cats appeared along the hall, two of them miaowing. They took up their place, gazing at the visitors, twirling gently round their mistress's skirts. At the same time a pervading smell of cat afflicted the nostrils of both men.

'I am Detective Inspector Hardcastle.'

'I hope you've come about that dreadful man who came to see me from the Prevention of Cruelty to Animals,' said Mrs Hemming. 'Disgraceful! I wrote and reported him. Saying my cats were kept in a condition prejudicial to their health and happiness! Quite disgraceful! I *live* for my cats, Inspector. They are my only joy and pleasure in life. Everything is done for them. Shah-Shah-Mimi. Not *there*, sweetie.'

Shah-Shah-Mimi paid no attention to a restraining hand and jumped on the hall table. He sat down and washed his face, staring at the strangers.

'Come in,' said Mrs Hemming. 'Oh no, not that room. I'd forgotten.'

She pushed open a door on the left. The atmosphere here was even more pungent.

'Come on, my pretties, come on.'

In the room various brushes and combs with cat hairs in them lay about on chairs and tables. There were faded and soiled cushions, and there were at least six more cats.

'I live for my darlings,' said Mrs Hemming. 'They understand every word I say to them.'

Inspector Hardcastle walked in manfully. Unfortunately for him he was one of those men who have cat allergy. As usually happens on these occasions all the cats immediately made for him. One jumped on his knee, another rubbed affectionately against his trousers. Detective Inspector Hardcastle, who was a brave man, set his lips and endured.

'I wonder if I could ask you a few questions, Mrs Hemming, about –'

'Anything you please,' said Mrs Hemming, interrupting him. 'I have nothing to hide. I can show you the cats' food, their beds where they sleep, five in my room, the other seven down here.

They have only the very best fish cooked by myself.'

'This is nothing to do with *cats*,' said Hardcastle, raising his voice. 'I came to talk to you about the unfortunate affair which happened next door. You have probably heard about it.'

'Next door? You mean Mr Joshua's dog?'

'No,' said Hardcastle, 'I do not. I mean at Number 19 where a man was found murdered yesterday.'

'Indeed?' said Mrs Hemming, with polite interest but no more. Her eyes were still straying over her pets.

'Were you at home yesterday afternoon, may I ask? That is to say between half past one and half past three?'

'Oh yes, indeed. I usually do my shopping quite early in the day and then get back so that I can do the darlings' lunch, and then comb and groom them.'

'And you didn't notice any activity next door? Police cars – ambulance – anything like that?'

'Well, I'm afraid I didn't look out of the front windows. I went out of the back of the house into the garden because dear Arabella was missing. She is quite a young cat and she had climbed up one of the trees and I was afraid she might not be able to get down. I tried to tempt her with a saucer of fish but she was frightened, poor little thing. I had to give up in the end and come back into the house. And would you believe it, just as I went through the door, down she came and followed me in.' She looked from one man to the other as though testing their powers of belief.

'Matter of fact, I would believe it,' said Colin, unable to keep silence any more.

'I beg your pardon?' Mrs Hemming looked at him slightly startled.

'I am much attached to cats,' said Colin, 'and I have therefore made a study of cat nature. What you have told me illustrates perfectly the pattern of cat behaviour and the rules they have made for themselves. In the same way your cats are all congregating round my friend who frankly does not care for cats, they will pay no attention to me in spite of all my blandishments.'

If it occurred to Mrs Hemming that Colin was hardly speaking in the proper role of sergeant of police, no trace of it appeared in her face. She merely murmured vaguely:

'They always know, the dear things, don't they?'

A handsome grey Persian put two paws on Inspector Hardcastle's knees, looked at him in an ecstasy of pleasure and dug his claws in hard with a kneading action as though the inspector was a pincushion. Goaded beyond endurance, Inspector Hardcastle rose to his feet.

'I wonder, madam,' he said, 'if I could see this back garden of yours.'

Colin grinned slightly.

'Oh, of course, of course. Anything you please.' Mrs Hemming rose.

The orange cat unwound itself from her neck. She replaced it in an absent-minded way with the grey Persian. She led the way out of the room. Hardcastle and Colin followed.

'We've met before,' said Colin to the orange cat and added, 'And *you're* a beauty, aren't you,' addressing another grey Persian who was sitting on a table by a Chinese lamp, swishing his tail slightly. Colin stroked him, tickled him behind the ears and the grey cat condescended to purr.

'Shut the door, please, as you come out, Mr – er – er,' said Mrs Hemming from the hall. 'There's a sharp wind today and I don't want my dears to get cold. Besides, there are those terrible boys – it's really not safe to let the dear things wander about in the garden by themselves.'

She walked towards the back of the hall and opened a side door.

'What terrible boys?' asked Hardcastle.

'Mrs Ramsay's two boys. They live in the south part of the crescent. Our gardens more or less back on each other. Absolute young hooligans, that's what they are. They have a catapult, you know, or they had. I insisted on its being confiscated but I have my suspicions. They make ambushes and hide. In the summer they throw apples.'

'Disgraceful,' said Colin.

The back garden was like the front only more so. It had some unkempt grass, some unpruned and crowded shrubs and a great many more laurels of the speckled variety, and some rather gloomy macrocarpas. In Colin's opinion, both he and Hardcastle were wasting their time. There was a solid barrage of laurels, trees and shrubs through which nothing of Miss Pebmarsh's garden could possibly be seen. Diana Lodge could be described as a fully detached house. From the point of view of its inhabitants, it might have had no neighbours.

'Number 19, did you say?' said Mrs Hemming, pausing irresolutely in the middle of her back garden. 'But I thought there was only one person living in the house, a blind woman.'

'The murdered man was not an occupant of the house,' said the inspector.

'Oh, I see,' said Mrs Hemming, still vaguely, 'he came here to be murdered. How odd.'

'Now that,' said Colin thoughtfully to himself, 'is a damned good description.'

CHAPTER 9

They drove along Wilbraham Crescent, turned to the right up Albany Road and then to the right again along the second instalment of Wilbraham Crescent.

'Simple really,' said Hardcastle.

'Once you know,' said Colin.

'61 really backs on Mrs Hemming's house – but a corner of it touches on 19, so that's good enough. It will give you a chance to look at your Mr Bland. No foreign help, by the way.'

'So there goes a beautiful theory.' The car drew up and the two men got out.

'Well, well,' said Colin. 'Some front garden!'

It was indeed a model of surburban perfection in a small way. There were beds of geraniums with lobelia edging. There were large fleshy-looking begonias, and there was a fine display of garden ornaments – frogs, toadstools, comic gnomes and pixies.

'I'm sure Mr Bland *must* be a nice worthy man,' said Colin, with a shudder. 'He couldn't have these terrible ideas if he wasn't.' He added as Hardcastle pushed the bell, 'Do you expect him to be in at this time of the morning?'

'I rang up,' explained Hardcastle. 'Asked him if it would be convenient.'

At that moment a smart little Traveller van drew up and turned into the garage, which had obviously been a late addition to the house. Mr Josaiah Bland got out, slammed the door and advanced towards them. He was a man of medium height with a bald head and rather small blue eyes. He had a hearty manner.

'Inspector Hardcastle? Come right in.'

He led the way into the sitting-room. It evinced several proofs of prosperity. There were expensive and rather ornate lamps, an Empire writing desk, a coruscated ormolu set of mantelpiece ornaments, a marquetry cabinet, and a *jardinère* full of flowers in the window. The chairs were modern and richly upholstered.

'Sit down,' said Mr Bland heartily. 'Smoke? Or can't you when you're on the job?'

'No, thanks,' said Hardcastle.

'Don't drink either, I suppose?' said Mr Bland. 'Ah well, better for both of us, I dare say. Now what's it all about? This business at Number 19 I suppose? The corners of our gardens adjoin, but we've not much real view of it except from the upper floor windows. Extraordinary business altogether it seems to be – at least from what I read in our local paper this morning. I was delighted when I got your message. A chance of getting some of the real dope. You've no idea the rumours that are flying about! It's made my wife quite nervous – feeling there's a killer on the loose, you know. The trouble is they let all these barmy people out of lunatic asylums nowadays. Send them home on parole or whatever they call it. Then they do in someone else and they clap them back again. And as I say, the rumours! I mean, what with our daily woman and the milk and paper boy, you'd be surprised. One says he was strangled with picture wire, and the other says he was stabbed. Someone else that he was coshed. At any rate it was a he, wasn't it? I mean, it wasn't the old girl who was done in? An unknown man, the papers said.'

Mr Bland came to a full stop at last.

Hardcastle smiled and said in a deprecating voice:

'Well, as to unknown, he *had* a card and an address in his pocket.'

'So much for that story then,' said Bland. 'But you know what people are. *I* don't know who thinks up all these things.'

'While we're on the subject of the victim,' said Hardcastle, 'perhaps you'll have a look at *this*.'

Once more he brought out the police photograph.

'So that's him, is it?' said Bland. 'He looks a perfectly ordinary chap, doesn't he? Ordinary as you and me. I suppose I mustn't ask if he had any particular reason to be murdered?'

'It's early days to talk about that,' said Hardcastle. 'What I want to know, Mr Bland, is if you've ever seen this man before.'

Bland shook his head.

'I'm sure I haven't. I'm quite good at remembering faces.'

'He hasn't called upon you for any particular purpose – selling insurance or – vacuum cleaners or washing machines, or anything of that kind?'

'No, no. Certainly not.'

'We ought perhaps to ask your wife,' said Hardcastle. 'After all, if he called at the house, it's your wife he would see.'

'Yes, that's perfectly true. I don't know, though . . . Valerie's not got very good health, you know. I wouldn't like to upset her. What I mean is, well, I suppose that's a picture of him when he's dead, isn't it?'

'Yes,' said Hardcastle, 'that is quite true. But it is not a painful photograph in any way.'

'No, no. Very well done. The chap might be asleep, really.'

'Are you talking about me, Josiah?'

An adjoining door from the other room was pushed open and a middle-aged woman entered the room. She had, Hardcastle decided, been listening with close attention on the other side of the door.

'Ah, there you are, my dear,' said Bland, 'I thought you were having your morning nap. This is my wife, Detective Inspector Hardcastle.'

'That terrible murder,' murmured Mrs Bland. 'It really makes me shiver to think of it.'

She sat down on the sofa with a little gasping sigh.

'Put your feet up, dear,' said Bland.

Mrs Bland obeyed. She was a sandy-haired woman, with a faint whining voice. She looked anaemic, and had all the airs of an invalid who accepts her invalidism with a certain amount of enjoyment. For a moment or two, she reminded Inspector

Hardcastle of somebody. He tried to think who it was, but failed. The faint, rather plaintive voice continued.

'My health isn't very good, Inspector Hardcastle, so my husband naturally tries to spare me any shocks or worry. I'm very sensitive. You were speaking about a photograph, I think, of the – of the murdered man. Oh dear, how terrible that sounds. I don't know that I can bear to look!'

'Dying to see it, really,' thought Hardcastle to himself.

With faint malice in his voice, he said:

'Perhaps I'd better not ask you to look at it, then, Mrs Bland. I just thought you might be able to help us, in case the man has called at this house at any time.'

'I must do my duty, mustn't I,' said Mrs Bland, with a sweet brave smile. She held out her hand.

'Do you think you'd better upset yourself, Val?'

'Don't be foolish, Josaiah. Of course I must see.'

She looked at the photograph with much interest and, or so the inspector thought, a certain amount of disappointment.

'He looks – really, he doesn't look dead at all,' she said. 'Not at all as though he'd been *murdered*. Was he – he can't have been strangled?'

'He was stabbed,' said the inspector.

Mrs Bland closed her eyes and shivered.

'Oh dear,' she said, 'how terrible.'

'You don't feel you've ever seen him, Mrs Bland?'

'No,' said Mrs Bland with obvious reluctance, 'no, no, I'm afraid not. Was he the sort of man who – who calls at houses selling things?'

'He seems to have been an insurance agent,' said the inspector carefully.

'Oh, I see. No, there's been nobody of that kind, I'm sure. You never remember my mentioning anything of that kind, do you, Josaiah?'

'Can't say I do,' said Mr Bland.

'Was he any relation to Miss Pebmarsh?' asked Mrs Bland.

'No,' said the inspector, 'he was quite unknown to her.'

'Very peculiar,' said Mrs Bland.

'You know Mrs Pebmarsh?'

'Oh yes, I mean, we know her as neighbours, of course. She

asks my husband for advice sometimes about the garden.'

'You're a very keen gardener, I gather?' said the inspector.

'Not really, not really,' said Bland deprecatingly. 'Haven't the time, you know. Of course, I know what's what. But I've got an excellent fellow – comes twice a week. He sees the garden's kept well stocked, and well tidied up. I'd say you couldn't beat our garden round here, but I'm not one of those real gardeners like my neighbour.'

'Mrs Ramsay?' said Hardcastle in some surprise.

'No, no, farther along. 63. Mr McNaughton. He just lives for his garden. In it all day long, and mad on compost. Really, he's quite a bore on the subject of compost – but I don't suppose that's what you want to talk about.'

'Not exactly,' said the inspector. 'I only wondered if anyone – you or your wife, for instance – were out in your garden yesterday. After all, as you say, it does touch on the border of 19 and there's just a chance that you might have seen something interesting yesterday – or heard something, perhaps?'

'Midday, wasn't it? When the murder happened I mean?'

'The relevant times are between one o'clock and three o'clock.'

Bland shook his head. 'I wouldn't have seen much then. I was here. So was Valerie, but we'd be having lunch, you know, and our dining-room looks out on the roadside. We shouldn't see anything that was going on in the garden.'

'What time do you have your meal?'

'One o'clock or thereabouts. Sometimes it's one-thirty.'

'And you didn't go out in the garden at all afterwards?'

Bland shook his head.

'Matter of fact,' he said, 'my wife always goes up to rest after lunch and, if things aren't too busy, I take a bit of shuteye myself in that chair there. I must have left the house about – oh, I suppose a quarter to three, but unfortunately I didn't go out in the garden at all.'

'Oh, well,' said Hardcastle with a sigh, 'we have to ask everyone.'

'Of course, of course. Wish I could be more helpful.'

'Nice place you have here,' said the inspector. 'No money spared, if I may say so.'

Bland laughed jovially.

'Ah well, we like things that are nice. My wife's got a lot of taste. We had a bit of a windfall a year ago. My wife came into some money from an uncle of hers. She hadn't seen him for twenty-five years. Quite a surprise it was! It made a bit of difference to us, I can tell you. We've been able to do ourselves well and we're thinking of going on one of these cruises later in the year. Very educational they are, I believe. Greece and all that. A lot of professors on them lecturing. Well, of course, I'm a self-made man and I haven't had much time for that sort of thing but I'd be interested. That chap who went and dug up Troy, he was a grocer, I believe. Very romantic. I must say I like going to foreign parts – not that I've done much of that – an occasional weekend in gay Paree, that's all. I've toyed with the idea of selling up here and going to live in Spain or Portugal or even the West Indies. A lot of people are doing it. Saves income tax and all that. But my wife doesn't fancy the idea.'

'I'm fond of travel, but I wouldn't care to live out of England,' said Mrs Bland. 'We've got all our friends here – and my sister lives here, and everybody knows *us*. If we went abroad we'd be strangers. And then we've got a very good doctor here. He really understands my health. I shouldn't care *at all* for a foreign doctor. I wouldn't have any confidence in him.'

'We'll see,' said Mr Bland cheerfully. 'We'll go on a cruise and you may fall in love with a Greek island.'

Mrs Bland looked as though that were very unlikely.

'There'd be a proper English doctor aboard, I suppose,' she said doubtfully.

'Sure to be,' said her husband.

He accompanied Hardcastle and Colin to the front door, repeating once more how sorry he was that he couldn't help them.

'Well,' said Hardcastle. 'What do you think of him?'

'I wouldn't care to let him build a house for me,' said Colin. 'But a crooked little builder isn't what I'm after. I'm looking for a man who is dedicated. And as regards your murder case, you've got the wrong kind of murder. Now if Bland was to feed his wife arsenic or push her into the Aegean in order to inherit her money and marry a slap-up blonde –'

'We'll see about that when it happens,' said Inspector Hardcastle. 'In the meantime we've got to get on with *this* murder.'

CHAPTER 10

At No. 62, Wilbraham Crescent, Mrs Ramsay was saying to herself encouragingly, 'Only two days now. Only two days.'

She pushed back some dank hair from her forehead. An almighty crash came from the kitchen. Mrs Ramsay felt very disinclined even to go and see what the crash portended. If only she could pretend that there *hadn't* been a crash. Oh well – *only two days*. She stepped across the hall, flung the kitchen door open and said in a voice of far less belligerence than it would have held three weeks ago:

'*Now* what have you done?'

'Sorry, Mum,' said her son Bill. 'We were just having a bit of a bowling match with these tins and somehow or other they rolled into the bottom of the china cupboard.'

'We didn't mean them to go into the bottom of the china cupboard,' said his younger brother Ted agreeably.

'Well, pick up those things and put them back in the cupboard and sweep up that broken china and put it in the bin.'

'Oh, Mum, not *now*.'

'Yes, now.'

'Ted can do it,' said Bill.

'I like that,' said Ted. 'Always putting on me. I won't do it if you won't.'

'Bet you will.'

'Bet I won't.'

'I'll make you.'

'Yahh!'

The boys closed in a fierce wrestling match. Ted was forced back against the kitchen table and a bowl of eggs rocked ominously.

'Oh, get out of the kitchen!' cried Mrs Ramsay. She pushed the two boys out of the kitchen door and shut it, and began to pick up tins and sweep up china.

'Two days,' she thought, 'and they'll be back at school! What a lovely, what a heavenly thought for a mother.'

She remembered vaguely some wicked remark by a woman columnist.

Only six happy days in the year for a woman.

The first and the last days of the holidays. How true that was, thought Mrs Ramsay, sweeping up portions of her best dinner-service. With what pleasure, what joy, had she contemplated the return of her offspring a bare five weeks before! And now? 'The day after tomorrow,' she repeated to herself, 'the day after tomorrow Bill and Ted will be back at school. I can hardly believe it. I can't wait!'

How heavenly it had been five weeks ago when she met them at the station. Their tempestuous and affectionate welcome! The way they had rushed all over the house and garden. A special cake baked for tea. And now – what was she looking forward to now? A day of complete peace. No enormous meals to prepare, no incessant clearing up. She loved the boys – they were fine boys, no doubt of that. She was proud of them. But they were also exhausting. Their appetite, their vitality, the *noise* they made.

At that moment, raucous cries arose. She turned her head in sharp alarm. It was all right. They had only gone out in the garden. That was better, there was far more room for them in the garden. They would probably annoy the neighbours. She hoped to goodness they would leave Mrs Hemming's cats alone. Not, it must be confessed, for the sake of the cats, but because the wired enclosure surrounding Mrs Hemming's garden was apt to tear their shorts. She cast a fleeting eye over the first-aid box which lay handy on the dresser. Not that she fussed unduly over the natural accidents of vigorous boyhood. In fact her first inevitable remark was: 'Now haven't I told you a hundred times, you are *not* to bleed in the drawing-room! Come straight into the kitchen and bleed there, where I can wipe over the linoleum.'

A terrific yell from outside seemed to be cut off mid-way and was followed by a silence so profound that Mrs Ramsay felt a real feeling of alarm spring up in her breast. Really, that silence was most unnatural. She stood uncertainly, the dust-pan with broken china in her hand. The kitchen door opened and Bill stood there. He had an awed, ecstatic expression most unusual on his eleven-year-old face.

'Mum,' he said. '*There's a detective inspector here and another man with him.*'

'Oh,' said Mrs Ramsay, relieved. 'What does he want, dear?'

'He asked for you,' said Bill, 'but I think it must be about the murder. You know, the one at Miss Pebmarsh's yesterday.'

'I don't see why he should come and wish to see me,' said Mrs Ramsay, in a slightly vexed voice.

Life was just one thing after another, she thought. How was she to get the potatoes on for the Irish stew if detective inspectors came along at this awkward hour?

'Oh well,' she said with a sigh. 'I suppose I'd better come.'

She shot the broken china into the bin under the sink, rinsed her hands under the tap, smoothed her hair and prepared to follow Bill, who was saying impatiently, 'Oh, come *on*, Mum.'

Mrs Ramsay, closely flanked by Bill, entered the sitting-room. Two men were standing there. Her younger son, Ted, was in attendance upon them, staring at them with wide appreciative eyes.

'Mrs Ramsay?'

'Good morning.'

'I expect these young men have told you that I am Detective Inspector Hardcastle?'

'It's very awkward,' said Mrs Ramsay. 'Very awkward this morning. I'm very busy. Will it take very long?'

'Hardly any time at all,' said Detective Inspector Hardcastle reassuringly. 'May we sit down?'

'Oh, yes, do, do.'

Mrs Ramsay took an upright chair and looked at them impatiently. She had suspicions that it was *not* going to take hardly any time at all.

'No need for you two to remain,' said Hardcastle to the boys pleasantly.

'Aw, we're not going,' said Bill.

'We're not going,' echoed Ted.

'We want to hear all about it,' said Bill.

'Sure we do,' said Ted.

'Was there a lot of blood?' asked Bill.

'Was it a burglar?' said Ted.

'Be quiet, boys,' said Mrs Ramsay. 'Didn't you hear the – Mr Hardcastle say he didn't want you in here?'

'We're not going,' said Bill. 'We want to hear.'

Hardcastle moved across to the door and opened it. He looked at the boys.

'Out,' he said.

It was only one word, quietly uttered, but it had behind it the quality of authority. Without more ado both boys got up, shuffled their feet and shuffled out of the room.

'How wonderful,' thought Mrs Ramsay appreciatively. 'Now why can't *I* be like that?'

But then, she reflected, she was the boys' mother. She knew by hearsay that the boys, when they went out, behaved in a manner entirely different from at home. It was always mothers who got the worst of things. But perhaps, she reflected, one would rather have it like that. To have nice quiet attentive polite boys at home and to have little hooligans going out, creating unfavourable opinions of themselves, would be worse – yes, that would be worse. She recalled herself to what was required of her, as Inspector Hardcastle came back and sat down again.

'If it's about what happened at Number 19 yesterday,' she said nervously, 'I really don't see that I can tell you anything, Inspector. I don't know anything about it. I don't even know the people who live there.'

'The house is lived in by a Miss Pebmarsh. She's blind and works at the Aaronberg Institute.'

'Oh, I see,' said Mrs Ramsay. 'I'm afraid I know hardly anybody in the lower Crescent.'

'Were you yourself here yesterday between half past twelve and three o'clock?'

'Oh, yes,' said Mrs Ramsay. 'There was dinner to cook and all that. I went out before three, though. I took the boys to the cinema.'

The inspector took the photograph from his pocket and handed it to her.

'I'd like you to tell me if you've ever seen this man before.'

Mrs Ramsay looked at it with a slight awakening of interest.

'No,' she said, 'no, I don't think so. I'm not sure if I would remember if I had seen him.'

'He did not come to this house on any occasion – trying to sell you insurance or anything of that kind?'

Mrs Ramsay shook her head more positively.

'No. No, I'm sure he didn't.'

'His name, we have some reason to believe, is Curry. Mr R. Curry.'

He looked inquiringly at her. Mrs Ramsay shook her head again.

'I'm afraid,' she said apologetically, 'I really haven't time to see or notice *anything* during the holidays.'

'That's always a busy time, isn't it,' said the inspector. 'Fine boys you've got. Full of life and spirits. Rather too many spirits sometimes, I expect?'

Mrs Ramsay positively smiled.

'Yes,' she said, 'it gets a little tiring, but they're very good boys really.'

'I'm sure they are,' said the inspector. 'Fine fellows, both of them. Very intelligent, I should say. I'll have a word with them before I go, if you don't mind. Boys notice things sometimes that nobody else in the house does.'

'I don't really see how they can have noticed anything,' said Mrs Ramsay. 'It's not as though we were next door or anything.'

'But your gardens back on each other.'

'Yes, they do,' agreed Mrs Ramsay. 'But they're quite separate.'

'Do you know Mrs Hemming at Number 20?'

'Well, in a way I do,' said Mrs Ramsay, 'because of the cats and one thing and another.'

'You are fond of cats?'

'Oh, no,' said Mrs Ramsay, 'it's not that. I mean it's usually complaints.'

'Oh, I see. Complaints. What about?'

Mrs Ramsay flushed.

'The trouble is,' she said, 'when people keep cats in that way – fourteen, she's got – they get absolutely besotted about them. And it's all a lot of nonsense. I like cats. We used to have a cat ourselves, a tabby. Very good mouser, too. But all the fuss that woman makes, cooking special food – hardly ever letting the poor things out to have a life of their own. Of course the cats are always trying to escape. I would, if I was one of those cats. And the boys are very good really, they wouldn't torment a cat in any way. What I say is cats can always take care of themselves very well. They're very sensible animals, cats, that is if they are treated sensibly.'

'I'm sure you're quite right,' said the inspector. 'You must have a busy life,' he went on, 'keeping those boys of yours amused and fed during the holidays. When are they going back to school?'

'The day after tomorrow,' said Mrs Ramsay.

'I hope you'll have a good rest then.'

'I mean to treat myself to a real lazy time,' she said.

The other young man who had been silently taking down notes, startled her a little by speaking.

'You ought to have one of those foreign girls,' he said. '*Au pair*, don't they call it, come and do chores here in return for learning English.'

'I suppose I might try something of that kind,' said Mrs Ramsay, considering, 'though I always feel that foreigners may be difficult. My husband laughs at me. But then of course he knows more about it than I do. I haven't travelled abroad as much as he has.'

'He's away now, isn't he?' said Hardcastle.

'Yes – he had to go to Sweden at the beginning of August. He's a constructional engineer. A pity he had to go just then – at the beginning of the holidays, too. He's so good with the children. He really likes playing with electric trains more than the boys do. Sometimes the lines and the marshalling yards and everything go right across the hall and into the other room. It's very difficult not to fall over them.' She shook her head. 'Men are such children,' she said indulgently.

'When do you expect him back, Mrs Ramsay?'

'I never know.' She sighed. 'It makes it rather – difficult.' There was a tremor in her voice. Colin looked at her keenly.

'We mustn't take up more of your time, Mrs Ramsay.'

Hardcastle rose to his feet.

'Perhaps your boys will show us the garden?'

Bill and Ted were waiting in the hall and fell in with the suggestion immediately.

'Of course,' said Bill apologetically, 'it isn't a very *big* garden.'

There had been some slight effort made to keep the garden of No. 62, Wilbraham Crescent in reasonable order. On one side there was a border of dahlias and Michaelmas daisies. Then a small lawn somewhat unevenly mown. The paths badly needed hoeing, models of aeroplanes, space guns and other representations of modern science lay about, looking slightly the worse for wear. At the end of the garden was an apple tree with pleasant-looking red apples on it. Next to it was a pear tree.

'That's *it*,' said Ted, pointing at the space between the apple and the pear, through which the back of Miss Pebmarsh's house showed clearly. 'That's Number 19 where the murder was.'

'Got quite a good view of the house, haven't you,' said the inspector. 'Better still, I expect, from the upstairs windows.'

'That's right,' said Bill. 'If only we'd been up there yesterday looking out, we might have seen something. But we didn't.'

'We were at the cinema,' said Ted.

'Were there fingerprints?' asked Bill.

'Not very helpful ones. Were you out in the garden at all yesterday?'

'Oh, yes, off and on,' said Bill. 'All the morning, that is. We didn't hear anything, though, or see anything.'

'If we'd been there in the afternoon we might have heard screams,' said Ted, wistfully. 'Awful screams there were.'

'Do you know Miss Pebmarsh, the lady who owns that house, by sight?'

The boys looked at each other, then nodded.

'She's blind,' said Ted, 'but she can walk around the garden all right. Doesn't have to walk with a stick or anything like that. She threw a ball back to us once. Quite nice about it she was.'

'You didn't see her at all yesterday?'

The boys shook their heads.

'We wouldn't see her in the morning. She's always out,' Bill explained. 'She usually comes out in the garden after tea.'

Colin was exploring a line of hosepipe which was attached to a tap in the house. It ran along the garden path and was laid down in the corner near the pear tree.

'Never knew that pear trees needed watering,' he remarked.

'Oh, that,' said Bill. He looked slightly embarrassed.

'On the other hand,' said Colin, 'if you climbed up in this tree.' He looked at both boys and grinned suddenly. 'You could get a very nice little line of water to play on a cat, couldn't you?'

Both boys scuffled the gravel with their feet and looked in every other direction but at Colin.

'That's what you do, isn't it?' said Colin.

'Aw, well,' said Bill, 'it doesn't hurt 'em. It's not,' he said with an air of virtue, 'like a catapult.'

'I suppose you used to use a catapult at one time.'

'Not properly,' said Ted. 'We never seemed to hit anything.'

'Anyway, you do have a bit of fun with that hose sometimes,' said Colin, 'and then Mrs Hemming comes along and complains?'

'She's always complaining,' said Bill.

'You ever get through her fence?'

'Not through that wire here,' said Ted, unguardedly.

'But you do get through into her garden sometimes, is that right? How do you do it?'

'Well, you can get through the fence – into Miss Pebmarsh's garden. Then a little way down to the right you can push through the hedge into Mrs Hemming's garden. There's a hole there in the wire.'

'Can't you shut up, you fool?' said Bill.

'I suppose you've done a bit of hunting about for clues since the murder?' said Hardcastle.

The boys looked at each other.

'When you came back from the cinema and heard what had happened, I bet you went through the fence into the garden of 19 and had a jolly good look round.'

'Well –' Bill paused cautiously.

'It's always possible,' said Hardcastle seriously, 'that you may have found something that we missed. If you have – er – a collection I should be much obliged if you would show it to me.'

Bill made up his mind.

'Get 'em, Ted,' he said.

Ted departed obediently at a run.

'I'm afraid we haven't got anything really good,' admitted Bill. 'We only – sort of pretended.'

He looked at Hardcastle anxiously.

'I quite understand,' said the inspector. 'Most of police work is like that. A lot of disappointments.'

Bill looked relieved.

Ted returned at a run. He passed over a grubby knotted handkerchief which chinked. Hardcastle unknotted it, with a boy on either side of him, and spread out the contents.

There was the handle off a cup, a fragment of willow pattern china, a broken trowel, a rusty fork, a coin, a clothes-peg, a bit of iridescent glass and half a pair of scissors.

'An interesting lot,' said the inspector solemnly.

He took pity on the eager faces of the boys and picked up the piece of glass.

'I'll take this. It may just possibly tie up with something.'

Colin had picked up the coin and was examining it.

'It's not English,' said Ted.

'No,' said Colin. 'It's not English.' He looked across at Hardcastle. 'We might perhaps take this, too,' he suggested.

'Don't say a word about this to anyone,' said Hardcastle in a conspiratorial fashion.

The boys promised delightedly that they wouldn't.

CHAPTER 11

'Ramsay,' said Colin, thoughtfully.

'What about him?'

'I like the sound of him, that's all. He travels abroad – at a moment's notice. His wife says he's a construction engineer, but that's all she seems to know about him.'

'She's a nice woman,' said Hardcastle.

'Yes – and not a very happy one.'

'Tired, that's all. Kids *are* tiring.'

'I think it's more than that.'

'Surely the sort of person you want wouldn't be burdened with a wife and two sons,' Hardcastle said sceptically.

'You never know,' said Colin. 'You'd be surprised what some of the boys do for camouflage. A hard-up widow with a couple of kids might be willing to come to an arrangement.'

'I shouldn't have thought she was that kind,' said Hardcastle primly.

'I don't mean living in sin, my dear fellow. I mean that she'd agree to be Mrs Ramsay and supply a background. Naturally, he'd spin her a yarn of the right kind. He'd be doing a spot of espionage, say, on our side. All highly patriotic.'

Hardcastle shook his head.

'You live in a strange world, Colin,' he said.

'Yes we do. I think, you know, I'll have to get out of it one day . . . One begins to forget what is what and who is who. Half of these people work for both sides and in the end they don't know themselves which side they are really on. Standards get gummed up – Oh, well – let's get on with things.'

'We'd better do the McNaughtons,' said Hardcastle, pausing at the gates of 63. 'A bit of his garden touches 19 – same as Bland.'

'What do you know about the McNaughtons?'

'Not much – they came here about a year ago. Elderly couple – retired professor, I believe. He gardens.'

The front garden had rose bushes in it and a thick bed of autumn crocus under the windows.

A cheerful young woman in a brightly flowered overall opened the door to them and said:

'You want? – Yes?'

Hardcastle murmured, 'The foreign help at last,' and handed her his card.

'Police,' said the young woman. She took a step or two back and looked at Hardcastle as though he were the Fiend in person.

'Mrs McNaughton,' said Hardcastle.

'Mrs McNaughton is here.'

She led them into the sitting-room, which overlooked the back garden. It was empty.

'She up the stairs is,' said the no-longer cheerful young woman. She went out into the hall and called, 'Mrs McNaughton – Mrs McNaughton.'

A voice far away said, 'Yes. What is it, Gretel?'

'It is the police – two police. I put them in sitting-room.'

There was a faint scurrying noise upstairs and the words 'Oh, dear. Oh, dear, what next?' floated down. Then there was a patter of feet and presently Mrs McNaughton entered the room with a worried expression on her face. There was, Hardcastle decided quite soon, usually a worried expression on Mrs McNaughton's face.

'Oh, dear,' she said again, 'oh, dear. Inspector – what is it – Hardcastle – oh, yes.' She looked at the card. 'But why do you want to see *us*? We don't know anything about it. I mean I suppose it *is* this murder, isn't it? I mean, it wouldn't be the television licence?'

Hardcastle reassured her on that point.

'It all seems so extraordinary, doesn't it?' said Mrs McNaughton, brightening up. 'And more or less midday, too. Such an odd time to come and burgle a house. Just the time when people are usually at home. But then one does read of such terrible things nowadays. All happening in broad daylight. Why, some friends of ours – they were out for lunch and a furniture van drove up and the men broke in and carried out every stick of furniture. The whole street saw it happen but of course they never thought there was anything wrong. You know, I did think I heard someone screaming yesterday, but Angus said it was those dreadful boys of Mrs Ramsay's. They rush about the garden making noises like space-ships, you know, or rockets, or atom bombs. It really is quite frightening sometimes.'

Once again Hardcastle produced his photograph.

'Have you ever seen this man, Mrs McNaughton?'

Mrs McNaughton stared at it with avidity.

'I'm almost sure I've seen him. Yes. Yes, I'm practically certain. Now, where was it? Was it the man who came and asked me if I wanted to buy a new encyclopedia in fourteen volumes? Or was it the man who came with a new model of vacuum cleaner. I wouldn't have anything to do with *him*, and he went out and worried my husband in the front garden. Angus was planting some bulbs, you know, and he didn't want to be interrupted and the man went on and on saying what the thing would do. You know, how it would run up and down curtains, and would clean doorsteps and do the stairs and cushions and spring-clean things. Everything, he said, absolutely everything. And then Angus just looked up at him and said, "Can it plant bulbs?" and I must say I had to laugh because it took the man quite aback and he went away.'

'And you really think that was the man in this photograph?'

'Well, no, I don't really,' said Mrs McNaughton, 'because that was a much younger man, now I come to think of it. But all the same I think I *have* seen this face before. Yes. The more I look at it the more sure I am that he came here and asked me to buy something.'

'Insurance perhaps?'

'No, no, not insurance. My husband attends to all that kind of thing. We are fully insured in every way. No. But all the same – yes, the more I look at that photograph –'

Hardcastle was less encouraged by this than he might have been. He put down Mrs McNaughton, from the fund of his experience, as a woman who would be anxious for the excitement of having seen someone connected with murder. The longer she looked at the picture, the more sure she would be that she could remember someone just like it.

He sighed.

'He was driving a van, I believe,' said Mrs McNaughton. 'But just when I saw him I can't remember. A baker's van, I think.'

'You didn't see him yesterday, did you, Mrs McNaughton?'

Mrs McNaughton's face fell slightly. She pushed back her rather untidy grey waved hair from her forehead.

'No. No, not *yesterday*,' she said. 'At least –' she paused. 'I don't *think* so.' Then she brightened a little. 'Perhaps my husband will remember.'

'Is he at home?'

'Oh, he's out in the garden.' She pointed through the window where at this moment an elderly man was pushing a wheelbarrow along the path.

'Perhaps we might go out and speak to him.'

'Of course. Come this way.'

She led the way out through a side door and into the garden. Mr McNaughton was in a fine state of perspiration.

'These gentlemen are from the police, Angus,' said his wife breathlessly. 'Come about the murder at Miss Pebmarsh's. There's a photograph they've got of the dead man. Do you know, I'm sure I've seen him somewhere. It wasn't the man, was it, who came last week and asked us if we had any antiques to dispose of?'

'Let's see,' said Mr McNaughton. 'Just hold it for me, will you,' he said to Hardcastle. 'My hands are too earthy to touch anything.'

He took a brief look and remarked, 'Never seen that fellow in my life.'

'Your neighbour tells me you're very fond of gardening,' said Hardcastle.

'Who told you that – not Mrs Ramsay?'

'No. Mr Bland.'

Angus McNaughton snorted.

'Bland doesn't know what gardening means,' he said. 'Bedding out, that's all *he* does. Shoves in begonias and geraniums and lobelia edging. That's not what I call *gardening*. Might as well live in a public park. Are you interested in shrubs at all, Inspector? Of course, it's the wrong time of year now, but I've one or two shrubs here that you'd be surprised at my being able to grow. Shrubs that they say only do well in Devon and Cornwall.'

'I'm afraid I can't lay claim to be a practical gardener,' said Hardcastle.

McNaughton looked at him much as an artist looks at someone who says they know nothing of art but they know what they like.

'I'm afraid I've called about a much less pleasant subject,' Hardcastle said.

'Of course. This business yesterday. I was out in the garden, you know, when it happened.'

'Indeed?'

'Well, I mean I was here when the girl screamed.'

'What did you do?'

'Well,' said Mr McNaughton rather sheepishly, 'I didn't do anything. As a matter of fact I thought it was those blasted Ramsay boys. Always yelling and screaming and making a noise.'

'But surely this scream didn't come from quite the same direction?'

'Not if those blasted boys ever stayed in their own garden. But they don't, you know. They get through people's fences and hedges. They chase those wretched cats of Mrs Hemming's all over the place. There's nobody to keep a firm hand on them, that's the trouble. Their mother's weak as water. Of course, when there's no man in the house, boys do get out of hand.'

'Mr Ramsay is abroad a good deal I understand.'

'Construction engineer, I believe,' said Mr McNaughton vaguely. 'Always going off somewhere. Dams, you know. I'm not swearing, my dear,' he assured his wife. 'I mean jobs to do with the building of dams, or else it's oil or pipelines or something like that. I don't really know. He had to go off to Sweden a month ago at a moment's notice. That left the boys' mother with a lot to do – cooking and housework and that – and, well – of course they were bound to run wild. They're not bad boys, mind you, but they need discipline.'

'You yourself didn't see anything – apart I mean from hearing the scream? When was that, by the way?'

'No idea,' said Mr McNaughton. 'I take my watch off always before I come out here. Ran the hose over it the other day and had quite a job getting it repaired afterwards. What time was it, my dear? You heard it, didn't you?'

'It must have been half past two perhaps – it was at least half an hour after we finished lunch.'

'I see. What time do you lunch?'

'Half past one,' said Mr McNaughton, 'if we're lucky. Our Danish girl has got no sense of time.'

'And afterwards – do you have a nap?'

'Sometimes. I didn't today. I wanted to get on with what I was doing. I was clearing away a lot of stuff, adding to the compost heap, and all that.'

'Wonderful thing, a compost heap,' said Hardcastle, solemnly.

Mr McNaughton brightened immediately.

'Absolutely. Nothing like it. Ah! The number of people I've converted. Using all these chemical manures! Suicide! Let me show you.'

He drew Hardcastle eagerly by the arm and trundling his barrow, went along the path to the edge of the fence that divided his garden from that of No. 19. Screened by lilac bushes, the compost heap was displayed in its glory. Mr McNaughton wheeled the wheelbarrow to a small shed beside it. Inside the shed were several nicely arranged tools.

'Very tidy you keep everything,' remarked Hardcastle.

'Got to take care of your tools,' said McNaughton.

Hardcastle was looking thoughtfully towards No. 19. On the other side of the fence was a rose pergola which led up to the side of the house.

'You didn't see anyone in the garden at Number 19 or looking out of the window in the house, or anything like that while you were at your compost heap?'

McNaughton shook his head.

'Didn't see anything at all,' he said. 'Sorry I can't help you, Inspector.'

'You know, Angus,' said his wife, 'I believe I did see a figure skulking in the garden of 19.'

'I don't think you did, my dear,' said her husband firmly. 'I didn't, either.'

'That woman would say she'd seen *anything*,' Hardcastle growled when they were back in the car.

'You don't think she recognized the photograph?'

Hardcastle shook his head. 'I doubt it. She just *wants* to think she's seen him. I know that type of witness only too well. When I pinned her down to it, she couldn't give chapter or verse, could she?'

'No.'

'Of course she *may* have sat opposite him in a bus or something. I'll allow you that. But if you ask me, it's wishful thinking. What do you think?'

'I think the same.'

'We didn't get much,' Hardcastle sighed. 'Of course there are things that seem queer. For instance, it seems almost impossible that Mrs Hemming – no matter how wrapped up in her cats she is – should know so little about her neighbour, Miss Pebmarsh, as she does. And also that she should be so extremely vague and uninterested in the murder.'

'She is a vague kind of woman.'

'Scatty!' said Hardcastle. 'When you meet a scatty woman – well, fires, burglaries, murders can go on all round them and they wouldn't notice it.'

'She's very well fenced in with all that wire netting, and that Victorian shrubbery doesn't leave you much of a view.'

They had arrived back at the police station. Hardcastle grinned at his friend and said:

'Well, Sergeant Lamb, I can let you go off duty now.'

'No more visits to pay?'

'Not just now. I must pay one more later, but I'm not taking you with me.'

'Well, thanks for this morning. Can you get these notes of mine typed up?' He handed them over. 'Inquest is the day after tomorrow you said? What time?'

'Eleven.'

'Right. I'll be back for it.'

'Are you going away?'

'I've got to go up to London tomorrow – make my report up to date.'

'I can guess who to.'

'You're not allowed to do that.'

Hardcastle grinned.

'Give the old boy my love.'

'Also, I may be going to see a specialist,' said Colin.

'A specialist? What for? What's wrong with you?'

'Nothing – bar thick-headedness. I don't mean that kind of a specialist. One in your line.'

'Scotland Yard?'

'No. A private detective – a friend of my Dad's – and a friend of mine. This fantastic business of yours will be just down his street. He'll love it – it will cheer him up. I've an idea he needs cheering up.'

'What's his name?'

'Hercule Poirot.'

'I've heard of him. I thought he was dead.'

'He's not dead. But I have a feeling he's bored. That's worse.'

Hardcastle looked at him curiously.

'You're an odd fellow, Colin. You make such unlikely friends.'

'Including you,' Colin said, and grinned.

CHAPTER 12

Having dismissed Colin, Inspector Hardcastle looked at the address neatly written in his note-book and nodded his head. Then he slipped the book back in his pocket and started to deal with the routine matters that had piled up on his desk.

It was a busy day for him. He sent out for coffee and sandwiches, and received reports from Sergeant Cray – no helpful lead had come up. Nobody at the railway station or buses had recognized the photograph of Mr Curry. The laboratory reports on clothing added up to nil. The suit had been made by a good tailor, but the tailor's name had been removed. Desire for anonymity on the part of Mr Curry? Or on the part of his killer. Details of dentistry had been circulated to the proper quarters and were probably the most helpful leads – it took a little time – but it got results in the end. Unless, of course, Mr Curry had been a foreigner? Hardcastle considered the idea. There might be a possibility that the dead man was French – on the other hand his clothes were definitely not French. No laundry marks had helped yet.

Hardcastle was not impatient. Identification was quite often a slow job. But in the end, someone always came forward. A laundry, a dentist, a doctor, a landlady. The picture of the dead man would be circulated to police stations, would be reproduced in newspapers. Sooner or later, Mr Curry would be known in his rightful identity.

In the meantime there was work to be done, and not only on the Curry case. Hardcastle worked without a break until half past five. He looked at his wrist-watch again and decided the time was ripe for the call he wanted to make.

Sergeant Cray had reported that Sheila Webb had resumed work at the Cavendish Bureau, and that at five o'clock she would be working with Professor Purdy at the Curlew Hotel and that she was unlikely to leave there until well after six.

What was the aunt's name again? Lawton – Mrs Lawton. 14, Palmerston Road. He did not take a police car but chose to walk the short distance.

Palmerston Road was a gloomy street that had known, as

is said, better days. The houses, Hardcastle noted, had been mainly converted into flats or maisonettes. As he turned the corner, a girl who was approaching him along the sidewalk hesitated for a moment. His mind occupied, the inspector had some momentary idea that she was going to ask him the way to somewhere. However, if that was so, the girl thought better of it and resumed her walk past him. He wondered why the idea of shoes came into his mind so suddenly. Shoes . . . No, one shoe. The girl's face was faintly familiar to him. Who was it now – someone he had seen just lately . . . Perhaps she had recognized him and was about to speak to him?

He paused for a moment, looking back after her. She was walking quite fast now. The trouble was, he thought, she had one of those indeterminate faces that are very hard to recognize unless there is some special reason for doing so. Blue eyes, fair complexion, slightly open mouth. Mouth. That recalled something also. Something that she'd been doing with her mouth? Talking? Putting on lipstick? No. He felt slightly annoyed with himself. Hardcastle prided himself on his recognition of faces. He never forgot, he'd been apt to say, a face he had seen in the dock or in the witness-box, but there were after all other places of contact. He would not be likely to remember, for instance, every waitress who had ever served him. He would not remember every bus conductress. He dismissed the matter from his mind.

He had arrived now at No. 14. The door stood ajar and there were four bells with names underneath. Mrs Lawton, he saw, had a flat on the ground floor. He went in and pressed the bell on the door on the left of the hall. It was a few moments before it was answered. Finally he heard steps inside and the door was opened by a tall, thin woman with straggling dark hair who had on an overall and seemed a little short of breath. The smell of onions wafted along from the direction of what was obviously the kitchen.

'Mrs Lawton?'

'Yes?' She looked at him doubtfully, with slight annoyance.

She was, he thought, about forty-five. Something faintly gypsyish about her appearance.

'What is it?'

'I should be glad if you could spare me a moment or two.'

'Well, what about? I'm really rather busy just now.' She added sharply, 'You're not a reporter, are you?'

'Of course,' said Hardcastle, adopting a sympathetic tone, 'I expect you've been a good deal worried by reporters.'

'Indeed we have. Knocking at the door and ringing the bell and asking all sorts of foolish questions.'

'Very annoying I know,' said the inspector. 'I wish we could spare you all that, Mrs Lawton. I am Detective Inspector Hardcastle, by the way, in charge of the case about which the reporters have been annoying you. We'd put a stop to a good deal of that if we could, but we're powerless in the matter, you know. The Press has its rights.'

'It's a shame to worry private people as they do,' said Mrs Lawton, 'saying they have to have news for the public. The only thing I've ever noticed about the news that they print is that it's a tissue of lies from beginning to end. They'll cook up *anything* so far as I can see. But come in.'

She stepped back and the inspector passed over the doorstep and she shut the door. There were a couple of letters which had fallen on the mat. Mrs Lawton bent forward to pick them up, but the inspector politely forestalled her. His eyes swept over them for half a second as he handed them to her, addresses uppermost.

'Thank you.'

She laid them down on the hall table.

'Come into the sitting-room, won't you? At least – if you go in this door and give me just a moment. I think something's boiling over.'

She beat a speedy retreat to the kitchen. Inspector Hardcastle took a last deliberate look at the letters on the hall table. One was addressed to Mrs Lawton and the two others to Miss R. S. Webb. He went into the room indicated. It was a small room, rather untidy, shabbily furnished but here and there it displayed some bright spot of colour or some unusual object. An attractive, probably expensive piece of Venetian glass of moulded colours and an abstract shape, two brightly coloured velvet cushions and an earthenware platter of foreign shells. Either the aunt or the niece, he thought, had an original streak in her make-up.

Mrs Lawton returned, slightly more breathless than before.

'I think that'll be all right now,' she said, rather uncertainly.

The inspector apologized again.

'I'm sorry if I've called at an inconvenient time,' he said, 'but I happened to be in this neighbourhood and I wanted to check over a few further points about this affair in which your niece was so unfortunately concerned. I hope she's none the worse for her experience? It must have been a great shock to any girl.'

'Yes, indeed,' said Mrs Lawton. 'Sheila came back in a terrible state. But she was all right by this morning and she's gone back to work again.'

'Oh, yes, I know that,' said the inspector. 'But I was told she was out doing work for a client somewhere and I didn't want to interrupt anything of that kind so I thought it would be better if I came round here and talked to her in her own home. But she's not back yet, is that it?'

'She'll probably be rather late this evening,' said Mrs Lawton. 'She's working for a Professor Purdy and from what Sheila says, he's a man with no idea of time at all. Always says "this won't take more than another ten minutes so I think we might as well get it finished," and then of course it takes nearer to three-quarters of an hour. He's a very nice man and most apologetic. Once or twice he's urged her to stay and have dinner and seemed quite concerned because he's kept her so much longer than he realized. Still, it is rather annoying sometimes. Is there something I can tell you, Inspector? In case Sheila is delayed a long time.'

'Well, not really,' said the inspector smiling. 'Of course, we only took down the bare details the other day and I'm not sure really whether I've even got those right.' He made a show of consulting his note-book once more. 'Let me see. Miss Sheila Webb – is that her full name or has she another Christian name? We have to have these things very exact, you know, for the records at the inquest.'

'The inquest is the day after tomorrow, isn't it? She got a notice to attend.'

'Yes, but she needn't let that worry her,' said Hardcastle. 'She'll just have to tell her story of how she found the body.'

'You don't know who the man was yet?'

'No. I'm afraid it's early days for that. There was a card in his pocket and we thought at first he was some kind of insurance agent. But it seems more likely now that it was a card he'd been given by someone. Perhaps he was contemplating insurance himself.'

'Oh, I see,' Mrs Lawton looked vaguely interested.

'Now I'll just get these names right,' said the inspector. 'I think I've got it down as Miss Sheila Webb or Miss Sheila R. Webb. I just couldn't remember what the other name was. Was it Rosalie?'

'Rosemary,' said Mrs Lawton, 'she was christened Rosemary Sheila but Sheila always thought Rosemary was rather fanciful so she's never called anything but Sheila.'

'I see.' There was nothing in Hardcastle's tone to show that he was pleased that one of his hunches had come out right. He noted another point. The name Rosemary occasioned no distress in Mrs Lawton. To her Rosemary was simply a Christian name that her niece did not use.

'I've got it straight now all right,' said the inspector smiling. 'I gather that your niece came from London and has been working for the Cavendish Bureau for the last ten months or so. You don't know the exact date, I suppose?'

'Well, really, I couldn't say now. It was last November some time. I think more towards the end of November.'

'Quite so. It doesn't really matter. She was not living with you here previously to taking the job at the Cavendish Bureau?'

'No. She was living in London before that.'

'Have you got her address in London?'

'Well, I've got it somewhere,' Mrs Lawton looked round her with the vague expression of the habitually untidy. 'I've got such a short memory,' she said. 'Something like Allington Grove, I think it was – out Fulham way. She shared a flat with two other girls. Terribly expensive rooms are in London for girls.'

'Do you remember the name of the firm she worked at there?'

'Oh, yes. Hopgood and Trent. They were estate agents in the Fulham Road.'

'Thank you. Well all that seems very clear. Miss Webb is an orphan, I understand?'

'Yes,' said Mrs Lawton. She moved uneasily. Her eyes strayed to the door. 'Do you mind if I just go into the kitchen again?'

'Of course.'

He opened the door for her. She went out. He wondered if he had been right or wrong in thinking that his last question had in some way perturbed Mrs Lawton. Her replies had come quite readily and easily up to then. He thought about it until Mrs Lawton returned.

'I'm so sorry,' she said, apologetically, 'but you know what it is – cooking things. Everything's quite all right now. Was there anything else you want to ask me? I've remembered, by the way, it wasn't Allington Grove. It was Carrington Grove and the number was 17.'

'Thank you,' said the inspector. 'I think I was asking you whether Miss Webb was an orphan.'

'Yes, she's an orphan. Her parents are dead.'

'Long ago?'

'They died when she was a child.'

There was something like defiance just perceptible in her tone.

'Was she your sister's child or your brother's?'

'My sister's.'

'Ah, yes. And what was Mr Webb's profession?'

Mrs Lawton paused a moment before answering. She was biting her lips. Then she said, 'I don't know.'

'You don't know?'

'I mean I don't remember, it's so long ago.'

Hardcastle waited, knowing that she would speak again. She did.

'May I ask what all this has got to do with it – I mean what does it matter who her father and mother were and what her father did and where he came from or anything like that?'

'I suppose it doesn't matter really, Mrs Lawton, not from your point of view, that is. But you see, the circumstances are rather unusual.'

'What do you mean – the circumstances are unusual?'

'Well, we have reason to believe that Miss Webb went to that house yesterday because she had been specially asked for at the Cavendish Bureau by name. It looks therefore as though someone had deliberately arranged for her to be there. Someone perhaps –' he hesitated '– with a grudge against her.'

'I can't imagine that anyone could have a grudge against Sheila. She's a very sweet girl. A nice friendly girl.'

'Yes,' said Hardcastle mildly. 'That's what I should have thought myself.'

'And I don't like to hear anybody suggesting the contrary,' said Mrs Lawton belligerently.

'Exactly.' Hardcastle continued to smile appeasingly. 'But you must realize, Mrs Lawton, that it looks as though your niece has been deliberately made a victim. She was being, as they say on the films, put on the spot. *Somebody* was arranging for her to go into a house where there was a dead man, and that dead man had died very recently. It seems on the face of it a malicious thing to do.'

'You mean – you mean someone was trying to make it appear that Sheila killed him? Oh, no, I can't believe it.'

'It is rather difficult to believe,' agreed the inspector, 'but we've got to make quite sure and clear up the matter. Could there be, for instance, some young man, someone perhaps who had fallen in love with your niece, and whom she, perhaps, did not care for? Young men sometimes do some very bitter and revengeful things, especially if they're rather ill-balanced.'

'I don't think it could be anything of that kind,' said Mrs Lawton, puckering her eyes in thought and frowning. 'Sheila has had one or two boys she's been friendly with, but there's been nothing serious. Nobody steady of any kind.'

'It might have been while she was living in London?' the inspector suggested. 'After all, I don't suppose you know very much about what friends she had there.'

'No, no, perhaps not . . . Well, you'll have to ask her about that yourself, Inspector Hardcastle. But I never heard of any trouble of any kind.'

'Or it might have been another girl,' suggested Hardcastle. 'Perhaps one of the girls she shared rooms with there was jealous of her?'

'I suppose,' said Mrs Lawton doubtfully, 'that there might be a girl who'd want to do her a bad turn. But not involving murder, surely.'

It was a shrewd appreciation and Hardcastle noted that Mrs Lawton was by no means a fool. He said quickly:

'I know it all sounds most unlikely, but then this whole business *is* unlikely.'

'It must have been someone mad,' said Mrs Lawton.

'Even in madness,' said Hardcastle, 'there's a definite idea behind the madness, you know. Something that's given rise to it. And that really,' he went on, 'is why I was asking you about Sheila Webb's father and mother. You'd be surprised how often motives arise that have their roots in the past. Since Miss Webb's father and mother died when she was a young child, naturally she can't tell me anything about them. That's why I'm applying to you.'

'Yes, I see, but – well . . .'

He noted that the trouble and uncertainty were back in her voice.

'Were they killed at the same time, in an accident, anything like that?'

'No, there was no accident.'

'They both died from natural causes?'

'I – well, yes, I mean – I don't really know.'

'I think you must know a little more than you are telling me, Mrs Lawton.' He hazarded a guess. 'Were they, perhaps, divorced – something of that kind?'

'No, they weren't divorced.'

'Come now, Mrs Lawton. You know – you must know of what your sister died?'

'I don't see what – I mean, I can't say – it's all very difficult. Raking up things. It's much better not raking them up.' There was a kind of desperate perplexity in her glance.

Hardcastle looked at her keenly. Then he said gently, 'Was Sheila Webb perhaps – an illegitimate child?'

He saw immediately a mixture of consternation and relief in her face.

'She's not *my* child,' she said.

'She is your sister's illegitimate child?'

'Yes. But she doesn't know it herself. I've never told her. I told her her parents died young. So that's why – well, you see . . .'

'Oh, yes, I see,' said the inspector, 'and I assure you that unless something comes of this particular line of inquiry there is no need for me to question Miss Webb on this subject.'

'You mean you needn't tell her?'

'Not unless there is some relevance to the case, which, I may say, seems unlikely. But I do want all the facts that you know,

Mrs Lawton, and I assure you that I'll do my best to keep what you tell me entirely between ourselves.'

'It's not a nice thing to happen,' said Mrs Lawton, 'and I was very distressed about it, I can tell you. My sister, you see, had always been the clever one of the family. She was a school teacher and doing very well. Highly respected and everything else. The last person you'd ever think would –'

'Well,' said the inspector, tactfully, 'it often happens that way. She got to know this man – this Webb –'

'I never even knew what his name was,' said Mrs Lawton. 'I never met him. But she came to me and told me what had happened. That she was expecting a child and that the man couldn't, or wouldn't – I never knew which – marry her. She was ambitious and it would have meant giving up her job if the whole thing came out. So naturally I – I said I'd help.'

'Where is your sister now, Mrs Lawton?'

'I've no idea. Absolutely no idea at all.' She was emphatic.

'She's alive, though.'

'I suppose so.'

'But you haven't kept in touch with her?'

'That's the way she wanted it. She thought it was best for the child and best for her that there should be a clean break. So it was fixed that way. We both had a little income of our own that our mother left us. Ann turned her half-share over to me to be used for the child's bringing up and keep. She was going to continue with her profession, she said, but she would change schools. There was some idea, I believe, of a year's exchange with a teacher abroad. Australia or somewhere. That's all I know, Inspector Hardcastle, and that's all I can tell you.'

He looked at her thoughtfully. Was that really all she knew? It was a difficult question to answer with any certainty. It was certainly all that she meant to tell him. It might very well be all she knew. Slight as the reference to the sister had been, Hardcastle got an impression of a forceful, bitter, angry personality. The sort of woman who was determined not to have her life blasted by one mistake. In a cold hard-headed way she had provided for the upkeep and presumable happiness of her child. From that moment on she had cut herself adrift to start life again on her own.

It was conceivable, he thought, that she might feel like that about the child. But what about her sister? He said mildly:

'It seems odd that she did not at least keep in touch with you by letter, did not want to know how the child was progressing?'

Mrs Lawton shook her head.

'Not if you knew Ann,' she said. 'She was always very clear-cut in her decisions. And then she and I weren't very close. I was younger than she was by a good deal – twelve years. As I say, we were never very close.'

'And what did your husband feel about this adoption?'

'I was a widow then,' said Mrs Lawton. 'I married young and my husband was killed in the war. I kept a small sweetshop at the time.'

'Where was all this? Not here in Crowdean.'

'No. We were living in Lincolnshire at the time. I came here in the holidays once, and I liked it so much that I sold the shop and came here to live. Later, when Sheila was old enough to go to school, I took a job in Roscoe and West, the big drapers here, you know. I still work there. They're very pleasant people.'

'Well,' said Hardcastle, rising to his feet, 'thank you very much, Mrs Lawton, for your frankness in what you have told me.'

'And you won't say a word of it to Sheila?'

'Not unless it should become necessary, and that would only happen if some circumstances out of the past proved to have been connected with this murder at 19, Wilbraham Crescent. And that, I think, is unlikely.' He took the photograph from his pocket which he had been showing to so many people, and showed it to Mrs Lawton. 'You've no idea who this man could be?'

'They've shown it me already,' said Mrs Lawton.

She took it and scrutinized it earnestly.

'No. I'm sure, quite sure, I've never seen this man before. I don't think he belonged round here or I might have remembered seeing him about. Of course –' she looked closely. She paused a moment before adding, rather unexpectedly, 'He looks a nice man I think. A gentleman, I'd say, wouldn't you?'

It was a slightly outmoded term in the inspector's experience, yet it fell very naturally from Mrs Lawton's lips. 'Brought up in the country,' he thought. 'They still think of things that way.'

He looked at the photograph again himself reflecting, with faint surprise, that he had not thought of the dead man in quite that way. Was he a nice man? He had been assuming just the contrary. Assuming it unconsciously perhaps, or influenced perhaps by the fact that the man had a card in his pocket which bore a name and an address which were obviously false. But the explanation he had given to Mrs Lawton just now might have been the true one. It might have been that the card did represent some bogus insurance agent who had pressed the card upon the dead man. And that, he thought wryly, would really make the whole thing even more difficult. He glanced at his watch again.

'I mustn't keep you from your cooking any longer,' he said, 'since your niece is not home yet –'

Mrs Lawton in turn looked at the clock on the mantelpiece. 'Only one clock in this room, thank heaven,' thought the inspector to himself.

'Yes, she is late,' she remarked. 'Surprising really. It's a good thing Edna didn't wait.'

Seeing a slightly puzzled expression on Hardcastle's face, she explained.

'It's just one of the girls from the office. She came here to see Sheila this evening and she waited a bit but after a while she said she couldn't wait any longer. She'd got a date with someone. She said it would do tomorrow, or some other time.'

Enlightenment came to the inspector. The girl he had passed in the street! He knew now why she'd made him think of shoes. Of course. It was the girl who had received him in the Cavendish Bureau and the girl who, when he left, had been holding up a shoe with a stiletto heel torn off it, and had been discussing in unhappy puzzlement how on earth she was going to get home like that. A nondescript kind of girl, he remembered, not very attractive, sucking some kind of sweet as she talked. She had recognized him when she passed him in the street, although he had not recognized her. She had hesitated, too, as though she thought of speaking to him. He wondered rather idly what she had wanted to say. Had she wanted to explain why she was calling on Sheila Webb or had she thought he would expect her to say something? He asked:

'Is she a great friend of your niece's?'

'Well, not particularly,' said Mrs Lawton. 'I mean they work in the same office and all that, but she's rather a dull girl. Not very bright and she and Sheila aren't particular friends. In fact, I wondered why she was so keen to see Sheila tonight. She said it was something she couldn't understand and that she wanted to ask Sheila about it.'

'She didn't tell you what it was?'

'No, she said it would keep and it didn't matter.'

'I see. Well, I must be going.'

'It's odd,' said Mrs Lawton, 'that Sheila hasn't telephoned. She usually does if she's late, because the professor sometimes asks her to stay to dinner. Ah, well, I expect she'll be here any moment now. There are a lot of bus queues sometimes and the Curlew Hotel is quite a good way along the Esplanade. There's nothing – no message – you want to leave for Sheila?'

'I think not,' said the inspector.

As he went out he asked, 'By the way, who chose your niece's Christian names, Rosemary and Sheila? Your sister or yourself?'

'Sheila was our mother's name. Rosemary was my sister's choice. Funny name to choose really. Fanciful. And yet my sister wasn't fanciful or sentimental in any way.'

'Well, good night, Mrs Lawton.'

As the inspector turned the corner from the gateway into the street he thought, 'Rosemary – hm . . . Rosemary for remembrance. Romantic remembrance? Or – something quite different?'

CHAPTER 13

COLIN LAMB'S NARRATIVE

I walked up Charing Cross Road and turned into the maze of streets that twist their way between New Oxford Street and Covent Garden. All sorts of unsuspected shops did business there, antique shops, a dolls' hospital, ballet shoes, foreign delicatessen shops.

I resisted the lure of the dolls' hospital with its various pairs of blue or brown glass eyes, and came at last to my objective. It was a small dingy bookshop in a side street not far from the

British Museum. It had the usual trays of books outside. Ancient novels, old text books, odds and ends of all kinds, labelled 3d., 6d., 1s., even some aristocrats which had nearly all their pages, and occasionally even their binding intact.

I sidled through the doorway. It was necessary to sidle since precariously arranged books impinged more and more every day on the passageway from the street. Inside, it was clear that the books owned the shop rather than the other way about. Everywhere they had run wild and taken possession of their habitat, breeding and multiplying and clearly lacking any strong hand to keep them down. The distance between bookshelves was so narrow that you could only get along with great difficulty. There were piles of books perched on every shelf or table. On a stool in a corner, hemmed in by books, was an old man in a pork-pie hat with a large flat face like a stuffed fish. He had the air of one who has given up an unequal struggle. He had attempted to master the books, but the books had obviously succeeded in mastering him. He was a kind of King Canute of the book world, retreating before the advancing book tide. If he ordered it to retreat it would have been with the sure and hopeless certainty that it would not do so. This was Mr Solomon, proprietor of the shop. He recognized me, his fishlike stare softened for a moment and he nodded.

'Got anything in my line?' I asked.

'You'll have to go up and see, Mr Lamb. Still on seaweeds and that stuff?'

'That's right.'

'Well, you know where they are. Marine biology, fossils, Antarctica – second floor. I had a new parcel in day before yesterday. I started to unpack 'em but I haven't got round to it properly yet. You'll find them in a corner up there.'

I nodded and sidled my way onwards to where a small rather rickety and very dirty staircase led up from the back of the shop. On the first floor were Orientalia, art books, medicine, and French classics. In this room was a rather interesting little curtained corner not known to the general public, but accessible to experts, where what is called 'odd' or 'curious' volumes reposed. I passed them and went on up to the second floor.

Here archaeological, natural history, and other respectable

volumes were rather inadequately sorted into categories. I steered my way through students and elderly colonels and clergymen, passed round the angle of a bookcase, stepped over various gaping parcels of books on the floor and found my further progress barred by two students of opposite sexes lost to the world in a closely knit embrace. They stood there swaying to and fro. I said:

'Excuse me,' pushed them firmly aside, raised a curtain which masked a door, and slipping a key from my pocket, turned it in the lock and passed through. I found myself incongruously in a kind of vestibule with cleanly distempered walls hung with prints of Highland cattle, and a door with a highly polished knocker on it. I manipulated the knocker discreetly and the door was opened by an elderly woman with grey hair, spectacles of a particularly old-fashioned kind, a black skirt and a rather unexpected peppermint-striped jumper.

'It's you, is it?' she said without any other form of greeting. 'He was asking about you only yesterday. He wasn't pleased.' She shook her head at me, rather as an elderly governess might do at a disappointing child. 'You'll have to try and do better,' she said.

'Oh, come off it, Nanny,' I said.

'And don't call me Nanny,' said the lady. 'It's a cheek. I've told you so before.'

'It's your fault,' I said. 'You mustn't talk to me as if I were a small boy.'

'Time you grew up. You'd better go in and get it over.'

She pressed a buzzer, picked up a telephone from the desk, and said:

'Mr Colin . . . Yes, I'm sending him in.' She put it down and nodded to me.

I went through a door at the end of the room into another room which was so full of cigar smoke that it was difficult to see anything at all. After my smarting eyes had cleared, I beheld the ample proportions of my chief sitting back in an aged, derelict grandfather chair, by the arm of which was an old-fashioned reading- or writing-desk on a swivel.

Colonel Beck took off his spectacles, pushed aside the reading-desk on which was a vast tome and looked disapprovingly at me.

'So it's you at last?' he said.

'Yes, sir,' I said.

'Got anything?'

'No, sir.'

'Ah! Well, it won't do, Colin, d'you hear? Won't do. Crescents indeed!'

'I still think,' I began.

'All right. You still think. But we can't wait for ever while you're thinking.'

'I'll admit it was only a hunch,' I said.

'No harm in that,' said Colonel Beck.

He was a contradictory man.

'Best jobs I've ever done have been hunches. Only this hunch of yours doesn't seem to be working out. Finished with the pubs?'

'Yes, sir. As I told you I've started on Crescents. Houses in crescents is what I mean.'

'I didn't suppose you meant bakers' shops with French rolls in them, though, come to think of it, there's no reason why not. Some of these places make an absolute fetish of producing French croissants that aren't really French. Keep 'em in a deep freeze nowadays like everything else. That's why nothing tastes of anything nowadays.'

I waited to see whether the old boy would enlarge upon this topic. It was a favourite one of his. But seeing that I was expecting him to do so, Colonel Beck refrained.

'Wash out all round?' he demanded.

'Almost. I've still got a little way to go.'

'You want more time, is that it?'

'I want more time, yes,' I said. 'But I don't want to move on to another place this minute. There's been a kind of coincidence and it might – only *might* – mean something.'

'Don't waffle. Give me facts.'

'Subject of investigation, Wilbraham Crescent.'

'And you drew a blank! Or didn't you?'

'I'm not sure.'

'Define yourself, define yourself, boy.'

'The coincidence is that a man was murdered in Wilbraham Crescent.'

'Who was murdered?'

'As yet he's unknown. Had a card with a name and address in his pocket, but that was bogus.'

'Hm. Yes. Suggestive. Tie up in any way?'

'I can't see that it does, sir, but all the same . . .'

'I know, I know. All the same . . . Well, what have you come for? Come for permission to go on nosing about Wilbraham Crescent – wherever that absurd-sounding place is?'

'It's a place called Crowdean. Ten miles from Portlebury.'

'Yes, yes. Very good locality. But what are you here for? You don't usually ask permission. You go your own pigheaded way, don't you?'

'That's right, sir, I'm afraid I do.'

'Well, then, what is it?'

'There are a couple of people I want vetted.'

With a sigh Colonel Beck drew his reading-desk back into position, took a ball-pen from his pocket, blew on it and looked at me.

'Well?'

'House called Diana Lodge. Actually, 20, Wilbraham Crescent. Woman called Mrs Hemming and about eighteen cats live there.'

'Diana? Hm,' said Colonel Beck. 'Moon goddess! Diana Lodge. Right. What does she do, this Mrs Hemming?'

'Nothing,' I said, 'she's absorbed in her cats.'

'Damned good cover, I dare say,' said Beck appreciatively. 'Certainly could be. Is that all?'

'No,' I said. 'There's a man called Ramsay. Lives at 62, Wilbraham Crescent. Said to be a construction engineer, whatever that is. Goes abroad a good deal.'

'I like the sound of that,' said Colonel Beck. 'I like the sound of that very much. You want to know about him, do you? All right.'

'He's got a wife,' I said. 'Quite a nice wife, and two obstreperous children – boys.'

'Well, he might have,' said Colonel Beck. 'It has been known. You remember Pendleton? He had a wife and children. Very nice wife. Stupidest woman I've ever come across. No idea in her head that her husband wasn't a pillar of respectability in oriental book dealing. Come to think of it, now I remember, Pendleton had a German wife as well, and a couple of daughters. And he also had a wife in Switzerland. I don't know what the wives were – his private excesses or just camouflage. He'd *say* of course that they were camouflage. Well, anyway, you want to know about Mr Ramsay. Anything else?'

'I'm not sure. There's a couple at 63. Retired professor. McNaughton by name. Scottish. Elderly. Spends his time gardening. No reason to think he and his wife are not all right – but –'

'All right. We'll check. We'll put 'em through the machine to make sure. What *are* all these people, by the way?'

'They're people whose gardens verge on or touch the garden of the house where the murder was committed.'

'Sounds like a French exercise,' said Beck. 'Where is the dead body of my uncle? In the garden of the cousin of my aunt. What about Number 19 itself?'

'A blind woman, a former school teacher, lives there. She works in an institute for the blind and she's been thoroughly investigated by the local police.'

'Live by herself?'

'Yes.'

'And what is your idea about all these other people?'

'My idea is,' I said, 'that if a murder was committed by any of these other people in any of these other houses that I have mentioned to you, it would be perfectly easy, though risky, to convey the dead body into Number 19 at a suitable time of day. It's a mere possibility, that's all. And there's something I'd like to show you. *This*.'

Beck took the earthstained coin I held out to him.

'A Czech Haller? Where did you find it?'

'I didn't. But it was found in the back garden of Number 19.'

'Interesting. You may have something after all in your persistent fixation on crescents and rising moons.' He added thoughtfully, 'There's a pub called The Rising Moon in the next street to this. Why don't you go and try your luck there?'

'I've been there already,' I said.

'You've always got an answer, haven't you?' said Colonel Beck. 'Have a cigar?'

I shook my head. 'Thank you – no time today.'

'Going back to Crowdean?'

'Yes. There's the inquest to attend.'

'It will only be adjourned. Sure it's not some girl you're running after in Crowdean?'

'Certainly not,' I said sharply.

Colonel Beck began to chuckle unexpectedly.

'You mind your step, my boy! Sex rearing its ugly head as usual. How long have you known her?'

'There isn't any – I mean – well – there *was* a girl who discovered the body.'

'What did she do when she discovered it?'

'Screamed.'

'Very nice too,' said the colonel. 'She rushed to you, cried on your shoulder and told you about it. Is that it?'

'I don't know what you're talking about,' I said coldly. 'Have a look at these.'

I gave him a selection of the police photographs.

'Who's this?' demanded Colonel Beck.

'The dead man.'

'Ten to one this girl you're so keen about killed him. The whole story sounds very fishy to me.'

'You haven't even heard it yet,' I said. 'I haven't told it to you.'

'I don't need telling,' Colonel Beck waved his cigar. 'Go away to your inquest, my boy, and look out for that girl. Is her name Diana, or Artemis, or anything crescenty or moonlike?'

'No, it isn't.'

'Well, remember that it might be!'

CHAPTER 14

COLIN LAMB'S NARRATIVE

It had been quite a long time since I had visited Whitehaven Mansions. Some years ago it had been an outstanding building of modern flats. Now there were many other more imposing and even more modern blocks of buildings flanking it on either side. Inside, I noted, it had recently had a face lift. It had been repainted in pale shades of yellow and green.

I went up in the lift and pressed the bell of Number 203. It was opened to me by that impeccable man-servant, George. A smile of welcome came to his face.

'Mr Colin! It's a long time since we've seen you here.'

'Yes, I know. How are you, George?'

'I am in good health, I am thankful to say, sir.'

I lowered my voice. 'And how's he?'

George lowered his own voice, though that was hardly necessary since it had been pitched in a most discreet key from the beginning of our conversation.

'I think, sir, that sometimes he gets a little depressed.'

I nodded sympathetically.

'If you will come this way, sir –' He relieved me of my hat.

'Announce me, please, as Mr Colin Lamb.'

'Very good, sir.' He opened a door and spoke in a clear voice. 'Mr Colin Lamb to see you, sir.'

He drew back to allow me to pass him and I went into the room.

My friend, Hercule Poirot, was sitting in his usual large, square armchair in front of the fireplace. I noted that one bar of the rectangular electric fire glowed red. It was early September, the weather was warm, but Poirot was one of the first men to recognize the autumn chill, and to take precautions against it. On either side of him on the floor was a neat pile of books. More books stood on the table at his left side. At his right hand was a cup from which steam rose. A tisane, I suspected. He was fond of tisanes and often urged them on me. They were nauseating to taste and pungent to smell.

'Don't get up,' I said, but Poirot was already on his feet. He came towards me on twinkling, patent-leather shod feet with outstretched hands.

'Aha, so it is *you*, it is *you*, my friend! My young friend Colin. But why do you call yourself by the name of Lamb? Let me think now. There is a proverb or a saying. Something about mutton dressed as lamb. No. That is what is said of elderly ladies who are trying to appear younger than they are. That does not apply to you. Aha, I have it. You are a wolf in sheep's clothing. Is that it?'

'Not even that,' I said. 'It's just that in my line of business

I thought my own name might be rather a mistake, that it might be connected too much with my old man. Hence Lamb. Short, simple, easily remembered. Suiting, I flatter myself, my personality.'

'Of that I cannot be sure,' said Poirot. 'And how is my good friend, your father?'

'The old man's fine,' I said. 'Very busy with his hollyhocks – or is it chrysanthemums? The seasons go by so fast I can never remember what it is at the moment.'

'He busies himself then, with the horticulture?'

'Everyone seems to come to that in the end,' I said.

'Not me,' said Hercule Poirot. 'Once the vegetable marrows, yes – but never again. If you want the best flowers, why not go to the florist's shop? I thought the good Superintendent was going to write his memoirs?'

'He started,' I said, 'but he found that so much would have to be left out that he finally came to the conclusion that what was left in would be so unbearably tame as not to be worth writing.'

'One has to have the discretion, yes. It is unfortunate,' said Poirot, 'because your father could tell some very interesting things. I have much admiration for him. I always had. You know, his methods were to me very interesting. He was so straightforward. He used the obvious as no man has used it before. He would set the trap, the very obvious trap and the people he wished to catch would say "it is too obvious, that. It cannot be true" and so they fell into it!'

I laughed. 'Well,' I said, 'it's not the fashion nowadays for sons to admire their fathers. Most of them seem to sit down, venom in their pens, and remember all the dirty things they can and put them down with obvious satisfaction. But personally, I've got enormous respect for my old man. I hope I'll even be as good as he was. Not that I'm exactly in his line of business, of course.'

'But related to it,' said Poirot. 'Closely related to it, though you have to work behind the scenes in a way that he did not.' He coughed delicately. 'I think I am to congratulate you on having had a rather spectacular success lately. Is it not so? The *affaire Larkin*.'

'It's all right so far as it goes,' I said. 'But there's a good deal more that I'd like to have, just to round it off properly. Still, that isn't really what I came here to talk to you about.'

'Of course not, of course not,' said Poirot. He waved me to a chair and offered me some tisane, which I instantly refused.

George entered at the apposite moment with a whisky decanter, a glass and a siphon which he placed at my elbow.

'And what are you doing with yourself these days?' I asked Poirot.

Casting a look at the various books around him I said: 'It looks as though you are doing a little research?'

Poirot sighed. 'You may call it that. Yes, perhaps in a way it is true. Lately I have felt very badly the need for a problem. It does not matter, I said to myself, what the problem is. It can be like the good Sherlock Holmes, the depth at which the parsley has sunk in the butter. All that matters is that there should *be* a problem. It is not the muscles I need to exercise, you see, it is the cells of the brain.'

'Just a question of keeping fit. I understand.'

'As you say.' He sighed. 'But problems, *mon cher*, are not so easy to come by. It is true that last Thursday one presented itself to me. The unwarranted appearance of three pieces of dried orange peel in my umbrella stand. How did they come there? How *could* they have come there? I do not eat oranges myself. George would never put old pieces of orange peel in the umbrella stand. Nor is a visitor likely to bring with him three pieces of orange peel. Yes, it was quite a problem.'

'And you solved it?'

'I solved it,' said Poirot.

He spoke with more melancholy than pride.

'It was not in the end very interesting. A question of a *remplacement* of the usual cleaning woman and the new one brought with her, strictly against orders, one of her children. Although it does not sound interesting, nevertheless it needed a steady penetration of lies, camouflage and all the rest of it. It was satisfactory, shall we say, but not important.'

'Disappointing,' I suggested.

'*Enfin*,' said Poirot, 'I am modest. But one should not need to use a rapier to cut the string of a parcel.'

I shook my head in a solemn manner. Poirot continued, 'I

have occupied myself of late in reading various real life unsolved mysteries. I apply to them my own solutions.'

'You mean cases like the Bravo case, Adelaide Bartlett and all the rest of them?'

'Exactly. But it was in a way too easy. There is no doubt whatever in my own mind as to who murdered Charles Bravo. The companion may have been involved, but she was certainly not the moving spirit in the matter. Then there was that unfortunate adolescent, Constance Kent. The true motive that lay behind her strangling of the small brother whom she undoubtedly loved has always been a puzzle. But not to me. It was clear as soon as I read about the case. As for Lizzie Borden, one wishes only that one could put a few necessary questions to various people concerned. I am fairly sure in my own mind of what the answers would be. Alas, they are all by now dead, I fear.'

I thought to myself, as so often before, that modesty was certainly not Hercule Poirot's strong point.

'And what did I do next?' continued Poirot.

I guessed that for some time now he had had no one much to talk to and was enjoying the sound of his own voice.

'From real life I turned to fiction. You see me here with various examples of criminal fiction at my right hand and my left. I have been working backwards. Here –' he picked up the volume that he had laid on the arm of his chair when I entered, '– here, my dear Colin, is *The Leavenworth Case*.' He handed the book to me.

'That's going back quite a long time,' I said. 'I believe my father mentioned that he read it as a boy. I believe I once read it myself. It must seem rather old-fashioned now.'

'It is admirable,' said Poirot. 'One savours its period atmosphere, its studied and deliberate melodrama. Those rich and lavish descriptions of the golden beauty of Eleanor, the moonlight beauty of Mary!'

'I must read it again,' I said. 'I'd forgotten the parts about the beautiful girls.'

'And there is the maid-servant, Hannah, so true to type, and the murderer, an excellent psychological study.'

I perceived that I had let myself in for a lecture. I composed myself to listen.

'Then we will take the *Adventures of Arsene Lupin*,' Poirot went on. 'How fantastic, how unreal. And yet what vitality there is in them, what vigour, what life! They are preposterous, but they have panache. There is humour, too.'

He laid down the *Adventures of Arsene Lupin* and picked up another book. 'And there is *The Mystery of the Yellow Room*. That – ah, that is really a *classic*! I approve of it from start to finish. Such a logical approach! There were criticisms of it, I remember, which said that it was unfair. But it is not unfair, my dear Colin. No, no. Very nearly so, perhaps, but not quite. There is the hair's breadth of difference. No. All through there is truth, concealed with a careful and cunning use of words. Everything should be clear at that supreme moment when the men meet at the angle of three corridors.' He laid it down reverently. 'Definitely a masterpiece, and, I gather, almost forgotten nowadays.'

Poirot skipped twenty years or so, to approach the works of somewhat later authors.

'I have read also,' he said, 'some of the early works of Mrs Ariadne Oliver. She is by way of being a friend of mine, and of yours, I think. I do not wholly approve of her works, mind you. The happenings in them are highly improbable. The long arm of coincidence is far too freely employed. And, being young at the time, she was foolish enough to make her detective a Finn, and it is clear that she knows nothing about Finns or Finland except possibly the works of Sibelius. Still, she has an original habit of mind, she makes an occasional shrewd deduction, and of later years she has learnt a good deal about things which she did not know before. Police procedure for instance. She is also now a little more reliable on the subject of firearms. What was even more needed, she has possibly acquired a solicitor or a barrister friend who has put her right on certain points of the law.'

He laid aside Mrs Ariadne Oliver and picked up another book.

'Now here is Mr Cyril Quain. Ah, he is a master, Mr Quain, of the alibi.'

'He's a deadly dull writer if I remember rightly,' I said.

'It is true,' said Poirot, 'that nothing particularly thrilling happens in his books. There is a corpse, of course. Occasionally more than one. But the whole point is always the alibi, the railway time-table, the bus routes, the plans of the cross-country roads. I confess I enjoy this intricate, this elaborate use of the alibi. I enjoy trying to catch Mr Cyril Quain out.'

'And I suppose you always succeed,' I said.

Poirot was honest.

'Not always,' he admitted. 'No, not always. Of course, after a time one realizes that one book of his is almost exactly like another. The alibis resemble each other every time, even though they are not exactly the same. You know, *mon cher* Colin, I imagine this Cyril Quain sitting in his room, smoking his pipe as he is represented to do in his photographs, sitting there with around him the A.B.C.s, the continental Bradshaws, the air-line brochures, the time-tables of every kind. Even the movements of liners. Say what you will, Colin, there is order and method in Mr Cyril Quain.'

He laid Mr Quain down and picked up another book.

'Now here is Mr Garry Gregson, a prodigious writer of thrillers. He has written at least sixty-four, I understand. He is almost the exact opposite of Mr Quain. In Mr Quain's books nothing much happens, in Garry Gregson's far too many things happen. They happen implausibly and in mass confusion. They are all highly coloured. It is melodrama stirred up with a stick. Bloodshed – bodies – clues – thrills piled up and bulging over. All lurid, all very unlike life. He is not quite, as you would say, my cup of tea. He is, in fact, not a cup of tea at all. He is more like one of these American cocktails of the more obscure kind, whose ingredients are highly suspect.'

Poirot paused, sighed and resumed his lecture. 'Then we turn to America.' He plucked a book from the left-hand pile. 'Florence Elks, now. There is order and method there, colourful happenings, yes, but plenty of point in them. Gay and alive. She has wit, this lady, though perhaps, like so many American writers, a little too obsessed with drink. I am, as you know, *mon ami*, a connoisseur of wine. A claret or a burgundy introduced into a story, with its vintage and date properly authenticated, I always find pleasing. But the exact amount of rye and bourbon that are consumed on every other page by the detective in an American thriller do not seem to me interesting at all. Whether he drinks a pint or a half-pint which he takes from his collar drawer does not seem to me really to affect the action of the story in any way.

This drink motive in American books is very much what King Charles's head was to poor Mr Dick when he tried to write his memoirs. Impossible to keep it out.'

'What about the tough school?' I asked.

Poirot waved aside the tough school much as he would have waved an intruding fly or mosquito.

'Violence for violence's sake? Since when has that been interesting? I have seen plenty of violence in my early career as a police officer. Bah, you might as well read a medical text book. *Tout de même*, I give American crime fiction on the whole a pretty high place. I think it is more ingenious, more imaginative than English writing. It is less atmospheric and over-laden with atmosphere than most French writers. Now take Louisa O'Malley for instance.'

He dived once more for a book.

'What a model of fine scholarly writing is hers, yet what excitement, what mounting apprehension she arouses in her reader. Those brownstone mansions in New York. *Enfin what is* a brownstone mansion – I have never known? Those exclusive apartments, and soulful snobberies, and underneath, deep unsuspected seams of crime run their uncharted course. It *could* happen so, and it *does* happen so. She is very good, this Louisa O'Malley, she is very good indeed.'

He sighed, leaned back, shook his head and drank off the remainder of his tisane.

'And then – there are always the old favourites.'

Again he dived for a book.

'*The Adventures of Sherlock Holmes*,' he murmured lovingly, and even uttered reverently the one word, '*Maître!*'

'Sherlock Holmes?' I asked.

'Ah, *non, non,* not Sherlock Holmes! It is the author, Sir Arthur Conan Doyle, that I salute. These tales of Sherlock Holmes are in reality far-fetched, full of fallacies and most artificially contrived. But the art of the writing – ah, that is entirely different. The pleasure of the language, the creation above all of that magnificent character, Dr Watson. Ah, that was indeed a triumph.'

He sighed and shook his head and murmured, obviously by a natural association of ideas:

'*Ce cher* Hastings. My friend Hastings of whom you have often heard me speak. It is a long time since I have had news of him. What an absurdity to go and bury oneself in South America, where they are always having revolutions.'

'That's not confined to South America,' I pointed out. 'They're having revolutions all over the world nowadays.'

'Let us not discuss the Bomb,' said Hercule Poirot. 'If it has to be, it has to be, but let us not discuss it.'

'Actually,' I said, 'I came to discuss something quite different with you.'

'Ah! You are about to be married, is that it? I am delighted, *mon cher*, delighted.'

'What on earth put that in your head, Poirot?' I asked. 'Nothing of the kind.'

'It happens,' said Poirot, 'it happens every day.'

'Perhaps,' I said firmly, 'but not to me. Actually I came to tell you that I'd run across rather a pretty little problem in murder.'

'Indeed? A pretty problem in murder, you say? And you have brought it to *me*. Why?'

'Well –' I was slightly embarrassed. 'I – I thought you might enjoy it,' I said.

Poirot looked at me thoughtfully. He caressed his moustache with a loving hand, then he spoke.

'A master,' he said, 'is often kind to his dog. He goes out and throws a ball for the dog. A dog, however, is also capable of being kind to its master. A dog kills a rabbit or a rat and he brings it and lays it at his master's feet. And what does he do then? He wags his tail.'

I laughed in spite of myself. 'Am I wagging my tail?'

'I think you are, my friend. Yes, I think you are.'

'All right then,' I said. 'And what does master say? Does he want to see doggy's rat? Does he want to know all about it?'

'Of course. Naturally. It is a crime that you think will interest me. Is that right?'

'The whole point of it is,' I said, 'that it just doesn't make sense.'

'That is impossible,' said Poirot. 'Everything makes sense. Everything.'

'Well, you try and make sense of this. I can't. Not that it's really anything to do with me. I just happened to come in on it. Mind you, it may turn out to be quite straightforward, once the dead man is identified.'

'You are talking without method or order,' said Poirot severely. 'Let me beg of you to let me have the facts. You say it is a murder, yes?'

'It's a murder all right,' I assured him. 'Well, here we go.'

I described to him in detail the events that had taken place at 19, Wilbraham Crescent. Hercule Poirot leant back in his chair. He closed his eyes and gently tapped with a forefinger the arm of his chair while he listened to my recital. When I finally stopped, he did not speak for a moment. Then he asked, without opening his eyes:

'*Sans blague?*'

'Oh, absolutely,' I said.

'*Epatant*,' said Hercule Poirot. He savoured the word on his tongue and repeated it syllable by syllable. '*E-pa-tant.*' After that he continued his tapping on the arm of his chair and gently nodded his head.

'Well,' I said impatiently, after waiting a few moments more. 'What have you got to say?'

'But what do you want me to say?'

'I want you to give me the solution. I've always understood from you that it was perfectly possible to lie back in one's chair, just think about it all, and come up with the answer. That it was quite unnecessary to go and question people and run about looking for clues.'

'It is what I have always maintained.'

'Well, I'm calling your bluff,' I said. 'I've given you the facts, and now I want the answer.'

'Just like that, hein? But then there is a lot more to be known, *mon ami*. We are only at the *beginning* of the facts. Is that not so?'

'I still want you to come up with *something*.'

'I see.' He reflected a moment. 'One thing is certain,' he pronounced. 'It must be a very simple crime.'

'Simple?' I demanded in some astonishment.

'Naturally.'

'Why must it be simple?'

'Because it appears so complex. If it has necessarily to appear complex, it *must* be simple. You comprehend that?'

'I don't really know that I do.'

'Curious,' mused Poirot, 'what you have told me – I think – yes, there is something familiar to me there. Now where – when – have I come across something . . .' He paused.

'Your memory,' I said, 'must be one vast reservoir of crimes. But you can't possibly remember them all, can you?'

'Unfortunately no,' said Poirot, 'but from time to time these reminiscences are helpful. There was a soap boiler, I remember, once, at Liège. He poisoned his wife in order to marry a blonde stenographer. The crime made a pattern. Later, much later, that pattern recurred. I recognized it. This time it was an affair of a kidnapped Pekinese dog, but the *pattern* was the same. I looked for the equivalent of the blonde stenographer and the soap boiler, and *voilà*! That is the kind of thing. And here again in what you have told me I have that feeling of recognition.'

'Clocks?' I suggested hopefully. 'Bogus insurance agents?'

'No, no,' Poirot shook his head.

'Blind women?'

'No, no, no. Do not confuse me.'

'I'm disappointed in you, Poirot,' I said. 'I thought you'd give me the answer straight away.'

'But, my friend, at present you have presented me only with a *pattern*. There are many more things to find out. Presumably this man will be identified. In that kind of thing the police are excellent. They have their criminal records, they can advertise the man's picture, they have access to a list of missing persons, there is scientific examination of the dead man's clothing, and so on and so on. Oh, yes, there are a hundred other ways and means at their disposal. Undoubtedly, this man will be identified.'

'So there's nothing to do at the moment. Is that what you think?'

'There is always something to do,' said Hercule Poirot, severely.

'Such as?'

He wagged an emphatic forefinger at me.

'Talk to the neighbours,' he said.

'I've done that,' I said. 'I went with Hardcastle when he was questioning them. They don't know anything useful.'

'Ah, tcha, tcha, that is what *you* think. But I assure you, that cannot be so. You go to them, you ask them: "Have you seen anything suspicious?" and they say no, and you think that that is all there is to it. But that is not what I mean when I say talk to the neighbours. I say *talk* to them. Let them talk to *you*. And from their conversation always, somewhere, you will find a clue. They may be talking about their gardens or their pets or their hairdressing or their dressmaker, or their friends, or the kind of food they like. Always somewhere there will be a word that sheds light. You say there was nothing in those conversations that was useful. I say that cannot be so. If you could repeat them to me word for word . . .'

'Well, that's practically what I can do,' I said. 'I took shorthand transcripts of what was said, acting in my role of assistant police officer. I've had them transcribed and typed and I've brought them along to you. Here they are.'

'Ah, but you are a good boy, you are a very good boy indeed! What you have done is exactly right. Exactly. *Je vous remercie infiniment.*'

I felt quite embarrassed.

'Have you any more suggestions?' I asked.

'Yes, always I have suggestions. There is this girl. You can talk to this girl. Go and see her. Already you are friends, are you not? Have you not clasped her in your arms when she flew from the house in terror?'

'You've been affected by reading Garry Gregson,' I said. 'You've caught the melodramatic style.'

'Perhaps you are right,' Poirot admitted. 'One gets infected, it is true, by the style of a work that one has been reading.'

'As for the girl –' I said, then paused.

Poirot looked at me inquiringly.

'Yes?' he said.

'I shouldn't like – I don't want . . .'

'Ah, so that is it. At the back of your mind you think she is concerned somehow in this case.'

'No, I don't. It was absolutely pure chance that she happened to be there.'

'No, no, *mon ami*, it was not pure chance. You know that very well. You've told me so. She was asked for over the telephone. Asked for specially.'

'But she doesn't know why.'

'You cannot be sure that she does not know why. Very likely she *does* know why and is hiding the fact.'

'I don't think so,' I said obstinately.

'It is even possible you may find out why by talking to her, even if she herself does not realize the truth.'

'I don't see very well how – I mean – I hardly know her.'

Hercule Poirot shut his eyes again.

'There is a time,' he said, 'in the course of an attraction between two persons of the opposite sex, when that particular statement is bound to be true. She is an attractive girl, I suppose?'

'Well – yes,' I said. 'Quite attractive.'

'You will talk to her,' Poirot ordered, 'because you are already friends, and you will go again and see this blind woman with some excuse. And you will talk to *her*. And you will go to the typewriting bureau on the pretence perhaps of having some manuscript typed. You will make friends, perhaps, with one of the other young ladies who works there. You will talk to all these people and then you will come and see me again and you will tell me all the things that they will say.'

'Have mercy!' I said.

'Not at all,' said Poirot, 'you will enjoy it.'

'You don't seem to realize that I've got my own work to do.'

'You will work all the better for having a certain amount of relaxation,' Poirot assured me.

I got up and laughed.

'Well,' I said, 'you're the doctor! Any more words of wisdom for me? What do you feel about this strange business of the clocks?'

Poirot leaned back in his chair again and closed his eyes.

The words he spoke were quite unexpected.

'"*The time has come, the Walrus said,*
To talk of many things.
Of shoes and ships and sealing wax,
And cabbages and kings.
And why the sea is boiling hot
And whether pigs have wings."'

He opened his eyes again and nodded his head.

'Do you understand?' he said.

'Quotation from "The Walrus and the Carpenter," *Alice Through the Looking Glass.*'

'Exactly. For the moment, that is the best I can do for you, *mon cher*. Reflect upon it.'

CHAPTER 15

The inquest was well attended by the general public. Thrilled by a murder in their midst, Crowdean turned out with eager hopes of sensational disclosures. The proceedings, however, were as dry as they could be. Sheila Webb need not have dreaded her ordeal, it was over in a couple of minutes.

There had been a telephone message to the Cavendish Bureau directing her to go to 19, Wilbraham Crescent. She had gone, acting as told to do, by entering the sitting-room. She had found the dead man there and had screamed and rushed out of the house to summon assistance. There were no questions or elaborations. Miss Martindale, who also gave evidence, was questioned for an even shorter time. She had received a message purporting to be from Miss Pebmarsh asking her to send a shorthand typist, preferably Miss Sheila Webb, to 19, Wilbraham Crescent, and giving certain directions. She had noted down the exact time of the telephone call as 1.49. That disposed of Miss Martindale.

Miss Pebmarsh, called next, denied categorically that she had asked for *any* typist to be sent to her that day from the Cavendish Bureau. Detective Inspector Hardcastle made a short emotionless statement. On receipt of a telephone call, he had gone to 19, Wilbraham Crescent where he had found the body of a dead man. The coroner then asked him:

'Have you been able to identify the dead man?'

'Not as yet, sir. For that reason, I would ask for this inquest to be adjourned.'

'Quite so.'

Then came the medical evidence. Doctor Rigg, the police surgeon, having described himself and his qualifications, told of his arrival at 19, Wilbraham Crescent, and of his examination of the dead man.

'Can you give us an approximate idea of the time of death, Doctor?'

'I examined him at half past three. I should put the time of death as between half past one and half past two.'

'You cannot put it nearer than that?'

'I should prefer not to do so. At a guess, the most likely time would be two o'clock or rather earlier, but there are many factors which have to be taken into account. Age, state of health, and so on.'

'You performed an autopsy?'

'I did.'

'The cause of death?'

'The man had been stabbed with a thin, sharp knife. Something in the nature, perhaps, of a French cooking-knife with a tapering blade. The point of the knife entered . . .' Here the doctor became technical as he explained the exact position where the knife had entered the heart.

'Would death have been instantaneous?'

'It would have occurred within a very few minutes.'

'The man would not have cried out or struggled?'

'Not under the circumstances in which he was stabbed.'

'Will you explain to us, Doctor, what you mean by that phrase?'

'I made an examination of certain organs and made certain tests. I would say that when he was killed he was in a state of coma due to the administration of a drug.'

'Can you tell us what this drug was, Doctor?'

'Yes. It was chloral hydrate.'

'Can you tell how this was adminstered?'

'I should say presumably in alcohol of some kind. The effect of chloral hydrate is very rapid.'

'Known in certain quarters as a Mickey Finn, I believe,' murmured the coroner.

'That is quite correct,' said Doctor Rigg. 'He would drink the liquid unsuspectingly, and a few moments later he would reel over and fall unconscious.'

'And he was stabbed, in your opinion, while unconscious?'

'That is my belief. It would account for there being no sign of a struggle and for his peaceful appearance.'

'How long after becoming unconscious was he killed?'

'That I cannot say with any accuracy. There again it depends on the personal idiosyncrasy of the victim. He would certainly not come round under half an hour and it might be a good deal more than that.'

'Thank you, Doctor Rigg. Have you any evidence as to when this man last had a meal?'

'He had not lunched if that is what you mean. He had eaten no solid food for at least four hours.'

'Thank you, Doctor Rigg. I think that is all.'

The coroner then looked round and said:

'The inquest will be adjourned for a fortnight, until September 28th.'

The inquest concluded, people began to move out of the court. Edna Brent who, with most of the other girls at the Cavendish Bureau, had been present, hesitated as she got outside the door. The Cavendish Secretarial Bureau had been closed for the morning. Maureen West, one of the other girls, spoke to her.

'What about it, Edna? Shall we go to the Bluebird for lunch? We've got heaps of time. At any rate, *you* have.'

'I haven't got any more time than you have,' said Edna in an injured voice. 'Sandy Cat told me I'd better take the first interval for lunch. Mean of her. I thought I'd get a good extra hour for shopping and things.'

'Just like Sandy Cat,' said Maureen. 'Mean as hell, isn't she? We open up again at two and we've all got to be there. Are you looking for anyone?'

'Only Sheila. I didn't see her come out.'

'She went away earlier,' said Maureen, 'after she'd finished giving her evidence. She went off with a young man – but I didn't see who he was. Are you coming?'

Edna still hovered uncertainly, and said, 'You go on – I've got shopping to do anyway.'

Maureen and another girl went off together. Edna lingered. Finally she nerved herself to speak to the fair-haired young policeman who stood at the entrance.

'Could I go in again?' she murmured timidly, 'and speak

to – to the one who came to the office – Inspector something.'

'Inspector Hardcastle?'

'That's right. The one who was giving evidence this morning.'

'Well –' the young policeman looked into the court and observed the inspector in deep consultation with the coroner and with the chief constable of the county.

'He looks busy at the moment, miss,' he said. 'If you called round at the station later, or if you'd like to give me a message . . . Is it anything important?'

'Oh, it doesn't matter really,' said Edna. 'It's – well – just that I don't see how what she said could have been true because I mean . . .' She turned away, still frowning perplexedly.

She wandered away from the Cornmarket and along the High Street. She was still frowning perplexedly and trying to think. Thinking had never been Edna's strong point. The more she tried to get things clear in her mind, the more muddled her mind became.

Once she said aloud:

'But it couldn't have been like that . . . It couldn't have been like she said . . .'

Suddenly, with an air of one making a resolution, she turned off from the High Street and along Albany Road in the direction of Wilbraham Crescent.

Since the day that the Press had announced that a murder had been committed at 19, Wilbraham Crescent, large numbers of people had gathered in front of the house every day to have a good look at it. The fascination mere bricks and mortar can have for the general public under certain circumstances is a truly mysterious thing. For the first twenty-four hours a policeman had been stationed there to pass people along in an authoritative manner. Since then interest had lessened; but had still not ceased entirely. Tradesmen's delivery vans would slacken speed a little as they passed, women wheeling prams would come to a four or five minute stop on the opposite pavement and stare their eyes out as they contemplated Miss Pebmarsh's neat residence. Shopping women with baskets would pause with avid eyes and exchange pleasurable gossip with friends.

'That's the house – that one there . . .'

'The body was in the sitting-room . . . No, I think the sitting-room's the room at the front, the one on the left . . .'

'The grocer's man told me it was the one on the right.'

'Well, of course it might be, I've been into Number 10 once and there, I distinctly remember the *dining*-room was on the right, and the sitting-room was on the left . . .'

'It doesn't look a bit as though there had been a murder done there, does it . . . ?'

'The girl, I believe, came out of the gate screaming her head off . . .'

'They say she's not been right in her head since . . . Terrible shock, of course . . .'

'He broke in by a back window, so they say. He was putting the silver in a bag when this girl came in and found him there . . .'

'The poor woman who owns the house, she's *blind*, poor soul. So, of course, *she* couldn't know what was going on.'

'Oh, but she wasn't *there* at the time . . .'

'Oh, I thought she *was*. I thought she was upstairs and heard him. Oh, dear, I *must* get on to the shops.'

These and similar conversations went on most of the time. Drawn as though by a magnet, the most unlikely people arrived in Wilbraham Crescent, paused, stared, and then passed on, some inner need satisfied.

Here, still puzzling in her mind, Edna Brent found herself jostling a small group of five or six people who were engaged in the favourite pastime of looking at the murder house.

Edna, always suggestible, stared also.

So that was the house where it happened! Net curtains in the windows. Looked ever so nice. And yet a man had been killed there. Killed with a kitchen knife. An ordinary kitchen knife. Nearly everybody had got a kitchen knife . . .

Mesmerized by the behaviour of the people round her, Edna, too, stared and ceased to think . . .

She had almost forgotten what had brought her here . . .

She started when a voice spoke in her ear.

She turned her head in surprised recognition.

CHAPTER 16

COLIN LAMB'S NARRATIVE

I

I noticed when Sheila Webb slipped quietly out of the Coroner's Court. She'd given her evidence very well. She had looked nervous but not unduly nervous. Just natural, in fact. (What would Beck say? 'Quite a good performance.' I could hear him say it!)

I took in the surprise finish of Doctor Rigg's evidence. (Dick Hardcastle hadn't told me that, but he must have known) and then I went after her.

'It wasn't so bad after all, was it?' I said, when I had caught her up.

'No. It was quite easy really. The coroner was very nice.' She hesitated. 'What will happen next?'

'He'll adjourn the inquest – for further evidence. A fortnight probably or until they can identify the dead man.'

'You think they *will* identify him?'

'Oh, yes,' I said. 'They'll identify him all right. No doubt of that.'

She shivered. 'It's cold today.'

It wasn't particularly cold. In fact I thought it was rather warm.

'What about an early lunch?' I suggested. 'You haven't got to go back to your typewriting place, have you?'

'No. It's closed until two o'clock.'

'Come along then. How do you react to Chinese food? I see there's a little Chinese restaurant just down the street.'

Sheila looked hesitant.

'I've really got to do some shopping.'

'You can do it afterwards.'

'No, I can't – some of the shops close between one and two.'

'All right then. Will you meet me there? In half an hour's time?'

She said she would.

I went along to the sea front and sat there in a shelter. As the wind was blowing straight in from the sea, I had it to myself.

I wanted to think. It always infuriates one when other people know more about you than you know about yourself. But old Beck and Hercule Poirot and Dick Hardcastle, they all had seen quite clearly what I was now forced to admit to myself was true.

I minded about this girl – minded in a way I had never minded about a girl before.

It wasn't her beauty – she was pretty, pretty in rather an unusual way, no more. It wasn't her sex appeal – I had met that often enough – had been given the full treatment.

It was just that, almost from the first, I had recognized that she was *my* girl.

And I didn't know the first damned thing about her!

II

It was just after two o'clock that I walked into the station and asked for Dick. I found him at his desk leafing over a pile of stuff. He looked up and asked me what I had thought of the inquest.

I told him I thought it had been a very nicely managed and gentlemanly performance.

'We do this sort of thing so well in this country.'

'What did you think of the medical evidence?'

'Rather a facer. Why didn't you tell me about it?'

'You were away. Did you consult your specialist?'

'Yes, I did.'

'I believe I remember him vaguely. A lot of moustache.'

'Oceans of it,' I agreed. 'He's very proud of that moustache.'

'He must be quite old.'

'Old but not ga-ga,' I said.

'Why did you really go to see him? Was it purely the milk of human kindness?'

'You have such a suspicious policeman's mind, Dick! It was mainly that. But I admit to curiosity, too. I wanted to hear what he had to say about our own particular set-up. You see, he's always talked what I call a lot of cock about its being easy to solve a case by just sitting in your chair, bringing the tips of your fingers symmetrically together, closing your eyes and thinking. I wanted to call his bluff.'

'Did he go through that procedure for you?'

'He did.'

'And what did he say?' Dick asked with some curiosity.

'He said,' I told him, 'that it must be a very *simple* murder.'

'Simple, my God!' said Hardcastle, roused. 'Why simple?'

'As far as I could gather,' I said, 'because the whole set-up was so complex.'

Hardcastle shook his head. 'I don't see it,' he said. 'It sounds like one of those clever things that young people in Chelsea say, but I don't see it. Anything else?'

'Well, he told me to talk to the neighbours. I assured him we had done so.'

'The neighbours are even more important now in view of the medical evidence.'

'The presumption being that he was doped somewhere else and brought to Number 19 to be killed?'

Something familiar about the words struck me.

'That's more or less what Mrs What's-her-name, the cat woman, said. It struck me at the time as a rather interesting remark.'

'Those cats,' said Dick, and shuddered. He went on: 'We've found the weapon, by the way. Yesterday.'

'You have? Where?'

'In the cattery. Presumably thrown there by the murderer after the crime.'

'No fingerprints, I suppose?'

'Carefully wiped. And it could be anybody's knife – slightly used – recently sharpened.'

'So it goes like this. He was doped – then brought to Number 19 – in a car? Or how?'

'He *could* have been brought from one of the houses with an adjoining garden.'

'Bit risky, wouldn't it have been?'

'It would need audacity,' Hardcastle agreed, 'and it would need a very good knowledge of the neighbourhood's habits. It's more likely that he would have been brought in a car.'

'That would have been risky too. People notice a car.'

'Nobody did. But I agree that the murderer couldn't know that they wouldn't. Passers-by would have noted a car stopping at Number 19 that day –'

'I wonder if they *would* notice,' I said. 'Everyone's so used to cars. Unless, of course, it had been a very lush car – something unusual, but that's not likely –'

'And of course it was the lunch hour. You realize, Colin, that this brings Miss Millicent Pebmarsh back into the picture? It seems far-fetched to think of an able-bodied man being stabbed by a blind woman – but if he was doped –'

'In other words "if he came there to be killed," as our Mrs Hemming put it, he arrived by appointment quite unsuspiciously, was offered a sherry or a cocktail – the Mickey Finn took effect and Miss Pebmarsh got to work. Then she washed up the Mickey Finn glass, arranged the body neatly on the floor, threw the knife into her neighbour's garden, and tripped out as usual.'

'Telephoning to the Cavendish Secretarial Bureau on the way –'

'And why should she do that? And ask particularly for Sheila Webb?'

'I wish we knew.' Hardcastle looked at me. 'Does *she* know? The girl herself?'

'She says not.'

'She says not,' Hardcastle repeated tonelessly. 'I'm asking you what *you* think about it?'

I didn't speak for a moment or two. What *did* I think? I had to decide right now on my course of action. The truth would come out in the end. It would do Sheila no harm if she were what I believed her to be.

With a brusque movement I pulled a postcard out of my pocket and shoved it across the table.

'Sheila got this through the post.'

Hardcastle scanned it. It was one of a series of postcards of London buildings. It represented the Central Criminal Court. Hardcastle turned it over. On the right was the address – in neat printing. Miss R. S. Webb, 14, Palmerston Road, Crowdean, Sussex. On the left hand side, also printed, was the word REMEMBER! and below it 4.13.

'4.13,' said Hardcastle. 'That was the time the clocks showed that day.' He shook his head. 'A picture of the Old Bailey, the word "Remember" and a time – 4.13. It *must* tie up with something.'

'She says she doesn't know what it means.' I added: 'I believe her.'

Hardcastle nodded.

'I'm keeping this. We may get something from it.'

'I hope you do.'

There was embarrassment between us. To relieve it, I said: 'You've got a lot of bumf there.'

'All the usual. And most of it no damned good. The dead man hadn't got a criminal record, his fingerprints aren't on file. Practically all this stuff is from people who claim to have recognized him.' He read:

> '"Dear Sir, the picture that was in the paper I'm almost sure is the same as a man who was catching a train at Willesden Junction the other day. He was muttering to himself and looking very wild and excited, I thought when I saw him there must be something wrong."

> '"Dear Sir, I think this man looks very like my husband's cousin John. He went abroad to South Africa but it may be that he's come back. He had a moustache when he went away but of course he could have shaved that off."

> '"Dear Sir, I saw the man in the paper in a tube train last night. I thought at the time there was something peculiar about him."

'And of course there are all the women who recognize husbands. Women don't really seem to know what their husbands look like! There are hopeful mothers who recognize sons they have not seen for twenty years.

'And here's the list of missing persons. Nothing here likely to help us. "George Barlow, 65, missing from home. His wife thinks he must have lost his memory." And a note below: "Owes a lot of money. Has been seen going about with a red-haired widow. Almost certain to have done a bunk."

'Next one: "Professor Hargraves, expected to deliver a lecture last Tuesday. Did not turn up and sent no wire or note of excuse."'

Hardcastle did not appear to consider Professor Hargraves seriously.

'Thought the lecture was the week before or the week after,' he said. 'Probably thought he had told his housekeeper where he was going but hasn't done so. We get a lot of that.'

The buzzer on Hardcastle's table sounded. He picked up the receiver.

'Yes? ... What? ... Who found her? Did she give her name? ... I see. Carry on.' He put down the receiver again. His face as he turned to me was a changed face. It was stern, almost vindictive.

'They've found a girl dead in a telephone box on Wilbraham Crescent,' he said.

'Dead?' I stared at him. 'How?'

'Strangled. With her own scarf!'

I felt suddenly cold.

'What girl? It's not –'

Hardcastle looked at me with a cold, appraising glance that I didn't like.

'It's not your girl friend,' he said, 'if that's what you're afraid of. The constable there seems to know who she is. He says she's a girl who works in the same office as Sheila Webb. Edna Brent her name is.'

'Who found her? The constable?'

'She was found by Miss Waterhouse, the woman from Number 18. It seems she went to the box to make a telephone call as her phone was out of order and found the girl there huddled down in a heap.'

The door opened and a police constable said:

'Doctor Rigg telephoned that he's on his way, sir. He'll meet you at Wilbraham Crescent.'

CHAPTER 17

It was an hour and a half later and Detective Inspector Hardcastle sat down behind his desk and accepted with relief an official cup of tea. His face still held its bleak, angry look.

'Excuse me, sir, Pierce would like a word with you.'

Hardcastle roused himself.

'Pierce? Oh, all right. Send him in.'

Pierce entered, a nervous-looking young constable.

'Excuse me, sir, I thought per'aps as I ought to tell you.'

'Yes? Tell me what?'

'It was after the inquest, sir. I was on duty at the door. This girl – this girl that's been killed. She – she spoke to me.'

'Spoke to you, did she? What did she say?'

'She wanted to have a word with you, sir.'

Hardcastle sat up, suddenly alert.

'She wanted to have a word with me? Did she say why?'

'Not exactly, sir. I'm sorry, sir, if I – if I ought to have done something about it. I asked her if she could give me a message or – or if perhaps she could come to the station later on. You see, you were busy with the chief constable and the coroner and I thought –'

'Damn!' said Hardcastle, under his breath. 'Couldn't you have told her just to wait until I was free?'

'I'm sorry, sir.' The young man flushed. 'I suppose if I'd known, I ought to have done so. But I didn't think it was anything important. I don't think *she* thought it was important. It was just something she said she was worried about.'

'Worried?' said Hardcastle. He was silent for quite a minute turning over in his mind certain facts. This was the girl he had passed in the street when he was going to Mrs Lawton's house, the girl who had wanted to see Sheila Webb. The girl who had recognized him as she passed him and had hesitated a moment as though uncertain whether to stop him or not. She'd had something on her mind. Yes, that was it. Something on her mind. He'd slipped up. He'd not been quick enough on the ball. Filled with his own purpose of finding out a little more about Sheila Webb's background, he had overlooked a valuable point. The girl had been worried? Why? Now, probably, they'd never know why.

'Go on, Pierce,' he said, 'tell me all you can remember.' He added kindly, for he was a fair man: 'You couldn't know that it was important.'

It wasn't, he knew, any good to pass on his own anger and frustration by blaming it on the boy. How should the boy have known? Part of his training was to uphold discipline, to make sure that his superiors were only accosted at the proper times and in the proper places. If the girl had said it was important or urgent, that would have been different. But she hadn't been, he thought, remembering his first view of her in the office, that kind of girl. A slow thinker. A girl probably distrustful of her own mental processes.

'Can you remember exactly what happened, and what she said to you, Pierce?' he asked.

Pierce was looking at him with a kind of eager gratitude.

'Well, sir, she just come up to me when everyone was leaving and she sort of hesitated a moment and looked round just as though she were looking for someone. Not you, sir, I don't think. Somebody else. Then she come up to me and said could she speak to the police officer, and she said the one that had given evidence. So, as I said, I saw you were busy with the chief constable so I explained to her that you were engaged just now, could she give me a message or contact you later at the station. And I think she said that would do quite well. I said was it anything particular . . .'

'Yes?' Hardcastle leaned forward.

'And she said well not really. It was just something, she said, that she didn't see how it could have been the way she'd said it was.'

'She didn't see how what she said could have been like that?' Hardcastle repeated.

'That's right, sir. I'm not sure of the exact words. Perhaps it was: "I don't see how what she said can have been true." She was frowning and looking puzzled-like. But when I asked her, she said it wasn't really important.'

Not really important, the girl had said. The same girl who had been found not long afterwards strangled in a telephone box . . .

'Was anybody near you at the time she was talking to you?' he asked.

'Well, there were a good many people, sir, filing out, you know. There'd been a lot of people attending the inquest. It's caused quite a stir, this murder has, what with the way the Press have taken it up and all.'

'You don't remember anyone in particular who was near you at the time – any of the people who'd given evidence, for instance?'

'I'm afraid I don't recall anyone in particular, sir.'

'Well,' said Hardcastle, 'it can't be helped. All right, Pierce, if you remember anything further, come to me at once with it.'

Left alone he made an effort to subdue his rising anger and self-condemnation. That girl, that rabbity-looking girl, had known something. No, perhaps not put it as high as *known*, but she had seen something, heard something. Something that had worried her; and the worry had been intensified after attending the inquest. What could it have been? Something in the evidence? Something, in all probability, in Sheila Webb's evidence? Had she gone to Sheila's aunt's house two days before on purpose to see Sheila? Surely she could have talked to Sheila at the office? Why did she want to see her privately? Did she know something about Sheila Webb that perplexed her? Did she want to ask Sheila for an explanation of whatever it was, somewhere in private – not in front of the other girls? It looked that way. It certainly looked like it.

He dismissed Pierce. Then he gave a few directions to Sergeant Cray.

'What do you think the girl went to Wilbraham Crescent *for*?' Sergeant Cray asked.

'I've been wondering about that,' said Hardcastle. 'It's possible, of course, that she just suffered from curiosity – wanted to see what the place looked like. There's nothing unusual about that – half the population of Crowdean seems to feel the same.'

'Don't we know it,' said Sergeant Cray with feeling.

'On the other hand,' said Hardcastle slowly, 'she may have gone to see someone who lived there . . .'

When Sergeant Cray had gone out again, Hardcastle wrote down three numbers on his blotting pad.

'20,' he wrote, and put a query after it. He added: '19?' and then '18?' He wrote names to correspond. Hemming, Pebmarsh, Waterhouse. The three houses in the higher crescent were out of it. To visit one of them Edna Brent would not have gone along the lower road at all.

Hardcastle studied the three possibilities.

He took No. 20 first. The knife used in the original murder had been found there. It seemed more likely that the knife had been thrown there from the garden of No. 19 but they didn't *know* that it had. It *could* have been thrust into the shrubbery by the owner of No. 20 herself. When questioned, Mrs Hemming's only reaction had been indignation. 'How wicked of someone to throw a nasty knife like that at my cats!' she had said. How did Mrs Hemming connect up with Edna Brent? She didn't, Inspector Hardcastle decided. He went on to consider Miss Pebmarsh.

Had Edna Brent gone to Wilbraham Crescent to call on Miss Pebmarsh? Miss Pebmarsh had given evidence at the inquest. Had there been something in that evidence which had aroused disbelief in Edna? But she had been worried *before* the inquest. Had she already known something about Miss Pebmarsh? Had she known, for instance, that there was a link of some kind between Miss Pebmarsh and Sheila Webb? That would fit in with her words to Pierce. 'It couldn't have been true what she said.'

'Conjecture, all conjecture,' he thought angrily.

And No. 18? Miss Waterhouse had found the body. Inspector Hardcastle was professionally prejudiced against people who found bodies. Finding the body avoided so many difficulties for a murderer – it saved the hazards of arranging an alibi, it accounted for any overlooked fingerprints. In many ways it was a cast-iron position – with one proviso only. There must be no obvious motive. There was certainly no apparent motive for Miss Waterhouse to do away with little Edna Brent. Miss Waterhouse had not given evidence at the inquest. She might have been there, though. Did Edna perhaps have some reason for knowing, or believing, that it was Miss Waterhouse who had impersonated Miss Pebmarsh over the telephone and asked for a shorthand typist to be sent to No. 19?

More conjecture.

And there was, of course, Sheila Webb herself . . .

Hardcastle's hand went to the telephone. He got on to the hotel where Colin Lamb was staying. Presently he got Colin himself on the wire.

'Hardcastle here – what time was it when you lunched with Sheila Webb today?'

There was a pause before Colin answered:

'How do you know that we lunched together?'

'A damned good guess. You did, didn't you?'

'Why shouldn't I have lunch with her?'

'No reason at all. I'm merely asking you the time. Did you go off to lunch straight from the inquest?'

'No. She had shopping to do. We met at the Chinese place in Market Street at one o'clock.'

'I see.'

Hardcastle looked down his notes. Edna Brent had died between 12.30 and one o'clock.

'Don't you want to know what we had for lunch?'

'Keep your hair on. I just wanted the exact time. For the record.'

'I see. It's like that.'

There was a pause. Hardcastle said, endeavouring to ease the strain:

'If you're not doing anything this evening –'

The other interrupted.

'I'm off. Just packing up. I found a message waiting for me. I've got to go abroad.'

'When will you be back?'

'That's anybody's guess. A week at least – perhaps longer – possibly never!'

'Bad luck – or isn't it?'

'I'm not sure,' said Colin, and rang off.

CHAPTER 18

I

Hardcastle arrived at No. 19, Wilbraham Crescent just as Miss Pebmarsh was coming out of the house.

'Excuse me a minute, Miss Pebmarsh.'

'Oh. Is it – Detective Inspector Hardcastle?'

'Yes. Can I have a word with you?'

'I don't want to be late at the Institute. Will it take long?'

'I assure you only three or four minutes.'

She went into the house and he followed.

'You've heard what happened this afternoon?' he said.

'Has anything happened?'

'I thought you might have heard. A girl was killed in the telephone box just down the road.'

'Killed? When?'

'Two hours and three quarters ago.' He looked at the grand-father clock.

'I've heard nothing about it. Nothing,' said Miss Pebmarsh. A kind of anger sounded momentarily in her voice. It was as though her disability had been brought home to her in some particularly wounding way. 'A girl – killed! What girl?'

'Her name is Edna Brent and she worked at the Cavendish Secretarial Bureau.'

'Another girl from there! Had she been sent for like this girl, Sheila what's-her-name was?'

'I don't think so,' said the inspector. 'She did not come to see you here, at your house?'

'Here? No. Certainly not.'

'Would you have been in if she had come here?'

'I'm not sure. What time did you say?'

'Approximately twelve-thirty or a little later.'

'Yes,' said Miss Pebmarsh. 'I would have been home by then.'

'Where did you go after the inquest?'

'I came straight back here.' She paused and then asked, 'Why did you think this girl might have come to see me?'

'Well, she had been at the inquest this morning and she had seen you there, and she must have had *some* reason for coming to Wilbraham Crescent. As far as we know, she was not acquainted with anyone in this road.'

'But why should she come to see me just because she had seen me at the inquest?'

'Well –' the inspector smiled a little, then hastily tried to put the smile in his voice as he realized that Miss Pebmarsh could not appreciate its disarming quality. 'One never knows with these girls. She might just have wanted an autograph. Something like that.'

'An autograph!' Miss Pebmarsh sounded scornful. Then she said, 'Yes . . . Yes, I suppose you're right. That sort of thing does happen.' Then she shook her head briskly. 'I can only assure you, Inspector Hardcastle, that it did *not* happen today. Nobody has been here since I came back from the inquest.'

'Well, thank you, Miss Pebmarsh. We thought we had better check up on every possibility.'

'How old was she?' asked Miss Pebmarsh.

'I believe she was nineteen.'

'Nineteen? Very young.' Her voice changed slightly. 'Very young . . . Poor child. Who would want to kill a girl of that age?'

'It happens,' said Hardcastle.

'Was she pretty – attractive – sexy?'

'No,' said Hardcastle. 'She would have liked to be, I think, but she was not.'

'Then that was not the reason,' said Miss Pebmarsh. She shook her head again. 'I'm sorry. More sorry than I can say, Inspector Hardcastle, that I can't help you.'

He went out, impressed as he always was impressed, by Miss Pebmarsh's personality.

II

Miss Waterhouse was also at home. She was also true to type, opening the door with a suddenness which displayed a desire to trap someone doing what they should not do.

'Oh, it's *you*!' she said. 'Really, I've told your people all I know.'

'I'm sure you've replied to all the questions that were asked you,' said Hardcastle, 'but they can't all be asked at once, you know. We have to go into a few more details.'

'I don't see why. The whole thing was a most terrible shock,' said Miss Waterhouse, looking at him in a censorious way as though it had been all his doing. 'Come in, come in. You can't stand on the mat all day. Come in and sit down and ask me any questions you want to, though really what questions there can be, I cannot see. As I told you, I went out to make a telephone call. I opened the door of the box and there was the girl. Never had such a shock in my life. I hurried down and got the police constable. And after that, in case you want to know, I came back here and I gave myself a medicinal dose of brandy. *Medicinal*,' said Miss Waterhouse fiercely.

'Very wise of you, madam,' said Inspector Hardcastle.

'And that's that,' said Miss Waterhouse with finality.

'I wanted to ask you if you were quite sure you had never seen this girl before?'

'May have seen her a dozen times,' said Miss Waterhouse, 'but not to remember. I mean, she may have served me in Woolworth's, or sat next to me in a bus, or sold me tickets in a cinema.'

'She was a shorthand typist at the Cavendish Bureau.'

'I don't think I've ever had occasion to use a shorthand typist. Perhaps she worked in my brother's office at Gainsford and Swettenham. Is that what you're driving at?'

'Oh, no,' said Inspector Hardcastle, 'there appears to be no connection of that kind. But I just wondered if she'd come to see you this morning before being killed.'

'Come to *see* me? No, of course not. Why should she?'

'Well, that we wouldn't know,' said Inspector Hardcastle, 'but you would say, would you, that anyone who saw her coming in at your gate this morning was mistaken?' He looked at her with innocent eyes.

'Somebody saw her coming in at my gate? Nonsense,' said Miss Waterhouse. She hesitated. 'At least –'

'Yes?' said Hardcastle, alert though he did not show it.

'Well, I suppose she may have pushed a leaflet or something through the door . . . There *was* a leaflet there at lunch time. Something about a meeting for nuclear disarmament, I think. There's always something every day. I suppose conceivably she might have come and pushed something through the letter box; but you can't blame me for that, can you?'

'Of course not. Now as to your telephone call – you say your own telephone was out of order. According to the exchange, that was not so.'

'Exchanges will say anything! I dialled and got a *most* peculiar noise, not the engaged signal, so I went out to the call box.'

Hardcastle got up.

'I'm sorry, Miss Waterhouse, for bothering you in this way, but there is some idea that this girl *did* come to call on someone in the crescent and that she went to a house not very far from here.'

'And so you have to inquire all along the crescent,' said Miss Waterhouse. 'I should think the most likely thing is that she went to the house next door – Miss Pebmarsh's, I mean.'

'Why should you consider that the most likely?'

'You said she was a shorthand typist and came from the Cavendish Bureau. Surely, if I remember rightly, it was said that Miss Pebmarsh asked for a shorthand typist to come to her house the other day when that man was killed.'

'It was said so, yes, but she denied it.'

'Well, if you ask me,' said Miss Waterhouse, 'not that anyone ever listens to what *I* say until it's too late, I should say that she'd gone a little batty. Miss Pebmarsh, I mean. I think, perhaps, that she *does* ring up bureaux and ask for shorthand typists to come. Then, perhaps, she forgets all about it.'

'But you don't think that she would do murder?'

'I never suggested murder or anything of that kind. I know a man was killed in her house, but I'm not for a moment suggesting that Miss Pebmarsh had anything to do with it. No. I just thought that she might have one of those curious fixations like people do. I knew a woman once who was always ringing up a confectioner's and ordering a dozen meringues. She didn't want them, and when they came she said she hadn't ordered them. That sort of thing.'

'Of course, anything is possible,' said Hardcastle. He said goodbye to Miss Waterhouse and left.

He thought she'd hardly done herself justice by her last suggestion. On the other hand, if she believed that the girl had been seen entering her house, and that that had in fact been the case, then the suggestion that the girl had gone to No. 19 was quite an adroit one under the circumstances.

Hardcastle glanced at his watch and decided that he had still time to tackle the Cavendish Secretarial Bureau. It had, he knew, been reopened at two o'clock this afternoon. He might get some help from the girls there. And he would find Sheila Webb there too.

III

One of the girls rose at once as he entered the office.

'It's Detective Inspector Hardcastle, isn't it?' she said. 'Miss Martindale is expecting you.'

She ushered him into the inner office. Miss Martindale did not wait a moment before attacking him.

'It's disgraceful, Inspector Hardcastle, absolutely disgraceful! You must get to the bottom of this. You must get to the bottom of it *at once*. No dilly-dallying about. The police are supposed to give protection and that is what we need here at this office. *Protection*. I want protection for my girls and I mean to get it.'

'I'm sure, Miss Martindale, that –'

'Are you going to deny that two of my girls, *two* of them, have been victimized? There is clearly some irresponsible person about who has got some kind of – what do they call it nowadays – a fixture or a complex – about shorthand typists or secretarial bureaux. They are deliberately martyrizing this institute. First Sheila Webb was summoned by a heartless trick to find a dead body – the kind of thing that might send a nervous girl off her head – and now this. A perfectly nice harmless girl murdered in a telephone box. You must get to the bottom of it, Inspector.'

'There's nothing I want more than to get to the bottom of it, Miss Martindale. I've come to see if you can give me any help.'

'Help! What help can I give you? Do you think if I had any help, I wouldn't have rushed to you with it before now? You've got to find who killed that poor girl, Edna, and who played that heartless trick on Sheila. I'm strict with my girls, Inspector, I keep them up to their work and I won't allow them to be late or slipshod. But I don't stand for their being victimized or murdered. I intend to defend them, and I intend to see that people who are paid by the State to defend them do their work.' She glared at him and looked rather like a tigress in human form.

'Give us time, Miss Martindale,' he said.

'Time? Just because that silly child is dead, I suppose you think you've all the time in the world. The next thing that happens will be one of the other girls is murdered.'

'I don't think you need fear that, Miss Martindale.'

'I don't suppose you thought this girl was going to be killed when you got up this morning, Inspector. If so, you'd have taken a few precautions, I suppose, to look after her. And when one of my girls gets killed or is put in some terribly compromising position, you'll be equally surprised. The whole thing is extraordinary, *crazy*! You must admit yourself it's a crazy set-up. That is, if the things one reads in the paper were true. All those clocks for instance. They weren't mentioned this morning at the inquest, I noticed.'

'As little as possible was mentioned this morning, Miss Martindale. It was only an *adjourned* inquest, you know.'

'All I say is,' said Miss Martindale, glaring at him again, 'you must *do* something about it.'

'And there's nothing you can tell me, no hint Edna might have given to you? She didn't appear worried by anything, she didn't consult you?'

'I don't suppose she'd have consulted me if she *was* worried,' said Miss Martindale. 'But what had she to be worried about?'

That was exactly the question that Inspector Hardcastle would have liked to have answered for him, but he could see that it was not likely that he would get the answer from Miss Martindale. Instead he said:

'I'd like to talk to as many of your girls here as I can. I can see that it is not likely that Edna Brent would have confided any fears or worries to you, but she *might* have spoken of them to her fellow employees.'

'That's possible enough, I expect,' said Miss Martindale. 'They spend their time gossiping – these girls. The moment they hear my step in the passage outside all the typewriters begin to rattle. But what have they been doing just before? Talking. Chat, chat, chitter-chat!' Calming down a little, she said, 'There are only three of them in the office at present. Would you like to speak to them while you're here? The others are out on assignments. I can give you their names and their home addresses, if you like.'

'Thank you, Miss Martindale.'

'I expect you'd like to speak to them alone,' said Miss Martindale. 'They wouldn't talk as freely if I was standing there looking on. They'd have to admit, you see, that they *had* been gossiping and wasting their time.'

She got up from her seat and opened the door into the outer office.

'Girls,' she said, 'Detective Inspector Hardcastle wants to talk things over with you. You can stop work for the moment. Try and tell him anything you know that can help him to find out who killed Edna Brent.'

She went back into her own private office and shut the door firmly. Three startled girlish faces looked at the inspector. He summed them up quickly and superficially, but sufficiently to make up his mind as to the quality of the material with which he was to deal. A fair solid-looking girl with spectacles. Dependable, he thought, but not particularly bright. A rather rakish-looking brunette with the kind of hair-do that suggested she'd been out in a blizzard lately. Eyes that noticed things here, perhaps, but probably highly unreliable in her recollection of events. Everything would be suitably touched up. The third was a born giggler who would, he was sure, agree with whatever anyone else said.

He spoke quietly, informally.

'I suppose you've all heard what has happened to Edna Brent who worked here?'

Three heads nodded violently.

'By the way, how did you hear?'

They looked at each other as if trying to decide who should be spokesman. By common consent it appeared to be the fair girl, whose name, it seemed, was Janet.

'Edna didn't come to work at two o'clock, as she should have done,' she explained.

'And Sandy Cat was very annoyed,' began the dark-haired girl, Maureen, and then stopped herself. 'Miss Martindale, I mean.'

The third girl giggled. 'Sandy Cat is just what we call her,' she explained.

'And not a bad name,' the inspector thought.

'She's a perfect terror when she likes,' said Maureen. 'Fairly jumps on you. She asked if Edna had said anything to us about not coming back to the office this afternoon, and that she ought to have at least sent an excuse.'

The fair girl said: 'I told Miss Martindale that she'd been at the inquest with the rest of us, but that we hadn't seen her afterwards and didn't know where she'd gone.'

'That was true, was it?' asked Hardcastle. 'You've no idea where she did go when she left the inquest.'

'I suggested she should come and have some lunch with me,' said Maureen, 'but she seemed to have something on her mind. She said she wasn't sure that she'd bother to have any lunch. Just buy something and eat it in the office.'

'So she meant, then, to come back to the office?'

'Oh, yes, of course. We all knew we'd got to do that.'

'Have any of you noticed anything different about Edna Brent these last few days? Did she seem to you worried at all, as though she had something on her mind? Did she tell you anything to that effect? If there is anything at all you know, I must beg of you to tell me.'

They looked at each other but not in a conspiratorial manner. It seemed to be merely vague conjecture.

'She was always worried about something,' said Maureen. 'She gets things muddled up, and makes mistakes. She was a bit slow in the uptake.'

'Things always seemed to happen to Edna,' said the giggler. 'Remember when that stiletto heel of hers came off the other day? Just the sort of thing that *would* happen to Edna.'

'I remember,' said Hardcastle.

He remembered how the girl had stood looking down ruefully at the shoe in her hand.

'You know, I had a feeling something awful had happened this afternoon when Edna didn't get here at two o'clock,' said Janet. She nodded with a solemn face.

Hardcastle looked at her with some dislike. He always disliked people who were wise after the event. He was quite sure that the girl in question had thought nothing of the kind. Far more likely, he thought to himself, that she had said, 'Edna will catch it from Sandy Cat when she does come in.'

'When did you hear what had happened?' he asked again.

They looked at each other. The giggler flushed guiltily. Her eyes shot sideways to the door into Miss Martindale's private office.

'Well, I – er – I just slipped out for a minute,' she said. 'I wanted some pastries to take home and I knew they'd all be gone by the time we left. And when I got to the shop – it's on the corner and they know me quite well there – the woman said, "She worked at your place, didn't she, ducks?" and I said, "Who do you mean?" And then she said, "This girl they've just found dead in a telephone box." Oh, it gave me ever such a turn! So I came rushing back and I told the others and in the end we all said we'd have to tell Miss Martindale about it, and just at that moment she came bouncing out of her office and said to us, "*Now* what are you doing? Not a single typewriter going."'

The fair girl took up the saga.

'And I said, "Really it's not *our* fault. We've heard some terrible news about Edna, Miss Martindale."'

'And what did Miss Martindale say or do?'

'Well, she wouldn't believe it at first,' said the brunette. 'She said, "Nonsense. You've just been picking up some silly gossip in a shop. It must be some other girl. Why should it be Edna?" And she marched back into her room and rang up the police station and found out it *was* true.'

'But I don't see,' said Janet almost dreamily, 'I don't see why *anyone* should want to kill Edna.'

'It's not as though she had a boy or anything,' said the brunette.

All three looked at Hardcastle hopefully as though he could give them the answer to the problem. He sighed. There was nothing here for him. Perhaps one of the other girls might be more helpful. And there was Sheila Webb herself.

'Were Sheila Webb and Edna Brent particular friends?' he asked.

They looked at each other vaguely.

'Not special, I don't think.'

'Where is Miss Webb, by the way?'

He was told that Sheila Webb was at the Curlew Hotel, attending on Professor Purdy.

CHAPTER 19

Professor Purdy sounded irritated as he broke off dictating and answered the telephone.

'Who? What? You mean he is here *now*? Well, ask him if tomorrow will do? – Oh, very well – very well – Tell him to come up.'

'Always something,' he said with vexation. 'How can one ever be expected to do any serious work with these constant interruptions.' He looked with mild displeasure at Sheila Webb and said: 'Now where were we, my dear?'

Sheila was about to reply when there was a knock at the door. Professor Purdy brought himself back with some difficulty from the chronological difficulties of approximately three thousand years ago.

'Yes?' he said testily, 'yes, come in, what is it? I may say I mentioned particularly that I was *not* to be disturbed this afternoon.'

'I'm very sorry, sir, very sorry indeed that it has been necessary to do so. Good evening, Miss Webb.'

Sheila Webb had risen to her feet, setting aside her note-book. Hardcastle wondered if he only fancied that he saw sudden apprehension come into her eyes.

'Well, what is it?' said the professor again, sharply.

'I am Detective Inspector Hardcastle, as Miss Webb here will tell you.'

'Quite,' said the professor. 'Quite.'

'What I really wanted was a few words with Miss Webb.'

'Can't you wait? It is really *most* awkward at this moment. Most awkward. We were just at a critical point. Miss Webb will be disengaged in about a quarter of an hour – oh, well, perhaps half an hour. Something like that. Oh, dear me, is it six o'clock *already*?'

'I'm very sorry, Professor Purdy,' Hardcastle's tone was firm.

'Oh, very well, very well. What is it – some motoring offence, I suppose? How very officious these traffic wardens are. One insisted the other day that I had left my car four and a half hours at a parking meter. I'm sure that could not possibly be so.'

'It's a little more serious than a parking offence, sir.'

'Oh, yes. Oh, yes. And you don't have a car, do you, my dear?' He looked vaguely at Sheila Webb. 'Yes, I remember, you come here by bus. Well, Inspector, what is it?'

'It's about a girl called Edna Brent.' He turned to Sheila Webb. 'I expect you've heard about it.'

She stared at him. Beautiful eyes. Cornflower-blue eyes. Eyes that reminded him of someone.

'Edna Brent, did you say?' She raised her eyebrows. 'Oh, yes, I know her, of course. What about her?'

'I see the news hasn't got to you yet. Where did you lunch, Miss Webb?'

Colour came up in her cheeks.

'I lunched with a friend at the Ho Tung restaurant, if – if it's really any business of yours.'

'You didn't go on afterwards to the office?'

'To the Cavendish Bureau, you mean? I called in there and was told it had been arranged that I was to come straight here to Professor Purdy at half past two.'

'That's right,' said the professor, nodding his head. '*Half past two*. And we have been working here ever since. Ever since. Dear me, I should have ordered tea. I am very sorry, Miss Webb, I'm afraid you must have missed having your tea. You should have reminded me.'

'Oh, it didn't matter, Professor Purdy, it didn't matter at all.'

'Very remiss of me,' said the professor, 'very remiss. But there. I mustn't interrupt, since the inspector wants to ask you some questions.'

'So you don't know what's happened to Edna Brent?'

'*Happened* to her?' asked Sheila, sharply, her voice rising. 'Happened to her? What do you mean? Has she had an accident or something – been run over?'

'Very dangerous, all this speeding,' put in the professor.

'Yes,' said Hardcastle, 'something's happened to her.' He paused and then said, putting it as brutally as possible, 'She was strangled about half past twelve, in a telephone box.'

'In a telephone box?' said the professor, rising to the occasion by showing some interest.

Sheila Webb said nothing. She stared at him. Her mouth opened slightly, her eyes widened. 'Either this is the first you've heard of it or you're a damn' good actress,' thought Hardcastle to himself.

'Dear, dear,' said the professor. 'Strangled in a telephone box. That seems *very* extraordinary to me. Very extraordinary. Not the sort of place I would choose myself. I mean, if I were to do such a thing. No, indeed. Well, well. Poor girl. Most unfortunate for her.'

'Edna – *killed*! But why?'

'Did you know, Miss Webb, that Edna Brent was very anxious to see you the day before yesterday, that she came to your aunt's house, and waited for some time for you to come back?'

'My fault again,' said the professor guiltily. 'I kept Miss Webb very late that evening, I remember. Very late indeed. I really still feel very apologetic about it. You *must* always remind me of the time, my dear. You really must.'

'My aunt told me about that,' said Sheila, 'but I didn't know it was anything special. Was it? Was Edna in trouble of any kind?'

'We don't know,' said the inspector. 'We probably never shall know. Unless *you* can tell us?'

'*I* tell you? How should I know?'

'You might have had some idea, perhaps, of what Edna Brent wanted to see you about?'

She shook her head. 'I've no idea, no idea at all.'

'Hasn't she hinted anything to you, spoken to you in the office at all about whatever the trouble was?'

'No. No, indeed she hasn't – hadn't – I wasn't at the office at all yesterday. I had to go over to Landis Bay to one of our authors for the whole day.'

'You didn't think that she'd been worried lately?'

'Well, Edna always looked worried or puzzled. She had a very – what shall I say – diffident, uncertain kind of mind. I mean, she was never quite sure that what she thought of doing was the right thing or not. She missed out two whole pages in typing Armand Levine's book once and she was terribly worried about what to do then, because she'd sent it off to him before she realized what had happened.'

'I see. And she asked you all your advice as to what she should do about it?'

'Yes. I told her she'd better write a note to him quickly because people don't always start reading their typescript at once for correction. She could write and say what had happened and ask him not to complain to Miss Martindale. But she said she didn't quite like to do that.'

'She usually came and asked for advice when one of these problems arose?'

'Oh, yes, always. But the trouble was, of course, that we didn't always all agree as to what she should do. Then she got puzzled again.'

'So it would be quite natural that she should come to one of you if she *had* a problem? It happened quite frequently?'

'Yes. Yes, it did.'

'You don't think it might have been something more serious this time?'

'I don't suppose so. What sort of serious thing could it be?'

Was Sheila Webb, the inspector wondered, quite as much at ease as she tried to appear?'

'I don't know what she wanted to talk to me about,' she went on, speaking faster and rather breathlessly. 'I've no idea. And I certainly can't imagine why she wanted to come out to my aunt's house and speak to me *there*.'

'It would seem, wouldn't it, that it was something she did not want to speak to you about at the Cavendish Bureau? Before the other girls, shall we say? Something, perhaps, that she felt ought to be kept private between you and her. Could that have been the case?'

'I think it's very unlikely. I'm sure it couldn't have been at all like that.' Her breath came quickly.

'So you can't help me, Miss Webb?'

'No. I'm sorry. I'm *very* sorry about Edna, but I don't know anything that could help you.'

'Nothing that might have a connection or a tie-up with what happened on the 9th of September?'

'You mean – that man – that man in Wilbraham Crescent?'

'That's what I mean.'

'How could it have been? What *could* Edna have known about that?'

'Nothing very important, perhaps,' said the inspector, 'but *something*. And anything would help. *Anything*, however small.' He paused. 'The telephone box where she was killed was in Wilbraham Crescent. Does that convey anything to you, Miss Webb?'

'Nothing at all.'

'Were you yourself in Wilbraham Crescent today?'

'No, I wasn't,' she said vehemently. 'I never went near it. I'm beginning to feel that it's a horrible place. I wish I'd never gone there in the first place, I wish I'd never got mixed up in all this. Why did they send for me, ask for me specially, that day? Why did Edna have to get killed near there? You *must* find out, Inspector, you must, you *must*!'

'We mean to find out, Miss Webb,' the inspector said. There was a faint menace in his voice as he went on: 'I can assure you of that.'

'You're trembling, my dear,' said Professor Purdy. 'I think, I really *do* think that you ought to have a glass of sherry.'

CHAPTER 20
....
COLIN LAMB'S NARRATIVE

I reported to Beck as soon as I got to London.

He waved his cigar at me.

'There might have been something in that idiotic crescent idea of yours after all,' he allowed.

'I've turned up something at last, have I?'

'I won't go as far as that, but I'll just say that you *may* have. Our construction engineer, Mr Ramsay of 62, Wilbraham Crescent, is not all he seems. Some very curious assignments he's taken on lately. Genuine firms, but firms without much back history, and what history they have, rather a peculiar one. Ramsay went off at a minute's notice about five weeks ago. He went to Rumania.'

'That's not what he told his wife.'

'Possibly not, but that's where he went. And that's where he is now. We'd like to know a bit more about him. So you can stir your stumps, my lad, and get going. I've got all the visas ready for you, and a nice new passport. Nigel Trench it will be this time. Rub up your knowledge of rare plants in the Balkans. You're a botanist.'

'Any special instructions?'

'No. We'll give you your contact when you pick up your papers. Find out all you can about our Mr Ramsay.' He looked at me keenly. 'You don't sound as pleased as you might be.' He peered through the cigar smoke.

'It's always pleasant when a hunch pays off,' I said evasively.

'Right Crescent, wrong number. 61 is occupied by a perfectly blameless builder. Blameless in our sense, that is. Poor old Hanbury got the number wrong, but he wasn't far off.'

'Have you vetted the others? Or only Ramsay?'

'Diana Lodge seems to be as pure as Diana. A long history of cats. McNaughton was vaguely interesting. He's a retired professor, as you know. Mathematics. Quite brilliant, it seems. Resigned his Chair quite suddenly on the grounds of ill-health. I suppose that *may* be true – but he seems quite hale and hearty. He seems to have cut himself off from all his old friends, which is rather odd.'

'The trouble is,' I said, 'that we get to thinking that everything that *everybody* does is highly suspicious.'

'You may have got something there,' said Colonel Beck. 'There are times when I suspect *you*, Colin, of having changed over to the other side. There are times when I suspect *myself* of having changed over to the other side, and then having changed back again to this one! All a jolly mix-up.'

My plane left at ten p.m. I went to see Hercule Poirot first. This time he was drinking a *sirop de cassis* (Blackcurrant to you and me). He offered me some. I refused. George brought me whisky. Everything as usual.

'You look depressed,' said Poirot.

'Not at all. I'm just off abroad.'

He looked at me. I nodded.

'So it is like that?'

'Yes, it is like that.'

'I wish you all success.'

'Thank you. And what about you, Poirot, how are you getting along with your homework?'

'*Pardon?*'

'What about the Crowdean Clocks Murder – Have you leaned back, closed your eyes and come up with all the answers?'

'I have read what you left here with great interest,' said Poirot.

'Not much there, was there? I told you these particular neighbours were a wash-out –'

'On the contrary. In the case of at least *two* of these people very illuminating remarks were made –'

'Which of them? And what were the remarks?'

Poirot told me in an irritating fashion that I must read my notes carefully.

'You will see for yourself then – It leaps to the eye. The thing to do now is to talk to more neighbours.'

'There aren't any more.'

'There must be. *Somebody* has always seen something. It is an axiom.'

'It may be an axiom but it isn't so in this case. And I've got further details for you. There has been another murder.'

'Indeed? So soon? That is interesting. Tell me.'

I told him. He questioned me closely until he got every single detail out of me. I told him, too, of the postcard I had passed on to Hardcastle.

'Remember – four one three – or four thirteen,' he repeated. 'Yes – it is the same pattern.'

'What do you mean by that?'

Poirot closed his eyes.

'That postcard lacks only one thing, a fingerprint dipped in blood.'

I looked at him doubtfully.

'What do you really think of this business?'

'It grows much clearer – as usual, the murderer cannot let well alone.'

'But who's the murderer?'

Poirot craftily did not reply to that.

'Whilst you are away, you permit that I make a few researches?'

'Such as?'

'Tomorrow I shall instruct Miss Lemon to write a letter to an old lawyer friend of mine, Mr Enderby. I shall ask her to consult the marriage records at Somerset House. She will also send for me a certain overseas cable.'

'I'm not sure that's fair,' I objected. 'You're not just sitting and thinking.'

'That is exactly what I am doing! What Miss Lemon is to do, is to verify for me the answers that I have already arrived at. I ask not for information, but for *confirmation.*'

'I don't believe you know a thing, Poirot! This is all bluff. Why, nobody knows yet who the dead man is –'

'I know.'

'What's his name?'

'I have no idea. His name is not important. I know, if you can understand, not *who* he is but who he *is.*'

'A blackmailer?'

Poirot closed his eyes.

'A private detective?'

Poirot opened his eyes.

'I say to you a little quotation. As I did last time. And after that I say no more.'

He recited with the utmost solemnity:

'*Dilly, dilly, dilly – Come and be killed.*'

CHAPTER 21

Detective Inspector Hardcastle looked at the calendar on his desk. 20th September. Just over ten days. They hadn't been able to make as much progress as he would have liked because they were held up with that initial difficulty: the identification of a dead body. It had taken longer than he would have thought possible. All the leads seemed to have petered out, failed. The laboratory examination of the clothes had brought in nothing particularly helpful. The clothes themselves had yielded no clues. They were good quality clothes, export quality, not new but well cared for. Dentists had not helped, nor laundries, nor cleaners. The dead man remained a 'mystery man'! And yet, Hardcastle felt, he was not really a 'mystery man'. There was nothing spectacular or dramatic about him. He was just a man whom nobody had been able to come forward and recognize. That was the pattern of it, he was sure. Hardcastle sighed as he thought of the telephone calls and letters that had necessarily poured in after the publication in the public press of the photograph with the caption below it: DO YOU KNOW THIS MAN? Astonishing the amount of people who thought they did know this man. Daughters who wrote in a hopeful vein of fathers from whom they'd been estranged for years. An old woman of ninety was sure that the photograph in question was her son who had left home thirty years ago. Innumerable wives had been sure that it was a missing husband. Sisters had not been quite so anxious to claim brothers. Sisters, perhaps, were less hopeful thinkers. And, of course, there were vast numbers of people who had seen that very man in Lincolnshire, Newcastle, Devon, London, on a tube, in a bus, lurking on a pier, looking sinister at the corner of a road, trying to hide his face as he came out of the cinema. Hundreds of leads, the more promising of them patiently followed up and not yielding anything.

But today, the inspector felt slightly more hopeful. He looked again at the letter on his desk. Merlina Rival. He didn't like the Christian name very much. Nobody in their senses, he thought, could christen a child Merlina. No doubt it was a fancy name adopted by the lady herself. But he liked the feel of the letter. It was not extravagant or over-confident. It merely said that the writer thought it possible that the man in question was her husband from whom she had parted several years ago. She was due this morning. He pressed his buzzer and Sergeant Cray came in.

'That Mrs Rival not arrived yet?'

'Just come this minute,' said Cray. 'I was coming to tell you.'

'What's she like?'

'Bit theatrical-looking,' said Cray, after reflecting a moment. 'Lots of make-up – not very good make-up. Fairly reliable sort of woman on the whole, I should say.'

'Did she seem upset?'

'No. Not noticeably.'

'All right,' said Hardcastle, 'let's have her in.'

Cray departed and presently returned saying as he did so, 'Mrs Rival, sir.'

The inspector got up and shook hands with her. About fifty, he would judge, but from a long way away – quite a long way – she might have looked thirty. Close at hand, the result of make-up carelessly applied made her look rather older than fifty but on the whole he put it at fifty. Dark hair heavily hennaed. No hat, medium height and build, wearing a dark coat and skirt and a white blouse. Carrying a large tartan bag. A jingly bracelet or two, several rings. On the whole, he thought, making moral judgements on the basis of his experience, rather a good sort. Not over-scrupulous, probably, but easy to live with, reasonably generous, possibly kind. Reliable? That was the question. He wouldn't bank on it, but then he couldn't afford to bank on that kind of thing anyway.

'I'm very glad to see you, Mrs Rival,' he said, 'and I hope very much you'll be able to help us.'

'Of course, I'm not at all sure,' said Mrs Rival. She spoke apologetically. 'But it did look like Harry. Very much like Harry. Of course I'm quite prepared to find that it isn't, and I hope I shan't have taken up your time for nothing.'

She seemed quite apologetic about it.

'You mustn't feel that in any case,' said the inspector. 'We want help very badly over this case.'

'Yes, I see. I hope I'll be able to be sure. You see, it's a long time since I saw him.'

'Shall we get down a few facts to help us? When did you last see your husband?'

'I've been trying to get it accurate,' said Mrs Rival, 'all the way down in the train. It's terrible how one's memory goes when it comes to time. I believe I said in my letter to you it was about ten years ago, but it's more than that. D'you know, I think it's nearer fifteen. Time does go so fast. I suppose,' she added shrewdly, 'that one tends to think it's less than it is because it makes you yourself feel younger. Don't you think so?'

'I should think it could do,' said the inspector. 'Anyway you think it's roughly fifteen years since you saw him? When were you married?'

'It must have been about three years before that,' said Mrs Rival.

'And you were living then?'

'At a place called Shipton Bois in Suffolk. Nice town. Market town. Rather one-horse, if you know what I mean.'

'And what did your husband do?'

'He was an insurance agent. At least –' she stopped herself '– that's what he said he was.'

The inspector looked up sharply.

'You found out that that wasn't true?'

'Well, no, not exactly . . . Not at the time. It's only since then that I've thought that perhaps it wasn't true. It'd be an easy thing for a man to say, wouldn't it?'

'I suppose it would in certain circumstances.'

'I mean, it gives a man an excuse for being away from home a good deal.'

'Your husband was away from home a good deal, Mrs Rival?'

'Yes. I never thought about it much to begin with –'

'But later?'

She did not answer at once then she said:

'Can't we get on with it? After all, if it *isn't* Harry . . .'

He wondered what exactly she was thinking. There was strain in her voice, possibly emotion? He was not sure.

'I can understand,' he said, 'that you'd like to get it over. We'll go now.'

He rose and escorted her out of the room to the waiting car. Her nervousness when they got to where they were going, was no more than the nervousness of other people he had taken to this same place. He said the usual reassuring things.

'It'll be quite all right. Nothing distressing. It will only take a minute or two.'

The tray was rolled out, the attendant lifted the sheet. She stood staring down for a few moments, her breath came a little faster, she made a faint gasping sound, then she turned away abruptly. She said:

'It's Harry. Yes. He's a lot older, he looks different . . . But it's Harry.'

The inspector nodded to the attendant, then he laid his hand on her arm and took her out again to the car and they drove back to the station. He didn't say anything. He left her to pull herself together. When they got back to his room a constable came in almost at once with a tray of tea.

'There you are, Mrs Rival. Have a cup, it'll pull you together. Then we'll talk.'

'Thank you.'

She put sugar in the tea, a good deal of it, and gulped it down quickly.

'That's better,' she said. 'It's not that I *mind* really. Only – only, well it does turn you up a bit, doesn't it?'

'You think this man is definitely your husband?'

'I'm sure he is. Of course, he's much older, but he hasn't changed really so much. He always looked – well, very neat. Nice, you know, good class.'

Yes, thought Hardcastle, it was quite a good description. Good class. Presumably, Harry had looked much better class than he was. Some men did, and it was helpful to them for their particular purposes.

Mrs Rival said, 'He was very particular always about his clothes and everything. That's why, I think – they fell for him so easily. They never suspected anything.'

'Who fell for him, Mrs Rival?' Hardcastle's voice was gentle, sympathetic.

'Women,' said Mrs Rival. 'Women. That's where he was most of the time.'

'I see. And you got to know about it.'

'Well, I – I suspected. I mean, he was away such a lot. Of course I knew what men are like. I thought probably there *was* a girl from time to time. But it's no good asking men about these things. They'll lie to you and that's all. But I didn't think – I really didn't think that he made a *business* of it.'

'And did he?'

She nodded. 'I think he must have done.'

'How did you find out?'

She shrugged her shoulders.

'He came back one day from a trip he'd taken. To Newcastle, he *said*. Anyway, he came back and said he'd have to clear out quickly. He said that the game was up. There was some woman he'd got into trouble. A school teacher, he said, and there might be a bit of a stink about it. I asked him questions then. He didn't mind telling me. Probably he thought I knew more than I did. They used to fall for him, you know, easily enough, just as I did. He'd give her a ring and they'd get engaged – and then he'd say he'd invest money for them. They usually gave it him quite easily.'

'Had he tried the same thing with you?'

'He had, as a matter of fact, only I didn't give him any.'

'Why not? Didn't you trust him even then?'

'Well, I wasn't the kind that trusts anybody. I'd had what you'd call a bit of experience, you know, of men and their ways and the seamier side of things. Anyway, I didn't want him investing my money for me. What money I had I could invest for myself. Always keep your money in your hands and then you'll be sure you've got it! I've seen too many girls and women make fools of themselves.'

'When did he want you to invest money? Before you were married or after?'

'I think he suggested something of the kind beforehand, but I didn't respond and he sheered off the subject at once. Then, after we were married, he told me about some wonderful opportunity he'd got. I said, "Nothing doing." It wasn't only because I didn't trust him, but I'd often heard men say they're on to something wonderful and then it turned out that they'd been had for a mug themselves.'

'Had your husband ever been in trouble with the police?'

'No fear,' said Mrs Rival. 'Women don't like the world to know they've been duped. But this time, apparently, things might be different. This girl or woman, she was an educated woman. She wouldn't be as easy to deceive as the others may have been.'

'She was going to have a child?'

'Yes.'

'Had that happened on other occasions?'

'I rather think so.' She added, 'I don't honestly know what it was used to start him off in the first place. Whether it was *only* the money – a way of getting a living, as you might say – or whether he was the kind of man who just *had* to have women and he saw no reason why they shouldn't pay the expenses of his fun.' There was no bitterness now in her voice.

Hardcastle said gently:

'You were fond of him, Mrs Rival?'

'I don't know. I honestly don't know. I suppose I was in a way, or I wouldn't have married him . . .'

'You *were* – excuse me – married to him?'

'I don't even know that for sure,' said Mrs Rival frankly. 'We were married all right. In a church, too, but I don't know if he had married other women as well, using a different name, I suppose. His name was Castleton when I married him. I don't think it was his own name.'

'Harry Castleton. Is that right?'

'Yes.'

'And you lived in this place, Shipton Bois, as man and wife – for how long?'

'We'd been there about two years. Before that we lived near Doncaster. I don't say I was really surprised when he came back that day and told me. I think I'd known he was a wrong 'un for some time. One just couldn't believe it because, you see, he always seemed so respectable. So absolutely the gentleman!'

'And what happened then?'

'He said he'd got to get out of there quick and I said he could go and good riddance, that I wasn't standing for all this!' She added thoughtfully, 'I gave him ten pounds. It was all I had in the house. He said he was short of money . . . I've never seen or heard of him since. Until today. Or rather, until I saw his picture in the paper.'

'He didn't have any special distinguishing marks? Scars? An operation – or a fracture – anything like that?'

She shook her head.

'I don't think so.'

'Did he ever use the name Curry?'

'Curry? No, I don't think so. Not that I know of, anyway.'

Hardcastle slipped the card across the table to her.

'This was in his pocket,' he said.

'Still saying he's an insurance agent, I see,' she remarked. 'I expect he uses – used, I mean – all sorts of different names.'

'You say you've never heard of him for the last fifteen years?'

'He hasn't sent me a Christmas card, if that's what you mean,' said Mrs Rival, with a sudden glint of humour. 'I don't suppose he'd know where I was, anyway. I went back to the stage for a bit after we parted. On tour mostly. It wasn't much of a life and I dropped the name of Castleton too. Went back to Merlina Rival.'

'Merlina's – er – not your real name, I suppose?'

She shook her head and a faint, cheerful smile appeared on her face.

'I thought it up. Unusual. My real name's Flossie Gapp. Florence, I suppose I must have been christened, but everyone always calls me Flossie or Flo. Flossie Gapp. Not very romantic, is it?'

'What are you doing now? Are you still acting, Mrs Rival?'

'Occasionally,' said Mrs Rival with a touch of reticence. 'On and off, as you might say.'

Hardcastle was tactful.

'I see,' he said.

'I do odd jobs here and there,' she said. 'Help out at parties, a bit of hostess work, that sort of thing. It's not a bad life. At any rate you meet people. Things get near the bone now and again.'

'You've never heard anything of Henry Castleton since you parted – or about him?'

'Not a word. I thought perhaps he'd gone abroad – or was dead.'

'The only other thing I can ask you, Mrs Rival, is if you have any idea why Harry Castleton should have come to this neighbourhood?'

'No. Of course I've no idea. I don't even know what he's been doing all these years.'

'Would it be likely that he would be selling fraudulent insurance – something of that kind?'

'I simply don't know. It doesn't seem to me terribly likely. I mean, Harry was very careful of himself always. He wouldn't stick his neck out doing something that he might be brought to book for. I should have thought it more likely it was some racket with women.'

'Might it have been, do you think, Mrs Rival, some form of blackmail?'

'Well, I don't know . . . I suppose, yes, in a way. Some woman, perhaps, that wouldn't want something in her past raked up. He'd feel pretty safe over that, I think. Mind you, I don't say it is *so*, but it might be. I don't think he'd want very much money, you know. I don't think he'd drive anyone desperate, but he might just collect in a small way.' She nodded in affirmation. 'Yes.'

'Women liked him, did they?'

'Yes. They always fell for him rather easily. Mainly, I think, because he always seemed so good class and respectable. They were proud of having made a conquest of a man like that. They looked forward to a nice safe future with him. That's the nearest way I can put it. I felt the same way myself,' added Mrs Rival with some frankness.

'There's just one more small point,' Hardcastle spoke to his subordinate. 'Just bring those clocks in, will you?'

They were brought in on a tray with a cloth over them. Hardcastle whipped off the cloth and exposed them to Mrs Rival's gaze. She inspected them with frank interest and approbation.

'Pretty, aren't they? I like that one.' She touched the ormolu clock.

'You haven't seen any of them before? They don't mean anything to you?'

'Can't say they do. Ought they to?'

'Can you think of any connection between your husband and the name Rosemary?'

'Rosemary? Let me think. There was a red-head – No, her name was Rosalie. I'm afraid I can't think of anyone. But then I probably wouldn't know, would I? Harry kept his affairs very dark.'

'If you saw a clock with the hands pointing to four-thirteen –' Hardcastle paused.

Mrs Rival gave a cheerful chuckle.

'I'd think it was getting on for tea-time.'

Hardcastle sighed.

'Well, Mrs Rival,' he said, 'we are very grateful to you. The adjourned inquest, as I told you, will be the day after tomorrow. You won't mind giving evidence of identification, will you?'

'No. No, that will be all right. I'll just have to say who he was, is that it? I shan't have to go into things? I won't have to go into the manner of his life – anything of that kind?'

'That will not be necessary at present. All you will have to swear to is he is the man, Harry Castleton, to whom you were married. The exact date will be on record at Somerset House. Where were you married? Can you remember that?'

'Place called Donbrook – St Michael's, I think was the name of the church. I hope it isn't *more* than twenty years ago. That *would* make me feel I had one foot in the grave,' said Mrs Rival.

She got up and held out her hand. Hardcastle said goodbye. He went back to his desk and sat there tapping it with a pencil. Presently Sergeant Cray came in.

'Satisfactory?' he asked.

'Seems so,' said the inspector. 'Name of Harry Castleton – possibly an alias. We'll have to see what we can find out about the fellow. It seems likely that more than one woman might have reason to want revenge on him.'

'Looks so respectable, too,' said Cray.

'That,' said Hardcastle, 'seems to have been his principal stock-in-trade.'

He thought again about the clock with Rosemary written on it. Remembrance?

CHAPTER 22

COLIN LAMB'S NARRATIVE

I

'So you have returned,' said Hercule Poirot.

He placed a bookmarker carefully to mark his place in the book he was reading. This time a cup of hot chocolate stood on the table by his elbow. Poirot certainly has the most terrible taste in drinks! For once he did not urge me to join him.

'How are you?' I asked.

'I am disturbed. I am much disturbed. They make the renovations, the redecorations, even the structural alteration in these flats.'

'Won't that improve them?'

'It will improve them, yes – but it will be most vexatious to *me*. I shall have to disarrange myself. There will be a smell of paint!' He looked at me with an air of outrage.

Then, dismissing his difficulties with a wave of his hand, he asked:

'You have had the success, yes?'

I said slowly: 'I don't know.'

'Ah – it is like that.'

'I found out what I was sent to find out. I did not find the man himself. I myself do not know what was wanted. Information? Or a body?'

'Speaking of bodies, I read the account of the adjourned inquest at Crowdean. Wilful murder by a person or persons unknown. And your body has been given a name at last.'

I nodded.

'Harry Castleton, whoever he may be.'

'Identified by his wife. You have been to Crowdean?'

'Not yet. I thought of going down tomorrow.'

'Oh, you have some leisure time?'

'Not yet. I'm still on the job. My job takes me there –' I paused a moment and then said: 'I don't know much about what's been happening while I've been abroad – just the mere fact of identification – what do you think of it?'

Poirot shrugged his shoulders.

'It was to be expected.'

'Yes – the police are very good –'

'And wives are very obliging.'

'Mrs Merlina Rival! What a name!'

'It reminds me of something,' said Poirot. 'Now of what does it remind me?'

He looked at me thoughtfully but I couldn't help him. Knowing Poirot, it might have reminded him of anything.

'A visit to a friend – in a country house,' mused Poirot, then shook his head. 'No – it is so long ago.'

'When I come back to London, I'll come and tell you all I can find out from Hardcastle about Mrs Merlina Rival,' I promised.

Poirot waved a hand and said: 'It is not necessary.'

'You mean you know all about her already without being told?'

'No. I mean that I am not interested in her –'

'You're not interested – but why not? I don't get it.' I shook my head.

'One must concentrate on the essentials. Tell me instead of the girl called Edna – who died in the telephone box in Wilbraham Crescent.'

'I can't tell you more than I've told you already – I know nothing about the girl.'

'So all you know,' said Poirot accusingly, 'or all you can tell me is that the girl was a poor little rabbit, whom you saw in a typewriting office, where she had torn the heel off her shoe in a grating –' he broke off. 'Where was that grating, by the way?'

'Really, Poirot, how should I know?'

'You could have known if you had *asked*. How do you expect to know *anything* if you do not ask the proper questions?'

'But how can it matter *where* the heel came off?'

'It may not matter. On the other hand, we should know a definite spot where this girl had been, and that might connect up with a person she had seen there – or with an event of some kind which took place there.'

'You are being rather far-fetched. Anyway I do know it was quite near the office because she said so and that she bought a bun and hobbled back on her stocking feet to eat the bun in the office and she ended up by saying how on earth was she to get home like that?'

'Ah, and how *did* she get home?' Poirot asked with interest.

I stared at him.

'I've no idea.'

'Ah – but it is impossible, the way you never ask the right questions! As a result you know nothing of what is important.'

'You'd better come down to Crowdean and ask questions yourself,' I said, nettled.

'That is impossible at the moment. There is a most interesting sale of authors' manuscripts next week –'

'Still on your hobby?'

'But, yes, indeed.' His eyes brightened. 'Take the works of John Dickson Carr or Carter Dickson, as he calls himself sometimes –'

I escaped before he could get under way, pleading an urgent appointment. I was in no mood to listen to lectures on past masters of the art of crime fiction.

II

I was sitting on the front step of Hardcastle's house, and rose out of the gloom to greet him when he got home on the following evening.

'Hallo, Colin? Is that you? So you've appeared out of the blue again, have you?'

'If you called it out of the *red*, it would be much more appropriate.'

'How long have you been here, sitting on my front doorstep?'

'Oh, half an hour or so.'

'Sorry you couldn't get into the house.'

'I could have got into the house with perfect ease,' I said indignantly. 'You don't know our training!'

'Then why didn't you get in?'

'I wouldn't like to lower your prestige in any way,' I explained. 'A detective inspector of police would be bound to lose face if his house were entered burglariously with complete ease.'

Hardcastle took his keys from his pocket and opened the front door.

'Come on in,' he said, 'and don't talk nonsense.'

He led the way into the sitting-room, and proceeded to supply liquid refreshment.

'Say when.'

I said it, not too soon, and we settled ourselves with our drinks.

'Things are moving at last,' said Hardcastle. 'We've identified our corpse.'

'I know. I looked up the newspaper files – who was Harry Castleton?'

'A man of apparently the utmost respectability and who made his living by going through a form of marriage or merely getting engaged to well-to-do credulous women. They entrusted their savings to him, impressed by his superior knowledge of finance and shortly afterwards he quietly faded into the blue.'

'He didn't look that kind of man,' I said, casting my mind back.

'That was his chief asset.'

'Wasn't he ever prosecuted?'

'No – we've made inquiries but it isn't easy to get much information. He changed his name fairly often. And although they think at the Yard that Harry Castleton, Raymond Blair, Lawrence Dalton, Roger Byron were all one and the same person, they never could prove it. The women, you see, wouldn't tell. They preferred to lose their money. The man was really more of a name than anything – cropping up here and there – always the same pattern – but incredibly elusive. Roger Byron, say, would disappear from Southend, and a man called Lawrence Dalton would commence operations in Newcastle on Tyne. He was shy of being photographed – eluded his lady friends' desire to snapshot him. All this goes quite a long time back – fifteen to twenty years. About that time he seemed really to disappear. The rumour spread about that he was dead – but some people said he had gone abroad –'

'Anyway, nothing was heard of him until he turned up, dead, on Miss Pebmarsh's sitting-room carpet?' I said.

'Exactly.'

'It certainly opens up possibilities.'

'It certainly does.'

'A woman scorned who never forgot?' I suggested.

'It does happen, you know. There *are* women with long memories who don't forget –'

'And if such a woman were to go blind – a second affliction on top of the other –'

'That's only conjecture. Nothing to substantiate it as yet.'

'What was the wife like – Mrs – what was it? – Merlina Rival? What a name! It can't be her own.'

'Her real name is Flossie Gapp. The other she invented. More suitable for her way of life.'

'What is she? A tart?'

'Not a professional.'

'What used to be called, tactfully, a lady of easy virtue?'

'I should say she was a good-natured woman, and one willing to oblige her friends. Described herself as an ex-actress. Occasionally did "hostess" work. Quite likeable.'

'Reliable?'

'As reliable as most. Her recognition was quite positive. No hesitation.'

'That's a blessing.'

'Yes. I was beginning to despair. The amount of wives I've had here! I'd begun to think it's a wise woman who knows her own husband. Mind you, I think Mrs Rival might have known a little more about her husband than she lets on.'

'Has she herself ever been mixed up in criminal activities?'

'Not for the record. I think she may have had, perhaps still has, some shady friends. Nothing serious – just fiddles – that kind of thing.'

'What about the clocks?'

'Didn't mean a thing to her. I think she was speaking the truth. We've traced where they came from – Portobello Market. That's the ormolu and the Dresden china. And very little help *that* is! You know what it's like on a Saturday there. Bought by an American lady, the stall keeper *thinks* – but I'd say that's just a guess. Portobello Market is full of American tourists. His wife says it was a man bought them. She can't remember what he looked like. The silver one came from a silversmith in Bournemouth. A tall lady who wanted a present for her little girl! All she can remember about her is she wore a green hat.'

'And the fourth clock? The one that disappeared?'

'No comment,' said Hardcastle.

I knew just what he meant by that.

CHAPTER 23
COLIN LAMB'S NARRATIVE

The hotel I was staying in was a poky little place by the station. It served a decent grill but that was all that could be said for it. Except, of course, that it was cheap.

At ten o'clock the following morning I rang the Cavendish Secretarial Bureau and said that I wanted a shorthand typist to take down some letters and retype a business agreement. My name was Douglas Weatherby and I was staying at the Clarendon Hotel (extraordinarily tatty hotels always have grand names). Was Miss Sheila Webb available? A friend of mine had found her very efficient.

I was in luck. Sheila could come straight away. She had,

however, an appointment at twelve o'clock. I said that I would have finished with her well before that as I had an appointment myself.

I was outside the swing doors of the Clarendon when Sheila appeared. I stepped forward.

'Mr Douglas Weatherby at your service,' I said.

'Was it *you* rang up?'

'It was.'

'But you can't do things like that.' She looked scandalized.

'Why not? I'm prepared to pay the Cavendish Bureau for your services. What does it matter to them if we spend your valuable and expensive time in the Buttercup Café just across the street instead of dictating dull letters beginning "Yours of the 3rd prontissimo to hand," etc. Come on, let's go and drink indifferent coffee in peaceful surroundings.'

The Buttercup Café lived up to its name by being violently and aggressively yellow. Formica table tops, plastic cushions and cups and saucers were all canary colour.

I ordered coffee and scones for two. It was early enough for us to have the place practically to ourselves.

When the waitress had taken the order and gone away, we looked across the table at each other.

'Are you all right, Sheila?'

'What do you mean – am I all right?'

Her eyes had such dark circles under them that they looked violet rather than blue.

'Have you been having a bad time?'

'Yes – no – I don't know. I thought you had gone away?'

'I had. I've come back.'

'Why?'

'You know why.'

Her eyes dropped.

'I'm afraid of him,' she said after a pause of at least a minute, which is a long time.

'Who are you afraid of?'

'That friend of yours – that inspector. He thinks . . . he thinks I killed that man, and that I killed Edna too . . .'

'Oh, that's just his manner,' I said reassuringly. 'He always goes about looking as though he suspected everybody.'

'No, Colin, it's not like that at all. It's no good saying things just to cheer me up. He's thought that I had something to do with it right from the beginning.'

'My dear girl, there's no evidence against you. Just because you were there on the spot that day, because someone put you on the spot . . .'

She interrupted.

'He thinks I put myself on the spot. He thinks it's all a trumped-up story. He thinks that Edna in some way knew about it. He thinks that Edna recognized my voice on the telephone pretending to be Miss Pebmarsh.'

'*Was* it your voice?' I asked.

'No, of course it wasn't. I *never* made that telephone call. I've always told you so.'

'Look here, Sheila,' I said. 'Whatever you tell anyone else, you've got to tell *me* the truth.'

'So you don't believe a word I say!'

'Yes, I do. You *might* have made that telephone call that day for some quite innocent reason. Someone may have *asked* you to make it, perhaps told you it was part of a joke, and then you got scared and once you'd lied about it, you had to go on lying. Was it like that?'

'No, no, *no*! How often have I got to tell you?'

'It's all very well, Sheila, but there's *something* you're not telling me. I want you to trust me. If Hardcastle *has* got something against you, something that he hasn't told me about –'

She interrupted again.

'Do you expect him to tell you everything?'

'Well, there's no reason why he shouldn't. We're roughly members of the same profession.'

The waitress brought our order at this point. The coffee was as pale as the latest fashionable shade of mink.

'I didn't know you had anything to do with the police,' Sheila said, slowly stirring her coffee round and round.

'It's not exactly the police. It's an entirely different branch. But what I was getting at was, that if Dick *doesn't* tell me things he knows about you, it's for a special reason. It's because he thinks I'm interested in you. Well, I am interested in you. I'm more than that. I'm *for* you, Sheila, whatever you've done. You came out of that house that day scared to death. You were really scared. You weren't pretending. You couldn't have acted a part the way you did.'

'Of course I was scared. I was terrified.'

'Was it only finding the dead body that scared you? Or was there something else?'

'What else should there be?'

I braced myself.

'Why did you pinch that clock with Rosemary written across it?'

'What do you mean? Why should I pinch it?'

'I'm asking you *why* you did.'

'I never touched it.'

'You went back into that room because you'd left your gloves there, you said. You weren't wearing any gloves that day. A fine September day. I've never seen you wear gloves. All right then, you went back into that room and you picked up that clock. Don't lie to me about that. That's what you did, isn't it?'

She was silent for a moment or two, crumbling up the scones on her plate.

'All right,' she said in a voice that was almost a whisper. 'All right. I did. I picked up the clock and I shoved it into my bag and I came out again.'

'But why did you do it?'

'Because of the name – Rosemary. It's my name.'

'Your name is Rosemary, not Sheila?'

'It's both. Rosemary Sheila.'

'And that was enough, just that? The fact that you'd the same name as was written on one of those clocks?'

She heard my disbelief, but she stuck to it.

'I was scared, I tell you.'

I looked at her. Sheila was *my* girl – the girl I wanted – and wanted for keeps. But it wasn't any use having illusions about her. Sheila was a liar and probably always would be a liar. It was her way of fighting for survival – the quick easy glib denial. It was a child's weapon – and she'd probably never got out of using it. If I wanted Sheila I must accept her as she was – be at hand to prop up the weak places. We've all got our weak places. Mine were different from Sheila's but they were there.

I made up my mind and attacked. It was the only way.

'It was *your* clock, wasn't it?' I said. 'It belonged to you?'

She gasped.

'How did you know?'

'Tell me about it.'

The story tumbled out then in a helter-skelter of words. She'd had the clock nearly all her life. Until she was about six years old she'd always gone by the name of Rosemary – but she hated it and had insisted on being called Sheila. Lately the clock had been giving trouble. She'd taken it with her to leave at a clock-repairing shop not far from the Bureau. But she'd left it somewhere – in the bus, perhaps, or in the milk bar where she went for a sandwich at lunch time.

'How long was this before the murder at 19, Wilbraham Crescent?'

About a week, she thought. She hadn't bothered much, because the clock was old and always going wrong and it would really be better to get a new one.

And then:

'I didn't notice it at first,' she said. 'Not when I went into the room. And then I – found the dead man. I was paralysed. I straightened up after touching him and I just stood there staring and my clock was facing me on a table by the fire – *my* clock – and there was blood on my hand – and then she came in and I forgot everything because she was going to tread on him. And – and so – I bolted. To get away – that's all I wanted.'

I nodded.

'And later?'

'I began to think. She said *she* hadn't telephoned for me – then who had – who'd got me there and put *my* clock there? I – I said that about leaving gloves and – and stuffed it into my bag. I suppose it was – stupid of me.'

'You couldn't have done anything sillier,' I told her. 'In some ways, Sheila, you've got no sense at all.'

'But someone is trying to involve me. That postcard. It must have been sent by someone who knows I took that clock. And the postcard itself – the Old Bailey. If my father was a criminal –'

'What do you know about your father and mother?'

'My father and mother died in an accident when I was a baby.

That's what my aunt told me, what I've always been told. But she never speaks about them, she never tells me anything *about* them. Sometimes, once or twice when I asked, she's told me things about them that aren't the same as what she's told me before. So I've always known, you see, that there's something *wrong*.'

'Go on.'

'So I think that perhaps my father was some kind of criminal – perhaps even, a murderer. Or perhaps it was my mother. People don't say your parents are dead and can't or won't tell you anything about those parents, unless the real reason is something – something that they think would be too awful for you to know.'

'So you got yourself all worked up. It's probably quite simple. You may just have been an illegitimate child.'

'I thought of that, too. People do sometimes try and hide that kind of thing from children. It's very stupid. They'd much better just tell them the real truth. It doesn't matter as much nowadays. But the whole point is, you see, that I don't *know*. I don't know what's *behind* all this. Why was I called Rosemary? It's not a family name. It means remembrance, doesn't it?'

'Which could be a nice meaning,' I pointed out.

'Yes, it could . . . But I don't feel it was. Anyway, after the inspector had asked me questions that day, I began to think. Why had someone wanted to get me there? To get me there with a strange man who was dead? Or was it the dead man who had wanted me to meet him there? Was he, perhaps – my father, and he wanted me to do something for him? And then someone had come along and killed him instead. Or did someone want to make out from the beginning that it was I who had killed him? Oh, I was all mixed up, frightened. It seemed somehow as if everything was being made to point at *me*. Getting me there, and a dead man and my name – Rosemary – on my own clock that didn't belong there. So I got in a panic and did something that was stupid, as you say.'

I shook my head at her.

'You've been reading or typing too many thrillers and mystery stories,' I said accusingly. 'What about Edna? Haven't you any idea at all what she'd got into her head about you? Why did she come all the way to your house to talk to you when she saw you every day at the office?'

'I've no idea. She couldn't have thought *I* had anything to do with the murder. She couldn't.'

'Could it have been something she overheard and made a mistake about?'

'There was nothing, I tell you. Nothing!'

I wondered. I couldn't help wondering . . . Even now, I didn't trust Sheila to tell the truth.

'Have you got any personal enemies? Disgruntled young men, jealous girls, someone or other a bit unbalanced who might have it in for you?'

It sounded most unconvincing as I said it.

'Of course not.'

So there it was. Even now I wasn't sure about that clock. It was a fantastic story. 413. What did those figures mean? Why write them on a postcard with the word: REMEMBER unless they would mean *something* to the person to whom the postcard was sent?

I sighed, paid the bill and got up.

'Don't worry,' I said. (Surely the most fatuous words in the English or any other language.) 'The Colin Lamb Personal Service is on the job. You're going to be all right, and we're going to be married and live happily ever after on practically nothing a year. By the way,' I said, unable to stop myself, though I knew it would have been better to end on the romantic note, but the Colin Lamb Personal Curiosity drove me on. 'What have you actually done with that clock? Hidden it in your stocking drawer?'

She waited just a moment before she said:

'I put it in the dustbin of the house next door.'

I was quite impressed. It was simple and probably effective. To think of that had been clever of her. Perhaps I had underestimated Sheila.

CHAPTER 24
COLIN LAMB'S NARRATIVE

I

When Sheila had gone, I went across to the Clarendon, packed my bag and left it ready with the porter. It was the kind of hotel where they are particular about your checking out before noon.

Then I set out. My route took me past the police station, and after hesitating a moment, I went in. I asked for Hardcastle and he was there. I found him frowning down at a letter in his hand.

'I'm off again this evening, Dick,' I said. 'Back to London.'

He looked up at me with a thoughtful expression.

'Will you take a piece of advice from me?'

'No,' I said immediately.

He paid no attention. People never do when they want to give you advice.

'I should get away – and stay away – if you know what's best for you.'

'Nobody can judge what's best for anyone else.'

'I doubt that.'

'I'll tell you something, Dick. When I've tidied up my present assignment, I'm quitting. At least – I think I am.'

'Why?'

'I'm like an old-fashioned Victorian clergyman. I have Doubts.'

'Give yourself time.'

I wasn't sure what he meant by that. I asked him what he himself was looking so worried about.

'Read that.' He passed me the letter he had been studying.

Dear Sir,

I've just thought of something. You asked me if my husband had any identifying marks and I said he hadn't. But I was wrong. Actually he has a kind of scar behind his left ear. He cut himself with a razor when a dog we had jumped up at him, and he had to have it stitched up. It was so small and unimportant I never thought of it the other day.

Yours truly,
Merlina Rival

'She writes a nice dashing hand,' I said, 'though I've never really fancied purple ink. Did the deceased have a scar?'

'He had a scar all right. Just where she says.'

'Didn't she see it when she was shown the body?'

Hardcastle shook his head.

'The ear covers it. You have to bend the ear forward before you can see it.'

'Then that's all right. Nice piece of corroboration. What's eating you?'

Hardcastle said gloomily that this case was the devil! He asked if I would be seeing my French or Belgian friend in London.

'Probably. Why?'

'I mentioned him to the chief constable who says he remembers him quite well – that Girl Guide murder case. I was to extend a very cordial welcome to him if he is thinking of coming down here.'

'Not he,' I said. 'The man is practically a limpet.'

II

It was a quarter past twelve when I rang the bell at 62, Wilbraham Crescent. Mrs Ramsay opened the door. She hardly raised her eyes to look at me.

'What is it?' she said.

'Can I speak to you for a moment? I was here about ten days ago. You may not remember.'

She lifted her eyes to study me further. A faint frown appeared between her eyebrows.

'You came – you were with the police inspector, weren't you?'

'That's right, Mrs Ramsay. Can I come in?'

'If you want to, I suppose. One doesn't refuse to let the police in. They'd take a very poor view of it if you did.'

She led the way into the sitting-room, made a brusque gesture towards a chair and sat down opposite me. There had been a faint acerbity in her voice, but her manner now resumed a listlessness which I had not noted in it previously.

I said:

'It seems quiet here today . . . I suppose your boys have gone back to school?'

'Yes. It does make a difference.' She went on, 'I suppose you want to ask some more questions, do you, about this last murder? The girl who was killed in the telephone box.'

'No, not exactly that. I'm not really connected with the police, you know.'

She looked faintly surprised.

'I thought you were Sergeant – Lamb, wasn't it?'

'My name is Lamb, yes, but I work in an entirely different department.'

The listlessness vanished from Mrs Ramsay's manner. She gave me a quick, hard, direct stare.

'Oh,' she said, 'well, what is it?'

'Your husband is still abroad?'

'Yes.'

'He's been gone rather a long time, hasn't he, Mrs Ramsay? And gone rather a long way?'

'What do you know about it?'

'Well, he's gone beyond the Iron Curtain, hasn't he?'

She was silent for a moment or two, and then she said in a quiet, toneless voice:

'Yes. Yes, that's quite right.'

'Did you know he was going?'

'More or less.' She paused a minute and then said, 'He wanted me to join him there.'

'Had he been thinking of it for some time?'

'I suppose so. He didn't tell me until lately.'

'You are not in sympathy with his views?'

'I was once, I suppose. But you must know that already . . . You check up pretty thoroughly on things like that, don't you? Go back into the past, find out who was a fellow traveller, who was a party member, all that sort of thing.'

'You might be able to give us information that would be very useful to us,' I said.

She shook her head.

'No. I can't do that. I don't mean that I won't. You see, he never told me anything definite. I didn't want to know. I was sick and tired of the whole thing! When Michael told me that he was leaving this country, clearing out, and going to Moscow, it didn't really startle me. I had to decide then, what *I* wanted to do.'

'And you decided you were not sufficiently in sympathy with your husband's aims?'

'No, I wouldn't put it like that at all! My view is entirely personal. I believe it always is with women in the end, unless of course one is a fanatic. And then women can be *very* fanatical, but I wasn't. I've never been anything more than mildly left-wing.'

'Was your husband mixed up in the Larkin business?'

'I don't know. I suppose he might have been. He never told me anything or spoke to me about it.'

She looked at me suddenly with more animation.

'We'd better get it quite clear, Mr Lamb. Or Mr Wolf in Lamb's clothing, or whatever you are. I loved my husband, I might have been fond enough of him to go with him to Moscow, whether I agreed with what his politics were or not. He wanted me to bring the boys. I didn't want to bring the boys! It was as simple as that. And so I decided I'd have to stay with them. Whether I shall ever see Michael again or not I don't know. He's got to choose his way of life and I've got to choose mine, but I did know one thing quite definitely. After he talked about it to me. I wanted the boys brought up here in their own country. They're English. I want them to be brought up as ordinary English boys.'

'I see.'

'And that I think is all,' said Mrs Ramsay, as she got up.

There was now a sudden decision in her manner.

'It must have been a hard choice,' I said gently. 'I'm very sorry for you.'

I was, too. Perhaps the real sympathy in my voice got through to her. She smiled very slightly.

'Perhaps you really are . . . I suppose in your job you have to try and get more or less under people's skins, know what they're feeling and thinking. It's been rather a knockout blow for me, but I'm over the worst of it . . . I've got to make plans now, what to do, where to go, whether to stay here or go somewhere else. I shall have to get a job. I used to do secretarial work once. Probably I'll take a refresher course in shorthand and typing.'

'Well, don't go and work for the Cavendish Bureau,' I said.

'Why not?'

'Girls who are employed there seem to have rather unfortunate things happen to them.'

'If you think I know anything at all about that, you're wrong. I don't.'

I wished her luck and went. I hadn't learnt anything from her. I hadn't really thought I should. But one has to tidy up the loose ends.

III

Going out of the gate I almost cannoned into Mrs McNaughton. She was carrying a shopping-bag and seemed very wobbly on her feet.

'Let me,' I said and took it from her. She was inclined to clutch it from me at first, then she leaned her head forward, peering at me, and relaxed her grip.

'You're the young man from the police,' she said. 'I didn't recognize you at first.'

I carried the shopping-bag to her front door and she teetered beside me. The shopping-bag was unexpectedly heavy. I wondered what was in it. Pounds of potatoes?

'Don't ring,' she said. 'The door isn't locked.'

Nobody's door seemed ever to be locked in Wilbraham Crescent.

'And how are you getting on with things?' she asked chattily. 'He seems to have married very much below him.'

I didn't know what she was talking about.

'Who did – I've been away,' I explained.

'Oh, I see. *Shadowing* someone, I suppose. I meant that Mrs Rival. I went to the inquest. Such a *common*-looking woman. I must say she didn't seem much upset by her husband's death.'

'She hadn't see him for fifteen years,' I explained.

'Angus and I have been married for twenty years.' She sighed. 'It's a long time. And so much gardening now that he isn't at the university . . . It makes it difficult to know what to do with oneself.'

At that moment, Mr McNaughton, spade in hand, came round the corner of the house.

'Oh, you're back, my dear. Let me take the things –'

'Just put it in the kitchen,' said Mrs McNaughton to me swiftly – her elbow nudged me. 'Just the Cornflakes and the eggs and a melon,' she said to her husband, smiling brightly.

I deposited the bag on the kitchen table. It clinked.

Cornflakes, my foot! I let my spy's instincts take over. Under a camouflage of sheet gelatine were three bottles of whisky.

I understood why Mrs McNaughton was sometimes so bright and garrulous and why she was occasionally a little unsteady on her feet. And possibly why McNaughton had resigned his Chair.

It was a morning for neighbours. I met Mr Bland as I was going along the crescent towards Albany Road. Mr Bland seemed in very good form. He recognized me at once.

'How are you? How's crime? Got your dead body identified, I see. Seems to have treated that wife of his rather badly. By the way, excuse me, you're not one of the locals, are you?'

I said evasively I had come down from London.

'So the Yard was interested, was it?'

'Well –' I drew the word out in a noncommittal way.

'I understand. Mustn't tell tales out of school. You weren't at the inquest, though.'

I said I had been abroad.

'So have I, my boy. So have I!' He winked at me.

'Gay Paree?' I asked, winking back.

'Wish it had been. No, only a day trip to Boulogne.'

He dug me in the side with his elbow (quite like Mrs McNaughton!).

'Didn't take the wife. Teamed up with a very nice little bit. Blonde. Quite a hot number.'

'Business trip?' I said. We both laughed like men of the world.

He went on towards No. 61 and I walked on towards Albany Road.

I was dissatisfied with myself. As Poirot had said, there should have been more to be got out of the neighbours. It was positively unnatural that *nobody* should have seen anything! Perhaps Hardcastle had asked the wrong questions. But could I think of any better ones? As I turned into Albany Road I made a mental list of questions. It went something like this:

Mr Curry (Castleton) had been doped – When?
ditto had been killed – Where?

> *Mr Curry (Castleton) had been taken to No. 19 – How?*
> *Somebody must have seen something! – Who?*
> *ditto – What?*

I turned to the left again. Now I was walking along Wilbraham Crescent just as I had walked on September 9th. Should I call on Miss Pebmarsh? Ring the bell and say – well, what should I say?

Call on Miss Waterhouse? But what on earth could I say to *her*?

Mrs Hemming perhaps? It wouldn't much matter what one said to Mrs Hemming. She wouldn't be listening, and what *she* said, however haphazard and irrelevant, *might* lead to something.

I walked along, mentally noting the numbers as I had before. Had the late Mr Curry come along here, also noting numbers, until he came to the number he meant to visit?

Wilbraham Crescent had never looked primmer. I almost found myself exclaiming in Victorian fashion, 'Oh! if these stones could speak!' It was a favourite quotation in those days, so it seemed. But stones don't speak, no more do bricks and mortar, nor even plaster nor stucco. Wilbraham Crescent remained silently itself. Old-fashioned, aloof, rather shabby, and not given to conversation. Disapproving, I was sure, of itinerant prowlers who didn't even know what they were looking for.

There were few people about, a couple of boys on bicycles passed me, two women with shopping-bags. The houses themselves might have been embalmed like mummies for all the signs of life there were in them. I knew why that was. It was already, or close upon, the sacred hour of one, an hour sanctified by English traditions to the consuming of a midday meal. In one or two houses I could see through the uncurtained windows a group of one or two people round a dining table, but even that was exceedingly rare. Either the windows were discreetly screened with nylon netting, as opposed to the once popular Nottingham lace, or – which was far more probable – anyone who was at home was eating in the 'modern' kitchen, according to the custom of the 1960's.

It was, I reflected, a perfect hour of day for a murder. Had the murderer thought of that, I wondered? Was it part of the murderer's plan? I came at last to No. 19.

Like so many other moronic members of the populace I stood and stared. There was, by now, no other human being in sight. 'No neighbours,' I said sadly, 'no intelligent onlookers.'

I felt a sharp pain in my shoulder. I had been wrong. There *was* a neighbour here, all right, a very useful neighbour if the neighbour had only been able to speak. I had been leaning against the post of No. 20, and the same large orange cat I had seen before was sitting on the gate post. I stopped and exchanged a few words with him, first detaching his playful claw from my shoulder.

'If cats could speak,' I offered him as a conversational opening.

The orange cat opened his mouth, gave a loud melodious miaow.

'I know you can,' I said. 'I know you can speak just as well as I can. But you're not speaking my language. Were you sitting here that day? Did you see who went into that house or came out of it? Do you know all about what happened? I wouldn't put it past you, puss.'

The cat took my remark in poor part. He turned his back on me and began to switch his tail.

'I'm sorry, your Majesty,' I said.

He gave me a cold look over his shoulder and started industriously to wash himself. Neighbours, I reflected bitterly! There was no doubt about it, neighbours were in short supply in Wilbraham Crescent. What I wanted – what Hardcastle wanted – was some nice gossipy, prying, peering old lady with time hanging heavy on her hands. Always hoping to look out and see something scandalous. The trouble is that that kind of old lady seems to have died out nowadays. They are all sitting grouped together in Old Ladies' Homes with every comfort for the aged, or crowding up hospitals where beds are needed urgently for the really sick. The lame and the halt and the old didn't live in their own houses any more, attended by a faithful domestic or by some half-witted poor relation glad of a good home. It was a serious setback to criminal investigation.

I looked across the road. Why couldn't there be any neighbours there? Why couldn't there be a neat row of houses facing me instead of that great, inhuman-looking concrete block. A kind of human beehive, no doubt, tenanted by worker bees who were out all day and only came back in the evening to wash their smalls or make up their faces and go out to meet their young men. By contrast with the inhumanity of that block of flats I began almost to have a kindly feeling for the faded Victorian gentility of Wilbraham Crescent.

My eye was caught by a flash of light somewhere half-way up the building. It puzzled me. I stared up. Yes, there it came again. An open window and someone looking through it. A face slightly obliterated by something that was being held up to it. The flash of light came again. I dropped a hand into my pocket. I keep a good many things in my pockets, things that may be useful. You'd be surprised at what is useful sometimes. A little adhesive tape. A few quite innocent-looking instruments which are quite capable of opening most locked doors, a tin of grey powder labelled something which it isn't and an insufflator to use with it, and one or two other little gadgets which most people wouldn't recognize for what they are. Amongst other things I had a pocket bird watcher. Not a high-powered one but just good enough to be useful. I took this out and raised it to my eye.

There was a child at the window. I could see a long plait of hair lying over one shoulder. She had a pair of small opera glasses and she was studying me with what might have been flattering attention. As there was nothing else for her to look at, however, it might not be as flattering as it seemed. At that moment, however, there was another midday distraction in Wilbraham Crescent.

A very old Rolls-Royce came with dignity along the road driven by a very elderly chauffeur. He looked dignified but rather disgusted with life. He passed me with the solemnity of a whole procession of cars. My child observer, I noticed, was now training her opera glasses on him. I stood there, thinking.

It is always my belief that if you wait long enough, you're bound to have *some* stroke of luck. Something that you can't count upon and that you would never have thought of, but which just *happens*. Was it possible that this might be mine? Looking up again at the big square block, I noted carefully the position of the particular window I was interested in, counting from it to each end and up from the ground. Third floor. Then I walked along the street till I came to the entrance to the block of flats. It had a wide carriage-drive sweeping round the block with neatly spaced flower-beds at strategic positions in the grass.

It's always well, I find, to go through all the motions, so I stepped off the carriage-drive towards the block, looked up over my head as though startled, bent down to the grass, pretended to hunt about and finally straightened up, apparently transferring something from my hand to my pocket. Then I walked round the block until I came to the entrance.

At most times of the day I should think there was a porter here, but between the sacred hour of one and two the entrance hall was empty. There was a bell with a large sign above it, saying PORTER, but I did not ring it. There was an automatic lift and I went to it and pressed a button for the third floor. After that I had to check things pretty carefully.

It looks simple enough from the outside to place one particular room, but the inside of a building is confusing. However, I've had a good deal of practice at that sort of thing in my time, and I was fairly sure that I'd got the right door. The number on it, for better or worse, was No. 77. 'Well,' I thought, 'sevens are lucky. Here goes.' I pressed the bell and stood back to await events.

CHAPTER 25

COLIN LAMB'S NARRATIVE

I had to wait just a minute or two, then the door opened.

A big blonde Nordic girl with a flushed face and wearing gay-coloured clothing looked at me inquiringly. Her hands had been hastily wiped but there were traces of flour on them and there was a slight smear of flour on her nose so it was easy for me to guess what she had been doing.

'Excuse me,' I said, 'but you have a little girl here, I think. She dropped something out of the window.'

She smiled at me encouragingly. The English language was not as yet her strong point.

'I am sorry – what you say?'

'A child here – a little girl.'

'Yes, yes.' She nodded.

'Dropped something – out of the window.'

Here I did a little gesticulation.

'I picked it up and brought it here.'

I held out an open hand. In it was a silver fruit knife. She looked at it without recognition.

'I do not think – I have not seen . . .'

'You're busy cooking,' I said sympathetically.

'Yes, yes, I cook. That is so.' She nodded vigorously.

'I don't want to disturb you,' I said. 'If you let me just take it to her.'

'Excuse?'

My meaning seemed to come to her. She led the way across the hall and opened a door. It led into a pleasant sitting-room. By the window a couch had been drawn up and on it there was a child of about nine or ten years old, with a leg done up in plaster.

'This gentleman, he say you – you drop . . .'

At this moment, rather fortunately, a strong smell of burning came from the kitchen. My guide uttered an exclamation of dismay.

'Excuse, please excuse.'

'You go along,' I said heartily. 'I can manage this.'

She fled with alacrity. I entered the room, shut the door behind me and came across to the couch.

'How d'you do?' I said.

The child said, 'How d'you do?' and proceeded to sum me up with a long, penetrating glance that almost unnerved me. She was rather a plain child with straight mousy hair arranged in two plaits. She had a bulging forehead, a sharp chin and a pair of very intelligent grey eyes.

'I'm Colin Lamb,' I said. 'What's your name?'

She gave me the information promptly.

'Geraldine Mary Alexandra Brown.'

'Dear me,' I said, 'that's quite a bit of a name. What do they call you?'

'Geraldine. Sometimes Gerry, but I don't like that. And Daddy doesn't approve of abbreviations.'

One of the great advantages of dealing with children is that they have their own logic. Anyone of adult years would at once have asked me what I wanted. Geraldine was quite ready to enter into conversation without resorting to foolish questions. She was alone and bored and the onset of any kind of visitor was an agreeable novelty. Until I proved myself a dull and unamusing fellow, she would be quite ready to converse.

'Your daddy's out, I suppose,' I said.

She replied with the same promptness and fullness of detail which she had already shown.

'Cartinghaven Engineering Works, Beaverbridge,' she said. 'It's fourteen and three-quarter miles from here exactly.'

'And your mother?'

'Mummy's dead,' said Geraldine, with no diminution of cheerfulness. 'She died when I was a baby two months old. She was in a plane coming from France. It crashed. Everyone was killed.'

She spoke with a certain satisfaction and I perceived that to a child, if her mother *is* dead, it reflects a certain kudos if she has been killed in a complete and devastating accident.

'I see,' I said. 'So you have –' I looked towards the door.

'That's Ingrid. She comes from Norway. She's only been here a fortnight. She doesn't know any English to speak of yet. I'm teaching her English.'

'And she is teaching you Norwegian?'

'Not very much,' said Geraldine.

'Do you like her?'

'Yes. She's all right. The things she cooks are rather odd sometimes. Do you know, she likes eating raw fish.'

'I've eaten raw fish in Norway,' I said. 'It's very good sometimes.'

Geraldine looked extremely doubtful about that.

'She is trying to make a treacle tart today,' she said.

'That sounds good.'

'Umm – yes, I like treacle tart.' She added politely, 'Have you come to lunch?'

'Not exactly. As a matter of fact I was passing down below out there, and I think you dropped something out of the window.'

'Me?'

'Yes.' I advanced the silver fruit knife.

Geraldine looked at it, at first suspiciously and then with signs of approval.

'It's rather nice,' she said. 'What is it?'

'It's a fruit knife.'

I opened it.

'Oh, I see. You mean you can peel apples with it and things like that.'

'Yes.'

Geraldine sighed.

'It's not mine. I didn't drop it. What made you think I did?'

'Well, you were looking out of the window, and . . .'

'I look out of the window most of the time,' said Geraldine. 'I fell down and broke my leg, you see.'

'Hard luck.'

'Yes, wasn't it. I didn't break it in a very interesting way, though. I was getting out of a bus and it went on suddenly. It hurt rather at first and it ached a bit, but it doesn't now.'

'Must be rather dull for you,' I said.

'Yes, it is. But Daddy brings me things. Plasticine, you know, and books and crayons and jigsaw puzzles and things like that, but you get tired of *doing* things, so I spend a lot of time looking out of the window with these.'

She produced with enormous pride a small pair of opera glasses.

'May I look?' I said.

I took them from her, adjusted them to my eyes and looked out of the window.

'They're jolly good,' I said appreciatively.

They were indeed, excellent. Geraldine's daddy, if it had been he who supplied them, had not spared expense. It was astonishing how clearly you could see No. 19, Wilbraham Crescent and its neighbouring houses. I handed them back to her.

'They're excellent,' I said. 'First-class.'

'They're proper ones,' said Geraldine, with pride. 'Not just for babies and pretending.'

'No . . . I can see that.'

'I keep a little book,' said Geraldine.

She showed me.

'I write down things in it and the times. It's like train spotting,' she added. 'I've got a cousin called Dick and he does train spotting. We do motor-car numbers too. You know, you start at one and see how far you can get.'

'It's rather a good sport,' I said.

'Yes, it is. Unfortunately there aren't many cars come down this road so I've rather given that up for the time being.'

'I suppose you must know all about those houses down there, who lives in them and all that sort of thing.'

I threw it out casually enough but Geraldine was quick to respond.

'Oh, yes. Of course I don't know their real names, so I have to give them names of my own.'

'That must be rather fun,' I said.

'That's the Marchioness of Carrabas down there,' said Geraldine, pointing. 'That one with all the untidy trees. You know, like Puss In Boots. She has masses and masses of cats.'

'I was talking to one just now,' I said, 'an orange one.'

'Yes, I saw you,' said Geraldine.

'You must be very sharp,' I said. 'I don't expect you miss much, do you?'

Geraldine smiled in a pleased way. Ingrid opened the door and came in breathless.

'You are all right, yes?'

'We're quite all right,' said Geraldine firmly. 'You needn't worry, Ingrid.'

She nodded violently and pantomimed with her hands.

'You go back, you cook.'

'Very well, I go. It is nice that you have a visitor.'

'She gets nervous when she cooks,' explained Geraldine, 'when she's trying anything new, I mean. And sometimes we have meals very late because of that. I'm glad you've come. It's nice to have someone to distract you, then you don't think about being hungry.'

'Tell me more about the people in the houses there,' I said, 'and what you see. Who lives in the next house – the neat one?'

'Oh, there's a blind woman there. She's quite blind and yet she walks just as well as though she could see. The porter told me that. Harry. He's very nice, Harry is. He tells me a lot of things. He told me about the murder.'

'The murder?' I said, sounding suitably astonished.

Geraldine nodded. Her eyes shone with importance at the information she was about to convey.

'There was a murder in that house. I practically *saw* it.'

'How very interesting.'

'Yes, isn't it? I've never seen a murder before. I mean I've never seen a place where a murder happened.'

'What did you – er – see?'

'Well, there wasn't very much going on just then. You know, it's rather an empty time of day. The exciting thing was when somebody came rushing out of the house screaming. And then of course I knew something must have happened.'

'Who was screaming?'

'Just a woman. She was quite young, rather pretty really. She came out of the door and she screamed and she screamed. There was a young man coming along the road. She came out of the gate and sort of clutched him – like this.' She made a motion with her arms. She fixed me with a sudden glance. 'He looked rather like you.'

'I must have a double,' I said lightly. 'What happened next? This is very exciting.'

'Well, he sort of plumped her down. You know, on the ground there and then he went back into the house and the Emperor – that's the orange cat, I always call him the Emperor because he looks so proud – stopped washing himself and he looked quite surprised, and then Miss Pikestaff came out of her house – that's the one there, Number 18 – she came out and stood on the steps staring.'

'Miss Pikestaff?'

'I call her Miss Pikestaff because she's so plain. She's got a brother and she bullies him.'

'Go on,' I said with interest.

'And then all sorts of things happened. The man came out of the house again – are you sure it wasn't you?'

'I'm a very ordinary-looking chap,' I said modestly, 'there are lots like me.'

'Yes, I suppose that's true,' said Geraldine, somewhat unflatteringly. 'Well, anyway, this man, he went off down the road and telephoned from the call-box down there. Presently police began arriving.' Her eyes sparkled. 'Lots of police. And they took the dead body away in a sort of ambulance thing. Of course there were lots of people by that time, staring, you know. I saw Harry there, too. That's the porter from these flats. He told me about it afterwards.'

'Did he tell you who was murdered?'

'He just said it was a man. Nobody knew his name.'

'It's all very interesting,' I said.

I prayed fervently that Ingrid would not choose this moment to come in again with a delectable treacle tart or other delicacy.

'But go back a little, do. Tell me earlier. Did you see this man – the man who was murdered – did you see him arrive at the house?'

'No, I didn't. I suppose he must have been there all along.'

'You mean he lived there?'

'Oh, no, nobody lives there except Miss Pebmarsh.'

'So you know her real name?'

'Oh, yes, it was in the papers. About the murder. And the screaming girl was called Sheila Webb. Harry told me that the man who was murdered was called Mr Curry. That's a funny name, isn't it, like the thing you eat. And there was a second murder, you know. Not the same day – later – in the telephone box down the road. I can see it from here, just, but I have to get my head right out of the window and turn it round. Of course I didn't really *see* it, because I mean if I'd known it was going to happen, I would have looked out. But, of course, I didn't know it was going to happen, so I didn't. There were a lot of people that morning just standing there in the street, looking at the house opposite. I think that's rather stupid, don't you?'

'Yes,' I said, 'very stupid.'

Here Ingrid made her appearance once more.

'I come soon,' she said reassuringly. 'I come very soon now.'

She departed again. Geraldine said:

'We don't really want her. She gets worried about meals. Of course this is the only one she has to cook except breakfast. Daddy goes down to the restaurant in the evening and he has something sent up for me from there. Just fish or something. Not a real dinner.' Her voice sounded wistful.

'What time do you usually have your lunch, Geraldine?'

'My dinner, you mean? This is my dinner. I don't have dinner in the evening, it's supper. Well, I really have my dinner at any time Ingrid happens to have cooked it. She's rather funny about time.

She has to get breakfast ready at the right time because Daddy gets so cross, but midday dinner we have any time. Sometimes we have it at twelve o'clock and sometimes I don't get it till two. Ingrid says you don't have meals at a particular time, you just have them when they're ready.'

'Well, it's an easy idea,' I said. 'What time did you have your lunch – dinner, I mean – on the day of the murder?'

'That was one of the twelve o'clock days. You see, Ingrid goes out that day. She goes to the cinema or to have her hair done and a Mrs Perry comes and keeps me company. She's terrible, really. She pats one.'

'Pats one?' I said, slightly puzzled.

'You know, on the head. Says things like "dear little girlie". She's not,' said Geraldine, 'the kind of person you can have *any* proper conversation with. But she brings me sweets and that sort of thing.'

'How old are you, Geraldine?'

'I'm ten. Ten and three months.'

'You seem to me very good at intelligent conversation,' I said.

'That's because I have to talk to Daddy a lot,' said Geraldine seriously.

'So you had your dinner early on that day of the murder?'

'Yes, so Ingrid could get washed up and go off just after one.'

'Then you were looking out of the window that morning, watching people.'

'Oh, yes. Part of the time. Earlier, about ten o'clock, I was doing a crossword puzzle.'

'I've been wondering whether you could possibly have seen Mr Curry arriving at the house?'

Geraldine shook her head.

'No. I didn't. It is rather odd, I agree.'

'Well, perhaps he got there quite early.'

'He didn't go to the front door and ring the bell. I'd have seen him.'

'Perhaps he came in through the garden. I mean through the other side of the house.'

'Oh, no,' said Geraldine. 'It backs on other houses. They wouldn't like anyone coming through their garden.'

'No, no, I suppose they wouldn't.'

'I wish I knew what he'd looked like,' said Geraldine.

'Well, he was quite old. About sixty. He was clean-shaven and he had on a dark grey suit.'

Geraldine shook her head.

'It sounds terribly ordinary,' she said with disapprobation.

'Anyway,' I said, 'I suppose it's difficult for you to remember one day from another when you're lying here and always looking.'

'It's not at all difficult.' She rose to the challenge. 'I can tell you everything about that morning. I know when Mrs Crab came and when she left.'

'That's the daily cleaning woman, is it?'

'Yes. She scuttles, just like a crab. She's got a little boy. Sometimes she brings him with her, but she didn't that day. And then Miss Pebmarsh goes out about ten o'clock. She goes to teach children at a blind school. Mrs Crab goes away about twelve. Sometimes she has a parcel with her that she didn't have when she came. Bits of butter, I expect, and cheese, because Miss Pebmarsh can't see. I know particularly well what happened that day because you see Ingrid and I were having a little quarrel so she wouldn't talk to me. I'm teaching her English and she wanted to know how to say "until we meet again". She had to tell it me in German. *Auf Wiedersehen.* I know that because I once went to Switzerland and people said that there. And they said *Grüss Gott,* too. That's rude if you say it in English.'

'So what did you tell Ingrid to say?'

Geraldine began to laugh a deep malicious chuckle. She started to speak but her chuckles prevented her, but at last she got it out.

'I told her to say "Get the hell out of here"! So she said it to Miss Bulstrode next door and Miss Bulstrode was *furious.* So Ingrid found out and was very cross with me and we didn't make friends until nearly tea-time the next day.'

I digested this information.

'So you concentrated on your opera glasses.'

Geraldine nodded.

'So that's how I know Mr Curry didn't go in by the front door. I think perhaps he got in somehow in the night and hid in an attic. Do you think that's likely?'

'I suppose anything really is possible,' I said, 'but it doesn't seem to me very probable.'

'No,' said Geraldine, 'he would have got hungry, wouldn't he? And he couldn't have asked Miss Pebmarsh for breakfast, not if he was hiding from her.'

'And nobody came to the house?' I said. 'Nobody at all? Nobody in a car – a tradesman – callers?'

'The grocer comes Mondays and Thursdays,' said Geraldine, 'and the milk comes at half past eight in the morning.'

The child was a positive encyclopaedia.

'The cauliflowers and things Miss Pebmarsh buys herself. Nobody called at all except the laundry. It was a new laundry,' she added.

'A new laundry?'

'Yes. It's usually the Southern Downs Laundry. Most people have the Southern Downs. It was a new laundry that day – the Snowflake Laundry. I've never seen the Snowflake Laundry. They must have just started.'

I fought hard to keep any undue interest out of my voice. I didn't want to start her romancing.

'Did it deliver laundry or call for it?' I asked.

'Deliver it,' said Geraldine. 'In a great big basket, too. Much bigger than the usual one.'

'Did Miss Pebmarsh take it in?'

'No, of course not, she'd gone out again.'

'What time was this, Geraldine?'

'1.35 exactly,' said Geraldine. 'I wrote it down,' she added proudly.

She motioned towards a small note-book and opening it pointed with a rather dirty forefinger to an entry. 1.35 *laundry came. No. 19.*

'You ought to be at Scotland Yard,' I said.

'Do they have women detectives? I'd quite like that. I don't mean police women. I think police women are silly.'

'You haven't told me exactly what happened when the laundry came.'

'Nothing happened,' said Geraldine. 'The driver got down, opened the van, took out this basket and staggered along round the side of the house to the back door. I expect he couldn't get in. Miss Pebmarsh probably locks it, so he probably left it there and came back.'

'What did he look like?'

'Just ordinary,' said Geraldine.

'Like me?' I asked.

'Oh, no, much older than you,' said Geraldine, 'but I didn't really see him properly because he drove up to the house – this way.' She pointed to the right. 'He drew up in front of 19 although he was on the wrong side of the road. But it doesn't matter in a street like this. And then he went in through the gate bent over the basket. I could only see the back of his head and when he came out again he was rubbing his face. I expect he found it a bit hot and trying, carrying that basket.'

'And then he drove off again?'

'Yes. Why do you think it so interesting?'

'Well, I don't know,' I said. 'I thought perhaps *he* might have seen something interesting.'

Ingrid flung the door open. She was wheeling a trolley.

'We eat dinner now,' she said, nodding brightly.

'Goody,' said Geraldine, 'I'm starving.'

I got up.

'I must be going now,' I said. 'Goodbye, Geraldine.'

'Goodbye. What about this thing?' She picked up the fruit knife. 'It's not mine.' Her voice became wistful. 'I wish it were.'

'It looks as though it's nobody's in particular, doesn't it?'

'Would that make it treasure trove, or whatever it is?'

'Something of the kind,' I said. 'I think you'd better hang on to it. That is, hang on to it until someone else claims it. But I don't think,' I said truthfully, 'that anybody will.'

'Get me an apple, Ingrid,' said Geraldine.

'Apple?'

'*Pomme! Apfel!*'

She did her linguistic best. I left them to it.

CHAPTER 26

Mrs Rival pushed open the door of the Peacock's Arms and made a slightly unsteady progress towards the bar. She was murmuring under her breath. She was no stranger to this particular hostelry and was greeted quite affectionately by the barman.

'How do, Flo,' he said, 'how's tricks?'

'It's not right,' said Mrs Rival. 'It's not fair. No, it's not right. I know what I'm talking about, Fred, and I say it's not right.'

'Of course it isn't right,' said Fred, soothingly. 'What is, I'd like to know? Want the usual, dear?'

Mrs Rival nodded assent. She paid and began to sip from her glass. Fred moved away to attend to another customer. Her drink cheered Mrs Rival slightly. She still muttered under her breath but with a more good-humoured expression. When Fred was near her once more she addressed him again with a slightly softened manner.

'All the same, I'm not going to put up with it,' she said. 'No, I'm not. If there's one thing I can't bear, it's deceit. I don't stand for deceit, I never did.'

'Of course you didn't,' said Fred.

He surveyed her with a practised eye. 'Had a good few already,' he thought to himself. 'Still, she can stand a couple more, I expect. Something's upset her.'

'Deceit,' said Mrs Rival. 'Prevari – prevari – well, you know the word I mean.'

'Sure I know,' said Fred.

He turned to greet another acquaintance. The unsatisfactory performance of certain dogs came under review. Mrs Rival continued to murmur.

'I don't like it and I won't stand for it. I shall say so. People can't think they can go around treating me like that. No, indeed they can't. I mean, it's not right and if you don't stick up for yourself, who'll stick up for you? Give me another, dearie,' she added in a louder voice.

Fred obliged.

'I should go home after that one, if I were you,' he advised.

He wondered what had upset the old girl so much. She was usually fairly even-tempered. A friendly soul, always good for a laugh.

'It'll get me in bad, Fred, you see,' she said. 'When people ask you to do a thing, they should tell you all about it. They should tell you what it means and what they're doing. Liars. Dirty liars, that's what I say. And I won't stand for it.'

'I should cut along home, if I were you,' said Fred, as he observed a tear about to trickle down the mascaraed splendour. 'Going to come on to rain soon, it is, and rain hard, too. Spoil that pretty hat of yours.'

Mrs Rival gave one faint appreciative smile.

'I always was fond of cornflowers,' she said. 'Oh, dear me, I don't know *what* to do, I'm sure.'

'I should go home and have a nice kip,' said the barman, kindly.

'Well, perhaps, but –'

'Come on, now, you don't want to spoil that hat.'

'That's very true,' said Mrs Rival. 'Yes, that's very true. That's a very prof – profumed – no I don't mean that – what do I mean?'

'Profound remark of yours, Fred.'

'Thank you very much.'

'You're welcome,' said Fred.

Mrs Rival slipped down from her high seat and went not too steadily towards the door.

'Something seems to have upset old Flo tonight,' said one of the customers.

'She's usually a cheerful bird – but we all have our ups and downs,' said another man, a gloomy-looking individual.

'If anyone had told me,' said the first man, 'that Jerry Grainger would come in fifth, way behind Queen Caroline, I wouldn't have believed it. If you ask me, there's been hanky-panky. Racing's not straight nowadays. Dope the horses, they do. All of 'em.'

Mrs Rival had come out of the Peacock's Arms. She looked up uncertainly at the sky. Yes, perhaps it *was* going to rain. She walked along the street, hurrying slightly, took a turn to the left, a turn to the right and stopped before a rather dingy-looking house. As she took out a key and went up the front steps a voice spoke from the area below, and a head poked round a corner of the door and looked up at her.

'Gentleman waiting for you upstairs.'

'For me?'

Mrs Rival sounded faintly surprised.

'Well, if you call him a gentleman. Well dressed and all that, but not quite Lord Algernon Vere de Vere, I would say.'

Mrs Rival succeeded in finding the keyhole, turned the key in it and entered.

The house smelled of cabbage and fish and eucalyptus. The latter smell was almost permanent in this particular hall. Mrs Rival's landlady was a great believer in taking care of her chest in winter weather and began the good work in mid-September. Mrs Rival climbed the stairs, aiding herself with the banisters. She pushed open the door on the first floor and went in, then she stopped dead and took a step backwards.

'Oh,' she said, 'it's you.'

Detective Inspector Hardcastle rose from the chair where he was sitting.

'Good evening, Mrs Rival.'

'What do *you* want?' asked Mrs Rival with less *finesse* than she would normally have shown.

'Well, I had to come up to London on duty,' said Inspector Hardcastle, 'and there were just one or two things I thought I'd like to take up with you, so I came along on the chance of finding you. The – er – the woman downstairs seemed to think you might be in before long.'

'Oh,' said Mrs Rival. 'Well, I don't see – well –'

Inspector Hardcastle pushed forward a chair.

'Do sit down,' he said politely.

Their positions might have been reversed, he the host and she the guest. Mrs Rival sat down. She stared at him very hard.

'What did you mean by one or two things?' she said.

'Little points,' said Inspector Hardcastle, 'little points that come up.'

'You mean – about Harry?'

'That's right.'

'Now look here,' said Mrs Rival, a slight belligerence coming into her voice; at the same time as an aroma of spirits came clearly to Inspector Hardcastle's nostrils. 'I've *had* Harry. I don't want to think of him any more. I came forward, didn't I, when I saw his picture in the paper? I came and told you about him. It's all a long time ago and I don't want to be reminded of it. There's nothing more I can tell you. I've told you everything I could remember and now I don't want to hear any more about it.'

'It's quite a small point,' said Inspector Hardcastle. He spoke gently and apologetically.

'Oh, very well,' said Mrs Rival, rather ungraciously. 'What is it? Let's have it.'

'You recognized the man as your husband or the man you'd gone through a form of marriage with about fifteen years ago. That is right, is it not?'

'I should have thought that by this time you would have known exactly how many years ago it was.'

'Sharper than I thought,' Inspector Hardcastle said to himself. He went on.

'Yes, you're quite right there. We looked it up. You were married on May 15th, 1948.'

'It's always unlucky to be a May bride, so they say,' said Mrs Rival gloomily. 'It didn't bring me any luck.'

'In spite of the years that have elapsed, you were able to identify your husband quite easily.'

Mrs Rival moved with some slight uneasiness.

'He hadn't aged much,' she said, 'always took care of himself, Harry did.'

'And you were able to give us some additional identification. You wrote to me, I think, about a scar.'

'That's right. Behind his left ear it was. Here,' Mrs Rival raised a hand and pointed to the place.

'Behind his *left* ear?' Hardcastle stressed the word.

'Well –' she looked momentarily doubtful, 'yes. Well, I think so. Yes I'm sure it was. Of course one never does know one's left from one's right in a hurry, does one? But, yes, it was the left side of his neck. Here.' She placed her hand on the same spot again.

'And he did it shaving, you say?'

'That's right. The dog jumped up on him. A very bouncy dog we had at the time. He kept rushing in – affectionate dog. He jumped up on Harry and he'd got the razor in his hand, and it went in deep. It bled a lot. It healed up but he never lost the mark.' She was speaking now with more assurance.

'That's a very valuable point, Mrs Rival. After all, one man sometimes looks very like another man, especially when a good many years have passed. But to find a man closely resembling your husband who has a scar in the identical place – well that makes the identification very nice and safe, doesn't it? It seems that we really have something to go on.'

'I'm glad you're pleased,' said Mrs Rival.

'And this accident with the razor happened – when?'

Mrs Rival considered a moment.

'It must have been about – oh, about six months after we were married. Yes, that was it. We got the dog that summer, I remember.'

'So it took place about October or November, 1948. Is that right?'

'That's right.'

'And after your husband left you in 1951 . . .'

'He didn't so much leave me as I turned him out,' said Mrs Rival with dignity.

'Quite so. Whichever way you like to put it. Anyway, after you turned your husband out in 1951 you never saw him again until you saw his picture in the paper?'

'Yes. That's what I told you.'

'And you're quite sure about that, Mrs Rival?'

'Of course I'm sure. I never set eyes on Harry Castleton since that day until I saw him dead.'

'That's odd, you know,' said Inspector Hardcastle, 'that's very odd.'

'Why – what do you mean?'

'Well, it's a very curious thing, scar tissue. Of course, it wouldn't mean much to you or me. A scar's a scar. But doctors can tell a lot from it. They can tell roughly, you know, how long a man has *had* a scar.'

'I don't know what you're getting at.'

'Well, simply this, Mrs Rival. According to our police surgeon and to another doctor whom we consulted, that scar tissue behind your husband's ear shows very clearly that the wound in question could not be older than about five to six years ago.'

'Nonsense,' said Mrs Rival. 'I don't believe it. I – nobody can tell. Anyway that wasn't when . . .'

'So you see,' proceeded Hardcastle in a smooth voice, 'if that wound made a scar only five or six years ago, it means that if the man *was* your husband he had no scar at the time when he left you in 1951.'

'Perhaps he didn't. But anyway it was Harry.'

'But you've never seen him since, Mrs Rival. So if you've never seen him since, how would you know that he had acquired a scar five or six years ago?'

'You mix me up,' said Mrs Rival, 'you mix me up badly. Perhaps it wasn't as long ago as 1948 – You can't remember all these things. Anyway, Harry had that scar and I know it.'

'I see,' said Inspector Hardcastle and he rose to his feet. 'I think you'd better think over that statement of yours very carefully, Mrs Rival. You don't want to get into trouble, you know.'

'How do you mean, get into trouble?'

'Well,' Inspector Hardcastle spoke almost apologetically, 'perjury.'

'Perjury. Me!'

'Yes. It's quite a serious offence in law, you know. You could get into trouble, even go to prison. Of course, you've not been on oath in a coroner's court, but you may have to swear to this evidence of yours in a proper court sometime. Then – well, I'd like you to think it over very carefully, Mrs Rival. It may be that somebody – suggested to you that you should tell us this story about the scar?'

Mrs Rival got up. She drew herself to her full height, her eyes flashed. She was at that moment almost magnificent.

'I never heard such nonsense in my life,' she said. 'Absolute nonsense. I try and do my duty. I come and help you, I tell you all I can remember. If I've made a mistake I'm sure it's natural enough. After all I meet a good many – well, gentlemen friends, and one may get things a little wrong sometimes. But I don't think I *did* make a mistake. That man was Harry and Harry had a scar behind his left ear, I'm quite sure of it. And now, perhaps, Inspector Hardcastle, you'll go away instead of coming here and insinuating that I've been telling lies.'

Inspector Hardcastle got up promptly.

'Good night, Mrs Rival,' he said. 'Just think it over. That's all.'

Mrs Rival tossed her head. Hardcastle went out of the door. With his departure, Mrs Rival's attitude altered immediately. The fine defiance of her attitude collapsed. She looked frightened and worried.

'Getting me into this,' she murmured, 'getting me into this. I'll – I'll not go on with it. I'll – I'll – I'm not going to get into trouble for anybody. Telling me things, lying to me, deceiving me. It's monstrous. Quite monstrous. I shall say so.'

She walked up and down unsteadily, then finally making up her mind, she took an umbrella from the corner and went out again. She walked along to the end of the street, hesitated at a call-box, then went on to a post office. She went in there, asked for change and went into one of the call-boxes. She dialled Directory and asked for a number. She stood there waiting till the call came through.

'Go ahead please. Your party is on the line.'

She spoke.

'Hallo . . . oh, it's you. Flo here. No, I know you told me not to but I've had to. You've not been straight with me. You never told me what I was getting into. You just said it would be awkward for you if this man was identified. I didn't dream for a moment that I would get mixed up in a murder . . . Well, of course you'd say that, but at any rate it wasn't what you told me . . . Yes, I do. I think you *are* mixed up in it in some way . . . Well, I'm not going to stand for it, I tell you . . . There's something about being an – ac – well, you know the word I mean – accessory, something like that. Though I always thought that was costume jewellery. Anyway, it's something like being a something after the fact, and I'm frightened, I tell you . . . telling me to write and tell them that bit about a scar. Now it seems he'd only got that scar a year or two ago and here's me swearing he had it when he left me years ago . . . And that's perjury and I might go to prison for it. Well, it's no good your trying to talk me round . . . No . . . Obliging someone is one thing . . . Well I know . . . I know you paid me for it. And not very much either . . . Well, all right, I'll listen to you, but I'm not going to . . . All right, all right, I'll keep quiet . . . What did you say? . . . How much? . . . That's a lot of money.

How do I know that you've got it even . . . Well, yes, of course it would make a difference. You swear you didn't have anything to do with it? – I mean with killing anyone . . . No, well I'm sure you wouldn't. Of course, I see that . . . Sometimes you get mixed up with a crowd of people – and they go further than you would and it's not your fault . . . You always make things sound so plausible . . . You always did . . . Well, all right, I'll think it over but it's got to be soon . . . Tomorrow? What time? . . . Yes . . . yes, I'll come but no cheque. It might bounce . . . I don't know really that I ought to go on getting myself mixed up in things even . . . all right. Well, if you say so . . . Well, I didn't mean to be nasty about it . . . All right then.'

She came out of the post office weaving from side to side of the pavement and smiling to herself.

It was worth risking a little trouble with the police for that amount of money. It would set her up nicely. And it wasn't very much risk really. She'd only got to say she'd forgotten or couldn't remember. Lots of women couldn't remember things that had only happened a year ago. She'd say she got mixed up between Harry and another man. Oh, she could think up lots of things to say.

Mrs Rival was a naturally mercurial type. Her spirits rose as much now as they had been depressed before. She began to think seriously and intently of the first things she would spend the money on . . .

CHAPTER 27

COLIN LAMB'S NARRATIVE

I

'You don't seem to have got much out of that Ramsay woman?' complained Colonel Beck.

'There wasn't much to get.'

'Sure of that?'

'Yes.'

'She's not an active party?'

'No.'

Beck gave me a searching glance.

'Satisfied?' he asked.

'Not really.'

'You hoped for more?'

'It doesn't fill the gap.'

'Well – we'll have to look elsewhere . . . give up crescents – eh?'

'Yes.'

'You're very monosyllabic. Got a hangover?'

'I'm no good at this job,' I said slowly.

'Want me to pat you on the head and say "There, there"?'

In spite of myself I laughed.

'That's better,' said Beck. 'Now then, what's it all about? Girl trouble, I suppose.'

I shook my head. 'It's been coming on for some time.'

'As a matter of fact I've noticed it,' said Beck unexpectedly. 'The world's in a confusing state nowadays. The issues aren't clear as they used to be. When discouragement sets in, it's like dry rot. Whacking great mushrooms bursting through the walls! If that's so, your usefulness to us is over. You've done some first-class work, boy. Be content with that. Go back to those damned seaweeds of yours.'

He paused and said: 'You really *like* the beastly things, don't you?'

'I find the whole subject passionately interesting.'

'I should find it repulsive. Splendid variation in nature, isn't there? Tastes, I mean. How's that patent murder of yours? I bet you the girl did it.'

'You're wrong,' I said.

Beck shook his finger at me in an admonitory and avuncular manner.

'What I say to you is: "Be prepared." And I don't mean it in the Boy Scout sense.'

I walked down Charing Cross Road deep in thought.

At the tube station I bought a paper.

I read that a woman, supposed to have collapsed in the rush hour at Victoria Station yesterday, had been taken to hospital. On arrival there she was found to have been stabbed. She had died without recovering consciousness.

Her name was Mrs Merlina Rival.

II

I rang Hardcastle.

'Yes,' he said in answer to my questions. 'It's just as they say.'

His voice sounded hard and bitter.

'I went to see her night before last. I told her her story about the scar just wouldn't jell. That the scar tissue was comparatively recent. Funny how people slip up. Just by trying to overdo things. Somebody paid that woman to identify the corpse as being that of her husband, who ran out on her years ago.

'Very well she did it, too! I believed her all right. And then whoever it was tried to be a little too clever. If she remembered that unimportant little scar as an *afterthought*, it would carry conviction and clinch the identification. If she had plumped out with it straight away, it might have sounded a bit too glib.'

'So Merlina Rival was in it up to the neck?'

'Do you know, I rather doubt that. Suppose an old friend or acquaintance goes to her and says: "Look here, I'm in a bit of a spot. A chap I've had business dealings with has been murdered. If they identify him and all our dealings come to light, it will be absolute disaster. But if you were to come along and say it's that husband of yours, Harry Castleton, who did a bunk years ago, then the whole case will peter out."'

'Surely she'd jib at that – say it was too risky?'

'If so, that someone would say: "What's the risk? At the worst, you've made a mistake. Any woman can make a mistake after fifteen years." And probably at that point a nice little sum would have been mentioned. And she says O.K. she'll be a sport! and do it.'

'With no suspicions?'

'She wasn't a suspicious woman. Why, good lord, Colin, every time we catch a murderer there are people who've known him well, and simply can't believe he could do anything like that!'

'What happened when you went up to see her?'

'I put the wind up her. After I left, she did what I expected she'd do – tried to get in touch with the man or woman who'd got her into this. I had a tail on her, of course. She went to a post office and put through a call from an automatic call-box. Unfortunately, it wasn't the box I'd expected her to use at the end of her own street. She had to get change. She came out of the call-box looking pleased with herself. She was kept under observation, but nothing of interest happened until yesterday evening. She went to Victoria Station and took a ticket to Crowdean. It was half past six, the rush hour. She wasn't on her guard. She thought she was going to meet whoever it was at Crowdean. But the cunning devil was a step ahead of her. Easiest thing in the world to gang up behind someone in a crowd, and press the knife in . . . Don't suppose she even knew she had been stabbed. People don't, you know. Remember that case of Barton in the Levitti Gang robbery? Walked the length of a street before he fell down dead. Just a sudden sharp pain – then you think you're all right again. But you're not. You're dead on your feet although you don't know it.'

He finished up: 'Damn and damn and damn!'

'Have you – checked on – anybody?'

I had to ask. I couldn't help myself.

His reply came swift and sharp.

'The Pebmarsh woman was in London yesterday. She did some business for the Institute and returned to Crowdean by the 7.40 train.' He paused. 'And Sheila Webb took up a typescript to check over with a foreign author who was in London on his way to New York. She left the Ritz Hotel at 5.30 approx. and took in a cinema – alone – before returning.'

'Look here, Hardcastle,' I said, 'I've got something for you. Vouched for by an eye witness. A laundry van drew up at 19, Wilbraham Crescent at 1.35 on September the 9th. The man who drove it delivered a big laundry basket at the back door of the house. It was a particularly large laundry basket.'

'Laundry? What laundry?'

'The Snowflake Laundry. Know it?'

'Not off-hand. New laundries are always starting up. It's an ordinary sort of name for a laundry.'

'Well – you check up. A *man* drove it – and a *man* took the basket into the house –'

Hardcastle's voice came suddenly, alert with suspicion.

'Are you making this up, Colin?'

'No. I told you I've got an eye witness. Check up, Dick. Get on with it.'

I rang off before he could badger me further.

I walked out from the box and looked at my watch. I had a good deal to do – and I wanted to be out of Hardcastle's reach whilst I did it. I had my future life to arrange.

CHAPTER 28

COLIN LAMB'S NARRATIVE

I

I arrived at Crowdean at eleven o'clock at night, five days later. I went to the Clarendon Hotel, got a room, and went to bed. I'd been tired the night before and I overslept. I woke up at a quarter to ten.

I sent for coffee and toast and a daily paper. It came and with it a large square note addressed to me with the words BY HAND in the top left-hand corner.

I examined it with some surprise. It was unexpected. The paper was thick and expensive, the superscription neatly printed.

After turning it over and playing with it, I finally opened it.

Inside was a sheet of paper. Printed on it in large letters were the words:

CURLEW HOTEL 11.30
ROOM 413
(Knock three times)

I stared at it, turned it over in my hand – what was all this?

I noted the room number – 413 – the same as the clocks. A coincidence? Or *not* a coincidence.

I had thoughts of ringing the Curlew Hotel. Then I thought of ringing Dick Hardcastle. I didn't do either.

My lethargy was gone. I got up, shaved, washed, dressed and walked along the front to the Curlew Hotel and got there at the appointed time.

The summer season was pretty well over now. There weren't many people about inside the hotel.

I didn't make any inquiries at the desk. I went up in the lift to the fourth floor and walked along the corridor to No. 413.

I stood there for a moment or two: then, feeling a complete fool, I knocked three times . . .

A voice said, 'Come in.'

I turned the handle, the door wasn't locked. I stepped inside and stopped dead.

I was looking at the last person on earth I would have expected to see.

Hercule Poirot sat facing me. He beamed at me.

'*Une petite surprise, n'est-ce pas?*' he said. 'But a pleasant one, I hope.'

'Poirot, you old fox,' I shouted. 'How did *you* get here?'

'I got here in a Daimler limousine – most comfortable.'

'But what are you *doing* here?'

'It was most vexing. They insisted, positively insisted on the redecoration of my apartment. Imagine my difficulty. What can I do? Where can I go?'

'Lots of places,' I said coldly.

'Possibly, but it is suggested to me by my doctor that the air of the sea will be good for me.'

'One of those obliging doctors who finds out where his patient wants to go, and advises him to go there! Was it you who sent me *this*?' I brandished the letter I had received.

'Naturally – who else?'

'Is it a coincidence that you have a room whose number is 413?'

'It is not a coincidence. I asked for it specially.'

'Why?'

Poirot put his head on one side and twinkled at me.

'It seemed to be appropriate.'

'And knocking three times?'

'I could not resist it. If I could have enclosed a sprig of rosemary it would have been better still. I thought of cutting my finger and putting a bloodstained fingerprint on the door. But enough is enough! I might have got an infection.'

'I suppose this is second childhood,' I remarked coldly. 'I'll buy you a balloon and a woolly rabbit this afternoon.'

'I do not think you enjoy my surprise. You express no joy, no delight at seeing me.'

'Did you expect me to?'

'*Pourquoi pas?* Come, let us be serious, now that I have had my little piece of foolery. I hope to be of assistance. I have called up the chief constable who has been of the utmost amiability, and at this moment I await your friend, Detective Inspector Hardcastle.'

'And what are you going to say to him?'

'It was in my mind that we might all three engage in conversation.'

I looked at him and laughed. He might call it conversation – but I knew who was going to do the talking.

Hercule Poirot!

II

Hardcastle had arrived. We had had the introduction and the greetings. We were now settled down in a companionable fashion, with Dick occasionally glancing surreptitiously at Poirot with the air of a man at the Zoo studying a new and surprising acquisition. I doubt if he had ever met anyone quite like Hercule Poirot before!

Finally, the amenities and politeness having been observed, Hardcastle cleared his throat and spoke.

'I suppose, M. Poirot,' he said cautiously, 'that you'll want to see – well, the whole set-up for yourself? It won't be exactly easy –' He hesitated. 'The chief constable told me to do everything I could for you. But you must appreciate that there are difficulties, questions that may be asked, objections. Still, as you have come down here specially –'

Poirot interrupted him – with a touch of coldness.

'I came here,' he said, 'because of the reconstruction and decoration of my apartment in London.'

I gave a horse laugh and Poirot shot me a look of reproach.

'M. Poirot doesn't have to go and see things,' I said. 'He has always insisted that you can do it all from an arm-chair. But that's not quite true, is it, Poirot? Or why have you come here?'

Poirot replied with dignity.

'I said that it was not necessary to be the foxhound, the bloodhound, the tracking dog, running to and fro upon the scent. But I will admit that for the chase a dog *is* necessary. A retriever, my friend. A good retriever.'

He turned towards the inspector. One hand twirled his moustache in a satisfied gesture.

'Let me tell you,' he said, 'that I am not like the English, obsessed with dogs. I, personally, can live without the dog. But I accept, nevertheless, your ideal of the dog. The man loves and respects his dog. He indulges him, he boasts of the intelligence and sagacity of his dog to his friends. Now figure to yourself, the opposite may also come to pass! The dog is fond of his master. He indulges that master! He, too, boasts of his master, boasts of his master's sagacity and intelligence. And as a man will rouse himself when he does not really want to go out, and take his dog for a walk because the dog enjoys the walk so much, so will the dog endeavour to give his master what that master pines to have.

'It was so with my kind young friend Colin here. He came to see me, not to ask for help with his own problem; that he was confident that he could solve for himself, and has, I gather, done so. No, he felt concern that I was unoccupied and lonely so he brought to me a problem that he felt would interest me and give me something to work upon. He challenged me with it – challenged me to do what I had so often told him it was possible to do – sit still in my chair and – in due course – resolve that problem. It may be, I suspect it is, that there was a *little* malice, just a small harmless amount, behind that challenge. He wanted, let us say, to prove to me that it was not so easy after all. *Mais oui, mon ami*, it is true, that! You wanted to mock yourself at me – just a little! I do not reproach you. All I say is, you did not know your Hercule Poirot.'

He thrust out his chest and twirled his moustaches.

I looked at him and grinned affectionately.

'All right then,' I said. 'Give us the answer to the problem – if you know it.'

'But of course I know it!'

Hardcastle stared at him incredulously.

'Are you saying you *know* who killed the man at 19, Wilbraham Crescent?'

'Certainly.'

'And also who killed Edna Brent?'

'Of course.'

'You know the identity of the dead man?'

'I know who he must be.'

Hardcastle had a very doubtful expression on his face. Mindful of the chief constable, he remained polite. But there was scepticism in his voice.

'Excuse me, M. Poirot, you claim that you know who killed three people. And why?'

'Yes.'

'You've got an open and shut case?'

'That, no.'

'All you mean is that you have a hunch,' I said, unkindly.

'I will not quarrel with you over a word, *mon cher* Colin. All I say is, I *know*!'

Hardcastle sighed.

'But you see, M. Poirot, *I* have to have evidence.'

'Naturally, but with the resources you have at your disposal, it will be possible for you, I think, to get that evidence.'

'I'm not so sure about that.'

'Come now, Inspector. If you know – really *know* – is not that the first step? Can you not, nearly always, go on from there?'

'Not always,' said Hardcastle with a sigh. 'There are men walking about today who ought to be in gaol. They know it and we know it.'

'But that is a very small percentage, is it not –'

I interrupted.

'All right. All right. *You know* . . . Now let *us* know too!'

'I perceive you are still sceptical. But first let me say this: To be *sure* means that when the right solution is reached, everything falls into place. You perceive that *in no other way* could things have happened.'

'For the love of Mike,' I said, 'get on with it! I grant you all the points you've made.'

Poirot arranged himself comfortably in his chair and motioned to the inspector to replenish his glass.

'One thing, *mes amis*, must be clearly understood. To solve any problem one must have the *facts*. For that one needs the dog, the dog who is a retriever, who brings the pieces one by one and lays them at –'

'At the feet of the master,' I said. 'Admitted.'

'One cannot from one's seat in a chair solve a case solely

from reading about it in a newspaper. For one's facts must be accurate, and newspapers are seldom, if ever, accurate. They report something happened at four o'clock when it was a quarter past four, they say a man had a sister called Elizabeth when actually he had a sister-in-law called Alexandra. And so on. But in Colin here, I have a dog of remarkable ability – an ability, I may say, which has taken him far in his own career. He has always had a remarkable memory. He can repeat to you, even several days later, conversations that have taken place. He can repeat them accurately – that is, not transposing them, as nearly all of us do, to what the impression made on *him* was. To explain roughly – he would not say, "And at twenty past eleven the post came" instead of describing what actually happened, namely a knock on the front door and someone coming into the room with letters in their hand. All this is very important. It means that he heard what *I* would have heard if I had been there and seen what I would have seen.'

'Only the poor dog hasn't made the necessary deductions?'

'So, as far as can be, I have the facts – I am "in the picture". It is your war-time term, is it not? To "put one in the picture". The thing that struck me first of all, when Colin recounted the story to me, was its highly *fantastic* character. Four clocks, each roughly an hour ahead of the right time, and all introduced into the house without the knowledge of the owner, or so she *said*. For we must never, must we, believe what we are told, until such statements have been carefully checked?'

'Your mind works the way that mine does,' said Hardcastle approvingly.

'On the floor lies a dead man – a respectable-looking elderly man. Nobody knows who he is (or again so they *say*). In his pocket is a card bearing the name of Mr R. H. Curry, 7, Denvers Street. Metropolis Insurance Company. But there is no Metropolis Insurance Company. There is no Denvers Street and there seems to be no such person as Mr Curry. That is negative evidence, but it *is* evidence. We now proceed further. Apparently at about ten minutes to two a secretarial agency is rung up, a Miss Millicent Pebmarsh asks for a stenographer to be sent to 19, Wilbraham Crescent at three o'clock. It is particularly asked that a Miss Sheila Webb should be sent. Miss Webb is sent. She arrives there at a few minutes before three; goes, according to instructions, into the sitting-room, finds a dead man on the floor and rushes out of the house screaming. She rushes into the arms of a young man.'

Poirot paused and looked at me. I bowed.

'Enter our young hero,' I said.

'You see,' Poirot pointed out. 'Even you cannot resist a farcical melodramatic tone when you speak of it. The whole thing is melodramatic, fantastic and completely unreal. It is the kind of thing that could occur in the writings of such people as Garry Gregson, for instance. I may mention that when my young friend arrived with this tale I was embarking on a course of thriller writers who had plied their craft over the last sixty years. Most interesting. One comes almost to regard actual crimes in the light of fiction. That is to say that if I observe that a dog has not barked when he should bark, I say to myself, "Ha! A Sherlock Holmes crime!" Similarly, if the corpse is found in a sealed room, naturally I say, "Ha! A Dickson Carr case!" Then there is my friend Mrs Oliver. If I were to find – but I will say no more. You catch my meaning? So here is the setting of a crime in such wildly improbable circumstances that one feels at once, "This book is not true to life. All this is quite unreal." But alas, that will not do here, for this *is* real. It *happened*. That gives one to think furiously, does it not?'

Hardcastle would not have put it like that, but he fully agreed with the sentiment, and nodded vigorously. Poirot went on:

'It is, as it were, the opposite of Chesterton's, "Where would you hide a leaf? In a forest. Where would you hide a pebble? On a beach." Here there is excess, fantasy, melodrama! When I say to myself in imitation of Chesterton, "Where does a middle-aged woman hide her fading beauty?" I do not reply, "Amongst other faded middle-aged faces." Not at all. She hides it under make-up, under rouge and mascara, with handsome furs wrapped round her and with jewels round her neck and hanging in her ears. You follow me?'

'Well –' said the inspector, disguising the fact that he didn't.

'Because then, you see, people will look at the furs and the jewels and the *coiffure* and the *haute couture*, and they will not observe what the *woman herself* is like at all! So I say to myself

– and I say to my friend Colin – Since this murder has so many fantastic trappings to distract one it must really be very simple. Did I not?'

'You did,' I said. 'But I still don't see how you can possibly be right.'

'For that you must wait. So, then, we discard the *trappings* of the crime and we go to the *essentials*. A man has been killed. Why has he been killed? And who is he? The answer to the first question will obviously depend on the answer to the second. And until you get the right answer to these two questions you cannot possibly proceed. He could be a blackmailer, or a confidence trickster, or somebody's husband whose existence was obnoxious or dangerous to his wife. He could be one of a dozen things. The more I heard, the more everybody seems to agree that he *looked* a perfectly ordinary, well-to-do, reputable elderly man. And suddenly I think to myself, "You say this should be a simple crime? Very well, make it so. Let this man be *exactly what he seems* – a well-to-do respectable elderly man."' He looked at the inspector. 'You see?'

'Well –' said the inspector again, and paused politely.

'So here is someone, an ordinary, pleasant, elderly man whose removal is necessary to *someone*. To whom? And here at last we can narrow the field a little. There is local knowledge – of Miss Pebmarsh and her habits, of the Cavendish Secretarial Bureau, of a girl working there called Sheila Webb. And so I say to my friend Colin: "The neighbours. Converse with them. Find out about them. Their backgrounds. But above all, engage in conversation. Because in conversation you do not get merely the answers to questions – in ordinary conversational prattle things slip out. People are on their guard when the subject may be dangerous to them, but the moment ordinary talk ensues they relax, they succumb to the relief of speaking the truth, which is always very much easier than lying. And so they let slip one little fact which unbeknown to them makes all the difference.'

'An admirable exposition,' I said. 'Unfortunately it didn't happen in this case.'

'But, *mon cher*, it *did*. One little sentence of inestimable importance.'

'What?' I demanded. 'Who said it? When?'

'In due course, *mon cher.*'

'You were saying, M. Poirot?' The inspector politely drew Poirot back to the subject.

'If you draw a circle round Number 19, anybody within it *might* have killed Mr Curry. Mrs Hemming, the Blands, the McNaughtons, Miss Waterhouse. But more important still, there are those already positioned on the spot. Miss Pebmarsh who could have killed him before she went out at 1.35 or thereabouts and Miss Webb who could have arranged to meet him there, and killed him before rushing from the house and giving the alarm.'

'Ah,' said the inspector. 'You're coming down to brass tacks now.'

'And of course,' said Poirot, wheeling round, '*you*, my dear Colin. You were also on the spot. Looking for a high number where the low numbers were.'

'Well, really,' I said indignantly. 'What will you say next?'

'Me, I say anything!' declared Poirot grandly.

'And yet *I* am the person who comes and dumps the whole thing in your lap!'

'Murderers are often conceited,' Poirot pointed out. 'And there too, it might have amused you – to have a joke like that at my expense.'

'If you go on, you'll convince *me*,' I said.

I was beginning to feel uncomfortable.

Poirot turned back to Inspector Hardcastle.

'Here, I say to myself, must be essentially a simple crime. The presence of irrelevant clocks, the advancing of time by an hour, the arrangements made so deliberately for the discovery of the body, all these must be set aside for the moment. They are, as is said in your immortal "Alice" like "*shoes and ships and sealing wax and cabbages and kings*". The vital point is that an ordinary elderly man is dead and that somebody wanted him dead. If we knew who the dead man was, it would give us a pointer to his killer. If he was a well-known blackmailer then we must look for a man who could be blackmailed. If he was a detective, then we look for a man who has a criminal secret; if he is a man of wealth, then we look among his heirs. But if we do *not* know who the man is – then we have the more difficult task of hunting amongst those in the surrounding circle for a man who has a reason to kill.

'Setting aside Miss Pebmarsh and Sheila Webb, who is there who might not be what they seem to be? The answer was disappointing. With the exception of Mr Ramsay who I understood was *not* what he seemed to be?' Here Poirot looked inquiringly at me and I nodded, 'everybody's *bona fides* were genuine. Bland was a well-known local builder, McNaughton had had a Chair at Cambridge, Mrs Hemming was the widow of a local auctioneer, the Waterhouses were respectable residents of long standing. So we come back to Mr Curry. Where did he come *from*? What brought him to 19, Wilbraham Crescent? And here one very valuable remark was spoken by one of the neighbours, Mrs Hemming. When told that the dead man did not live at Number 19, she said, "Oh! I see. He just came there to be killed. How odd." She had the gift, often possessed by those who are too occupied with their own thoughts to pay attention to what others are saying, to come to the heart of the problem. She summed up the whole crime. *Mr Curry came to 19, Wilbraham Crescent to be killed.* It was as simple as that!'

'That remark of hers struck me at the time,' I said.

Poirot took no notice of me.

'"*Dilly, dilly, dilly – come and be killed.*" Mr Curry came – and he was killed. But that was not all. It was important *that he should not be identified.* He had no wallet, no papers, the tailor's marks were removed from his clothes. But that would not be enough. The printed card of Curry, Insurance Agent, was only a temporary measure. If the man's identity was to be concealed *permanently*, he must be given a false identity. Sooner or later, I was sure, somebody would turn up, recognize him positively and that would be that. A brother, a sister, a wife. It was a wife. Mrs Rival – and the name alone might have aroused suspicion. There is a village in Somerset – I have stayed near there with friends – the village of Curry Rival – Subconsciously, without knowing why those two names suggested themselves, they were chosen. Mr Curry – Mrs Rival.

'So far – the plan is obvious, but what puzzled me was why our murderer took for granted that there would be no *real* identification. If the man had no family, there are at least landladies, servants, business associates. That led me to the next assumption – this man was *not known to be missing*. A further assumption was that he was not English, and was only visiting this country. That would tie in with the fact that the dental work done on his teeth did not correspond with any dental records here.

'I began to have a shadowy picture both of the victim and of the murderer. No more than that. The crime was well planned and intelligently carried out – but now there came that one piece of sheer bad luck that no murderer can foresee.'

'And what was that?' asked Hardcastle.

Unexpectedly, Poirot threw his head back, and recited dramatically:

> 'For want of a nail the shoe was lost,
> For want of a shoe the horse was lost,
> For want of a horse the battle was lost,
> For want of a battle the Kingdom was lost,
> And all for the want of a horse shoe nail.'

He leaned forward.

'A good many people *could* have killed Mr Curry. But *only one person* could have killed, or could have had reason to kill, the girl Edna.'

We both stared at him.

'Let us consider the Cavendish Secretarial Bureau. Eight girls work there. On the 9th of September, four of those girls were out on assignments some little distance away – that is, they were provided with lunch by the clients to whom they had gone. They were the four who normally took the first lunch period from 12.30 to 1.30. The remaining four, Sheila Webb, Edna Brent and two girls, Janet and Maureen, took the second period, 1.30 to 2.30. But on that day Edna Brent had an accident quite soon after leaving the office. She tore the heel off her shoe in the grating. She could not walk like that. She bought some buns and came back to the office.'

Poirot shook an emphatic finger at us.

'We have been told that Edna Brent was worried about something. She tried to see Sheila Webb out of the office, but failed. It has been assumed that that something was connected with Sheila Webb, but there is no evidence of that. She might only have wanted to consult Sheila Webb about something that had puzzled her – but if so one thing was clear. She wanted to talk to Sheila Webb *away* from the bureau.

'Her words to the constable at the inquest are the only clue we have as to what was worrying her: She said something like: "I don't see how what she said can have been true." Three women had given evidence that morning. Edna could have been referring to Miss Pebmarsh. Or, as it has been generally assumed, she could have been referring to Sheila Webb. But there is a third possibility – *she could have been referring to Miss Martindale*.'

'Miss Martindale? But her evidence only lasted a few minutes.'

'Exactly. It consisted only of the telephone call she had received purporting to be from Miss Pebmarsh.'

'Do you mean that Edna knew that it *wasn't* from Miss Pebmarsh?'

'I think it was simpler than that. I am suggesting that there was *no* telephone call at all.'

He went on:

'The heel of Edna's shoe came off. The grating was quite close to the office. She came back to the bureau. But Miss Martindale, in her private office, did not know that Edna had come back. As far as she knew there was nobody but herself in the bureau. All she need do was to *say* a telephone call had come through at 1.49. Edna does not see the significance of what she knows at first. Sheila is called in to Miss Martindale and told to go out on an appointment. How and when that appointment was made is not mentioned to Edna. News of the murder comes through and little by little the story gets more definite. Miss Pebmarsh *rang up* and asked for Sheila Webb to be sent. But Miss Pebmarsh says it was not she who rang up. The call is said to have come through at ten minutes to two. *But Edna knows that couldn't be true*. No telephone call came through then. Miss Martindale must have made a mistake – But Miss Martindale definitely doesn't make mistakes. The more Edna thinks about it, the more puzzling it is. She must ask Sheila about it. Sheila will know.

'And then comes the inquest. And the girls all go to it. Miss Martindale repeats her story of the telephone call and Edna knows definitely now that the evidence Miss Martindale gives so clearly, with such precision as to the exact time, is untrue. It was then that she asked the constable if she could speak to the inspector. I think probably that Miss Martindale, leaving the Cornmarket in a crowd of people, overheard her asking that. Perhaps by then she had heard the girls chaffing Edna about her shoe accident without realizing what it involved. Anyway, she followed the girl to Wilbraham Crescent. Why did Edna go there, I wonder?'

'Just to stare at the place where it happened, I expect,' said Hardcastle with a sigh. 'People do.'

'Yes, that is true enough. Perhaps Miss Martindale speaks to her there, walks with her down the road and Edna plumps out her question. Miss Martindale acts quickly. They are just by the telephone box. She says, "This is very important. You must ring up the police at once. The number of the police station is so and so. Ring up and tell them we are both coming there now." It is second nature for Edna to do what she is told. She goes in, picks up the receiver and Miss Martindale comes in behind her, pulls the scarf round her neck and strangles her.'

'And nobody saw this?'

Poirot shrugged his shoulders.

'They might have done, but they didn't! It was just on one o'clock. Lunch time. And what people there were in the Crescent were busy staring at 19. It was a chance boldly taken by a bold and unscrupulous woman.'

Hardcastle was shaking his head doubtfully.

'Miss Martindale? I don't see how she can possibly come into it.'

'No. One does not see at first. But since Miss Martindale undoubtedly killed Edna – oh, yes – only she could have killed Edna, then she *must* come into it. And I begin to suspect that in Miss Martindale we have the Lady Macbeth of this crime, a woman who is ruthless and unimaginative.'

'Unimaginative?' queried Hardcastle.

'Oh, yes, quite unimaginative. But very efficient. A good planner.'

'But why? Where's the motive?'

Hercule Poirot looked at me. He wagged a finger.

'So the neighbours' conversation was no use to you, eh? I found one most illuminating sentence. Do you remember that after talking of living abroad, Mrs Bland remarked that she liked living in Crowdean *because she had a sister here. But Mrs Bland was not supposed to have a sister.* She had inherited a large fortune a year ago from a Canadian great-uncle because she was the only surviving member of his family.'

Hardcastle sat up alertly.

'So you think –'

Poirot leaned back in his chair and put his fingertips together. He half closed his eyes and spoke dreamily.

'Say you are a man, a very ordinary and not too scrupulous man, in bad financial difficulties. A letter comes one day from a firm of lawyers to say that your wife has inherited a big fortune from a great-uncle in Canada. The letter is addressed to Mrs Bland and the only difficulty is that the Mrs Bland who receives it is the wrong Mrs Bland – she is the second wife – not the first one – Imagine the chagrin! The fury! And then an idea comes. Who is to know that it is the wrong Mrs Bland? Nobody in Crowdean knows that Bland was married before. His first marriage, years ago, took place during the war when he was overseas. Presumably his first wife died soon afterwards, and he almost immediately remarried. He has the original marriage certificate, various family papers, photographs of Canadian relations now dead – It will be all plain sailing. Anyway, it is worth risking. They risk it, and it comes off. The legal formalities go through. And there the Blands are, rich and prosperous, all their financial troubles over –

'And then – a year later – something happens. What happens? I suggest that someone was coming over from Canada to this country – and that this someone had known the first Mrs Bland well enough not to be deceived by an impersonation. He may have been an elderly member of the family attorneys, or a close friend of the family – but whoever he was, he will *know*. Perhaps they thought of ways of avoiding a meeting. Mrs Bland could feign illness, she could go abroad – but anything of that kind would only arouse suspicion. The visitor would insist on seeing the woman he had come over to see –'

'And so – to murder?'

'Yes. And here, I fancy, Mrs Bland's sister may have been the ruling spirit. She thought up and planned the whole thing.'

'You are taking it that Miss Martindale and Mrs Bland *are* sisters?'

'It is the only way things make sense.'

'Mrs Bland did remind me of someone when I saw her,' said Hardcastle. 'They're very different in manner – but it's true – there *is* a likeness. But how could they hope to get away with it?' The man would be missed. Inquiries would be made –'

'If this man were travelling abroad – perhaps for pleasure, not for business, his schedule would be vague. A letter from one place – a postcard from another – it would be a little time before people wondered why they had not heard from him. By that time who would connect a man identified and buried as Harry Castleton, with a rich Canadian visitor to the country who has not even been seen in this part of the world? If I had been the murderer, I would have slipped over on a day trip to France or Belgium and discarded the dead man's passport in a train or a tram so that the inquiry would take place from another country.'

I moved involuntarily, and Poirot's eyes came round to me.

'Yes?' he said.

'Bland mentioned to me that he had recently taken a day trip to Boulogne – with a blonde, I understand –'

'Which would make it quite a natural thing to do. Doubtless it is a habit of his.'

'This is still conjecture,' Hardcastle objected.

'But inquiries can be made,' said Poirot.

He took a sheet of hotel notepaper from the rack in front of him and handed it to Hardcastle.

'If you will write to Mr Enderby at 10, Ennismore Gardens, S.W.7 he has promised to make certain inquiries for me in Canada. He is a well-known international lawyer.'

'And what about the business of the clocks?'

'Oh! The clocks. Those famous clocks!' Poirot smiled. 'I think you will find that Miss Martindale was responsible for them. Since the crime, as I said, was a simple crime, it was disguised by making it a fantastic one. That Rosemary clock that Sheila Webb took to be repaired. Did she lose it in the Bureau of Secretarial Studies? Did Miss Martindale take it as the foundation of her rigmarole, and was it partly because of that clock that she chose Sheila as the person to discover the body –?'

Hardcastle burst out:

'And you say this woman is unimaginative? When she concocted all this?'

'But she did not concoct it. That is what is so interesting. It was all there – waiting for her. From the very first I detected a pattern – a pattern I knew. A pattern familiar because I had just been reading such patterns. I have been very fortunate. As Colin here will tell you, I attended this week a *sale of authors' manuscripts*. Among them were some of Garry Gregson's. I hardly dared hope. But luck was with me. *Here* –' Like a conjuror he whipped from a drawer in the desk two shabby exercise books ' – it is all *here*! Among the many plots of books he planned to write. He did not live to write this one – but Miss Martindale, who was his secretary, knew all about it. She just lifted it bodily to suit her purpose.'

'But the clocks must have meant something originally – in Gregson's plot, I mean.'

'Oh, yes. His clocks were set at one minute past five, four minutes past five and seven minutes past five. That was the combination number of a safe, 515457. The safe was concealed behind a reproduction of the Mona Lisa. Inside the safe,' continued Poirot, with distaste, 'were the Crown jewels of the Russian Royal Family. *Un tas de bêtises*, the whole thing! And of course there was a story of kinds – a persecuted girl. Oh, yes, it came in very handy for la Martindale. She just chose her local characters and adapted the story to fit in. All these flamboyant clues would lead – where? Exactly nowhere! Ah, yes, an efficient woman. One wonders – he left her a legacy – did he not? How and of what did he die, I wonder?'

Hardcastle refused to be interested in past history. He gathered up the exercise books and took the sheet of hotel paper from my hand. For the last two minutes I had been staring at it, fascinated. Hardcastle had scribbled down Enderby's address without troubling to turn the sheet the right way up. The hotel address was upside down in the left-hand bottom corner.

Staring at the sheet of paper, I knew what a fool I had been.

'Well, thank you, M. Poirot,' said Hardcastle. 'You've certainly given us something to think about. Whether anything will come of it –'

'I am most delighted if I have been of any assistance.'

Poirot was playing it modestly.

'I'll have to check various things –'

'Naturally – naturally –'

Goodbyes were said. Hardcastle took his departure.

Poirot turned his attention to me. His eyebrows rose.

'*Eh bien* – and what, may I ask, is biting you? – you look like a man who has seen an apparition.'

'I've seen what a fool I've been.'

'Aha. Well, that happens to many of us.'

But presumably not to Hercule Poirot! I had to attack him.

'Just tell me one thing, Poirot. If, as you said, you could do all this sitting in your chair in London and could have got me and Dick Hardcastle to come to you there, why – oh, why, did you come down here at all?'

'I told you, they make the reparation in my apartment.'

'They would have lent you another apartment. Or you could have gone to the Ritz, you would have been more comfortable there than in the Curlew Hotel.'

'Indubitably,' said Hercule Poirot. 'The coffee here, *mon dieu*, the coffee!'

'Well, then, *why*?'

Hercule Poirot flew into a rage.

'*Eh bien*, since you are too stupid to guess, I will tell you. I am human, am I not? I can be the machine if it is necessary. I can lie back and think. I can solve the problem so. But I am human, I tell you. And the problems concern human beings.'

'And so?'

'The explanation is as simple as the murder was simple. I came out of human curiosity,' said Hercule Poirot, with an attempt at dignity.

CHAPTER 29

Once more I was in Wilbraham Crescent, proceeding in a westerly direction.

I stopped before the gate of No. 19. No one came screaming out of the house this time. It was neat and peaceful.

I went up to the front door and rang the bell.

Miss Millicent Pebmarsh opened it.

'This is Colin Lamb,' I said. 'May I come in and speak to you?'

'Certainly.'

She preceded me into the sitting-room.

'You seem to spend a lot of time down here, Mr Lamb. I understood that you were *not* connected with the local police –'

'You understood rightly. I think, really, you have known exactly who I am from the first day you spoke to me.'

'I'm not sure quite what you mean by that.'

'I've been extremely stupid, Miss Pebmarsh. I came to this place to look for you. I found you the first day I was here – and I didn't know I had found you!'

'Possibly murder distracted you.'

'As you say. I was also stupid enough to look at a piece of paper the wrong way up.'

'And what is the point of all this?'

'Just that the game is up, Miss Pebmarsh. I've found the headquarters where all the planning is done. Such records and memoranda as are necessary are kept by you on the micro dot system in Braille. The information Larkin got at Portlebury was passed to you. From here it went to its destination by means of Ramsay. He came across when necessary from his house to yours at night by way of the garden. He dropped a Czech coin in your garden one day –'

'That was careless of him.'

'We're all careless at some time or another. Your cover is very good. You're blind, you work at an institute for disabled children, you keep children's books in Braille in your house as is only natural – you are a woman of unusual intelligence and personality. I don't know what is the driving power that animates you –'

'Say if you like that I am dedicated.'

'Yes. I thought it might be like that.'

'And why are you telling me all this? It seems unusual.'

I looked at my watch.

'You have two hours, Miss Pebmarsh. In two hours' time members of the special branch will come here and take charge –'

'I don't understand you. Why do you come here ahead of your people, to give me what seems to be a warning –'

'It *is* a warning. I have come here myself, and shall remain here until my people arrive, to see that nothing leaves this house – with one exception. That exception is you yourself. You have two hours' start if you choose to go.'

'But why? *Why?*'

I said slowly:

'Because I think there is an off-chance that you might shortly become my mother-in-law . . . I may be quite wrong.'

There was a silence. Millicent Pebmarsh got up and went to the window. I didn't take my eyes off her. I had no illusions about Millicent Pebmarsh. I didn't trust her an inch. She was blind but even a blind woman can catch you if you are off guard. Her blindness wouldn't handicap her if she once got her chance to jam an automatic against my spine.

She said quietly:

'I shall not tell you if you're right or wrong. What makes you think that – that it might be so?'

'Eyes.'

'But we are not alike in character.'

'No.'

She spoke almost defiantly.

'I did the best I could for her.'

'That's a matter of opinion. With you a cause came first.'

'As it should do.'

'I don't agree.'

There was silence again. Then I asked, 'Did you know who she was – that day?'

'Not until I heard the name . . . I had kept myself informed about her – always.'

'You were never as inhuman as you would have liked to be.'

'Don't talk nonsense.'

I looked at my watch again.

'Time is going on,' I said.

She came back from the window and across to the desk.

'I have a photograph of her here – as a child . . .'

I was behind her as she pulled the drawer open. It wasn't an automatic. It was a small very deadly knife . . .

My hand closed over hers and took it away.

'I may be soft, but I'm not a fool,' I said.

She felt for a chair and sat down. She displayed no emotion whatever.

'I am not taking advantage of your offer. What would be the use? I shall stay here until – they come. There are always opportunities – even in prison.'

'Of indoctrination, you mean?'

'If you like to put it that way.'

We sat there, hostile to each other, but with understanding.

'I've resigned from the Service,' I told her. 'I'm going back to my old job – marine biology. There's a post going at a university in Australia.'

'I think you are wise. You haven't got what it takes for this job. You are like Rosemary's father. He couldn't understand Lenin's dictum: "Away with softness".'

I thought of Hercule Poirot's words.

'I'm content,' I said, 'to be human . . .'

We sat there in silence, each of us convinced that the other's point of view was wrong.

Letter from Detective Inspector Hardcastle to M. Hercule Poirot

Dear M. Poirot,

We are now in possession of certain facts, and I feel you may be interested to hear about them.

A Mr Quentin Duguesclin of Quebec left Canada for Europe approximately four weeks ago. He has no near relatives and his plans for return were indefinite. His passport was found by the proprietor of a small restaurant in Boulogne, who handed it in to the police. It has not so far been claimed.

Mr Duguesclin was a lifelong friend of the Montresor family of Quebec. The head of that family, Mr Henry Montresor, died eighteen months ago, leaving his very considerable fortune to his only surviving relative, his great-niece Valerie, described as the wife of Josiah Bland of Portlebury, England. A very reputable firm of London solicitors acted for the Canadian executors. All communications between Mrs Bland and her family in Canada ceased from the time of her marriage of which her family did not approve. Mr Duguesclin mentioned to one of his friends that he intended to look up the Blands while he was in England, since he had always been very fond of Valerie.

The body hitherto identified as that of Henry Castleton has been positively identified as Quentin Duguesclin.

Certain boards have been found stowed away in a corner of Bland's building yard. Though hastily painted out, the words SNOWFLAKE LAUNDRY *are plainly perceptible after treatment by experts.*

I will not trouble you with lesser details, but the public prosecutor considers that a warrant can be granted for the arrest of Josiah Bland. Miss Martindale and Mrs Bland are, as you conjectured, sisters, but though I agree with your views on her participation in these crimes, satisfactory evidence will be hard to obtain. She is undoubtedly a very clever woman. I have hopes, though, of Mrs Bland. She is the type of woman who rats.

The death of the first Mrs Bland through enemy action in France, and his second marriage to Hilda Martindale (who was in the N.A.A.F.I.) also in France can be, I think, clearly established, though many records were, of course, destroyed at that time.

It was a great pleasure meeting you that day, and I must thank you for the very useful suggestions you made on that occasion. I hope the alterations and redecorations of your London flat have been satisfactory.

Yours sincerely,
Richard Hardcastle

Further communication from R.H. to H.P.

Good news! The Bland woman cracked! Admitted the whole thing!!! Puts the blame entirely on her sister and her husband. She 'never understood until too late what they meant to do'! Thought they were only 'going to dope him so that he wouldn't recognize she was the wrong woman'! A likely story! But I'd say it's true enough that she wasn't the prime mover.

The Portobello Market people have identified Miss Martindale as the 'American' lady who bought two of the clocks.

Mrs McNaughton now says she saw Duguesclin in Bland's van being driven into Bland's garage. Did she really?

Our friend Colin has married that girl. If you ask me, *he's mad.*
All the best.
Yours,
Richard Hardcastle

BIOGRAPHY

- [ ] **Agatha Christie's Hercule Poirot** by Anne Hart 0-00-649957-0 £7.99
- [ ] **Agatha Christie's Miss Marple** by Anne Hart 0-00-649956-2 £6.99
- [ ] **Come, Tell Me How You Live** by Agatha Christie Mallowan
  0-00-653114-8 £7.99
- [ ] **An Autobiography** by Agatha Christie 0-00-635328-2 £8.99
- [ ] **Agatha Christie: A Biography** by Janet Morgan
  0-00-636961-8 £7.99
- [ ] **The Life & Crimes of Agatha Christie** by Charles Osborne
  0-00-653172-5 £8.99

AGATHA CHRISTIE READERS – BOOK & CD

- [ ] **1: The Bloodstained Pavement and other stories**
  0-00-716378-9 £10.99
- [ ] **2: Death by Drowning and other stories** 0-00-716379-7 £10.99
- [ ] **3: Witness for the Prosecution and other stories**
  0-00-716380-0 £10.99
- [ ] **4: Double Sin and other stories** 0-00-716381-9 £10.99

Total cost _____

10% discount _____

Final total _____

To purchase by Visa/Mastercard/Switch simply call
08707 871724 or fax on 08707 871725

To pay by cheque, send a copy of this form with a cheque made payable to
'HarperCollins Publishers' to: Mail Order Dept. (Ref: BOB4),
HarperCollins Publishers, Westerhill Road, Bishopbriggs, G64 2QT,
making sure to include your full name, postal address and phone number.

From time to time HarperCollins may wish to use your personal data
to send you details of other HarperCollins publications and offers.
If you wish to receive information on other HarperCollins publications
and offers please tick this box [ ]

Do not send cash or currency. Prices correct at time of press.
Prices and availability are subject to change without notice.
Delivery overseas and to Ireland incurs a £2 per book postage and packing charge.